HE HAD TO HAVE HER

From the moment Temujin—known to his followers as Genghis Khan—saw the Princess Azara, he knew that he must have her. Women he had enjoyed in plenty, from the earliest years of his young manhood, but none like this beautiful flower of a ripe and decadent civilization.

Little did the elegant, mocking princess realize that for the taste of her lips, armies of men would die . . . that for the touch of her flesh, a hundred great cities would fall . . . until her whole world lay prostrate before the flashing sword and iron will of the conqueror.

"A huge historical canvas—magnificent . . . blood spurts from the knife; beads of sweat stand out on straining flesh; lusts are consummated and revenges achieved"
—*New York Herald Tribune*

"Overpowering"—*Kansas City Star*

"Taylor Caldwell's finest novel"
—*New York Mirror*

"The lofty peaks of best-sellerdom are traditionally difficult to scale. . . . But there are three American novelists who have climbed to the top not once or twice but over and over again. In so doing they have established themselves as an elite among U.S. fiction writers. . . . All three are women: Edna Ferber, Frances Parkinson Keyes and Taylor Caldwell."

Life Magazine

Novels by Taylor Caldwell in Pyramid editions

TIME NO LONGER
LET LOVE COME LAST
THE EARTH IS THE LORD'S
THERE WAS A TIME
THE BALANCE WHEEL
THE STRONG CITY
THE EAGLES GATHER
THE TURNBULLS
MELISSA
THE WIDE HOUSE
DYNASTY OF DEATH

Glory & the Lightening

THE EARTH IS THE LORD'S

TAYLOR CALDWELL

PYRAMID BOOKS NEW YORK

To
Lois Dwight Cole

THE EARTH IS THE LORD'S

A PYRAMID BOOK
Published by arrangement with Charles Scribner's Sons

Scribner's edition published January 1941
Literary Guild edition published January 1941
Pyramid edition published January 1965
Ninth printing, February 1976

ISBN: 0-515-04062-2

Printed in the United States of America

Pyramid Books are published by Pyramid Communications, Inc. Its trademarks, consisting of the word "Pyramid" and the portrayal of a pyramid, are registered in the United States Patent Office.

Pyramid Communications, Inc.,
919 Third Avenue, New York, New York 10022

Any resemblance between the characters of this novel and personages living today is indignantly denied by the author! Ghost of Genghis Khan should notify author if such libelous rumor begins to circulate.

LIST OF PRINCIPAL CHARACTERS

(In order of appearance)

Kurelen	Uncle of Temujin
Houlun	Sister of Kurelen
Kokchu	Shaman (priest)
TEMUJIN (Genghis Kahn)	Son of Houlun and Yesukai (Mighty Manslayer)
Yesukai	Khan of the Yakka Mongols, husband of Houlun
Kasar	Brother of Temujin (Genghis Khan)
Bortei	Wife of Temujin
Paladins of Genghis Khan	*Subodai*, cavalry leader *Chepe Noyon* *Belgutei*, half-brother of *Temujin*
Bektor	Half-brother of *Temujin*
Jamuga Sechen (Jamuga the Wise)	Sworn brother of *Temujin*
Toghrul Khan (Prester John; Wang Khan)	Karait Turk, Nestorian Christian, ruler of the Karait Empire
Azara	Daughter of *Toghrul Khan*
Taliph	Son of *Toghrul Khan*

Book One

THE LAST HARVEST

With Earth's first Clay They did the Last Man Knead,
And there of the Last Harvest sow'd the Seed:
And the First Morning of Creation wrote
What the Last Dawn of Reckoning shall read.

—OMAR KHAYYAM

chapter 1

Houlun sent the old serving-woman, Yasai, to the yurt of her half-brother, the crippled Kurelen. As she scuttled through the raw pink light of the sunset, the old woman wiped her hands, which were covered with blood, on her soiled garments. The dust she raised, scuttling so among the yurts, turned gold, followed her like a cloud. She found Kurelen eating as usual, smacking his lips over a silver bowl full of kumiss, fermented mare's milk. After each filling of his mouth he would lift the silver bowl, which had been stolen from a wandering Chinese trader, and squint at it with profound admiration. He would rub a twisted and dirty finger over its delicate traceries, and a sort of voluptuous joy would shine on his dark and emaciated features.

Yasai mounted to the platform of Kurelen's yurt. The oxen were unyoked, but they stared at her with blank brown eyes, in which the terrible sunset was reflected. The old woman paused at the opened flap of the yurt, and peered within at Kurelen. Every one despised Kurelen, because he found so many things amusing, but every one also feared him, because he hated mankind. He laughed at everything and detested everything also. Even his greed and his enormous appetite had something contemptuous about them, as though they were not a part of him, but loathsome qualities belonging to some one else, and about which he was never silent, but openly mocking.

Yasai stared at Kurelen and glowered. She was only a Karuit slave, but even she had no respect for the brother of the chieftain's wife. She knew the story; even the herd-boys knew the story, and the shepherds, who were as stupid as the animals they drove out to pasture. Houlun had been stolen on her wedding day from her husband, a man of another tribe, by Yesukai, the Yakka Mongol. A few days later her crippled brother, Kurelen, had come to the ordu, or tent village, of Yesukai, to plead for his sister's return. The Merkit, the clan to which Kurelen and his sister, Houlun, belonged, were shrewd folk, forest-dwelling and active traders. In sending Kurelen to Yesukai they sent a messenger who was clever and loquacious, and was possessed of a beautiful and persuasive voice. He, if any one, might be successful. If he were killed, his clan was prepared to be very philosophical about the sad event. He was a trouble-maker, and a laugher, and was disliked and hated by his people. The Merkit might not get back Houlun, but there was a fine likelihood that they might rid themselves of Kurelen. Had he been a strong and stalwart man, they might have killed him in their incomprehension and dislike. But as a cripple, and the son of a chieftain, they could not kill him. Besides, he was an exceedingly shrewd trader, and a wonderful artisan, and he could read Chinese, which was very useful in dealing with the subtle traders of Cathay. His father had said that had he been a stalwart man his people would not have killed him, for he would not have been the sort of man who deserved killing. At which sage remark the tribe had laughed heartily, but Kurelen had just made his silent wry mouth, which was singularly infuriating to simple men.

Houlun was not returned to her father's ordu nor to her husband, for she was exceedingly beautiful and Yesukai had found her delightful in his bed. Neither did Kurelen return. It was a very uncomplicated story. He had been led to Yesukai's tent, and the young arrogant Yakka Mongol had glowered at him ferociously. Kurelen had not been disturbed. In a mild and interested voice he asked to be shown the ordu of the young Khan. Yesukai, who had expected pleas or threats, was exceedingly nonplussed and surprised. Kurelen had not even asked for his sister, had not expressed a desire to see her, though through the corner of his eye he had observed her peeping at him behind the flap of her new husband's yurt. Nor did he seem to be alarmed by the glowering and ominous presence of a number of young warriors, who were eyeing him fiercely.

Yesukai, who was not subtle, and thought very slowly when he thought at all, found himself leading his wife's brother through the tent village. The women and children stood on the platforms or at the open flaps of the yurts, and stared. A profound silence filled the village. Even the horses and the home-coming cattle seemed less vociferous. Yesukai led the way, and Kurelen, limping and smiling his curious twisted smile, followed. Behind them trailed the young warriors, scowling more fiercely than ever, and wetting their lips. The dogs forgot to bark. It was a long and ludicrous journey. At intervals, Yesukai, who was beginning to feel foolish, would frown over his shoulder at the limping and following cripple. But Kurelen's expression was artless, and had a pleased and open quality about it, like a child's. He kept nodding his head, as though happily surprised, and muttering unintelligible comments to himself. "Twenty thousand yurts!" he said once, in a loud and musical voice. He beamed at Yesukai admiringly.

They came back to Yesukai's yurt. At the door, Yesukai paused and waited. Now Kurelen would demand the return of his sister, or at least some large payment. But Kurelen was apparently in no hurry. He seemed thoughtful. Yesukai, who feared nothing, began to shift uneasily from foot to foot. He glowered ferociously. He fingered the Chinese dagger at his belt. His black eyes glowed with a savage fire. The warriors were tired of glowering, and began to exchange glances. Somewhere, near a distant yurt, a woman laughed openly.

Kurelen lifted one dark twisted hand to his lips and thoughtfully chewed the nails. Had he not been bent and crippled, he would have been a tall lean man. His shoulders were broad, if awry. His good leg was long, though the other was gnarled like a desert tree. His body was flat and emaciated, and the bones bent out of shape. He had a long thin face, dark and mischievous and ugly, with narrow flashing teeth, as white as milk. His cheekbones stood out like sharp shelves under slanting and glittering eyes, which were full of the light of mockery. His hair was black and long. His smile was amused and venomous.

He addressed Yesukai at last, with profound respect, in which the mockery shimmered like threads of silver. "Thou hast a lordly tribe, most valiant Khan," he said, and his voice was soft and soothing. "Let me speak to my sister, Houlun."

Yesukai hesitated. He had decided heretofore that Houlun was not to see her brother. But now he was impelled to grant the other's request, though he did not know why. He waved his arm curtly at the serving-women who were standing on the platform of his yurt. They brought out Houlun, and made her stand between them. She stood there, tall and beautiful and proud and hating, her gray eyes red and swollen with tears. But when she saw her brother, she smiled at him, and made a swift and involuntary movement towards him. But it was more his expression than the restraining hands of the serving-women which made her halt abruptly. He was regarding her with bland unconcern and reticence. She stood and stared at him, blinking, turning pale, while all watched. He was much loved by her, for they were the wisest and the most understanding of their father's children, and few words were necessary between them.

He spoke to her gently, yet with a sort of mild and icy contempt. "I have seen the ordu of thy husband, Yesukai, my sister. I have walked through the village. Remain here, and be a dutiful wife to Yesukai. His people stink less than ours."

The Mongols, who loved laughter in spite of their harsh life, at first stared at this astounding speech, and then burst into loud and roaring laughter. Yesukai laughed until the tears ran down his cheeks to his bearded lips. The warriors fell into each other's arms. The children whooped; the women shrieked with mirth. The cattle lowed and the horses neighed and the dogs barked wildly. The herdboys and the shepherds stamped until clouds of thick dust filled the raw brightness of the desert air and made them choke.

But Houlun did not laugh. She stood there on the high platform and gazed down at her brother. Her face was as white as the mountain snows. Her white lip quivered and arched. Her eye began to flash with scorn and repudiation. And Kurelen stood below her, smiling upwards through his slanting eyes. Then at last, without a word, she turned proudly and went back into the yurt.

When the laughter subsided to a point where he could be heard, Kurelen said to Yesukai, who was openly wiping his eyes: "All men stink, but thine the least of all I have seen. Let me live in thy ordu and be one with thy people. I speak the language of Cathay; I am a bigger thief than a Bagdad Turk. I am a shrewder trader than the Naiman. I can make shields and harness, and can hammer metal into many useful shapes. I can write in the speech of Cathay and the Uighurs. I have been within the Great Wall of Cathay, and know many things. Though my body is twisted, I can be useful to thee in countless ways."

Yesukai and his people gaped, amazed. Here was no enemy, demanding and threatening. The Shaman was angrily disappointed, and came to Yesukai's elbow, as he hesitated, biting his lip. He whispered: "The cattle have been dying of a mysterious disease. The spirits of the Blue Sky need a sacrifice. Here is one at thy hand, O Lord. The son of a chieftain, the brother of thy wife. The spirits demand a noble sacrifice."

The superstitious Mongol was unhappy. He needed craftsmen, and he had not been unsensible to the light of affection and joy in the eye of his beautiful and unwilling wife, Houlun, when she had seen her brother. He had been thinking that she might be more amenable if he were gracious and kindly to her brother, and that she might be happier among strangers with one of her own blood near her. But the Chief Shaman, the priest, was whispering in his ear, and he listened.

Kurelen, who hated priests, knew what was transpiring. He saw the young Khan's hesitant eye glitter and darken as it rested on him. He saw the malignant profile of the Shaman, the cowardly and cruelly drooping lip. He saw the sly and malevolent glances, full of greed for torture and blood. He saw the suddenly dilated nostrils of the warriors, who were no longer smiling, but were drawing in closely about him. He knew he must show no fear.

He said, with amusement: "Most holy Shaman, I know not what thou art whispering, but I know that thou art whispering folly. Priests are the emasculators of men. They have the souls of jackals, and must use silly magic because they are afraid of the sword. They swell out their bellies with the meat of animals they have not hunted. They drink milk they have not taken from the mares. They lie with women they have neither bought nor stolen, nor won in combat. Because they have the hearts of camels, they would die but for their cunning. They enslave men with gibberish, in order that men may continue to serve them."

The warriors did not like the Chief Shaman, who they suspected had an impious eye for their wives, and grinned. The Shaman surveyed Kurelen with the most malignant hatred, and his crafty face flooded with scarlet. Yesukai had begun to smile, for all his uncertainty. Kurelen turned to him.

"Answer me truly, O noble Khan: Canst thou dispense easier with one warrior than thou canst dispense with this silly priest?"

Yesukai, in his simplicity, answered at once: "A warrior is better than a Shaman. A craftsman is not as good as a warrior, but he is still better than a priest. Kurelen, if thou wilt be one of my people, I welcome thee."

So Kurelen, who had lived all his precarious life by his wits, and his intelligence, which was very great, became a member of the tribe of Yesukai. The Shaman, who had been worsted by him, became his most terrible enemy. The warriors, who despised the defeated, no longer listened to the Shaman. But only the women and children listened.

For a long time Houlun would have nothing to do with her brother, who had betrayed and mocked her. She became pregnant by Yesukai. She tended his yurt and lay in his bed, and seemed reconciled, for she was a sagacious woman and wasted little time in grief and bewailing. Like all wise people, she made the best of circumstances, and compromised with them for the advancement of her comfort and well-being. But she would not see her brother. It was not until the hour of her labor that she sent for him. She was having a difficult time, and was afraid, and wanted the only creature she truly loved near at hand, even though he had mocked her. Her husband was away on a hunting and marauding excursion, and she had no love for him, anyway.

She knew Kurelen was detested and feared by her husband's people. But he had been detested by his own, and she knew why. She, too, hated her kind, and despised them. But because she was cold and haughty and reserved, she was respected. Kurelen was not respected, for he was loquacious and mingled freely with the tribesmen, and was sometimes ingratiating. They thought him inferior, in consequence, and even the shepherds spoke of him contemptuously, and laughed at his cowardice. Had he not acquiesced in the rape of his sister?

The old serving-woman, Yasai, having come to the open flap of Kurelen's yurt, stood there and stared at him. He looked up and saw her, and then lapped up the last of the kumiss, and admired, for the final time, the beautiful chasings of the silver bowl. He carefully deposited the bowl on the skin-strewn floor of the yurt, wiped his wide, thin, twisted mouth on his dirty sleeve, and smiled. "Well, Yasai?" he asked amiably.

She scowled. He was the son of a chieftain, and he spoke to her as to an equal. Her withered lips curled in uneasy contempt. They made a spitting motion, and she grunted in her old throat. Kurelen continued to eye her blandly, and waited. He folded his hands in his wide sleeves and sat there, on the floor, only his evil and mischievous eyes glinting in the hot gloom of the yurt. His amiability and lack of pride did not deceive the old woman, as they did not deceive the others, that he believed the members of the tribe of Yesukai his equals. Had he displayed pride and a consciousness of his superiority, as well as democratic amiability, they would have been flattered and grateful, and would have adored him. His very pridelessness, his very air of equality, were, they knew, merely mocking half-disguises for his awareness of their inferiority, and his mortal hatred and contempt for them.

She said curtly: "Thy sister, the wife of the Khan, wishes thee to come to her yurt."

He raised his eyebrows, which slanted upward like black streaks. "My sister," he said meditatively. He grinned. He got to his feet with an astonishing agility. Yasai regarded him with aversion. The simple Mongol barbarians were revolted by physical deformity. "What does she want with me?" he added, after a pause.

"She is in labor," answered the old woman, and climbed down from the platform. She left him alone, standing in the center of his small yurt, his eyebrows dancing up and down over his eyes, his lips twisted in a half smile. His head was bent; he seemed to be thinking curious thoughts. In spite of his deformity, and his restless eyes, and his smile, he was strangely pathetic. He went out into the raw hot light of the pink sunset.

chapter 2

The shepherds and the herdboys were bringing in their flocks of goats and cattle. Clouds of gray and golden dust exploded about them, and the burning and glittering desert air was full of their hoarse shouts and shrill cries. The cattle complained in deep and melancholy voices, as they galloped through the winding passageways between the black, dome-shaped yurts on their wooden platforms. The tent village was pitched near the River Onon, and it was towards this yellow-gray river that the guardians of the flocks were driving their charges. Children, naked and brown, played in the gravelly dust near the yurts, but upon the thundering approach of the herds they scrambled up upon the platforms, and jeered at the shepherds as they came running by in the midst of churning hoofs and hot dust. Like phantoms the flocks went by; here and there a tossing head, a cluster of horns, a sea of tails, a plain of rumps, a forest of hairy legs, went by in this swirling and all-enveloping dust, which sparkled in the frightful glare of the sunlight.

Women, anxious about their offspring, came to the gaps of the yurts. Some had been nursing their babies, and their brown breasts hung down, full and swelling and naked. They added their shrill threats and calls to the clamor of the herdboys and the cries of the beasts. Others emerged from the yurts with copper and wooden pails, for the animals would be milked after their return from the river. Now other shepherds were approaching, with wild and lashing stallions and mares and young colts, and the stragglers of the village prudently scurried up upon the yurt platforms. One might risk the charge of goats, but never the charge of stallions. Their savage eyes gleamed in the dust; their shaggy bodies were coated with a gray pall. Their shepherds, on horseback, cursed and shouted, and struck at the animals with long staffs. These shepherds were more savage than the stallions, and wilder. Their eyes glinted with untamed light. Their dark faces ran with sweat, and their black lips were cracked with dust. The uproar was deafening, and the stench, observed Kurelen, wrinkling his nose, was insupportable.

The hunters followed on their short and agile Arabian horses, carrying the fruits of the hunt slung before them: hares and antelopes, hedgehogs and birds and foxes, martens and other small furry animals. The hunters whooped triumphantly, and made their mounts cavort and whirl, and when they collided with others they laughed like maniacs. They waved their short swords and their bows, and dug their hard heels into the sides of their horses, and galloped in circles. Their women did not approve of this childish display, and as the hunters entered their yurts the sound of women's voices could be heard, contemptuous and scolding and quelling. Great scarlet campfires began to burn between the rows of the yurts, and spluttering torches began to move between these rows, for the mighty sky above was rapidly turning purple in the desert evening.

The herds had passed, and Kurelen emerged from a small space between two yurts, and began to make his way towards the largest yurt of all, where his sister dwelt. The bright yellow dust was still thick in the air, and the black yurts could be discerned only dimly through it, like huge beehives floating unattached in a fog. The campfires were burning high and vivid, like banners, and the torches moved here and there in the dusk. Voices were muffled, and sounded seemingly at a great hollow distance. The gravelly and powdered earth under Kurelen's feet was still hot from the day's heat, and felt like velvet. He looked at the dimming sky. The west, in the direction of the yellow-gray river, whose boundaries were marked with irregular grayish-green verdure, was a terrible spectacle. It flamed alone in its frightful isolation, illuminating the west, but giving no light to the earth. The horizon was an unbearable and pulsing crimson, bitten into by miles of little sharp black hills, like teeth. Above this enormous pulsing, which was like the beating of a monstrous heart, were bands of pale fire, hundreds of miles in width, and blowing in silent and gigantic gales, as yet unheard and unfelt on the earth. And above these bands were serrated layers of green and gold and red and blazing blue, rising to the zenith, which was the color of hyacinths. And the earth below was dark and unformed and chaotic, lost and empty, in which the tiny red spots of the fires burned in pathetic helplessness.

Kurelen looked at the east. Here the endless heavens were a dim and spectral pink. Arched against them, purple and vague, was the immense shadow and curve of the earth, the tent of night, reaching into the skies that reflected it. And now the winds, descending from heaven like a vast and invisible horde, assaulted the earth, and filled it with the sound of their huge voices. But they made the great silence of the Gobi night only the deeper, only more awful. Now the earth itself belonged to the night and the winds, and was lost in them, and there was only the west, and its most horrible splendor, and its eternal loneliness.

Kurelen, forgetting his sister, left the tent village, and moved through the swelling darkness to a little space beyond it. It had suddenly become bitterly cold, and he shivered in his cloak of goatskins. His eyes sparkled in the gloom, as though possessed of some malevolent life of their own, or a reflection of the falling light of the western skies. He was alone. He drew deep breaths of the gale-filled darkness into his nostrils. Now the zenith was sprinkled with the mighty sparkling of new stars, fierce and icy and imminent. He thought to himself, standing in the wind and the silence: Here man hath not ruined for his avarice. Here no cursed footstep falls, no breath befouls the night. Here are the stars, and here the earth, and only wind and I between!

Somewhere in one of the yurts, at a far distance, the camp flutist had taken up his flute. All at once the enormous Gobi night was pierced with the most heart-rending and sweetest sounds, wild and savage and lonely, touching the soul with aching fire. Kurelen felt his heart squeezing and expanding, until all his spirit throbbed with unbearable pain, and the bitterest longing. And yet with his pain was a sense of majesty and peace that was at once tortured and rimmed with joy. Tears ran down his sunken cheeks; he could taste their salt on his lips. Here he had no need of irony, no shield of mockery against the hideousness of living. He had turned his back to the village, and did not see the little flickering banners of the campfires. He saw only the east, and the dark drifting shadow of the earth.

I should never have gone to Cathay, he thought. I should never have seen of what man is capable, if he wills. If a man drinks of the flaming cup of knowledge, there is no peace henceforth for him, but only loneliness and longing, hatred and sadness. He must walk among his fellows like a leprous dog hating and hated, yet filled with pity and madness, knowing much and knowing little, but understanding only that he can never know anything. He must see his stature dwindle to nothingness, yet be tortured with an awareness of infinity, without bounds.

The voice of the flute wailed, but its wailing rose and at last it was triumphant, its thin flame assaulting and piercing the heavens, not lighting them but entering them. It entered the chaos of eternity, and burned there, not illuminating it, but apart from it, beautiful and sad and defiant. It was the soul of man, besieged and alien, lost and little and bright, assailed by all the winds of heaven and hell, seeking the fragile and living. Its trembling voice spoke of love and God and futility and pain, but always of hope, even under its despair.

When it ceased, Kurelen was overwhelmed with sorrow. He went on his way to his sister's yurt. When he mounted the platform, and bent his head to enter the yurt, he was smiling ironically once more, and his tilting eyes were full of mischief.

The dome-shaped yurt was made of thick black felt, stretched over a framework of wattled rods. There was a hole in the top, which allowed the egress of smoke. A brazier of charcoal was burning brightly under this hole, and furnished the only source of light. The curved walls of the yurt had been coated with white lime, and a skillful Chinese friend of Yesukai had ornamented it with elaborate and decadent figures, delicately colored. These corrupt postures, these subtle faces, these frail colors, were a strange contrast to the barbaric Mongols, who seemed to gain in strength and virility and power by their juxtaposition. The yurt's wooden floor was colored with silken carpets from Kabul and Bokhara; the luster of these carpets made a warm shimmer in the gloom. Standing on these carpets were three chests of teakwood, looted from some Chinese caravan. Exquisitely and weirdly carved, depicting forests of bamboo, grottoes, arched and fretted bridges, herons and toads, Buddhist monks with long sleeves and pointed hats, lovers and flowers, they had a grotesque and alien air in this yurt of the barbarian. One of the chests stood open, and revealed silken and embroidered women's garments, also taken from caravans, or bought from some crafty Arab trader, and articles of inlaid silver, such as small jewel boxes and daggers and bowls. On one side of the felt wall, which had not been decorated by the Chinese artist, hung two or three round leather shields, gilded and lacquered and colored, bamboo and ivory bowcases, Turkish scimitars gleaming like lightning, arrows and short Chinese swords, and two broad silver belts, the intricate and lacelike work of the best of the Chinese artisans, studded with irregular turquoises.

Houlun lay on a wide bed strewn with embroidered Chinese silks and soft furry skins. Squatting on the carpets about the bed were several women, rocking back and forth on their hams, their eyes shut tightly, muttering prayers to the spirits. Their hands were folded in their long wide sleeves; their long cotton robes fell over their thighs and arms and shoulders in statuesque folds. When Kurelen entered, they stared at him with hostile eyes, not rising, though this was the brother of the chieftain's wife, and the son of a chieftain. Houlun lifted her head a little from her bed at his entry, and she gazed at him unsmilingly, and in silence.

It was evident that she was suffering. The red and wavering light of the brazier showed her pale drawn face, her gray tormented eyes. Even her lips were the color of lead. Her long black hair, like strands of lustrous glass, fell over her arms and over the bed, to the floor. Her full breasts rose like hills under her thin silken robe, which was a shining white and embroidered with scarlet, green and yellow Chinese figures. Her belly was enormously swollen, and she had clasped her hands convulsively over it. Her long rounded legs were drawn up in her pain.

She regarded her brother with pride and dignity and extreme coldness. They had not spoken since the day he had betrayed her, though he had seen her at a distance, and once or twice she had passed near him, proud and unseeing, her beautiful features rigid with aversion. Now, as he stood beside her bed, smiling down at her wryly, his slanted eyes shining with a curious light, her own eyes filled with angry and suffering tears, and she turned her face aside.

Kurelen smiled. "Thou hast sent for me, Houlun?" he asked softly.

She kept her face averted, rigidly, the tears thick on her lashes, her face prouder and colder than ever, for all her pain. Her legs drew up, tightened. Kurelen thoughtfully bit his upper lip with his lower teeth, an odd habit of his. He looked at the hostile women surrounding the bed, and they turned their gazes away, contemptuously. He rubbed his chin with his thumb. He returned his attention to his sister. He saw that her forehead was gleaming with beads of tortured sweat, and that there were purple lines about her bitten lips.

"Hast thou sent for the Shaman?" he asked her, and smiled again, sardonically.

She turned her head on her pillows, her eyes filled with dark wrath. "Even in my suffering, thou dost mock me!" she cried.

The women muttered. They shifted their hams away from him. But they seemed uncertain. One spoke to Kurelen, out of the side of her mouth.

"She will not have the Shaman, though he stood at the door of the yurt all day."

"Ah," said Kurelen, meditatively. Houlun had begun to weep, and her weeping angered her, shamed her. She strained her face away from him, away from the light of the brazier, and proudly made no effort to wipe away her tears. He lifted a corner of a thin silken robe, and gently touched her cheek and eyes. She made no gesture of repudiation, but all at once she sobbed aloud, as though his touch had broken down her defenses.

"Leave me," she said brokenly. But he knew she did not mean it. He turned to the women. "Thou hast heard thy mistress," he said. They stood up, surprised and more uncertain than ever, staring at Houlun. But she was weeping, and did not look at them. Slowly they filed from the yurt, muttering. They closed the flap after them. Brother and sister were alone.

The charcoal in the Chinese brazier crackled; the red dim light rose and fell. The ornamented walls of the yurt were buffeted by the terrible winds outside. The colored figures on the walls swayed, bellied in, were sucked outwards. Some of the corrupt and subtle faces seemed to wear evil and sardonic smiles. The tall woman on the bed writhed and wept in her pain and loneliness. The Turkish scimitars glittered, as they moved.

Kurelen sat down on a chest near his sister, and waited. Finally, she wiped her eyes simply on the back of her hands, and turned her face to him. Again, it was proud and cold, but her gray eyes were soft and stricken.

"Why hast thou not left me?" she asked.

He replied gently: "Thou dost know, Houlun, that I have never left thee."

She became, all at once, greatly agitated. She raised herself on her elbow. Her round arms were clasped about with broad Chinese bracelets of silver and turquoise. Her breast heaved, her eyes flashed. "Thou didst betray me, and leave me to my enemy!" she cried out. About her neck was clasped a broad Chinese collar of silver, inlaid with wide flat crimson stones. They glowed like fire, with her uneven breath. Her silken garments fell back from her breast and thighs, and Kurelen thought how beautiful she was.

He answered her with increasing gentleness: "I considered thee at all times to be very wise, Houlun. Not childish, not womanish. I believed that thou didst believe with me that not to struggle, always to accept, always to seize the advantage from disadvantage, was the mark of a man who had risen above the other beasts. I never thought thee the victim of foolish pride and smallness of vision. What didst thou desire from life? A husband? Thou didst have one, and he ran away and deserted thee, and a stronger one took thee. Are not all men alike in the darkness? And is it not better to have one who is strong, ambitious, and a great hunter?"

He reached over and fingered the delicate silk of her garments.

She regarded him, breathing stormily, the jewels about her neck and her eyes equally passionate with light. He shrugged, released the silk.

"Thou didst wear cotton and rough wool, before. Now thou dost wear silks. Thou hast a strong husband. Thou hast soft garments, and food, and chests and silver. Thou hast the passion of a virile man, and he treats thee gently. He is master of thirty thousand yurts, and his followers grow daily. He hath protected thee. None could take thee from him. What more dost thou wish?"

She did not answer. Her breath was as stormy as ever. Anger glared upon her features. But she had nothing to say.

Kurelen, still smiling, sighed. He glanced about the yurt. On a carved and inlaid Chinese tabouret of teakwood was a silver bowl full of Turkish sweetmeats and dates. He helped himself, chewing stickily, and sucking on the stones of the dates. He spit out the stones, licked his lips appreciatively. And all the time his sister watched him, more furious than ever, but with growing embarrassment.

He regarded her with amusement, wiping his lips on his sleeves. "Do not be a fool, Houlun," he said.

She burst out in a loud and stammering voice: "Thou art a coward, Kurelen!"

He stared at her, as though astounded. The smile left his subtle face. He seemed genuinely outraged and amazed.

"Why? Because I, a lone man, and a cripple, did not engage thy husband in combat? Because I did not deliberately throw myself upon his lance, or his dagger, in some monstrous folly?"

She glared at him with enraged contempt. "Hast thou never heard of honor, Kurelen?"

His stare became wider, more incredulous, more astounded. "Honor?" He burst into laughter. He rocked on the chest. He seemed convulsed with uncontrollable mirth. Houlun watched him, blinking her eyes, flushing. She listened to him as he laughed. Her rage increased, because she felt more foolish than ever.

Finally he became quieter, but he had to wipe his eyes. He kept shaking his head.

"The dead," he remarked, "have no need of honor or dishonor. But I, Kurelen, have need of my life. Had I died, thou wouldst still have been retained by Yesukai. But thou wouldst have worn my 'honorable' death on thy breast, like a bauble. I have mistaken thee, Houlun. Thou art a fool."

He rose. He shook out his woolen garments. He put his

hands in his sleeves. He stood beside her, tall, misshapen, bent, his long dark face subtly smiling, his eyes ironic. His white teeth flashed in the light of the brazier. He bent his head sardonically, then moved toward the flap of the yurt, as if to leave.

She watched him until he had reached the flap and was about to raise it. Then in a heartbroken and despairing voice she called out to him: "Kurelen, my brother, do not leave me!"

He paused, but did not turn. She swung her legs with difficulty over the side of the bed. She groaned. She staggered towards him. He turned, and she fell into his arms. He held her to him as she trembled and sobbed, her black hair falling over her hands and breast. He felt the shaking and swelling of her bosom against his chest; he felt the pressure of her limbs. He pressed his lips to the crown of her head, and held her to him more tightly. He smiled, but it was with a strange passion and tenderness, which no one had ever seen before on his lips.

"I have never left thee, Houlun," he repeated, very gently. "I have loved only thee, in all the world."

"And I," she wept, "have loved only thee."

He was strong, for all his deformity, and he lifted her in his arms and carried her back to her bed. He straightened the silks and the furs upon it. He smoothed her long hair, and pushed it back from her wet face. He covered her feet with a red fox robe. She allowed him to minister to her, watching him with streaming and humble and adoring eyes. And then he sat beside her again, and took her hand. He smiled at her, but his smile was odd and wry and bitter.

"It was an evil day when the gods gave us the same father," he said.

She did not reply, but she pressed her pale cheek against the back of his hand. He sighed. He put his other hand on her head, and they remained like this, not moving, but looking at each other deeply, daring not to say the things they thought.

The gales of the night rose to the sound of thunder. The floor of the yurt trembled; the walls shook and swelled and were sucked in and out. The carpets on the floor were agitated, and their lustrous colors shimmered as though with life. The wattled rods of the yurt groaned and squeaked. The deep lowing of the disturbed cattle and oxen mingled with the wind. A horse neighed at a distance, and other stallions answered him, neighing with distress and fear. But Kurelen and Houlun were in a sad and passionate world of their own, looking deeply in each other's eyes.

Then, very gently, Kurelen released his hand, which was

under Houlun's cheek. And as he did so, she writhed convulsively, seized with her pains again. He watched her, wrinkling his narrow high brow, distending his nostrils.

"It goes too long," he said aloud, but as though speaking to himself.

Houlun clasped her hands over her writhing belly. She bit her lips, but could not keep her groans in her throat. She flung her legs about. The flap of the door was lifted, and a serving-woman peered within.

"Mistress, the Shaman is here again," she said.

Kurelen made a motion of admission, and a moment later the Shaman, his enemy, entered sullenly, his gray woolen robe falling around his gaunt legs, his dark and wicked face full of enmity for Kurelen. He had a nose like a vulture's beak, and fierce glinting eyes. Kurelen smiled at him artlessly.

"Ah, Shaman, we have need of thy prayers tonight."

The Shaman regarded him with black hatred, curling his thin lips. He was a handsome man, for all his gauntness. The fierceness of the desert was in his eyes, the wildness of the plains in his face. But his mouth was the mouth of a furtive coward.

He disregarded Kurelen. He stood beside Houlun, and he saw her dishevelled beauty. The sockets of his eyes flamed. He dropped his lids. He folded his hands in his sleeves, bent his head, and his lips moved in silent prayer. Kurelen, crouching on his chest, watched him, and slowly his smile grew broader and broader. He caught Houlun's glance, and he winked at her. She attempted to appear scandalized, but could only smile in return.

The priest prayed aloud now. He lifted his eyes to the aperture of the yurt, through which the smoke of the brazier was coiling, like a gray and nebulous snake.

"O ye spirits of the sacred Blue Sky, deliver this woman's womb of its fruit in short order, and let her sufferings be done! For she is the wife of our Khan, the noble Yesukai, and this is her first-born son, who will rule over us in good time! Let the blessed darkness of release fall over her eyelids; let her womb throw out its burden, and let her have peace."

His voice was vindictive, for he had seen Houlun's furtive smile at her brother. His hands clenched and unclenched in their sleeves. His face twisted with hatred.

He bent over her. He laid his shaking hands, gaunt and roped with veins, on her head and eyes. He drew his hands slowly and lingeringly over her breasts, stopped them upon her belly. He kneaded her belly gently, and she moved restlessly in her pain, watching him closely, meanwhile. Kurelen's brow wrinkled; his mouth drew up under his nose. He leaned forward, his shoulders rising about his ears.

Suddenly the Shaman, bending over Houlun, glanced fiercely over his shoulder at her half-brother.

"It is not good for an unbeliever to be in this yurt, while I pray," he said. "The spirits will not hear me."

The two men regarded each other with fiery eyes. Houlun, interested, waited.

Then Kurelen rose. He took the Shaman by the arm. He smiled. "Get out," he whispered.

Again they regarded each other with those fiery eyes. The Shaman sucked in his lips, but did not move. His nostrils flared out.

Kurelen slipped his hands within his garments, and drew out a short Chinese dagger, broad and sparkling, its hilt encrusted with turquoises. He pressed its point delicately against his finger. A drop of red blood sprang out under it. His glittering eyes fixed themselves upon the priest. Nothing could have been gentler than his expression.

The Shaman stood upright. He looked at Houlun, and then looked at her brother. Something in Kurelen's face and smile terrified him. He bit his lips; rage contorted his gaunt features. He tried to assume a manner of dignity, but his breath, hoarse and hurried, could be heard plainly.

"If this woman dies, then I shall tell Yesukai that it was because of thee, and thy blasphemy, and because thou wouldst not allow me to be with her," he said, his voice breaking in fury.

Very slowly and smilingly, Kurelen lifted the dagger, and placed its point against the priest's breast. The Shaman tried not to wince as he felt its needle-point. Terror flared up into his eyes, like the reflection of a fire. He backed away, then, unable to look away from Kurelen, he moved backwards towards the flap of the yurt. He stumbled, fell backwards through the aperture, caught himself by clutching the sides of it. But to the last he looked only at Kurelen. His legs shook as he clambered down from the platform. The serving-women stood there, and they stared at him, and fell back from him. As he stalked away he heard Kurelen's laughter, and Houlun's, and he muttered curses upon them in the darkness.

Inside the yurt Kurelen said to his sister: "The filthy priest! What a tribe are they! But it is necessary, I suppose, that we allow them to exist. Otherwise, there would be no kings, and no oppressors of the people, to keep them in subjection."

But Houlun's pains had her again. Kurelen took her hand, and spoke seriously: "During my two years in Cathay, I sat in their academies. I listened to the dissertations of their physicians. Wilt thou trust me to deliver thee, Houlun?"

Houlun regarded him for a long moment, deeply, out of her dark pain and exhaustion. Then she answered simply: "Yes, I will trust thee."

He bent over her, and kissed her on the forehead. Then he went to the door and called in the serving-women, who entered, muttering and apprehensive. He ordered them to give their mistress a large cup of wine. One of the women filled a silver Chinese cup with Yesukai's hoarded Turkish wine, and Houlun obediently drank. Her eyes fixed themselves upon her brother over the chased rim. Again he ordered the cup filled, though the old serving-woman, Yasai, protested. And again Houlun drank. And yet again, and again.

A dim golden fog enveloped Houlun's tormented senses. She lay back on her bed, and found her pains not only endurable, but dreamlike, as though another suffered, and not herself. The lime-coated walls of the yurt expanded, became a vast hall peopled with colored faces and bright robes, and music, and smiles and laughter. She relaxed, laughed, spoke loving nonsense to her brother, made fun of the painted Chinese figures which her drunkenness had endowed with febrile and fascinating life. The three serving-women, huddled together at the foot of the bed, muttered to each other, and eyed Kurelen menacingly. They listened to Houlun's laughter, stared at her brilliant eyes and parted smiling lips.

Then Kurelen lifted a Baghdad lamp, which had been burning on a tabouret, and held it in his hands. He sat on his sister's bed. He lifted the lamp so it gleamed vividly in his eyes. He began to speak very gently, and in a low monotonous voice:

"Do not look away from my eyes, Houlun. Thou canst not look away. So. Thou hast no pain. Thou art happy, and at peace. Dost thou hear me?"

She looked at his lighted eyes. Everything else fell away into vague and shifting confusion, but his eyes grew more vivid, more flame-filled. There was nothing else in all the world. His form, his face, were lost in shadow, did not exist. But his gaze compelled her, held her in hypnotic power. Somewhere she could hear the passionate beating of a drum, and did not know it was her own heart. The red light of the brazier, refreshed with dried animal droppings, flared up and faded, flared up and filled all the yurt with its bloody reflection. The serving-women were stricken immobile and silent with fear. They could not move, could look only at the deformed black-faced man sitting on the bed, the bright lamp in his hands, and the beautiful woman with her tranced face, her long body covered with the embroidered film of her silken robe. And the great winds outside, as though mysteriously enchanted, fell into silence also.

Houlun spoke in a clear but faint voice, not looking away from her brother's eyes. "Yes, Kurelen, I hear thee."

He spoke again, monotonously, gently: "Soon thou wilt sleep, and wilt not awaken until I call thee. Thou wilt dream dreams of our home, and our father. Thou wilt ride again with me, over the snow-covered steppes, on our Turkoman ponies, and we will see the northern lights flashing in the black sky. And when thou dost awake, thou wilt be refreshed and happy, remembering no pain, and having only joy in thy son."

His illuminated eyes expanded before her dreaming and transfixed gaze, until they filled all the universe. Her soul seemed to stream out of her body like wisps of cloud, rushing towards him with a passion of love, desiring only to be lost in him. His eyes were like suns to her, in boundless and chaotic darkness.

Her arms relaxed, fell to her sides. One hand drooped over the side of the bed; the long fingers brushed the carpet. Her hair and red lips gained an intense life in the gloom.

Very slowly, still murmuring, Kurelen laid aside the lamp. He bent over his sister, took her face between his two hands, and gazed into her half-closed eyes.

"Sleep, Houlun," he whispered. "Sleep."

Her lids dropped. They lay on her cheeks, like fringed scimitars. He laid her head on the bed. She breathed gently, as if profoundly asleep. Kurelen sat and watched her. He heeded the serving-women no more than if they had been the painted figures on the walls. Nor did they move more than if they had been those figures, for they were paralyzed with terror at this strange scene.

Then Kurelen inserted his thin dark hands into his sister's body and seized the head of her child, which had become wedged in the ring of her pelvis. The serving-women, horrified, but still full of terror, sucked in their breath. Very delicately he moved the pulsing head; the bones and flesh relaxed about it. Blood and water gushed forth. Then Kurelen, moving so delicately, so carefully, brought forth the child, inch by inch. It was not half-freed from its mother's body before it wailed aloud, lustily, and threshed its strong arms. Houlun slept, dreaming, smiling, her lips parted, her teeth glistening in lamp and firelight, her garments stained with blood. The women leaned forward, peering and blinking.

"It is a son," said Kurelen, aloud.

The child lay on the bed now, kicking and screaming, still tied to his mother by his cord. Kurelen sat and admired the child, playfully moved its head from side to side. "It is a fine fellow," he remarked. In one of the child's fists was clenched a lump of congealed blood.

He called to Yasai, without glancing at her. "Wash the child, and cover it. And first, cut the cord."

Yasai snatched up the infant, and glowered at Kurelen, as though he threatened it. Another woman cut the cord, and ministered to Houlun. But Houlun still slept. Rugs covered her feet; her cheek was pressed to her bed, and she continued to smile, as though absorbed in the sweetest dreams. The child wailed and screamed. And now the winds returned, fiercer and wilder than ever.

Kurelen stood up. All at once he appeared exhausted. He seemed broken, drained of vitality. While the women busied themselves with the child, exclaiming and clucking, and ignoring the man, he stood beside his sister and watched her for a long time. Finally one of the women plucked him impertinently by the sleeve of his long woolen coat.

"Wilt thou not wake her now, and let her see her son?"

Kurelen was silent for so long that the woman believed he had not heard her. His face was strange and dark, full of meditative sadness, and something grim besides. His hands were folded in his sleeves.

"No," he said at last, "I shall not wake her yet. Let her dream. That is the best of life."

chapter 3

Yesukai rode in just after the red and purple desert dawn, accompanied by his wide and savage riders, his captives and his loot.

Kurelen, standing at the door of his sister's yurt, watched his brother-in-law ride in. He had no particular aversion or liking for Yesukai. Nor did he have disdain, for he thought Yesukai's kind extremely useful. His was rather the lazy and amused tolerance of the intelligent man for the simple, oxlike man, who provided sustenance whereby the intelligent person might live without undue labor. There was even a kind of indifferent gratitude in him for Yesukai. He professed to take his sister's husband seriously, thereby assuring himself of continued moderate comforts and peace of mind. Sometimes he baited Yesukai, but with discretion, for, as he said, only a foolish horse quarrels with his oat-bag. A clever man contrived to pass his life with as little exertion as possible and as little pain. Existence was a painful affair; only a fool complicated it with strife and dissension, for the evanescent comfort of occasionally speaking his mind or fighting. If Kurelen spoke his mind at all, publicly, it was in such euphemistic terms that only his sister, and perhaps the Shaman, understood. Yesukai was too elemental, too guileless to comprehend at all; Kurelen had first made sure of this.

Kurelen, who loved beauty, and the rhythm that was beauty itself, commented to himself again, as always, that there was a flow and poetry about the person and movements of this petty noble of the endless steppes. There he rode into his ordu on his fierce stallion, his lithe young body clad in a long wool coat, his pointed hat high on his proud-held head, a Turkish scimitar stuck through his blue leather belt. It was always evident that he thought, in his simplicity, that he was a great khan, and that his tiny confederation of tribes and smoldering clans was a terrible nomadic empire. Kurelen, who knew the mighty civilization of Cathay, suave and beautiful and adult and decadent, smiled at the pride of this baghatur, this childlike adventurer of the plateaus and the desert. The theatres of Cathay often produced deft and corrupt comedies, in which the ridiculous buffoon, decked out in a prodigious number of yak tails, was one of these "corporals," one of these turbulent and amusing barbarians. Yet Kurelen admitted to himself that all the involved beauty of Chinese paintings, depraved and painted and gilded though they were, was not half so splendid as one of these barbarians. Under Yesukai's high pointed hat, which was made of felt, was a youthful and handsome face as untamed, yet as simple, as an innocent beast's. The restless eyes were savage and uncivilized, but there was the clarity of the desert in them. The skin was dark and bronzed, but it was the color of desert hills with the sun fallen behind them. He had a nose like the beak of a bird of prey, but it gave his expression a primitive fierceness that possessed something of grandeur. His back was straight, his waist slender. As he wheeled and cavorted in the dust, Kurelen admired the perfect magnificence of his posture, so unaffected, so artlessly proud.

Yesukai was a reserved man, but this morning it was evident he was excited, for all his efforts at composure. His warriors and hunters whooped and screamed, and brandished whips, lariats, and weapons. Their garments blew back; they waved their hats; their dark bearded lips grinned joyously. Their haul had been excellent. They had encountered a Tatar caravan, which they had discovered was a convoy for Karait and Naiman traders on the way from Cathay to a Karait town. The caravan consisted of horses and camels, laden with tea, spices, silver, silk, carpets, manuscripts and musical instruments, embroidered garments, jewelry, turquoises, and jewel-encrusted weapons, and many other luxurious items, the excreta of civilization. Among the traders were a Buddhist monk and a Nestorian Christian priest, the first as a missionary and teacher, the second the last of a band of missionaries which had been slaughtered coming from India to Hsi-Hsia. He had begged, in Cathay, to be allowed to go along with some caravan to his home near the Sea of Aral, and as he agreed to carry his own food and supplies, the permission had been granted.

The Mongols had dispatched Tatars and traders with great facility, after a ferocious fight. The Tatars and Karaits were brave fighters, but they were outnumbered. Yesukai had spared the priests, for he was even more superstitious than the average Mongol, and besides, the Buddhist asserted, upon questioning, that he was a deft weaver, and the Nestorian that he was an excellent tanner of hides. Many of the traders had brought their wives with them, and Yesukai carefully picked the fairest and youngest, and dispatched the rest with their husbands. He had selected an extraordinarily beautiful Karait girl for himself, his second wife, and he had brought her back to his ordu, along with his other loot, on the back of a camel. The girl wept without ceasing, and wept loudest whenever Yesukai looked at her, which was often. But he was not deceived that she was inconsolable.

All the Mongols who had not taken the flocks to pasture swarmed out to greet the returning lord and his warriors, and exclaim over the loot. The Mongol women fingered the silks and put on the silver bracelets, and snatched, and quarrelled with each other, jealously. The old men cackled sensually over the women, licking their lips and rubbing their bodies, enviously, for they knew that these women were for the warriors, and not for them. One of them was a woman of the Turkomans, and she sat proudly on her camel, unspeaking, her veil fallen thickly over her face. The warriors, their shoulders and backs loaded, began to carry their portions into their yurts, where their women could soon be heard exclaiming gleefully. The children seized on the musical instruments, and soon the ordu resounded with the din of discordant sounds, which mingled with the screams of the camels, the shrilling of the horses, the hoarse and jubilant voices of the men, and the excited barks of the dogs. The frightful heat of the desert was already shimmering over the tent village and the red and jagged distant hills; the river glittered, yellow-gray and sluggish, wild birds fluttering over it, and over its narrow strips of grayish fertile borders. Campfires were burning, and the odors of cooking mutton filled the dry air.

Yesukai, momentarily forgetting the Karait girl, came straight to the yurt of his wife. Kurelen met him on the platform. The crippled man smiled into the face of the dust-stained barbarian. "Thou hast a son," he said. "It is a memorable day, this birth of the son of a great khan, in the year of the Swine, in the Calendar of the Twelve Beasts." He smiled again, reverently, for Kurelen considered flattery the cheapest yet most efficacious coin with which to buy ease and freedom from labor. Had he not said: "The fool prepares; the wise man eats"?

Yesukai's broad tight mouth opened in a smile of childlike gratification. He thrust past Kurelen, who was obliged to step aside. He entered the yurt. Houlun still slept, her cheek in her hand. She, too, was smiling, strangely, deeply. A serving-woman squatted on the floor, the swaddled and screaming child in her arms. Yesukai brought force and turbulence into the yurt with him; in the gloom his barbarian's eyes sparkled fiercely. He looked only at his son; with a shout he raised it high in his arms. He looked about him with a savage smile. He cried out, lifting the child towards the roof of the yurt, as one who presents a treasure to a god, for the god's amazed delight, thought Kurelen, who was standing in the aperture of the door.

Yesukai exultantly called upon the gods to witness the strength and beauty of his firstborn, descendant of the Bourchikoun, the Gray-eyed Men, and more ancient descendant of the blue wolf who had conceived the Yakka Mongols. This was the descendant of Kabul Khan, who had laughed in the face of the Emperor of Cathay, and had impudently tweaked him by the beard. This child would be the greatest of them all, for was not his father's sworn brother the mighty Khan of the Karaits, Toghrul, most formidable of the desert hordes, the one known among the Christians as Prester John? The whole Gobi would tremble at his tread; the red and white hills would melt before him; the rivers would rise and make new pastures for his herds, where only desert smoldered before! The treasures of Cathay, the fairest women of Tibet and India and Samarkand and Baghdad, would all be his. Cities would fall before him! Ah! Yesukai's eyes grew fiercer and wilder. He replaced the bellowing infant in his nurse's arms. He must see the Shaman at once, for surely the Chief Shaman, Kokchu, would testify that he spoke truth. No doubt, observed Kurelen wryly to himself. He regarded Yesukai with detached curiosity. The barbarian's vitality and passion seemed to fill the yurt with a wind, so that Kurelen would not have been surprised had the felt separated itself from the wattled rods and been violently blown to the heavens.

Yesukai called for the Shaman, but before the serving-woman could rise to her feet and obey, he rushed impetuously from the yurt, himself, shouting at the top of his voice. Kurelen remarked to himself that Yesukai would, without doubt, be delayed far longer than he expected. The Shaman would have many a word with him, before returning to the yurt. So Kurelen prudently decided that he must awaken Houlun.

He stood beside her bed. The serving-woman scowled at him, covered the screaming infant's face. But Kurelen was not interested in the child; he saw only Houlun. He laid his hand on her forehead, bent over her. His face took on an inscrutable expression, sad and somber, and very dark. He said aloud, in a quiet and steadfast voice: "Awake, my sister. Awake."

She did not move. The scowling serving-woman bent forward avidly, a look of malicious pleasure on her face. Houlun did not move; her smile only deepened, almost imperceptibly. He has enchanted her, thought the woman, and if she does not awaken, they will kill him. She licked her lips; her eyes gleamed with malignant hatred.

Kurelen continued to bend over his sister, his hand on her forehead. He was silent. The inscrutable expression deepened on his face. His eyes narrowed. A terrible struggle was taking place in that yurt. A struggle between the wills of the sleeping woman and the man who sought to wake her. Above the bed two invisible antagonists clenched each other in their arms, and stood locked, immobile, staring into the other eyes. The struggle went on, moment after moment. Something in the air stilled the child's cries, and he fell to whimpering softly, as though terrified. Beads of sweat burst out on Kurelen's wrinkled forehead; they rolled slowly down his cheeks, like drops of quicksilver. The serving-woman lifted her shoulders to her ears in thin and unholy glee.

Kurelen said silently, to the will of his sister: Awaken. Thou must awaken. Thou canst not triumph over me. Houlun, awaken.

But Houlun slept. A subtle smile curved her lips.

Kurelen lifted his head alertly. There was an approaching commotion. It was Yesukai, accompanied by Kokchu, Kurelen's deadly enemy, and several of the rejoicing warriors. The barking of the dogs preceded them like the fanfares of an army. Kurelen's wet lips suddenly parched; salt water filled his mouth. Anger and terror rose up in him. His eyes dilated, flashed.

He bent over his sister again, in a rage. He seized her hands, bent them inwards, and there was a faint cracking of bones, loud in the breathless stillness of the yurt. Then he pressed his thumbs against her eyelids, and forced them open. Haste and panic and greater rage were in his gestures. He said in his mind to his sister, with contempt and fear: Thou art a coward, because thou wilt not awaken. But awaken for me. They are at the door of the yurt, and are about to enter. If thou dost not awaken, they will kill me. I command thee in the name of our love to awaken, Houlun. I hate life, but I hate death more, and greater than these, I hate pain. (Her glazed dull eyes seemed to regard him like the eyes of the dead.)

Yesukai's face appeared at the door, dark and ominous. He was entering. A faint moan rose like a bubble in Houlun's throat. She moved her head. The serving-woman drew in a breath of acrid disappointment. She cried out eagerly to Yesukai, who was approaching the bed, his short curved sword in his hand: "He hath enchanted her!" Behind Yesukai loomed the tall lean figure of the robed Shaman, his long face smiling with evil anticipation.

Kurelen stood upright. His features were pallid and sickly with exhaustion. He looked at his sister; he knew he had won. He said aloud, in a quiet voice: "She hath suffered much, and slept profoundly. But she is awakening now, to greet her lord."

Yesukai did not speak; he stood beside his wife's bed. He fixed his menacing eyes on Kurelen. Then Houlun moaned again, moved her head on her pillow as though she were suffering, then opened her eyes. They were still glazed, but now there was a faint light of recognition in them. And she, too, looked only at Kurelen.

He smiled at her, as one smiles at a child who has come back along the dim road to death. "Thou hast slept long, my sister," he said in the gentlest of voices.

The Shaman came forward now, in a fury of disappointment and hatred. "Thou didst enchant her!" he accused. "It is not thy fault she did not die!"

But Kurelen ignored him as a noble might ignore the clamor of a herdsman. He said to Yesukai, with an indulgent smile: "She will live long to bear thee other mighty sons."

Yesukai scratched his ear, uncertainly. He began to tuck his sword within his belt. He regarded Houlun, and began to smile foolishly. He loved her very much. He bent over her and kissed her passionately upon the lips. "I have brought back many treasures, and thou shalt have the pick of them, Houlun, for thou hast given me the greatest treasure of all."

The Shaman grimaced contemptuously. He turned and stared at Kurelen with fury. But Kurelen only grinned, and poked him in the holy chest with one long crooked finger.

"Again, thou must sacrifice only mutton, or horse meat, on this auspicious occasion, Kokchu," he said. "But, go to! Thou are skillful with the knife, and doubtless thou canst delicately prolong the agony of the beast."

Enraged, Kokchu struck aside that crooked finger. He stepped back with a violent gesture, as though repelling a sacrilegious and unclean touch. Hatred and madness contorted his features. His eyes blazed. Kurelen burst out into a scream of laughter.

"Waste not thy imagination upon me, Kokchu! Go out and think awhile, and prophesy greatly concerning this noble son of the Yakka Mongols! But thou wilt, I know, be able to conjure up the most amazing things in the manner of priests!"

And he went out of the yurt, laughing louder than ever.

chapter 4

He was much elated, and exquisitely amused, and kept laughing aloud to himself as he wound his crippled way through the aisles of the yurts. He did not seem to see the scowls that greeted him on every hand. Finally he stopped. Two of the captives, the Buddhist monk and the Nestorian Christian priest, were sitting disconsolately on the piles of their belongings, wiping their dusty faces with their sleeves. No one noticed them particularly, though a ring of dogs barked at them threateningly. Kurelen kicked at the leader of the dogs, and sent him howling on his way, accompanied by his followers.

Kurelen regarded the captives with interest. The Buddhist monk had a mild and gentle face, the color of yellow ivory. His slanting eyes were full of patience. His woolen robe was in tatters, and his feet were bare and bleeding, and crusted with dirt. He had removed his pointed hat, and the bitter sun gleamed like a halo of fire about his bald pate. At his belt hung his beads and his prayer wheel. His hands were folded in his lap; he seemed to be sunken in some melancholy and supernatural revery. The Christian priest, however, had a bolder air. Kurelen commented to himself that this man was a barbarian, not a member of the civilized race of Cathay, such as was the monk. He had a dark and angry face, and a questing and hungry eye. He kept scratching his ragged beard and hair impatiently, and destroying the lice he found there, with a petty vindictiveness. His woolen robe was not tattered; the pile of his belongings was much larger than that of the monk's. Moreover, he wore a respectable dagger in an ivory sheath. He was a bigger man, a more virile man, than the monk, and a younger. At his belt, on a rope, swung a wooden cross.

Kurelen could not place him immediately. He said: "What is thy country, priest?"

The man stared at him bellicosely for so long a time that Kurelen began to believe he did not understand his language. But finally he answered shortly, in Kurelen's tongue, but with an unfamiliar accent: "I come from the land of the Sea of Aral."

Kurelen smiled. "Thou wilt be excellent friends with our Shaman," he remarked. He turned to the Buddhist monk, who had not heeded him, so deep was he fallen in his melancholy revery. He spoke to him in the tongue of Cathay, and at that beloved sound the monk lifted his head, and he smiled, and his eyes filled with tears.

"Do not be cast down," said Kurelen, softly. He squatted beside the monk and gazed at him with a humorous smile. "We are not bad men. Go thy way, and hold thy tongue, and no harm will befall thee."

The priest, however, had lived in Cathay, and understood some of the language. He made an angry sound. "My father is a prince!" he cried.

Kurelen glanced at him whimsically over his shoulder.

"The whole accursed place is full of princes," he observed. "Be wise; accustom thyself. But, as I said, no doubt thou wilt be excellent friends with our Shaman. There is a blood brother for you!"

Again he turned his attention to the monk, who had begun to weep. Kurelen lifted his eyebrows curiously. The monk rocked on his belongings, and mourned. "The Lord sent me forth, to bring light into the heathen and the lost, and hath delivered me into the pit of the desert, where no lamp falls."

Kurelen shrugged. "Well, then, shed thy lamp. But I warn thee, do not compete with the Shaman. He hath nasty manners."

The priest had the most profound contempt for the Buddhist, and kept darting disdainful glances at him.

"Thy god is an evil spirit, but mine is the Way of Truth. Here shall I set up his standard and his cross, and call these dwellers in the darkness into the Eternal Light."

Kurelen smiled at him contemplatively. The priest shifted with rage on his belongings, pulled his beard, glared about him, snorted. "Where is the chief?" he shouted. "I shall not be treated thus! I am the son of a prince!"

Kurelen said: "Wert thou not driven out of Cathay? If I remember rightly, thou and thy kind kicked up a foul stink in that land, and the emperor courteously ejected ye."

But the priest only snorted again, disdainfully refusing to answer.

Kurelen inquired as to the names of the monk and priest. The Buddhist informed him that his name was Jelmi, and that he came from an ancient family of Mandarins. Ah, thought Kurelen, that accounts for his gentleness and courtesy, his modesty and forbearance. Only the truly noble, of mind and flesh, had these qualities. The priest at first ignored Kurelen's question, and then haughtily announced that his name was Seljuken, and repeated more loudly that his father was a prince. Kurelen grinned. He knew these wild "princes" of steppe and salt lake, these tiny potentates who ate half-cooked meat and depended for livelihood on raids and murder.

Another lively commotion in the distance informed Kurelen that Yesukai had left his wife's yurt, and was proceeding about the business of disposing of the loot. His new wife, the Karait girl, was assigned to a yurt, and serving-women given her. Yesukai disappeared into this yurt, and did not emerge again. Kurelen, who had begun to wander about again, kicking at the dogs, and inquisitively inspecting the piles of stolen goods, grimaced as he passed the yurt of the new wife. He paused to listen. There was no sound from behind the fastened flap.

He went back to his sister. She was holding her son in her arms, and he was sucking her naked breast. Her face was cold and averted, and she held the child carelessly. But when her brother entered, her eyes warmed, and she smiled at him. He patted her shoulder, bent over the little one, and pinched one hard rosy cheek. The child made an impatient flapping movement with one strong hand, but in spite of the pain of the pinch he continued about his strong and earnest business.

"Ah," said Kurelen, "it is a fine fellow. Dost thou think he looks like me, perhaps?"

Houlun laughed. She regarded the child with some interest, and slowly a look of pride reluctantly appeared on her face. "I think not. He hath not thy sweetness of expression." They chuckled together. She twisted a tendril of the child's hair about her fingers. "Look at this hair! As red-gold as the evening sunset! And his eyes are as gray as the desert sands." Then in a hesitant voice, from which she tried to keep the newly awakened pride, she said: "Surely he will be a great man?"

"Oh, I have no doubt," he answered largely. She glanced at him with quick suspicion, but nothing could have been blander than his look. She pressed the child fiercely to her breast, and cried:

"Thou shalt teach him to read, and thou shalt take him to strange lands, Kurelen! Surely he will be a great man, for he is my son, and he is all my life!"

Kurelen pursed his lips thoughtfully. He pinched the baby's ear. He playfully pulled the small round face away from the mother's breast. At this insult the little one raised a great and infuriated shout, and threw his naked limbs about in a frenzy of anger. Kurelen laughed delightedly. He pushed the child's face against the swelling breast, and after a few outraged snufflings, the child resumed his tugging.

Then Kurelen spoke quietly, in a peculiar voice: "He is all thy life, thou dost say. But, perhaps he is also his father's life. Do not teach him to hate his father, Houlun. It is a terrible thing for the soul of a son, if he hateth his father. I know."

And then he turned and went out of the yurt. Houlun watched him go, frowning. She held the child closely to her. She felt his strong lips at her breast. "He is my life," she muttered, and frowned again.

chapter 5

Yesukai exultantly celebrated his triumph and the birth of his son with a great feast, and his people celebrated joyously with him. Life was harsh for these people, these inhabitants of the mighty snowy steppes, the terrible empty plains, the red and glittering mountains, the deserts which were as dry and colorless as an old man's beard. Wind and lightning, dust and hail, thunder and barrens, ice and tempests, were the familiars of their lives. They knew no settled home, these nomads, but must travel with the seasons, fleeing before the gale-filled white onslaughts of the most frightful winters, and fleeing, in the summer, from drought and sand, from desert heat and desert storms. Hunger was the specter that sat with them at every meal, no matter how plentiful an occasional one might be. The ease and security of the townsmen was not theirs; often they surged up to the great Wall that protected the people of Cathay from their barbarian influence, but few, except traders, ever entered within that stony guardian. Sometimes these hordes squatted outside the Walls, and looked enviously at the fat men who came and went through the gates on business. They would squat there disconsolately, when pastures had been arid, and cattle and horses had died, and they would rub their lean and empty bellies, hating the townsmen. But when the pastures had been good, and raids profitable, they despised the suetty inhabitants of the towns, and spoke ringingly of the glory of freedom, and the wild steppes with the pale shadows of the sun flying across them, and the northern lights which wheeled magnificently across the winter skies for the joy of free men, and of untrod valleys where the city men never ventured.

Only those who live dangerously can rejoice fully. So each marriage or death or birth was the occasion for unrestrained levity and festivity. Then they killed their fat horses and sheep, and filled their cups with kumiss and rice wine, and danced, and shouted, and clapped their hands, and laughed uproariously. The laughter of the nomad was the laughter of ferocious beasts, freed for the moment of the exigencies of his life, and its constant fear and danger and strife. The townsmen, fat and fastidious and bored, did not laugh like this, for ease does not breed great laughter that rises simultaneously from the belly and the soul. The laughter of townsmen, as Kurelen said, came thinly from the brain, and was as acrid as desert water, and as brackish. The mirth that came from the brain was acid and malicious, and rose mostly from the contemplation of the folly of mankind. It was not good mirth, though amusing to the initiated, who hated other men. Kurelen had observed that pain and suffering, privation and uncertainty, hardship and struggle, were the fuel that made the tremendous fires of revelry, and made the very earth dance in joyous sympathy, as she never danced for the luxurious and the peaceful.

As night approached the campfires began to burn with a vivid orange flame in the plum-colored twilight. The flaps of the dome-shaped yurts were open, and the braziers blazed red within. The vault of heaven was lost in immense mauve mists, but to the east the hills, carved and turreted, jutting and falling, were inexorable ramparts hewn of a brilliant and rosy jade, rippling with heliotrope. Above the hills, the curve of the earth, colossal and diffused, was a bow of purple. The west streamed tremendously with violent yellow banners, as raw as new gold, slashed with an icy and translucent green. The earth floated like a mirage, and took on strange colors, the broken windswept plains imbued with shadows of gray and lavender, blue and umber. The immense and lonely silence of the Gobi seemed to fall out of infinitude upon the earth, and even the voice of the gray-yellow river was lost in that silence. Brighter and brighter, with a pathetic bravery, the orange flames of the little campfires soared upwards, and the voices of the people were frail and tenuous in the unearthly and luminous air of the desert, the chirping of crickets in the face of a universal dream. Like tiny black crickets, they moved between and behind the fires, seemingly endowed with a febrile and pointless life, leaping and moving. In the near distance the spined and twisted desert trees, contorted as though tortured beyond endurance, seemed to be moving upon the ordu like aisles of menacing monsters, bristling with strange and brandished weapons, voiceless monster nightmares invading that universal dream.

All at once the earth and the sky were blighted in a darkness that was like the dropping of a veil. And then into this intense night sprang a colossal and blazing moon, seemingly from behind a western hill, without warning, without the milklike diffusion attendant on moons of more humid climates. Earth and sky were illuminated in sharp spectral light, colorless but intense; distances lost vagueness, advanced into the foreground, distinct and imminent. Ranges of chaotic and broken hills, scores of miles away, seemed but a few moments' walk. Every pebble, every piece of gravel, on the desert floor, gleamed in a frail and bitter radiance. Huge globular stars appeared within reach of a horseman's hand; their fiery shining was not dimmed even by the moon. In this universe of blackness and blazing whiteness, these transparent grays and sharp-edged shadows, the dung-fires, orange and red, were little fantastic banners. And again, the ice-laden winds fell upon the earth, hollow-voiced, laden with mysterious echoes, blowing with moonlight, coming winged with awfulness from heaven.

Men were already laughing hoarsely about the fires, for this was to be a noble ikhudur, the finest festival in many a day. The superstitious Mongols were greatly excited over the story of the congealed lump of blood in the fist of the first-born of Yesukai. Clearly, it was a sign from the spirits of the air and sky. Clearly, it indicated that this was no ordinary child of a chieftain. This was to be some great Khan, perhaps a kha khan, who would win enormous pasturage for his people, and humble the fat townsmen to their knees. Warriors, completely armed with bows and arrow-cases, short curved swords and lances, dressed in thick felt coats and sheepskins, tanned leather jackets, lacquer breastplates, their lean dark faces coated with grease, were drinking heavily and excitedly laughing, or repeating the story of the lump of blood. Old men wandered from fire to fire, playing on one-stringed fiddles, and droning tales of mighty heroes and tribal forebears in thin and wavering voices. Cups of rice wine were lifted to them as reward, and they drank, wiping their wet beards with the backs of their gnarled hands. All was blackness and moonlight beyond the fires, but here the orange fires were rudely carved on dark and savage cheek and lip, on a jut of chin, in the sockets of fierce and open eyes. Here the crude colors on a round lacquered shield of leather suddenly were revealed to the minutest detail; here the blade of a scimitar or a sword blazed; here there was a glitter and flash of white teeth. Beyond the fires were the smooth black beehive mounds of the yurts, through the flaps of which the women came and went, laden with wine and mutton and sweetmeats. The women were allowed to sit behind the warriors near the fires, but the young children skirmished and fought, and struggled with each other and the dogs for morsels of food. The uproar and the laughter and music assaulted the dark arching caverns of the limitless skies, and the winds answered, thundering, and tossed the fires.

It was very cold, and almost time to move on to winter pastures. The dung fires had to be continually replenished, and the warriors put on extra coats of embroidered felt, and rubbed their hands. Cattle and sheep and camels and horses, disturbed, could be heard in their uneasiness.

The songs of the savage and wild were rarely songs of love, but songs of courage, of heroes, of valiant deeds, of the friendship of man for man. To these the warriors listened, sometimes joining in the chorus with hoarse and exultant voices. Near one fire an old man, strumming on his fiddle, sang:

"Khan of forty-thousand tents is our noble lord.
Son of the blue wolf is our khan, the blue wolf
Who ran on the white steppes like a shadow, voiceless.
Who shall defy our lord, he who stands before the moon,
Brighter than the moon, with his lance and his banners?
Who shall defy his son, the beloved of his people?"

And the warriors shouted exultantly:

"Who shall defy our lord, and the son of our lord?
His eyes are the color of the gray desert. His heart
Is iron. Who shall defy the lord, the kha khan?"

Kurelen, squatting in his sister's tent while she wrapped the baby in some soft silken stuff, sewn with precious stones, helped himself to Turkish sweetmeats from a silver box. The sweetmeats were made of the fragrance and substance of roses, and they filled the fire-lighted yurt with heavenly odors. Kurelen, appreciative, licked his fingers, ate some more. He began to hum in his singularly beautiful voice:

"Who shall defy our lord, and the son of our lord?"

And burst out laughing, shaking his head, stuffing his mouth.

Houlun frowned. In the past it had not displeased her for Kurelen to mock Yesukai. In fact, she had laughed also; but now she was displeased. Her eye gleamed angrily as she glanced at her brother. She said:

"Thou art disturbing the child, Kurelen, with thy noise."

Kurelen grinned at her, raised his eyebrows. "Surely not," he said mockingly. "What a superb song that is: Hark:

" 'Khan of forty thousand tents is our noble lord.
His tents are full of riches and beautiful women.
His cattle roam the plains and the cloud-touched hills.
Great is the lord, the kha khan, the blessed of heaven!' "

Houlun affected to be absorbed in wrapping the boy. "Thou art so silly, Kurelen," she remarked, without looking at her brother. "Besides, why art thou always eating?"

Kurelen, grinning again, shrugged. "What else is there left in the world for a sensible man?" And he sucked his fingers with a loud noise.

He looked about for something more to eat. There was a silver plate of boiled mutton and herbs. He picked up a large section and ate it with relish, biting at it with his long white teeth. Houlun stopped her work to stare at him distastefully, then, catching his teasing eye, she was forced to laugh herself. She put down the child, and, still sitting, reached over to a tabouret and poured her brother a cup of rice wine, and thrust it at him indulgently. Her long black hair fell across her bare arms; her beautiful gray eyes were full of love. He took the cup, but did not drink. An inscrutable shadow fell across his face as he contemplated her. Lying beside his mother on the bed, the baby kicked furiously at the confining swathes of the gleaming silken stuff. There was sudden silence in the yurt, but the songs and the laughter and the shouting outside were louder than ever. The yurt trembled in the gales of wind.

Then Kurelen looked at the baby and seemed to muse. "Ah, yes," he said, softly, "it is indeed a fine fellow."

Houlun, startled, turned her head slowly and regarded her son. A slow and ineffable smile touched her lips. She lifted him in her arms and pressed him against her breast. The swaddling clothes had been intended for a Turkoman princess's wedding gown; they were the color of roses, and had a petal-like gleam. The gems with which they were embroidered glittered red and blue. The hems were sewn with pearls.

"No doubt," said Kurelen, "it will be a kha khan."

The intelligent Houlun was no longer intelligent. She gazed at Kurelen with brilliant eyes. "Oh, dost thou think so, truly?" she cried.

Kurelen was about to laugh again, but the laugh died, aborted. His eyelids drew together. He nodded. "No doubt," he repeated, and his sister did not hear his irony.

Yesukai and his warriors were coming for the child for the naming ceremony. Houlun was not to be present, not only because she was a woman, but because she was still weak from the birth. The child was closely swaddled now, and red in the face with infantile rage. Houlun wrapped him in a short coat of sables, to protect him from the night air. Yesukai, drunk and excited, wild-eyed, young and glorious, appeared at the flap, and shouted for his son. He wore the treasured sable coat of his father; beneath it he wore a white woolen coat, richly embroidered with red and blue. The flaps of his fur hat were turned upwards, and Kurelen could see his sweating forehead.

He took the child from Houlun's arms. She surrendered the infant as though the gesture wounded her. Yesukai ignored Kurelen. He was at the door when he heard Kurelen's mild ingratiating voice:

"I have said the child will be at least a kha khan, Yesukai."

Yesukai turned. His handsome and simple face lighted with ecstasy and pride. "Dost thou think so? But what else could be expected of a son of the gray-eyed men, Kurelen?"

Kurelen rose indolently. He scratched his chin, and affected to be engrossed in studying the infant, who had begun to bellow.

"Ah, yes," murmured Kurelen. He seemed to be struck with a thought. "I had a strange dream last night. I saw a man on a golden throne, sitting in a great yurt, surrounded by hundreds of noble warriors with circlets about their heads. At his side sat princesses of Cathay and Samarkand. It was the greatest of all khans. And I knew it was thy son, Yesukai."

Yesukai beamed. He seemed to swell with egotism. He jiggled the child in his arms. He could hardly contain himself. He made a faint deprecating sound. And then he started to go again. And again Kurelen's voice halted him.

"Yesukai, one of thy captives is a priest, and another a holy man from Cathay. I saw the priest haranguing some of thy people. This is very bad. It will create dissension. Tell those two to close their mouths on pain of death."

Yesukai frowned haughtily. "My father had many religions among his people, without harm."

Kurelen shook his head gently. "But not this kind. I have seen them in Cathay. What dissensions they created! The emperor was courteous and tolerant, for he was a wise man. But wisdom is sometimes mistaken for weakness by arrogant men. It was necessary for the emperor to resort to massacres to put down those of his people incited against him by the Christians. It is said he wept. Then, I was in Samarkand, and there I saw, too——"

"Thou hast seen too many things," interrupted Yesukai rudely and went out with his son.

There was a little silence in the tent. Then Kurelen, as though remembering the last words of Yesukai, said gently and musingly to himself: "No doubt. No doubt." And shook his head, and smiled, mockingly.

Kurelen wandered about among the yurts and the fires, looking for a space where he could secure warmth and food and wine. But as he was so disliked, no one made room for him, but instead, closed up what little space there was. The women grimaced at him, for they were concerned only with comeliness of the body, and they believed, too, that Kurelen despised them. He limped from fire to fire, shivering in his felt coat, the hood pulled about his long dark face with the long white teeth and the glittering, cynical eyes. Finally, he came on the smallest dung fire of them all, and here, practically deserted, crouched the priest, Seljuken, and the Buddhist monk, Jelmi. A pot of boiling horse meat was on the fire, and there was a plenitude of wine, for the Mongol law of hospitality was an important one. Seljuken was eating sullenly, tearing the bits of meat from the bone with a vicious air. But Jelmi drank only a small quantity of wine. He sat, gazing with gentle melancholy into the fire, and seemed to have forgotten where he was. At intervals he sighed, rubbed his torn and swollen feet. Seljuken ignored him, kept leaning rudely across him to fill his cup from the sack of kumiss.

Kurelen squatted on the other side of the fire, and greeted the two holy men with friendly words. Seljuken grunted over stuffed jowls, but Jelmi answered the Merkit's words with great courtesy and gentleness. His melancholy lightened; he smiled. When Kurelen began to speak to him in the language of Cathay, the thin tired face of the monk beamed with delight, and his eyes filled with tears.

Kurelen spoke to him of Cathay, of its temples and its bells, its mighty buildings, its streets, its scholars and its great learning, its philosophers and musicians and teachers, its academies and its palaces. Jelmi glowed with pride; his tears fell. "My father was a friend of the old emperor," he said, "and his manuscripts are still the treasures of the palaces. He was a poet. His name was Ch'un Chin."

"Is that so, in truth?" exclaimed Kurelen. "I know many of his poems. Was not one called 'The Polished Bowl Upturned'?"

Jelmi smiled deprecatingly and shook his head. "My father was a great cynic. And a great lover. He believed nothing, not even that he believed nothing. One must make allowances —"

Kurelen chuckled, in remembrance. "The Persian poets cannot equal him. The Persians declare that nothing is of importance. But only the Chinese believe that. Poetry without belief is only strings of bright and empty beads strung on worthless gut. They shine and attract the eye, but are without value."

Seljuken, listening to this extraordinary conversation in the voiceless immensity of the Gobi desert, stared, his mouth open, his teeth slowly chewing. An expression of contempt finally came over his face, and he dismissed these imbeciles with a shrug. He thought to himself with pride: My father is a prince.

Kurelen continued to converse with the monk. He laughed continually, and his teeth glistened; his shoulders rose about his ears. His hands flew about, with vehement gestures. There was a singular vitality about him, which manifested itself in the thin acrid smile, the sudden gleam of his sardonic eyes. Jelmi laughed softly at Kurelen's witticisms; his melancholy lifted, and as is the way with all scholars and wise men, he forgot the misery of his present state in the exaltation and ecstasy of words that emanate from the brain and not the belly. He might have been in his father's house again, a house filled with ivory and teakwood, with precious rugs and silken stuff, with gold-encrusted ceramics and jade and incense, and Kurelen might have been one of those gay and cynic philosophers of whom his father was so fond.

He cried at last: "But how strange for thee to remain here, in this wilderness, when thou art so learned!"

Kurelen grimaced. "I am not so learned. I have merely a facility for words, a quick mind that has memorized the gestures and the phrases of wisdom. But I have no real learning. I am too lazy. I prefer to eat," and he helped himself to a tender morsel on Jelmi's plate. Nevertheless, he was pleased. Jelmi shook his head with gentle denial of Kurelen's deprecating assertions.

Kurelen, his mouth full, regarded the monk thoughtfully. "But I have one word of wisdom, however, for both of you. Our Chief Shaman, Kokchu, is a vengeful man. I observed him watching you today, with no pleasant expression, when ye were speaking to our people. I advise you to remain subservient to him. He has knowledge of many poisons."

Seljuken snorted disdainfully. "We Christians are bidden to go to the ends of the world, and dispense the words of the Lord, even though threatened with death and torture."

Kurelen raised his eyebrows. "Speak not so loosely about torture. Thou dost not know the inventiveness of the Shaman. Nevertheless, I have warned thee."

"I shall dispense the truth!" said Seljuken, angrily, though he glanced about him with an uneasy eye.

Kurelen chewed meditatively, and when he replied, he looked

at Jelmi, dismissing the priest as an unlearned man. "Truth," he said, "wears many different coats, and is the harlot of many masters. One of thy father's poems, I remember, was a rollicking affair about truth, which he declared was the mercenary of any prince. I trust thou, at least, wilt confine thy version of the truth to thine own thoughts."

He made a sweeping gesture, indicating the many fires, and the throngs of warriors sitting beside them.

"These are strong men, my friend, and rude, and savage. They do not discourse; they take. What need have they for logic, or philosophy? They live these things; they do not converse about them."

"But thou," said Jelmi, with a sweet smile, "dost converse about them."

Kurelen shrugged, swallowed some wine. "I have told thee, my friend: I am lazy."

"But why dost thou not return to Cathay?"

"In Cathay," replied Kurelen, grinning, "I am a fool among wise men. Here, I am a man among beasts. The beasts feed me. In Cathay, they are wiser." He licked his fingers appreciatively, and then smiled blandly at the monk. "Do not forget: I have said they are beasts. Their beasthood is predictable, but civilized men are unpredictable, except in their villainy. Expect evil of every man, and thou wilt not be disappointed."

The uproar about the fires became louder, so that voices were drowned out. Kurelen rose. "My nephew," he said, "is about to be named. I must join the ceremonies." And he walked away. Jelmi watched him with his melancholy eyes. But the priest had eyes for no one; he was pleasantly drunk. Jelmi had not touched the wine in the cup which he held in his hands. The priest rudely took the cup, drank the contents, exhaled noisily, wiping his beard. Jelmi did not notice. His face fell into deep sadness.

Kurelen advanced upon the great fire where Yesukai stood, the infant in his arms. The Shaman was examining the child, and exclaiming over its beauty, and prophesying. When the two men saw Kurelen, they scowled, but said nothing.

The Shaman was saying that as Yesukai's biggest loot had been taken on the day of the child's birth, he ought to be called by the name of the chief that Yesukai had conquered and killed. The name was Temujin. Yesukai was delighted, and the child was immediately named Temujin. The warriors crowded about to look at the little one, and marvelled at his thick golden hair, his fierce gray eyes. The Shaman, excited, promised that that night he would summon a spirit from the Blue Sky, and proffer the child for its custody and protection. Kurelen began to laugh, and the Shaman regarded him with black hatred.

"The last spirit thou didst conjure up, Shaman, appeared in the form of a bear, and killed two handsome children."

The Shaman turned his back on the scoffer, but Yesukai became uneasy. He rewrapped the infant in the sable cloak, and seemed uncertain.

"Perhaps," said Kurelen, who was slightly drunk, "we ought to have other conjurers, too, on this momentous occasion. Call the monk and the priest to attend. Perhaps their spirits will be less murderous."

Yesukai thought this an excellent idea, and sent a herdsman to bid the captives to attend. While they all waited, Kurelen turned to the Shaman. He spoke with cynical ingratiation: "I have warned Yesukai that he must not allow these two holy men to distract the minds of our people with strange doctrines."

The Shaman was amazed; his look of hatred melted away, but his eyes remained wary. Kurelen nodded. "Strange doctrines breed strange feuds. Thou art enough for our people."

Kokchu smiled darkly, but he was still wary. "Thou art wise, Kurelen. But not all men are so wise."

"I think," said Kurelen, "that they ought to be joined to the next caravan, and sent on their way. Especially the monk. I am convinced of his holiness, and perhaps the spirits might be annoyed if he is murdered. But the priest does not impress me as being under the guardianship of any important god— Besides, the winter is coming, and we must move on, and each extra mouth is an extra burden."

Kokchu nodded, smiling evilly. He wet his lips.

Kurelen enlarged on the subject. "The Year of the Swine is not considered a very propitious one for the Yakka Mongols. Perhaps the spirits need placating—a worthy sacrifice. Eh, Kokchu?"

The Shaman replied gravely, but his eyes gleamed: "I am certain thou dost speak truth, Kurelen."

Yesukai had been listening with truculent bewilderment. He said ironically: "The heavens will surely fall, observing you both in agreement."

Kurelen regarded him with immense gravity: "Wise men may disagree on matters of no importance, but on serious things they are of one thought." He poked the Shaman in the belly, and the holy man winced. "Eh, Kokchu?"

The Shaman rubbed the sore spot, shot a fiery look at Kurelen, but answered at once: "Again, thou dost speak truth."

The herdsman returned with Jelmi and Seljuken. The latter was reeling, but the monk walked with serene dignity and quietness. The Shaman examined both men closely. Finally his eye lingered on Jelmi, whom he hated upon sight. And then, very slowly, his eye travelled to Kurelen and back to Jelmi, and the most evil smile lit up his sallow features.

Yesukai wanted the goodwill and the friendship of all gods on this occasion, so he greeted the captives heartily, and assigned them to the warmest places near the fire. The choicest morsels were urged on them, and brimming cups. Jelmi smiled courteously, tried to eat and drink. Seljuken gorged, became boastful. The warriors, amused, kept egging him on to fresh extravagances, and roaring with laughter, poking him with their fists, and refilled his cup. Kurelen squatted near by, grinning, his chin on his knees. The old men twanged their fiddles, the fires glowed brighter, some of the warriors, completely drunken, did an uncouth dance. Against the background of the black night the savage faces were splashed with vivid orange fire, and the crowding eyes were the glittering eyes of savagery. Hoarse voices and cries mingled with the wind, bodies swayed with the songs and the fiddles. Warriors smote the hilts of daggers upon their shields, so that the ice-cold air vibrated like drums. The laughter was like the bellowing of wild beasts.

And like beasts, too, were the warriors, with their huge shaggy coats of marten and fox and bear, the furred hats high over wrinkling foreheads, the bared teeth with their wolf-like glisten. Brothers to the mountain lion and the bear of the ravines, the eagles of the white peaks. Simple and ferocious, mercy to them was an unheard word, and gentleness a sound in an unknown tongue. Kurelen was of their flesh and their land and desert, yet he felt to them as alien as a denizen of that languid and golden civilization behind the Great Wall. He felt corrupt and old, smiling and decadent, lazy and amused, subtle and impotent. He found a place beside Jelmi, and instinctively the two drew together, as men who find themselves in danger. Both constantly shivered, for each moment the air grew more like rarefied ice, and that part of them not turned to the fire slowly became numb, in spite of padded garments of felt and fur. In that air sounds came clear and sharp and imminent, and the cough or laugh at a distant fire intruded into the laughter and shouts of a nearer fire.

Some one remembered that Kurelen had a beautiful voice, and Yesukai commanded him to sing. By this time he was quite drunk. He struggled to his feet, and the firelight fell full on him. His hood had fallen back on his broad and twisted shoulders; his dark face had a gleam and flash on it as from some unseen lightning. The red firelight lay in the folds of his stiff felt coat, and his eye-sockets were full of the lurid redness. He looked at the warriors, and they looked back at him, and their foreheads wrinkled; they muttered to themselves. From other fires hurried other men, hearing that Kurelen was to sing, and three old men, grinning, began to twang their fiddles tentatively. Kurelen flung out his arms with a smile that was at once ribald and sinister, and he laughed. No one laughed with him. The priest, Seljuken, had collapsed in a drunken sleep.

Kurelen bowed to Jelmi, who was gazing at him earnestly and with sadness. "I shall sing one of thy father's songs, translating it roughly for these rude ears," he said. "They will not understand. We shall be amused, thou and I."

"I understand some of thy people's tongue," responded Jelmi in his soft voice. "I have worked among them before this." An eagerness had come into his face, and he waited.

Houlun, lying exhaustedly on her bed, heard, through the clear and icy air, her brother's voice. She sat up. She pulled a fur robe over her shoulders, and painfully made her way to the door of the yurt. There she sat, listening, all her heart fixed on the sound, hearing nothing else. She heard each word, but she listened mostly to his voice, so strong and sweet and full, and round with laughter, accompanied by the weird high strumming of the fiddles.

"By misery and human want betrayed,
Bright Inspiration plays the wench to fear,
And Courage on her ardent lips has laid
Her own cold hands. No Art draws near
When Wisdom for a bone applauds the clown.
Before the Belly even gods go down.

"It would be sweet, if any truths remain,
That man, tormented, can recall his soul,
That tasteless porridge never can sustain
Unless 'tis offered in a polished bowl.
But this be truth, however fools may frown:
Before the Belly even gods go down."

His voice fell into silence, and left a throbbing in the night behind it, like the vibration of a struck note. But no one applauded; the warriors, puzzled, stared at each other. They were disappointed. They had not understood a single word. Only

Jelmi had understood, and the Shaman with his subtle face. Jelmi had been entranced by the singer's voice. Truly, he thought, it is the voice of the Lord Buddha, Himself. It seemed to him that the immense emptiness of the Gobi night had magnified that voice until it had reached the stars, who had stood still in amazement. It seemed to him that the black ramparts of the hills had been filled with an answering choral of angels. The Shaman smiled. His expression was no longer hostile, and he regarded Kurelen as a man might regard another man in the company of soulless animals. Curled before the fire, the priest snored.

Then the Shaman clapped his hands. It was the only applause. The warriors licked their lips, and scowled. "Hast thou no songs of valor, Kurelen?" one of them shouted, contemptuously.

"Valor?" repeated Kurelen, meditatively, as though he had never heard the word before.

Yesukai spit, to show his disdain.

"Doubtless a meaningless word to thee," he suggested, amid laughter.

"Valor," said Kurelen, "is the fool's answer to wisdom."

And again only Jelmi and the Shaman understood, and the Shaman laughed with subtle delight.

"Sing us a song, then, of love," said another warrior. The others bellowed with jeering laughter, and struck each other on the chest and shoulders, and rolled before the fire. Kurelen and love! The combination was too delicious for their simple souls. They laughed until their ribs protested, and then their mirth exuded from their grinning lips in animal grunts.

But Kurelen waited, smiling, for their attention. On his lips and his forehead appeared drops of shining sweat.

"Yes," he said gently, "I shall sing you a song of love."

Again they laughed. The old man twiddled the strings, and a sweet fair sound fluttered out into the night. Kurelen began to sing. His voice was fierce and mournful, full of despair and wild hopelessness. The grins on the faces of the warriors faded, leaving them with expressions of wonder and enchantment; they leaned towards the singer, as though loath to miss the faintest inflection in that strong and marvellous voice, so pure and passionate:

"Who may sing of my heart's beloved?
A thousand men in a thousand songs,
The winds of night and the winds of the morning,
The long blue heron in the lake of silver,
The desert's voice on the scarlet mountains,

The jade-green forest in the arms of the tempest,
The herdsman's pipes and the drums of a king.

'Tis only I, 'tis only I, who dare not sing!"

His voice, so beautiful, so strong, yet so unbearably sweet, rose like a wild bird from an abyss of dark chaos and torment, its wings lighted, and its heart visibly beating. All the universe seemed to be listening; one could imagine that the outer borders of space were transfixed with wonder and poignant sadness, and that even the turreted mountains wept in unendurable delight and sorrow. The eyes and the mouths of the warriors stood open, and the shadowy shapes standing beyond the light of the fires were entranced. Even the dogs were silent, and the herded cattle and camels. A strange expression moved over the people's faces, so that their beasthood was lost, and they were men in their emotion.

The strange unseen lightning glimmered unceasingly on Kurelen's face as he sang; his eyes were upraised, and filled with an unearthly dazzle, so that the pupils were lost. He smiled, but it was a smile of torture. His hands lifted and moved, the gestures of a dying but convulsed body. No one saw his deformity; he had acquired splendor, so that he towered like a god, standing in the red firelight.

"Who may gaze on my heart's beloved?
The fox and the marten, the bear and the snake,
The caliphs of Baghdad, the Prince of Cathay,
The rat in his hole, and the god in the skies,
The red-eyed camel, the red-beaked vulture,
The priest in the temple, the rag-covered beggar!

'Tis only I, 'tis only I, who dare not gaze!"

Tears fell over the bearded cheeks of the warriors, and lingered a moment in the corners of their savage lips. The Shaman drew back from the firelight; he was seen to wipe his eyes on his sleeve. Jelmi listened to the rude translation of his father's song. He knew that the translation lost by conversion; it was not the words that so moved the people. It was Kurelen's voice that struck men's hearts with sounds too lovely, too sweet, too tragic for endurance. That voice expressed all the sorrow of all men, all their inarticulate yearning, their fumbling hands in the universal darkness, which was lighted only feebly by the dim candle of their souls, and inhabited only by their unsleeping terror. Here was man's cry against the gods, against his own torment, against his lostness and his eternal loneliness.

Drawn by her brother's voice, Houlun crept weakly from her yurt, wrapped in her dragging furs. She stayed far from any fire, but she could hear him clearly. She saw his face, haloed in the red light. It was turned towards her, as though he knew she was there. And it seemed to her that only she and he stood in that desert vastness and silence and night.

"Who may dream of my heart's beloved?
The lowliest shepherd, the khan of all men.
'Tis only I, 'tis only I, who dare not dream!
Blind must mine eyes be, and frozen my tongue,
Dark are my dreams, as empty as silence,
And lonely my bed, and cold as the shut grave.

'Tis only I, 'tis only I, who dare not dream!"

On the last word Kurelen's voice broke on a cry. His arms dropped; his head dropped on his concave chest. He stood, unhearing, while a storm of riotous shouts and applause exploded about him. Yesukai was beside himself with admiration and excitement. He ordered that one of the captive women be brought out. The applause still roared about Kurelen when the girl was conducted to the fire. She was a small, plump, pretty thing, and very frightened, and her eyes were big and black as plums, and her mouth tiny and puckered, like a red berry. Yesukai, with a loud laugh, thrust her into Kurelen's lax arms, and shouted: "Here, take her! I had intended her for myself, but she is thine. Take her to thy tent, and let her comfort thee."

But Kurelen made no effort to retain the girl in his arms. Yesukai ordered her to go to Kurelen's yurt, and a herdsman went with her to show her the way. Yesukai shook his wife's brother jocosely by the arm.

"Go to, Kurelen! She was a fat morsel, and thou didst not look at her. But thou art always shivering, and she will keep thee warm, at least."

The warriors shouted in a friendly fashion. Kurelen looked about him, bemused. He smiled faintly. "Give me more wine," he said.

Half a dozen cups were held up for him. He drank from them all, and the warriors' new admiration for him mounted prodigiously. Room was made for him, but he went back to his seat beside Jelmi. He hugged his legs, his long chin on his knees. His smile was wider and more grotesque than ever;

he kept up a constant shivering, and his teeth chattered, for all his nearness to the fire. He trembled with a convulsive inner mirth, but his eyes were turned inward.

Houlun sat on her bed. Her child had been brought back to her, and lay on her knees, wailing. But she appeared not to hear him. Her eyes, enormous and full of tragedy, stared out into the darkness.

In the meantime, the revelry continued.

chapter 6

It was in the darkest hour just before morning when the Shaman began his great prophecies about the young child, Temujin. One mighty central fire had been piled high with dried animal-droppings and gnarled wood of the desert pines. Around this fire gathered all the people, to listen to the prophecies, and to see the strange things which the Shaman would conjure into their vision. Kokchu was reputed to be a remarkable wizard, but so far few had witnessed his marvels, and there had even been some scepticism about him. Now that the dark dawn was approaching, the rumor had spread that Kokchu would conjure mightily, and every one from all the other fires came, so that one by one the deserted fires flickered slowly out, like red stars, and there was just this fire.

Kurelen had drunk more deeply than ever before in his life, but he could not retain his drunkenness. Finally, the more rice wine he drank the more his mind cleared, until he was afflicted by a sharp clarity of perception which rapidly became agony. Sound impinged on him physically, as though he had been flayed, and hot irons applied to raw nerves and bleeding tendons. Sight became unendurable. He dropped his forehead to his knees and closed his eyes. But he had no desire to rise and go away. Inertia had him in numb chains, and besides, he was very cold, colder than he had ever been before. He did not know that the monk, Jelmi, had removed his own felt coat, and had thrown it over his shoulders. The priest, Seljuken, had begun to stir in his sodden drunken sleep, and was now sitting upright, blinking, rubbing his beard and his eyes, beginning to eat again.

Now a deep silence fell about the smoldering and leaping fire. Kokchu, the Chief Shaman, had arisen. He was standing in the crimson circle of light, and had fixed his eyes on the lightless heavens. His father had been a great Mongol chieftain, of noble family and passionate pride; Kokchu, himself, was a handsome, and even magnificent, man. He was very tall and thin, and had burning black eyes, large and compelling and ferocious. His face was long and brown, his nose beaklike, with flaring nostrils, which gave him a savage look. His large mouth, heavy and drooping, was possessed of a cruel, stubborn and melancholy expression, the mouth of the barbarian. His thick black eyebrows sprang from the inner corner of his eyes upward, like wings, so that his whole face took on a wild ferocity at once intimidating and beautiful. Yet, for all this, he had a subtle and crafty look, as though decadence had come on him before his savagery had been dissolved. On his head he wore a high pointed hood, very narrow and stiff; the scarflike ends framed his face and lay on his shoulders, as did the two thick braids of his black hair. His body, to the waist, was clad in a short coat of creamy woolen, elaborately embroidered in blue and red and yellow in esoteric symbols; the sleeves were long and full, and he kept his hands folded in them. From the waist down he wore a voluminous skirt of blue wool, the folds heavy and dragging. They hid his felt boots, which some enamored woman had richly embroidered. When he removed his hands from his sleeves, his thin dark wrists jangled with gold bangles set with turquoises.

Kurelen opened his eyes and studied the Shaman with interest. He smiled. There, he thought, with admiration, is I, under more fortunate circumstances. At times he enjoyed conversing with Kokchu, who had a mind like glittering jet, and no compunctions whatsoever. Had Kurelen not laughed at the spirits (in which Kokchu had absolutely no belief), the two would have been the most genial of friends. But when Kurelen laughed, the Shaman felt himself endangered. Nevertheless, at intervals, they enjoyed each other, for all their instinctive hatred. For, as Kurelen said, they were the only two men of sense in Yesukai's ordu. Kurelen said openly, to the Shaman, that he had no objection if Kokchu made swines of men with his conjurings. But he reserved to himself, he announced, the right to laugh both at the Shaman and his believers. The laughter was the eternal sword of enmity between them.

Tonight, Kokchu determined that he would silence Kurelen's laughter forever, if not with his conjurings, then with another method. He felt very gloomy, for Kurelen, watching him in the firelight, had begun to smile and look interested.

Kokchu placed the palms of his hands piously together, and regarded the sky solemnly. His lips moved; his expression became one of intense awe. All the watchers fell into awe, also, except Kurelen and Jelmi. Eyes were raised so high that the foreheads over them wrinkled like crushed parchment, and fur hats fell far back on skulls. Between parted lips, teeth glistened like the teeth of beasts of prey.

Kurelen bent towards Jelmi, chuckling: "Thou hast never seen the like! Observe closely."

Jelmi smiled with his perfect gentle courtesy, and fixed his eyes on the Shaman, ringed about with scores of glittering eyes and entranced faces. He held his prayer-wheel in his hands, and spun it absently. He whispered: "God appears in many forms, and whatsoever this man produces is part of the eternal manifestation."

Kurelen pursed his lips, but did not answer. He watched Kokchu with enjoyment, proof against any witchery or magic. Yet he was not insensible to the mysterious silence that stood over everything, as though the universe held its breath and waited.

Kokchu lifted his arms slowly; his dark face had turned the color of lead, and upon it lay drops of quicksilver, starting from every pore. The cords of his throat rose like ropes under his skin. There was no sign of physical struggle about him, yet every one was aware of enormous strain and conflict within the Shaman. He began to pray, first in a whisper, then in a mounting voice, high and hysterical:

"O ye Spirits of the Eternal Blue Sky! I call upon ye; I command ye! Ye have given unto us a man-child of great beauty and strength, and have put in his hand an omen. It is not always given unto men to see the future, but because we desire to accord this child his proper honors, we pray that ye give us a sign of his greatness and his mystery!"

The quicksilver drops slowly moved down his face; red veins sprang out in the whites of his eyes. He shuddered; his fists clenched. He fixed his unblinking and somehow terrible gaze unmovingly on the heavens. Now he was silent, but the struggle within him flowed out to infect the watchers with an eerie restlessness and vague fright. The huge fire had suddenly died down, so that only a vast ring of fiery shifting coals lay on the earth. These coals threw out a blood-red light, a ring in which the Shaman seemed to stand, the upper part of his body in semidarkness, his feet and knees seemingly burning.

All at once a faint groaning came from the watchers. Kurelen leaned forward, and gazed at the fire, which the warriors were watching with expression of fixed horror and fear and superstition. He saw nothing, nothing but the red, radiant coals. He glanced humorously at Jelmi, but to his surprise Jelmi was looking at the coals solemnly, his face pale and transfixed. The priest, Seljuken, was staring, too, mouth and eyes agape. His hair was slowly rising.

"It is impossible," Kurelen muttered, shrugging. And then he was silent. For in the falling ring of coals something was taking shape. A cool thrill ran down Kurelen's twisted spine; a tingling invaded his hands and feet. Slowly the Things within the fire brightened into outline. Slowly the form of a mountain lion, crouching on his belly, manifested itself. It was an enormous lion; its head was lifted with pride and courage and ferocity; its red eyes glittered in the incandescent light. Kurelen could see its flexed paws, its white fangs and white claws. About its rippling body was coiled a thick scarlet serpent; Kurelen could see the markings on the serpent's scaly skin. But it was not crushing the lion; rather, its coils were quiet, its long flat head resting on the head of the beast. Its evil eyes, green and opalescent, shone; between its jaws a tongue flickered incessantly. Beast and serpent lay together in peace, frightful eyes full of mystery and unearthly meditation. They appeared to breathe together, coils and body rising together in unison. And near them, looking only at the sky, stood the Shaman, the leaden tint of his flesh deepening, the sweat coursing down his face, his lips open and gaping.

Kurelen felt his hair rising. His body, affrighted, recoiled. But his mind repudiated what he saw. "It is not possible," he said aloud, enraged. He leaned forward, the better to see the beast and the serpent. And slowly, as if they felt the infuriated impact of his eyes, the Things turned their heads together in unison in the fire and gazed at him. He saw the pointed slash of their dilated pupils; he heard their hissing breath; he saw their wet fangs. His heart began to beat like a struck cymbal with terror and anger.

The Shaman began to speak in a low droning voice, broken by gasps.

"O ye Spirits, eternal and terrible, ye have answered my prayers, and have given us a sign! Strong and fierce as the mountain lion is this child, and wise and all-embracing as the serpent! What man shall withstand him? What creature of air and earth and mountain shall defy him?"

Kurelen's body was running with ice-cold sweat. He was leaning forward farther than ever. He was looking directly into the eyes of the awful Things that regarded him so steadfastly from the fire. He felt that they saw him and understood him, yet they saw and understood with a horrible indifference, with a supernatural awareness which was yet as aloof and impersonal as death. He felt himself face to face with monstrous things beyond the pale rim of reality and sanity, things of madness before which men were impotent and threatened and which, once seen, would drive them to madness, also.

Every one else vanished from Kurelen's consciousness.

There were only himself and these ghastly visitants that had moved from nightmare into reality. Dimly, in the background, he heard the Shaman's droning voice, his weird incantations. But he looked only into the shimmering incandescent eyes of the Things and they looked back only at him, breathing steadily, the coals faintly seen through their transparent bodies. He thought to himself, numbly: I must defy them, and declare they do not exist, that they are foul emanations from the Shaman's own soul. And as he thought this thought, the Things seemed to gaze at him the more intensely, and now with enmity and fearful menace.

Slowly, with an almost superhuman effort, he turned his eyes from the fire and glanced at the Shaman. His heart plunged foolishly, for he saw that Kokchu was watching him obliquely, and that the Shaman was smiling as though with gloating irony.

Kurelen's pale lips twisted into a faint grin. He turned to Jelmi, who was watching the Things with profound gravity. "They do not exist," he made himself say. But Jelmi did not turn his head. An expression of deep sorrow and despair moved like a cloud over his yellowed features.

"Yes," he whispered, "they do exist, it is true they come from the soul of an evil man. But evil lives apart and in men, and can be conjured into the eye. 'Tis only goodness which is a dream."

The Shaman was exhausted; he was trembling visibly. He said faintly : "We have seen, O ye Spirits!" His hands fell to his sides; his head dropped on his chest.

Slowly, before Kurelen's incredulous gaze, the Things stirred a little, then began to pale. Their outlines dimmed; lion and serpent dissolved again to red coals. But to the last their incandescent eyes were fixed on Kurelen in an obscene but awful warning, and long after the coals were black he felt their influence in his soul.

A deep subterranean groan burst from the warriors. Superstitious terror filled them. They emitted hysterical cries and incoherent words. Kokchu smiled. He sat down on the other side of the fire, folded his hands in his sleeves, seemed to give himself up to meditation. But he met Kurelen's eyes, and again he smiled, subtly. Thou art a fraud, said Kurelen to him, in his mind, and his own eyes flashed with the message. He had no doubt that the Shaman read the message, and was maddened by the other's answering the contemptuous look.

Yesukai was beside himself with joy. He wept and beamed. The cups of wine were handed about, again. The fiddlers played hysterically, their fingers flashing up and down the strings in an ecstasy of rejoicing. Then some one suggested that the captive monk and priest be induced to prophesy in behalf of the child, Temujin. The drunken Nestorian priest, full of wine, meat and bombast, was only too willing. His inflamed mind was intoxicated by what he had seen. Verily, he had witnessed a holy miracle! His mind became confused; legends and strange tales, gleaned from his own faith, swam through his chaotic consciousness. He was helped to his feet. His bearded face shone with exaltation, though he swayed in the arms of those who held him upright. He flung out his own arms, and so violent was the gesture that he would have fallen into the fire but for the firm grip of the two Mongol warriors who held him.

He began to shout. He had seen a vision in his soul! God had vouchsafed to him the sight of wonders and miracles! What glories had he seen, what secrets of past and future! His protruding eyes gleamed like wet stones in the firelight: froth appeared on his bearded lips. His chest heaved and shuddered, and sweat ran down from his forehead. He panted. Every one regarded him with awe and fear, except the Shaman, who had begun to frown, and Kurelen, who was laughing silently.

The priest flung up his arms and now his whole expression took on the aspect of madness. He stood rigid, unmoving, like a statue, or rather like a tree that had been stricken with lightning, and now vibrated. His voice, when it emerged again from his foam-lined lips, was shrill and broken.

"What a vision is this! Darkly through the mists do I see a virgin, clothed in garments of the moon, standing on a red star! Upon her head is a crown of fire, and in her hands she holdeth a sphere of flame! The sphere bursts into fragments, and behold! they form into seven stars! But one of these stars is the largest, and it too bursts, and forms itself into glowing letters! What is that sacred name, that terrible name, that most dreadful and holy name!"

The crowding warriors leaned forward, lips dropping, eyes glazed with terror and joy. A mad and frenetic ecstasy lit up the priest's ghastly face. He seemed to be regarding something wondrous written in the sky. Slowly, one by one, the warriors followed his fixed gaze, as if they, too, might see something there, some wonder written by the finger of a god.

The priest, in that pent silence, suddenly howled, and every man jumped violently. He howled again. The Shaman and Kurelen winced, and then exchanged a wry glance.

"I see the name!" shrieked the priest. "It is the name of the Child which was born before the rising of the sun! It is the name of Temujin!"

The warriors groaned joyfully. Many wept, wiping away their tears with the backs of their hands. Yesukai was white and stricken with emotion.

The priest's madness increased. He leaped into the air in his drunken rapture. He clapped his hands with a sharp sound. His beard and hair flew together.

"The Child born of a Virgin!" he screamed. "Seven generations have passed, but it is as only yesterday! Seven stars and seven generations, and this Child is born! This is he, the Conqueror, the King of all men, the sword and the whip of God!"

Kurelen leaned towards Jelmi, and whispered: "I have heard this tale before, in Cathay, from the Christians. But the name they named was not Temujin!"

Jelmi, without looking at Kurelen, smiled faintly. He seemed painfully intent upon the priest.

The priest was shouting again, but incoherently now, and all at once he pitched towards the fire, and would have fallen in it but for the alert hands of the warriors. But he was unconscious, from wine and emotion. They laid him down, carefully, and some one threw a blanket over him. He began to snore. But the warriors were full of excitement. The seventh generation rising from a virgin! No wonder such signs and portents had surrounded the birth of this child! Each warrior began to relate, in turn, several curious things he had observed lately, which he had been at a loss to explain. The more imaginative had strange tales. A hawk had been observed scattering eagles. The sun had stood still in the heavens a day or two ago, far beyond his sojourn. Flowers, far out of season, had been seen growing along the river, whose edge had been frozen hard in the morning. Others had seen red shadows drifting across the moon. The excitement became more vociferous and incoherent.

Jelmi whispered to Kurelen, with his slight smile: "It is a strange story, but an old one. It is said even of the Lord Buddha, by some of his worshippers, that he is descended from a virgin. It was suggested for Lao-Tse, but he repudiated it, angrily. I have heard that our present emperor regarded it kindly, for himself, but my father and others laughed him out of it. It is a very unwholesome idea, but there are some, perverted and unclean, who admire it."

Kurelen shrugged. "It will do no harm, and may insure their loyalty to my sister's child. But I can see that our Shaman is green with envy. He wishes he had thought of it first."

But Jelmi now observed that many of the warriors were looking and pointing at him eagerly. Then all at once a concerned shout arose that this holy man must prophesy also. Jelmi paled and tried to shrink back from the firelight. But hands were already seizing him, thrusting him to the front.

"Prophesy! Prophesy!" cried the warriors, and many of them struck their lacquered shields with the hilts of their daggers.

The poor monk stood, uncertain and bewildered, before the fire. He looked at all the wild dark faces ringed about him. Kurelen tugged the hem of his yellow robe and urged, with a laugh: "Thou surely hast as much imagination as that foul priest!"

Jelmi regarded the warriors humbly. He said, in his soft and gentle voice: "I am only the lowliest of the lowliest. Who am I, that God should speak unto me? I dare not even pray; I must only stand in His presence, like a worm deserving of a crushing foot. How will the Lord see me, who am smaller than a grain of sand, of less worth than a drop of water?"

Each ferocious face wrinkled in perplexity, not comprehending. A low muttering rose from the warriors. "Prophesy!" they shouted again, impatiently.

Jelmi hesitated, his expression becoming more sad than ever. He folded his hands together, with great humility. His face emerged from the shadow of his hood like a delicately carved image of the most fragile ivory. He closed his eyes, and whispered: "I can only wait."

Kurelen was alarmed. The warriors were in no mood to be balked. He felt some anger against Jelmi. Surely the man was not a fool; he was not without wit. A few shouts, a few disordered gestures, a scream or two, some idiot extravagance, and the warriors would be satisfied. It was necessary for holy men to treat others like imbeciles, otherwise of what use were they? If they could not excite the people with happy and delirious lies, they might as well go back to labor and sheep-herding. Priests and philosophers were buffoons, but like buffoons, they must mystify and terrify and entrance, to earn the bread for which they had not honestly worked.

But Jelmi stood in humble silence, his head bent, his eyes closed, his hands clasped, his lips moving. All at once he seemed to become rigid; his lips stopped their silent movements. He turned as pale as death. He seemed to be listening to some frightful and portentous message. His head fell on his chest, as though he had been mortally struck. Kurelen smiled, relieved. The warriors leaned forward again, waiting for the words of mystery and prophecy.

Then very slowly, Jelmi lifted his head, opened his eyes,

and gazed at the sky. He seemed to have aged; his yellowed skin was taut and dry as bleached sheepskin. In his eyes stood an awesome expression, horrified and stricken and appalled, as though he were seeing a vision too terrible for the mind to endure. He began to speak in so low a voice that it was almost a whisper:

"It is not possible that I have seen so awful a vision, and it is not possible that it is true! Who could endure such a sight, or such knowledge, and not die at the contemplation? Who can contemplate such agony and such despair, such fire and such ravishment, and hear such cries, without madness! Why hast thou afflicted me so, Lord Buddha? Why hast thou given me such a vision?"

Kurelen's smile widened. Jelmi was a clever man after all. But surely he hardly needed such extravagance— At this, some thought wiped the smile abruptly from Kurelen's face. This was a strange prophecy, indeed, spoken of in such a despairing and agonized voice! He stared at Jelmi, piercingly. The monk's face was wet with tears; he was wringing his hands as though overcome with frantic sorrow. It is not possible! thought Kurelen, amazed. The man believes he has seen a vision!

Jelmi wept; the warriors gazed at him, wetting their lips, glancing at each other, alarmed and mystified. The Shaman spat contemptuously at the fire, and subsided into gloom.

In a broken voice, the monk resumed: "Better had it been for me to have died, then to see this. Better had I never issued from the womb and drawn breath. For who can contemplate the monstrous soul of man, and live again? Who can endure the light of the sun, with this knowledge? What days remain to me must be days of grief and torment, and unending suffering."

The warriors muttered; the muttering increased to a dull roar. Every man turned to his neighbor, with an astounded question in his eyes. Face after face began to scowl. Kurelen, greatly alarmed, tugged urgently at the monk's hem. The Shaman brightened; his smile was a smile of intense amusement. Yesukai, whose simple soul was bewildered, stood in silence, grimacing, plucking at his lip.

But Jelmi paid no heed to any one. His weeping became more violent; he wrung his hands over and over as though in the utmost extremity of despair.

"For what has God given His sons to the earth? For what have they died? Their voices are lost in the winds; their footsteps are covered over with sand. The streams lose the mark of their passing; the rocks reveal no sign. Over their dust move the bloody legions of the mad and the wicked, the haters of men and the destroyers of men. Where they have trod are planted the banners of the damned; where they have spoken is the screech of the vulture, seeking for the dead. The fires of hatred have destroyed the harvests they have planted. The iron foot has trod out the grapes they tended, and has squeezed forth a poisonous brew. For what is good is dissolved in the earth, but what is evil is an immortal sword."

His voice, sorrowful and passionate, and full of grief, rose stronger and stronger upon the suddenly quiet air, like a lamentation addressed only to the ear of God. He raised his face; he flung out his arms as though he saw the face of the Inscrutable One, who listened.

"Why hast Thou given us Thy sons, O Master of Chaos? We have destroyed them, and have poured out their blood, and have given adulation to monsters and worshipped them because they have willed us death and agony! Thy sons gave us love, and we have cried out that we hate love, and desire hatred, which delivereth our helpless brother into our murderous hands! We are an abomination unto Thine eyes, and a foul noise unto Thine ears. We are the breeders of the cursed, the lovers of the despoilers, the adorers of madmen and mountebanks. Generation after generation, we spew forth a fiend, each fouler than the last, until all reason and all love and goodness are stamped into the dust, and the bones of innocent men lie crumbling in the sun. Generation after generation, the bloody dream is born again, until the skies are reddened, and the convulsed earth groans in her loathing!"

His voice dropped to a deep mourning sound. And from the mountains the sound seemed to echo until all the universe lamented dimly with this man. No one appeared to breathe about the fire. Every hand was stilled. Bodies were lost in shadow, but each face was crimson with light. Every eye gleamed steadfastly, like the eye of an enchanted wild animal.

Jelmi's head dropped upon his breast; he sobbed aloud. And then he was silent, as though exhausted. After a long moment, he began to speak again, very softly.

"I hear Thy holy voice, O Lord, but it is just a murmur in my ears, like the sound of distant wind in the forests——"

Suddenly he flung up his head, and an expression of unearthly joy blazed on his yellowed features. His eyes flashed with supernatural ecstasy; his mouth opened in an ineffable smile.

"I hear Thee, O Lord! I hear Thy words! O beautiful words of hope and love! For Thou dost say that though evil liveth, and the monster doth flourish, and the lamentations of the helpless resound from every mountain and every hill, Thou shalt forever prevail! The madmen come and go, but to the end the Earth is the Lord God's, the Earth is still the Lord's, the Earth is eternally the Lord's!"

His voice was like a trumpet, sonorous and triumphant. His frail body appeared to expand, to swell, to vibrate with an inner power and rapture. He seemed to grow taller. Even when he no longer spoke, the air was filled with the echo of his words, so that every man shivered without knowing why.

Kurelen did not move. He stared steadily at the fire. His thin dark face wore a cryptic expression.

Neither did the Shaman move. He sat like a graven image, but in his eyes, as he regarded Jelmi, was the most baleful light.

The warriors were stupefied. Slowly, after a long time, they looked questioningly at each other. Yesukai was completely bewildered. He fixed his eyes hopefully upon the Shaman, awaiting an interpretation of this extraordinary prophecy. And then, smiling, the Shaman stood up, full of dignity and portentousness. He bowed to the oblivious monk, with great and ironic ceremony.

"He sayeth that he hath heard the words of the Great Spirit who lives in the Blue Sky. He who heareth the words of the Great Spirit standeth on the threshold of death. The Great Spirit hath indicated that He desireth that this holy man enter His presence, otherwise He would not have allowed His servant to hear His voice."

Kurelen had been only half listening, but all at once the meaning of the Shaman struck him like a physical impact. He paled. His lips dried. His brows wrinkled, and drew together, alertly.

"It is true!" cried the warriors, vociferously.

The Shaman smiled sweetly.

"And as for the Christian priest, he, too, hath had a vision which we have not seen, and hath heard a voice we did not hear——"

"It is true!" shouted the warriors, full of ferocious delight.

The Shaman carefully and delicately put his fingers together. He lifted his eyes piously.

"Shall we bring down the wrath of the Great Spirit upon us and upon the child who was born today, by refusing to dispatch to Him the servants He desireth? Shall we refuse Him this sacrifice?"

"No!" roared the warriors. They began to struggle to their feet. They exhaled an odor like wild beasts about to kill, an odor so strong that it was a stench. They struck their shields.

Their eyes had a phosphorescent glow of lust and madness. The Christian priest snored blissfully on, his feet to the fire. But Jelmi did not move. He seemed lost in a profound meditation, his head on his breast.

Then Kurelen, misshapen and bent, got to his feet, his face ghastly. He regarded the Shaman with a sick rage. "O thou stinking priest!" he cried. "Thou wouldst destroy this holy man in thy envy and littleness——"

"What holy man?" asked the Shaman, with mild wonder. "This?—" and he touched the Christian disdainfully with the tip of his sandal, "or this?—" and he pointed derisively at Jelmi. The warriors muttered ominously.

Kurelen was beside himself with fear. "Thou knowest it is forbidden to harm holy men——"

"Harm them?" repeated the Shaman, raising his eyebrows in gentle rebuke. "I have not suggested they be harmed. Holy men are sacred. And what could be more appropriate, on this auspicious occasion, than sacrificing these holy ones to the Great Spirit? Besides, hath He not indicated He desireth such a sacrifice?"

Without waiting for Kurelen's answer, he turned to the warriors and Yesukai. "But after all, I am only a meek and priestly man. I can only interpret according to the wisdom which has been mysteriously given me. What is finally ordained must come from the Khan, himself."

Kurelen looked despairingly from one fierce and sanguinary face to another; he saw the cruel and animal-like eyes, the untamed and barbarous wrinkling of foreheads. Once he had heard the phrase, in Cathay:—"beyond good and evil." His lightninglike thought was that these creatures, lusting for blood, were truly beyond good and evil, and any appeal for mercy to them would have a meaningless sound. He became frantic. He turned impetuously to his sister's husband, and cried:

"I have served thee well, Yesukai! But I have been lonely, for I have longed for no wife, and have none. Neither shall I have children, such as thou shalt have, to comfort me. But in this holy man, Jelmi, I have found a friend, and one with whom I can converse. Give me his life, as a gift!"

The Shaman's smile became gloating. He radiated his glee. But he addressed Kurelen in a stern voice:

"And for thy small and selfish pleasure, thou wouldst sacrifice the good fortune, and perhaps the line, of the son of the Khan?"

The warriors shouted their anger at Kurelen, and brandished their weapons almost in his face. Yesukai stood in silence, doubt, uncertainty, the desire to accord Kurelen this favor, and superstition, all mingling on his handsome and simple countenance. He looked at the Shaman, and looked at Kurelen, and sank deeper into perplexity. Kurelen seized his arm, and cried pleadingly:

"Yesukai! I have never asked a favor of thee, but this——!"

Yesukai regarded the Shaman pleadingly.

"It is not possible, Kokchu?"

The Shaman shrugged. He replied respectfully, but with sorrow: "It is not possible, my lord."

Yesukai sighed. He put his hand on Kurelen's misshapen shoulder. He smiled placatingly. "Look thee, Kurelen, thou shalt have whatever else thou dost desire. I have a sable cape, which I took today, and new silver. If the girl I gave thee doth not please thee, thou shalt have the pick of any of them save one. Thou shalt have the best mare, the finest silks and jade —"

Kurelen shook off his hand. "I want nothing but this man, Jelmi!" He threw himself at the feet of his brother-in-law; he embraced his knees. Tears ran down his face. "I desire nothing but this man!"

He felt a touch on his shoulder. He turned his head and looked up. Jelmi was smiling down at him, tenderly and sadly.

"It, too, is my wish, that I die, Kurelen," he said, very gently. "I am tired. Life hath become insupportable to me. I desire to rest."

"Thou seest, my lord," said the Shaman to Yesukai. "The holy man, himself, hath heard his own summons."

"No!" cried Kurelen, in despair, seizing the monk by his robe. The warriors, diverted from their desire, regarded the crippled man in astonishment. The ribald and mocking Kurelen was lost in this weeping wretch. They could scarce believe it. Deep satisfaction finally pervaded them, and they grinned.

"Let me go in peace," said Jelmi, in his gentle and pleading voice.

Kurelen got to his feet. He put his hand on the hilt of his dagger, which was thrust through his belt. But even as he did so, he thought bitterly to himself: I would not die, even for him. Nothing, at the end, is valuable to me but myself. This is only a gesture, fit for laughter.

The Shaman saw the movement, and subtle man that he was, he saw the thoughts running through Kurelen's dark mind. He was quick to take advantage, however, and cried loudly: "Strike him down! He would murder the Khan!"

One of the warriors leaped upon Kurelen with a growl like

the growl of a beast. He struck him full in the face with his fist, and Kurelen went down like an ox under a hammer. Blood spurted from his nose and lips, and seeing this the warriors burst into shouts of laughter and ridicule. They kicked the fallen man, crowding about him for the pleasure. But Kurelen, as though insensible to his bodily anguish, groped for the robe of the monk. His fingers twined themselves in it. He saw only Jelmi's face, looking down at him with tender compassion. And then, like water, the robe slipped through his fingers, and blackness fell over his eyes.

chapter 7

When Kurelen awoke, he became aware that he had been conscious of movement for a long time, and that the movement had now ceased. He also became aware that he had suffered much, and that the torment he was now enduring was nothing to what he had already endured. But these awarenesses were vague, faint gleams of consciousness in an after-darkness from which he was slowly and painfully emerging.

He lay with his eyes shut. He heard a faint dry hissing accompanied by a hollow and somber moaning and a vast tremor and shaking. These he dimly recognized; they were snow and sand and wind. He thought to himself: winter has come. We are on our way. And as he thought this, he opened his eyes abruptly, the past and present rushing together in a whirlpool of bewilderment and readjustment. Instantly, as he opened his eyes, the vague awareness of torment and lapse of time and unconscious darkness became sharper and more intolerable.

He discovered himself lying on his bed, covered with thick layers of fur and coarse felt. The yurt was filled with dimness and the odor and presence of dung smoke which emerged from the sultry brazier in the center. He saw the shadowy outlines of his cherished carved Chinese chests and tabourets. He saw the livid gleam of his pale silk Chinese paintings on the walls of the yurt. He saw the flash of the Turkish scimitars hung between the billowing banners. But confusion still had him, and he wondered dismally if he were still engrossed in the half-forgotten nightmares of his suffering dreams. Everything was very still about him, in the yurt, but he could hear distant shouts of the tribesmen, the irritable cries of camels and horses, the lowing of cattle and the bleating of sheep, in the wintry twilight outside. He heard the creaking and rumbling of yurts, being moved into better positions for the night's camp, the curses of men, the abusing voices of women and the squalls of children. All these were old familiar sounds, rapidly slipping into place in the midst of his bewilderment. The thundering wind, assaulting the yurt, the hiss of mingled snow and sand upon its black felt walls, were familiar, too, and told him accurately what was transpiring and approximately the position of the ordu.

He attempted to move, and was immediately plunged into

sharp agony. His right arm was bound with strips of cloth and held closely to his side. His entire body screamed out its protest in lightninglike pains and crushing aches. His head seemed to fly into tortured fragments, and scarlet lights pierced his eyes. Astonishment was in his groan as well as pain. And then he remembered the night when he had attempted to save the life of the Buddhist monk. He panted aloud in his misery and dismay.

He heard a slight sound near him, and slowly, and with agony, turned his head. Squatting beside him, and seemingly part of the shadows, was the huddled form of a woman. His heart leaped feebly. "Houlun!" he murmured. The form moved again, bent over him. And then he saw that it was not Houlun, his beloved sister, but another woman. The dung fire brightened, and by its dull red light he was able to see that this was the girl whom Yesukai had largely flung into his arms on that distant night. He saw her enormous black eyes with their thick fringes of lashes, the roundness of her pale dark cheek, the pursed tininess of her red mouth. She smiled at him, and laid her hand on his forehead. At this movement of her body and garments she exhaled the pungent odor of hot femaleness and youth, unwashed and primitive, like the earth in fecund spring. For some reason, Kurelen was nauseated, and he drew in his nostrils for protection.

"What is thy name, girl?" he asked.

"Chassa," she answered, shyly.

Kurelen was never vicious with the simple or innocent, and delicately refrained from offending them. Therefore, though the rank female smell revolted him in his weakness, he made himself smile at the author of it.

"Have I been—like this—very long, Chassa?"

"Yes, Master, very long. Three moons have come and gone, and we have been far on our way, since they carried thee into thy yurt." She added: "Thou wert sorely hurt, Master."

"So I imagine," said Kurelen kindly, wincing at the pain it caused him to speak. The noises outside increased in intensity. Inside, Kurelen was suddenly overpowered by odor and smoke and heat. "Open the flap," he gasped.

The girl obediently opened the flap, and the dark winter wind rushed in, making the brazier flare into crimson, and forcing the smoke out in the form of gray coiling ghosts. The opening was a rectangle of dim blue light in the darkness, shaking with snow. Very faintly he could discern the blurred outlines of animated cattle and men in that snow-filled spectral blue light, as they passed and repassed the opening of the yurt. The air had a strangeness about it, pure and fierce and sterile, as if it had been blown from the transfixed mountains of the frozen moon, and Kurelen breathed it deeply into his laboring chest. Chassa crouched beside the flap, looking at the man over her shoulder, patiently and anxiously. Feathers of snow gathered on the floor of the yurt, near the flap, or scurried backwards into the interior, like white moths.

Suddenly the yurt lurched and shuddered. Yesukai's people were on their way again, deciding to move on a little more. The shouts outside were redoubled; wood shafts creaked and strained. The cattle lamented; the heavy wooden wheels groaned, and then squeaked over the virgin snow and ice. The wind increased in fury. Kurelen rocked and rolled on his couch, his eyelids wrinkling with pain, his teeth chewing into his lips. The girl closed the flap, and resumed her place by his side. The dung fire smoldered and crackled, throwing off golden sparks.

Kurelen opened his eyes again, and smiled kindly at Chassa. "Hath my sister, Houlun, been with me?" he asked.

"Oh, yes, Master! When I slept she was beside thee, with the little one."

"Ah." Some of the deathly pallor lessened on Kurelen's face, and was replaced by a look of shadowy contentment.

"And the Shaman, Master—he was often with thee, with his spells and conjurings."

At this, Kurelen burst into weak laughter; the blood rushed achingly through his veins at the involuntary convulsion. But he felt much better, and was able to think about matters with interest. He cautiously investigated his injuries, and reflected that only excellent nursing had saved his life. Chassa was bending over him anxiously, and when he suddenly fixed his piercing eyes on her childish face she blushed, and averted her head. He took one of her hands in his feverish grasp.

"I am not worth thine efforts, Chassa," he said. But he smiled internally, amused that he did not believe this maudlin sentiment. However, he observed to himself, it rarely did harm to say or do what was expected of one. Life was thus made more pleasant for the liar and the lied-to.

The girl was overcome with confusion and joy, and gazed at Kurelen with her innocent primitive soul in her eyes. And then an odd thing happened to him: he was faintly ashamed.

The multitude of yurts, lumbering and heaving and groaning all about Kurelen's yurt, lumbered and heaved and groaned to another stop, and the shouting was renewed. Chassa opened the flap and peered out to discover the cause. Night had shut down into black and impenetrable chaos, in which torches were thin and streaming red banners illuminating only immediate dark faces, or the wet side of an animal or the flap of a yurt. Chassa asked a passing man the meaning of the stop, and he hoarsely replied, pausing a moment, that the ordu was halting for the night. The storm made it too dangerous to continue in that country of broken craters smoothly filled with snow, and showing only the rims of black teeth to warn the wanderer.

Again the dark and swirling air was filled with the noise and uproar of men and beasts, making ready for the night's camp. Chassa shovelled more dung upon the fire, and blew upon it, crouching shapelessly in her thick felt garments. The fire shone in her eyes, and Kurelen observed that they were the eyes of some shy wild animal, purely savage and unhuman and untouched. The pupil was a fierce and pulsing point swimming in untamed and electric radiance. She had cupped her hands about her mouth, to concentrate her breath. Her tangled hair fell about her round cheeks and over her brow.

Some one was tugging at the flap, and, when Chassa went to answer, Kurelen's heart leaped expectantly. But it was not Houlun who entered, but the Shaman, bending his head, with its pointed hood. He was wrapped in furs, and appeared to be a tall bear standing on its hind legs. He came to Kurelen's bed, and when he saw that the sick man was conscious, he smiled darkly. Kurelen grimaced with amusement.

"Thou dost see, Kokchu, that thy conjurings did not kill me after all."

The Shaman, still smiling, did not answer. He sat down on the floor near the bed. The two men regarded each other in the silence of enjoyment. At length Kokchu spoke, gravely and with mock solicitude.

"I am a healer beyond mine own expectation, and thou art the proof. It will be many days, however, before thy recovery is complete. Rest, and think of nothing." He added, leaning towards Kurelen: "Art thou in much pain?"

"Pain," answered Kurelen, with deliberate sententiousness, "is the price of consciousness."

Again they regarded each other with enjoyment.

"My nephew," said Kurelen. "The spirits were propitiated?"

Kokchu raised his eyes piously and solemnly to the rounded roof of the yurt. "I can assure thee of that," he said with fervor.

Kurelen winced. "How thou must have enjoyed thyself," and bit his tongue for the childishness of his words.

But Kokchu merely inclined his head seriously. He hesitated.

Kurelen could detect no particular hostility in this man. But all at once he did detect loneliness. Kokchu's loneliness was suddenly as poignant and as imminent as his own; it had the same smell, the same presence. For a moment he felt compassion, followed by a curious and cunning hatred, as though he were hating himself. He knew he had been correct in his surmise, for Kokchu's next words were revealing.

"Thou and I, Kurelen: we are men of understanding. We are men among animals. We could laugh together."

Kurelen smiled. "But thou wouldst deny me the pleasure of laughing at thee, also."

Kokchu pursed his lips in amusement. "Nay, thou mayest laugh, for all of me. I ask only that thou dost laugh in secret."

"And not at thy dupes?"

Kokchu's lip curled; he seemed to gaze at Kurelen as though both surprised and dissillusioned. He leaned over him, plucked at the cloth on his breast.

"Look thee, Kurelen: thou hast lived in Cathay, where there are men. But these are only beasts. Why dost thou not seek worthier objects for thy laughter?" His voice was scornful, his eyes full of contempt.

Kurelen stared, and then his sallow and shrunken features were suffused with mortification. He was speechless. The Shaman stood up, shook out his furs and his felt garments, fastidiously. He glanced at Chassa, who still crouched by the fire. The girl turned her head over her shoulder, and gazed back at the priest with the eyes, humility and fear of a dog. Kokchu picked up a strand of her long hair, and curled it about his fingers as one curls the hair of a child. "Thou hast done well by thy master, Chassa," he said, in his rich voice.

Without another word to Kurelen, he left the yurt. He left behind him a peculiar blankness, as though some essence, some power, had been withdrawn from the air. Kurelen closed his eyes; he was burning with rage and humiliation. When Chassa approached him, timidly proffering him a bowl of hot mare's milk, he thrust aside her hand and shook his head.

He must have slept, for when he opened his eyes again he discovered that Chassa was gone, and that it was Houlun who sat beside him, motionless and watchful. Her hood lay on her shoulders; her glittering hair hung like black spun glass about her beautiful face. Her gray eyes were soft and smiling. She had been bathing his face, and he could smell the fragrance of the scent with which the warm water had been perfumed. When she saw he was conscious, she leaned over him and laid her warm full cheek against his for a moment. His heart seemed to rush to the spot which she had touched, and beat there, madly and painfully.

"Ah, Houlun," he murmured faintly. He took her hand; he held it against his breast with both of his. She could feel the pounding of his heart, which raced under her palms. She laughed softly, and shook her head at him.

"It is well for thee that I had just given my husband a son, and so could prevail upon him with my pleadings," she said. Kurelen saw that the fur-wrapped bundle near by, much agitated, was his sister's child.

Houlun continued: "But he was certain thou would have had his life, and it took many days to persuade him to the contrary. Ah, Kurelen, thou must have a care!"

"What didst thou tell him, Houlun?"

She began to laugh lightly. Her face shone like a pearl in the uncertain firelight.

"I told him it was impossible! I told him thou didst not have the courage to kill a mouse."

They laughed together, then. All at once the interior of the yurt seemed warm and full, as though joy and contentment pervaded it.

"But thou must have a care, my brother," repeated Houlun, ceasing her laughter. "The next time I might fail. But thou wilt never learn to hold thy tongue, I fear."

She picked up the squirming bundle, which had begun to emit protesting roars. When Kurelen looked at the child, after Houlun had carefully unwrapped several layers of wool, he realized how long he had been ill. The boy was vigorous, and had an angry light in his great gray eyes. Though less than three moons old, he struggled to raise himself in his mother's arms. His red hair was a tangle of raw gold over his large round head, and his lips were the color of pomegranates. Houlun laid him beside Kurelen, and the baby and the man regarded each other with passionate solemnity. Kurelen's expression reluctantly changed. He appeared to be embarrassed, after a few moments. He shut his eyes.

"Take him away," he said with a half laugh. "The eyes of children see too much."

Houlun lifted the child. She exposed the full moon of her breast, and the infant began to suck with loud noises. Houlun's head drooped over him; the firelight outlined the immobile figures, and Houlun's face was hidden by her falling hair. Kurelen felt that he was being drawn into the profound circle of mysterious life and strength which appears to surround a mother and her suckling child. Contentment and peace flowed over him like cool water over burned flesh.

Houlun informed him, after she had tended to the needs of the child, that she lived in comparative quiet. Yesukai rarely plagued her with his demands, for he was engrossed with his second wife, the Karait girl. She was already with child, and the Shaman had promised another son. But Houlun had refused to have her in her own yurt, as was the custom with wives. Yesukai, remembered Kurelen, stood in some awe of Houlun; this was usually the way of things between the simple and the imperious.

Again, the child was laid beside Kurelen, and again the two looked at each other with passionate intensity, and in deep silence. Then suddenly dogs began to bark savagely outside; the clamor rose to a deafening crescendo. Kurelen felt the child wince at the noise; the little lips parted, and he whimpered. Fear, stark and adult, made the child's gray eyes wide and intent in the dusky light.

"He is afraid of dogs," said Houlun, smiling. "Young as he is, he crouches in mine arms, at the sound of their barking."

But Kurelen did not hear her. He was absorbed in something terrible and unhuman which he was glimpsing behind the gray curtain of the infant's eyes, and which was not concerned with the clamor of the dogs.

chapter 8

Many times, as the seasons revolved, had Kurelen made this prodigious journey across mountain and desert, steppe and plateau, river and plain, fleeing the winter, seeking warmer winds and green pastures. But each time it were as though he had never experienced this before. The frightful vastness, the immense loneliness, the sensation that only this small band of wanderers were alive in the universal chaos of gale and snow and ridge and wilderness, had a breathless fascination for him. Some of the chronic and distant pain within him was lifted and dissipated, as though the mighty struggle and passion of the elements outside had drawn out his own torment, as a great sea sucks into its anonymity the little trickles of tiny streams. He lost the misery of individual consciousness for an hour; his consciousness was part of the dim consciousness beyond him, and so lost the sharp edges of awareness.

Moreover, no scene was so savage, so awful, so crushing, that it frightened him. At times he was seized with a desire to howl with unseen wolves, to scream with the hurricanes, to roar with the roaring of the dead forests of poplars, tamarisks, firs and reeds. When a disordered string of wild shaggy camels raced grotesquely against the gray and swirling sky-line, he shouted with glee, feeling himself one with them, feeling the bitter cut of sleet and wind through matted hair, feeling long stringy muscles pulling against suffocating air, experiencing the endless struggle between the animate and inanimate.

As his strength increased, he would weakly wrap himself in layers of felt and fur, pull his hood over his head, and limp out upon the platform of the yurt. He would sit there, while Chassa, standing before the closed flap, would guide the oxen. The girl, choking in the tearing wind, which was full of sand and ice and snow, would bend her head so that her face was partially protected by hair and hood. The yurts were all linked together, moving as a fluid unit, one shaft fastened to the axle of another vehicle. There, in the shadowy dusk of the enveloping and pursuing winter, would sit Kurelen for hours, not talking, not moving, hardly breathing, all his consciousness in his eyes and the scenes upon which they untiringly gazed.

Sometimes he would think: It is good to be a townsman before one's secure fire and amid secure walls. It is good to have all one's effort and soul concentrated on the smallness of perfection, to feel that nothing matters but that a leaf be delicately painted on a square of yellow silk. It is good to believe that exquisiteness is more valuable than life, and that the sole purpose for which man is created is to perfect his manners, or to admire the tracery on a silver bowl, or to listen to pretty verses and to converse with friends who are interested in the dead manuscripts of philosophy. Perhaps it is delightful to feel rapture over a phrase which cannot be surpassed, or a strain of music which has reached pure excellence and beauty. But now I verily believe that the pursuit of perfection leads only to death. The arts are only pallid excrescences of the soul. The phrasemaker and the philosopher are the priests of dissolution. Man the Spectator is Man the Corpse. Man the Individual is Man the Lost. Only by surrender to the universal Soul doth man gain true life, and in understanding the universe about him, and in partaking of it, doth he acquire the fullness of joy.

He would think: here is the substance of living, the raw spring of being. Danger and strife are the natural states of man. He who deprives his fellow of them, and shuts him safely within walls, hath made of his brother a chattering ape clad in silk, a eunuch both impotent and sterile, a blind fashioner of gold bracelets, an unbreathing polisher of stone.

The moving ordu, beehives of rounded black felt on wooden platforms and drawn by gasping oxen, rumbled and heaved and shuddered its way southward. Slowly, awful panoramas formed and sank and dissolved and shifted before Kurelen's eyes. Ranges of black and broken mountains rose upon the horizons of the snow-filled steppes, marbled with livid ice and cracked asunder with falling chasms. The ranges would curve like a scimitar in their path, then move aside, to ring them in immense rams' horns. They would rise upon an endless plateau, upon which not a tree or a stone was visible, and upon which tall gray grasses, dry and withered, moved with a deathly sound in the dropping snow. They would pass gray and moaning forests, whose naked trees and dried river-beds showed mutely where fertile civilizations had lived and had died, and been abandoned to the marten and the desert lizard. Aisles of black firs moved upon them menacingly, the floor about them white as bone, their hairy limbs laden with tufts of snow. They entered, lumberingly, labyrinths of desolate hills, as bare as the palms of one's hands. They passed black skeletal walls of stone, sculptured by the unceasing wind, descended into broad latitudinal valleys cracked with frozen watercourses, strewn with gray-green tamarisks, made chaotic with boulders and jagged pillars and volcanic rocks. Here and there, like shattered mirrors, were strewn frozen sheets of water the color of polished lead, and reflecting in them the dull cloud-shapes or the image of a twisted column of stone. At long intervals a lonely hawk or other bird of prey would cut the gaseous sky with a curving wing, and then sink out of sight. But it moved without sound. Even the wind, resistless and omnipresent, seemed less a sound than a terrific presence. It rolled and swept over the deathly immobility of rock and hill and valley like a tremendous shadow of doom, increasing and enhancing the transfixed silence.

The ordu was the only moving thing in this colossal wilderness, and it became a sluggish trickle of ants creeping through mountain passes and struggling over the enormous plateaus. Lost and tiny, it disappeared between scarified ramparts, emerged upon plains of utter desolation, crept towards a horizon vanishing into vaporous sky. There was something awesome in its courage, its grim determination. One by one the yurts would tilt into vast shallow caldrons, lurch over rocks hidden by the snow, painfully climb the opposite side. And then onward moved the ordu, defiant of the wilderness, its tiny collection of hearts beating warmly and strongly in the universal tomb, undaunted by crystalline schists, by gigantic layers of rock sliding with snow, tilted up like great platters, and showing, in the livid light of full day, scars of crystal and scarlet and vivid blue; not to be turned back by empty steppes and gorges and ravines and torrents fanged with glittering ice. In the soul of the nomads was an irresistible urge, the urge found in migratory birds who fly by instinct rather than by reason.

At intervals ice-storms raged, coating shaft and yurt and wheel with faint thick crystal, fringing the eyes of the oxen and breaking under the wheels with the echoing sound of shattering glass. The storms would flay the faces of the Mongols, for often they would be laden with sand. Sometimes the awful silence would be convulsed with detonations of thunder, and the nomads, superstitiously terrified, would halt in their tracks and cover their deafened ears, muttering prayers.

But as they crept southward, they left the tides of winter increasingly behind. Now they would come out upon bleached terraces, huge and shallow and tilted, going up into the sky or downwards to the valleys, like the vast ruined stairways of giants. Here there was little snow, and the gales screamed as though released. The skies were less vaporous. Sometimes, in a heaven the pale delicate hue of turquoises, the clouds would pile up lightly, ballooning immensely, layer upon layer, their upper reaches burnished with silver. The deformed and stunted vegetation would thaw at noon, and could be eaten by the cattle and horses and camels. The moving ranges of mountains, sinking and rising and curving, were sometimes flooded with purple and yellow, and at sunset, with bright pink. Gullies, wind-eroded and ribbed and winding, had snow only at the bottoms. Boundless areas of earth, dry and crumbling, were mixed with gravel and covered with desert scrub. Oases, weedy and forlorn, were increasingly encountered. Foot by foot, the Mongols moved onward, quickening their pace, now, laughing occasionally. Networks of greenish-gray and yellow lakes and rivers, frozen except at noon, were encountered and could be crossed on ice-bridges.

Nothing missed Kurelen's hypnotized eye in all this enormity of sky and wilderness and silence. Long after others were asleep, he would sit on the yurt platform, his lashes bristling with ice, and watch the measureless streaming of the Northern Lights, and listen to their crackling. Ribbon by ribbon, leagues in length, they would explode and uncurl against the black sky, hurting the eye with their blazes of scarlet and blue and dazzling white. False rainbows, vivid and incredible, would arch against the lightless darkness, pulsing and flaming. Crowns, hundreds of miles in diameter, would glitter and burn, their ragged points gemmed with stars. Sometimes, at vast distances, Kurelen would hear the melancholy howling of wolves, the voices of the wilderness.

And now he knew that soon they would encounter other ordus moving southward. The grasslands to which all were headed were just north of the Gobi sands, and as yet there had been no real contest for them. There was room to spare, many thought, tolerantly. So other ordus, regarded as enemies during the journey, could be greeted with polite reserve. The boys of other tribes would fish with those of Yesukai's, breaking the morning and evening ice on the rivers to catch the fat fish. Sometimes one ordu would help another with diminishing supplies. The young warriors would engage in wrestling, and often, if intermarriage was permitted, there would be wedding feasts and much revelry. There was a feeling of escape from imminent danger, which added luster to gaiety.

In these fertile valleys between the rivers Onon and Kerulon the winters were fairly endurable, and there was often nearly adequate sustenance for the herds. The grazing lands of Yesukai's people extended vaguely from Lake Baikul eastward, and here the wild antelope and the hare and the fox and lizard and marten, and sometimes the bear, could be hunted. It was a life of harshness, and sometimes when the herds had been consumed to the danger point, the people were compelled to live on kumiss and millet. Hunters desperately went far afield, sleeping in the snow without a fire, searching for elusive game. Towards the spring, the earlier intercourse between tribes became infrequent, and there was sullenness and fighting, often breaking out into bloody violence. Then raids were organized, and the boys spent sleepless nights, watching for robbers, or hunting for stray cattle. A fast of three days was not rare. Sometimes, during a severe period of bad weather, many froze to death. But in the spring the mares and the cows, feasting on freshened and more abundant pasture, gave large quantities of milk, and young foals and calves and lambs were born, and the tribesmen stuffed to capacity, and gorged. Then came the long journey back to the summer pastures, gayer this time, and less arduous.

The chieftains sternly shared the miseries and hungers with their people. The warriors, it is true, fared better than the others, for upon their strength and fortitude depended the very existence of the tribe. Women with child had a larger share of supplies than usual, but otherwise they and their children had only the leavings of the pots. It was a happy time for all when the spring journey began; amity was restored between passing tribes. Hunger, the great destroyer of love and friendship and tolerance, had been drowned in the flood of new milk and trampled in the cavorting of new life. It is true that the warriors, feeling strong again, and exceedingly lustful, would raid other tribes for women, and gallop into their ordus with them weeping behind them on the saddles. But not too much ill temper was aroused by this. Women were born for the beds of strong men, and the victor was more or less condoned. The women expected this, and felt badly used if they were not eventually carried off, or at least vigorously fought for.

The winter of violent red sunsets gleaming over frozen lakes and white barrens was over. The stars were softer at night, now, and the moon gentler. On their way to the summer pastures, they saw that the scarlet walls and ramparts and cliffs glowed against deep blue skies, and that the rivers were sometimes the color of blood from the silt of the red soil. Grass and scrub and tamarisk were the hue of brilliant green jade, and the desert blossomed with leagues of flowers. Sometimes miles of white flowers bent before the fresh strong wind, and blue and golden and rosy petals flowed over plateau and ridge and gulley like an enormous Turkish carpet. Birds cut hot white skies with vivid wings, and their voices, exultant, filled the desert with exciting song. The journey back was slow, for the herds must fill out their ribs, and the people must feast. Often at nights the heavens would be ripped with the flame of lightning, and the earth would roar and tremble with thunder. Vegetation, from the stunted and deformed trees of the Gobi, to the thick grass and the flowers, burst overnight into an orgy of life, and all the air was full of the sound of feverish growing. Almost within a few hours, it seemed, the lush grass was knee-high, and the yurts tossed and heaved and lumbered over horizonless steppes which resembled blowing green seas. The winds were laden with fecund smells. When the torrential rains fell, gray as spears and gleaming like impassable glassy walls, the odors were sometimes suffocating. It was as if the endless land and desert were exhaling clouds of steam, overpoweringly filled with the hot emanations of thousands of miles of orgiastic fruitfulness. Shining dark-green lakes and streams and rivers and pools were streaked with white threads, like liquid marble. Now the campfires at night were centers of revelry and song and laughter, and incredible stories and boastings.

Kurelen found the journey back no less exalting than the journey southward. The child, Temujin, strong of back, gray of eye, and wiry and vigorous of limb, would sit on his knee now, on the platform. He would laugh often, and appeared fond of his mother's brother. Houlun would join them contentedly, though she had lately complained. For she was with child again, the spring having been too much for Yesukai, who had acquired one or two extra wives.

The sun would lie warmly on Kurelen's twisted back. The child would scramble on his knees, or laugh over the handfuls of rank-smelling and pungent flowers gathered for him. But sometimes, in the gray childish eyes there would be a dark shadow, in spite of the blinding sun. And something of the primitive ferocity of the barrens, the mountains and the deserts, would transfix his little features.

There was a place on the way back which Kurelen had seen many times. He always watched for it eagerly. Among the red cliffs and chasms and ramparts, among the pointed pyramids and the pillared natural temples as red as blood, he would finally find a high hill of steel-colored granite. Its profile, against the passionately blue sky, was the profile of a sleeping giant, a giant who never awakened, whose face was turned upwards eternally to wind and heaven and storm. There was something terrible in that fixed and ageless repose, something appalling, Kurelen would think. It was like the spirit of the desert, the spirit of death or fatefulness, waiting for eons, perhaps never to awaken, or if awakening at long intervals, to turn frightful eyes for one awful moment upon the world, before sleeping again.

Many years later, he thought of this sleeping doom when he looked upon the face of Temujin.

chapter 9

The shallow bowl of the earth was filled with purple, floating, deep and tenuous. Streaks of fiery yellow splintered the west. In another moon, the winter migration would begin. The air was already chill as a frozen mountain stream. The purple of the earth lightened, and now the world was lost in vagrant shadows of pale orange, violet, dusky blue and gray, having lost its solid quality and become but a dream of chaos.

In his yurt, Kurelen warmed his hands at his dung fire. The three young boys at his side were still unsatiated. They would have more stories about Baghdad and Samarkand and the cities of Cathay. But Jamuga was interested excessively in the accounts of the strange mailed men whom Kurelen had seen once on a time, destined to an even stranger land. Kasar was inclined to be dubious. He never believed in the existence of anything which he had not himself tasted, smelled, touched or heard or seen.

"If thou wouldst have been born blind, Kasar, thou wouldst have called men liars if they spoke of the sun," said Kurelen.

Jamuga had replied, in his soft and steadfast voice: "Kasar would not have been so great a fool, in truth. If he could not have seen the sun, then the sun, for him, could not exist."

Kurelen smiled. He liked Jamuga. But this did not keep him from teasing the boy. Part of his malice arose from his old discovery that Jamuga did not trust him, and had a cold small contempt for him. Jamuga, he would tell Temujin, had eyes which were incapable of glancing sideways.

But Temujin was impatient. He was not an imperious boy. But he detested idle talk. He also hated obscurity. But this was not because he was a fool. He understood most of the abstruse talk between Kurelen, and his anda, Jamuga, but he thought abstract conversation folly because it was not accompanied by action. This aversion of his did not extend to heroic tales, or strange ones. They carried with them the aroma and the violence of things which had happened and were done.

"Tell us more of the men with the pale faces, and with the coats of mail," said Kasar, the brother of Temujin, sceptically.

Kurelen chuckled. "They were not so fair of face when we came upon them, lost in the Gobi sands! Their flesh was the color of raw entrails, from the heat of the sun and the flailing of the sandstorms and wind. They wore coats of silvery mail, not like our armor, which is of hard lacquered leather, and their swords were better than the Turkish swords. Their horses had long since been killed and eaten. They numbered about fifty, though they explained that many, many times that number had died in the long journey, including their leader, whom they called a great prince. We were able to understand them, for some of our people were Nestorian Christians, and two of them had been beyond the mountains into a far country called Russia, where men of many languages congregate, especially at the western borders. It seems they were lost, and far out of their way. Upon questioning, they declared that they had originally set out from their native countries far to the west for the purpose of going to a strange country, there to engage in mortal combat to rescue that strange country from those they called 'infidels.' "

He added reflectively: "We finally understood that these 'infidels' were Turkomans, or a kindred race, who lived in the strange country, where the god of these pale-skinned men once dwelt, and where he died. It was all very stupid, and very confusing. Men must fight for women and food and pasture lands, and perhaps, sometimes, for things of beauty. It is worthy that they fight if suffocated for room. But for none of these things were these imbeciles fighting. Their language and gestures were very noble, and many of us were impressed, though puzzled and contemptuously pitying. From the first, I doubted very seriously the story they told us. When they were fed, and ointment put upon their raw flesh, and when they were given quantities of Turkish wine, they lost their nobility very quickly. They began to boast. They told us the real reason for their seeking and fighting. They desired to find some one they called Prester John, the Old Man of the Mountain, a fabulous being who lived in a gigantic city whose tents were made of cloth of gold, and who had many treasures. Moreover, I gathered from their confused accounts, that they had heard of Cathay. The streets and temples, they condescendingly informed us, were made of gold, and the doors of the temples and the palaces were studded with turquoises and many other precious stones. Even the horses were harnessed with silver and gems, and the women were of surpassing loveliness. When they spoke of these things their eyes glowed and they licked their lips and scratched.

"I said to them: 'It is true that in Cathay are many treasures, but not what ye seek. They are treasures of the mind, the jewels of philosophy, the gems of fine manners and gracious living.'

But of these things they had never heard, and stared at me with scornful amazement, as men might stare at an idiot. It was most evident that they were what the people of Cathay call us: barbarians. In truth, they were even less civilized than we, for they tried to repay our hospitality with treachery and theft, for all their fine words about their god, and our women were not safe with them. One morning we awoke and discovered that they had made off with our father's best horses, and two of my sisters. We pursued them, and found them with little trouble. We left their bodies for the vultures to pick to the bones. My father said to me, for I was a youth then 'Beware of him who cometh with holy words and eyes that are piously lifted, and mouth that is piously drawn down, for surely he is a thief and a liar and a traitor.' Then he ordered the Nestorian Christians among us to be tortured and killed, for they had seemed to understand something of what the pale men had said, though somewhat puzzled."

Kurelen stuffed his mouth with a choice piece of young mutton, and chewed with a pleasant expression on his face, as though his thoughts pleased him.

"My father was a wise man. He preferred murder to argument. I often thought he had an envious eye on the Christians' swords and chains of mail, and was grateful for their treachery. Otherwise, he would have been hard put to it to find a way to violate the laws of hospitality."

The boys laughed. Jamuga had listened with passionate intensity. Kurelen glanced at him. "As thou dost know, Jamuga, thy mother is the wife of Lotchu, half-brother to Yesukai. She cometh from the Naiman, and was one of their fairest maidens. But before she married Lotchu she was with child by one of the pale men. Thou wert that child. Yet, it is strange: thou art neither mealy-mouthed nor pious, treacherous nor crafty. That proveth that good blood can drown out black."

Jamuga smiled with reserve; he was a youth without humor, and suspected those guilty of it. He was certain that Kurelen was mocking him. Nevertheless, he was secretly proud. The bitter suns and winds of the Gobi could not completely darken his fair skin. His eyes were as blue as the mirage waters of the Lake of the Damned, which he had seen once on a time. This blueness of his eyes was not fierce or hot, but rather misty and fragile and very pale. Though Temujin, his anda, had the gray eyes of the Bourchikoun, and hair the color of raw red gold, he seemed darker than Jamuga, whose fine hair was the color of an autumn leaf. Moreover, Jamuga's body was lighter and more delicate, his eye-sockets wide and straight instead of slanting, his nose smaller and tilted, his mouth gentle and reserved. There was no ferocity about him, no anger that was wild and untamed. When angry, he felt as cold as death, and only the rigidity of his fine features betrayed his emotion. Too, though courageous, he did not care for wrestling, which was the chief amusement of the young Yakka Mongols. On the other hand, he was not liked, except by those of subservient spirit, for he was of a peculiar temperament, almost sullen, aloof, haughty, imperious, yet at times kind and sensitive. When the hunters returned with the spoils of their raids, he was not interested in the swords and the lances and scimitars and bow-cases and the arrows of various weights, nor in the lacquered shields and the cattle and camels. He did not care for the bags of silver coins, mixed with gold. But he was his mother's favorite, and also beloved of his stepfather, Lotchu, who was afraid of him, and he was always able to coax and wheedle the things he desired from their shares of the loot. In the yurt which he shared with his half-brothers he had a strong Chinese chest of his own, made of the hardest black wood, and in that chest he had gathered lengths of silvery cloth, ivory figurines exquisitely carved, rolled manuscripts painted with strange characters of tiny lovely faces and gracious Chinese landscapes, silver cups beautifully traced and shaped, daggers with ivory sheaths inlaid with silver, and small rugs which glowed like jewels, and even strings of turquoises and pearls, and silver and ivory flutes. No one laughed at him to his face, partly because Lotchu was a fierce warrior, and partly because there was something mysterious and odd in Jamuga himself, which made laughter sound foolish. He had long ago discovered that men laugh only at those who have been guilty of familiarity, and that if a man sits at your side and eats with you in equality, and drinks from your cup, he will consider himself your equal, or even your superior. Jamuga secretly thought no one his equal or superior, yet he had no contempt in him except for those like Kurelen, who laughed when laughter was not indicated. To the end of his life, Jamuga suspected those who laughed with their eyes, only, and especially those who laughed internally. This was because he was enormously egotistic, but had the wit to be able to conceal this egotism from the simple. But from Kurelen, and from the Shaman, who detested him, he had not been able to conceal it.

Moreover, though generous to a few, and especially to the helpless, he was avaricious and selfish and secretive. Rarely did his eye warm with human emotion and tenderness, except for Temujin (whom he considered not too intelligent) and for his mother. He suspected, with truth, that Kurelen understood this about him, also, and with his dislike for the crippled man was mingled cold apprehension.

But Kurelen was fond of him, for he knew that Jamuga never lied nor cheated, nor was consciously cruel, and that his word, once given, was even more rigid than the word of the Mongols, if that were possible. He knew he had honor almost beyond belief, and that he was brave and steadfast. Kurelen had taught him to read the language of Cathay, and even as much as he knew of the language of the Turkomans, the inhabitants of Baghdad and Samarkand. He had taught him philosophy and the religions of other men. But never had he been able to teach him that delicate laughter at others, which is without brutality, and filled only with wry cynicism and mirth at oneself. Jamuga, thought Kurelen, with some regret, was too egotistic for humor, for above all things he had a passion for his own pride, and a deep love for himself. In that pride and that love, Kurelen suspected, sprang his bitter honor, his hatred for ferocity, his contemplative mind.

Kurelen, who had lived in more or less amity with his old enemy, the Shaman, for some years now, once said to him: "Kokchu, when thou hast eventually disposed of me, thou wilt have another with whom to converse. Jamuga. And a far more comfortable other, for, lacking the ability to laugh, he will be no asp in thy hand."

But the Shaman had smiled his dark subtle smile, and had replied: "Men of mind who laugh are dangerous, but more dangerous are men of mind who do not laugh." He had tapped Kurelen on the chest: "Thou and I, Kurelen, are rascals, therefore we can enjoy each other. But this youth is no rascal, and I have no love for him."

Jamuga, Kurelen observed, grinning, had no love for the Shaman, either. But Jamuga did not condescend to tease the Shaman, nor argue with him, nor give him tribal honor. He merely ignored him. Jamuga's mother was a simple woman, and a comely one, and Kokchu had long enjoyed her; otherwise Jamuga might have long ago been found with a knife in his back, or mysteriously left upon the desert for the vultures. In him, Kokchu had long ago recognized a mortal enemy.

"Men of thought," said Kurelen, "who are without mirth and humor, are vigorous enemies of all charlatans, whereas men of thought and humor tolerate them and are grateful for their buffoonery in a tiresome world."

Once or twice he had wished that Jamuga liked him. That was because he was the anda of Temujin, whom Kurelen loved with all his heart, as he loved Houlun. At first he had feared that Jamuga might injure Temujin's affection for his uncle, and then he had lost his fear. Jamuga was incapable of tampering with the loyalties of others, even of his friend.

Once Jamuga had complained fastidiously of some of the cruder cruelties and debaucheries of the Yakka Mongols. Their lustiness offended him; their ruthlessness and savagery revolted him. Then it was, to his own profound surprise, that Kurelen had said:

"It is these things which make our people invincible and strong and undefeated. Townsmen, whom thou dost admire, are weak. Temples are places for eunuchs, and academies the houses of castration. The man who sits on his hams and contemplates hath the soul of a slave, and he who writeth in books and he who readeth the books, is a man without bowels."

While Jamuga was interested profoundly in the subject of the wandering Christians, Temujin was interested only in Kurelen's accounts of the great riches and power of Cathay, its decaying grandeur, its cynical decadence, its generals, ministers, princes and emperors. He liked to hear his uncle tell about the Northern Kins and the native Sung dynasty of Cathay, and the tragic chaos which internal conflict was inducing in that magnificent empire. Above all, Kurelen observed, the youth was minutely absorbed in every account of the military weaknesses of Cathay, and the strength of the Turkish towns and cities in the vicinity of the Orkhon River. As he listened to these accounts, Temujin's dilated nostrils would expand still more, as though with contempt, and there would be an eager gleam in his tilted gray eyes.

Temujin was a handsome youth, though not quite as tall and impressive of stature as Bektor, his hated half-brother, nor quite as broad as Belgutei, Bektor's brother. But he was alert, and swift as a fox, and never tired, and his step was swifter than that of the others, his glance quicker and more piercing, his manner shorter and more decisive. His face was bronzed by wind and sun, and his cheekbones were broad and harsh, framed by two thick braids of red hair. His mouth, straight and hard, rarely laughed, though he could smile occasionally, and then with a sort of impatience. His gleaming eyes, his expanded nostrils in his jutting nose, his broad darkened face and grim chin caught the most casual glance and held it. For there was a fateful ferocity about him, which had nothing of primitive innocence and simple animalism. Rather, it was a ferocity which was completely aware, and as implacable as stone, and as cruel and impersonal as death.

Jamuga might consider Temujin not overly subtle or intelligent, but Kurelen knew that Jamuga was never a good judge of other men. Such as Jamuga spent their lives in a confused and resentful quandary, because others upon whom they had passed early judgment failed to justify that judgment in later days. Jamuga, to the end of his life, never understood the deeps in Temujin, and when the day came for him to die he could only die in despair and weariness, still not understanding. In his own soul there was always this weariness, this tired impotence, even in youth, and Temujin's restless energy, his avid seeking, his lust for life, his exuberant passion for all things, offended him. Once he had called Temujin a barbarian, and then when Temujin had stared, and had laughed loud and long, Jamuga was affronted as though by some subtle insult. When, towards the end of his life, he dimly guessed what lay beneath the surface of Temujin's impatient nature and rough hard manner, Jamuga was so appalled, so stricken down, that he turned to death as one turns to opium, loathing himself, and full of hatred and misery. He told himself he might have known, had he not been a fool, but his own egotism, his own necessity to condescend, had made it impossible to discern in Temujin what Kurelen and a few others had discerned from the beginning.

Kurelen had known. He had tried to make his sister understand, when she had demanded of him that he teach Temujin to read and to write. But she, too, was egotistic, and for a long time there was the most acrimonious dispute between the brother and sister because of Kurelen's refusal.

"Thou dost teach that pale-lipped Jamuga, that white-faced camel!" she would cry, hotly. "But my son, my Temujin, thou wilt not teach."

And he said to her, over and over: "Houlun, Temujin hath no need for written words. There is in him such a thing that words would despoil. He is greater than words, more powerful than written folly. I dare not teach him."

And he added, often: "Take thy son behind the walls of Cathay, to those who make eunuchs of men. And then I will teach him."

Kurelen thought again of this, watching the violent play of crude light and shadow on Temujin's face, as he listened to his uncle's accounts of the weakness and impotence and splendor of the mighty empire of Cathay. He thought to himself, wryly: I am the only one who remembereth the prophecies that attended his naming, and I, at the last, am the only one who believeth in them. For surely, on this youth's high broad brow, in his restless and rapacious eyes, the color of granite, in his mouth, with its protruding under lip, in all his expression, at once savage, wild and cold, in his voice, not loud but strong and measured, was something greater than other men, something which made small souls uneasy and afraid, and which made larger souls even more uneasy and more afraid. This uneasiness was always present in Jamuga's face, when he spoke or turned his eyes in the direction of his beloved anda, and he tried to hide it in an assumption of indulgent superiority, or, at times, in captious irritability.

Turning from these two, as he related his stories, Kurelen found it some relief to gaze at Kasar, Temujin's younger brother. Here was such a simple, uncomplicated spirit, without the dark chasms in that of Temujin's, and the petty fastidiousness of Jamuga's. Short, broad, powerful and direct, this was a youth upon which one could look with a sensation of restfulness, for there was no rapacity in him, no envies, no uneasiness, no lusts except those of the animal-body, no seekings, no miseries of the mind. He loved his mother and his brother, Temujin. He hated Bektor, because Bektor hated Temujin. He loved Kurelen because Kurelen loved Temujin. He was the enemy of the Shaman, because he had discerned that the Shaman disliked Temujin. It was all as simple as this, to this loyal and simple youth. There was only one deviousness in all his emotions, and that was his emotion for Jamuga, who was more beloved of Temujin than himself. For Jamuga he had a hatred as pure and primitive as a beast's. But he hid it deeply in his heart, fearful that Temujin would cast him out if he discovered this.

His face was as full and flat as the full moon, and as faintly yellow. Above the wide shelf of his broad cheekbones were set his fixed black eyes in their slanting sockets. His nostrils were so broad, his nose so shallow, that he had a slightly porcine look. His wide mouth was full and red, and somewhat sullen. This unoriginal boy, with the doglike heart, had only one originality: he cut his coarse black hair closely to his big round skull.

Jamuga wanted to know more of that mysterious continent to the west, from which his father had come. Kurelen had to draw much on what he had heard to enlarge the little he had seen. But he had the gift of winnowing the false from the true and his stories were strikingly accurate. Moreover, Jamuga, who knew nothing beyond the desert and the mountains of the Gobi, had the incomprehensible faculty of discerning falseness, without experience. So Kurelen, who might have colored his narrative with fantasy for the sake of Temujin and Kasar, found himself adhering to what he believed to be the truth.

"Jamuga Sechen," he said, "thou art a hole in the sand, which is never filled. The stories I have told thee are all I know."

Jamuga smiled his faint and frigid smile. "Tell them again, Kurelen. Know that I could hear them hourly, and still be unsatisfied."

Kurelen shrugged his shoulders with resignation. Temujin frowned slightly, and then listened attentively. Kasar yawned, investigated Kurelen's pot for left-over morsels. He thrust his finger deeply into the pot, secured some fragments of meat and gravy, and licked his fingers with simple and unaffected appreciation. Chassa was with the other women tonight, so Kasar stood up on his strong short legs and replenished the dung fire. Kurelen cast him a grateful glance, glad to rest his eyes upon him as a relief from the exigent Jamuga Sechen. The fire replenished, Kasar stood near it, his legs spread out, his hands on his hips, an expression of boredom on his features. The red fire was like a fan of light radiating up Kasar's body, its extended circle ending just below his eyes which glistened like those of a mountain wolf's. His long full robe of coarse gray wool was banded at his thick waist with a belt of red leather, in which were thrust a curved Turkish scimitar and his short dagger. He looked only at Temujin, and there was a doglike devotion on his face. The wind sounded like muffled drums on the walls of the yurt.

Kurelen spoke mechanically: "It is a strange land to the westward, Europe, a land of many nations, and many climates. But more fertile than High Asia, it is said. There are forests there, of trees such as we have never seen, and mountains as high as ours, and blue as the twilight, each gazing over the other's head, and crowned with snow. There are steppes like ours, countless leagues of them, and then there are rivers that never end, as green as grass or golden. And lakes like seas of flat silver. There are places that are dark and gloomy, filled with giants with yellow hair and eyes like hawks, men as untamed as eagles. There are nations that are hot and languorous, full of odd fruits and laughing people. There are many cities scattered in those lands, but none so fair, so beautiful, so gracious as the cities of Asia. They are cities of gray stone and mud and rotting wood, filthy beyond imagination. And those who live in them are as crude as their cities and as ugly and dirty. I have this on the best authority. They have no civilization, these people, and their stupidity and ignorance are matched only by their craftiness and cowardice. Their temples are reflections of their souls, and are uncouth and peculiar and squat. The cities are far apart, and there are no fine courier-roads between them, but only thorny wilderness and black forests and malignant rivers. Each people struggles with another people, and all their battles are marked by the most virulent hatred and treachery and cruelty. The Turkomans would disdain their crudities and violences. There is no generosity among them, no honor, no loyalty, no friendship. Look not incredulous, Jamuga Sechen. I know all this to be true. Most of them are followers of Christianity, which must be a parlous creed, in truth, if it breeds such monsters. As for their women, it is said that they are bowed of leg and rotten of teeth, and have a most insupportable stench."

The young men laughed. Kasar, standing over the fire showed his wet white teeth.

"They have no music, no culture, no men of learning, no philosophies and no academies of any moment," went on Kurelen. "The meanest slave in the streets of Cathay would spit at them contemptuously. Their poetry is the boasting of pusillanimous children, and their songs are the crude strumming of wandering minstrels. Their kings cannot compare with the sultans of Persia and Bokhara and Kunduz and Balkh and Samarkand, for they are like bears that walk about on their hind legs, and roar thickly. Before the servants of Islam, before the Persian imam and sayyid, the priests of these Christians are mumbling and dirty clowns, without learning or knowledge. At times they have had the audacity, I am told, to send some of their priests to the splendid courts of Cathay, where the emperor, a man of folly in that he believed in kindness and tolerance, received them with fool's courtesy. And there they would sit, these barbarians in their rope-belted robes of cotton and wool, their dirty feet laced with leather thongs, their beards and hair swarming with lice, their breath as foul as that of a carrion bird's, and gaze about them arrogantly, condescending to the high-born ladies and lords of the emperor's court, shedding their vermin on rich carpets, laying down their filthy bodies on couches of silk and cloth of gold, thrusting their unclean fingers into porcelain bowls. Indeed, the emperor was a fool! But I have already told ye how these priests betrayed the emperor."

"I have never seen men from those strange lands," said Temujin. "But I despise them."

Kasar yawned. He lifted the flap of the yurt and gazed out. "Chepe Noyon and Bektor are wrestling," he said, eagerly.

"Bektor is not obeying the laws. He is trying to kick Chepe Noyon in the belly."

Temujin rose to his feet with one swift unfolding of his legs. He peered over Kasar's shoulder, and shouted. "The offal! It is so, Kasar. Let us go out and teach Bektor the first rule of good manners."

The two youths sprang out of the yurt, leaving Jamuga and Kurelen alone. Kurelen wiped his hands, and remarked that he had nothing more to tell. Jamuga regarded him gravely, his distrust and dislike of Kurelen chilling his eyes with reserve.

"There is but one more thing, Kurelen, that I wish to know. What was the name or rank of those men of whom my father was a brother?"

Kurelen chuckled. "They called themselves Crusaders, or rescuers. They would bring to Asia, they said, the ennobling beauty of their creed, the civilizing gentleness of their god. They brought nothing, but they did not return empty-handed. They took the Saracens' disease to their wives, and to the beds of all their women."

chapter 10

Chepe Noyon, a sweet, brave but fiery youth of passionate tempers and erratic emotions, was much beloved of Temujin, who regarded him as a younger brother. He was somewhat small and delicate and wiry of body, and had the bright innocent face of a child, with laughing mouth and dancing eyes. He was noted for his wit and his gaiety and his love for the maidens. Temujin frequently swore that Chepe Noyon understood the language of the horses, for he had but to approach them for them to neigh at him eagerly, their eyes glittering and rolling. He apparently gave them no audible commands, yet they obeyed instantly, moving as though part of his small body. Because of his wit, which could be as sharp as a sliver of crystal ice, he was not a favorite with all his tribe, and especially not with the jealous Jamuga, who tolerated him because of Temujin, but distrusted him for his laughter and his tongue. But he was admired by all men for his prodigious courage, amazing in so slight and feminine a body, and for his unerring aim with the bow, and his mad ferocity in a battle or a raid. Though still very young, he could astonish the old men with his craftiness and his knowledge. He was beloved of the women, for he deigned to be aware of them, and flattered them, and he would be certain at all times that his mother and sisters and their friends would reserve for him the choicest morsel from the pots.

Bektor, Temujin's half-brother, hated Chepe Noyon as he hated all that loved Temujin and was beloved of him. He was a strong, square, dark-faced youth, with overhanging brows, triangular cheekbones, and thick sulky lips. Though he was a bully, he was no coward. His dark body was the body of a wrestler and a warrior, and there was a primal splendor about him which fascinated even his enemies, of which he had no small number. There was none he loved, except his younger brother, Belgutei, who at times displayed a disconcerting admiration for Temujin, and a desire for his company. None saw the pathos of Bektor's love for Belgutei, and the sullen eagerness he displayed for Belgutei's careless affection. Somber, short of speech, irritable, formidable of face and expression, splendid and without fear, his heart was full of bitterness and hatred, especially for Temujin. It was he, he thought, that ought to have been the first-born of his father, Yesukai, and not this gray-eyed, red-haired son of Houlun, who mocked him at every encounter. For each knew what was in the heart of the other, and knew what an adversary he had.

He had no friends. Not even Belgutei was his true friend, for Belgutei disliked darkness and gloominess, and preferred the gaiety of those who surrounded Temujin. But Belgutei was an affable and generous youth, amiable and accommodating, and at all times not to be trusted overmuch. He was too selfish. He would remain devoted and loyal to a leader and a victor, and even sacrifice his life for such a man. But let that leader and victor be once defeated, and Belgutei would be among the first to aid in his destruction. Though he was still a boy, he would speculate reflectively upon the merits of his brother, Bektor, and his half-brother, Temujin, and wonder to whom he would eventually dedicate his final loyalty. In the meantime, he was friends with both, and was much liked by Temujin.

When Temujin and Kasar hurried to the central campfire, they learned, through the huge laughter of the old men and the warriors who were watching, that Chepe Noyon had been tormenting Bektor for his lack of popularity with the maidens of the tribe, and had been giving him some ribald advice. Bektor, admitted the happy watchers, had withstood the gibes nobly, until at last his black patience had broken, and he had attacked Chepe Noyon, who was much his inferior in weight and skill.

It was not good to the Mongols that a stronger should attack a weaker, and there had been a murmur of anger. But after a moment, they ceased their murmuring, and shouted with delight. For Chepe Noyon, recovering from the first assault, had returned Bektor's blows courageously, fighting like a small fox against the onslaughts of a wolf. Bektor was disconcerted. Only the Shaman saw that he had been moderating his blows, and that it was only his rage which gave him so formidable an aspect. Finally, in order to end a combat which he knew would be unequal if he exerted himself, he had lifted his foot and plunged it into Chepe Noyon's belly. It was this gesture which Kasar had seen, and which had aroused his passionate indignation. By the time he and Temujin arrived, Bektor, in haste to end the struggle, of which he was already ashamed, had seized Chepe Noyon about the waist and was bending him backwards. The small youth's backbone had begun to crack. An expression of agony distorted his girlish but fearless face; there was an intense look of concentration in his tormented eyes, as though his will alone was resisting death. He had thrust his thumbs into Bektor's nostrils, and thin trickles of blood glittered in the firelight as they ran down Bektor's chin and lips.

Temujin, after a swift glance, uttered a loud shout and sprang upon his half-brother. He struck down Bektor's arms; Chepe Noyon fell in a heap at his feet. Some one dragged the half-conscious youth from the fire. An utter silence fell on the assembled warriors and old men. Yesukai fixed his eyes sternly upon his two sons, and bit his lips. Beyond the range of the men's heads the faces of women and children appeared, open-mouthed and open-eyed. Houlun was there, and beside her stood the Karait woman, the mother of Bektor. Between the two women was the most venomous enmity, and as they gazed upon the two youths facing each other like colored and barbaric statues, bending forward from their hips and their teeth sparkling, their nostrils distended, their hands flexed into claws, each woman held her breath and prayed to her particular spirit for help for her son. No one noticed Kurelen limping up, nor Jamuga, silent and still, his pale face paler than ever as he watched.

Wild and somber black eye gazed savagely into wild and dilated gray eye. They could smell each other's hot breath. The firelight gave them a violent and beastlike aspect. Bektor's distorted face, filled with hatred and rage, was dark as midnight, his lips drawn back over his teeth in a soundless snarl. Temujin's face was the color of Chinese lead, his eyes the hue of silver with lightning upon it. Kurelen reflected that here was primitive beauty at its most perfect. Both youths were tall, though Bektor was larger and broader than Temujin. But Temujin was quicker and fleeter. They were well matched. And between them was a hatred that was as pure as the hatred of one animal for another, free of subtlety and treachery.

They faced each other, waiting for the first move, and no one spoke nor moved. Every warrior's brow wrinkled eagerly with expectation. Every nostril drew in a hot breath. There was no sound but the crackling of the high and blazing fire. It was soon evident that Bektor would not strike the first blow.

Then, almost too quick for eye to follow, Temujin sprang upon his enemy. He seized him about the waist. He intended to hurl him into the fire. Fury like a black storm swirled in him. Chepe Noyon was forgotten. The festering detestation of years swelled in his heart, poured its poison into his brain. There was in him an exultation, the passionate lust to kill.

After the first onslaught, they stood motionless, locked in each other's arms, their feet sunken into the gravelly earth, their muscles rising all over their bodies. Face was thrust into face; they could see each other's shining pupil swimming in the glistening iris. They could see each other's wet teeth, feel each other's scorching breath. As they gazed like this at each other, each felt that there was nothing else in the world but this combat, and only they two were alive in a dead universe. They forgot where they were, and who they were. They were elemental forces in the midst of a static chaos. They felt only one lust, one desire: to kill.

But they were so evenly matched that they stood as motionless as stone. But no one was deceived; every man knew that here was a gigantic struggle. They saw the two young faces slowly turn purple with exertion. They saw the veins rising on forehead and neck. They saw the glare slowly turn to flame in the eyes which saw nothing but the other eyes. They saw how white as chalk became the fingernails, and how the feet in their sandals arched and flexed. Kurelen thought: They should be painted on porcelain, in raw red and black and white and yellow, with the scarlet firelight outlining them, and filling every furrow of skin and gray robe. But no: not on porcelain, glazed and delicate, but on smooth stone, set in the desert, surrounded by pink hills and sand the color of bone.

The warriors suddenly raised a shout. Temujin had flung his leg about the thighs of his brother, Bektor. Body was pressed against body, as though fused together. Then, very slowly, with audible crackings of bone, Bektor was thrust backwards, his inclination followed by the bending body of Temujin. Slowly, almost imperceptibly, Bektor's spine bent. Yet never for an instant did wild eye leave wild eye. But Temujin had begun to grin like a wolf.

A moment later, with a groan, Bektor collapsed. He became limp in his brother's arms. Foam appeared on his lips. His eyes rolled upward, showing the red-threaded whites; they became fixed, like dead eyes. But still Temujin bent him backwards. In a moment more, he would break his back.

Suddenly there was a thin and piercing scream. Bektor's mother pushed her way through the crowding warriors with superhuman strength. She flung herself upon Temujin. She sunk her teeth into his neck, and hung on to him like a weasel upon the throat of a wolf. She uttered no sound after that first anguished cry, but her teeth bit in deeper, her head thrust between Temujin and her fainting son, her long hair hiding his contorted face.

Temujin, shocked by the attack, experienced excruciating pain in his throat. He felt his blood oozing about the murderous teeth of the woman, who seemed to have become a part of him, a vampire who would never let go. He staggered. His arms became weak as water. He heard a faint crash, and weight upon his feet, as Bektor fell upon them. Now he was concerned only with freeing himself from this loathsome thing, which filled him with horror rather than fear. His heart beat with sickening and choking disgust. He felt that any moment he would spew up vomit. He swung his head from side to side, staggering drunkenly. But the woman hung on, as though all her life was concentrated in her teeth. His hands plucked at her, striking her, squeezing her, his breath gone from his chest. But she would not let go.

Dimly, he heard a shout, followed by others, and then screams of rapturous delight. Darkness fell over his eyes. He felt himself sliding down the slope of a dark hill, into blackness. He was conscious of a burning anguish in his neck, and an emotion of intense loathing and shame. Then, the shouts and screams of ecstatic laughter became louder in his ears. He opened his eyes dully.

He was lying on his back, his head almost in the fire. But no one was looking at him. Whooping, striking each other with delight and huge mirth, rolling on their haunches, the warriors were watching the mad scrambling, scratching, tearing, shrieking, tumbling mass that was Houlun and the Karait woman. They rolled over and over on the ground, scattering the fire, their feet flailing into the faces of the helpless warriors, who were weeping in the excess of their laughter, their bodies rapidly becoming denuded. Now a naked leg appeared in the ball of their entwined bodies. Now a nude breast was exposed, now a thigh, and finally a torso. They had clenched their hands into each other's long and streaming hair. Their teeth were busy. They emitted growls like she-bears, and they worried each other, sinking their fangs into bare shoulder, throat or arm. They howled like wolves. Houlun would wrench herself to her knees, striking and scratching; then the Karait woman would drag her down and under. Their faces were distorted out of all semblance to humanity, and streaming with blood. Their eyes were swollen and black. A struggle which had portended death was ending in a farce.

Finally, they were totally naked, breast crushing into breast, covered only intermittently by their disordered hair. Leg twined about leg; arms like snakes wound about each other. Their hoarse breath whistled in their throats. Their expressions were mad. The warriors rolled helplessly upon the ground, panting with groans of laughter, wheezing like old men. Temujin sat up, shaking his head free of the splinters of red light that pierced his eyes. Bektor had been dragged away from the seat of the combat of the women. And then when Temujin saw his mother like this, naked and covered with blood, her face almost unrecognizable, he was pierced by the deepest shame and degradation. He burst into tears.

He heard renewed shouts. Yesukai had entered the fray, wielding a camel whip. He stood over the rolling women, lashing indiscriminately. His whip tore red, bleeding welts into their naked flesh, caught strands of their streaming hair and wrenched them from their scalps. They released each other, rolling apart, trying to protect their bodies with their hands, doubling up their legs. Their buttocks winced under the blows; they folded their arms across their tender breasts, and bent their heads between their shoulders. Temujin, weeping, closed his eyes.

He felt himself carried away. When he opened his eyes again, he was in Kurelen's yurt. The crippled man was spent with laughter, and exhausted. But Jamuga, his face pale with disgust, was gravely laving his anda's face with cool water, and wiping away the clotted blood on his throat.

"A she-wolf hath bitten thee," he said quietly.

Temujin raised his voice in lamentations for the disgrace of his mother. Kurelen shook his head, laughing deeply in his chest.

"Regret nothing that doth give occasion for laughter, Temujin," he said.

But Jamuga fixed his eyes upon him with stern loathing.

"Thou art wrong, Kurelen. There are times when laughter is more bitter than death, and less endurable."

chapter 11

Bektor wept also, learning of his mother's disgrace.

"I shall never lift my face again, and look straightly into another's eyes, knowing that it was my mother, a weak woman, who saved me from death," he lamented.

He would not see his mother, though bruised and broken and torn, she stood outside the yurt he occupied with his brother, Belgutei, waiting humbly to speak to him. He could not forgive her. He would allow only the Shaman, who was his elder adviser and friend, to attend him, and his brother. When his father, Yesukai, entered and upbraided him harshly in vague terms, he hid his face for shame. Even when Yesukai kicked him savagely, he offered no resistance. He realized that the chieftain had been disgraced also, and knew no other way of avenging himself. Yesukai professed to be outraged that his sons should attack each other. But he would not have been so exercised, Bektor knew, if one had killed his enemy. A Mongol accepted grief simply; it was one of the aspects of living. But disgrace he never accepted. His sons, he cried, might have been ennobled by death; alive, they were occasions for the laughter of the meanest of the herdboys and the slaves.

Bektor accepted this abuse and the kicking with humility, acknowledging the truth of his father's words. He kissed Yesukai's feet in an access of regret and sorrow. Better had he died, and been forgotten, than lived and be remembered with mirth and ridicule, he said.

Yesukai listened darkly. Then he said: "The day must come when this must be settled in blood and death. Prepare for that day, Bektor."

To Temujin, whom he also kicked and upbraided, he said the same thing. Soon it was noised about through the whole ordu that Yesukai had commanded his sons to engage in a mortal combat, for the sake of his honor. But they would wait, until time had given them strength of sufficient dignity.

In the meantime, the Shaman attempted to console Bektor. "Temujin is older than thee by almost a year," he told his favorite, who was partly in his favor because of real liking, and partly because of Kokchu's own hatred for Temujin. "Too, he hath craft. Thou hast only strength."

"But he fighteth fairly!" exclaimed Bektor, quickly.

The Shaman exchanged a glance of contempt with the pliant and furtively smiling Belgutei. These two understood each other with remarkable insight.

"Know, Bektor, that a combat must be won at any cost. Thou hast told me before that victory is not true victory, if it be stained with guile or treachery. That is the belief of the fool. A victor, however he doth obtain his victory, is always justified by his followers, and by time. It is only the vanquished, at the last, who is judged a knave."

Bektor regarded him with some fear and distrust and uncertainty. But he was essentially of a simple nature. He also had the humility of that nature, and a belief in the superiority of any one of a smooth and subtle tongue. He gnawed his swollen lip, and knitted his brows. Surely, he was wrong, and the Shaman right. Nevertheless, he could not rid himself of uneasiness.

He said: "Mayhap I could waylay him, and slay him with a knife in the back, when he is unsuspecting."

"True," said the Shaman, frowning thoughtfully. "But that would bring thee little honor. The craft must be so artfully disguised that it appeareth valor. Let me judge for thee, and advise thee, Bektor. The folly of fools, however despised, must be considered."

Bektor, in his simplicity, consented. But still he was uneasy.

When the Shaman had departed, after anointing Bektor's back with a magic ointment to relieve the torn muscles and ligaments, Belgutei began to laugh. Bektor watched him a moment, then, his face turning crimson, he forced himself to a sitting position and hurled a basin at his brother. Belgutei rolled out of the way of the missile, and renewed his laughter.

"Thou art too serious!" he cried. "It was a brave fight, until the women came. Nevertheless, I am glad they did interfere. Otherwise, I would have lost my brother."

Bektor scowled. But he was touched pathetically at these affectionate words. Finally he smiled. He said, in an almost placating voice:

"Thou dost prefer me to Temujin, Belgutei?"

Without a moment's hesitation, the wily youth replied: "Thou art my brother. It is thou who shouldst be the khan when our father is dead, and not Temujin. Thou hast only to do what the Shaman would have thee do."

"Dost thou trust him?"

Belgutei widened his eyes. He smiled slightly. "I trust no one, Bektor, not even thee. Thou art too simple. But the others are too guileful. Trust the Shaman only to the extent of the advancement of his own interests. Beyond that, trust no one."

A feeling of ineffable sadness came over Bektor. Despite his dark and formidable features, he looked wounded. He was the simple man, distressed that other men could be devious and treacherous, and envying them a little in his heart for their ability to deceive.

The Shaman, upon leaving Bektor, went to Temujin's yurt. Kurelen, who was becoming bored by his nephew's lamentations, and Jamuga's melancholy and mortification, greeted the Shaman with pleasure, though he eyed him keenly, knowing his predilection for Bektor.

"Ah, now, Kokchu, thou canst give these womanish youths some fortitude. They wail like girls."

The Shaman pursed his lips, and without replying, examined Temujins injuries. "A woman's bite is like a dog's bite," he commented. "There is a venom in their slaver."

Kurelen made a wry grimace. He narrowed his eyes. He did not like the serious expression on the face of his old enemy, which he knew was hypocrisy.

Kokchu passed his long dark hands, as flexible as serpents, over the throat of Temujin, and muttered an incantation. Kurelen began to smile. Jamuga watched with cool reserve, the bloody cloth in his hand.

Having done with his incantations, the Shaman regarded Temujin severely.

"It is not good for kinsmen to quarrel," he said. "I have come from Bektor, and he is properly ashamed. I said to him: 'Know that every man doth need every friend, and every brother his brother, for this is a fierce world without mercy or hope for the vanquished.' Make up thy quarrel with thy brother, Temujin. It is an evil day when the blood of kindred floweth."

Kurelen raised his brows at these moral sentiments. But Kokchu, without a glance at him or at Jamuga, walked with a stately step from the yurt, every movement of his body expressing his reproach and indignant coldness. When he had gone, Kurelen exchanged a look with Jamuga, who was pale with anger.

"When a serpent speaketh of brotherly love, it is time for honest men to flee," he said.

Temujin did not speak. His features settled in a mask of obstinate sullenness. But Jamuga replied eagerly:

"It is so, Kurelen. If Bektor had killed Temujin, the Shaman would not have engaged in such fine talk of kindred blood. Kokchu is ambitious."

Kurelen nodded. "Let men beware when one of lust appeareth among them, but let all men arm themselves when a priest coveteth power."

chapter 12

Temujin and his friends, Jamuga Sechen, Chepe Noyon and Subodai, and his brother, Kasar, came in at sunset, jubilant. Temujin loved white stallions, and his father had given him one on an occasion when he was pleased with him. The youth had come upon a huge bear unexpectedly, and had slain him with his short dagger, a prodigious feat. The white stallion was a gift. Henceforth, Temujin would ride no other sort of horse. But Jamuga Sechen preferred black horses, small and fleet and compact, with his own narrow grace. Chepe Noyon loved gay horses, that would cavort in high spirits. His steed was a young mottled mare with a knowing and flirtatious eye, and an arched tail. Subodai, whom Kurelen called the distillation of pure virtue, rode a gray mare who could drift like a spectral shadow, almost unseen, through herds and through groups of men.

Yesukai's ordu had reached the winter pastures. The greenish-gray steppes were rimed at sunset with gray drops of frozen crystal. Beyond this dim sea of tall and whispering grass were far and floating masses of violet hills, scuttled out by ghostly rose. But the west was a lake of dark and savage scarlet, and the figures of the five young horsemen loomed against it, black and sharp and featureless, as they rode swiftly, shouting, through the bending grasses. The hunt had been good, that day. Each youth rode his horse as though part of it, straight young back swayed lightly with the movement of the animal, strong straight legs stiffened in the stirrups. Their high pointed hats cut the sunset like black daggers; their felt coats were belted about their narrow hard waists; their bow-cases were slung on their backs. But featureless and colorless though they were, Kurelen knew each youth by his silhouette against the burning sky. There was Temujin, taller than the others on his taller horse, riding with a wild and quiet pride, like a horseman running down the slope of the heavens from some mysterious other world. About him rode his friends, young paladins of a king, a kind of savage dignity about them, splendor in the poise of their heads and the straightness of their shoulders.

Kurelen reflected that Temujin had the ability to inspire devotion in good and brave and valorous men, and often, in men nobler than himself. Among those who loved him sincerely were none of flawed and cunning character, none who followed him for sheer self-gain. Kurelen wondered at this, for Temujin was a somber and furious youth at times, hasty, harsh and implacable, unbending and often inexorable. He had little patience in small matters, and could be most brutal and exigent. Yet in him was the best of Mongol generosity and fearlessness, and his word, once given to a friend, would never be broken. He was honest with Mongol honesty, which was simple and primitive. If he were ever subtle, it was not with the sublety of Jamuga, but with the deep and innocent subtlety which was yet more profound than the other's. In time, Temujin would be a wise and ferocious man, magnificent, endowed with primal and heroic dignity. But it was not all these things which inspired the devotion of his friends. It was something in the glance of his gray eye, steadfast and eaglelike, something in his lifted profile, with its slumbering aspect of awful power and ageless strength. This was a youth fashioned by the mysterious agents of supernatural power to be a king among men, an instrument made by the gods for some dreadful but splendid purpose of their own. And it was all this that Temujin's friends knew without conscious awareness.

He could inspire devotion in men like Kasar, childlike and unthinking, like the greater mass of mankind. He could inspire love in those like Jamuga, who loved philosophy and wisdom and thought. He could draw the affection of those like Chepe Noyon, gay adventurers, courageous, laughing, eager and resistless. And then, strangest of all, this youth without pure virtue could seize the passionate adherence of those like Subodai, silent, thoughtful, brave, pure, devoted and lofty. In truth, here was an embryo khan of all men, to whose banner of the yak tails would flock every kind of spirit, including those like Belgutei, who followed a victor in order to share in the spoils.

Kurelen often remarked that in the presence of unsullied virtue, like that of Subodai, men were crestfallen and uneasy, or inspired with selfless love, or convulsed with remorseless malignancy and hatred. Subodai had the face and body of a young god, beautiful and quiet and meditative. His smile was a gleam, his glance like a shaft of light. His voice was low and sweet. He had never been known to do a cruel thing, or a treacherous one. Yet none was braver than he, none more without fear, none swifter with the sword nor more graceful on a horse. Sometimes Kurelen suspected that he was more profound than Jamuga, with his wan and bitter lip, and his deep and jealous eye. But Subodai spoke very simply, so that the dullest man could comprehend. His enemies were more venomous than the enemies of Temujin, and those who loved him loved him even more deeply than they loved the young son of the Khan. Kurelen had taught him to read. Jamuga was free and lucid with comments during the lessons, but Subodai listened in silence, his still, dark-blue eyes fixed lambently on Kurelen's lips, his face like pale and burnished bronze. To the end of his life, no one ever knew what he thought, not even Kurelen, who could only guess. The Shaman hated him more than he did Jamuga Sechen, who might at times be beguiled by a clever phrase.

Subodai knew more about horses than did Chepe Noyon, who understood their language. When he sat his shadowy gray mare, with the morning light upon his face, it seemed to many that this was some beautiful and majestic spirit who communicated his thought to his steed by a mere breath or sigh or touch. He had a genius for organizing potent cavalry, and though he was still very young, Yesukai had already appointed him the master of the younger horsemen, which Chepe Noyon had copiously and humorously resented. But no one, not even the most ambitious, could long be resentful of this chivalrous youth, who offended none except by the very effulgence of his nature and his soul, and the beauty of his aspect.

Kasar was jealous of him, as was Jamuga Sechen, for at times it appeared to them that Temujin loved Subodai more than themselves. But at other times Temujin was uneasy with Subodai, and seemed impatient, and would avoid him. These were the times, commented Kurelen, when Temujin's actions would not conspicuously bear the light of day.

For the rest, Subodai was a flutist of marvellous accomplishment, and when he played it seemed to many that it was not a silver instrument he held in his lips, but that it was the very voice of his spirit that they heard. Through the medium of his flute Subodai's heart was made manifest, so poignant and thrilling in every note that solemn tears would rise to the eyes of those who heard.

When Subodai was amused, he did not laugh outright like the hearty Mongols, who loved laughter almost as much as they loved hunting and raiding. But his entire face, from his eyes down to his lips, became illuminated, and at once he seemed the very soul of mirth and lightness.

It was significant, thought Kurelen, as the young men rode so gallantly into the tent village, that they had assumed the appropriate places about Temujin, who rode in the center of his followers. On his right hand was his anda, Jamuga Sechen, on his left, Subodai, the chivalrous. Behind him trotted the simple and faithful Kasar. Cavorting wildly back and forth, making forays, falling behind, galloping up and circling, with shouts, came the gay adventurer Chepe Noyon. But always, like a lodestone, Temujin drew about him, magnetically and irresistibly, the bodies and hearts of his followers. This vehement and tempestuous youth, with the angry gray eyes and the violent profile, had a mysterious and nameless power which none could oppose.

The spoils of the hunt having been distributed, the spirits of the young men were still high. The moon had risen now, and the distant hills had turned as black as polished ebony under its argent light, their rounded tops plated with bright silver. The long grasses of the steppes had become luminously gray, rolling like a spectral sea before the wind. The limitless sky was flooded with a milky radiance, and the air, sharp and clear as crystal, had an exciting quality in it.

The young men raced, shouting and screaming, over the steppes, cracking their whips furiously, standing up in their stirrups, their belted coats floating stiffly behind them. The dogs scampered after them, barking wildly, nipping at the heels of the galloping and rearing horses. The old men came to the doors of their yurts, and grinning, watched the race, their faded eyes bright with envy. The maidens clapped and laughed, the children shrieked. The women beside the orange campfires stirred the pots and smiled with excitement. The camels screamed thinly, tugging at their ropes; the other horses, mad with jealousy, neighed and reared. Even the cattle and the sheep lowed and bleated. When the young men finally returned to the ordu, their horses were white with foam.

Temujin and his followers gathered around Kurelen's fire, ably tended by the mute and devoted Chassa. It was not only love that brought them. They had long ago learned that in Kurelen's pot could be found the choicest meat and the richest gravy. In some way, he always contrived to have Turkish and Chinese sweetmeats in his silver boxes. His leather bags were always bursting with wine and kumiss. If milk were short in the ordu, it could always be found about Kurelen's fire. Then, after dining to the point of bursting, the young men usually could persuade him to sing them the strangest songs, which stirred their blood and filled them with mysterious longing. Here they could laugh and joke and box and wrestle freely, confident of sympathy and friendship. They knew that Kurelen loved youth, however wry his tongue, and that he admired them profoundly for their beauty, strength and fearlessness. Kurelen had no dogs, for he detested them. Temujin, who had never rid himself of his terror of them, could come here and not be forced to conceal that terror from the eyes of his followers. When the young men boasted, Kurelen did not eye them with the quizzical jocoseness and acid smiles of the old men, who hated them, and envied them. Rather, he listened, one eyebrow streaking up towards his long black hair, a smile of mingled affection, interest and amusement on his long lean face. Even when he spoke venomously, they could laugh, knowing that it was mostly venom directed against himself, or at the worst, it was good-natured.

Temujin ate with a monster appetite this night. Some inner fire and excitement seemed to devour him. He drank until Kurelen was obliged to take the sacks away from him, with a ribald and pointed remark. He insisted that each of his followers wrestle with him, and even when he threw them, one after another, the flame that consumed him did not seem quenched or lessened. His eyes glittered in the mingled firelight and moonlight. His breath was hard and audible and quick. He could not sit down, but stood near the fire, his legs straddled, his hands on his hips, his mouth stretched in panting laughter. Despite the coldness of the air, he had opened his coat and his wool robe, and his bronzed chest was damp and glistening with hot sweat.

"Sing us a song!" he cried to his uncle, and stirred up the fire to a roaring blaze.

So Kurelen sang, and those about all the near and distant campfires became quiet, as that supernal voice floated strongly and sweetly to the stars. He first sang one of Temujin's favorite songs:

> "I shall die in the saddle all booted and spurred,
> I shall die with my sword in my hand.
> Though oft have I faltered and oft have I erred,
> As the great and the small in the land—
> This be my story, wheree'er man hath trod:
> He died in the saddle, he died like a god!"

"Yes, yes!" shouted Temujin, panting. "I shall die in the saddle! I shall die like a god! But not before I am Emperor of all men, the Perfect Warrior, the Mighty Ruler!"

His followers screamed with laughter at this grandiloquent

statement. Chepe Noyon cried: "Khan of forty thousand tents! It is a brave empire!"

Temujin thrust out with his leg, and Chepe Noyon rolled out of his way. Then Temujin, the laughter gone from his face, glared about at his surprised friends, his dark face wrinkling and grimacing with tempestuous fury, his eyes flaming. Kurelen, about to rebuke him, suddenly was silent. He narrowed his own eyes, and thoughtfully bit his lip.

"Who is the camel who wisheth to laugh now?" cried Temujin.

Jamuga Sechen said quietly, with distaste: "Sit down, Temujin. Thou hast too much kumiss in thy belly."

Temujin swung on him with rage. "It is said of thee, Jamuga, that thy liver is yellow, and that it spews bile into thy blood."

Jamuga said nothing, but all at once his pale and rigid face became like bleached stone. He lifted his eyes quietly, and fixed them with a steadfast and piercing look upon the face of his anda. All the others were suddenly silent.

Temujin's eyes were caught and held by Jamuga's, and then his cheek flushed with shame and confusion. Kurelen thought it time to interfere.

"For a 'Perfect Warrior' thou hast the tongue of a windbreaking old woman, Temujin. Thou art as swollen as an overfilled bladder. Go quietly and relieve thyself, and we will wait for thee."

The young men grinned. Temujin, panting again, his face the color of congested blood, glared at them. But Jamuga was not smiling. He had averted his head. His eyes, fixed upon the distant hills, were cold and inscrutable.

As if the words came from him without his will, and tempestuously, Temujin exclaimed: "Forgive me, Jamuga."

Jamuga, without turning to him, without moving his eyes from the hills, said quietly: "I have already forgiven thee."

Temujin, with an amazing drop of his spirits, sat down. He looked at his friends. Chepe Noyon was laughing a little. Kasar was glancing about, fiercely, ready to defend his brother from any ridicule, now that he was chastened. But Subodai was regarding him gravely and in silence, his beautiful face calm. It was that look that struck most sorely on Temujin's heart, and he vowed again, as he had vowed a thousand times before, that he must better control his unruly tongue, which was like a sword that wounded his friends. He resolved that tomorrow he would give Jamuga his most cherished possession, a Chinese dagger whose silver hilt was rough with turquoises.

But he reflected miserably that Jamuga's feelings were not quickly soothed and healed. It would be several days before confidence would be restored between them. In the meantime, he, Temujin, would suffer intensely. It was during times like these that he realized how deep was his love for his anda. He loathed himself.

Subodai had asked Kurelen for his own favorite song, and now Kurelen's voice rose again, passionate and melancholy, and again the distant campfires listened, and even the herds were silent.

"And unto me a radiant angel came,
With wings of light within a silver rain,
And in his hands, as shining as the moon,
He held the brimming wine of goblets twain.

In tones like sweetest flute he gently spake:
'Of these two goblets thou a choice must make.
And never more, though endless suns will roll,
Canst thou recant, and of its mate partake.

In this bright cup, I hold within this hand,
Is joy eternal, in a crystal land,
Where love and life, like two immortal flames,
Burn high together from a single brand.

Thyself shalt live, where mirth alone abides,
Untouched, unchanged, while all the tides
Of change and ruin and death turn earth to dust,
And lonely in the heavens the dark sun rides.

But in this nether cup is only peace,
And only darkness and the pale release
That follows on the grave. Here is no pain,
But endless silence when thy heart doth cease.

No joy is here, no ecstasy sublime,
No sweet awareness of a scented clime.
No love, no laughter, only marble eyes
And marble lips forever mute in time,'

And troubled did I raise my glances up,
And said unto the angel, 'I shall sup
Without regret, but with a weary sigh,
Of that pale wine within the nether cup.'"

Only the loveliness of his voice held the interest of the listeners, save for Jamuga, Subodai and Temujin. For no one understood, but these three, and then with curious and various understanding. Subodai's beautiful face became more sad and grave; a wan restlessness moved like the shadow of rippling water over Jamuga's eyes. But Temujin's face darkened and tightened, as though he felt some secret contempt. He said: "That is the song of old men."

He stood up. He looked about him with an eye that was suddenly wild and dark. And then he lifted his head and gazed piercingly at the sky. The firelight illuminated with a red glow the lower part of his face. But over this red shadow his eyes were in shadow, yet strangely, more potent because of this.

No one saw Bektor moving silently near by. No one saw him pause, nor saw his features assume an expression of black bitterness and gloomy hatred.

chapter 13

Yesukai called his son, Temujin, to him. He sat in his yurt, with the Shaman at his side, and two old men. Temujin, impatient, stood before his father, while Yesukai surveyed him thoroughly from head to foot.

"Thou art old enough to be betrothed, my son," he said at last. "I have it in my mind to take thee to the tents of the Olhonod, where they have fair maidens with good dowries. Make thyself ready. For, as thou dost know, thou wilt remain with the parents of thy betrothed. Thou mayest take with thee two friends who will remain with thee for a time, to comfort thee so that thou wilt not regret thy home."

His lined brown face softened for a moment, as he gazed at his son. Surely no man had a more comely. But Temujin was scowling with dismay.

"Am I to go now, my father?"

"This hour. Make haste, Temujin. Our horses are already saddled."

Temujin went to the yurt of his mother. Being a practical woman, she would hear no complaints from him. "Thou art old enough to be betrothed," she said, repeating Yesukai. "But when thou art married, thou wilt return to the ordu of thy father, and when he hath died, thou wilt be the khan."

She gave him a little silver box of perfumed ointment for his bride. She smiled at him, her gray eyes bright with indulgent affection. "Give me many grandsons, my child," she said. She put her long palms against his cheeks in a swift embrace. It pleased her and aroused her pride that he was so tall and handsome. "No man liveth to himself alone. At the appointed hour he must take up the sword of duty. He who shirks must die. It hath always been so."

Kurelen listened to Temujin's angry plaint philosophically. The crippled man thrust his finger with a ribald gesture into the other's breast. "What! Art thou not a man? If thou art not, return to thy father, and plead for more time."

Temujin flushed with fury. He looked at Kurelen's grinning face, and for the first time in his life he was seized with a desire to strike it. While he struggled with the impulse, Kurelen, still laughing, opened one of his chests and withdrew from it two wide bracelets of silver, cunningly cut. The silver seemed spun of cobwebs, so fine was it, so delicately fashioned. The design was of a climbing and flowering vine, and the petals were made of turquoises and dark red stones. Kurelen hung them lovingly on his fingers, and forgetting his brief rage, Temujin squatted on his haunches and admired the trinkets.

"Ah," said Kurelen, softly, and dropped them off his fingers into Temujin's eager hands. His eyes narrowed a little with regret, but he smiled. Then he put his hand into the chest again, and brought out a wide and heavy necklace to match. Temujin could not repress a cry of pleasure as the necklace tinkled and clashed over his fingers.

"May she be sufficiently fair to add luster to these baubles," said Kurelen. "And may her virtue be as precious. It is said she who weareth these will never lack for sons."

He added, while Temujin thrust the bracelets over his fingers to study the effect: "May thy wife love thee above all other things. Our people scorn the love of women as a worthless thing. We ask only they be pleasant in our beds and bear us many children. But that is because we are barbarians. Know that, in truth, Temujin, nothing is more precious than the love of the woman we desire, and that that love is water in a desert, a horse among enemies, a sword in battle, and a warm hearth. It is a fortress and a refuge. He who hath such a woman hath a jewel above all price, and all heaven with it."

Temujin was surprised. He looked up, expecting to see a quizzical smile on his uncle's face. But Kurelen's expression was somber and weary.

"Hast thou ever loved, Kurelen?" he asked, astonished. He looked about him. Chassa sat near by, weaving hair into a rope. But she answered Temujin's glance with a strange smile, and bent her head.

"Yes," answered Kurelen, tranquilly. His face was as bland as new milk, and as without expression. "But, go thou: thy father is calling thee."

When Temujin had gone, Kurelen sat in deep silence for a long time, his hands hanging limply between his knees. Finally he looked up, and caught Chassa regarding him with an aspect of sorrowful yearning. He reached out and took her hand, and as he did so, a scarlet flood ran over her face.

"I should have given thee to a virile man a long time ago, Chassa," he said, gently.

She burst into tears. She laid her head on his knees. "Nay,

master! Nay, master," She kissed his feet in a frenzy of humble passion and grief.

He laid his hand gently on her head, and a look of wonder and gratitude brightened in his eyes. Love is not to be despised, he thought, almost with humility, even when it is made manifest in a poor creature like this, or even in a dog. It is wine of priceless vintage, and becometh no less intoxicating in an earthen cup than in a golden one.

Temujin chose Subodai and Chepe Noyon and Jamuga Sechen to accompany him and his father to the ordu of his betrothed. After their first dismay, the youths became hilarious and eager for adventure. Even Jamuga laughed more than usual. Temujin teased him because he was not betrothed, and Jamuga vowed that he would be married before him. But Subodai only smiled, and rode a little faster, his eyes fixed ahead.

They rode towards the sunset, their hoods pulled over their heads, for the air was rapidly cooling. They had long ago left the fertile meadows, and were now riding slowly over the broken floor of the desert, which was flooded with the blood-red light of the dying sun. Here were tossed huge boulders, black as ebony, crusted with prophyritic sparks. Two great smooth pillars of stone stood before them, like the ruined gateways of a temple. In the distance reared shattered ramparts with ribbed and flattened tops and sides, black against the consuming heavens. The Mongols encountered no other living creatures in this awful universe of red fire and black boulders and sparkling crimson earth and frightful loneliness. Soon they were overcome with awe, their eyes glancing, appalled, at the limitless flaming sky and the limitless ruined earth, which were imbued with the supernatural light of hell, and the unshaking silence of death. Their horses felt their apprehension, and shied when their hooves struck with a ringing sound on some smaller rock, and shattered it into fragments. The whites of their eyes caught the red radiance, and blazed, rolling.

And then, as they rose upon a shallow terrace, an unearthly scene met their eyes at the left. A great misty lake, shadowy blue and violet, lay in a sunken valley, its vague shores strewn with dark purple pyramids of stone. There it floated, cool and lost, catching no red light from the red heavens, its outlines nebulous and pale, its waters as fixed as shadow-filled glass. There was something terrible in the aspect of this remote and motionless water, which had the appearance of a dream in the fiery twilight. Immobile yet drifting, it seemed almost at hand, and then again, a hundred leagues away, deepening and paling in its hues of dim turquoise and amethyst. Its margins mingled with and faded into the red desert, without vegetation.

Temujin uttered a stunned cry at the sight of this lake. Jamuga murmured. Subodai sat on his horse and gazed in silence. But Yesukai looked upon the water without perturbation.

"It cannot be!" exclaimed Temujin. He inhaled a deep breath, but the acrid and burning air was not filled with the fresh smell of water.

Yesukai nodded. "It is not, in truth," he said. "It is but a desert mirage, a dream. But it doth appear at every sunset like this, in this very place, unchanging, and men call it the Lake of the Damned, for many have lost their lives seeking to approach it. When it is full day, and the sun is high in the sky, there is nothing there but a whitish plain, strewn with greenish stones. The old wise men say that once on a time, many ages ago, a lake did verily lie there, in a fertile land filled with the clamor of cities and the comings and goings of a vast populace. This is but the specter of that lake, an evil illusion, leading men to death."

The youths fell into deeper silence as they gazed upon the lake, which moment by moment enhanced its aspect of an unearthly dream. A sensation of dim horror seized them. Temujin felt an irresistible urge to ride down to it. His whole soul was pervaded with that urge, which had in it a kind of terror. He looked at the low pyramids of purple stone scattered about the margins. One was the shape of a temple, and the broken pillars of it were vividly discernible. Temujin shook his head. His heart was beating violently, and in that deathlike silence he could hear the throbbing sound of it.

Suddenly the reserved Jamuga cried out in the loud and echoing voice of fear: "Let us go on!" And without waiting for a reply, he spurred his horse so fiercely that it reared back on its haunches, and then plunged ahead. Temujin began to laugh, as did Yesukai. They followed Jamuga. When they had gone a little distance, they missed Subodai. They saw him, a black silhouette against the red sky, watching the lake. He was like a statue carved of ebony, motionless on his horse. They shouted to him. It was not until they had shouted several times that he seemed to hear, and then he followed them in a tranquil canter. When he came up to them, they saw that his face had taken on itself something of the weird and dreamlike quality of the accursed lake.

The burning sky rapidly paled and faded, and almost in a twinkling the desert night had fallen. They camped as soon as the last rays had gone.

That night, as he lay wrapped in his furs and felts near the campfire, Temujin had a strange and preternatural dream. He dreamt that he and Jamuga were sitting on their horses near the margin of the Lake of the Damned. It had a terrible fascination for him; he could not take his eyes from it. He was conscious of a wild exultation in him, and he could feel the hot sweat pouring down his back and face. But when he looked at Jamuga, it was as though he looked at a dead and suffering face. Jamuga's eyes were distended, and filled with an anguished light. He pointed at the lake. His lips moved, and though Temujin could hear no sound, he knew that Jamuga was warning him, solemnly and with agony.

And then as Temujin, bewildered, watched, Jamuga opened his coat and revealed his breast. There was a bleeding wound in it, ghastly to see, and in its spongy depths he could see Jamuga's heart, beating and dying, spouting thick red fountains of blood.

chapter 14

But the next day the lake and the dream were forgotten, for the desert floor was like cracked sheets of pure gold in the sun, and the broken hills and ramparts and temples and pillars shimmered with the color of delicate jade against a sky of bright pearl. The unceasing wind, brilliant and strong, blew like waves over the rubble on the floor of the desert, which appeared formed of fragments of polished brass. The young men raced, shouting, ahead of Yesukai, circled back, cracking whips and spurring their horses, leaping over boulders, rearing and swinging about, their voices echoing back from the sides of the cliff and hill.

At noon it was so hot that they were forced to find shelter against the flank of a bleached natural wall, which resembled the enormous skeleton backbone of some prehistoric monster. Now the sky was an arch of pulsing and burning blue flame against which the shattered hills in the distance had turned a fiery bronze, and the desert floor was the color of crumbled topaz. The place where they rested was a little cauldron-shaped valley, scattered with dry jade-green tufts. A fierce white glare lay over everything, so that all things made the eye water with the unbearable brilliance. The horses stood with their heads below their knees, panting, while the Mongols covered everything but their eyes with the folds of their hoods. Temujin, stunned by the heat, languidly watched desert scorpions and lizards creeping from the shelter of one small stone to another, their sharp black shadows crawling with them. Nothing else moved in that blazing and petrified world of rock and sun and desert.

Then all at once, in that merciless inferno, a tiny figure on horseback appeared, a mere black fly in the glare, creeping carefully across the yellow floor of the desert. Yesukai and the youths became alert, feeling for their daggers and their bowcases. The horses lifted their heads and whinnied. The men sat with their backs against the crumbling cream-colored ribs of the wall, and waited. In the sunlight, Temujin's eyes were the hue of lighted emeralds.

It took a long time for the horseman to approach them, for distances are deceptive on the desert. Shadows were longer when he finally rode down into the cauldron. When he saw the waiting men, he reined in his horse and regarded them intently. He was an old man, dry and brown, with a cunning face like that of an aged monkey. Under the drooping edge of his hood his eyes gazed out at them, bright and crafty. In the lines of his wrinkled face the sweat ran like trickles of water. He smiled.

"I give thee greetings, brothers," he said courteously. He looked from one to the other, and finally his look fastened closely on Temujin, and remained there. He added: "I am Dai Sechen."

Yesukai and the youths rose, and answered the old man with equal courtesy. "I," said Yesukai, "am khan of the Yakka Mongols. This is my son, Temujin, for whom I am about to secure a bride from the clan of Olhonod, his mother's people. And this is Subodai, of the reindeer people, whose father is now a member of my tribe. And this is Chepe Noyon, whose father belonged to a hostile clan, but who now serves me." He put his hand on the shoulder of Chepe Noyon, and smiled with affection. "None is braver than Chepe Noyon, not even his father. He, himself, alone, raided Gutchluk of Black Cathay and stole a vast drove of white-nosed horses, which he presented to me as a gift and a token of reconciliation. And this is Jamuga, the anda of my son."

But Dai Sechen, though he smiled politely in acknowledgment of Yesukai's introductions to Subodai and Jamuga and Chepe Noyon, continued to regard Temujin intently. Finally he said:

"Eyes like fierce green stone hath thy son, and a face like the sky at noon. Last night I had a vision of a white hawk descending from heaven, carrying the sun and the moon. He stood before me, brighter than day, and his eyes were the eyes of Temujin. And then, as my daughter, Bortei, emerged from the yurt, the hawk flew unto her and perched on her hand. Brother-in-law, my tribe is not hostile to thine. Bring thy son to my ordu and let him gaze on my daughter, who is fairer than any other maiden."

Yesukai hesitated. But Temujin said eagerly: "It will do no harm to look upon the girl, and we can rest overnight at the least."

Seeing Yesukai's hesitation, Dai Sechen went on: "It is an omen. The gods have sent thy son in my path. I am something of a conjurer, for my uncles were shamans. Thy son shall reign over many peoples and many ordus."

Yesukai, the superstitious, was not able to resist this flattery. So they accompanied Dai Sechen as soon as the sun sloped in a flaming arc to the west. They arrived at a large but weedy oasis about which a tent village of over twenty thousand yurts was gathered. Dai Sechen led them to his yurt through a crowd of curious women and children and yapping dogs. Hearing the dogs, Temujin's face paled and the corners of his lips shook. Subodai, who never laughed at his friend's fear, rode protectingly beside him, lashing his whip at the curs, while Chepe Noyon ridiculed him gayly.

The five guests were received with great cordiality by the warriors. Water in silver basins was brought to them to lave their burning hands and faces. A great feast was summoned. When the night had fallen and the campfires were roaring high, Dai Sechen took Temujin by the hand and led him to the yurt where lived his first wife and her only child, Bortei the Fair. He called the women, and they came out slowly, dressed in soft cream-hued robes of wool. About Bortei's waist was a twisted silver serpent, with eyes of red stones. Over her shoulders lay a magnificent sable cloak, her betrothal gift from her father.

Temujin was followed by his father and his friends. But when he saw Bortei no one else existed for him in all the world. He saw a small girl, hardly more than a child, with a little straight nose and slender arms. But slight of stature though she was, she was surrounded with an aura of ineffable and unshakable dignity and pride. Her small head, with its falling masses of dark burnished hair, was held as high as though she were the daughter of an emperor instead of the child of a shaggy baghatur of the lonely steppes. Her eyes, large and quiet, were gray as winter wind and as cold, and set in black silken lashes so thick that they cast a shadow on her cheek. In her smooth pale face her mouth bloomed as suddenly as a red flower, giving to her expression a look of passion, for all its aloofness. Temujin could see her small rounded breast, the virginal swell of her hip, under the creamy robe.

Dai Sechen's wife bent her head very low in greeting to the visitors, but Bortei looked straightly and coolly into Temujin's eyes. It seemed to him that a flame ran over his body, invading his blood, consuming his bones. He felt that his heart had become enormous in his breast, and thick. It was beating so violently that he was certain that its pulsing was visible in his throat and temples. His knees trembled under him. He was seized with a sensation of joy and rapture, of hunger and desire and passionate yearning. When the girl's red lips parted, and she gave him a distant and faintly disdainful smile, he wanted to seize her in his arms and force his mouth furiously upon her own.

Dai Sechen, smiling his cunning smile at the evidences of

the young man's overwhelmed emotion, took his daughter's hand and placed it in Temujin's. As he felt the touch of the girl's fingers, Temujin felt that his heart was bursting. He moved his head and panted slightly, unable to look away from her mouth and her throat.

Yesukai studied the girl critically, as though she were a young mare he contemplated purchasing, and then he turned to Dai Sechen and began to argue with him about the dowry. His son was no son to a herdsman, but to a khan of forty thousand tents. Dai Sechen must understand that. Dai Sechen nodded, scratching himself uneasily. Over Temujin's shoulder Chepe Noyon peered curiously at Bortei, and he made a faint, approving smacking-sound with his smiling lips. Subodai regarded her gravely. But Jamuga, the eternally jealous, looked at her with shadowy reserve and icy coldness.

Bortei was pleased with Temujin, though he stood there like a great calf, clutching her hand, his gray-green eyes fixed so devouringly yet so imploringly upon her. She told herself that she was fortunate to be betrothed to the oldest son of a khan, for she had a secret lust for power in her girl's body. She had always been her father's pet, and when first her young beauty had manifested itself clearly, he had promised her that he would wed her to no mere tribesman, but to a khan, a king, with a mighty ordu. Now the young khan had come, and he was handsome and strong and bold, for all his strange and somewhat uncanny face and look. She saw that he was courageous and fierce, and she felt the grip of his hand, masterful and inexorable. A thin flamelike thrill ran over her legs and her breast, and she smiled again, languorously, now, and her lips bloomed scarlet.

Hers was an imperious, proud and wilful nature, and she was a woman, with all a woman's understanding of a man. She knew that here was one she could rule by the very power of her body and her arms and lips. She would bend him to her will, and he would run to answer her commands. And then, as she looked him fully again in his eyes, a cold stab entered her heart. Then she was no longer certain, but even a little afraid.

To recover her startled poise again, she looked away from him, and her eyes rested on Subodai. An expression of astonishment stood on her face, and her lips fell open. She forgot Temujin, became unconscious of the hand that still held hers. It was as though complete awareness rushed to the windows of her eyes, and gazed out, fascinated. Never had she seen such beauty in a youth, such pride and sweetness and majesty.

A wave of color ran over her features and her lips grew moist as though with sudden dew. She smiled at him, a most unmaidenly act, and her flesh glowed as if she had voluntarily loosened her robe and stepped from it, naked. Her breast seemed to swell, and her thighs moved in an irresistible impulse towards him.

Temujin saw nothing, except her loveliness, and was conscious of his desire. But Chepe Noyon pursed up his lips soundlessly. Subodai, unaware as a statue, returned her gaze with gentle gravity. He seemed not to see her, but to be filled with some inner removed contemplation.

Bortei's red tongue appeared daintily and she ran it over her lips. Her nostrils distended. She looked like an embodied and delicate lust. And then, as though inexorably called by a stern voice, she was impelled to remove her eyes from Subodai and turn them to Jamuga.

And then it was that all the light and fire and color seemed to go from her, and leave her a small and colorless shape of woman-flesh. For when her eyes met Jamuga's, she knew that here was a mortal enemy who understood her, and hated her with all his soul. His eyes were the color of hard stone, and his rigid lips were set in granite.

Even when he turned away abruptly, and left them all, she followed him with her hating gaze, and her heart felt full of venom, as though a serpent has fastened its fangs upon her breast.

chapter 15

Yesukai, who was secretly pleased with the bride of his son, pretended to find her dowry inadequate.

"My sworn brother is Toghrul Khan of the Karait," he boasted. "He will bestow great gifts upon my son, if his bride pleaseth him."

Dai Sechen exclaimed: "And my daughter cometh of as noble people as thine, Yesukai. The Gray-eyed people are hers as well as Temujin's." Nevertheless, he grudgingly added more treasures to the girl's dowry.

"When my son sitteth on the white horseskin, a score of tribes and clans will pay him homage," continued Yesukai, exultant.

He left Temujin in the evening of the second day. Jamuga and Chepe Noyon and Subodai offered to accompany him, but he saw the wistfulness on his son's face and urged the friends to remain for a few days longer. He bade farewell to Dai Sechen and his tribe, and laid his hands on Bortei's head in blessing. "A sensible wench," he thought.

And he was not far wrong. Bortei, enamored of Subodai, nevertheless understood that Temujin, who excited her, was the son of the khan of the Yakka Mongols and Subodai was only his follower. Had it been possible for her to defy usage and her father and all the laws of her tribe, and marry Subodai, she would not have done so. Like Houlun, she had sagacity and intelligence. But when she thought of Subodai she smiled to herself, and the tip of her tongue touched her lips delicately.

She avoided Jamuga, who never spoke to her even when encountered. She thought to herself: Thou pale-faced scorpion! Not long shalt thou be the anda of Temujin, when I am his wife in his tent.

For in Jamuga she recognized unending enmity, distrust and hatred. If she were to rule Temujin's ordu as a queen, and have unquestioned influence over her husband, she must rid herself of this malignant foe who watched over Temujin like an unsleeping eagle. No matter where she went in the ordu with her betrothed, there she saw those steadfast and vigilant eyes fixed upon her darkly and contemptuously. Sometimes her body trembled with her loathing. And sometimes, she felt the cold fingers of fear clutch her throat. She was aware that there is no vengefulness like the vengefulness of a reserved and passionless man. Once or twice she attempted to win him with gracious smiles, looking up at him with eyes deliberately artful and luminous. But always he turned away from her without speaking or smiling.

Sometimes she was afraid that he would speak to Temujin and persuade him to abandon her. In order to prevent this, she flaunted Temujin's passion in Jamuga's face, reduced him to humility with petulance, raised him to rapture with her touch and laughter. Besides, she had done nothing upon which any one could place a finger.

Yesukai, singing joyously to himself, rode away from the tribe of Dai Sechen. He passed the Lake of the Damned at sunset, and stopped for a moment to regard it. More than ever tonight, it had the aspect of an evil dream floating in the vast silence of the desert. For some reason he, the unimaginative, shivered, and rode quickly away. It seemed to him that the sun darkened more rapidly tonight than usual. He no longer sang. The wind was harsher and more violent than ever, when the sun sank down behind the black and broken ramparts to the west. Used to solitude and desolation, as he was, he could not keep his heart from beating uneasily. When he saw a campfire, as he rounded the flank that resembled a backbone, he could hardly keep from shouting with relief.

More and more campfires flared in the dark purple twilight, and he halted, vaguely apprehensive, when he saw that he had come upon a camp of Tatars. After a few moments, before the dogs discovered him, he took heart, remembering the inexorable law of the steppes, that hospitality must be given freely when asked even by an enemy. Between his people and the Tatars was an immortal hostility. He rode up the camp, conscious of great weariness, and when the chief came out he demanded hospitality for the night.

He looked at the dark and sullen faces ringed about his horse, and held his head high and fearlessly. After a moment of heavy silence, the chief invited Yesukai to be his guest.

They filled his enamelled plate over and over, and gave him large quantities of wine. The chief listened with somber smiles to his stories of the betrothal of Temujin and Bortei, and exchanged glances with his warriors when Yesukai began to boast prodigiously. Yesukai's courage had returned. He became quite patronizing to the chief, who pretended to be much impressed.

He left at dawn. He did not feel particularly well, and laid this to the fact that he had eaten and drunk far too much. He did nót detect the irony in the smiles and the salutes of his hosts, as he rode away. But when he glanced back, to wave his arm at them in farewell, they merely stood and watched him, without replying.

The sun rose high and hot, and all at once Yesukai realized that he was mortally ill. The sweat that rolled down his cheeks was cold as ice. Violent cramps seized his middle. He leaned over on his horse and vomited. The fiery desert swung about him in circles, and there were a score of raging suns in the scarlet sky.

He thought to himself, simply: They have poisoned me. He fastened his rope lariat tightly about his waist and tied himself to his horse. He leaned his head on his horse's neck and gave himself up to black suffering. Blood began to trickle and writhe from his mouth. Finally, he lost consciousness.

When he next opened his eyes, he saw that he was in his own ordu, and that they had laid him on his own bed. He saw the grief-stricken faces of his people, and the gray eyes of Houlun. The Shaman was muttering his incantations. Unable to endure his torment, Yesukai gripped his lower lip with his teeth, and then cried out for his son, Temujin.

Kurelen came to him and knelt by his bed. Sincere sorrow stood on the face of the crippled man. Yesukai smiled at him faintly.

"Counsel my son, Kurelen. Thou art a wise man, though oft-times a foolish one."

He closed his eyes. A courier had already been dispatched for Temujin, and this courier was Kasar.

But when Temujin arrived, his father was already dead.

chapter 16

"Loyalty?" Kurelen shrugged his shoulders, and looked at his nephew with ironic compassion. "There is but one way to secure the undying loyalty of thy followers: Make it to their best advantage to be faithful unto thee."

"That is not just," said Jamuga with bitterness and anger.

Chepe Noyon laughed lightly, but he regarded Temujin with sparkling eyes as hard as gems. "As for myself, Temujin, know that thou hast my life if need be."

Kasar was so overcome with emotion, that he made his face as fierce as a bear's, to hide the tears in his eyes. He could not speak. He could only keep beating the fist of one hand in the other, and looking at his brother with passionate love.

But Subodai said gravely, his brow seemingly touched with light: "Thou knowest me, Temujin."

Temujin, whose eyes were red with weeping for grief for his father, flung out his arms wildly. "But what are we, after all? Who are my followers? A cripple, a woman, and you, who are but children?" His voice was harsh. He regarded them with helpless fury.

No one spoke for a moment. Their faces were somber as they contemplated the truth of Temujin's words. Then Temujin, more infuriated than ever, exclaimed:

"Even the Shaman hath deserted me. He standeth with Bektor. I believe they plot my life."

"I am sure of it," said Kurelen, without mockery, and in such a quiet voice that Temujin, who always relied on Kurelen's irony and ridicule to hearten him, felt his heart fall into a pit of coldness.

"Then, I shall go forth and kill Bektor at once!" cried Kasar, in his simplicity. He wrenched his scimitar from his belt, and ran his finger lightly over its edge.

"That would be folly," said Kurelen. "Kokchu would only find another sword against you. To destroy an enemy, it is a waste of time to knock the sword from his hand. The enemy himself must be destroyed."

Chepe Noyon drew out his dagger, and said with quick resolution: "I shall kill the Shaman."

Kurelen shook his head, smiling: "Nay, that is a pleasure

I reserve for myself, in the future. In the meantime, I enjoy his conversation. Besides, ye are all young fools. Ye may kill a people's king; ye may destroy them and enslave them, and throw down their heroes. And even then, if ye are powerful enough they will submit and forgive, and even offer their love. But lay a hand upon their priests, and they will rise up and overthrow ye. Such is the power of superstition. At the end, men are afraid of their gods, no matter how they laugh at them. Secure the loyalty of a people's priests, and ye have nothing to fear from them. I suggest thou secure the Shaman, Temujin."

"But how?"

"By making it valuable to him to be faithful to thee."

They fell into gloomy silence.

The situation of Temujin was truly formidable. He looked at his followers with helpless rage, his face dark, his eyes the translucent green eyes of a wolf in the night.

Yesukai had been dead two days when Temujin had arrived home. Before his arrival, the leading and discontented men of the clan had thoroughly discussed the whole matter. Much more than half, thereafter, resolved that they would desert the banner of the yak tails and seek new and stronger chieftains to adhere to and serve.

After all, they argued, they had wives and families and herds of their own to protect and for whom to find sustenance and protectors: Who was left in Yesukai's ordu now? A weak woman and her children; a youth without experience. Poor staffs to sustain them. A shattered sword to guard them. A rent banner to follow.

"The strong wheel is broken," they said. "The horsemen have lost their horses. The sustaining water hath been swallowed in the sand. Let us go."

They were inarticulate people, but the Shaman had subtly put words into their mouths. Bektor, he had hinted, was a strong and resolute youth. He would lead them to new protectors. But what was Temujin? A youth of fiery and uncertain character, given to passions and rages without point. It was good for men to be faithful, but after all, what was faithfulness if it lead to death? A mirage, sought only by fools. It was the business and wisdom of men to live.

So nearly two-thirds of the clansmen decided to desert. Even while Temujin discussed the desperate state of affairs in his uncle's yurt, the people were harnessing their oxen and calling in their herds and horses. It was spring, and the journey to summer pastures had already begun. Around the yurts of Temujin and his family there was a bare ring of desertion and silence. Even the dogs had left them.

The flap of the yurt opened, and bending her head Houlun entered. Her quiet face was stern, but her gray eyes flashed with bitter lightning and affront. The hood of her fur cloak had fallen on her shoulders, and her head emerged, strong and heroic, for all that her hair was streaked with threads of steel. She stood a moment, looking at her sons and her brother, and her lip lifted rigidly with scorn.

"Ye sit here, like whipped dogs, while the wife of the dead khan is insulted in her own ordu! But the strong stone is broken, and there is left nothing but gravel!"

They were abashed by her sudden appearance, and her look of majestic anger and cold sternness. Then Kurelen stood up and took her hand, pressing it between his palms. He was concerned at its coldness and its fixed tremor.

"What meanest thou, Houlun? We are here, consulting as to what best is to be done. Who hath offended thee?"

Her stern anger seemed to increase, but Kurelen saw the hard tears rising in her eyes.

"The Shaman hath just told me that I have been refused admission to the sacrifices. I protested, and the women set upon me with screams of contempt, and have ordered me to leave their camp and pastures. 'Thou art an alien woman,' they said to me, with disdain. 'Our husbands shall not follow thee, and thou art an outcast, with thy children, among us. Get thee gone.' "

Her sons and their friends stood about her, shaking with rage. Their breath filled the yurt with its hoarse sound. Kurelen gazed piercingly into his sister's eyes. Then he lifted her right hand. It was clenched about a whip, and caught in that whip were strands of hair. He smiled, dropped her hand. He said: "My sister, thou art a master among women. Fear not we shall leave thee on the field alone."

He went out of the yurt alone. His hands were folded in his sleeves, for he carried certain objects in them. The ordu was in a state of great confusion, he observed wryly. Running cattle were being chased and gathered by shouting herdboys and shepherds. Preparation for departing was in evidence everywhere. A long line of camels and yurts, cattle, sheep and horses, was already strung out towards the horizon. Campfires were being stamped out, children gathered up. Few took time to glance at Kurelen, and those who did spat openly and contemptuously, and turned away. But he went serenely on to the yurt of Kokchu, the Shaman. Two warriors rose up at his approach, and warned him away. He eyed them humbly, and spoke to them in a deprecating voice:

"I wish only a moment with the Shaman, to bid him farewell."

"Bah," said one warrior, spitting at Kurelen's feet. "He will have nought to do with the kinsman of an alien woman and her beggar brats. Besides, the Shaman is preparing to go, and cannot be hindered by idle chatter."

Kurelen lifted his voice loud enough to be heard within the yurt. He knew very well that behind the flap the Shaman was listening intently.

"Nevertheless, if it please him, I should like a single word with him. It is a matter of extreme importance." He sighed. "However, grave matters are ofttimes overlooked for trivial affairs. If he will not see me, he will not."

He turned away. The flap opened, and not at all to his surprise, the Shaman appeared on the platform, suspicious, cold and formal, with eyes like pieces of hard jet. He looked down at Kurelen with disdainful composure.

"How now, Kurelen, what wouldst thou have with me?"

Kurelen, smiling to himself, glanced about diffidently at the hurrying and departing tribesmen.

"Forgive me, Kokchu. I see thou art in the midst of confusion. I will not keep thee."

He lifted his eyes to the Shaman, and they were as soft and bright as the simple eyes of a doe. Kokchu gazed at him searchingly, and then suddenly he smiled cynically, with inner amusement. "Come into the yurt," he said, and re-entered, himself, abruptly.

The warriors, muttering with dark surprise, stood aside while Kurelen mounted the platform. He fastened the flap carefully behind him. Kokchu was already sitting cross-legged on the floor, his hands in his sleeves, waiting.

Kurelen said: "It would be of no use to speak to thee of loyalty to the son of Yesukai?"

Kokchu smiled still more. "Let us waste no time in the language of fools, Kurelen. We are men of sense. Sit down."

Kurelen sat down. The Shaman graciously filled a cup with wine and handed it to his old enemy. Kurelen thanked him, drank deeply.

"I shall miss thee, Kurelen. From this night on, I must confine my conversation to the camels."

Kurelen shook his head sadly. "I have written to Toghrul Khan. He is sworn brother to Yesukai, and will assist his son. Moreover, he is a man of wit and much fame. I have promised him edifying conversations with thee."

The Shaman raised his eyebrows in deprecating surprise. He heard the threat behind Kurelen's words, but pretended to hear only the words.

"Express my regret to the khan. But mayhap I shall meet him some day in the future."

"Kokchu, I am certain of that."

He held out his cup to the Shaman, who refilled it. But as he did so, he fixed his subtle eyes motionlessly on the other man.

"Tell the khan, Kurelen, that even priests must live, and that the gods themselves despise the fallen."

"But the gods frequently make mistakes," said Kurelen, with an indulgent smile for the folly of them. "They would make a grave error today, for instance." He withdrew his hands from his sleeves, and Kokchu, with amazement, saw that they were full of gold and silver trinkets, studded with jewels. Kurelen, watching him closely, saw his face pale.

"A mere handful of the gifts which Toghrul Khan sent to Temujin, for his bride. But they were so many, and the promise of more so generous, that my nephew gave these handfuls to me. I am sad to see thee go, Kokchu. In token of my esteem, and as a remembrance, take thy choice of any of them."

He extended his hands to the Shaman, who could only stare, paling even more.

Kurelen laughed softly. "With any of these, thou couldst buy a fair woman, or a white horse, or the swords of a hundred men."

Kokchu lifted his head and looked at him with a dark frown. "Thou art a liar, Kurelen."

Kurelen laughed. "Mayhap."

"Toghrul Khan is famed for his greediness and avarice. I know this."

Kurelen shook his head indulgently.

"Nevertheless, take thy choice, Kokchu. I have much more."

The Shaman carefully and lingeringly selected a string of golden beads alternating with beads of turquoise. "Thou art also a thief," he observed.

"Mayhap. But, as thou dost say, the gods love a clever man."

The Shaman lovingly laid aside the necklace. Again, he fixed his eyes on Kurelen.

"What hast thou to offer?" he asked, almost with contempt.

Kurelen sighed with relief. "Ah, now we begin to speak like honest men. It is true that Toghrul Khan will assist Temujin, and avenge him, if necessary. But that is beside the point. I have faith in the destiny of Temujin. Thou, thyself, didst prophesy what he would become." And he grinned.

The Shaman smiled darkly. But he said nothing, merely waiting.

"I believe myself a judge of men," Kurelen went on. "Swear allegiance to Temujin, and thou shalt be a khan among priests. Desert him, and thou shalt not prosper. This is not an opinion or a superstition. It is a fact."

"Bah," said the Shaman. But he frowned, and examined his fingernails.

Kurelen jingled his treasures. He selected a string of golden coins, and tossed them lightly onto Kokchu's knee. "Another token of my regard," he said.

The Shaman slowly lifted his eyes. The black balls were immobile in their glistening whites. His dark face darkened even more.

"There is fate in Temujin," said Kurelen. "Whosoever follows, shall follow him to power."

Kokchu smiled, and then suddenly he laughed aloud. He laid the string of gold coins with the gold and turquoise necklace. He leaned towards Kurelen and laid his hand upon the other's shoulder, and shook him.

"Kurelen, I cannot dispense with thy conversation! Come with me."

The two men, smiling amiably, went out of the yurt together. The warriors regarded them with astonishment. To the east, the clouds of dust following on the desertion of many of the tribesmen billowed up like golden vapor. Only a handful was left, and this was already preparing to follow the others. As the Shaman strode among them, followed by Kurelen, they ceased their feverish preparations, and stared after him. He went to the center of the almost deserted plot where the great village had stood, and shouted aloud. His tall and majestic figure, his magnificent head, were outlined like the figure of some celestial being against a burning yellow sunset. Within a few moments all that remained of Yesukai's ordu was there, except Houlun, who had unaccountably disappeared. Bektor, sullen and confused, stood beside his brother, Belgutei, and his mother. Temujin stood among his friends, his face black with anger and despair. The hubbub of disconcerted voices fell before the fierce and contemptuous glance of the Shaman, and every one listened to what he had to say.

"Where are ye going?" cried the Shaman. "Art ye deserting your khan, the son of Yesukai, ye craven dogs? Is there no loyalty in your hearts, no faithfulness in your souls? Are ye like the weak wheel that breaks on a small stone, a sword of lead that bends at the first blow? Are your loins the loins of men, or the thighs of women?"

The tribesmen gaped at him, astounded, their eyes blinking, their faces wrinkling with bewilderment. He looked at each man in turn, at each bronzed, lined face and their staring eyes. Before his fiery glance each man's glance finally fell away, and each man asked himself, confused, if he had heard the Shaman rightly yesterday.

The Shaman smiled with grim scorn.

"I know ye believe ye will be welcomed by the khan of the Taijiuts. But ye believe wrongly, to your death. For the khan will say to himself: 'What manner of traitors are these, who desert their leader when he needeth them, and come yowling like curs to the feet of another? Men like these must die, for they are a stone of flour in the walls of a fortress, a sword of bamboo in a conflict, a horse with a broken leg in a battle.'

"Know that the khan will not have you. But, if ye believe it not, go. For your young khan will have no traitors among his people, no camel-hearts riding beside him."

Belgutei, who had avoided Temujin, believing his star fallen, now glanced at him with a friendly and heartening smile. Bektor gnawed his lip. Temujin's eyes widened with surprise, and Jamuga turned aside with disgust. But the other tribesmen rubbed their bodies and looked uneasily at each other, flushing.

Slowly and portentously, the Shaman fixed his eyes upon the bleached area beyond the ordu. Then, still slowly and portentously, he turned back to his people, and like a man who goes in an orchard and gathers up the fruit piece by piece, so did he gather up each eye and hold it. An intense silence fell, full of a nameless fear, while every man looked at the face of the Shaman, which seemed illuminated with strange lightning.

"Look!" exclaimed Kokchu, in a low and thrilling voice. "The spirits have sent an omen!"

Then every one looked, and a deep and terrified cry broke from every throat. Kurelen stared, then pursed his lips. His eyes lighted with mirth and admiration. At first there had been nothing to see but the golden vapor that followed on the vast departure of herds and camels and horses and yurts. Then this vapor parted like a curtain, rolling aside, and there, where nothing but wilderness had been before was a host of shadowy and giant horsemen, standing in enormous silence, their upheld lances streaming with ghostly banners, their faces as fateful and somber as the profile on the hills, which Kurelen had seen. There was something frightful in their immense silence, something awful in their portentous waiting. Their heads seemed to reach higher than the hills; their horses, gray and spectral, were three times the size of living horses. The ghostly banners blew in an unearthly wind, seemingly in the very clouds. Pale lightning fluttered among them, and each man, in his extreme terror, thought he heard the far and terrible sound of horns and drums.

The Shaman lifted his arm, and cried out in a fearful voice: "The Spirits of the Blue Sky have come to the aid of Temujin, son of Yesukai!"

A single groan of utter panic rose from the people. They fell on their faces, and covered their heads with their arms. The cattle and camels and horses, who saw nothing, moved and reared, uneasily, smelling the acrid scent of human fear. But Temujin and his friends, and Kurelen, did not fall on their faces. Kurelen smiled. He thought to himself: The rascal hath as much imagination as I!

Slowly the host faded, the vapor moved back like a golden cloud. One by one, the people rose, cowed and trembling. One by one, they fell on their knees about Temujin and pledged their faith and allegiance. Across their bent heads, Kokchu and Kurelen exchanged a faint smile. Kurelen touched his brow mockingly, and with admiration. Smugly, Kokchu acknowledged the salute with a gratified bend of his head.

But only a handful, after all, were these who remained with Temujin. The young khan was full of gloom. Nothing could console him. He went to look for his mother, and soon he came running from her yurt, shouting: "My mother hath disappeared, and is nowhere to be found!"

When darkness fell, Houlun returned, and the people were more astonished than ever. For that intrepid woman had slipped away from the ordu on a horse, and, carrying the banner of the yak tails, had pursued the deserting tribesmen, and coming upon them, had harangued and shamed some of them into returning and renewing their allegiance to her son. She rode into the camp, her black hair streaming about her, her heroic head upheld, proudly carrying the banner high in her hand, the sheepish tribesmen following her in their yurts, and surrounded by their herds.

Kurelen looked upon his sister, and for once, his smile was not ironic. But Temujin, after one glance, turned a furious crimson. He swung upon his heel and went to his yurt. His heart was bitter against his mother. For the second time she had shamed him.

chapter 17

"Thou art a fool," said Kurelen, mildly.

Temujin regarded him with rage. All the violence of his nature showed in the lividity of his lips and in the vivid greenness of his eyes, which changed color with his mood.

"I am shamed forever, by my mother!" he cried.

Kurelen shrugged. "I repeat, thou art a fool. Because of thy mother, thou dost still have a people about thee, and thou art still alive. But perhaps thou wouldst prefer to have been left helpless, and then been killed? A hero's death? Bah. I thought thou didst have some wit. Remember this: it matters not how a man surviveth, except that he survive. It matters not how his victory is obtained, except that he be the victor. Be sensible. Recall only that thou art still khan of the Yakka Mongols, and set thyself to the task of consolidating thy gains and sagaciously planning for the future. For thou art still in dire peril of losing thy clan and also thy life."

"Kurelen is right," said Jamuga, slowly, thoughtfully knitting his brows. "Thou art in no position to be heroic, or strike a figure. Thy people need thee."

Chepe Noyon began to laugh. "Let the people sing of the memory of heroes. I prefer to sing with them, and not be the object of the song."

Subodai said again, to his leader: "Temujin, I am glad thou art living, and not dead."

But Kasar, who echoed all Temujin's moods, in his adoration, exclaimed: "Thou dost not understand my brother! Ye all see but the opportunity and the gain. Ye do not see the dishonor."

Kurelen looked at him kindly, but with indulgent disdain. "It is well that Temujin hath a heart like thine at his side, Kasar. But for his sake, refrain from counselling him." He turned to Temujin, who was breathing rapidly. "Sit down. Thou art ridiculous. Let me give thee some advice. Make friends with thy brother, Bektor, at least outwardly. Thou dost not dare have division in thy ordu at this time. Woo the Shaman, and convince him of thy resolution. If a king have the priests with him, it is better than a thousand warriors. He can do what he will with his people. And he can be certain of the loyalty of the priests if he keepeth them fat and secure. Give the fairest woman of the next raid to Kokchu. Flatter him. Thou wilt not deceive him as to thy real sentiments, but he will be pleased that thou dost consult him, for that will convince him of his own power. Flattery is ofttimes better than gifts. And a smooth tongue maketh faster friends than all the virtues."

"Men are fools," replied Temujin, contemptuously.

Kurelen nodded. "Wise men know this, but never say it." He went on: "But save subtleties for later. Thou and thy people are in grave danger. Thy father's kinsmen, Targutai-Kuriltuk and Todyan-Girte, the two Taijiut chiefs, know that so long as thou dost live they must face a foe, and a holder of the pasture lands thy covet, they know it is to their advantage to kill thee, and absorb thy people in their own clans and tribes. Moreover, thy father was a brave man, and defied them successfully, for all he was so much smaller and weaker. They suspect (and whether this is true or not thou knowest best) thou art his worthy successor. They have already taken the greater part of thy people as vassals, and would have them all, but for thy mother and Kokchu. What hast thou in mind to do?"

"I will appeal to Toghrul Khan."

Kurelen lifted one shoulder. "Toghrul Khan. That foxlike Nestorian Christian, who is known for his craftiness, treachery and sly cowardice! But mayhap thou wilt please him, but only if thou dost convince him thou art worth sponsoring. The test must come first, before he will assist thee."

"Let me take breath," said Temujin. He went out into the dark wind of the night. Lightning was playing in the east, and there was a mutter of thunder behind the hills, which the lightning made incandescent at intervals. The campfires were already low. Most of the tribesmen were asleep. Only the watchmen of the herds were awake, and some of them were nodding over their feeble fires. This enraged Temujin. He lifted his whip and struck the drowsers viciously. But he never wasted words. The blow was struck in silence, and then he went on. The aroused men rubbed their backs and shoulders and stared after him, blinking with awed amazement, as he strode through the camp, the folds of his coat blowing about him. The next day many of them said to their wives: "The youth became the young khan in a twinkling. He grew a foot in stature. He walked like a king. When he looked at me, his eyes glowed like the eyes of a wolf in the darkness, and I was afraid."

Temujin, for all his gloomy and angered preoccupation that night, learned his first and most significant lesson: that some men can be won with words, a few with love, many with gifts, but all with the threat of force. He learned that a strong whip in the hand of a master is greater than any philosophy, and that a stern boot is more feared than all the gods. He was yet to learn that a few, if only a very few, can be won by reason, and that even less fear nothing except their own consciences. But even when he learned that, he knew that these few were insignificant in influence provided the master never lost belief in his mastery.

He left the ordu, and stood alone under the stars, with the dark wind in his face, and his eyes fixed on the hills that leaped in the lightning. He kept lashing his boots with his whip, and his face was set somberly. When a dog came sniffing at his heels, and growling, he struck the beast savagely, and sent him howling on his way. At this, his expression lightened. His feeling of impotence grew less. He went on, found a flat boulder, and sat down on it. He rested his chin in his palm, and thought.

His anxious thoughts grew larger, more diffused, and finally, like a cloud, they lifted. Tranquillity slowly returned to him. He felt the strength of his young body, felt the strong beating of his heart. He lifted his head, and again looked at the stars.

Some dim intuition made his spirit stir, and his pulses began to sing with exultation. Who can conquer me, he thought, if I refuse to be conquered? Kurelen would laugh at me for this. But let him have his subtleties. Philosophies were invented by the weak; in their laughter, which acquiesces to everything, is the ointment for the wound which the strong inflict upon them. I shall not laugh. I shall live.

He got up and went to the yurt of his half-brothers, Bektor and Belgutei. The youths were sleeping, but Temujin drummed imperiously on the flap of the yurt, and awakened them. Belgutei stirred up the fire, and by its dusky red light he regarded Temujin amiably. But Bektor sat on his heap of furs and waited sullenly. Temujin looked slowly from one to the other with sparkling eyes.

"We are brothers," he said, quietly. "And as your older brother, and khan, I demand your loyalty. If I fall, you fall. Give me your faithfulness, not because of our blood or because I ask your love. But only because of expediency. If you fail me, I shall kill you with mine own hands. If you stand with me, you shall have no reason to complain."

"I am no traitor," said Bektor, in a loud, morose voice.

"And thou hast always had my allegiance. And love," said Belgutei, in a soothing voice, which he managed to make admiring. His knowing eyes shone with assumed affection.

Temujin was silent. He continued to look slowly from one to the other. He thought to himself: Bektor hateth me, but he will not betray me. But because of his hatred, he is a temptation to those who would use him. He is simple, and a fool. He is a slave to words. But Belgutei will follow faithfully where I lead, so long as he is assured I will not fail in the long run. He is not so dangerous as Bektor. He distrusteth words, because, wordy himself, he knows how little they are worth.

Then and there he resolved that Bektor must die. He resolved this with no twinge or pang. His situation was too desperate, and never in his life was he to hesitate for sentimental or personal reasons.

"I shall never fail," he said aloud, addressing himself to Belgutei.

He went out, sprang lightly down from the platform of the yurt. He went to his mother. She opened the flap for him, and he entered her tent. She looked at him with an eager smile, knowing how angered he was against her. But after one look at his face, she was silent, knowing that he was a man at last. He bent and kissed her forehead.

"I thank thee, my mother. Thou art a woman of great sagacity. I will look to thee always for advice. Thou art the mistress of my yurts. Tomorrow I shall bring my wife to thee, and do thou counsel her in the ways that will be worthy of my spouse and the mother of my children."

She was deeply touched, but filled with respect and joy.

"Temujin, long ago I knew that thy destiny was greater than other men's. Thou hast a long and bitter road before thee, but thou wilt travel it with courage, to power and glory. Thou hast no one to fear but thyself. Remember that man is not so much the slave of his fellow-men, as he is of his consciousness of his own inferiority. Believe thou art greater than others, and thou shalt be greater than others."

"I have always believed so," replied Temujin, and he believed this to be true.

He went to Kokchu, who was busy with some potion that he was mixing. He received Temujin with elaborate ceremony. But the youth observed that there was considerable amusement and mockery in this. He caught Kokchu's eye and held it sternly.

"Kokchu," he said, "I know thee for a rascal and a traitor. Thou dost see, I talk to thee straightly, for I have no time for flattery. Thou hast always preferred Bektor; he listens to thee, and I do not. Moreover, thou hast dreamed of using him to destroy me, because of thy hatred. It is strange that thou dost admire men of thine own kind, but hatest them in thy heart! Too, thou dost conspire for the very love of conspiracy, which is the way of priests. But I tell thee now that I need thee, for thou art a wise and knowing man. Serve me well, and some day thou shalt crown me as a kha khan. Betray me, and I will disembowel thee. Dost thou understand?"

Kokchu looked at him piercingly, his eyes narrowed, his lips faded to a leaden hue. He thought to himself: Thou son of a simple fox! I shall match wits with thee yet, and shall have the laugh on thee. He who defies and threatens a priest knoweth not what an enemy he makes.

Nevertheless, as he looked at Temujin, he was strangely excited. Perhaps, he thought, this is no mere silly youth, full of bombast. But we shall see. But that all dependeth on whether my desire for power is greater than my desire for revenge.

He assumed an expression of fatherly regret and love.

"Temujin, thy words are harsh, but it is my mission to forgive and counsel, and to pledge my loyalty to my khan. Let us hope we shall understand each other better as we travel together. Thy threats fill me with sorrow, but I remember that thou art young and untried, and bear no malice to thee for them."

They fixed their eyes intently on each other in a hard silence. Then, very slowly, Temujin began to smile, grimly. He laid his hand on the Shaman's shoulder.

"Live up to thy words, Kokchu, as well as say them. That is all I ask."

He left the Shaman. Kokchu stood immobile for a long time afterwards. Many thoughts and emotions drifted across his dark and crafty face. Finally he began to laugh.

"I must remember that revenge is less sweet than self-gain. But still, we shall see." He added, a moment later: "Is it possible that Kurelen hath schooled him in these words? If so, I know what I must do. If not, then I must rechart my course."

The next day Temujin called all his people together. He stood before them, tall, fierce, resolute, with a face that had grown harder and older. He said:

"Our position is desperate. But nothing can touch me. If ye betray me, we shall all perish. Follow me, and nothing can resist us. I speak no idle words."

Thought Kurelen with amazement: He believeth this!

chapter 18

Temujin went for his bride.

Dai Sechen, who had heard of the disorganization of Temujin's ordu, demurred. Better that Temujin consolidate his people, and become stronger, before he took his young wife to his poor camp, among a frightened and poverty-stricken people. But when Temujin turned to him quickly, and he saw his face, the old man fell into uneasy silence. Finally he said: "I did not look for thee to be alive."

He made a great marriage feast. All the young warriors gathered, clad in their sheepskins, lacquer breast-plates weirdly painted, tanned leather jackets loose and red and embroidered, their lances slung over their shoulders and their bow-cases filled with sharp arrows. Their bitten faces shone with layers of grease, which protected them from the fierce winds of the Gobi. The women arrayed themselves in their best woolen robes and hung bracelets and necklaces about their persons and braided their hair with bright threads. The fattest horses and sheep were killed, and soon the rich odors of cooking meat permeated the ordu. The warriors piled their weapons at the entrances to their yurts, as a token of their friendship, and sat at the right hand of the elders. Drinking was prodigious. Before each drink, each warrior poured libations to the four corners of the earth. The minstrels, the old men with their fiddles of one string, sang heroic songs and the songs of marriage, and wandered from fire to fire, sampling the contents of the pots, and quaffing wine.

The warriors drank and clapped their hands, and shouted, and sang. Fermented milk and rice wine flowed like water. Soon they were dancing awkwardly in their deerskin boots, beating their hands in time on their leather shields. When night came, the revelry increased. The bronzed and bony faces shone in the red firelight, which glistened on laughing mouths and wet white teeth, making grotesque the clumsy dancers, so that they seemed like furry animals, cavorting. Beyond them the dark plains and the stars spread in limitless vistas.

The festivities continued for three days, and then Bortei was brought to sit at the left hand of her bridegroom. She was clad in a gown of white felt, embroidered with scarlet and blue and yellow and silver, and upon her head, heavily braided with silver coins and round blue turquoises, was fitted a cone-shaped head-dress, formed of bark covered with embroidered silk. She sat there, demure and silent, her eyes cast down so that the lashes were silken scimitars upon her cheeks, and her lips were full and pouting and red and soft, like a poppy bud. Upon her shoulders hung her sable coat; upon her wrists hung heavy bracelets of silver coins and tiny silver figures.

Temujin sat, looking at his bride, his nostrils flaring and his eyes full of flame. His upper lip was beaded with sweat, and he breathed hoarsely and unevenly. When she glanced up at him from under her lashes, and a faint smile curved the corners of her red mouth, and her breast moved a little, he clenched his hands together and looked about him fiercely, as though defying any watcher to find him demoralized and full of unmanly emotion. Near him sat the tranquil Subodai, upon whom all Bortei's passionate attention was fixed, and Chepe Noyon, gayly drunk as usual, and the wan-lipped and rigid Jamuga with the stony eyelids, who drank nothing and saw everything. Sometimes Bortei, impelled by that immobile gaze, looked at Jamuga, and it seemed to her that her heart turned over with fear and rage and loathing, and she vowed to herself, again and again, that Jamuga must be ruined and sent away from her husband. At these moments the color in her lips grew less warm, and a blue shadow pinched her nostrils.

An old minstrel paused before the young couple and sang:

My beloved is she who sitteth by my side.
Arrayed in the blue girdles and the robe of marriage.
She will be my comfort from my youth to my age,
When my beard is grayer than the steppes, and my heart
Is slower than the ice-held waters. She will bear
My sons, each stronger than the last. She will crown
My life with fruitfulness and sweetness like pure honey.
She will warm my cold bed and my cold heart. Her hands
Will lay upon my neck like a circlet of tender fire.
She will bind up my wounds and shepherd my flocks,
Will beat felt for my yurt, and sew my garments,
And make my boots of deerskin. Where'er I go,
Where'er I die, there will my wife be, my comfort,
My refuge, my hearth and my hope. Blessed is she
Above all other women. Ah, blessed is she, my wife!

Bortei looked at Subodai, and her breast swelled, and her

breath came quicker. Temujin reached for her hand, and when she felt it, she quailed.

Dai Sechen, however, was still uneasy. He called Temujin to him in his yurt, at the height of the festivities. He was no forthright man, but cunning and devious, and crafty, all the things that Temujin despised. After much hesitation and thoughtful humming, the old man said, wincing a little from the expression in Temujin's eyes:

"I have heard of all the travail that hath followed thee, and all the prodigious things done by thee and thy mother to retain thy seat on the white horseskin. I have heard how thou wast hunted, and how thy people fell away. I know thy miseries and thy dangers are not done——"

Temujin interrupted with contempt: "Thou dost know too much, Dai Sechen, and thou dost weary me with thy recital of my woes. Thou hast something to suggest. Say it, and have done."

Dai Sechen's old eyes narrowed slyly. He said, softly: "Ah." And then he pulled his beard. He went on: "I would feel calmer in my heart about my daughter if thou wouldst appeal for protection to thy father's anda, his sworn brother, Toghrul Khan, the chieftain of the Karait Turks. Do thou ride over to the walled cities of the Karaits, and demand of Toghrul Khan the assistance he is sworn to render thee on demand."

He stopped abruptly, for Temujin was regarding him with rage. The young man stood up and began to stride from one end of the yurt to the other, as though he could not contain himself. Finally he stopped before his father-in-law, and shouted at him furiously:

"Thou hast no wisdom, Dai Sechen, if thou dost not know that one must not appeal to a friend with empty hands, if thou desirest not to be met with scorn or hesitation or excuses. Come strongly, on horseback, with treasures, and a friend will greet thee gladly and offer all manner of assistance. If I came today to Toghrul Khan, he would say to himself: 'This is a weak and whining youth, who will take from any coffers without hope of return, and endanger me because of my assistance.' He would not be wrong. The strong aid the strong. I must prove to my foster-father that I am worth helping, before I ask for help, or expect it."

Dai Sechen pondered this, his face wrinkling with disappointment and obstinacy. He thought to himself: Even now I can refuse my daughter, saying that she goeth inevitably to death or starvation, and that her husband must have a secure place for her before she leaveth her father's tent. If he will not agree, he is, at the last, but a helpless youth, with but three youths with him, and I can easily destroy him. Neither can his people avenge him, for they are much weaker than mine.

Temujin watched the old man, as he sat crouched cross-legged on the floor before him. His face darkened, and his lips drew together in a cruel and ferocious line. He began to speak so quietly that it was a moment or two before Dai Sechen became aware of his words:

"Do me treachery, Dai Sechen, and thou wilt have no more tomorrows. It was said of me at my birth that I would be the ruler of all men. How canst thou defy the spirits, who have ordained this?"

Dai Sechen lifted his eyes and studied the hard young face above his. Then, very slowly and craftily, he began to smile. "Thou dost not believe the prophecies, Temujin. But thou hast resolved to fulfil them."

He stood up, and took Temujin by the arm. "Mayhap I am a fool, in my dotage, but there is something of fatefulness in thee. I look upon thy face, and I see in it a strange thing, like a destiny. Look thee: I will send with my daughter not only her servants, but ten warriors and their yurts and families." He paused, sighed. "It is said of Toghrul Khan that his people are very rich, possessed of gold and silver and many weapons, and even the fire-that-flies of the Chinese, and that their cities are invincibly walled. Thou wilt not reconsider?"

"No," said Temujin, quietly. "When I go to him, I shall go as an ally, not a supplicant. I shall overcome the Taijiuts with mine own hand. Trust me."

Dai Sechen said thoughtfully: "Thy words are vainglorious, like those of all young men, but I verily believe thou art not vainglorious."

Temujin smiled, grimly. "I am no longer young. Years do not age, but only knowledge. I have learned many things, but the greatest I have learned is that a man must not use reason to become powerful and invincible. He must use promises of gain to some men. But those promises of gain are for his paladins, only. For his people he must use force and terror. His will must become a divine will, for them. He must not be a man among them, but a god, with death in his hand. He must be compounded of mystery and ruthlessness and superstition; he must wear a frightful crown, and carry a merciless sword in his hand. A good king is a weak king, and his people must inevitably despise him."

His face was suddenly contorted, as though with a fury of contempt and black understanding.

"Many things have I learned, but I have also learned that the soul of man is the soul of a camel, who heedeth only a whip! But I shall temper my implacability with generosity to those who serve me well, and no man shall ever say that Temujin's word is water. For these things will my people love me, and who shall stand against us! As for myself, so long as I trust no man so shall I be unconquerable." Dai Sechen smiled a little, and pulled his beard. Then he linked his arm with Temujin's, and said: "Well, then, we have understood each other. Let us return to thy bride."

And now Bortei must retire among her half-sisters and her women, and Temujin must pursue her through the tents, as though he seized her by force from her father's ordu. He must struggle with the women for her, as they blocked his pursuit, and she fled from yurt to yurt. It was a happy game, in which every one joined with laughter and ribald advice. Temujin's path was also blocked with singing and drunken warriors, who tusselled with him, shouting. He threw off many of them, kicked others out of his way. His blood sang; his teeth glittered. Now his eyes were the fierce blue of a flame.

Bortei, hearing his tumultuous approach, ran from the yurt in which she was hiding, and scampered for another, almost deserted and in a quieter spot. She had reached it, and was about to climb the platform, when a gray shadow in the gray light of dawn rose up before her. She put her hands to her mouth to smother a startled scream. And then she saw that the shadow was Jamuga.

They stood like statues, voiceless, motionless, and looked at each other. Moments passed, and the sound of the seeking tumult came nearer. But neither the youth nor the girl spoke. Their eyes were locked together like wrestlers. Silvery fire ran along the eastern horizon, and the earth floated in a milky sea. Yet still these two did not move, but as the light brightened, they saw the hatred between them. And Bortei knew that Jamuga was warning her, and challenging her, and that she had an enemy who would know no mercy at the end.

The hunting party burst into full view. Bortei, whose face was as pale as death, glanced at the approaching Temujin and those who followed him on a run. And then she looked at Jamuga once more. But he was gone. It was as though the earth had swallowed him up, so completely had he vanished.

When Temujin seized her with a cry of triumph, she lay supine in his arms, smiling fixedly. But her heart was thundering like a drum, and a coldness lay along her spine.

chapter 19

With a cynical compassion, Kurelen observed the triumphant return of Temujin with his bride. There was an exultant and turbulent defiance in his manner, a hasty largeness which at first seemed the boastfulness of youth. But, after a moment's thoughtful study, Kurelen, with amazement, decided that he was wrong. I must be aging, he thought, with attempt at self-derision, for I believe in portents.

He was pleased with the beauty of Bortei, but after the first pleasure he saw how ambitious she was, how imperious and vain and wilful. She brought a cloak of black sable skins to Houlun, a precious gift, but she presented it with supercilious respect, and allowed no one to doubt that she thought Temujin's people poor and defenseless, and that she, herself, came from a richer clan and a more easy life. Her father's pastures had been settled and fatter; he was not hunted, but rather respected, by other chieftains. She had already heard the sordid story of Temujin's recent flight from murder at the hands of Targoutai, who had announced he was now overlord of the Gobi northern pastures. Temujin had told her, with rage and mortification. But even his explanation that he had had to flee for a little while, because he was unable to fight back and retain his people's pastures, had not reduced the ignominy, in her opinion. A man who had to flee was, to her, a poor creature. However, she did not regret her marriage. Temujin was still a khan, though khan of a miserable handful of people, and she was a very astute girl. She believed in him, though she feared rather than loved him. She had decided from the first that he would become a kha khan, and had diligently planned out the proper steps in her own mind. She remembered, with conceit, that her father had often bewailed the fact that she was not a man, for her wit was so superior. The only thing necessary was to get him entirely under her influence, in order to guide him rightly. To do this, she had to rid herself of Jamuga, who she suspected was not ruthless nor exigent. To her dismay, she found herself confronted not only with Jamuga, but with Houlun and Kurelen also.

She had approached Kurelen with misgiving and hatred. She had sounded him out as to his own desires for Temujin. To her sudden delight and pleasure, she discovered in him her own cynicism and realistic philosophy. But she also perceived that though her own objectives were acceptable to him, he was not serious about them. It would be good, he had said to her frankly, if Temujin became what she willed. But if he did not, and merely survived in peace and comfort, then it would still be good. After all, it was enough for a man if he lived with a minimum of pain.

"Thou thinkest so because thou art impotent," said the young girl, looking at him with brutal candor. Her eyes were as gray as a frozen lake, thought Kurelen, even while he smiled and raised his eyebrows with indulgent malice.

"Well, what wouldst thou with Temujin, child?"

The gray eyes had glinted as though lightning had touched them. "I would have him lord of all the Gobi," she answered, not loudly, but with a sort of cold fierceness.

"Because thou lovest him?"

She had hesitated. And then she thought to herself that Kurelen loved candor, for it made him laugh, and if he laughed, that cleansed him of venom and she would not need to fear him.

"Nay," she replied, with an enchanting smile. "Because I love myself."

They understood each other, were wary of each other, but no longer disliked each other. If Kurelen opposed her, shrewdly concluded the girl, it would be merely to tease her. He would watch her with intense interest, and assist her when needful. For long ago she had perceived that under his derision for those who loved power was an unquenchable lust for it, himself. Only his great humor had kept him from being a conspirator; only his self-evaluation had made him refrain from envious plotting. He knew his limitations. But he was wise in that he did not seek revenge for them. He, as he often explained, preferred to eat, and he also preferred that what he ate be untainted by bitterness.

But Houlun, recognizing one like herself, immediately hated the young wife, who threatened her own dominion. The two women had looked into each other's eyes. Houlun had thought, with fury: I am no longer young. And Bortei had thought: Thou hast ruled too long. Thus began a struggle for Temujin which was to end only in death, and a hatred that was to be unremitting and remorseless.

One by one, she studied those who could aid or oppose her. She was not concerned about Kasar, and gave him her sweetest smiles when she discovered his idolatry of his brother. He was brave, simple and devoted, a good henchman. She soon convinced him that she adored Temujin, also, and wished only his good, and was ambitious for him. He gave her a measure of worship and blind devotion, in return. Nothing, henceforth, would shake his allegiance to her.

Chepe Noyon, she knew, extravagantly admired her beauty. But he was shrewd. He might be beguiled by her eyes and her lips, but only lightly, and he would cheerfully cut her throat if he discovered her in any treachery against her husband. The throat-cutting would proceed with dispatch, and without any personal animosity. She set herself to win him, and pretend to an artlessness which did not deceive but only amused him. This amused her, also. They became great friends, gay and impudent. She could count on him not to oppose her in anything that would advance Temujin's interests, however devious and sly her methods were. He was supremely loyal, but had little personal integrity, she observed with relief. She was too clever to be amazed at paradoxes.

She soon knew that the Shaman was a formidable force which she must not under-evaluate. She perceived he was extremely susceptible to female loveliness and flattery, but only so far as his own interests extended. He would sacrifice or risk nothing because of any feminine beguilements. At first she was concerned. But later she was heartened. She had only to show him that his own gain lay with Temujin, and then she had him completely. But then she discovered Bektor.

She saw that Bektor was innocently the most dangerous foe with whom she would have to contend, because of Kokchu and others who hated Temujin. Without regret, she decided he must die. She had only to prepare the way. Once Bektor was dead, the Shaman would have no choice but to follow Temujin. And the murder must take place soon, she concluded. Poison, perhaps. Her own mother had taught her the most potent toxins. She would think about it in a few days, and plan the proper occasion.

Jamuga, too, must die, or be rid of in some other way. Perhaps not death; that would cement his influence with Temujin, who would never believe in any accusation of disaffection, unless he saw it himself. He must be made to see it, and by Jamuga. That would take planning. Bortei methodically laid the idea aside, to be worked upon at leisure. For it would require great cleverness. In the meantime, she would study Jamuga, and discover the way to make him ruin himself.

And then there was Subodai, the chivalrous, the pure and the beautiful, whose soul was like clear water in a silver cup. Her lust for him grew daily, so that it seemed to her that liquid fire instead of blood ran in her veins. If she were to seduce him, she must do it with all skill and wit, for there were too many eyes upon her. She wondered if Kurelen and the Shaman had already guessed her passion. Kurelen, she decided, would not interfere, unless she swerved from her duties to Temujin. Once he had said to her: "Among us, adultery is a crime. Among the civilized, it is an art." However, she was not yet certain that his tolerance would extend to her, in spite of his smile of ridicule when he spoke of his own people's simplicity. She saw that Kurelen, at the last, would ask only that she not force him to see her physical betrayal of Temujin. As for the Shaman, she must be careful not to offend his vanity. She must save her most delicate flatteries for him.

But Subodai, himself, was the greatest obstacle in the path of his own seduction. He was a veritable white knight, selfless, brave and truthful. He would never be seduced by passion, but only by a great love. And there must be no shadow on that love. She decided that he must be made to love her secretly; she did not seriously believe that any man could resist passion at the last, provided it had been stimulated enough. But her task, she felt, would be long and arduous. She must present herself in his eyes as a pure and devoted and heroic wife, full of tenderness and all the virtues. Then he would love her. His capitulation would then be only a matter of time. He would never begin with lust; he would only end with it. Sometimes she felt a wondering contempt for him, and doubted his virility. And then her own desire would sweep it away, and she knew that nothing mattered but this desire and its fulfilment; and then there was a perverse respect in her for a man who would love a woman only because she was virtuous and devoted to her husband.

But always, at every devious turn of her labyrinthian nature, she came face to face with the stony eyes of Jamuga, Temujin's anda, whom he loved above all others, even his wife. The obstacle that must be destroyed, before any of her desires could be fruitful.

She had not learned, and perhaps never would learn, that Temujin, at the very last, was influenced only by himself, and did, finally, only what he had always decided to do. If others believed that they had influenced him, they had the blind gratification of their own vanity. He never bothered to disillusion them. He found deluded people advantageous, and their delusion cemented their loyalty to him. He had long ago realized that men are devoted to a leader in whom they believe they see their own leadership and desires in influence. Their own conceit is the spring of their devotion. To betray him would be to betray themselves. And only saints and madmen betray themselves.

Kurelen, alone, suspected Temujin's true nature, and because of this, he was careful to dilute his advice with laughter, so that his nephew might not be made uncertain by it.

In the meantime, he, Kurelen, found life very interesting. He saw everything, and found everything full of excitement and mirth.

chapter 20

Kurelen had told Temujin: "The day a man doth realize that he hath no friends is the day he is delivered from his swaddling clothes."

Temujin believed this, with reservations. He believed that it is given to few men to have a true friend, and then only one. He might have devoted followers like Chepe Noyon and Kasar and Subodai. But only if he is singularly blessed will he have a friend like Jamuga Sechen, his spiritual anda as well as his mere sworn brother.

A man might have a noble mother like Houlun. He might have a beautiful and industrious and clever wife like Bortei. He might have an adviser who loved him, like Kurelen. But rarely will he have a friend, who is above mother and wife and children and priest and kin.

Even later, he never doubted Jamuga's love and devotion to him. Nor, in spite of many things, did he ever doubt Jamuga's fundamental loyalty. Only to Jamuga could he ever talk freely and simply. There was in Temujin an eternal thirst for freedom and simplicity, untainted by laughter and subtleties and all other wearinesses. He came back to them like a man returning to an oasis after long forays. Whatever other lusts there were in him, there was this deeper thirst. He satisfied it in Jamuga.

He could talk to Jamuga. They did not often agree. They were too dissimilar, and liked opposing things. But they trusted each other, and understood each other. Temujin said to Jamuga that all the devotion of others was based on individual illusions as to his real self. But Jamuga knew his anda completely, and so could love him completely. He, Jamuga, would never be long shocked nor disconcerted by Temujin, no matter what he did. Not because of love, but because of comprehension, even when it was a distasteful comprehension, alien to his own nature.

Sometimes others were offended and jealous because of the young men's habit of riding off alone together. But it was a necessity for Temujin, who felt that when he was with Jamuga he was truly alone, an alter ego accompanying him with whom he need not pretend. Often he had to lie. Lying was tedious for him, for it was a waste of time. With Jamuga he never needed to lie. There was joy in being himself, as though he had stripped off hot and cumbersome clothing, and plunged, naked, into cool water.

Because of his enemy, Targoutai, who had declared himself overlord of the northern Gobi since Yesukai's death, Temujin's people had had to deviate considerably from their usual course in their travels from winter to summer pastures. Temujin had at first raged, but it was not in his nature to rage long against the inevitable. Only fools wasted the substance of their soul in unavailing fury. It embittered him to have to lead his people stealthily into poor pastures, in order not to infuriate Targoutai. But he recognized the necessity of convincing Targoutai that Temujin was no longer a foe that had to be annihilated. He knew that his best weapon against Targoutai was Targoutai's own contempt for him. Let Targoutai say to himself: "This young khan is a small yellow dog not worthy of mine enmity and my hunt." Thus would Temujin continue to live, and grow strong. In the meantime, he had sent a tribesman to Targoutai, pretending treachery. The tribesman, allegedly deserting to Targoutai, had been schooled to say:

"Temujin hath realized he is no true leader, and wisheth in his heart to swear allegiance to thee. But he hath a little pride, and desireth to attain some strength, in order to present himself proudly to thee saying: 'I am worthy to be one of thy vassals, one of thy noyon.' "

Later, it was reported to Temujin that Targoutai had laughed scornfully, and had said: "He, then, hath more sense than I believed possible for a son of Yesukai. Let him prove his worth, and mayhap I shall later allow him to swear allegiance to me."

Temujin, turning pale with wrath, was yet able to smile grimly at this report. Despite his tumultous nature, he had the terrible patience of the nomad. But he did not have the nomad's pliability and fatalism. He could not shrug, and forget. He might shrug, but he never resigned himself to inexorableness. Fate, to him, was never inflexible, but only a sword that could be seized by a strong man.

In the meantime, his people complained because of their increasing poverty and the poorness of their pastures. Temujin was apparently resigned to the little leader of a miserable ordu. He heard their mutterings, and his lips tightened. But he said nothing, only looking at them in silent balefulness, so that they were filled with terror of him.

One evening, near sunset, he rode off with Jamuga to be alone for a while. Sometimes, in spite of himself, his anger and gloom were too much for him. He had to go away where he could think.

Because of their fear and poverty, the people had had to skirt about the good pastures, and in their travels they had been forced to enter the foothills of great mountains, where pasture was scarce and the country harsh and rugged. Here there was good hunting for antelope and bear and fox, but little good grass.

The air was fresh and cool, and ageless, impregnated with the pungency of fir and the purity of rock. Temujin rode a little ahead of Jamuga with sudden impatience, as though some sharp thought spurred him. His white stallion leaped lightly to a stony ledge, and then stood like a statue, his long white mane and tail rippling slightly in the wind. Against a background of bright pale sky and intense blue mountain, horse and rider stood motionless, something impelling and fateful in their attitude. Temujin's dark and violent profile was full of somber melancholy; planes of faint but vivid light lay on his cheek, like a reflection of snow. The sun, far and cold and shining, glimmered on his harness and the hilts of his dagger and scimitar. His eye had borrowed the hue of the sky, and sparkled like hard blue stone. His shoulders, broad and thin and straight, and his back, were the form of a soldier. His uncovered red hair glinted with threads of fiery gold. Savage, wild and grim, his bronzed skin lined and harsh, he was part of this enormous landscape of blue and white, this tremendous vista of sky and mountain.

Of what was he thinking? Jamuga asked of himself, watching his friend with deep gravity. He remembered the younger Temujin, turbulent and vehement, laughing and tumultuous. It seemed to him that Temujin was like a vivid and moving being, full of impetuous movement, imbued with flame and passion, which had suddenly frozen into eternal immobility, caught in the moment of an heroic attitude. His youth had gone forever, and something terrible had taken its place.

Jamuga, seized with a sudden vague fear, spurred his narrow black horse, and reached Temujin's side. They stood together for a long time without speaking, while Temujin's eye ranged the mountains and the water-threaded valleys with a dark hunger. There were nothing but silence and pallid sunlight, and the wind moved without sound.

Then Temujin said: "We must have pastures. Many pastures. Or we die. My people are afraid of me, but they are more afraid of death. At the end, this fear will win. Somehow, I must overcome Targoutai in open combat. I must be lord of the northern Gobi."

"Why not offer to join him?"

Temujin did not move for a moment nor reply, and then he turned to Jamuga and regarded him with an eye that blazed. But his voice was quiet:

"No. I must overcome him. I must invoke the aid of Toghrul. But first, I must make Toghrul value me as an ally. I have thought of something. I shall take the cloak of black sable to him, and convince him I am worthy of his aid."

"How canst thou do that?"

Temujin smiled. He flicked his white stallion with his whip, and the horse flung up his head so that his snowy mane rose like a foaming crest over it.

"Look thee, Jamuga: At the best, what are we, and what was my father? Beggarly robbers—quarrelsome hunters of good pasture. One of thousands of the little aristocrats of the steppes, which fight bloodily among themselves, and are no better at the end. Raiders, hunters, fighters, boasters, slaves to poverty and hardship, constantly fearful of annihilation. Yet, all together, bonded and sworn, they would be formidable, a powerful menace to the towns and the cities, who could be made to yield tribute."

Jamuga knitted his brows. His wan lip became rigid.

"Tribute," he murmured. "But we seek only pastures. And peace."

Temujin smiled again, this time with contempt. He regarded Jamuga with a sparkling eye. He went on, as though Jamuga had not spoken:

"A man who seeketh peace is a rabbit among foxes. Only he who hath fought well and conquered deserveth peace, and only he shall have it.

"Look thee, again: each of our little lords seeketh to attract followers, in order that he might be strong enough to raid weak tribes. Each little noyon must succeed or die. This constant success and failure doth destroy the small aristocrats, the tiny khans. Each man must prove himself strong by force of arms, and not by gifts, as is the way of townsmen. A weak man who giveth gifts is an object of contempt. Only the strong dare offer presents. Men will follow a strong man who is generous. Therefore, it is necessary that raids be continual, and warfare among us unremitting. A strong leader doth attract many followers. Why not, then, a single strong leader, a kha khan, exacting obedience and loyalty from all the dwellers of the steppes, instead of such like Toghrul Khan and Targoutai, who hate each other, and who bring about anarchy and disorder with their constant struggles with each other, and others like them?"

Jamuga gazed at him earnestly. "And thou dost think that by uniting all the little khans and leaders under one resistless man thou canst bring about harmony and peace, and all men, thereafter, can dwell together without fear, and in comfort?"

Again Temujin smiled, but this time he looked away from his anda and stared at the mountain. His voice, strong and hoarse, dropped to a low note:

"Peace! The man who desireth peace is a man who looketh at his grave!"

He spurred his horse, and it sprang down from the ledge. Temujin suddenly shouted, lifted his whip and struck the stallion fiercely. It leaped into the air, swung about, rearing on its hind legs, and Temujin stood against the sky like a statue come suddenly and violently to life. His face had taken on itself that wild and fateful quality which filled Jamuga with a nameless terror. His eyes were green flame. Then the horse, fallen to his four feet again, raced off like a mad thing down into the valley, leaping from ledge to ledge, sliding in a cloud of golden dust down a steep incline. The noise of their going awakened echoes, until all the air was filled with a near thunder.

After some time, Jamuga followed thoughtfully on his light black horse. He coughed in the yellow dust. Temujin had stopped below, in a level crevice between the mountains. His horse was panting. But when Jamuga came up, Temujin looked at him with the sweet and magnetic smile which no one could resist. Yet, there was amusement in his eyes, as well as indulgent affection for his anda.

"If thou wert not so brave, Jamuga, I would suspect thee of being one of the eunuchs of the city, of which Kurelen doth tell us."

Jamuga flushed. His rare color came reluctantly into his pale face, and only when he was deeply angered or disturbed.

"I do not understand thee, Temujin!" he exclaimed. But he felt faintly ill, as though with premonition.

But Temujin had already forgotten what he had said, and the mood which had caused it. He lifted his whip and pointed.

"Over there lieth the Khwarizmian Empire of Central Asia. And over there, the Kin Empire of Cathay. Both rich and elegant and vast, full of academies and universities and temples and libraries and palaces, and white streets tree-bordered and jewelled with pools and gardens. Kurelen hath told me. He hath also told me that these empires are rotten, like fat old lustful men with diseased bowels. They sit in their gardens, with singing women about them, their fingers covered with jewels, their many chins sunken on their breasts, their slothful bodies clothed in cloth of gold and embroidered silk, their feet as soft as their pallid hands, and puffed as bladders. They move only to eat and drink; they listen to philosophy, and converse with scholars. They lust after weak strange pleasures, when they are infrequently stirred to motion. They smile with sleepy delight at the music of many languid singers. Their bellies droop with fat. Wealth and degraded lusts and safety have made them eunuchs in soul, as well as body. They are ready for destruction, for death by the clean strong sword."

He paused. He fixed his smiling eyes, which were now innocently blue, upon Jamuga, who was frowning in his efforts to understand.

"Jamuga, dost thou remember the stories the Persians tell, which Kurelen hath spoken of, about a strange conqueror who came from the west, and who was called Alexander of Macedon, the godlike, the Conqueror?"

Jamuga, believing he was being made game of by Temujin, in his incomprehensible mood, assumed an expression of dignity to hide his confusion.

"But what hath all this to do with seeking protection for our people from Targoutai, and finding and keeping good pastures for them?"

But Temujin only smiled. His breath was short and quick, as he stared at Jamuga.

Jamuga, still affronted, said: "Thou dost speak of one ulus, or confederation. That is impossible. The Tatar, the Merkit, the Turk, the Urghur, the Naiman, the Taijiut—these can never dwell together in harmony under one leader." He paused, then said in a low voice: "But can they not?" He added, in a louder voice: "I have always loved peace. But where is the man who can bring it about?"

He looked questioningly at Temujin, whose eyes had begun to glitter with restless impatience. But Temujin did not reply. He, even as he stared at his anda, seemed absorbed in some vague and enormous dream, whose outlines were slowly becoming clearer to him.

Jamuga, raising his voice as though Temujin were deaf, asked:

"But what hath all this to do with good pastures for our herds?"

His horse suddenly shied, for Temujin had burst into a savage shout of laughter.

"Nothing! Nothing!" he cried.

And then again, he reined in his horse, so that the stallion stood again on his hind legs. And then, swinging about, he raced away so swiftly that Jamuga, sitting motionless on his horse, despaired of catching up with him. He stood in silence, a strange sad dejection upon him, a cold premonition about his heart. He watched Temujin winding furiously through the narrow valley below. And then he spoke aloud, in a voice of increasing bewilderment and fear:

"But no one could ask more than pastures and peace!"

chapter 21

For some reason he could scarcely name, Jamuga avoided Temujin that night. He ate quietly with his half-brothers at the campfire before their yurt. They were all young boys, gay and boisterous. The youngest one had to be caught from hurtling into the fire at intervals. But there was a simple animalism about them that Jamuga, for all his fastidiousness and silence, found refreshing and soothing tonight. A painful suspicion was awakening in him that there was something secret and menacing in Temujin which he had never suspected before, and that the youth he had thought all turbulence and vehement speech and gestures was some one he did not know. His lack of perspicacity troubled him more than the thing he learned about his anda, for his egotism, for all it was not aggressive, was only the deeper and he could not endure any affront to it.

In the midst of his disturbed thoughts he glanced up to see that the pliant and amiable Belgutei had joined the group about the fire. Upon catching his eye, Belgutei smiled, caught the youngest child deftly from his latest surge towards the fire, and set him on his feet. He sat down, and began to joke humorously with the children, who responded to him enthusiastically. Jamuga, frowning perplexedly, watched the youth in his play with the children. He seemed to see Temujin's younger half-brother for the first time. Belgutei was slight and active, and had an affable and responsive face, and no enemies. That seemed sinister to Jamuga, yet he could not help but admit to himself that the reason might be because Belgutei offended no one, was never aggressive or arrogant or fierce, but always ready for laughter and friendship, and amiably disposed to any one who made overtures to him. Still, Jamuga doubted. Open looks frequently hid devious hearts. Pleasant smiles were sometimes the smooth door behind which villainy waited. Moreover, he had always had the feeling that Belgutei never said anything he meant. He laughed without venom, but sometimes venom was too crafty to betray itself.

Jamuga's mother now came scolding for the young children, and Jamuga and Belgutei were left alone. Then it was that Jamuga thought with pale contempt: It is not mere friendliness that bringeth him here. For, out of the corners of his eyes he saw that Belgutei was studying him speculatively. When he looked fully at the other youth, Belgutei immediately broke into an artless smile, which Jamuga did not return.

"I have heard it rumored that Temujin will soon seek the aid of Toghrul Khan," said Belgutei, in his agreeable voice.

Jamuga shrugged. "Who knoweth?" he answered, coldly.

Belgutei eyed him with pleasant reflectiveness, knowing him undeceived.

"I have always loved Temujin," he said, candidly. "I have always believed in his destiny."

For some reason this irritated Jamuga, and he said impatiently:

"What destiny? It is strange that every one is mouthing that word, like a camel eating thorns. But thou didst not come here to me, Belgutei, merely to discuss Temujin's vainglorious dreams." When he said that, he was conscious of a feeling of slight sickness, as though he had been self-caught in treachery. But there was a sore and aching spot in him, which he had to rub.

Belgutei laughed lightly and good-temperedly. "Thou art right, Jamuga. I did not come to discuss Temujin's plans. I only came from motives of brotherly concern. Last night, an attempt was made to poison Bektor, my brother."

Jamuga was startled. He turned and faced Belgutei fully and hastily. "But Temujin would not stoop to the wickedness of poisoning Bektor! Thou art a fool, Belgutei! What quarrel there is between them will be settled openly and fairly." But to himself, with mounting sickness, he thought: How do I know this? Do I know Temujin at all?

Belgutei shrugged placatingly. "I am glad that thou dost believe this, Jamuga. It doth relieve my mind of many apprehensions. I love Bektor. Nevertheless, though I am inclined to believe thee, an attempt was made to poison him. He hath not been in good spirits the last few days, and could eat little. Therefore, his life was saved."

Quickening with anxiety, Jamuga exclaimed: "Tell me!" His very lips felt cold.

Belgutei said, new gravity darkening his friendly face: "Last night Bektor was passing Temujin's yurt. Bortei was stirring the pot, in which she was cooking a fine antelope stew. Temujin was dining with Kurelen, as he often doth, and Bortei, seeing Bektor, assumed an air of affection and kindness and offered to share the meal with him, calling him 'brother.' "

He paused, and fixed his eyes, suddenly piercing, upon the silent Jamuga.

"She did declare to Bektor that she was much annoyed at Temujin's fondness for Kurelen, and that he often left her lonely. My brother—he is a simple and tormented soul. He doth respond to friendliness like a wounded dog. Under all his formidable and sulky appearance, he longeth for kindness and peace. All his fierceness doth spring from his aching desire to be accepted. His bullying manner doth conceal his bewilderment. Men like this can be tamed to loyalty and generosity; misunderstood, none can be more terrible."

Again he paused. Jamuga was still silent, but a deep furrow appeared between his pale eyes.

Belgutei sighed. "Bektor sat with Bortei, not censuring her for her forward ways. He was very lonely. She filled his plate and hers, from the pot. She urged him to eat. But all at once his somber sadness clutched his vitals, and only courtesy made him swallow a little. As soon as he could, he left her."

Belgutei shrugged slightly. "He told me that there was something about the woman which revolted him, though she hath great beauty."

He waited. But still Jamuga did not speak.

Belgutei went on quietly, all the merriment gone from his eyes.

"Bektor lay down to sleep. And then suddenly woke with a cry, clutching his belly. He called for the Shaman. When Kokchu came, he cried out that my brother had been poisoned. He mixed him a foul brew, and forced it upon him. Bektor vomited. The food he had eaten spewed through his mouth, bright red with his blood."

Jamuga grew frigid with horror and disgust. He began to speak in a stammering voice: "But, thou didst say that Bortei ate from the same pot, sitting beside Bektor!"

Belgutei nodded gravely. "That is true. I questioned Bektor closely. The woman did go in and out of the yurt, bringing cups and kumiss and millet. At any time, she had the opportunity to mix poison separately with the food she was placing on Bektor's plate. He recalled that it had a dimly strange flavor. Or, mayhap, she mixed the poison in his cup."

Jamuga bent his head and stared at the fire.

"Look thee, Jamuga," said Belgutei, reasonably. "Bortei would have no reason to poison Bektor, except by command of Temujin."

Jamuga spoke in a low voice, not looking at him: "Doth it occur to thee that she might have been moved by loyal fervor to Temujin, and undertook this herself?"

Belgutei threw back his head and laughed. "Hah! She hath

the eye of a wanton! I am amazed that she hath not heretofore attempted to poison Temujin, himself, for it is open for any one to see that she lusteth after Subodai! Nay, she poisoned Bektor by Temujin's command——"

He stopped abruptly, for Jamuga's eyes were filled with fire. The reserved youth seemed imbued with a frantic passion and rage, and Belgutei could do nothing but stare at him, astounded.

"It is a lie!" cried Jamuga. "In truth, she attempted to poison Bektor, but by her own desire. And in my heart, I know her motive."

He got to his feet. He was visibly trembling. He struggled to control himself. When he spoke again, his voice was unnaturally quiet.

"Fear no more treachery against Bektor, such as this. And now, do thou leave me."

When Belgutei had left him, Jamuga stood, rigidly trembling, for a long while. Then, pulling his hood over his head, he slipped along the rear of the yurts and made his way to that of Temujin. Bortei was sitting before her fire, with Houlun, and when they perceived Jamuga, they stared up at him, wonderingly. Houlun greeted him with reserve, but Bortei said nothing, only paling a trifle. Jamuga did not answer Houlun's greeting, but said directly to Bortei, looking down at her with hatred and loathing:

"Thou didst attempt to poison Bektor!"

Houlun uttered a concerned exclamation, but Bortei, turning white as tallow, looked at him boldly, and answered:

"It is a lie."

Jamuga shook his head at her with a sort of cold ferocity. "It is not a lie, and thou knowest it. Look thee, Bortei—Temujin hath a quarrel to settle with Bektor. If thou dost settle it for him, for thine own motives which I know, he will be a mockery among his people. I shall not tell Temujin, for he might kill thee for thy foul craftiness. But lift thy hand against Bektor again, and thy husband shall know everything about thee."

Houlun looked at him with quickening and passionate interest: "What dost thou know of Bortei, Jamuga?"

But he looked only at Bortei, whose lips had become livid, and whose eyes, enormously distended, were filled with hatred and terror. And then he turned away, and left them. Soon, he heard the acrimonious voices of the two women, upbraiding each other, accusing and counter-accusing, until a scream assured him that Houlun had smacked her daughter-in-law across the face.

He went back to his yurt. His young brothers were asleep. He lay down on his bed of furs and felt, and closed his eyes. But he could not sleep.

There was a great sickness in him, but he was not thinking about Bortei.

Over and over, he thought: Is it possible it was by Temujin's command?

chapter 22

But Jamuga underestimated Bortei tragically when he believed that he had frightened her, or set her aside from her purpose. He had merely shown her that she must be more careful, and proceed along a different way.

Extremely guileful and without conscience or scruple, she knew how to win the confidence of others, even of one like Houlun, who was jealous, and disliked her intensely. It was not long before she convinced Houlun that her concern with the safety and well-being of Temujin was sincere and all-engrossing. At first, Houlun was inclined to be jealously resentful. But later, she was touched.

One day Bortei said to her mother-in-law: "I have no enmity for Bektor, half-brother of my husband. But I can readily see that he is a danger."

Houlun, surprised and taken aback by the astuteness of this young girl, agreed. But what could one do? Bortei gazed at her mother-in-law's perplexed face very reflectively. She listened to Houlun's honest defense of Bektor, and nodded gravely when the older woman suggested that the best course was a reconcilation between the two young men. But Houlun, later, had the uneasy sensation that the grave nod had been merely diplomatic, and Bortei had not believed this at all.

Bortei believed in herself that there are some natures which can never be reconciled nor comprehended by each other. Or, at best, the reconciliation could be only tentative. This was not a matter to cause worry, if there were not some external and dangerous circumstances to be considered, also. But in the matter of Temujin, there were external and dangerous circumstances. Moreover, Bortei believed reconciliations were very good, provided that they did not take undue time. If the reconciliations demanded a long period of finesse and delicacy, then the intelligent man ruthlessly refused to consider them. He must eliminate his enemy. Life was too short to take circuitous routes, even in the cause of mercy and sweetness. It was better to hack down a flowering tree that impeded one's path than to go laboriously around it. Thus, coldly, she reasoned.

She knew that Temujin had no time to spare. Moreover,

very shrewdly, she began to guess that he would make haste upon a plan suggested by another, if he had already decided on this plan heretofore. So, tactfully and carefully, she approached him upon the danger inherent in the very existence of Bektor. She pretended to speak reluctantly, giving him to understand that it was only her intense love and devotion to him which impelled her to speak. After all, she said, gazing at Temujin with the frozen gray of her eyes, a man must resent any innuendoes about his own brother, even if they came from his wife. The gray of her eyes became artless; she was very careful not to let Temujin suspect that she knew of the enmity between him and his brother.

Temujin listened with interest, his face gloomy and suspicious. But his eyes softened in spite of himself, as he looked at his beautiful wife, whom he loved with intense passion and lust, and yet with something stranger and deeper than these. She sat at his feet as she talked in her soft, loving and regretful voice, and she let him twine his fingers awkwardly in her red-tinged dark hair. She leaned forward a little so that he could see the modelling of her high and lovely breasts with their conical nipples. Versed in the ways of women, she had carelessly extended one leg, and the wool of her robe sculptured it, revealing the round thigh and the slenderness of dainty calf. She talked reason with him, but artfully colored that reason with an invitation to desire. She knew that the arguments of a woman are more potent if accompanied by lustful suggestion, and that even wisdom is received without resentment when it comes with the face of youth and the odor of femaleness. Mingled with her primal knowledge was her contempt for men, whose strength and resolution become as water at the rise of a woman's breast, and whose knowledge becomes impotent before surrendering thighs.

Temujin, who all his life was abnormally susceptible to women, looked at her restlessly, and turned aside his eyes. He distrusted his susceptibility. Yet he had to acknowledge that she was a wise and astute woman. He had already decided upon the death of Bektor. When Bortei hinted its necessity, she gave him the final thrust towards its accomplishment. Nevertheless, he would tell her nothing. To the end of his life, he never told her everything. There was only one, to whom he told all.

There was, in Jamuga, something of which Temujin was secretly afraid or, better, something which he feared and was abashed before. He, himself, was not above unscrupulous and devious things, for first of all he believed that nothing mattered but the end, and that a thing was good if it survived and was successful, however it was attained. But in Jamuga he knew there was not this exigency, not this cold ruthlessness of spirit. Kurelen might disapprove a given action and raise his right eyebrow quizzically. But if it were finally successful, he would laugh, as at some ironic jest. Chepe Noyon, who loved adventure for its own sake, would be amused, too, provided the thing had been accomplished with cleverness and color. Subodai, the stainless, saw no evil in any man. Kasar adored Temujin under any circumstances, found nothing dark in him. But Jamuga would acknowledge no good in a result if the means used to attain it were evil or treacherous or ignoble. It was this somber rigidity with which Jamuga abashed Temujin, this narrow clarity of eye, this simple and lofty certainty of right and wrong. And sometimes when Jamuga gazed sternly at Temujin with his light and inexorable eyes, accusing and faintly disdainful, Temujin felt both anger and shame.

Yet, he was not able to keep matters that concerned him deeply from Jamuga. However he vowed to accomplish what he had in mind in secret from Jamuga, until it was an unchangeable fact and not to be lamented over incontinently, he always discovered himself hinting to Jamuga, as though to ascertain beforehand the results of his acts to his anda.

Now he knew that he must kill Bektor. There must be no subtle dilly-dallying, such as Kurelen suggested, with his squeamishness. It must be a clean and ruthless kill, cleansed of enmity, dictated by necessity. So Temujin told himself. Yet, when he faced Jamuga, wishing to tell him, he would fall silent, his face the very color of rage. Each day he said to himself: Today, I shall tell Jamuga that I must kill Bektor. And each day, looking into Jamuga's reserved remote eyes, which waited, his lips would become cold and voiceless. So, as usual, he approached the subject in a circumambient manner.

And Jamuga, guessing that Temujin had something of the most immense gravity to tell him, was afraid. But this time, he knew that Temujin would not accomplish the thing ruthlessly, telling him later, as he sometimes did. It was too important. In that he felt both comfort and fear. But he was too sensitive to precipitate the telling. He had the feeling that the longer the matter was delayed, the longer would be his own peace of mind.

Then, on a certain day when Temujin casually suggested they ride off alone together, Jamuga thought: He will tell me today. He did not know whether to be relieved or more alarmed.

They rode into the fiery red hills. They had moved away from the blue mountains deeper into the territory of Toghrul Khan, where rich but narrow green pastures could be found. Here, at least, they would not be unduly harassed.

Stopping at last near a huge volcanic boulder which offered them some shade from the monstrous heat, Temujin smiled at his anda with that simple artlessness which never failed to arouse apprehension in Jamuga. They dismounted, sat down in the sharp black shade thrown onto the fierce whiteness of the desert. Temujin urged rice wine on his friend. He was talkative today, and laughed more than customary. His laughter had a harsh and boisterous sound, as though he were uneasy beneath it. Jamuga made himself smile. Temujin had little wit, but that little was acrid and cruel. A fever seemed to burn in him. His inner turmoil betrayed itself in the bitter green sparkle of his eyes, in the very hot color of his broad-cheeked face, in the flash and glitter of his large white teeth. In the center of his large and barbarian ferocity the uneasiness glowed like a coal. It was nothing so complicated and effete as the conscience of the townsman, but simply an angry and irritated necessity for the approval of his anda.

He said at length, in a voice too careless: "Within a few days I must visit Toghrul Khan, with my suggestions and my demands. Thou shalt go with me, and Chepe Noyon and Subodai and Kasar, so that he will see I have noble paladins. There is but one thing: who shall keep order and unity among my people while I am gone? Thou knowest they are as nervous as a mountain antelope, and might scatter. This is a grave thing to consider."

For a moment Jamuga was relieved. The matter, then, was not so grave——

He said: "Surely Kurelen, and thy mother, have experience and wisdom. And thy wife is clever and resolute. Then, there is the Shaman, who knowest his duty, or, at least, his security."

Temujin's face darkened, and his eyes became slits of blazing emerald. He gnawed his lip. He looked away, and said quietly: "The Shaman! That is my difficulty. I do not trust him. Who can trust a priest? When I am gone, he will plot against me, out of his hatred and ambition. I shall not be there to impress upon him mine invincibility. Priests have short memories, when their own gain is concerned."

Jamuga said thoughtfully: "Kurelen is a match for him." A faint trembling went along his nerves, and he felt chilled, as though with presentiment. "Or take him with us."

Temujin suddenly got up, as though propelled by some inner

force. He leaned his hand against the huge black boulder, which stood jagged and enormous against the hot blue sky. His back was turned to Jamuga, and his voice came muffled.

"Without the priest to control them, as well as Kurelen and my mother, the people cannot be trusted." He paused. "Thou knowest Kokchu's fondness for Bektor——"

Terror, vivid and all-seeing, clutched Jamuga. He got to his feet. He stood beside Temujin. He said, in a loud sharp voice:

"Take Bektor with us! Oh, I know thou dost hate him, but he is a harmless youth, and doth desire only loyalty to thee, if thou wouldst only see it! Thou wouldst say he hateth thee, but only because of thy hatred. Let him prove his loyalty to thee—give him a sign of brotherly reconciliation——"

Temujin broke into a loud and infuriated laugh. "Dost thou not know that there are enmities that are part of the blood and the sinew, and can never be reconciled? When I look upon Bektor, I see my natural enemy, who must be destroyed. Even Kurelen doth see that."

In Jamuga's throat was a lump that was like a piece of cutting rock. He swallowed. He made his voice light as he said, through lips chilled as ice:

"Kurelen is not all-wise, though thou hast always thought it. Moreover, he doth talk loosely, not knowing that a potent man never talketh except as a preliminary to action." He smiled acidly. "That is why I, myself, am not potent. Like Kurelen, I speak as an antidote to exertion. If—any harm—came to Bektor, Kurelen would be the first to be disgusted."

Temujin did not speak. Jamuga saw only that violent profile, as remorseless and savage as the outlines of the volcanic boulder against which he leaned.

Jamuga raised his voice. "There are no enmities that cannot be reconciled, no jealousies which cannot be satisfied, no foe who cannot be made a friend."

Temujin turned to him with fury, and Jamuga saw that the fury was partly against himself. "I have no time!" he cried. "I cannot dally! I must do what I must do!"

Jamuga asked quietly, holding down his trembling: "And what is that?"

But Temujin did not answer him immediately. His breath was short and tumultuous. Then, in a voice strangely composed and low, he said: "Bektor must be removed."

Jamuga kept down any agitation in his tone, when he said: "But how?" He remembered the poison of Bortei, and closed his eyes on a sickened spasm. But when Temujin did not reply, he opened his eyes again. A mask of stone had fallen over the face of his anda, and behind it, unseen but terrible, his spirit looked out.

Jamuga forced his stiff lips into an amused smile. "Thou wouldst not kill him, Temujin?" And when Temujin still did not speak, Jamuga's voice came out in a thin cry: "Thou wouldst not murder thy brother?"

He fell back, for the spirit of Temujin had come from behind his mask, and it was awful to the eyes of Jamuga. For a long moment the two young men gazed at each other. Jamuga was fascinated by what he saw as he would be fascinated by some overwhelming horror, which paralyzed him.

Then in a soft voice, and smiling evilly, Temujin said: "Art thou not mine anda?"

And again the two young men looked at each other. Jamuga's face was the color of stone which had been blasted by lightning. His heart was beating with a strange disorder, which was excruciatingly painful.

He whispered: "I am thine anda. Who can take that away? Even thee?"

Temujin still smiled. And then, without another word, he turned away and deliberately mounted his horse. He rode off as though he were alone, and had always been alone, without a backward glance.

Jamuga watched him go. He was so faint and weak that he had to lean against the boulder for support. He closed his eyes. He heard Temujin's going, until at last there was only silence.

Temujin rode back to the ordu, without haste, but only with an inexorable and unhurried purpose. He sought out Kasar, who, because of his skill, was known as the Bowman. He said to him, looking into his eyes:

"Where is Bektor?"

Kasar was a simple youth, but when he saw Temujin's face, he knew his purpose. His own face paled a little, but its simple lines did not alter. He answered: "Bektor is out with the horses, to the east. Belgutei is with him."

Temujin said: "Come with me!"

First he went into his yurt, and slung his bow and arrow case over his shoulders. When he came out, Kasar was already armed. They mounted their horses and rode away, still without hurry. Temujin rode ahead, and Kasar a little behind. Temujin rarely had much to say to his brother, and spoke little more to him than he spoke to his white stallion, in whom he felt the same simple devotion and unquestioning obedience.

The cream-colored clay of the desert, hard and dry, rang to their horses' hoofs. Lizards scuttled across their path, like slim jewelled creatures. The red hills in the distance were a low broken ring. The sky grew hotter and bluer. There was no shade anywhere, except that like inky pools beside the scattered boulders, which stood ageless and immobile, over the desert floor. Once a desert bird rose with a shrill and dreadful cry from some tufts of dry grass, and floated over their heads, menacingly. The wind moved like an invisible flow of water over them, not dimming the eternal and blinding glare.

They descended a shallow terrace of stone and clay, and there below them lay the vivid and dazzling green of a narrow fertile valley, an oasis, in which were a clump of palms with thin leaves like scimitars. The small herd of horses grazed here, with bent absorbed heads, their manes fluttering in the wind. On a stone, under the palms, sat Belgutei and Bektor.

Belgutei saw Temujin and Kasar first, and raised a shout in greeting. He came out to meet them, waving his arm. The horses lifted their heads, and shrilled to the approaching beasts. But Bektor got up slowly and reluctantly, and emerged from the palms. Even at a distance, his figure was embued with dark bitterness and silence.

Belgutei reached Temujin's horse, smiling. He began to speak, lifting his head. But when he saw Temujin's face, his voice died in his throat. He lifted his hand as though to clutch Temujin's bridle, and then it fell to his side, nerveless. His color became the yellowish tint of the desert. He did not move. A curious expression moved over his features, and his eyes glinted inscrutably. He was like a man confronted with a remorseless destiny.

Temujin passed him. Kasar paused for a moment, and took an arrow from his bowcase. Then, he, too, had passed Belgutei. Temujin held his sword in his hand. He rode up to Bektor, who waited, scowling. He looked down at Bektor, and their eyes fastened together.

Instantly, the hapless Bektor knew what had brought Temujin here. His face became the color of iron. His body bent backwards. But his lips grew hard and still, and his eyes were unflinching and quiet. Above the high collar of his coat a purple pulse sprang out.

Kasar came up to Temujin. The arrow was fitted to his bow. All at once, a frenzy seized him. He could not bear the look on Bektor's face. It was a gesture of self-defense, almost as if he threw up his arm to hide the sight, that made him draw back the string of his bow and let fly an arrow at Bektor. One arrow was usually sufficient to kill, for he was exceedingly skillful, but at the last moment his hand shook and the arrow pierced Bektor in the belly.

The poor youth staggered backwards. His hands flew to the quivering shaft sunken deep in his entrails. Instantly, blood welled up through his fingers. He bent double. He sank to his knees. But he did not groan. Nor did his eyes shift from Temujin's.

Temujin looked at Kasar with a terrible expression. "Thou fool, thou bungling fool," he said quietly. He seized the bow from his brother's nerveless hands, and with calm deliberation he fitted one of his own arrows to it. Then he paused. He looked down at the kneeling and bleeding form of his half-brother. Bektor was bent double. From between his clutching fingers the bright red blood dripped down to the thirsty earth.

"I would have spared thee this," said Temujin.

For the last time, they stared at each other. An awful quietness held them. Belgutei stood at a distance, watching. Kasar's head was bent. They might all have been statues of stone in the passionate and burning glare of the sunlight.

Bektor's eyes were already glazing with death and agony. Bubbles of blood appeared at the corners of his white lips. Blood trickled from one nostril. His hands were wet and scarlet, about the shaft of the arrow. Yet, he could look at Temujin like this, steadfastly and silently.

Temujin drew back the string. The bow bent. Like a flash of light the arrow left the bow, and sank itself in Bektor's heart. Without a sound, he fell forward on his face, rolled impotently to his side. Yet, to the very last, as his eyes rolled upward, transfixed in death, he looked at Temujin.

Temujin returned the bow to his brother. He wheeled his horse about. The animal's nostrils flared at the smell of blood and death, and he trembled. Kasar followed. He had begun to retch. Temujin rode up to Belgutei, and stood, looking down at him. Belgutei returned his look, without fear, and even smiling faintly with his pale lips.

"Am I to die, also?" he asked at last, almost indifferently.

Temujin was silent for a long moment, then he said in a low voice:

"Follow me."

He rode on. Kasar trailed him, slowly. Belgutei mounted

a horse, called to the herd, which followed, making a wide and skittish circle about the dead Bektor.

Temujin rode ahead, faster now, and yet, not as one who flees. To Kasar, watching him with dim eyes, he loomed like a figure from some other world, straight and baleful and gigantic, followed with a shadow of doom.

chapter 23

Kurelen said, coldly and with disgust: "Thou must be exceedingly proud, to kill a defenseless boy."

Temujin replied quietly: "Had he been defenseless, I should not have killed him."

Kurelen was unwillingly silent a moment, considering this, and angrily acknowledging its truth to himself. Then he said, his eyes still averted from his nephew:

"Thou couldst have betrothed him to a girl of another tribe, and so have gotten rid of him that way."

Temujin smiled grimly. "That, too, would have taken time. I have no time."

Then Kurelen looked at him curiously and attentively. He said to himself: That is true. Nevertheless, he was seized with a fear rare with him. He had flattered himself that he had had an enormous influence over Temujin, and that, in anything of importance, his nephew would have consulted him in his circuitous way. Yet, Temujin had not consulted him. Therefore, he, Kurelen, had lost his influence. And if he had lost his influence, he, in reality, did not know Temujin at all. This was a stranger standing before him, locked in the black fortress of his own soul, which could be entered by no one. Kurelen's vanity smarted. The interpreter of men was no interpreter. He knew no more than the veriest simpleton. He thought: I have been wrong. There is no scale with which to measure and weigh all men. Each man is a law and a type unto himself. He who sayeth he understandeth men is without understanding, and is only a conceited fool. An attempt at understanding resolveth only in confusion and bafflement.

He had believed for a long time that there was a strange and frightful force in Temujin. Now he knew it. He was always appalled at tremendous force, which seemed reasonless and terrifying, a sort of cataclysm of nature before which men must stand, impotently aghast. Yet, as he looked now at Temujin, he knew this force in him was not reasonless, not stupidly cataclysmic. It was even more terrible, for it was deliberate and reasoning. He was not merely ruthless by nature; he was ruthless by intention. And that was the most appalling violence.

He said, lamely and somewhat incoherently: "Go. I cannot

bear to look at thee." But he knew that it was his own futility, his own broken vanity, at which he could not bear to look. He said to himself, bitterly: "I know nothing at all."

Houlun, learning that night of Temujin's foul deed, wrapped herself in her cloak and pulled her hood over her head. She went to the tent of Bektor's mother. The poor woman was stricken tearless with grief. When she saw Houlun, she could only stare at her with bright dry eyes. Houlun knelt before her, and kissed her feet, weeping.

She cried: "Forgive me, that I have given birth to a murderer!"

The Karait woman was illiterate and simple and stupid. Yet, with a simplicity deeper than intelligence, she raised Houlun up and embraced her. She said: "Thou hast deeper reason to mourn than I. Let me comfort thee."

The enmity between the two women was washed away in their tears.

In death, this poor woman still retained her son. But Houlun knew that she no longer had Temujin. She knew that never again would she completely love him, for she could never trust him. Between them, this murder would stand like a bloody shadow. And all at once, with a sickening and frenzied certainty, she thought of her daughter-in-law, and hated her with a murderous hatred.

She went to Temujin, sitting alone in his yurt with Kasar. Her terror and grief and despair distorted her face, made her expression wild and filled her eyes with fire. Her hair, as though catching the disorder of her mood, was dishevelled. Her breast heaved with anguished breath. She looked down at the two youths with passionate scorn and fury. But she spoke to Temujin, who looked up at her with eyes dark and inscrutable and cold as ice.

"Thou coward and monster!" she cried. "The man who lifteth his hand against his brother is accursed! Take heed for thyself! Guard thy shadow, lest it rise up and smite thee down! Guard thy heart, for no other man's heart will beat trustingly for thee again. Hold close thy whips, for no other man's whip will rise in thy defense. Sharpen thy sword, for thou hast only this one to protect thee. Call in the Shaman, to stand guard before thy yurt, for the spirits shall seek vengeance on thee!"

Temujin listened in silence, but when his mother had finished he smiled slightly. For some reason this slight smile afflicted her more than his deed had done, and filled her with a greater terror.

He answered her at last, in a quiet voice:

"Go to thy yurt, Mother, and calm thyself. Thy words are extravagant. I do only the things which I must do, and there was no anger in me against Bektor. But thou art only a woman, and cannot understand. Go."

And paralyzed and bewildered by her terror, she went, her lips cold and her eyes blind. Later, when the Karait woman came to her yurt, she threw herself in this woman's arms and wept wildly.

Temujin sat alone, with Kasar, whose face was white but resolute. He waited. And then, one by one, his friends came to him, as he knew they would come. Subodai came. The beautiful youth's eyes were intensely bright, his expression calm. He looked at Temujin in silence for a long moment. Then he knelt down before him, lifted Temujin's hand and placed it on his head.

He spoke in his dulcet voice: "To the end, I will ward off thy foes. I will be thy sword. I will be the yurt that protecteth thee from the wind. That, to the end of my life, is what I shall be to thee."

Temujin was unendurably touched. For he knew that this loyalty, which was not blind, was the greatest loyalty of all.

Then Chepe Noyon came, pale but brilliantly smiling. It was evident that he had rehearsed what he would say to Temujin. But once in the yurt, and confronted with the man whose hands were still red with the blood of his brother, he could not speak for a moment or two, and could only smile his false and determined smile. Then all at once, the smile vanished from his face, and a look of intense gravity and sternness replaced it—a strange look for the gay adventurer. He knelt before Temujin, but he looked him straightly in the eye.

"Thou art my khan," he said, and his upper lip lifted as though the words were painful to him.

Temujin thought: He will still be loyal to me, for I have convinced him I will stop at nothing.

He made himself smile, and touched Chepe Noyon lightly on the shoulder. "And thou art Chepe Noyon, my paladin," he said. With profound wisdom, he knew that only the light touch, the light smile, were the approach to Chepe Noyon.

And then Belgutei came. The others were dimly surprised at this, but Temujin was not surprised. He held out his hand to Belgutei, and said: "My brother! Sit by my side."

Belgutei, with a smooth expression that none could read for all the faint redness about his eyelids, sat down at Temujin's left hand. He, as well as Chepe Noyon, acknowledged the perfection of Temujin's words and gestures. Less penetration would have made a mortal enemy of Belgutei. But now Belgutei knew beyond all doubt that Temujin was worth loyalty.

They all continued to wait, in unspeaking silence. Each knew why they waited. They were waiting for Jamuga, the anda of Temujin. As time passed, and Jamuga Sechen did not come, Kasar's simplicity glowed with anger. How dared his brother's anda affront him this way? He looked about him, his nostrils distended, his eyes glaring, as though he challenged them all. But Temujin's expression was tranquil. None knew the perturbation that quickened his heart. He thought to himself: If Jamuga hath not come before the dawn, then I know he hath violated our brotherhood. But this realization saddened instead of enraging him. If Jamuga did not come, he would suffer the greatest loss he could ever suffer. Sorrow grew heavier in him, like lead. He could not endure the thought of losing the love and friendship of Jamuga. At last, all the power of his nature was concentrated in a wordless cry that Jamuga come to him, if only to reproach him. He no longer cared for Jamuga's forgiveness; he did not want his understanding. He wanted only Jamuga's physical presence.

The dawn was already running in a pale ragged fire along the eastern horizon when Jamuga finally came. He came so silently that they were not aware of his presence until he stood among them.

Temujin was aware of him first. When he looked up at his anda, standing there so motionlessly before him, his heart gave a quick leap. And then he saw that Jamuga was whiter than a corpse and that he looked like a man who had been suffering intolerably over a long period. His own lips moved several times before he could speak, for there was something in Jamuga's dry and steadfast eyes that shamed him.

He said: "Jamuga, I had no enmity against Bektor."

Jamuga continued to gaze at him unmovingly. Then in a faint voice, he asked:

"Temujin, didst thou try to poison Bektor a night or two ago?"

Temujin stared at him with unfeigned astonishment.

"Poison Bektor? Art thou mad, Jamuga?"

He stopped, for Jamuga had suddenly burst into tears. He waited, still astounded, as Jamuga slowly knelt before him. Jamuga gazed at him with his streaming eyes.

He said simply: "Thou art mine anda."

And he took his place at Temujin's right hand.

Again they waited, in silence. Temujin waited for the Shaman.

At first, he had thought of going to Kokchu himself. And then a moment's swift reflection pointed out the danger. If he went to Kokchu, then Kokchu would be the final victor. Dawn was bright in the skies, when Temujin said to Chepe Noyon:

"Go to the Shaman and tell him to come at once to me."

chapter 24

When the Shaman entered the yurt, he was very calm, though his face was lined and gray and wizened. Yet he had never been more dignified, more magnificent. He did not know what to expect. Was it death? How much did Temujin know? Was the young man too violent for reason? But though there was a possibility of death by torture, the punishment of traitors, Kokchu walked with quiet dignity, and if he felt fear, he did not betray it.

He did not look at any one but Temujin, sitting arrogantly and silently in the midst of his young heroes. But when he saw Temujin's eyes, eyes now as soft and gray and luminous as a dove's, he prepared himself for the worst. Craft turned Temujin's eyes innocently blue; rage colored them with blazing emerald. But murder threw a dim soft shadow of gray over them.

Kokchu did not kneel. He thought to himself: If he hath decided to kill me, he shall not first enjoy my humiliation. But he inclined his head gravely, and waited.

Temujin began to speak in a gentle voice, the tender gray deepening in his eyes:

"I know thou didst love Bektor, Kokchu, and that his death is grievous to thee."

Kokchu's eyelids quivered, but he answered in a low voice:

"Thou art the khan, Temujin, and a poor priest hath no choice but to find all acts of his khan virtuous and just."

Temujin smiled. He affected an air of kingly gratification. But now the gray was deepening to emerald in his eyes.

"Because thou didst love Bektor as a son, I feel constrained to explain mine act. And because thou art so simply loyal, I need thine assistance with the people. I have heard reports they are stunned and horrified at a deed which was necessary."

Kokchu was silent. But he fixed his gaze unwinkingly on Temujin. He asked himself: Is it possible he is afraid? But a moment later he regretfully decided that Temujin was not afraid.

Temujin said, his voice still ominously soft:

"Had there not been traitors among my people, I should not have killed Bektor, who might have been a sword in their hands against me. So, I found it necessary to slay him. The odium of the deed, therefore, lieth not with me, but the traitors. On their hands is his blood."

Despite his calm, Kokchu's heart leapt, then settled down to a fearful trembling.

"However," continued Temujin, in a voice of sad reason: "I wish to have done with violence. I hope the death of Bektor will be a warning to the traitors." He paused, then loudly and harshly he added: "Dost thou understand, Kokchu?"

Through pale steady lips the Shaman replied: "I understand, O my khan."

Temujin relaxed, smiled his terrible smile. "Thou art a man of sense, Kokchu, as well as a priest. But mine uncle hath often said that priests are men of sense. They inevitably support the strong against the weak. I am not weak, Kokchu."

The Shaman inclined his head reverently. He thought: I am not to die, then? He was contemptuously amazed at the sudden weakening of his legs with a profound relief.

Temujin went on, watching him with those brutal and evil eyes:

"I hate treachery. I shall not hesitate to kill again, with mine own hands. Thou shalt tell the people this, Kokchu. Thou shalt tell them that Bektor was a traitor, and deserved his death, as all traitors deserve death. But the next time, a traitor shall not die so mercifully."

Again, the Shaman inclined his head with submissive reverence.

"Thou shalt also tell the people, Kokchu, that thou didst advise the death of Bektor, for thou wert warned of his treachery in a dream."

Kokchu raised his bent head slowly. His lips became the color of stone. Then, after a long moment, he answered almost inaudibly:

"Thou hast commanded, Temujin."

Temujin removed a huge ring of green and violet stones set in gold from his finger. Kurelen had given it to him. But now he reached up for Kokchu's hand and placed it upon the other's finger. Kokchu stared at it, and a little color came back into his lined and sunken cheeks.

"Kings without priests may prosper. But priests without kings must disappear from the earth," said Temujin.

Kokchu touched his forehead and bowed almost to his knees. Temujin glanced at his silent paladins with a smile of triumphant contempt.

"Go, now, Kokchu, and remember my commands."

The Shaman left the yurt. The east was silver and pearl. The women were already building the campfires, and the smoke rose darkly and straightly in the pure morning air.

Kokchu stood in silence, and gazed at the sky. His face was contorted. He lifted his clenched fist passionately, as though to utter savage imprecations. The first light of the rising sun struck the green and violet stones of the ring which Temujin had given him, and it blazed. Kokchu stared at it with dilated eyes. Slowly, his clenched fist opened, slowly, his hand dropped to his side. Slowly, a crafty smile widened his cracked lips.

He went on his way, preparing in his mind the most placating things to say to the people.

Temujin went to the tent of his wife. Hearing him as he mounted the platform (for she had not slept all night), she unfastened her robe of white wool. When he entered, she rose from her couch, and the robe fell about her. In the dim red light of the brazier she stood, naked, her arms outstretched to him, a smile of ineffable seduction on her lovely red mouth. He stood for a moment, feasting himself on the vision of her small moonlike breasts and her hips and thighs which were like rosy transparent alabaster. She looked at his face, and the fearful shivering of her heart slowed down to a steady, triumphant beat. She flung herself into his arms, and with a cry of mingled lust, love and exultation, he fastened his lips on hers.

Book Two

THE PHANTOM CARAVAN

A Moment's Halt—a momentary taste
Of Being from the Well amid the Waste—
And Lo!—the phantom Caravan has reached
The Nothing it set out from—Oh, make haste!

—OMAR KHAYYAM

chapter 1

"My people," said Temujin, "have been beaten and scattered. They have been made afraid, and covered with shame and humiliation. They are poor and wretched. I am khan of a handful of frightened children and old women, and men whose bowels have turned to water with fear. But I shall avenge them! I shall lead them from the wilderness to wide pastures, and they shall cast their tents in peace beside the leaping waters."

Thus did he speak to his people before leaving with Chepe Noyon, Jamuga Sechen, Subodai and Kasar, for his visit to his father's sworn brother, the powerful but crafty and cowardly Toghrul Khan, the Nestorian Christian, the Karait Turk.

He appointed his uncle, Kurelen, to take his place in his absence, and gave the care of the women and children to his mother, Houlun. At Kurelen's right hand he artfully placed the Shaman, and on his left, his half-brother, Belgutei. His wife, he said, was a queen. Her commands must be obeyed.

He looked at his poverty-stricken and ragged people, a mere handful, as he said. He saw their poor yurts, their miserable herds of horses and cattle and goats and sheep and camels. For a moment he was full of dismay. But they guessed nothing of this from his stern and implacable face and his fiery eyes. For the sanguine light of dawn was pouring upon him all its splendor. His hand was resolute on his lance. He sat his horse like an emperor, with his paladins about him. Over the pommel of his saddle was his greatest treasure, a heavy robe of dark sable skins, the gift for Toghrul Khan.

He thought to himself: Out of these wretches, what can I make? Out of dismal poverty, how can I emerge, a mighty ruler? I was resolved to become an emperor: what is needful? Are mine arm, my courage, my hatred, my lust and my greed sufficient? Is their miserable heart strong enough to follow me? Can I make conquerors of hungry nomads, unlettered and afraid?

To Jamuga, he said, looking at his anda with eyes turned as innocently blue as a child's: "My people must have room and pastures and hunting grounds and peace." To Chepe Noyon, he said: "No man is alive who is not an adventurer. I shall give my people adventure." To Kasar, he said: "My people love me. I love my people. They are simple men, and simple men are always wise and good. I seek only to serve my people."

To Subodai, he said: "I must make my people strong, for only the strong can survive. But I will make them generous, also, and excellent neighbors, full of virtue." To Kurelen, he said: "We must survive."

But to himself, he said: "I alone matter."

He was all things to all men. He was the image every man saw in his own reflection, but glorified and invincible and mighty. He deceived even Jamuga, who was passionately willing to believe. But he deceived neither Kurelen nor Kokchu. Kurelen hoped for the best. Kokchu hoped only for reflected power.

He set out, grim and unshakable, followed by his paladins. Kurelen offered some of his treasures as gifts to Toghrul Khan, but Temujin said:

"No. A man who is too heavily laden with gifts inspires suspicion that he is not strong."

He would not allow any one to guess how perturbed he was about the loyalty of his people. He knew they were aghast at the murder of Bektor, rude and simple though they were. Had he been challenged by Bektor, and they had been engaged in an open and honorable struggle, though ending in death, there would have been no horror, no odium. But his attack, accompanied by that of Kasar's upon a defenseless youth who had been given no time to defend himself, but had been brutally murdered without challenge by his own brother, appalled the people.

But Temujin told himself that he had had no time. Besides, he had already a vague inkling that horror opens the way to power, and terror is its henchman. Had he openly challenged Bektor, that would have taken time; too, Temujin was none too certain that he would have won the combat, for he was not so strong as Bektor had been. Later, he was to attain a reputation for the most stupendous audacity. But, in truth, he was never audacious. Conquerors, he was to say, must appear bold. But their ruin began when they stupidly followed their own advice. Boldness impresses the masses; but it is enough that a ruler be gifted with histrionic talents and make dramatic gestures.

The mighty Toghrul Khan, of whom it was said that he possessed forty tents made of cloth-of-gold, occupied the river lands near the Great Wall of Cathay. The Karait occupied many walled cities of their own, the houses made of mud and clay, but powerful. Composed in great part of the Turkish race, they were excellent and prosperous traders, and their wealthier men lived in luxury in the cities. Toghrul Khan, now old, was a man of pleasant address, and smooth smiling face. His voice was gentle and ingratiating, and he was given to great piety. But his piety was flexible; when it pleased him, he loved Islam, and gave honor to Mohammed. Again, when it was necessary, he was full of Christian sweetness. His people had, in large part, been converted by Saints Andrew and Thomas to Christianity, and more and more, as he aged, and found it expedient, he leaned towards this religion. He was a great rascal, a liar, a hypocrite, full of craft and treachery and self-seeking, never quailing from murder, but able, at all times, to attach a Christian phrase to a monstrous deed.

But so engaging was his extraordinary charm of manner that he was able to secure the allegiance and sworn brotherhood of scores of poor and petty chieftains like Yesukai. He frequently broke his most solemn promises. But the simple and credulous chieftains never held it against him, for his excuses were so sorrowful, his explanations so valid, that they believed everything he said. They would look into his wide innocent eyes set in his old grave face, and listen to his soft voice, and be won again to an allegiance that gave him everything and frequently gave them nothing.

Once he cynically said to his son: "Be a man of great virtue and honor and courage; be a hero before whom all obstacles disappear. Be noble and just and brave. And all this will be as nothing to win the faith and love of others. But speak thou words of honey, argue with no man but agree with all; smile sweetly and tenderly. Be full of promises, which are not necessary to fulfill. Let thine eye dwell with affection on every man, even if thou hatest him. And I tell thee that the people, who have only the souls of dogs, will hang upon thy footsteps and die gladly for thee. A pliable tongue costs nothing, but it will bring treasures to its owner."

His son asked him if great conquerors possessed pliable tongues and sweet smiles. And Toghrul Khan, pursing up his lips, tentatively shook his head. He said: "There is another way to win allegiance, the harsher way, and that is the way of terror. But that is too exhausting. I prefer the lesser but easier way, and am content with security. Men who take the way of terror come not more than once a century. They are the frightful gods who do not need sweetness."

At this time he was dwelling temporarily on the banks of the Tula, near the tremendous blue pine forests. Nomad in his soul, as he was, he could not long endure the confines of his rich Karait cities, and though he was old, he still had an occasional longing for the spaces and the steppes and the deserts.

But he always brought with him his most luxurious tents and his strongest men and fairest women, to make comfortable his stay under the wild stars of his birth.

He was already rife in the legends of the Europeans, who called him Prester John, and these Christians often visited him in his cities, and partook of his hospitality. At these times his chambers were hung with golden and silver crosses, and great Christian piety prevailed. He gave the visitors many gifts, and displayed his luxuries to them. They never guessed the contempt this artful and treacherous old man had for them, these barbarians from the lands to the west. Sometimes, if they came richly themselves, merchants hoping to broaden the caravan routes from the treasures of the east to the starkness of the west, a whispered word went from Prester John to his men, and this whisper went out far to the west of the Karait cities. And so it was that at these times the merchants never returned to their own lands, but left their skeletons to bleach in the deserts, and their treasures to find their way over devious routes to the coffers of Prester John.

Temujin knew Toghrul Khan only from the stories of his father. Yesukai, like all the little chieftains of the steppes, adored Toghrul Khan, spoke of him with passionate reverence and awe and love. But Temujin had already learned to distrust report. He went to his father's sworn brother with an open eye and a sharp open mind. He listened to the stories of his paladins in silence. Jamuga was aroused to his rare pale enthusiasms. He remembered that Toghrul Khan had the reputation of being a just and kindly prince, devoted to his followers, and heedful of their well-being. Moreover, he was not lustful, it was said, but preferred peace and civilization, and had a reputation for learning. One of his wives was a Persian woman, the daughter of a great noble. She was well versed in music and literature and painting, and was the best beloved of all the women of her husband. It was said that he had learned much from her. Jamuga promised himself fine conversations and feasts of beauty and philosophy. How splendid it would be, to enter the presence of men of culture and civilization!

Chepe Noyon declared that he would smother in cities. But he was excited, in spite of himself. Kasar cared only that Temujin secure aid from Prester John. As for Subodai, he, as usual, said nothing, and no one knew what he thought.

Slowly, as they all rode briskly towards the Tula River, some prescience came mysteriously to Temujin, and though he had never seen Toghrul Khan he knew him. All through his terrible life he was to have these deep and uncanny premonitions, and sometimes he was to speak of them, thus giving rise to the legend among his people that he was in communication with the spirits. He had started out with the resolution to invoke the aid of the old man. Now, he revised his resolution. He would subtly force Toghrul Khan to renew the ancient pledge, himself.

In these last few weeks he had rid himself of superstition. But young as he was, he knew the value of superstition in controlling others. However, he was still too close to the earth from which he had sprung not to feel the influence of portents, despite his intelligence.

Three days and three nights had passed in the long journey. At dusk on the third day a most awful storm vented itself over the broken and chaotic desert. Temujin was not frightened, but the others, even the cold Jamuga, were appalled. They found a hollow place at the bottom of a red and crumbling rampart, and crouched in it, waiting and watching with eyes distended with fear.

A darkness, like that of a supernatural and premature night, fell over the earth, so that it seemed to be brimming with a dim and shadowy sea. But the limitless sky boiled and rolled and twisted with baleful green clouds, continually torn by scarlet flames, parting the heavens to emit deafening thunder, which shook the earth savagely. This lightning lit up the desert for miles, burning up the dark shadows, and revealing volcanic hill and skeletal rampart in stark and horrible clarity. Sometimes everything glowed with a rosy incandescence, so that the smallest stone was visible at a great distance, and the hills and ramparts seemed formed of petrified flame. It was a landscape of the moon, not of the earth, cratered and chaotic and convulsive, illuminated by the fire of an exploding sun.

There was no rain, only an awful wind, which seemed, in its strength, to be imminently about to shatter the rampart under which Temujin and his friends were crouching. At times they believed the earth must dissolve and go up in a pillar of fire under this supernatural onslaught. The gale was laden with dust and sand from far places, and small crystalline fragments, which tore their faces and their hands and choked their breath. Finally, unable to endure sight and sound and wind, they turned their faces away and faced the rock, closing their eyes.

But Temujin was not frightened. He gazed at everything, though he was blinded and deafened. The leaping conflagration of the skies fascinated, but did not appall him. He covered his mouth with a part of his cloak, and narrowed his eyes against the flailing wind. And then in his heart a twin fury rose to answer the fury of insensate heaven and earth. It was a fury of exultation, invincible and almost mad.

He said to himself: It is a portent. Like this am I, and like this shall I ever be!

When the storm had gone raging and blazing over the distant ramparts the others laughed weakly in their relief, congratulating themselves that they were still alive. They rose to comfort their shrilling and trembling horses, which they had tied together under the shelter of an overhanging ledge. But Temujin looked at his companions in silent contempt. They seemed strange and petty to him. As for himself, he had lost the last of his youth.

He was no longer apprehensive about his visit to Toghrul Khan. He faced the future with stupendous calm and fatefulness.

They arrived in a sweet and lucid dawn at the huge camp of the old man.

The camp, orderly and immense, composed of thousands of huge yurts, with here and there an immense tent of cloth-of-gold or cloth-of-silver, elaborately decorated and pennanted, was gathered in a low green valley beside the purple river Tula, whose waters were shot with restless quicksilver. Behind the camp the mountains rose, range above range, peering, shading from the most delicate crystalline blue to the most misty violet, and then to the deepest of shining amethyst with incandescent caps against the pellucid skies. Forests of blue pine wound solemnly over the mountains, filling the pure air with a strong and pungent scent. It was a lovely, silent and majestic spot, this in which Toghrul Khan held his temporary court far from his hot and crowded cities. The sweet morning wind was filled with the lowing of cattle, and the far calls of the shepherds, driving forth their flocks to pasture.

As Temujin rode towards the camp with his companions, a clear and ringing sound rent the dawn quiet—the warning notes of a horn. Instantly, a number of warriors appeared before the camp, astride the finest stallions. The horn had been a warning. To Temujin, riding quietly forward, it seemed like the horn announcing the advent of a conqueror. He did not slow down his pace. He approached resolutely, quickening his horse, riding ahead of his friends. A priest, clad in a brown wool robe, appeared among the warriors, advanced towards the visitors. When Temujin rode up, and then halted, the priest lifted his right hand and made the sign of the cross.

"Peace be with ye," he said, and looked at them suspiciously.

The salutation was a strange one to Temujin, but he lifted

his hand gravely in a dignified salute. "Peace be with thee," he answered. "I wish to speak to my foster-father, Toghrul Khan. Tell him that Temujin, son of Yesukai, doth ask an audience of him."

The priest and the approaching warriors stared uncertainly. They consulted among themselves. Then the warriors galloped up and surrounded Temujin and his companions, and the leader announced that they would be taken to Toghrul Khan at once. They were no longer suspicious, but disdainful, recognizing in Temujin another one of the petty and poverty-stricken nobles of the steppes and the desert.

chapter 2

But first they were led to one of the yurts reserved for visitors. There servants brought them clean fresh water in silver and porcelain bowls, beautifully enamelled, and cloths of the whitest fabrics on which to wipe their hands and faces. Then they were given loaves of sweet bread and mares' new milk, and a basin of plump and fragrant dates. This was hospitality for all visitors, but again, to Temujin, this was also a portent.

A warrior, no longer suspicious, but increasingly scornful, then came to them and announced that the Khan would see them. He led them to the largest tent of all, fully twenty feet across, and glittering in its costliness of cloth-of-gold. They entered, and their feet sank into rich Bokhara carpets. Along the slanting walls, on carved tabourets of teakwood, porcelain, gold and silver lamps burnt softly. On a couch covered with robes of silk and embroidered wool and fur reclined the old Khan, drinking a goblet of fresh milk.

Temujin entered alone, bidding his followers remain outside. He stood there in the lamplit dimness, weather-stained, dark-faced, tall and resplendent with youth and courage. Toghrul Khan, lifting his eyes with the fatherly smile reserved for visiting little chieftains, suddenly stopped smiling, and he gazed at Temujin with a sudden sharpness. His eyes narrowed. Very slowly, he handed the cup to a kneeling woman-slave, and motioned her from the tent.

Still without speaking, Temujin knelt before the old man and touched his forehead to the floor, without humility, but even with a sort of arrogance. Then he said, lifting his head and looking at Toghrul piercingly:

"Thy son hath come to thee, my foster-father, to swear the allegiance of his father, Yesukai."

He saw before him a little old man, bald and emaciated, with a smooth and gentle face and tiny vivid eyes, like a bird's. He saw the golden bracelets on the withered wrists, the many twinkling rings on the gnarled fingers. He saw the richness of the silken robes. But more than all these, he saw the khan, and knew that his prescience had not lied to him. A lesser eye might have seen a little aged man with a sweet expression and a kindly, paternal manner, and no more. But Temujin saw behind all these, and what he saw made his lips tighten grimly and all his senses become acute and wary.

Then, after a long moment, Toghrul Khan extended his hand and said in a voice of great affection and gladness:

"Welcome, my son! Mine eyes are filled with joy at thy coming. Sit beside me at my right hand, and let me have the pleasure of knowing thou art near me."

His voice was dulcet and caressing. He laid his hand on Temujin's shoulder, and feigned to be tenderly delighted with him. He asked him if he had partaken of his morning meal. He asked him the details of his father's death, and shook his head with sorrow and regret. No one could have been kinder. No father could have displayed more affection and interest. But even while he listened to the old man, and felt the weight of his loving hand on his shoulder, Temujin was watching him closely, and knowing moment by moment that this was the most deadly being he had ever encountered, the most avaricious and cruel and treacherous.

All at once, under his watchfulness, he felt a profound contempt. Had the Khan been all he was, and curt and brutal and cold besides, Temujin would have honored him and admired him. But above all things he loathed hypocrisy. To him the foulest of all things was an evil soul that spoke in the sweet words of love and peace and piety.

But he masked his knowledge of Toghrul Khan, and presented him with the sable cloak. At first, seeing all the splendor of the camp and the tent, he had thought that the cloak would be a poor gift. But now he knew that everything was welcome to this greedy Karait vulture. And in truth, it was a good gift, the skins beautiful and soft and full. Toghrul Khan, with little cries of pleasure, sank his fingers in the fur, smoothed it lovingly, lifted a corner and pressed it delicately to his cheek. Temujin, watching him, felt revulsion. There was something unclean in the sight of the dead old fingers lustfully fingering the living warmth of the skins, something repulsive in the vision of them against the sunken old cheek. He remembered how he had last seen the cloak, on the full young shoulders of Bortei, and he experienced a pang of rage and disgust. It were as though the licentious old hands had seized wantonly on the very flesh of Bortei.

And then he knew that Toghrul Khan, for all his wealth and his power, envied him his handsome youth and strength, the color of his young eyes, the leanness of his waist and the broadness and straightness of his shoulders. And he knew that envy is always the twin brother of hatred. He said to himself: I have an enemy.

But he had felt, on the way, that Toghrul Khan would be an enemy. It was his task, now, to appease that enmity, but to make the old man desire him as an ally. Even enmity must step back from the presence of profit.

He looked about him at all the evidences of luxury which the tent contained. He felt no lust for them, and was vaguely surprised at this. He glanced at the old man's bracelets and robes and rings, and thought to himself how fair they would look upon Bortei. He had seen the fat herds, and desired them for his people. As for himself, he desired something greater. A vast excitement filled him.

He listened as Toghrul Khan promised him a fine feast. There would be great festivities in honor of his coming.

"I have had no pleasure like this for many days!" said the old man. "But now my foster son hath come to me, and filleth mine eyes with joy. God hath remembered mine age, and hath brought me another son."

He lifted his eyes reverently, and Temujin, following his gaze, saw that a large golden cross hung over the couch, beautifully inlaid with enamel, and shining and sparkling in the lamplight. Temujin eyed it curiously. One or two of his people were Nestorian Christians, but he had never felt any cleavage from them. Kokchu resented them, but Kokchu always resented anything that might threaten his own influence. Temujin had believed with his father that a man might hold any faith he wished, provided it did not interfere with his loyalty to his leader. But now, strangely, he felt that the golden cross was a very part of Toghrul Khan, and that the old man's enmity was somehow involved with it.

Toghrul called for one of the servants who were waiting in a smaller tent attached to this large one. He told the servant to lead Temujin's paladins to other yurts, where every pleasure and comfort was to be given them.

"As for thyself, my son," he said, turning to Temujin again, and putting his hand lovingly on his arm, "thou wilt remain with me for a while, and tell me more of thyself, and how I may help thee."

Temujin gazed at him for a long moment, and Toghrul Khan, who made his pleasing and affectionate remark with his usual glib courtesy which meant nothing, was startled, when, looking again at Temujin in the silence, he saw the young man's strange expression and sparkling emerald eyes. His first uneasy thought, wary as ever, was that Temujin had taken him seriously and might have some disconcerting request to make. His second thought, more uneasy and touched with suspicion, was that he had no request. One of his axioms was that a man must never cease watching other men, and that the clever man watched without giving evidence of his watching. He saw that Temujin was watching him, and was entirely indifferent as to whether he was discerned in this or not. This was not lack of cleverness, reflected the old man with a vague feeling of angry humiliation, but merely a disdainful disregard for the devious craft of such cleverness. All at once, the old man gnawed his under lip with a sensation of hostile helplessness. Then he smiled again, pressed Temujin's arm with his hand.

"But I have been remiss!" he exclaimed, with a gay laugh at himself. "My daughter, Azara, should have welcomed thee, at my side! Her mother was a Persian lady, and she, herself, is a follower of the Lord Jesus. But I have had tutors and teachers for the wench, for she is possessed of much wisdom, and I enjoy her presence. Ah, that she had been a man! I shall send for her."

He called a servant from the other tent, and requested the presence of his daughter. When he had done this, he was surprised and annoyed. He had never expected to display his daughter to this petty and ragged chieftain. But he had experienced confusion, and to cover it, he had called for the girl. He fumed internally, as they waited, and tried to cover his angry discomfiture with renewed smiles and words of affection. He thought to himself: What have I done? Why should I do this, for this mongrel of the steppes, this shabby barbarian of the desert? And then all his annoyance was lost in wonder at himself, and hatred.

The flap of the great tent parted and Azara entered. Temujin, always eager for the sight of beautiful women, looked at her and felt a stunning amazement. For never had he seen such a lovely face, such a perfect figure.

For Azara was taller than any other woman he had ever seen, almost as tall as himself. He thought: She is like a young birch tree, white and slender, bending a little in the wind. The girl was clad, below the waist, in some filmy white stuff, almost diaphanous, caught about her narrow hips with a coiling circle of thin gold. Her breasts, high and pointed and virginal, were covered with circles of jewelled gold. Her arms and throat and neck were whiter than milk, and luminous, like pearls. Her face, a pure and delicate oval, covered with the milky mist of her veil, was also pearl-like, and flushed with tender rose upon the lip and cheek. Her eyes, black and sparkling as jet, were fringed in golden lashes, as soft as silk, and her long streaming hair was also golden, but of so pale a tint, and so bright, as to be almost incredible. She was laden with gems, necklaces and bracelets and rings, so that she blazed in the beams of the lamps.

Her manner was calm and dignified, but so remote as to give the impression that she moved mechanically, and in a dream. Even when she smiled modestly, and bowed before her father and his guest Temujin told himself that she was but half awake. His sensation of astonishment increased. He thought: What a prize is this, what glory, what beauty! His heart beat thickly, and sweat appeared on his brow and upper lip.

Toghrul Khan laid his hand lovingly on the head of his daughter and sat her at his left side. He played with the pale golden strands of her silken hair.

"Before the moon has waned, she will be betrothed to the Caliph of Bokhara, who hath heard of her great beauty," he said, all his craftiness momentarily lost in paternal pride. He looked at her with delight, as one would look at a beautiful mare, who cannot understand the language of men, but is only a comely and submissive beast. The girl bent her head, and a deep blush covered her cheeks and throat and bosom.

Temujin forgot Bortei. All his body swelled and strained in his lust for this wonderful creature. He had heard of the Caliph of Bokhara, an old lecherous man with a huge harem. Suddenly he had a vision of Azara, naked, in the arms of the Caliph, and all his blood rushed to his head so that his face became crimson with rage. His flesh was as hot as a stone under the sun, and yet moist with his sweat. He looked at the girl's hands, as delicate and white as flowers, and covered with jewels, and involuntarily he remembered Bortei's hands, short and square and hard, accustomed to the work of weaving and sewing and milking.

The girl breathed as one who sleeps, deeply and slowly, the breastplates barely moving with her breasts. Her head had fallen, also as one who sleeps, overcome with dreams. This seemed no living creature, but a painted vision, hardly come to life. She belonged to the great effete cities, in a silk-hung chamber dimly glowing with lamps, and filled with soft couches. From her body there exhaled an odor of jasmine and rose, intoxicating as strong drink.

Toghrul Khan watched Temujin. He saw the varying shades of red and crimson rushing across the young man's face as he gazed at the girl and lusted. He saw him suddenly pale, so that he looked like death itself. He saw him tremble, saw him bite his lip so that the blood left it. And then he knew that he had sent for his daughter with a wish for revenge. And he was overcome with astonishment that he could condescend to revenge himself on this miserable Mongol from the burning desert. So astonished was he, so disconcerted, that the fixed smile on his face disappeared, and was replaced with a blank expression of outrage.

He made himself speak, lightly, forcing his smile back onto his lips.

"Tonight, my son, thou shalt tell me what thou dost desire of me, and I tell thee beforehand, that it is already granted!"

He could hardly believe he had said these words, and stood aghast before them, wondering what had made him give them utterance. He had hardly spoken them when his whole soul retreated in confusion to its inner fortress of craft and treachery.

But Temujin, speaking to him but not looking away from the dreaming girl, said: "I want nothing from thee, my father. I have come to give allegiance, and to offer thee any assistance thou dost desire."

These extraordinary words, spoken in a loud firm voice without arrogance but with limitless strength, aroused Azara. She slowly lifted her heavy and beautiful head, as a water lily lifts itself to the sun. Slowly, over the edges of her filmy veil, her eyes focussed themselves upon Temujin, and then, like the dawn, a light broke over their darkness and she saw him fully.

They gazed at each other in a passionate silence. An expression, startled and frightened, yet fascinated, passed over the girl's face, like one who has been awakened suddenly from sleep by an exigent and somehow terrible stranger. He saw her rosy lips part, heard the quick inhaling of her caught breath. She paled, and he thought of a white flower in the moonlight. And then, all at once, as she gazed at him so fixedly, tears rose like a mist over her black eyes, and her expression became soft and sweetly alarmed, and poignantly confused. Her breast heaved, then trembled. She smiled suddenly, with a kind of wild and fragile joy, modest, but unbearably beautiful. She seemed like a maiden caught in her virginal bedchamber by one for whom she had dimly longed.

And then, without asking permission, she rose with one movement to her feet. She bent her head, turned, and went, as one fleeing, from her father's golden tent. She had gone, like a white dove, on silent wings.

Toghrul Khan, who always saw everything, smiled viciously. He was not concerned with his daughter's emotion, for after all, she was only woman-flesh, and had no real soul. She was but a lovely body, fit for the bed of a Caliph. His only concern was with Temujin, and what he saw comforted and gratified his venomous soul.

And then he stopped smiling, for Temujin had turned to him, and his pale face was fierce, his eyes sparkling with green fire. Never had Toghrul seen such a face and such eyes, and he thought to himself, involuntarily: This is one the like of which I have never seen before, and one who is like a wolf, to be greatly feared. A moment later, he said to himself, with an almost murderous hatred: But he is only a miserable wretch from the barrens, and I shall crush him under my foot like a worm!

He was alarmed. He made himself smile tenderly at Temujin. But over his smile his eyes, in their network of wrinkles, were wicked.

Temujin said calmly, his fierce expression brighter than ever on his face: "Tonight, I shall tell thee momentous things, my father."

When he had gone, the old khan sat alone, sunken in his thoughts. And then he looked up and said aloud: "Thou shalt never return home, thou insolent son of a starving desert rat!"

And then he stopped, abruptly, and the tent was filled with his brittle and disordered breathing, and his eyes were full of malignant fire.

He glared about him, his nostrils distended. He shrieked for a servant, and demanded wine. When it was brought to him he drank deeply.

The cup shook in his hands.

He wiped his lips with a kerchief of white silk. And then his eyes, raging, fell on the golden cross. He lifted his fist.

"I shall be avenged!" he cried. And then, as though his words were so preposterous even to his own ears, he burst into shrill and discordant laughter.

chapter 3

Temujin feasted by the side of Toghrul Khan, and looked at all the licentious splendors displayed before him, and thought contemptuously: Do men struggle and die for such things, such softnesses of the body that kill all desire?

He could drink prodigiously, without becoming drunk. Strong drink only intensified the ferocity of his nature, only magnified his colossal will to power. When he drank he knew all things were possible to him. His vision enlarged; his heart beat stronger with fierce resolution. He felt himself more than human. He seemed to stand alone on a mountain top, surveying a boundless realm. All his stonelike implacability grew greater. He knew then, while he drank, that he had always believed that he would be a kha khan, and understood how he had never experienced awe of any other man, or any respect or reverence. He had understood how he had felt only contempt, such contempt as he felt now for the mighty Toghrul Khan, who lusted only for the things of the body and was content with softness under his buttocks. He felt his destiny grow large in him, as a woman feels the enlarging and growing of the child in her womb. He looked about him with inexorable strength, and slowly, like a lion among jackals.

Toghrul Khan, impelled by his hatred, and wishing to awe this presumptuous beggar from the steppes and the barrens, had outdone himself in the splendor and luxury of his feast. Even while he did so, he asked himself, with a frenzied fury and wonder: Why do I do this? Why do I give him what I reserve for princes?

He did not know. He thought that he had degraded himself, and marvelled at his own pettiness. He was like a king who had set himself out to dazzle a mendicant.

The tents, with their flaps open, blazed with lamps. Golden and crystal and silver lamps hung from poles sunken in the pungent grass. Great bonfires, upon which had been flung handfuls of myrrh and sandalwood, burned furiously, filling the clear mountain air with intoxicating scents. Pots boiled on the fires, attended by women clad in scarlet and blue and white. Poultry roasted over spits. Mutton and horse-flesh simmered in rich gravies. Loaves made of flour as white as snow were heaped on silver platters, and other platters were heaped with rare and rosy fruits, like jewels. Jugs and sacks of wine were as plentiful as water. Plates were piled with Turkish sweetmeats, which gave off the odor of roses. Pastries, flaky and delicate, were to be found in endless varieties. Herbs were stewed in fragrant and exotic sauces. There was fish from the mountain streams, dripping with wine. The bowls were of silver, the plates of the most exquisite enamel. Banners, silken and painted with colorful Chinese emblems, fluttered everywhere in the dark mountain wind. There was a constant coming and going of male and female servants, jingling with silver bracelets, and out of sight, a score of musicians played sweetly and entrancingly, and women sang in high melodious voices.

Cloths of white silk exquisitely embroidered were spread over low tables. And at these low tables, seated on silken cushions stuffed with down, sat Temujin and Toghrul Khan and Azara, and Temujin's friends.

Behind them, black and looming, stood the mighty mountains, silent under the blazing stars and the riding moon. The pines gave off their pungent scents. The air was as fresh and pure as water. The revelry and song and laughter became deafening. Toghrul Khan's generals and chiefs sat near him, drinking and shouting, and, at intervals, glancing with furtive contempt and hidden laughter, at Temujin and his poor and shabby followers. For these generals and chiefs, like the khan, were arrayed in silken robes, and glittered with gems. They were literate men, acquainted with the cities, leaders of armies and regiments. They had caught the enmity of Toghrul Khan, and though he had not spoken, they knew that this was a death feast. When they spoke to Temujin and his friends, their voices were filled with mocking respect and elaborate irony.

But Temujin, who had the nose of an animal accustomed to danger, knew everything. He was quite calm. He pretended to be impressed by all he saw. But Toghrul Khan, after a little while, knew that the young chieftain was not impressed, and that he had already smelled the menace in the air. So he set himself out, with excessive affection and amiability, to allay Temujin's suspicions.

He said, in a tone of paternal sympathy: "Thy father's kinsman, Targoutai, is thine enemy now, I have heard, and hath taken unfair advantage of thy state. I offer thee any assistance thou mayest desire."

Temujin smiled with a hard tightening of his lips. "I thank thee, my father, for thy kindness. But I shall fight Targoutai myself. I have brave heroes at my sides, youthful paladins who would give their lives for me. As for myself, I know in my heart that no man shall conquer me or destroy me." And he looked fully into Toghrul's eyes with a bland and open expression, like a child's, and his own eyes were boyishly blue and simple.

Toghrul looked into those eyes, and he thought: This is a panther from the deserts!— He smiled gently, and laid his withered hand sympathetically on Temujin's for a moment. He was astounded that his heart had begun to beat painfully.

Temujin gazed boldly at Azara, who had been listening intently. But when he caught her eyes like this she flushed, and bent her head. Clad in robes of glistening gold, with her wonderful hair braided with pearls, she was a dream of beauty. When he saw her blushes, Temujin smiled to himself, like a conqueror.

There was a sudden clash of cymbals, which sent shivering echoes to the stars. And then out upon a cleared place among the tables there danced almost a score of beautiful slave women dressed in harem trousers of blue and scarlet and snowy silk, their feet in jewelled sandals. But their warm and rounded breasts were uncovered, and glistened in the crowding light of the many lamps. Their black hair flowed loosely about their young shoulders, and was crowned with golden circlets glittering with gems. About their upper arms were clasped jewelled circles of broad gold. Their red lips revealed shining teeth, as white as milk. Their eyes were large and soft and dark, like the eyes of does. They danced in an aura of intoxicating perfumes, like a fragrant hot wind.

They danced simply and dreamily at first, to the gentle strains of flutes and the soft persistent muttering of drums. They might have been innocent maidens, moving in the motion of innocent dreams of love, instead of houris accustomed to licentious pleasures and shameful joys. Their arms and breasts and shoulders shimmered like silk; their jewels blazed restlessly; their feet, moving through the intricate mazes of the dance, twinkled like stars. They smiled as a sleeper smiles, sunken in blissful visions. They seemed unaware of the hundreds of lecherous eyes fixed upon them, and the hungry smiles like the grimaces of starved animals. The music dreamed its dreams, as though unconscious of those who danced to its strains.

And then, the music quickened, the drums lifted their hoarse voices. The dancers uttered a light provocative cry, as though the visions they saw became unendurably rapturous. They flung up their arms; their breasts began to pant. Quicker and quicker screamed the pipes and the flutes; faster and deeper and more impelling thundered the drums. The naked torsos began to gleam with sweat, and the odor of it mingled with the heated perfumes until the scent was overpowering. Eyes flashed wildly; the red lips were wet and drawn back from the white teeth. The women seemed caught by the flutes and the drums irresistibly, as though they were being involuntarily whirled up to a shameful surrender and orgasm. Now the warriors began to shout, to sway on their haunches, to clap their hands. Sweat rolled down their swarthy faces. They reached out hands like talons towards the women, who were panting audibly and moaning softly, their flexible wet bodies swaying like serpents. Their eyes flashed like lightning upon the warriors, full of bestial laughter and invitation; their breasts seemed to swell. Now all the air was pierced and torn by the unbearable sweetness and ecstasy of the flutes, and the drums leaped in maddening thunder. The women swung their buttocks with a wanton movement, looking over their shoulders as they laughed deeply, and shaking their bosoms. Many of the warriors leapt to their feet and snatched at them, trying to grasp hair or arm, but with shrieks of mirth the women would dodge or bend and then dance away. It was a wild and dissolute scene; the flutes and the drums and the fragrances overwhelmed the senses.

Then there was another clash of cymbals, and like a wind the dancers were gone, their laughter trailing behind them. The warriors looked at each other's crimson faces with foolish smiles, then sat down again and began to drink as though to drown out the memory of what they had seen.

But Temujin looked only at Azara, who had covered her face with her veil.

Toghrul Khan said to Temujin: "Even the caliphs of Bokhara and Samarkand have no fairer women than these. Didst thou notice that each was an exact replica of the others? Even I cannot distinguish between them. The slave markets of all the cities were winnowed to match. Every lip and eye is a duplicate, and even their hair is the same color and texture. I have been offered a fortune for them."

And Temujin, looking only at Azara, said in a loud firm voice: "I have seen nothing more beautiful."

His voice pierced into the confusion of the girl's senses. She lifted her head and turned her face to him. She blushed, then smiled, shyly and sweetly, understanding him. And then again, she bent her head and drew her veil more closely. All her gestures were covered with confusion and modesty. Her hands trembled; the veil stirred with her breath.

Toghrul Khan saw all this, and his smooth face wrinkled

into nutlike lines as he smiled malignantly. He motioned to a slave, who refilled Temujin's cup. The young man had never ceased to drink, but he never became intoxicated. His glance was as steadfast as ever; his gestures calm and controlled.

The drinking and the feasting went on, accompanied by the distant and provocative music and voices. The floating silken banners caught firelight and lamplight, and shimmered in the wind. The fires rose higher, so that the trunks and branches of the circling pine forests were bathed in rosy light.

Toghrul Khan thought: He hath much to say to me. Why, then, doth he not say it? For what is he waiting? And he studied the young Temujin furtively, admiringly moved, in spite of himself, by his control and his bearing. But even this admiration heightened his hatred.

A slave bent and whispered in the old khan's ear, and Toghrul nodded. He turned to Temujin and said: "There is a messenger bringing me news of import. I must leave thee for a moment." Temujin stood up and courteously assisted him to rise. As Toghrul felt the strong and resistless grip upon his arm, his heart raged and he felt his age and impotence. When he walked away to speak to the messenger, his feet stumbled, and he thought with fury: I am an old man!

Temujin slipped deftly onto the cushion vacated by his host. He leaned towards Azara. His nostrils distended, and he inhaled the fragrance of her body, which seemed to have a sweet and virginal smell. He saw that she trembled at his nearness, and his pulses rose strongly. He whispered: "When I look at thee mine eyes are dazzled, and I am filled with bewilderment. Who can compare with thee, O beautiful maiden?"

Overcome with his emotion, he seized her arm; his hot breath fanned her silken veil. He muttered wildly: "Look at me, Azara!"

Her head was still bent, and then, as though impelled, she lifted it and turned her face to his. Over her veil her eyes, filled with mist, looked at his, and as they did so, they dilated and shone. He saw the rosy shadow of her lips through her veil; he saw how her breast lifted. He drew her closer, and his urgent body leaned against hers.

"I love thee, Azara!" he murmured in her ear, his mouth against it.

She shivered violently. She gazed, fascinated, at his blazing emerald-colored eyes, at his brown throat. She seemed overcome with terror. But her eyes implored him to continue, as though he were uttering words of incomparable delight.

"Naught shall come between us, Azara!" he muttered through

teeth clenched on his passion. "I shall come again, some day, and claim thee."

At this, she suddenly paled until her face was as white as her veil. Her trembling ceased. Her eyes lost their mist and shone brightly, as though with extreme fear. She cast a quick glance over her shoulder, and now she shivered again, as if stricken with a mortal chill. Startled, Temujin released her arm. She leaned towards him, and for the first time he heard her voice, whispering and hurried:

"When my father offereth thee a cup of wine on a silver salver, standing beside his, and asketh thee to drink a toast to your mutual pact of help, thou must take it, but on no account must thou drink it!"

He gasped at her, his lips opening. And then, as his eyes fixed themselves sharply on hers, which were filling with tears, he smiled darkly, and his eyelids narrowed. And then the girl, pressing the veil thickly over her face, rose before he could stop her, and had gone like a doe fleeing from the hunter.

Temujin lifted his wine cup thoughtfully, and slowly sipped his wine. He glanced at his companions at the other table. They were watching him alertly. He inclined his head, reassuring them, for they had seen the girl's emotion and her flight. Chepe Noyon, grinning mischieviously, nudged Subodai, believing Azara had fled before the urgency of Temujin's advances.

Toghrul Khan returned, and seeing Azara's empty place, he asked: "Where is my daughter?"

Temujin said tranquilly: "She asked me to beg thy pardon for her, but she was weary, and hath retired to her couch."

"Ah," said the old Khan, thoughtfully, his yellow skin wrinkling. He sat down. Temujin seemed absorbed in the delicious taste of his spiced wine. Toghrul thought with malicious satisfaction: Azara hath fled from his importunities, and now he doth pretend to an artless unconcern!

Pleased, his voice was richer than ever as he leaned towards Temujin and said: "But thou hast much to say to me, my son, and when will be a better time?"

Temujin put down his cup and inclined his head courteously: "Yes, my father, I have much to say to thee, and if it will not weary thee I shall say it to thee now."

His face became stern, his lips as grave as stone. He said quietly:

"First, I must call thy attention to many things.

"Thou art rich and powerful, in thy cities with their walls and fortresses. But even thou art insecure, because of the dark insecurity and struggles and conflicts and lawlessness of the thousands of nomad tribes ranging the barrens and the mountains. Only three out of five of thy caravans reach their destined places. Each little chieftain is the head of his own little nation, attracting followers from one tribe or another to him, when his repute for robbery and rich raids hath become prodigious enough. Robbery and murder are, in these circumstances, inevitable, and the traders of the cities suffer in consequence. When hunger forces, tribes assault the smaller towns under thy jurisdiction, and are laid waste. This cannot be changed under the system of these days, under a patriarchal society roaming independently and ferociously over High Asia."

Toghrul Khan had begun to listen with a half smile and a heart full of crafty ridicule. But now, despite his hatred and the plan he had laid, he was overcome with amazement at the astuteness and clarity of tone of this illiterate barbarian. His smile faded; his eyes narrowed. He looked into Temujin's face, and said quietly:

"Go on." He was suddenly enormously excited.

Temujin smiled. His eyes were the color of hard jade.

"We nomads have a rude military society. But because we are separated from each other by feuds and envies and lusts, we war against each other, destroying each other. We despoil and ruin each other. In the old days, my father told me, we were craftsmen of no mean repute, making bronze and iron, and pottery, and our carpenters and smiths made our own weapons. But now we must secure our weapons from Khorasan and Cathay, for we have no time for adequate production."

Toghrul said, whispering: "Go on."

Temujin sipped his wine. He said calmly: "I seem to wander, but thou knowest I do not wander. Bear with me a little.

"It is said that ye rich townsmen help us no longer. Ye pick out no strong man who can weld the tribes together. As a consequence, out of your own cupidity and smallness of mind and lack of understanding, there is no leader, and our tribes are filled with liars, murderers, robbers, thieves and raiders. Each chieftain must do as he does, if he is to survive, and ye suffer because of his necessity."

Toghrul Khan's head and face had become like a death's head. His skull shone wetly in the lamplight. His features grimaced like an ape's.

Temujin calmly filled his cup, raised it to his lips. He drank deeply and slowly. He removed the cup from his mouth, wiped the latter, and smacked loudly. "I have not before tasted such nectar," he said, with a boyish smile at his foster father.

Toghrul Khan seized his arm in fingers like pincers. They sank through the hard flesh almost to the bone, and Temujin was surprised at their febrile strength. The old man's eyes blazed like dying coals, redly.

"Go on!" he muttered through his teeth.

Temujin raised his eyebrows artlessly. "Methinks I have drunk enough," he said.

"Not enough!" cried the old khan fiercely. "Go on!"

Again, Temujin filled his cup, and drank without hurry, while Toghrul Khan's eyes blazed upon him. The generals and officers at the other tables, attracted by their khan's face, leaned forward, trying to catch a word. But the music, and the shouts and laughter defeated them.

Temujin put down the cup, and again wiped his lips. He turned to Toghrul Khan, and his eyes glittered in spite of his light smile.

"No security, no safety, no guarantees, no law, no order," he said softly. "And ye townsmen bite your fingers in impotent wrath because of the loss of your caravans. You Urgurs and Karaits and Moslem merchants, losing your vast rich caravans on the north roads from Cathay, from Samarkand or Bokhara, from the routes south of the Altai mountains! You townsmen sitting fatly in your gardens, and lamenting your losses! And why?" His voice rose on a harsh note of contempt, and he flung away the gripping fingers on his arm. "Because ye have no minds with which to think, but only lust for profits. Because ye cannot know that among all the tribes that roam the barrens, hungrily, there is a passionate desire for unity, for a leader who will guarantee them sufficient food and security and comfort. We do as we do, in our terrible necessity. And ye merchants pay through the nose, because ye will not call a leader to your aid, who will unite all the nomad tribes and control them, and give them security from your own pockets."

Toghrul held his withered lip between his teeth, and he spoke mumblingly: "Go on!" His eyes sparkled beneath their wrinkling lids.

Temujin shrugged. "I have told thee. There must be an end to the ceaseless quarrelling and turbulence and anarchy among our starving beggared nomads. There must be safety from them on the caravan routes. But only a single strong man, a leader, supported by your wealth, supplied with limitless arms and horses, can unite these tribes, and guarantee your caravans. I have already told thee." He reached up his hand and helped himself to the pastries held out to him by a servant. He stuffed the whole delicacy into his mouth and began to crunch on it, making sounds of appreciation. He seemed to have dismissed everything else from his mind.

Toghrul Khan sunk into himself on his thick cushion. He was as still as an image. But his eyes were terribly alive. He wet his lips. He moved his head as though he were choking. He could hear the brittle hammering of his own pulses. Then he put his hand on Temujin's arm, and smiled with revolting sweetness.

"Thy conversation is most fascinating, my son. Go on. Thou dost delight mine ears, for thou art full of astuteness and wisdom."

Temujin raised his brows. He affected to be touched with modesty and vanity. He spoke again.

"Mine uncle, Kurelen, hath told me that the goodness of the world resides in its poets and its philosophers and wise men. But who is concerned with goodness? Thou, thyself, knowest that the world belongeth to the merchants, to the shopkeeper, to the manufacturer of arms, and stuffs." And now he grinned malevolently, and his eyes shone with sardonic contempt. "I honor you merchants, for who am I but a beggarly nomad, not knowing what day I shall feast and what day I shall starve? Nothing matters, after all, but the profits of the merchant, and a world of men is well sacrificed for these profits. Thou knowest all this. But thou hast not known, heretofore, that only a single strong man can protect thee from the lusts and hungers of countless insecure men."

He wiped his sticky hands on the white embroidered napkin. He said so quietly that at first Toghrul did not hear the ferocity under his words, and the hatred:

"I hate ye merchants. But I hate more the anonymous mass of mankind, who cannot think except with their bellies and their genitals. But ye must reckon with them soon, or die. Ye must give support to a leader who hateth them, but who hath the skill and intelligence to unite them and subjugate them and lead them. For the protection of yourselves, and the maintenance of your profits. They desire only a little bread and wine, and a single hatred. Such can a leader give them."

The silence that fell sharply between them was only enhanced by the laughter and uproar of the others. But they looked into each other's eyes unwinkingly, Temujin with infinite stonelike calm and immobility, and Toghrul with the eyes and expression of an intent serpent.

Then Toghrul Khan whispered, leaning towards the young

man until the latter was struck in the face by his hot and fetid breath:

"But where is there such a leader?"

Temujin continued to stare into his eyes. And then, after a long moment, he shrugged. "Who knoweth?" he replied indifferently.

And still again, he filled his cup, and drank deeply. And Toghrul watched him, panting dryly, his face grimacing as though he grinned.

A servant now approached them, carrying two golden cups encrusted with jewels upon a silver salver. He bowed before Toghrul Khan. "Here, lord, are the cups which thou didst request," he said.

Toghrul Khan turned sharply and looked at the goblets. Temujin turned his bland face towards him with simple interest. Toghrul continued to stare at the goblets, and then, at last, he slowly turned his head and gazed piercingly at Temujin. For a long time they looked at each other.

Then Toghrul Khan smiled a sweet and evil smile. He shook his head and motioned the wine away.

"Nay," he said, "I like not this wine, Chaffa. Take it hence."

The servant bowed, went away.

Temujin smiled grimly to himself. Toghrul Khan gazed at him with intense affection.

"Thou art a strange youth, Temujin, but I love thee! And I wish to give thee a small gift to reveal my love." He reached within his robes and withdrew a cloth bag. He opened it. The lamplight glittered on coins of gold. He retied the bag, flung it upon Temujin's knee. And then he pulled off a ring from his finger, and thrust it upon Temujin's finger.

"There, my son! Now thou knowest how I love thee! I am thy foster father, and I remind thee now, with all solemnity, of our sacred pledge to aid each other! Never must thou forget it, I adjure thee!"

And he fell upon Temujin's shoulder and embraced him.

Seeing this, the generals and officers gaped with astonishment. Temujin's friends burst into wild cries of exultation, and raised their hands and shook them in the air. But the generals and officers looked at each other in dumb stupefaction.

A little later, before they retired, Toghrul Khan said to Temujin:

"I have thought much of what thou didst say, Temujin. But how can even a strong man unite all the murdering and marauding tribes?"

Temujin raised his hand above his head, then slowly clenched his fist, as though he were crushing something in it.

He said quietly, almost whisperingly, but his eyes were full of a terrible light:

"By force. Only by force."

chapter 4

The companions of Temujin were jubilant over the success of his visit. As they rode homewards, they sang and shouted. Even the silent Subodai laughed inordinately, with love, happy that his leader had not been slighted by the mighty Toghrul Khan. Temujin rode placidly, smilingly watching the gay antics of his friends. But Jamuga did not race, nor laugh, nor shout. He rode beside Temujin, his head bent thoughtfully, his wan lip bitten.

Temujin well knew these moods of his anda, and was aware that they were partially rooted in uneasiness, distrust and disapproval, stemming from his, Temujin's, actions. Sometimes these moods irritated him, and he would engage in heated argument with Jamuga, defending himself, and giving vent to extravagant language in which he threatened even more heinous and doubtful conduct. Sometimes they embarrassed him, and he would argue reasonably with Jamuga, seeking for approval and understanding and consent. And sometimes (and these occasions were ominously becoming more frequent) he was tranquilly indifferent and indulgently impatient.

Jamuga, who had been hoping that Temujin would provoke him into angry argument by inquiring as to the reason for his moody silence, felt a dismay which was becoming familiar with him. He glanced swiftly at Temujin's bronzed and metallically hard profile, which was maturely calm and composed. As he did so, his heart sank.

He was the first to speak. "Temujin, thou wert boastful with Toghrul Khan. Thou dost promise extravagantly and foolishly. But thou didst not ask him for the assistance for which we made this visit. Thou hast upon thy finger a new ring, yet we have no warriors behind us from the camp of Toghrul. Why is this so?"

Temujin smiled, without turning his head to his anda. "I did not ask him for warriors, nor did I ask him for assistance."

Jamuga's pale face flushed with anger, but he kept his voice even: "But why, Temujin? Is this not folly? We return as poor as we came, and as helpless. Except," he added with sardonic bitterness, "for the ring upon thy finger, which will not buy us pastures, and will not protect our women and our children."

Temujin flicked his stallion lightly with his whip, and the animal leaped forward a step or two. He regarded the pale and vivid sky tranquilly. He spoke as though addressing himself: "There is an auspicious occasion for asking, and there is an inauspicious occasion. This was not auspicious."

Jamuga exclaimed, his light voice hard and cold: "But Toghrul Khan's last words were to remind thee that thou must not forget the oath that bound you two together! Was that not auspicious?"

"No. More than any other time, this was most inauspicious." He gazed over his shoulder blandly at Jamuga. "Thou art a man of wisdom, but like most wise men, thou dost know nothing of mankind. Thou dost live in a world where words are valid, acts forthright, smiles honorable, where, in truth, all things are simple and have little under the surface. Alas! Such is not the real world, where there is nothing but duplicity, treachery, greed, lies, cruelty and rapine. I deal with this real world, and watch each player as he casteth his dice, knowing that even the spots he doth turn up are lies, that his every smile is mask for another meaning, where his voice is but a cloud that hideth his real face."

"And thou dost not think that Toghrul Khan would have assisted thee?" asked Jamuga, incredulously.

Temujin shook his head. "Perhaps he might have. I am sure, at the last, that he would have given me what I desired. Nevertheless, the occasion was inauspicious, and because he offered, it was the more necessary that I refuse."

"But what will Kurelen say? He will upbraid thee for this? He knoweth how sorely we need help."

Temujin smiled slightly. "But Kurelen, who is subtle, will understand, more than any other man."

But Jamuga was bitterly disappointed, and full of dismay.

"Thou didst disdain to ask, because thou didst wish to impress a wench with golden hair!" he cried. "Oh, I saw thee! Simpering and posturing and fixing thine eyes and grinning, and cutting a figure! Thou canst leave no woman alone, if she hath not the face of a camel!"

Temujin burst into loud laughter. "It is true that I love women, and that the softness of a woman's thighs is worth an empire. But, nevertheless, they cost an empire, and so, I seek to acquire one."

"Thou dost boast like a child," said Jamuga, with scorn. "I heard thee! 'A strong leader,' thou didst say to Toghrul Khan, and he laughed in his sleeve at thee, thou, a shaggy nomad with eight geldings and five stallions to thy name, and a starving band of women and children and miserable warriors! Thou didst talk like a kha khan, when thou hast nothing but the little bag of gold he flung at thee as he would fling a bone at a dog! Thou dost dream the dreams of a madman, and thy belly is as flat as a stone, and as full of nourishment!"

Temujin answered him with such mildness that a cold chill struck at Jamuga's heart, as though with premonition:

"Toghrul Khan did not laugh in his sleeve. And thou art right: I dream dreams, but out of their frail stuff I shall build an empire. I shall, indeed, be a Kha Khan!"

Jamuga tried to laugh acridly, but the sound died in his throat. But finally, in a stifled voice he said:

"Think, rather, how to alleviate the lot of thy people. They are poor and wretched. They are hungry and lost. A good leader is he who speaketh with gentleness and pity, and liveth only that his people are comforted and sheltered. Once a chieftain was father to his clan, feeding them and guiding them. But the old blood tie hath vanished. We have a new society. Each of our men must maraud for himself, like a wild dog leaving the pack——"

"I have said, that we must have unity," remarked Temujin with indifference.

"But thou dost not mean what I mean!" cried Jamuga, coloring. "Thou dost seek unity for conquest. I seek it for peace and security, and the comfort of the poor and homeless."

Temujin turned his face to him, and it was as smooth and expressionless as polished stone. "I must remind thee, Jamuga, that thou hast said, thyself, that I am poor and shabby, and that I must not dream vast dreams."

Jamuga looked at him in silence, then cried out: "I must breathe!"

He raced his narrow black horse ahead, and soon had outstripped the others. Soon his figure was a tiny racing one along the rim of the desert horizon, weaving its way through tamarisk and desert shrub and boulder. The others, seeing this, came back to Temujin. Kasar asked anxiously: "What troubleth thee, my brother?"

"Nothing," replied Temujin placidly. "Jamuga merely wished to breathe purer air." And he laughed with lightness.

It was not until they stopped for the night in the shadow of an overhanging cliff that Jamuga returned. And then he was pale and morose, and hardly spoke. It was in vain that he reminded himself insistently that Temujin must toil for years to provide sustenance for his people, and that the odds against his mere personal survival for a year were overwhelming. He was young; he had been abandoned by over two-thirds of his tribe; he was poor and had no allegiances, and no man was his friend. No powerful khan had taken him as a vassal, and promised him help and support. It was inevitable that within a short time even the remnant of his people would desert him for some more powerful chieftain who would be able to lead them and maintain them. And then, he, like a hunted dog, would be destroyed by stronger leaders of other tribes, unless he would become as a humble member of the anonymous mass. Therefore, he, Jamuga, was foolish to entertain this immense vague fear, which was without form, and had only drifted from the strange and fateful face of a youth who had nothing but the coat upon his back. But it was all in vain. The fear remained, and when the night came he could not sleep. Near him, he heard Temujin's deep and steadfast breathing, and thought him asleep.

But when the moon, moving across the heavens, sent a long cold beam into the hollow of the cliff, and it fell upon Temujin's face, Jamuga saw that his anda's eyes were open and fixed, and that he was not asleep at all. He leaned on his elbow, and called softly: "Temujin!" all his sore yearning in his voice, all his desire for peace between them urgent on his face.

Temujin slowly turned his head, and smiled with friendly affection. "Canst thou not sleep either, Jamuga? Come, let us walk out under the moon." He got up and Jamuga followed him, wrapping his cloak about him against the night air, which was as sharp and clear as ice.

They left the sleeping companions, wrapped in their cloaks. They walked past the horses, who slept with bent heads, their saddles spread out upon low rocks. They walked slowly and softly over a black earth plated with bright silver, and under a sky like an inverted silver bowl, polished to dazzling radiance. The weird and soundless silence of the desert engulfed them. In the distance there was a black wall, like a man-made rampart, and on every hand they had the mysterious and uneasy impression that thousands of spectral eyes were watching them. High shrub and dead and lonely fir seemed like a malignant and waiting presence, about to leap into life. They had the feeling of unreality, not a dreamlike unreality, but of a supernatural awareness, as though they had been transported to a far planet where men had never been before. Their shadows, black and sharp as jet, writhed behind them on the desert floor, endowed with an occult life.

Temujin halted and gazed at the sky. His voice was hushed: "On nights like these, Jamuga, on the thousands of nights of the desert, I feel in strange communication with another world, a world of malevolence and horror and vivid life. I cannot explain it. I cannot see this world, but I feel that I breathe its air, that my body brusheth its inhabitants, and that I feel the beatings of their hearts in and about me. Sometimes I am afraid, conscious of awful terrors which I cannot discern. And sometimes, like this, I feel that I understand everything!"

He was silent a moment, then he cried out in the strangest voice: "O ye mysterious spirits who live in the air of men, and hateth them! I am one with you! I implore your presence and your help! I have known from all time that ye and I comprehend each other, as ye comprehend men who cometh like me, out of wind and terror and flame, and returneth to them! I know I come, but I know not why. Only ye know! I ask not to pierce the mystery, but only to invoke its powers! Abandon me not, for I know ye, and I am the sword in your hands!"

His face, uplifted, was a mask of black stone cut into angles with a silver knife. His eyes glittered like the eyes of a madman. He flung up his arms, and his cloak fell in heavy folds about him. He stood there, under the moon, tall, vibrant, a statue of dark marble illuminated with the light of another and more terrible world.

Jamuga said to himself: He is mad. And again: He is mad! But he knew he lied in his heart, and he was full of dread and fear. He gazed awfully at the sky. For a frightful moment or so he was certain that some fearful Malignancy had halted, had paused to listen, and with its all-seeing eyes, was gazing at Temujin. Perhaps some demon, thought Jamuga, his reason failing; perhaps some Presence which by its touch could shatter the whole earth to dust.

Temujin dropped his arms. He turned his head and smiled at Jamuga. "Let us go on," he said in a normal voice.

Jamuga followed him. He spoke at last, painfully:

"What dost thou intend to do now, that thou hast not asked the assistance of Toghrul Khan?"

Temujin shrugged, smiled again:

"I know the end of the journey. I know what awaiteth me. I am like a man who travelleth a road destined for him, but can see only a length before him. I shall go on from point to point, knowing only that I am on the road. My destiny guideth me, and knowing this, I am content."

He put his arm about Jamuga's shoulder and said: "Come with me, mine anda. Let us go on together."

Then Jamuga, against all the arguments of reason and scepticism, heard himself (to his own dull amazement), cry out violently:

"No, no! Never! Unto the end of the world—never!"

chapter 5

As they rode home towards the little river Tungel, where the Yakka Mongols were encamped, Temujin thought with pleasure of his young wife, Bortei, to whom he was returning. He recalled that he had not thought of her once during his sojourn with Toghrul Khan, and was amused. The beautiful Azara, whom he had not seen since the night of her desperate warning, had occupied his desires and dazzled his senses. When he brought her face before his inner vision it seemed to him that he was remembering a dream of paradise, which all his life he must strive to seize.

There was something more than mere huge lust in his desire for her. She was the glory which all men dream of—a glory more than woman-flesh. He had looked into her eyes and had seen radiance and tenderness and understanding. Never would he forget her, and someday she would be his. In the meantime, she was the lofty moon that sailed in silver light over the dark cliffs and caves where he had his daily being. And in these caves and in the shadow of these cliffs he could live quite comfortably and affectionately with Bortei. In his mind, the two women never approached. They were distinct creatures, one of heaven, the other of earth.

He had only to accelerate his plans, before Azara was given in marriage to the Caliph of Bokhara. He thought to himself: She is the mate of my heart and my soul, and naught can divide us. Of Bortei he thought: She is the mate of my flesh, the mother of my sons, and the comforter of my bed.

The closer he came to Bortei, the more pleased he was. He was like a man returning to a warm hearth after a journey to far and glorious places which he would never forget. Yet the memory of Azara hung in his thoughts like a sweet perfume, intoxicating and exhilarating.

They were riding rapidly homewards, now, over the smooth desert floor, where the broken red pillars stood beside their fallen black shadows in the molten light. The burning wind tightened the skins of the young men over their facial bones, and they drew their hoods over their heads and brows to protect them. About the bits in the horses' mouths foam gathered, and they panted in the heat. They saw the yellow gleam of the little river in the distance, and hastened their pace. They wound about the flank of a shattered red cliff, and uttered a loud cry to warn their people of their approach. They saw the black yurts clustered near the river, and the barking dogs rushed out to greet them.

Suddenly Temujin reined in his horse with a low exclamation to his companions. They reined in their horses, also, and they stood in rigid and immobile silence, staring at the little tent village in the valley below. Everything was enormously silent in the bitter and magnifying glare of the molten sun, save for the barking of the dogs, which had a thin and metallic sound. But there was no movement about the village, no sign of horses or herds, no running child or woman or campfire. It were as though all life except that of the dogs had fled. They saw the yurts in the inky pools of their shadows; they saw the fitful sluggish golden gleam of the river; they saw the fantastic scarlet hills and the green desert shrubs on the yellow floor of the earth. But there was nothing else.

Temujin, with a wild cry, struck at his horse savagely, and the animal leaped forward as if about to rise in the air. Still striking at his horse, the young man galloped towards the village, his companions following, crying aloud in their distress and apprehension. Behind them raced the howling dogs, nipping at the heels of the horses.

In a cloud of hot dust Temujin plunged into the center of the village, flung himself from his stallion, rushed towards the yurts where lived his mother, his uncle and his wife. Not a soul met him; the doors of all the other yurts stood open, idly flapping in the smoldering wind. But as he approached the yurts of his family, he heard a faint and dismal wailing and sobbing. He sprang up upon the platform of Houlun's yurt, thrust himself through the flap.

Kurelen lay unconscious upon his couch with a face like a mask of death. Near him crouched Houlun, grimly silent, with a face no less pale. She was laving his face and misformed chest with steadfast hands; all her attention was fixed upon him, as though her life lay there, ebbing away. On the floor about her crouched Chassa, two old serving-women, and three or four younger women with their children in their arms. From them came a constant moaning, as they rocked from side to side on their buttocks. On the other side of Kurelen's couch stood the Shaman, his face dark and fixed, his arms folded upon his chest. Only he looked up as Temujin entered, and then his eyes gleamed a little with a malignant light.

"It is time thou didst return," he said in an ominous voice. "But it will do thee no good now."

Temujin paled; his nostrils flared out. He went to his mother and put his hand on her shoulder. But she did not look up at him. Her heart was in her eyes, as she bathed and tended the unconscious Kurelen. She was conscious of nothing else. Her son shook her, at first gently, then violently. Still receiving no response from the tranced woman, he turned savagely to the Shaman, who was smiling evilly.

"What has happened? Where is my wife? Where are my people?"

His companions, who had now arrived, stood outside on the platform and tried to see within.

Again, Kokchu smiled with the malice of hatred.

"When thou wert away, the second day, the Merkit came, the barbarians of the white frozen world. Our warriors tried to defend the ordu; all but six were killed, and these six fled, to save their lives. Among them was Belgutei. The Merkit seized many of the women and the children." He paused, and his fixed eyes became malevolent as they studied Temujin: "They entered the yurt of thy wife, Bortei, and they seized her. Kurelen attempted to defend her. One of the Merkit thrust him through the shoulder with his lance, and left him for dead." He shrugged. "I pleaded with them to spare Bortei, but they shouted at me with contemptuous laughter, saying they were clansmen of thy mother, Houlun, who was stolen from her husband. And now, they said, they would give her as a slave to a kinsman of thy mother's first husband, as a recompense and a revenge. They also took our herds, and the mother of Belgutei."

While he had been speaking, Temujin had turned even paler than before, until it seemed that all his blood had left his body. He stood without movement, though Chepe Noyon, Subodai and Jamuga cried aloud in grief and despair, and ran from the platform of this yurt to seek unavailingly among the other yurts for their mothers and sisters. Still, though moment after moment passed in the hot gloom of the yurt, filled with the wailing of the wretched women and children, Temujin did not move. His head was bent; his face was whiter than snow. And the Shaman watched him, darkly smiling with his wicked triumph, delighted, even in this predicament of his people, that Temujin should be so stricken.

What art thou thinking of, thou vainglorious dreamer? he thought viciously. Art thou not beaten down, thou boaster, thou kha khan, thou emperor of all men? Happy am I that thou art reduced to this, a hunted starveling on the face of the desert! Thou hast failed, for none of the men of Toghrul

Khan are with thee, and thou hast no one but these miserable women and thy hungry beggars who call themselves thy heroes! Where wilt thou go now, thou wild dog? Every man's hand is against thee, and before the night begins, thy body will be an offering to the vultures.

Then, slowly, as though hearing these virulent thoughts, Temujin lifted his head and fixed his terrible eyes upon the Shaman. And involuntarily Kokchu recoiled, wetting his lips with a vague terror, as though he were confronted with a frightful beast suddenly sprung up before him. But Temujin's voice was very quiet when he spoke:

"But thou, Kokchu, art still alive."

The Shaman trembled. He opened his lips, but it was a moment or two before he could reply, and then only faintly:

"I am not a warrior. I am only a priest."

Temujin's lips writhed, and he said:

"Ah, yes. It is true that when good men die the priest liveth."

Kokchu recoiled still another step, and again he wet his lips. But he could not speak again.

Kurelen, lying so motionless on his couch, moved his head and groaned dimly. Temujin bent over him, and laid his hand on his uncle's forehead. The hot sweat on it startled him. And now Houlun, as though aware for the first time of her son, looked at him with hollow eyes filled with anguish. She uttered a choked cry, and burst into tears. She leaned her head against his hip, and abandoned herself to her grief, her long black hair falling over her face.

Temujin fastened his compelling attention on his uncle's shrunken eyelids. "Kurelen," he called in a loud, urgent voice. "Kurelen! It is I, Temujin, come to avenge thee!"

Kurelen stirred again, as though deep in the fastnesses of his dying body he heard Temujin, and was striving to come up through the depths to him. Kasar knelt beside his mother, drew her head to his chest, and silently and awkwardly attempted to console her. Her cries and sobs were heartbreaking. But Temujin looked only at his uncle, and his will impelled him, forced him to come to the surface of the black sea which was drowning him.

The shrunken eyelids flickered; the cracked lips quivered. And then, almost imperceptibly, the eyelids opened, and the glazed eyes fixed themselves upon Temujin. And then Kurelen smiled, attempted to lift his hand. The other arm and shoulder were covered with cloths, which were stained with dried blood.

Temujin put his ear to his uncle's mouth, for it was evident that the cripple was trying to speak to him. He felt the dry flutter of Kurelen's lips, and heard his leaflike whisper:

"Ha, so thou hast returned! And now, I shall live."

Temujin smiled at him through his white lips.

"Most certainly thou shalt live, mine uncle. More than ever, I need thee now. But sleep, and recover." He laid his hand on Kurelen's forehead, drew it down gently, and pressed closed the eyes. A faint tinge of color had come into Kurelen's waxlike features. He drew a deep breath, turned his head, and slept. Then Temujin turned to his mother, knelt down, and took her into his arms.

"Weep not, my mother, for Kurelen shall not die. I promise thee that. And I promise that I shall avenge thy grief and thy suffering."

She wept on his shoulder, then relaxed, and kneeling there, slept in his arms, overcome with profound exhaustion. After a little while he gave her over to the serving-women, who laid her gently on the floor beside her brother, and fanned her with their sleeves.

In the meantime, weeping sternly, the others had returned. Temujin went out into the blinding sun, and, standing on the platform, looked down at them as they stood below. They saw his face, graven like stone, and his eyes, the color of blazing emeralds.

"My companions," he said, quietly, "great misfortune hath come to all of us. But we must waste no time in bewailing. We must be avenged. I must recover my wife, my bride, and you, your mothers and sisters. We dare not stop for grief, nor be overcome with despair, lest we, too, be lost. Chepe Noyon, do thou return at once to Toghrul Khan and demand his help of me, without delay. Subodai, Kasar, and Jamuga will remain with me."

Chepe Noyon, turning quite white, touched his forehead with his hand. He went to his mother's deserted yurt, and filled his sacks with kumiss and millet, supplies for himself and his exhausted horse. Then, the others heard him leaving the village on a gallop, and saw his figure rising over the rim of the valley. A moment later it had disappeared around the flank of the red cliff. Yet, for some time afterwards, they could hear the sharp echo of his going as he raced over the cracked earth.

Temujin let his mother sleep for a while, and then he awakened her, and commanded that she and the other women prepare what little food remained, as he and his companions were hungry. He knew that activity was the anodyne of despair. Soon two or three campfires were burning. In the meantime, Kasar and Jamuga and Subodai had gone hunting, and brought back a few foxes and martens and rabbits. Their herds had been stolen by the Merkit, and there was no other food but what they could kill in the desert and the hills. It was a small and dejected, but somewhat cheered little gathering which sat about the fires that night, eating the sparse food and drinking what remained of the kumiss and wine. Temujin had embued them with some of his fierce resolution and courage. After they had eaten, he commanded Kasar and Subodai to make music, and Kasar sang in his strong boyish voice, and Subodai made beautiful lilting sounds with his flute. Beyond the fires the flaps of the deserted yurts blew in the desert wind, and the stars rose, huge and cold. In his yurt, Kurelen, awake and less fevered now, listened and smiled, and held his sister's hand. But the Shaman, frightened, hid in his yurt and kept to himself.

Jamuga was grief-stricken, not only because his stepfather had been murdered by the Merkit and his mother, young brothers and his little sister had been stolen, but also because his chest of treasures had been carried off by the raiders. They were as dear to him as those of his flesh were dear, and as he sat by the fire he could scarcely eat, famished though he was. He remembered each ivory statuette, each inlaid dagger, each enamelled cup and plate, each pointed manuscript, and it seemed to him that his heart was full of wounds. He thought: When beauty and sweetness are gone, what remains on the earth? And he wiped away his tears with the hem of his sleeve.

That night Temujin lay in his bed alone, Bortei's place empty beside him. He stared at the black walls of his yurt, and his mouth was still and tight. But he told himself that he must sleep, for tomorrow there was much to do.

He sternly closed his eyes, and so intense was his will that in a short time he was sleeping peacefully, his sword in his hand.

chapter 6

The next morning Temujin told his friends that they must hunt through the desert and the mountains for the half dozen warriors and Belgutei who had escaped the Merkit. He and Jamuga would go together through the most dangerous country where the Taijiut ranged, and Subodai and Kasar would go to the north and west, respectively. But first they all hunted for food for the women and children, and when this was supplied, enough for several days, they left on their search for their warriors.

Temujin and Jamuga rode side by side for a long time, only stopping to replenish themselves, and to search each foot of the menacing country. But only the silence of the barrens greeted them, in spite of their ringing shouts when they entered a place of caves and hollow cliffs and sunken valleys. Only the blinding sun and the searing wind met them everywhere, except for the hoarse calling of a few desert birds, and the scurrying of frightened lizards over the hard earth. They avoided oases and streams by day, fearing the Taijiut, and seeking water only at night, and in silence.

By the third day, Jamuga was possessed by stark fear, for it seemed to him that it was not Temujin who rode so silently and inexorably beside him, but an implacable stonelike fury, exhaustless. Temujin spoke less and less, and rode on rapidly when Jamuga was certain that he, himself, would fall from his horse prostrated. His profile, lifted against the burning blue sky, was the profile of a bird of prey, sharp and bronzed and haggard, which could never be turned back, but would go on, pursuing until avenged. Each hour found him leaner, and darker of skin, and grimmer of lip. The two young men no longer conversed with each other, saving their strength for their periodic shouts and calls. And then, as they penetrated deeper and deeper into the Taijiut country, they used their eyes more than their voices, and searched for signs in the gravelly earth. Once, in the violet twilight, they saw the distant orange fires of a camp of the Taijiut, and they drifted far away in a circle, like shadows.

At last Jamuga said: "It is not possible, Temujin, that they have come so far away, into this dangerous country. Let us turn back."

Temujin did not answer for a long time, and then he said: "It is true. Tonight, if we have not found them, we shall turn back. Yet, I have a premonition that they are not far away from us today."

They had come onto a vast steppe, and standing knee-deep in the green grass, Temujin looked about him and said: "These are the pastures of my people. I shall seize these places for them."

"They were once ours," replied Jamuga, sadly. "The Taijiut do not need all these pastures. Why do men seize more than they need? Surely, there is enough space in all the world for all men."

Very slowly, Temujin turned his face to him, and the dark contempt on it struck Jamuga like a blow. But Temujin did not speak, but only swung himself up on his horse again, and loped away. I do not understand him any longer, thought Jamuga with deep dejection. But, did I ever understand him, in truth?

Yet, later, when he caught up with Temujin, nothing could have been gentler than the young khan's smile. They rode side by side in a warm silence, Temujin leaning towards his anda, and resting his hand lightly on his shoulder. To Jamuga, this was peace and happiness, and he thought to himself that he would be content to ride like this into eternity, with Temujin's hand on his shoulder and the sun in their faces. Surely, surely, he thought, with a sort of passion, there could be nothing sweeter than friendship and trust and love, and men who had them not were men who walked in blindness armed only with hatred, dangerous men whom other men must kill in order to save the world.

They camped that night in a high pine forest, sleeping under one blanket. At least, Temujin slept, but Jamuga did not. Sleep was never a familiar of his, for his thoughts were always too sad and melancholy. But he could marvel at the stern will of Temujin, who could slumber at the very threshold of enemies, and who never allowed himself the miserable luxury of anxiety and despair. He lay on his back, his quiet harsh face upturned to the moon, and Jamuga remembered the colossal and fateful profile which Kurelen had pointed out to him, saying that it was the profile of Temujin. It was true. This sleeping man's face was the face of the sleeping giant, portentous and full of power of doom. And again, Jamuga's heart sank into a pit of sadness, and he knew that he had been riding in an illusion, and that he did not know Temujin at all.

He leaned on his elbow, and stared at his anda. And as he did so, his mind became confused, and it seemed to him that all the brightness of the moon had come to a focus in Temujin's sleeping face, and that beyond it there was nothing but nebulous unreality. He was appalled and fascinated and terrified; he kept shaking his head, as though to rid it of its mounting confusion. And the moon burned brighter with its argent light, and gave a look of wild ferocity to Temujin even while he slept, a fatal look. A lock of his red hair blew softly across his brow. But it did not alter his expression; it might have been a butterfly fluttering over stone.

The next morning Jamuga said: "We must turn back. They are not here in this country."

Temujin agreed. But there was a curious light in his eye, and Jamuga knew that he was thinking of something else. His eye had the stillness of a gray lake over which his thoughts hovered like clouds, but could not be discerned. At last he said:

"These are wonderful pastures, unknown to us. But I shall have them for my people."

They stood on a vast green plain filled with quiet radiance. For scores of miles they could see nothing but this immense green flatness, which was like a sea rippling gently in the wind. To the north there was a single white peak, incandescent in the sun, blazing like crystal. The air was as pure as mountain water, and as clear, and the wind was laden in the fresh scents of earth and grass.

When Jamuga did not answer, Temujin turned to him with a smile:

"Thou dost think I am boastful. Thou dost not believe me."

Jamuga regarded him for a moment in pale silence, then he said bitterly: "I do believe thee!"

And then, overcome with his sad and distracted thoughts, he rode ahead, followed by Temujin's light and indulgent laughter.

At noon, Temujin said: "Thou art right. We must turn back now."

They swung their horses about, and rode away from the great white peak, which had seemed to approach no nearer to them. They left the steppe towards evening, and rose over a swelling terrace. And then stricken with fear, they stood for a moment, immobile. For advancing towards them was a detachment of horsemen, the Taijiut.

At length Jamuga uttered a low cry. "The Taijiut! They have seen us! Let us flee!"

But the horsemen had already seen them. They were led by Targoutai, Temujin's old enemy, and instantly he recognized the young man by his fiery red hair and the straight tall way he sat his horse. He gave vent to a shrill and triumphant shout, and, followed by his men, he galloped towards Temujin, brandishing his lance.

"Come," said Temujin in a low voice, and they turned their horses about and rushed away with the fleetness of shadows. They heard singing sounds, and saw arrows flying past them. The horsemen were gaining on them, filling the sunlit air with hoarse shouts, for their horses were fresh and Temujin's and Jamuga's were already tired. Temujin reined in his horse. He looked at Jamuga fiercely.

"Go on, Jamuga, and I will try to halt them for a moment, to give thee time."

Jamuga looked into his eyes, and replied steadfastly: "Nay. I will stand with thee, and if thou diest, then I shall die by thy side."

"Thou fool!" exclaimed Temujin, but even then he could smile at his anda.

He pulled on his reins, and his horse reared on his hind legs, swung about. Temujin balanced his lance in his hand, and Jamuga fitted an arrow to his bow. They stood against the blue sky, ready and unmoved.

The Taijiut, surprised at this unexpected stand, reined in their horses and slowed their speed. But Targoutai, who wished only to kill Temujin, came on, thinking his men still at his heels. Temujin narrowed his eyes, lifted his lance, measured the narrowing distance between himself and his old enemy. Targoutai came on like an avenging shadow, racing over the green grass. And then Temujin lifted his lance, pointed it, and let it fly forward with all the power of his young strength behind it. A second later it buried its head in Targoutai's thigh, and another second later, Jamuga's arrow had hurled itself into the neck of Targoutai's horse.

The horse, with a scream of agony, reared upwards, and Targoutai, with a shriek of pain, grasped futilely at the reins, fell backwards, and rolled off the horse, crashing heavily on the ground. The horse lost his balance and fell also, his shoulder striking Targoutai in the belly. The horsemen, coming up at an accelerated pace, swerved, but two of them stumbled over the fallen man and his horse, and were flung headlong. The air was filled with the cries of men and horses.

"Come!" said Temujin, and again he and Jamuga fled. The fear of death spurred them on, and they struck at their horses viciously. They galloped at a furious speed, leaning forward and standing in their stirrups, not caring about direction but only hoping to outrun their enemies. And their horses, imbued with their own terror, forgot their weariness and raced onwards, bellies almost level with the grass.

Temujin glanced back over his shoulder. What he saw made him laugh with exultation. For the Taijiut had fallen far behind. Only three were following now, and without much enthusiasm, swinging their lariats half-heartedly, and pursuing the two young men with hoarse threats. Only a short time later Temujin had lost his pursuers. He and Jamuga were running now over the lower level of the valley towards the incandescent white peak, the mountain Burkan.

Temujin fixed his eyes steadily on the peak. There lay comparative safety for a time at least. The horses were panting; their hides were covered with foam. But still they spurred them on, anxiously scanning the sky, hoping for the swift twilight of the steppes.

It came, a purple curtain dropping over the earth. Now the white peak had turned to a glowing rose against the amethyst sky. The wind mounted to a deep and thundering sound like the voice of a tremendous drum. Over the mountain appeared the tremulous face of the moon, brightening momentarily. They were alone on the earth, slackening their pace. The horses panted heavily. To rest them for a while, the young men dismounted, and led them by the bridles.

The ground was no longer grassy, but broken by boulders and low stones. And then the earth dipped and rose in steep hollows. In the shelter of a shelf of mingled earth and stone, the two young men stopped for the night, not daring to build a fire though the air had become as cold as ice. They wrapped themselves in their cloaks, huddled together under their blankets. And instantly, they were asleep from exhaustion, even Jamuga whose mind was always a battlefield for distressful thoughts. Above them towered the mountain Burkan, like a gigantic protection, black and silver against the milky heavens.

The dawn came, all pearl and blue and gold. Temujin said: "The mountain hath saved my life. Unto the end of my days I shall make sacrifice here, and command my children to the least one to do it also, in my name."

He folded his arms on his breast, and bowed deeply, three times, before the mountain, which the morning had turned to white flame. And then he bowed to the sun, and called upon the eternal Blue Sky to guard him forevermore.

A little later, having drunk of a cold mountain stream and swallowed a handful of dried millet, they circled about and cautiously began the journey homeward, avoiding as much as possible any open stretches of land during the day, and riding across them only at night.

It took them several days to reach the little river Tungel again, and the Mongol camp. And there, to their great joy, they discovered that Belgutei and the others had been found, and had returned.

Kurelen was out of danger, now, and listened with eager attention to Temujin's account of his flight from the Taijiut, and that night the Shaman, after a short hint from Temujin, made sacrifice to the Blue Sky because of the young khan's escape.

Two nights later Chepe Noyon arrived, triumphant, and followed by a large and formidable detachment of Karait warriors, sent to aid Temujin, by Toghrul Khan.

chapter 7

Kurelen, watching the exhaustless activity of Temujin, as he exhorted his own warriors and the Karait upon their conduct of the proposed raid on the Merkit, and oversaw every detail of the complicated plan, marvelled. He knew that this was to be something more than an avenging raid, and dimly, he began to perceive what it was. For Temujin was giving orders that only those among the Merkit who resisted were to be killed. Captives were to be seized, and the whole ordu of the Merkit, if possible, was to be taken intact. He was particularly insistent that the women of the Merkit be spared, and all the young children, and the warriors, especially, were merely to be disarmed and subdued. He added, with some irony, that the Shaman was not to be harmed, nor the old fathers of families.

He did not mention his young wife, Bortei, and somewhat curious, Kurelen summoned his nephew to his yurt. It was most extraordinary, he said, that Temujin apparently sought no bloodthirsty revenge for the rape of his bride and the murder and captivity of so many of his people. Perhaps, he suggested, with a malicious look, Temujin's heart had become soft; or again, perhaps he was indifferent to Bortei, who might think him a poor creature for not avenging her humiliation.

Then Temujin said the thing which was to be repeated for countless ages:

"Men are more than revenge, and unity more than personal desire."

Kurelen bit a fingernail meditatively, and smiled a little.

"It is nothing to thee that thy wife, then, hath been raped by a Merkit, and mayhap become the mother of his child?"

Temujin's dark face paled, but he replied quietly:

"I have said that there are things greater than a woman, and more portentous than one man's heart."

"Brave words," remarked Kurelen, with cynical reflectiveness. "It would seem thou hast no human passions, and instead, art the coldest of realists."

"What I have to do hath no place in it for human passions, which are insignificant."

"What dost thou desire?" asked Kurelen, curiously.

Temujin smiled briefly. "The world," he answered, and went away.

Alone, Kurelen burst into laughter. "The world!" he exclaimed. "Young fool! And yet, I do believe he will have it!"

He went to the door of his yurt, leaning on the shoulder of Chassa. He peered out. Temujin was mounted on his white stallion with Kasar, Jamuga, Chepe Noyon, Belgutei, and Subodai about him. Behind him, on fresh horses, sat the remnant of his warriors, and behind them, the dark-faced inscrutable warriors of the Karait, who watched Temujin with wary curiosity and interest. He had already convinced them of his courage, intelligence and resolution, and these, combined with the commands of Toghrul Khan, had persuaded them to follow and obey him to the end.

Temujin sat there on his horse, the red sunlight of evening like an aura of flame about him. His stallion kept throwing up his white-maned head, and pawing the ground and wheeling. But Temujin's voice, as he gave his final commands, was quiet and penetrating. Even the dogs, as though understanding something momentous was afoot, merely sniffed at the heels of the horde. And above them the evening sky blazed in august conflagration, and from this Temujin's vivid hair caught a fiery reflection.

Then he lifted his lance, wheeled, and plunged away. With hoarse shouts and exultant cries the horde followed, riding in close formation. The ground trembled under their going. They rode into the sunset, blackly silhouetted against it, raising crimson clouds of dust behind them.

Kurelen dropped the flap of his yurt, and turned away with a strange smile. He laid his hand against Chassa's cheek.

"Dost thou know, Chassa, that thou hast seen the beginning of the convulsion of the earth?" And then: "Laugh at me, Chassa, for a foolish old cripple, who doth babble insanities. And yet, even while thou dost laugh, know thou that I have spoken the truth."

The moon rose, flooding earth and heaven with silver light. Now Temujin and his horde rode as silently as possible, only the jingling of their harness to be heard, and the soft pounding of the horses' hoofs. No one spoke. They moved drifting, under the moon, straight and wary and ready, their lances in their hands, their shadows gliding with them. They wound through narrow passes between looming and overhanging cliffs, descended into craters, rose on terraces. When the moon was at its highest they rounded the flank of a smooth hill, and saw below them the campfires and luminous smoke of the Merkit camp.

Temujin reined in his horse, and carefully studied the situation of the camp, which was very large, consisting of over five thousand souls. The black yurts crowded together in a vast circle, the fires in the center. They could hear the disturbed lowing of herds, and could hear faint sounds of laughter and music. And now the dogs, scenting their presence, began to howl.

"Come!" said Temujin. He lifted his lance, and shouted menacingly, and the horde took up the shouts. The horses shrilled, threw up their heads. And then, like a vengeance, the horde rode down to the camp in a surge of noise and shouts and clattering hoofs.

The Merkit had not expected this, certainly not that Temujin would come, greatly reinforced. They were caught unprepared. They had scarcely time to glance up and to perceive this mighty battalion of fierce warriors, when it had broken like a wave into the camp. The warriors ran to their yurts to seize their weapons, but the enemy blocked them, striking at them with whips, pinioning them with lariats, riding them down with their horses. Those who resisted were run through, and these were many, for the dour Merkit were valorous fighters, and did not surrender easily. The screaming of horses, the shrieking of women and children, the shouts and calls of men, the barking of dogs and the plunging of the herds, filled the moonlit night with confusion and uproar.

Temujin, fighting off defenders, kicking at them from his stallion, slashing at them with his sword, fought a way through the disordered throngs. He rode through the village of the yurts, calling desperately for his wife. And now he was no longer an avenging warrior, but a husband searching for his bride.

"Bortei!" he called. "Bortei, my beloved, it is I, Temujin!"

Some one reached up and seized his reins, swung from them. He lifted his fist to strike this creature down, when he saw it was Bortei, herself. With a cry of joy he reached forth his arm, seized her about the waist, and swung her up before him. She wound her arms about his neck, leaned against his bosom, and wept.

"My husband! My husband! Thou hast come at last!"

Her hair covered his face; her weight was sweet and precious against him. He could, even in those moments of wild confusion and death and struggle, fasten his mouth down upon hers, hold her tightly in his arms, and comfort her.

"Didst thou doubt I would come, beloved?"

In the meantime his warriors had rapidly subdued the Merkit.

They were driving them before them with whips, men and women and children, raiding the yurts and dragging forth the terrified occupants. And then when all had been herded into an open place, the horde mounted about them, Temujin rode up with Bortei and addressed them.

His voice was mild and firm:

"Look ye, Merkit, I have not come solely for vengeance, though he who hath taken my wife shall die, and that as terribly as possible.

"But I have come to ye as a friend and as a conqueror. Henceforth ye shall be my vassals and my people, and I, your lord. Hasten, then, and yoke your oxen to your yurts, and follow me."

He looked down at the white and contorted faces, and smiled. Silence answered him. He saw only strange and obstinate looks and tears. But he was satisfied.

At dawn he rode back to his own ordu, the thousands of captives and his warriors behind him, and behind them, the fat herds and the many horses. Behind him trundled the hundreds of yurts, filled with weeping women and children. But the warriors of the Merkit rode dourly and darkly, looking about them with fierce glances.

That night the man who had raped Bortei was slowly and methodically burned to death, with appropriate ceremonies.

chapter 8

Temujin, victorious, had acquired his first vassals. But if he felt exultation, this was not evident in his calm and inscrutable bearing, his strong quiet voice, his controlled movements. The banner of the nine yaktails stood outside his yurt, triumphantly. But no one knew what he thought.

He well knew the uses of terror. So he called the Shaman to him.

Kokchu came at once, subservient and subtle. When he looked at Temujin his eyes were full of malicious respect. But his voice was humble when he bowed before the young lord, who lolled indolently on his couch with his young wife beside him. Temujin played with her long dark locks as he stared at the Shaman.

"Kokchu, today I shall have a great feast celebrating my first victory. And after that feast thou shalt talk to my people. Thou shalt tell them of a vision thou didst have last night."

The Shaman bowed low again. "And what was that vision, lord?" he asked softly, only the faintest note of irony in his tones.

Temujin smiled. "That I was born to be lord of the Gobi, and that he who followeth me followeth me to glory and victory and much riches. And that he who faileth me shall die horribly and without mercy, and that the spirits of the Blue Sky shall eternally damn him."

Kokchu smiled in answer. "But I have already told the people this."

"Tell them again! Terror must be their familiar. Terror of me, my glance, my voice, my hand. Invoke the spirits."

Kokchu's subtle eyes glinted. "Better still, I shall have the lord of the spirits descend to earth and tell them, himself."

He glanced at Bortei, who was smiling, and bowed in her direction. When he had gone, Temujin burst into laughter.

"Verily, the man who hath the priests on his side is a man whom none dare resist!"

He kissed Bortei passionately, and she returned his kisses. But between them there was a wedge of darkness. A moon had waxed full, and had waned, and had gone, and Bortei knew she was with child. And Temujin knew. But neither could know if this child was Temujin's. It was not a matter of extreme moment to him, Temujin persuaded himself. For the Mongols loved and valued children as evidences of tribal power, and children were, with the herds, the first prizes of warfare. Men, as Temujin often said, were more valuable than chests of gold. Still, when he held Bortei in his arms, and knew that another man had held her like this in the black hot intimacy of the night, his heart rose like a searing flame and burned all his flesh. But in the day the matter became one of insignificance. He loved Bortei. She amused and thrilled him, and he was delighted with her shrewd wit and intelligence, and the beauty of her young body. He was more influenced by her than he knew, for his susceptibility to women was enormous.

And Bortei, who was extremely wise, held down her disappointed bitterness and knew she must wait. She hoped, before her seizure by the Merkit, that a child would cement her hold upon Temujin, and he would henceforth be more easily guided. But now this child would come under a cloud. She knew she must wait for another child, incontestably Temujin's. In the meantime, she must prepare the way she meant him to go very delicately and subtly, and without too much pressure.

Her lust for Subodai had increased, rather than decreased. She had won his respect and admiration with her devotion to Temujin. Often, when he came into Temujin's yurt, and found her with her husband, he would look at her gently with his beautiful tranquil eyes, and often he would be amused at her wit, and laugh with innocent heartiness.

She had need of much consolation and courage, for Houlun, who had not forgiven Temujin the murder of Bektor, and his subsequent insulting remark to her, did all she could to discipline the young wife harshly and make her life hard. Here was a younger woman who must bow before her, and give her honor and respect, and she exercised her privilege with unremitting sternness and coldness. It was as though she was avenging herself for all her humiliations and despairs and griefs. It was not until it was definitely established that Bortei was to bear a child that Houlun laid aside her actual whip, and refrained from striking the girl as was her custom when she displeased her.

Beneath the glittering surface of Temujin's triumph all sorts of small dark passions writhed, unseen. But because he was not of the order of ordinary men, he stood on that glittering surface and refused to care what lay beneath. He had laid out the road he must travel, and pettinesses must not interfere.

The feast he had ordered was a hearty and tumultuous one. The Merkit were reconciled to their new lord, for the law of the Gobi was the law of the survival and triumph of the fittest, a natural edict before which all men sensibly bowed. They were confident that Temujin would provide security and pastures for them. These were all they desired. If a stronger lord took them, then they would serve him with equal loyalty and simple devotion. The Karait warriors which Toghrul Khan had sent Temujin remained with him, and Toghrul dispatched their wives and children and yurts to join them. And with them he also sent a silver coffer filled with shining golden coins, and a kibitka loaded with swords and lances and shields and scimitars. And a day or two later he sent Temujin another gift: twenty of the finest brood mares and their foals, and a fat herd of sheep.

Temujin smiled grimly on receiving these gifts. He smiled with even more grim satisfaction when a caravan passed near him, and a messenger came to him with messages of praise and offers of support from the merchants who had dispatched the caravan. And then the messenger gave Temujin another coffer, a larger one, filled with silver coins, and precious stones. Then Temujin, to show his gratitude, sent one hundred of his picked warriors to guard the caravan across the most dangerous stretches of the Gobi. Commanding them was Chepe Noyon, the artful and clever, the best of all strategists, who could be relied upon to convoy the rich caravan within sight of its destination. Subsequently, Chepe Noyon, for a long time, and with an increased horde of warriors, was assigned these tasks. And never did a caravan pass through without a rich gift for Temujin, and letters of gratitude and offers of unlimited support. Sometimes the gifts were slaves, skilled in the making of saddles and bridles, carpenters and smiths and sword-makers and weavers.

Temujin formed the new institution of nokud, picked companions of chivalry, courage and devotion and intelligence. Kurelen watched with intense admiration and surprise. He questioned Temujin about this new military nucleus which he was forming, and wondered aloud how his nephew had thought of it.

And Temujin replied:

"The clever man, the lord, doth not always make circumstance. He doth seize on change and necessity, and make them his servants. He must bend inevitable events to his purpose. The world doth change constantly, even here on the Gobi, as though change were mysteriously ordained by the gods. The victor is he who doth foresee the changes, and ride them, at their head."

He swore each nokur to him personally, impressing upon him that his devotion was more than any devotion to other tribe or family or wife or child or friend. The nokur was entirely free, not a vassal, not a toiler like a slave. He was a military servant, a commander, an organizer in command of lesser men. He had his own dignity and pride, and because Temujin did not interfere (wisely) with these things, and demanded nothing but the most implicit obedience and allegiance to himself, the nokud served him like a god and would not hesitate to give up their lives for him. They shared the first fruits of the raids, the fairest women, the finest horses. Fluid but disciplined, fierce and devoted, bold and obedient, they were the first military caste of the desert and the barrens. And Temujin, as always, seemed to inspire in all of them an almost superstitious worship and love. He never broke his word, for he had said that the first law a leader must impose upon himself was to observe his promises implicitly, whether they were promises of punishment or reward.

Before long, the rumor of his laws flew over the barrens to other tribes, and it was said of him that he was a man with a country. He was a prince who demanded almost superhuman devotion, but in return he was devoted to his people, and was the first servant of all.

Jamuga Sechen watched the formation of this new military caste with dismay. To him, the nokud appeared parasites, who lived by the enslaving of the weak and poor and helpless. Heretofore, each member of the tribe was an individual unto himself, giving service when demanded to his lord, but proud of his intense personal life in which the lord did not interfere. The lord provided him with pasture, asking only that the man help him protect this pasture. But now every member was the servant of some nokud, and his life was filled with constant obligations and toil. No longer was the old free and independent life possible, with every man keeping what he had seized for himself. Each lowly man was the complete slave and servant of his nokur, and he must submit all that he seized into a common heap, which the nokur would divide as he saw fit and just. He had no life of his own. His duties were rigid, and done for the good of all. His obedience was demanded, and the slightest infringement resulted in severe punishment and even death. For the nokud were harsh and merciless, if just, and they impressed upon the people that the first law of survival was obedience, and he who disobeyed in the smallest thing was an enemy of the whole clan. He who demurred or complained was called a traitor, and his punishment descended upon him like a sword.

Temujin's nokud consisted of many commanders, and among them were Chepe Noyon, Jamuga, Subodai and Kasar and Belgutei. He formed them into a personal military bodyguard for himself, and by so doing removed himself from the trivial affairs of the tribe, which the nokud managed, and reserved himself for greater things.

Jamuga admitted to himself that order and discipline had appeared for the first time in any tribe, and that the whole ordu moved as a single unit, strong and formidable and obedient, each member only a link in a chain, only a spoke in a wheel. But this seemed terrible to him, this violation of the ageless integrity and individual pride of the nomad, when each man served his lord only for his own protection, and was a law unto himself, when immediate service was no longer demanded of him. But now there were no proud individuals, no self-respect. There were only slaves under the whip and voice of the nokud, with no personal life.

Temujin increasingly became strange to him. Temujin still showed his anda his old affection and confidence, but Jamuga felt that some frightful stranger had taken possession of Temujin's body and voice, and the spirit that looked through his eyes was some malignancy which could never be placated. He could not be at ease with this stranger, this malignancy; he could not speak to him fully. His own bitterness and dejection darkened his face and voice, and more and more he avoided Temujin.

One day he went to Kurelen, in his despair, forgetting his old suspicion. He began to speak of the nokud, the stern military caste, the commanders who treated those under them like soulless dogs. He stammered in his dismay and grief, and his voice died away. Kurelen lifted one of his tilted black brows and smiled.

"I see law and order for the first time, Jamuga," he said.

"But at what cost!" exclaimed the young man.

Kurelen shrugged. "Know thee, Jamuga, that I do not value law and order above the hearts of men. But that is because I have always hated ruthless discipline. However, that doth not mean that law and order are not desirable, with the security and oneness they bring. Before this, we had unrest and unruliness and discontent. I grant thee that these things are subdued by fear. But mayhap fear is necessary in this new world which Temujin hath seized, and made." He added, with a quizzical smile: "When, before this, were we so safe, so secure? We must give all honor to Temujin."

Jamuga regarded him with bitterness. "Then it is useless to point out to thee that our people are slaves, and no longer free men?"

Again Kurelen shrugged. "Freedom! Not all men are capable or deserving of it. It doth make them no happier. They prefer obedience and security. Our people appear more contented, more at ease. Each man doth know he will not starve, for the nokud portion out loot to every one. Life is short. It doth seem to me that the surrender of freedom is a small price to pay for a comfortable life." He added: "Long ago I decided that. Let another make the decision for me, so long as I may eat at regular intervals."

Jamuga stared at him with icy violence. "Thou hast the soul of a slave, Kurelen! But I prefer to make mine own decisions, and for the sake of mine own peace, I wish to see other men also make theirs."

Kurelen smiled, but did not answer. Jamuga did not see the cynicism and irony in that smile, the self-disdain and ridicule. He turned and went away.

Driven by his misery, he at last sought out Temujin one night. Temujin was already asleep, but appeared pleased when Jamuga entered his yurt. He lifted a lamp and threw its light on Jamuga's pale face. He saw the light blue eyes, heavy-rimmed and somber. For a long moment the two young men regarded each other in silence. Then Temujin put the lamp on its tabouret, and motioned Jamuga to sit beside him. But Jamuga remained standing, thin and tall, like a steel blade.

"Temujin," he began in a low voice, "I have come unto thee out of my wretchedness and despair, and my feeling of helpless strangeness. I come because I feel deprived and lost."

Temujin looked at him intently. His eyes were as blue and kind as a summer sky. He said sympathetically:

"Deprived, Jamuga? That is most strange! I thought the treasures thou didst lose to the Merkit had been replenished a hundred times. I believed that thou didst receive thy pick of the most delicate jewels and ivories and silvers which Toghrul Khan and the other traders sent to me as a gift."

Jamuga opened his lips to reply disgustedly, thinking that Temujin had misunderstood him. And then his mouth became rigid. For he saw only too clearly that Temujin had understood him perfectly. A sensation of complete impotence overcame him. He felt physically sick. But his was an obstinate and tenacious nature, and he would not give up. He knelt before Temujin, and began to speak in a hurried and eager voice, which was filled with anxious despair.

"Look thee, Temujin, thou dost not need to mock me. Thou dost know my heart. And I have come to thee out of our old love, which thou hast forgotten."

Temujin was silent. A hard and curious expression tightened his fixed smile. But his eyes were still kind; he shifted them a little, so that they did not gaze directly at his anda.

Jamuga, as though by laying a physical touch upon Temujin he might bring back his friend, seized his arm. But his confusion grew.

"Temujin, once thou didst have honor and courtliness and pride. Now thou hast none of these, and my heart faileth me. And because I love thee I must come with prayers and censure ——"

Then Temujin looked at him directly, and his eyes were like green polished jade, and as expressionless. But his voice was still sympathetic.

"Jamuga, thou dost think too much. Get thee a wife, several wives. Look thee, tomorrow thou shalt have the pick of my women. There is one who hath hair the color of a raven's wing, and eyes as blue as spring water. When men's souls do trouble them they need only a woman, and not philosophy."

Jamuga gazed at him with dumb and sorrowful silence. Temujin shook him lightly and affectionately.

"Men who develop their souls wither their bodies, Jamuga. Thou dost pore too much over those Chinese manuscripts of thine, which are full of enervating subtleties. Men lose their reason in a forest of words, and their swords rust in the stagnant waters of thought. Thou hast begun to substitute conversation for action, and art losing thy virility. I tell thee again: take a woman."

He smiled with affectionate amusement. But inwardly he was irritated by Jamuga's dark fixed sorrow.

Jamuga said simply: "I live only to serve thee, Temujin. I love none but thee. I am dedicated to thy life. Thou hast always known this. Thou dost think many love thee: Kurelen, Houlun and Bortei. But none love thee as I love thee. And that is why I come without fear to thee, and must speak."

Temujin yawned. "Thou dost discover strange times to speak, Jamuga. That is thy peculiarity. But speak, and then go, and let me sleep again."

Jamuga lifted his hands in a heavy and despairing gesture, and let them drop. But he continued to speak in low quiet tones:

"Since thou didst become khan, Temujin, thou art strange

to me. Thy father had his nomad honor. Thou hast none. For instance, those caravans whose owners pay thee flattery and tribute are protected by thee, even at the cost of many of the lives of our people. But those caravans who come without gifts through thy territory are raided, the men enslaved, the treasures seized. Is that honor?"

Temujin laughed lightly. "Wouldst thou have me raid and rob without discrimination?"

But Jamuga replied steadfastly: "There is no honor in discrimination, when it is bought. I grant thee we must live. But not by such means."

Temujin said impatiently: "Thou art becoming subtle, Jamuga. I despise subtlety. But go on; thou hast more to say."

"Yes, much more. Temujin, I hate thy nokud. Our people are enslaved, robbed of personal integrity. Robbed of their souls."

Temujin looked at him with eyes like a savage beast's. "What souls?" he asked contemptuously. "Go to, Jamuga! Thou dost whine like a Buddhist monk, or a silly woman. What is the purpose of man? To survive! I survive, my people survive. Less than three moons ago, I was a hunted beggar, robbed of ordu and herds. Now, I am strong. I have seized over ten weaker tribes, and welded them to mine. I am a khan in truth, not a starving fugitive. My people have good pastures again, and security. Where is there security in honor? My nokud are my warrior bodyguard, mine officers. I have instituted order and discipline, for the good of all. All these are little to pay for what we have become."

Jamuga's head dropped wearily on his chest. "I prefer peace," he murmured sadly.

"Peace!" Temujin burst into scornful laughter. "Did we have peace when we were hunted?"

"Thou dost not understand, Temujin."

Temujin smiled with disdain. "Jamuga, thou didst always underestimate me. I understand thee well. But peace is not for men of action. Peace is for the conqueror, when he can afford it. I cannot afford it. Dost thou understand?"

"Thou dost not want it, Temujin."

"Perhaps not. I am still virile, Jamuga."

Then Jamuga lifted his head and looked at him straightly.

"What dost thou want, Temujin?"

And Temujin replied, with a smile, as he had replied to Kurelen, "The world."

Jamuga got to his feet, and in silence went to the flap of

the yurt. He had reached it, when Temujin's voice, peremptory and harsh, stopped him.

"Jamuga, thou art mine anda."

Jamuga turned slowly and gazed at him with grief.

"It is not I who have forgotten it, Temujin, but thou."

He went out. Temujin did not lie down immediately, and sleep again. He scowled to himself in the yurt. He remembered that once Jamuga had told him that men of great dissimilar aims cannot be friends in truth, but have only hatred, especially if those aims collide with the conscience of one. He shook his head irritably. Surely Jamuga did not hate him! He knew Jamuga too well, he told himself. There was no treachery in that stern cold heart, no craftiness in that narrow conscience! He could trust Jamuga to the end of his life, despite his anda's predilection for philosophy and peace.

Yet, fragments of other voices joined his angry thoughts. He remembered that Bortei had said only that morning:

"There is much behind that pale still face of Jamuga's. He loveth the old slow ways, and hateth and suspecteth the new. What place is there for a man who clingeth to the past, in a world that is changing? Men like this have a tenacious hold on the things which are dead, and fear that which is living. And because of this, they cannot be faithful to the new way, for they suspecteth it, and find no good in it. Temujin, my love, I do not ask thee to break thy sworn oath of brotherhood to Jamuga, but because I worship thee I must warn thee to trust Jamuga little, and to watch him ever."

Houlun had heard these words, and her face had become inscrutable as she looked at her son. But she said only: "Bortei sayeth well."

Temujin had then gone to Kurelen, and had told him what his wife and mother had said. And Kurelen, after a long silent moment, had asked: "Dost thou truly suspect Jamuga?"

"Nay," Temujin had replied impatiently, but involuntarily looking away.

Kurelen had smiled and shrugged. "I know thee well, Temujin. Thou dost listen to others only if thou hast already agreed with them in thy heart. I have nothing more to say."

Temujin lay down on his couch, and continued to scowl in the darkness. He never lied to himself. He thought: Am I ready to distrust Jamuga because he doth irritate me? Am I ready to find him treacherous, because he doth irritate me? Am I ready to find him treacherous, because his ways do not coincide with mine? Have I become so foolish that I find faithfulness only in those who say to me: "Yea, lord"? Who is there to trust?

And his heart replied honestly: Jamuga, only.

He made an impatient gesture, and forced himself to sleep.

Jamuga slowly walked under the stars. Their fiery white light illuminated all the vast grassy steppe. He saw the mounted sentries against the heavens, motionless like statues. Another horseman was in conversation with one of them, and he saw that it was the nokud, Chepe Noyon. Chepe Noyon greeted him with his gay dimpled smile. Jamuga halted and looked at him earnestly.

"Thou hast returned, then, Chepe Noyon. How many of our warriors died in defense of the last caravan which paid us tribute?"

Chepe Noyon smiled, but his merry eyes narrowed. He looked at Jamuga from his horse's back.

"Ten, Jamuga. But why?"

But Jamuga did not answer. He bent his head and went on. Chepe Noyon followed him with a speculative glance, pursing his lips. He thought Jamuga rather stupid, but had no personal animosity towards him, knowing the singleness of his devotion. He said aloud: "There is trouble in that heart. And when a man hath trouble in his heart, let his friends beware."

He added thoughtfully: "There are many who envy Jamuga's place." He felt no regret. Gay and affable and opportunistic, he, like so many charming men, was completely selfish. He knew the malicious rumors about Jamuga, and knew they were lies. But for his own advancement he would not brand them as falsehood. He had, he told himself, his own progress to consider. Let events take their course.

Jamuga returned to his solitary yurt. He lit the beautiful silver and crystal lamp which Temujin had given him. He opened his carved chest and withdrew his most treasured Chinese manuscript, and began to read, sitting cross-legged on a low cushioned stool, his face bent and brooding, carved in light and shadow by the lamp.

"Let a man seek virtue, and he will find wantonness. Let him seek honor among men, and he will discover himself in a den of thieves. Let him seek God in the world, and he will find nothingness. Let him search for a just man, and he will find a bloody sword. Let him cry for love unto the hearts of men, and hatred will answer. Let him seek in the places of mankind for peace, and he will find himself among the dead. Let him call unto the nations for truth, and falsehood and treachery will echo him. But let him seek all goodness in himself, in humility and gentleness and faith, and he will see the face of God, and will find all the world arrayed in light and mercy. And then, at last, he will no longer fear any man."

Jamuga closed the manuscript. He gazed somberly before him into space. And then, one by one, the tears slowly filed their way down his cheeks. But his quiet eyes were full of sad tranquillity.

He said aloud: "I agree with Temujin that unity is necessary among the warring tribes. But it need not be a unity forged by force and violence, but by trust and honor, and the voluntary consent of all, seeking only pastures and peace, and not conquest and tribute."

chapter 9

Targoutai-Kirltuk and Todoyan-Girte, brothers and Taijiut chiefs, held a consultation together, filled with alarm and fury.

"That young red-haired dog, our kinsman, hath become wondrously arrogant and powerful. It is said that Toghrul-Khan, the old plotting fox, is aiding him. Before he groweth more in power, we must destroy him."

Targoutai, as he spoke, rubbed the old aching wound in his thigh, which Temujin had inflicted.

Todoyan-Girte scowled. "It is we who are old, and have not seen an opportunity. Why did we not seek support from the traders and townsmen and merchants, and offer to protect their caravans? We lacked wit, Targoutai. Let us, as thou dost say, destroy Temujin, and make treaties with the cities, as he hath done. We are still stronger than he. Oh, Targoutai, thou art to blame, thyself, for not slaying him when thou didst have the chance."

Targoutai gritted his teeth. "Let us go. I ask only that Temujin be left for mine own hand, and I promise thee he shall not escape again!"

Todoyan-Girte bit his lip reflectively. "We could, mayhap, secure him as a vassal, for he hath intelligence and valor, and knoweth how to rule men. Well, scowl at me not so fiercely, brother. He shall be thine to do with as thou wilt." He added: "But will not Toghrul-Khan then become our enemy, if we murder his loving foster-son?"

Targoutai laughed harshly. "I know the pious old wolf! He will greet us as brothers, no matter what we do, if we are all-powerful, and can protect his caravans!"

The Yakka Mongols now consisted of fourteen thousand warriors, powerful and single-hearted and devoted with idolatry to Temujin. Never had a chieftain inspired such love, such superstitious worship, such profound obedience. For he was just if cruel, and they knew his word could be trusted. And he had made them believe that at the last he was only their servant, and lived only for their welfare.

Within a short space of time he had attacked, conquered and absorbed small weak clans belonging to the Merkit, the Naiman, the Uighur, the Ongut, the Turkomans, and even the

Karait and the Taijiut tribes. Resistance had been slight, for his energy, his ruthlessness, his courage and ferocity travelled before his horde, like the scent of a beast travelling on the wind. There had been little sullenness, little rebellion and hatred because of his conquest of these small clans. For he was kind and just to those who swore allegiance to him, and he frequently assured them that he had conquered them not to enslave them, but to unite them in one formidable and resistless whole. Generous, never breaking his word, chivalrous when the purpose served him, meting out punishment and reward with equal impersonalness, handsome and vigorous and sleepless, the new members of his increasing ordu soon came to regard him with idolatry. Here was a strong leader who always knew what he wanted, and feared no man. Here was a man who made promises, and fulfilled them. Soon they felt overwhelming pride that they belonged under the banner of the yaktails. Soon they boasted arrogantly that their new lord was a lord indeed, who had conquered them because of his love for them, and his solicitude for their security and fatness. They would have died for him, and constantly sought out occasions to prove their faithfulness and affection.

Too, his system of the nokud served, by removing him from intimate contact with his people, to endow him with a remote and superstitious aura. He came among them each day, but surrounded by the lances and swords of his military bodyguard, a king moving among bronze-faced princes, his glance like that of an eagle, his bearing like that of a great conqueror. He knew that familiarity dulled the edge of the strongest sword, that when a king laughs with his people they end by laughing at him. So he was aloof from them, and never laughed with them, never joined in a common feast. And therefore, they adored him. Even their knowledge that he would not hesitate to order their death for the slightest infraction of tribal rules merely served to intensify their awe and worship. He knew that above all other things the simple must have an idol, and it must be an idol they can see and hear, and not some abstract and invisible spirit which their childish imaginations could not encompass.

He knew now that Jamuga's belief in the innate integrity and sanctity of each man was the dream of one removed from reality, and without the understanding of men. He told himself that only a fool believed that the simple man had a deep human pride and independence and inaccessibility, and was possessed of reasoning virtue. Experience had convinced him that men wished a stronger man to decide all things for them, to command them and not consult them, to say "Thou shalt," and not "Shall we?" He knew that individual responsibility irked and confused and frightened the simple mass of men, and that all they wished was guidance, protection, duty and an idol. The leader who consulted his people was a leader who is not respected, but even regarded with contempt. His reasonableness marked him among his people as a weak creature, not deserving of honor and fidelity. Law and not reason was this dais upon which the real king set his throne, knowing that the sword has more power when it is wielded without explanation.

Years later he said to a Persian historian: "I was but a youth when I realized that capriciousness is the fatality of a ruler. At all times his people must know that his laws are undeviating, and that a certain action will bring a fixed and certain result. This doth bestow upon them peace of mind and tranquillity. Like children, the capriciousness of an unpredictable ruler doth afflict them with bewilderment and fear, and by demanding of them the act of thinking, doth make them feel that they stand on shifting sands covered with treacherous water. Let a ruler despise the souls of his people, and drive them with his whip into good pastures, and they will bow down before him and call him lord indeed."

Kurelen continually marvelled and smiled at the amazing prescience of this youth of little experience. Finally, he spoke about it to the Shaman. Kokchu inclined his head, and smiled also.

"Kurelen, I must thank thee much, in truth, that thou didst persuade me to remain and enjoy thy conversation. For I have discovered that Temujin is a man of power and destiny, as thou once didst say. But thou hast asked me how he knew all the things he must do, and in return I can only answer that mayhap there are gods in reality, and that they whisper their wisdom to him. Once a Persian priest told me: 'God doth decree the tides that sweep over the souls of men, and doth set on those tides the soul of one great man, like a ship that rideth on mighty waters to some predestined land.' "

Kurelen said: "Thou didst prophesy what he would do. And now thou dost believe thy prophecy."

Kokchu, with a straight face, replied: "Mayhap the spirits put the prophecy in my mouth."

Kurelen ordered wine, and they drank a toast to the young khan.

Kurelen then said: "Once I told Temujin that he had the

light of destiny in his eye. He believed me. Mayhap opportunity is merely the handmaid of belief. He who believeth in himself hath won the first and the last battle."

"He is master of men and priests," remarked Kokchu, with malice. "Nay, do not believe that I am resentful because I am the first of his servants, and he doth tell me the decree of the spirits of the Blue Sky. When a priest is master of a people, then that people is both treacherous and impotent. I prefer to serve rather than to be served. It doth bring me more peace of mind, and at the end, more pleasure."

Kurelen, smiling, said: "The first desire of man was pleasure. And, if he is wise, that is always his desire."

One morning Temujin was breaking his fast with Kasar, Subodai, Chepe Noyon and Jamuga, whom men called "the four Knights of Temujin, the four silver hounds." A messenger, spent and bleeding and panting, was admitted to his yurt, and threw himself, breathless, at Temujin's feet. When he could speak, he cried:

"Lord, the Taijiut, led by the two brothers, Targoutai and Todoyan, with thirty thousand horsemen, are moving down upon thee, swearing that this day thou shalt die!"

The four knights paled, sprang to their feet. Then instinctively, they glanced at Temujin, awaiting orders. But Temujin had tranquilly resumed the breaking of bread. He held out his cup to Chepe Noyon, who, amazed, filled it. Then Temujin gave the cup to the fainting messenger, and forced him to drink. He said at last: "How far are they from us?"

The messenger wept. "Before the sun is high in the heaven, but near the zenith, they will be upon us."

Temujin shrugged, lifted his eyes, and smiled palely at his disturbed nokud.

"Then, why do we not finish our meal?"

One by one, still pale, they resumed their places about him. He gestured to them, and they forced themselves to be quiet, and to continue their meal. He helped himself to more food, and seemed engaged in peaceful thought. Finally, he looked at them again, and said:

"Last night it was unseasonably cold. We must move faster to our winter pastures, lest the snow and ice be upon us like wolves. Though this valley is sheltered, there was a web of ice upon the stream even when the sun was high yesterday."

No one spoke. They exchanged perturbed looks. But the discipline of their lord had eaten into their souls, and they waited. Jamuga was whiter than any of the others, and the eye he fixed upon Temujin was sad but resolute and calm.

The meal finished, Temujin rose and went out under the high colorless sun. The grass of the long valley was already turning brown. Thousands of horses, sheep, goats, and cattle, and a few camels, were pasturing upon the grass. Morning campfires burned before the city of tents. The cries of the herdsmen rose in the clear air to the clear wan sky. As far as the eye could see, there were only the peaceful herds, the peaceful women, the playing children, and the busy warriors sharpening their swords, wrestling, grooming their stallions and mares, and practising marksmanship with their bows, and laughing boisterously. Temujin looked at it all, and reflectively cleaned his teeth with a straw. Behind him stood his four knights, composed but ready, and awaiting his orders.

No one knew what he was thinking. But in reality his brain was roiled with sharp thoughts. At first he contemplated flight, knowing how he was outnumbered. But to fly meant the abandoning of the herds, the treasures of the clan, the women and children—the loss of everything he had gained. To remain and fight would probably result in being completely surrounded, his warriors murdered, and himself taken prisoner for a worse fate. He faced almost inevitable destruction, however he decided. He glanced at the sun. Within a short time, now, the Taijiut would be upon him, and he must act at once. Instantly, his tall composed figure seemed imbued with fiery life. He turned to the nokud and issued a brief command.

The nokud inclined their grave heads, ran from him, calling commands in loud peremptory shouts. He then went quickly, but without particular haste, to the yurt of his mother. There he found Houlun supervising the preparation of the morning meal for her women servants and the young wife, Bortei. For Bortei was experiencing the wretched nausea of her condition; too, she cared little for household affairs, and believed that she must reserve the energies of her mind for more important matters. At this moment, she was still in her yurt, next to Houlun's, fast asleep.

Houlun, seeing her son, frowned at him coldly, and said: "Thy wife is still aslumber, while I prepare what thou wilt eat, and thy haughty nokud. If thou wert not still enamored of her body, thou wouldst go to her and deal with her severely."

Temujin smiled slightly, and laid his hand with affection on his mother's arm, admiring, even in that moment, her queenly carriage, her beautiful head and smooth face, and neatly braided gray-and-black hair. Widow and mother of a lord of a barbarian horde, she conveyed the impression of noble bearing and blood and great dignity. When Temujin touched her, she winced a little, and withdrew from him, remembering Bektor who had been killed for no reason which seemed valid to her.

"What wouldst thou have with me, Temujin?" she asked. Never again would she call him son, and never again would her eyes warm with love for him. But her astuteness warned her that he came to her now on no trivial mission.

"Mother, we face the gravest crisis of our life. Within an hour the Taijiut and my loving kinsmen will be upon us. Before the sun doth slope to the west, we shall be conquerors, or conquered, and I shall be dead. Listen carefully to my commands, and do thou gather up the women and tell them what to do."

She bowed her head in haughty submission, and then listened attentively. But even while one part of her alert brain listened, she thought with another, and with fear: My brother! This thought made her face pale, her eyes distend and her lips dry.

When Temujin had done, she fixed her gaze intently upon his face, which the strong pale light of the morning seemed to illumine. He had loosened the neck of his coat, and she saw, below the skin bronzed by sun and wind, the milk-white flesh which had been sheltered from them. She saw how his eyes, usually gray and opaque, had turned to the green-blue color of a winter sky. And she marvelled at his calm expression, his calm unhurried voice as he issued his commands. Involuntarily, she thought: This is no ordinary man to which I have given birth! And she saw how his red hair flamed beneath the round fur hat, and how like dark stone were his broad cheekbones, and the harsh planes of his strong face, and how firm and vital was his slender tall body.

"What thou dost command shall be done at once," she said, and though her words were humble, her tone was not. She watched him walk away, and bit her lip.

He sprang up upon the platform of his wife's yurt, and entered. Bortei slept on her fur-strewn couch, her little hand under her cheek, her hair streaming over her shoulders and over the bed. She smiled as she slept, wantonly, and with a sort of voluptuousness. He stood beside her and looked down at her for a long moment, watching how her high and rounded breast moved with her breath, and how lovely was the curve of her small thigh, and how thick were her black lashes as they lay on her childish cheek. And then he looked away from her and sighed, remembering a woman who had never left his thoughts, a woman with golden hair and red lips and misty eyes.

He withdrew his dagger and held it in his hand. Then he gently awakened his wife. She woke simply, and completely, like a child. She smiled at him, languorously lifted her arms. He knelt beside her and kissed her throat, and then her mouth. But seeing his eyes, she ceased to smile, and sat upright.

"What ailest thee, my lord?"

He told her. And as she listened, she turned white, even to the lips. He laid the dagger beside her, and she looked at it, as though fascinated.

"If I am killed, and thou and the other women are made captive, thou must give me thy promise now that thou wilt sink this dagger into thy heart, and that thou, my wife, shalt never occupy another's bed, and that my child, which thou dost carry in thy womb, shall never be the slave of the Taijiut."

Her eyes widened; she paled even more. She could not look away from the dagger.

He took her into his arms with a passionate movement, and kissed her wildly. "Bortei, my love, my wife!" And yet, under his lips he dreamt that he kissed another woman. After a moment, she returned his kisses abstractedly, looking sideways at the dagger.

He released her. "Bortei! Thy promise!"

She smiled at him, rested her arms on his shoulders, and looked clearly and candidly into his eyes.

"My lord, didst thou think I would do otherwise, even if thou hadst not commanded me?"

"Thou hast spoken like the wife of a khan, Bortei, and I love thee!"

He picked up the dagger and put it into her hand. Her fingers winced from the touch of it, but she assumed a brave and resolute expression, and gazed at him fearlessly.

He kissed her again, then left her abruptly. She sat alone for some moments after he had gone, smiling fixedly. Then she glanced at the dagger. Her face changed, became cruel and contemptuous. She flung the weapon from her and it fell at some distance; she grimaced.

"I am the wife of a fool!" she exclaimed aloud. She lay back on her bed, and stared at the rounded roof of the yurt. Through its opening she could see the fierce blue sky, shining with the sun. She smiled. She moved voluptuously on her bed. She twined a strand of her hair about her fingers. Her smile widened, became languid and wanton. She smoothed her hands over her beautiful young breasts, and wondered if Targoutai would admire her, and whether he would make her the chief of his wives.

In the meantime, Temujin had gone to the yurt of his uncle, Kurelen. The Shaman was with him. They seemed excellent friends these days. They were enjoying breakfast, and chaffing each other. When Temujin entered swiftly, they looked up at him, and smiled, but seeing his face, they smiled no longer.

He told them the story. Kurelen's face seemed to wither; his lips twitched. He laid his hand on his dagger. The Shaman paled; his eyes dropped before Temujin's. But neither he nor Kurelen spoke.

Then Temujin said to his uncle: "If I never see thee again, Kurelen, remember that I have loved thee."

Kurelen replied gently, looking at him steadfastly: "Thou shalt see me again, Temujin. Never have I regretted so much until this day that I can give thee nothing but my blessing. It is not worth much, but thou hast it."

Temujin knelt before him and took his hand, pressing it. "I know I have it, mine uncle." And he lifted the dark and twisted hand to his lips. Kurelen's contorted mouth quivered. He had not shed tears since his childhood, but now tears rose to his eyes, like liquid fire. He felt like a father whose only son was about to face death. And he thought: In spirit, he is indeed my son.

Temujin rose to his feet again, and turned to Kokchu. "Do thou come with me at once."

The Shaman, still without speaking, rose and followed Temujin out of the yurt into the blazing sun of approaching noonday.

The valley was long, if somewhat narrow. Now the pillared red hills in the distance, and the terraced bleached white ramparts to the east, quivered in the intolerable light. The nokud had not been idle. Each had his standard, and under this standard, which differed in color only from Temujin's banner of the nine yaktails, he had gathered the men under his command. Great activity was prevailing. The kibitkas with their yurts were in rapid motion, and hot yellow dust hung over everything. The herds filled the sharp bright air with deafening cries.

Behind the camp was a dense wood of fir and dead poplars. This formed one side of a rough square. On another side of the square one nokud had drawn up his men into a squadron, the first rank wearing heavy plates of iron armor, fastened together with thongs. They wore helmets of armor or of lacquered leather. Their horses also wore breastplates of armor, and their chests, legs and necks were covered with leather. The warriors carried little round shields of leather, and lances, and hard sticks bearing curved hooks on the ends. Their lariats hung from their saddles. Behind this first rank were the other warriors, lighter and quicker, and not armored with iron, but protected by leather, and carrying javelins and bows. Their horses were small and nimble, and between the ranks of the armored men were open spaces, through which the quicker and lighter-clad warriors could break upon signal. These men, also at a signal, were to ride ahead, leaving the heavy-weighted warriors to protect the village. Each rank numbered five hundred men.

Each nokud had drawn up his men on the other two sides in like manner. In the center of this square of living warriors had been driven the herds, the women and children, the herdsmen and the kibitkas. The boys had been given arrows and lariats.

Outside the square, Temujin now gathered up his own picked men, double squadrons of a thousand, ten deep. These squadrons rode ahead to the neck of the narrow valley, and were prepared to meet the first onslaught. There were only thirteen units of them, and the Taijiut, Temujin knew, had sixty bands. But these sixty bands had first to face the bottleneck of the valley, guarded by Temujin's dense squadrons. Here numbers would not count so much as courage.

All was now ready. Everything had been accomplished with amazing speed and a minimum of confusion. Dust hung over everything like a yellow pall. But there was little noise. Temujin saw only stern dark resolute faces wherever he looked. Behind the living armored walls of the square he saw the thick city of the yurts.

Temujin left his squadrons, and rode swiftly on his white stallion towards the square. He saw how the sun was splintered on the lances and the swords and javelins and sabers. The warriors looked at him in hard alert silence as he rode by them, flashing his fierce green eye upon them, noting everything. In his hand he carried a curved Turkish scimitar. He approached a nokud, Subodai. He smiled at him briefly.

"I rely much on thine excellent cavalry, Subodai."

Subodai returned his smile with his clear and beautiful look.

"Thy trust will not be betrayed, O lord," he answered quietly. Temujin hesitated a moment, then leaned towards Subodai and kissed him upon the cheek. Every one was utterly silent. Tears rose to Subodai's eyes.

Then, in this deep waiting silence, Temujin galloped to

another side of the square, the hoofs of his horse loud in the dusty stillness. He came up to Chepe Noyon, whose gay face dimpled and whose eyes smiled. Temujin smiled also, a smile quite gay for him.

"Thou wilt play no pranks, Chepe Noyon," he said, laying his hand on the neck of the other's horse.

Chepe Noyon pursed up his lip humorously. "But I like to play with the Taijiut, lord," he answered, making his voice high and effeminate, like that of a petulant woman's. The dark faces of his warriors relaxed in a faint smile.

Temujin laughed shortly. He patted the neck of Chepe Noyon's horse and rode on.

He came to the last side of the square. Here his simple brave brother, the bowman, Kasar, stood mounted before his men. Temujin was silent for a moment, looking deeply and affectionately into his brother's eyes. But neither spoke. Temujin laid his hand momentarily on Kasar's hand, glanced swiftly at the warriors. Kasar fixed his gaze upon Temujin's face as one who gazes, rapt and fearless, at a god.

Then Temujin rode away. In a wide open space stood the Shaman, unmounted, waiting. Temujin nodded to him curtly. "Speak thou now to my warriors."

Kokchu faced the square. He lifted his hand solemnly. He stood there, tall, broad, magnificent, in his blue-and-white robes, his high pointed hat on his head. His eyes flashed in the sun; hie severe and handsome face was stern.

"Warriors of the lord, Temujin!" he began, and his voice echoed in the intense silence. "Today we face an ordeal of fire and sword and death. But ye must not falter, ye must not doubt, nor feel terror. For ye cannot be conquered. The spirits of the eternal Blue Sky have ordained that no man shall be victor over Temujin, their servant, their soldier. He who doubts, who turns and runs, shall be destroyed by the lightning of the spirits. For I tell ye again, that ye cannot be overcome, nay, not even if the Taijiut number a hundred thousand, and not thirty."

He lifted both his arms now, and blessed them somberly. They bowed their heads, and then, lifting their eyes, they looked devoutly at the shining blue glass of the heavens.

Temujin smiled wryly to himself, then galloped away to join his squadrons. He had, as his immediate officers, the nokud Belgutei and Jamuga. Belgutei smiled at him lightly as he came up. "We are ready, lord," he said to his half-brother.

Temujin nodded. "I see that. Thou hast done well, Belgutei."

He put his hand on the other's shoulder, and shook him affectionately.

He turned to Jamuga, and the two young men looked at each other in sudden silence. Jamuga's wan face remained impassive; his pale blue eyes were quiet and deep with reserved courage. He sat his horse straightly. In his hand was a naked sword.

Temujin thought: The man of peace is prepared to fight and die for me, with faithfulness and bravery as always, but his heart is not in it.

He was both irritated and touched, recognizing that Jamuga did not hesitate to violate himself, however he loathed doing so. He inclined his head before necessity, with bitterness and resolution. Fidelity was more to him, at least just now, than his own integrity and belief. He would fight for love of Temujin only.

Yet, for an instant, Temujin, influenced in spite of himself by the innuendoes of his mother and his wife, and the Shaman, doubted that love. And he thought to himself that men may die grimly for duty and necessity, but not as passionately as they would die for love. He asked himself: Why doth not mine anda love me as he loved me before?

He looked into Jamuga's pale eyes questioningly, and Jamuga looked back at him straightly. But Temujin could read nothing in those brave and quiet eyes. What would he have me do? he asked himself with contemptuous anger. And then he remembered Jamuga's words: "A man who doth make himself powerful doth become infested with enemies, as a camel becometh infested with lice."

He leaned a little towards Jamuga, and said lamely, merely for the sake of saying something to that grave, unspeaking face:

"We have a hard battle before us, Jamuga."

Jamuga's colorless lips moved, and he replied quietly: "There will always be battles, Temujin." Only he these days called his anda by his name, and not saying, "lord." Even Belgutei, his half-brother, did not address him by his own name.

Temujin nodded with gravity at Jamuga's words. And then, feeling somewhat nonplussed, he rode on. Jamuga followed him with his eyes, and in them was a great and mournful sadness.

Temujin rode to the head of his squadrons.

And now they waited in utter silence. The square walls of the warriors behind the squadrons of Temujin did not move. They might have been armored and colored mounted statues. Even the women and children and boys within the square were quiet. Nothing moved but the banners, fluttering in the wind, and the clouds, casting their rounded shadows fleetingly over the valley. Shadows ran over the red-and-white ramparts, and at times they looked like the huge façades of terraced, windowed and pillared temples and walls.

Everything seemed to wait. Even the horses, panting a little, and lifting and dropping their heads, appeared to know what portended. The sun glittered on the lifted lances and the swords and armor. Now the sun wheeled to its zenith, and the whole earth was inundated with light, unbearable and unshaking.

Suddenly there was a distant cry, the thunder of hoofs. All at once, between the passes of the cliffs, appeared the dark and galloping hordes of the Taijiut, the only things of motion in that vast raw radiance. They came on their swift stallions, brandishing their swords and lances and javelins, swinging their lariats, fixing arrows to their bows. Temujin watched them pour down into the narrow bottleneck of the valley. He marvelled at the endless stream of them, riding under the banner of the two chiefs, Targoutai and his brother. They came like waves of black ants, crowding up together, surging downwards. And then, all at once, they stopped. Their cries of triumph were halted. And again, the awful silence of the wilderness fell over everything.

For the Taijiut were struck dumb with confused amazement. They had expected to find a peaceful city of tents, unprepared and unsuspecting, the herds scattered, the campfires burning, the warriors unarmed. And now down below them they saw the huge thick square of waiting warriors and, ahead of this square, the massed squadrons of Temujin. Targoutai and his brother leaned forward on their horses, blinking their eyes unbelievingly, their mouths falling open, their foreheads wrinkling with rage. Behind them, in the narrow passes, halted by those before, stood the rest of the thirty thousand Taijiut. Seeing nothing but the backs of their silent comrades, they muttered bewildered questions to each other, and reared their horses.

At last Targoutai turned to his brother. "But after all, there are only fourteen thousand, or less, of them. Let us go on!"

He lifted his arm and shouted hoarsely. His officers answered in a wave of ferocious shouts, and lifted their swords. The shouts rang back from rampart and cliff. The horses struck down their hoofs in muffled thunder.

And then, like a flood of death, the hordes of the Taijiut roared down towards Temujin's squadrons, spurring their mounts, screaming like eagles. The sun flashed on thousands of dilated eyes, on thousands of naked swords, which were like mirrors reflecting the blinding light.

Temujin glanced at his two nokud, Belgutei and Jamuga. "Ready!" he said in a low voice.

Instantly, the lighter-armored men on their nimble horses sprang forward as though winged. A moment later they had mingled with the first onslaught of the Taijiut. Cataracts of arrows blazed through the air, which was filled with the scream of roaring horses and men, the thud of falling bodies, the clash of swords, the dull crash of weapon upon lacquered shield. The scent of blood rose like a stench. The confusion was indescribable. The dust rose over everything, so that one could hardly tell if the wild face and glittering eyes in the midst of it was foeman or friend.

Behind the squadrons, the nokud had given their orders to the warriors in the square. Now the lighter-armored men rode irresistibly through the gaps of their comrades, and advanced to the aid of the squadrons. Behind them, heavier, moved the iron-armored warriors, advancing at an implacable trot. The men ahead leaned back on their horses, swinging their lariats, bending bows strengthened with powerful horn, or launching swift light lances. No bow was bent or weapon wielded or lance sent on flight except at a particular object, and inevitably that object was reached and the foeman sent flying, shrieking, from his horse, to be trampled upon, or to be finished by one lightning swing of a scimitar.

The Taijiut, dismayed and confused, were at a disadvantage. For the thousands behind them were choked in the passes by those ahead, and the increasing mounds of those who had fallen. But because of their immense numbers, thousands managed to enter the valley and spread out. The Taijiut light cavalry, under the command of Targoutai's brother, wheeled orderly into position, and roared onwards in a mass, at a gallop.

They were met by the heavily armored Mongols, who were mystically without fear, and who knew they dared not retreat. They were armed with faith in the aid of the spirits. The Taijiut were armed only with lust and hatred, and courage.

Now the hills threw back waves of cries and thunder. The Taijiut, who had ridden far, had not been able to bring heavily armored men with them. Protected only by thick layers of leather, they were no match for Temujin's warriors. The Mongols, fleetly separating into small bands, whirled and wheeled, loosing arrows and lariats, dragging down foemen with their bare hands when at too close quarters for sword or rope or bow. Nothing could resist them. Up and down the narrow valley the struggle raged, the earth boiling with men and horses and banners. Alone in their yurts, the women huddled and prayed, and pressed their crying infants' faces to their breasts. The herds, resolutely guarded by the boys and shepherds, screamed and tried to stampede, but were held in check.

Temujin had given his orders long before. His men spread out, to encompass the Taijiut hordes in a thin battling circle. Implacably, they narrowed the circle, driving the enemy in on himself, so that he was choked by the crushing bodies and presence of his own men, and rendered impotent.

Temujin was in the very center of the battle. His arm, cutting down the Taijiut, did not seem to tire. He was a superhuman warrior, swinging his sword, standing up in his stirrups to strike down the oncoming hordes. He had a flesh wound in the shoulder, and his white coat ran with trickles of red blood. His cap had fallen from his head, and his red hair was like a flame in the sunlight. But whenever he glanced at his right, Jamuga was beside him, his sword flashing blindingly to protect him, his horse trampling those who had fallen, but who were rising on elbows to hamstring Temujin's horse with a sword.

Even then, in the midst of all that welter of death and blood and steel, and stumbling horses and shrieking men, Temujin could think: I was mistaken. He loveth me still. And the thought was like an exultation to him, and he laughed a little to himself, wondering at his own emotion. Once his eye met Jamuga's and Jamuga smiled faintly. There was color on his wan cheekbones, a light in his pale blue eye. And again, Temujin was touched by a small curiosity as to what this strange man of peace and thought was thinking.

Then all at once Targoutai appeared before him, wild-eyed and savage, a middle-aged man full of the kinsman's hatred for a younger man who was stronger and bolder than he. Targoutai knew that he would have no victory as long as Temujin lived, and that there could be no peace between them. The lordship of the barrens and the steppes was the prize, and one must die.

Temujin saw the mad gleam in the eyes in the narrow, bearded face, the mad glitter of teeth. Targoutai had courage and fierceness beyond other men, and he was also armed with furious hatred. Temujin saw the lifted arm with its bloody sword. He was so surprised at his kinsman's sudden appearance, and the madness in his face, that his own arm became momentarily paralyzed. He heard nothing, saw nothing, but Targoutai. He saw Targoutai's sword advancing towards his breast, and he knew that now nothing could save him, for he had wasted a precious moment.

Then, he sat, stupefied, in the welter of men and horses. For there sat Targoutai one moment, grinning insanely and swinging his sword, and the next instant a headless horsemen sat on his horse, his severed neck spouting little fountains of blood, the sword still in his hand. And then, slowly and with immense dignity, the spouting torso leaned sideways, and ponderously fell from the horse.

Temujin glanced to his right, his mouth dropping open with amazement. Jamuga was beside him, his sword dripping. And again Jamuga smiled faintly, wiped the blood away on the side of his gray mare.

"Again, thou hast saved my life!" exclaimed Temujin.

Jamuga did not reply. He merely swung his sword dexterously at those who continued to come on. But Temujin could see that he still smiled, as at some sad and ironic thought.

All at once the air was filled with crescendos of wild and exultant shouts. Temujin blinked, shook his head. The Taijiut, mysteriously knowing of the death of Targoutai, were in wild flight. As one man, thousands of them raced towards the passes between the ramparts, leaning forward upon their terrified horses, spurring their sides cruelly. The victorious Mongols shrieked with joy, pursued the fleeing foemen, cutting them down, dragging them from their horses with lariats, thrusting them through with swords, loosing arrows at them. Now terror had the enemy completely. Each man sought only to save his own life. Hundreds threw down their swords, and held up their arms in token of surrender. Only a few got completely away. As one, they believed that they had been conquered by demons, and not by men.

Five thousand Taijiut had been killed. Ten thousand and more were wounded, and still more thousands were taken prisoner. Among the prisoners was the brother of Targoutai, Todoyan-Girte. Three thousand of Temujin's best warriors had been killed. Kasar, himself, was terribly wounded. Several of the lesser nokud had died. And other thousands of Temujin's men had been injured.

Twilight had come, the west slashed with pallid and dazzling silver and scarlet fire. Tides of amethyst were running over the battlefield, which was heaped with the dead and dying.

Temujin had won his first major victory. The overlordship of the northern Gobi steppes and barrens was his. He had won because of the mystical superstition of his warriors, and because of their selfless courage and desperation. But more than anything, he had won because they loved him.

chapter 10

Temujin was wise, in that he never continued on from one important act to another without sleeping between them. That night he and his warriors and his people, and all the captives, slept the deathlike sleep of utter exhaustion. And during the night the vultures were busy with those who lay dead on the battlefields, and the wolves, and all the other denizens of the barrens.

Imitating Toghrul Khan, Temujin had a yurt fully twenty feet across, which he used for consultations with his officers, and the transaction of momentous business. Tonight, he slept there, and about his couch slept his five chief nokud, Kasar, Belgutei, Chepe Noyon and Jamuga and Subodai. Jamuga, his anda, slept beside him on the broad couch, under the same blankets. And this was for the first time in many moons.

Belgutei had said to Kasar: "The coldness between our lord and his anda is done and gone. Henceforth, nothing shall rise between them."

Kasar had replied, with a sour, jealous expression on his broad and simple face: "Jamuga hath no blood, but only milk in his veins, albeit he is valiant. But it is the valor of stone, which resisteth because it can do nothing else."

Belgutei had remained in thoughtful silence for some moments, and then he had said in the soft voice of a man who reflects:

"Men without blood are men without true loyalty."

Kasar, who out of his jealousy was inclined to listen to anything against Jamuga, exclaimed: "Thou dost not think he would betray our lord in the smallest thing?"

And again Belgutei affected to meditate. But he saw the face of his dead brother, Bektor. And then he replied: "Jamuga is ambitious."

He never said this to any one else, for he knew they would laugh in his face, at least so would laugh the nokud. But he had already said this to Houlun and Bortei, recognizing that where there is envy and dislike, there is always the eager willingness to believe. Now, he had said this to another such a one, knowing that jealousy is the handmaid of violence.

Kasar had gritted his teeth, and had said between them: "Let me suspect him in the slightest thing, and I shall cut him down with mine own hand!" And his simple face had become contorted with feverish hatred.

Before they slept, Jamuga had cleansed and anointed Temujin's wound. He had hands as deft and delicate as a woman's, and Temujin hardly felt any pain. For Jamuga was endowed with the gift of healing. There was some magic in his touch. After he had done, Temujin had smiled up in his face, as one who is greatly moved.

"The love and bodies of women are precious as rich perfume, Jamuga. But the love between a man and his friend surpasseth the things of the flesh."

Jamuga had paused only an instant in his ministrations. His head was bent. Finally he said in a strange, quiet voice: "I have never forgotten that, Temujin. I ask thee only to remember."

A sudden dark color had risen into Temujin's cheeks, but he had not replied. For a while he appeared disturbed. But later he had lifted the blanket on his bed, and had said, looking at Jamuga only, though his other nokud were there:

"As we slept under the shadow of the Mountain Burkan, let us sleep this night, for thou didst save my life again."

And that night Jamuga felt the soreness leave his heart, not entirely, but in a large measure. Temujin slept, but he did not. For, as he lay there, he thought: I must not sleep this night, but be happy, for my spirit doth tell me that never again shall I be flesh of his flesh as I am now."

He could rejoice, for Temujin had not gone to his mother, nor his wife, nor his uncle. He had gone only to his friend for ministrations.

But even while Jamuga lay unsleeping in the darkness, thinking his thoughts, sadness like the weight of a stone pressed down upon him.

The next morning Temujin appeared before the ranks of his victorious warriors, and received their triumphant and loving ovation. Beside him stood Jamuga Sechen, silent and wan as always, and behind him stood his chief nokud, and behind them, the array of his other officers.

Temujin, with dignity and calm, thanked his people for their devotion and loyalty and courage. "We are no longer a small clan, but a great tribe. My glory is your glory. My triumph, yours also. Ye have proved to me and yourselves that naught can resist us, for the spirits of the Blue Sky have given us their blessing. I, like you, await their further commands. In the meantime, let us rejoice. I ask no part of the spoils of this battle. It is all yours."

He ordered a tremendous feast. He knew the value of relaxation and gaiety, after struggle. Always was he solicitous for the welfare of his people, though only Jamuga suspected that this was expediency, and not from his heart. For once Temujin had said to him: "A General who doth not spare his men when they have had enough, and hath no care for the lighter things which they desire, is a General without understanding, and one to whom his warriors will give only sullen loyalty."

Seventy Taijiut chiefs, among them Todoyan-Girte, had been taken prisoner. They sat with their own warriors, in dark and despairing silence, listening to the rejoicing of the feast that night. They all believed that death would await them.

The next day, as Temujin sat in consultation with his nokud and his uncle, Kurelen, the Shaman came into his yurt, and made his obeisance.

"Lord," he said humbly, "the spirits have blessed thee indeed. It is only just that thou givest them a sacrifice in return."

Temujin winked slyly at his friends, but answered seriously: "And what dost thou suggest, Kokchu?"

Kokchu fixed his subtle eye upon him. "The lives of the seventy chiefs which thou has taken, lord." His thin red tongue touched his lips and wet them, as though he were relishing a good morsel.

Temujin frowned, and meditated to himself. The nokud exchanged glances. Then Subodai said:

"These seventy, particularly Todoyan-Girte, are a danger to thee, lord." He said this gravely, and with distaste.

Chepe Noyon shrugged. "It is always well to destroy the leaders of a pack, and allow the pack to witness the destroying. Then, they are terrorized. Unless thou dost desire to murder all of them, lord?"

Temujin did not answer. He turned his head slowly. His eye touched Kasar, who was eagerly waiting to speak. But Temujin's eye left him, and went to Jamuga. At this, Kasar's teeth and fists clenched.

"And thou, Jamuga, what dost thou say?"

Jamuga looked him full in the face and answered: "There hath been enough death. These seventy chiefs are brave and valorous. Reconcile them to thee."

Kasar had been about to say this very thing, but jealousy inflamed him now. He cried out, though Temujin was not looking at him: "A reconciled enemy is a treacherous friend! Kill them, lord!"

But Temujin was still gazing at Jamuga, who said quietly:

"Only a man who knoweth in his heart that he is weak killeth the enemies who have fallen into his hands. It is his own impotence which he feareth, and the violence he wreaketh on his captives is only an attempted violence on his own cowardice."

Temujin smiled, and Jamuga, looking on that smile which had something a little terrible about it, felt his heart sink wearily.

Temujin spoke with amusement: "Art thou suggesting I am a coward, Jamuga?"

The others murmured. Belgutei smiled secretly, and exchanged a glance with the silently raging Kasar. The Shaman, amazed and delighted, showed his teeth between his lips. But Kurelen, alarmed, frowned and bit a fingernail.

Jamuga saw no one but Temujin, and Temujin saw no one but Jamuga. They looked at each other in a silence that seemed to glitter like a bared sword. All color had left Jamuga's face. His light blue eyes seemed to sink far back in their sockets, as though with sudden exhaustion of the soul.

At last he said, almost inaudibly: "I have never said that, Temujin."

Temujin laughed a little. "But thou didst imply it, mine anda."

Jamuga's pale lips moved, but he was silent. He said to himself: Of what use is it that I speak?

Kurelen said, in a contemptuous voice: "Thou knowest well enough, Temujin, that Jamuga implied nothing of the sort. The man who playeth with the heart of a friend will soon discover that he is playing with a heart that hath died."

"Or with the heart of an enemy," smiled the Shaman.

Kurelen glanced at the Shaman, and shrugged. "At times thou are not the least subtle, Kokchu. Sometimes thou dost forget that thou art no longer the shabby, dirty shaman of a band of beggars." He turned to Temujin, and fixed his tilted eyes sternly upon him. "A real prince hath no time for cat-and-mouse games, Temujin, and he who doth indulge in them should confine himself to a little hearth fire."

Temujin laughed good-naturedly, though no one else would have dared speak so to him. He rested his arm on Jamuga's shoulder, which for the first time in his life did not respond to his touch. He smiled at his anda's cold and averted profile, which had become like stone.

"Jamuga, thou hast no sense of the ridiculous. I was but rallying thee. Learn to laugh. Thou knowest how I love thee."

Slowly, Jamuga lifted his head and turned his face to him. It was full of pale sadness and heavy despair.

"I know nothing," he answered.

A thick silence of consternation and surprise fell in the yurt. Temujin continued to lean his arm on Jamuga's shoulder, and Jamuga continued to gaze unsmilingly into his eyes. But Temujin's smile had become a little fixed. And then, at last, he removed his arm and looked away.

All at once Kasar sprang to his feet and drew his sword. He trembled visibly. He glared at Jamuga.

"Thou white-bellied coward and traitor! Thou hast affronted our lord, and for this thou must die!"

Temujin looked at his brother and began to laugh loudly, and after a moment all joined in the laughter except Kokchu. Temujin slapped his thigh. His laughter became raucous. He pushed his brother's side, as one pushes a silly child. Then, still choking with mirth, he said:

"Kasar, this is a momentous consultation, and not a yurt full of children. Go outside and play with the other little ones."

Panting, Kasar glared about him, from one laughing face to another. His breath became stronger; he trembled even more. He returned his eyes to his brother, looked down at him, the sword still in his hands. And then, touchingly, there were tears in his blazing eyes. He replaced his sword, bent his head, and left the yurt.

Temujin looked after him, his face sparkling with laughter. Then he turned to Kurelen:

"Thou alone hast not been heard from. What shall we do with the seventy chiefs, Kurelen?"

Kurelen lifted his brows, and looked at him with amusement.

"Temujin, thou hast already decided what to do, and thou need not flatter us that thou art really consulting us. But if thou hast decided to murder these seventy brave men, then I ask only that thou wilt spare me the revolting sight. I am getting old, and my stomach is not what it used to be." He turned to Kokchu, and tapped him on the arm. "It is strange, that the older a priest doth become, the more he lusteth for blood."

Kokchu replied coldly: "I am concerned only with fitting sacrifice."

"Then sacrifice that handsome Merkit wench of whom thou art so fond. The spirits, who are masculine, prefer a juicy morsel like this rather than the knotty flesh of hard-bitten warriors." He waited a moment, while the Shaman regarded him with alarmed and baleful eyes. "What! Thou art not willing to sacrifice a woman in gratitude for the victory of thy lord?"

Temujin, highly amused, forced his face to assume an expression of waiting sternness, and turned to the Shaman. Kokchu flushed a deep crimson hue. He began to stammer, addressing himself to Temujin:

"Lord, it would be an insult to the spirits to offer up a slave woman."

Temujin laughed, and all laughed with him. He rose and said: "Let us be done with this bandying. We have work to do." Kurelen and the Shaman were the last to leave. Kurelen turned to the Shaman with a quizzical smile.

"Dost thou still enjoy my conversation, Kokchu?"

Kokchu replied sourly: "Thou art always clever, Kurelen."

Kurelen tapped him familiarly on the shoulder-blade. "Be thou not too clever, my friend. When a priest doth err like that, he endeth up with a rope about his neck, the self-same rope he knotted for another."

Temujin had all the captives brought before him, the thousands of them, and their seventy chiefs. He stood before them, carefully scanning their faces, the sun like a flame on his red head, his gray-green eyes sparkling like sunlit water. At first they returned his scrutiny with looks of defiance and resignation and assumed contempt. And then, in spite of themselves, in that deep silence, they were impressed and afraid. They saw that this bronzed, lined face, though young, was the face of a king, harsh and powerful and full of inexorable strength. Too, each man felt that when Temujin looked at him he drew his soul in sudden slavish answer, despite himself.

Temujin began to speak, quietly and strongly, without hurry:

"Ye are my captives, overcome in fair battle. I hold naught against you, for struggle for existence and power is the first law of the barrens and the steppes, and only he who is victor doth deserve to live and rule. I am that victor.

"Search your souls, O Taijiut, in silence, and ask yourselves if you will enter my service with loyalty, selflessness and devotion. Ye are brave and fearless men, without hypocrisy or cowardice, and the answer ye give me I will know is true. Those who will not be mine must die. But fear of death is not one of your vices, and though ye know death may confront you, ye will answer me honestly."

He waited a moment, looking at those ranks of dark, inscrutable faces. Then he resumed:

"Thou knowest I have never broken my word to any man who was my friend and follower. I live only for my people. I am their servant. I conquer that they may be conquerors. Whosoever followeth me shall never be betrayed, and never regretful. The power of kings lies in their men. I desire men, not riches."

He now turned to the seventy chiefs. Foremost among them was his father's cousin, Todoyan-Girte, and he of all his people looked at Temujin with quenchless hatred and rage. His brother had been very dear to him. With his sorrow was mingled a burning humiliation and despair.

Temujin addressed each chief separately, saying: "Wilt thou swear allegiance to me?"

And one by one, after a momentary hesitation, each chief knelt before him and bowed his head in submission to his feet. As each man did this, their captive warriors murmured, until the murmuring was a dull thunder in the air. And slowly, as their chiefs knelt, so the squadrons of the Taijiut knelt, giving their submission with that of their chiefs.

Soon, the thousands were kneeling, and were silent, looking at Temujin with quiet, proud eyes, telling him with those eyes that he had conquered them because he was a great lord and they wished to follow him, and not because they were afraid.

But Todoyan-Girte did not kneel. He stood before Temujin, his face black with fury and contempt. They fixed their eyes upon each other in an intense silence, and every one watched them.

Temujin asked at last: "Thou wilt not give me thine allegiance, O kinsman?"

"Never!" cried the Taijiut with shrill violence. "Never, thou red-headed dog of a Mongol! Nor will I stoop to the shamefulness of pretense, and for the sake of my life give the scurvy son of Yesukai honor!"

Temujin slowly turned to the kneeling ranks of the Taijiut, to see how they were taking this feverish defiance and brave despair. But they were like men who were hypnotized, hearing nothing and seeing nothing but their master.

He bit his lip and knitted his brows as he turned again to Todoyan-Girte, who was panting heavily, his eyes full of black sparks. A look of admiration stood on the young khan's face, and also regret. He heard a whisper near his ear. It was Jamuga, and he was saying urgently: "Free him, and send him back to his ordu. He is a brave and honorable man."

Temujin looked at the others. Subodai's beautiful face was stern but unreadable. Chepe Noyon was smiling. Kasar was glaring at Todoyan-Girte. Kurelen's eyebrows were lifting, and he inclined his head. But Kokchu was wetting his lips avidly as he stared at the Taijiut chief.

Then Temujin withdrew his own dagger from his belt, and handed it by the hilt to the Taijiut. He smiled at him.

Todoyan-Girte stared stupidly at the dagger in his hand, and then at Temujin. His features jerked. For one moment he seemed overcome with despair. Then, still looking at Temujin, he deliberately raised the dagger and sank it into his heart. To the last, before he fell, his expression was one of indomitable hatred and contempt.

There he lay, dead and bleeding, in the wild, fierce sunlight that streamed down from the fiery blue sky. Thousands looked at him. The Taijiut were not disturbed or moved. More than ever, their slavish admiration for Temujin grew. They thought he had done a gallant and chivalrous thing. Only Jamuga, whose face was like marble, and Kurelen, who was pursing his lips quizzically, averted their heads.

Temujin, standing beside the body of the dead brave chief, lifted his arms and cried to all his people:

"Ye are mine, and I am yours! Follow me unto the ends of the earth!"

chapter 11

Temujin sent his old foster father, Toghrul Khan, the head of Targoutai, wrapped in silk in a basket of wrought silver. With this engaging gift was enclosed a letter, which Temujin had dictated to the literate Jamuga Sechen.

"Greetings, O venerable and revered father! It hath been many moons since I last sat at thy side, but in truth it doth seem many years, and I gaze back across the arid waste of time to those resplendent hours I spent with thee."

Reading this, Toghrul Khan made a wry face. He glanced distastefully at the silk-wrapped head, and pushed it aside with his foot. He continued to read, and as he did so, his features became sharpened and more wizened, as though sucked together by an acrid fluid. "Hah," he remarked, as he read.

"Thou didst have faith in me, and I have not betrayed thine astuteness. Thy power and thy glory have come from thy knowledge of men. Thou didst know me, O my father! And now I am overlord of the Northern Gobi, and have just begun.

"Thou knowest how safe are thy caravans. None hath been seized by marauders, because of my endless efforts. Thy last gift was munificent. For this I thank thee.

"I am sending thee the head of my kinsman, Targoutai, as a symbol that the sword of the Taijiut raiders and murderers and robbers hath been broken, and new caravan routes may be reopened through their former territory."

Toghrul Khan raised his brows, and mused with pleasant surprise at this. The new routes would save time and men for the traders and merchants, exceedingly much time. New markets would be obtained. New riches for his coffers. He absently lifted a sweetmeat from the gold and enamel bowl at his side and chewed with slow pleasure. "There is something in all this," he reflected. "Nevertheless——"

He continued to read. "Ofttimes caravans were about to be attacked, and then the word went forth: 'Temujin has guaranteed these!' And the marauders scattered like dust in wind, with cries of terror. My name is worth a thousand warriors to those who travel on thy business, and the business of those who have been kind and astute enough to trust, and reward me.

"I salute thee, O my father. I am thine to command. Thy son, Temujin."

Toghrul Khan sat in a deep aura of thought after he had finished this letter. Then his eye fell again on the silver basket containing the head of Targoutai. He grimaced. He thrust at the head again with his foot, and said to one of his servants: "Take it away. And, ah yes, fill it to the brim with silver coins. Nay, half silver, half gold, and a necklace of pearls wrapped in five lengths of cloth of silver embroidered with turquoises, for the wife of Temujin Khan. And tell my scribe to come to me at sunset, for a letter to my noble son, Temujin."

As the servant bowed deeply and was about to go, Toghrul Khan added: "And a herd of three hundred stallions for my son, also, to accompany the messenger and his bodyguard. One hundred fifty of the black, one hundred fifty of the white."

A gift for a prince, thought the slave, as he left the wide cool apartment of the old khan.

Toghrul Khan was spending the cool winter months in one of the larger Karait towns, for his rheumatism was annoying him again, and he was lamed by it. His palace was small, but perfect, for it had belonged to a bankrupt Persian noble, who liked women and gambling much too well. It was built in graceful, somewhat effeminate lines, of white marble, and its green gardens, filled with heavy trees and fronded palms and emerald pools and white bridges and many flowers, were the gardens of a poet. Awnings of striped red and white silk made spots of coolness on the hottest day, and the air was full of the singing of fountains and the soft laughter of the women of the harem. Toghrul Khan was a lover of silken black cats, and also of the fluffy gray Persian variety; they ran everywhere, meticulously attended by slaves.

One of them, huge and gray as a soft cloud, lay at Toghrul's feet, as he sat among his silken cushions in his own shaded apartments. Though the air in the gardens was balmy, and the sun hot, there was yet an edged breeze, and this his malady could not endure. His old withered legs were covered with woolen robes and furs, and a brazier burned warmly near him, upon which a slave would occasionally throw handfuls of myrrh and other sweet scents. The room was large and airy, the floor of blocks of alternating black and white marble, glinting dimly in the gloom. Behind him was a little colonnade of fluted white pillars, for the Persian noble had pretensions of old Greek elegance. This colonnade was open to the sun, and the light was a dazzling curtain through which shone the intense blue sky. The tops of green trees could be seen by the old man on his cushions, and he liked to watch them sparkling and moving in the wind. He could hear the gay laughter of the women, disporting themselves in the gardens, and the sweet and merry tinkling of music. Other rooms were partitioned off by thick curtains of crimson silk, fringed with gold. Behind the khan stood a beautiful brown female slave with rings of gold in her ears, which were reflected on her round cheeks. She was naked to the waist, and clothed downward therefrom in diaphanous silk spangled with jewels. She held a fan of ostrich plumes in her flexible hand, and moved them languidly, to keep the smoke of the brazier, and the flies, from the head of her master. Her reflection in the marble floor moved with her, and the jewels on her garment sparkled faintly. Her brown breast shimmered with her breath; her black eyes rolled and caught the reflected light. Sometimes she lifted a bare foot, and little golden bells jangled. When she yawned, her red, full lips revealed teeth as white and glistening as an animal's.

The room was filled with carved chests, heavy carved teakwood tables with legs cut to resemble the legs and claws of dragons, soft couches draped with silk, and cabinets of ebony and ivory. There were also small stools and tabourets of ebony. Scarlet banners hung against walls of marble. And on one wall hung Toghrul Khan's favorite cross, huge and gold and intricately pierced. At this particular time he was a Christian, though yesterday, upon the visit of a little sultan, he had been the most devout son of Islam. This morning a rich Nestorian bishop had called upon him, to discuss the condition of those of his people who were Christians. Toghrul Khan reflected that tomorrow he must be a Mohammedan again, for the first envoys of the Caliph of Bokhara were to call upon him to make the final arrangements for the marriage of Azara, which was to take place in four weeks.

Toghrul ordered the brown girl to draw the crimson curtains over half of the aperture that led to the little colonnade. He complained that the wind had veered, and was blowing upon his bald and yellow skull. When she had obeyed, he lay back on his cushions, and again gave himself up to thought. He held his cat in his arms, and stroked the pampered beast absently, with voluptuous touches. His eye wandered over the great room, and seemed to be interested in the jade-colored Chinese porcelain vases with their twisted arms, and the sparkling gold and silver boxes, and the crystal and silver lamps on the tables. One huge porcelain vase, half the height of a man and almost as wide, and exquisitely enamelled in lustrous green, gold and scarlet, stood against one section of a marble wall, and was filled with white and rosy flowers. This was Azara's loving task: to keep it filled for the delight of her father. The flowers exhaled a scent at once delicate and poignant, which could be discerned over the odors of the incense on the brazier.

Toghrul's eye continued to wander. Now it dropped to the floor, and appeared concerned with the rich shimmering hues of the small Turkish and Persian rugs scattered over the marble. But in reality he saw nothing but his own thoughts. Finally he clapped his hands with a dry, impatient sound, and a eunuch, huge and fat and naked to the waist, with a scimitar thrust through his silver belt, entered and bowed his head to the old man's feet.

"Send my son, Taliph, to me, at once."

Taliph was his oldest and favorite son, the first-born of Toghrul's first and favorite wife. He soon came to his father, a tall, thin, dark man, still youthful, with a narrow, sleek head and the crafty face of a priest. He imagined himself a graceful poet, but all his poetry was plagiarized from Persian poets, especially Omar Khayyam. But it was very skillfully plagiarized, and sometimes there would be a line, or a verse, that was original and clever, and so cunningly mixed with the borrowed phrases and stanzas that his erudite friends could praise it without too much hypocrisy. His dress was elaborate and somewhat effeminate, and he was given to many rings. But Toghrul Khan forgave him the poetry and the dress, for Taliph was evil and unscrupulous and wise and witty, and exceedingly subtle. Moreover, he pleased his father by his greediness and expediency, and because the old man could never deceive him.

Toghrul made him sit by his side, and himself poured a crystal goblet for him of spiced wine. As his son drank, he gazed at him with his usual fond amusement. He greatly admired the dark, narrow face, elongated and quick, and the alert and jerking black eyes, deep-sunken under a high, thin forehead. The cheeks were concave and heavily lined, giving him an ascetic and avid look, almost of interesting illness. Even in repose, the thin, wide mouth seemed twisted in a cruel and ironical smile. His rings glittered in the semi-darkness, and under the wide sleeves Toghrul suspected that there were gemmed bracelets. But he could even forgive this, looking at the competent dagger at his belt, and the strong, lean hands, so dark and long.

"What wert thou doing? Playing with the women, or writing poetry as usual?" he asked, trying to make his fond voice disdainful.

Taliph smiled, delicately wiped his lips. He regarded his father with disrespectful affection.

"Neither. I was taking a bath."

Toghrul elaborately sniffed, and grimaced. "Hah! So that is the source of the attar of roses! Why dost thou not try verbena for a change? I prefer it."

Taliph shrugged. "I still prefer attar of roses. They coincide with my moods."

"Azara doth like violets. I have discovered that women who love violets are much more to be desired than women who love roses. That is, if one only careth to gaze upon them. But wantons worship roses. Just at present, I prefer that Azara confine herself to violets. But then, she will never change to attar, I fear."

Taliph yawned. "Didst thou disturb me in my bath to discuss the preferences of Azara, and to comment upon her chastity?"

"Nevertheless, obliquely, Azara is concerned with my news. Here: read this letter I have received from Temujin, that barbarian and sweaty baghatur of the barrens."

Taliph read the letter. He began to laugh.

"Dost thou know what I think? This animal from the Gobi doth condescend to thee!"

Toghrul showed no resentment. He smiled with genuine amusement. "I thought that, also. Thou shouldst see him! But then, thou couldst not endure the smell. Even if he bathed in thy perfumed bath, he would still stink of horses and manure and sour milk and the arms of unwashed women. But yet there is something splendid about him. Splendor is often an attribute of strong wild beasts, who lurk in deserts and stony mountains. He hath a terrible eye of jade, and hair as red as a sunset, and a voice one must listen to, however reluctant and contemptuous."

Taliph cocked an eyebrow. "Nevertheless, he hath made thy caravans safe, and so enriched thee to twice thy former condition. My friends tell me that their fathers swear by him superstitiously. And from this letter, I would gather that he hath made himself a power among the hordes." He twisted his lips. "Pah! Those hordes! They are not men, but beasts. Once I thought I would compose an epic poem about them, but just at that time I smelled a score of the petty nobles visiting in one of the bazaars. Sometimes I wish I had not so sensitive a nose." He sighed regretfully. "It would have been a fine poem. The hordes against a red evening sky, on the gray and purple desert! Campfires, and primitive songs. Beautiful wild women on white stallions. But now I must admit they are but animals, who call themselves men by our courtesy. Once I thought I would visit them, and feel the winds of the barrens in my face, and afterwards compose a poem that would be sung down the ages."

Toghrul laughed. "If one wisheth to be sentimental, one must first hold the nose. But still, Temujin doth smell no worse than the small sultan who visited me yesterday. I should like thee to see him. From a distance, of course."

Taliph waited. He fixed his eyes intently on his father.

Toghrul sighed. "I have been trying to make up my mind whether or not I should have him murdered. Thou art astute. Thou hast already discerned what he is. He will continue to go on. Who knows but what he may eventually control all the Gobi? Who can then prophesy what may happen? I have encouraged and helped him, and so have my friends, because of our caravans. But will he be content merely with the barrens?"

"I think not," answered Taliph, coolly. "But thou canst secretly encourage other petty khans against him, and so keep him busy defending himself. Never let a vassal become too strong. The balance of power must remain with the master. But it doth take critical wisdom and judgment to know just how far to hamper a vassal. On one hand, he may be so enfeebled as to lose the master the gains he hath given him. On the other hand, his busy encounters with others secretly encouraged by the master may make him even stronger, and the final conqueror. Thou must be careful thou dost make a nice balance. Perhaps a peaceful confederation and agreement and exchange among all the petty nobles of the steppes? Confederations are excellent for the master, if they all throng under his banner for mutual protection and gain."

Toghrul shook his head. "Thou dost not know the hordes! Peaceful confederations cannot exist among them, except by violence and force. And the one who finally doth form them with such violence and force into a confederation is their real master. Then we of the towns will have good reason to be apprehensive. Remember, we are not dealing with civilized men, but with barbarians."

"There is really little distinction," observed Taliph. "All are amenable to profit. Why not suggest to this Temujin that thou art now well satisfied with what he hath done, and that he may now rest on his victories? Or his women? Tell him thou wilt see that he is maintained in his lordship over the northern Gobi, but that thou canst guarantee him no assistance if he doth endeavor to extend his domain. Thou dost know him: perhaps thou canst also suggest, with a little hint of reproof, that thou wilt countenance no further conquests, and that if he doth not obey thee, thou mayest even remove the support thou art already giving him."

Toghrul looked at him admiringly. "How astute thou art, Taliph. But what of the other merchants and townsmen? Will they follow me on this? Or will they, out of envy or enmity, continue to encourage Temujin if I remove my support? Can they be made to understand the potential danger of his unrestricted conquests?"

"There I can offer thee little encouragement, my father," replied Taliph frankly. "Fat merchants and tradesmen have no imagination. They are like overfed and avaricious sheep, without eyes. They see only the immediate profit, and will slavishly support him who doth promise them continued revenue. Most of them hate thee. They may make a deal with this smelly Temujin, and so engage him to seize thy caravans, and divide the spoils with him. There is no honor among merchants."

Toghrul was silent, but his little eye brightened. He and his son looked at each other vividly. Then Taliph laughed regretfully, and shook his head. "I am afraid that would do no good, my father. Once suggest to Temujin that he seize other caravans for thee, and he will have thoughts of thine, also. But I have an idea he is too clever to make enemies of thy competitors. He is apparently looking ahead to something else."

"That is what I am afraid of. Pah. What am I saying? Our towns and cities are well fortified, and our soldiers well trained. He cannot make himself that strong in one generation. And after I am dead, I will not care."

Nevertheless, he was uneasy. He gnawed his lip.

"I still think thou canst continue to give him rich gifts, and bind him to thee," said Taliph, after a long reflection. "Who knows? We have imagination, and can extend our horizon. The extending of horizons is easy in the cities, among townsmen. But this Temujin probably is incapable, after all, of far-sighted vision. Strong animals rarely realize their strength, and can always be stroked into submission by a skillful hand that doth also feed them well."

Again his father was silent. Taliph regarded him thoughtfully, and finally he smiled with delicious amusement.

"But thou dost hate him personally, dost thou not, my father?"

Toghrul's small and wizened face contorted into a malignant

if somewhat sheepish smile. But he said: "Thy subtlety doth imagine too many things. I can see, though, after this conversation with thee, that I dare not murder him. Our caravans would no longer be safe from the hordes. I have a thought: I shall invite him to be a guest at the marriage of Azara. Then thou canst study him at thy leisure."

Taliph affected to be alarmed. "But thou dost know I cannot endure stenches! Do not have him in the palace. Set up his tent outside thy grounds." He stood up and laughed lightly. "How absurd we are, in truth! We have vast armies of soldiers. Behind us, we have the huge empire of Cathay, with her legions. We have been indulging in daydreams. However, bring this Temujin to me, and let me see him. Mayhap I may write a poem after all. About him, with my finger and thumb on my nose."

And so it was that the next day Temujin's messengers were dispatched with the rich gifts, and a gracious letter of invitation for Temujin to attend the wedding ceremony of Azara of the wondrous pale hair.

Toghrul Khan, laughing to himself at the nightmares his imagination had conjured up, thought: The Gobi is vast. No one can conquer the extent of it. No one man in his own lifetime. And even if he could, what barbarian chieftain would dream of attacking mighty Cathay, and the Khwarismian Empire, and all our mighty Turkoman cities? He would be crushed like a presumptuous fly. I am an impotent old man, and have grandiloquent dreams of what I, myself, might like to do. if God gave me countless legions.

But nevertheless, he slowly resolved in himself that the day would soon come when he must destroy Temujin, not because of any fear of him, but because of his hatred.

We arm those we hate with supernatural weapons, and cower before them, he thought. And so, at the last, it is not they who conquer us, but ourselves.

chapter 12

On a certain day Temujin had two reasons for rejoicing and exultation. The most important, for the moment, was the birth of Juchi, son of Bortei. The second was the arrival of the jubilant messengers with the gifts of Toghrul Khan.

It was dawn when Houlun, her graying hair covered with her hood, aroused her son and told him that his wife had given birth to a man-child. She stood there as she told him, a lamp in her hand, her gaunt heroic face carved into black harsh planes by the dim light. Her gray eyes looked out at him gravely and inscrutably, from under the narrow ledge of her brow. Her tall magnificent body was held with her old pride and dignity, the heavy folds of her garments following each line of thigh and breast. She was a priestess announcing strange things.

Temujin, with a cry of joy, rose at once and threw a fur cloak over his shoulders. Bare-headed, he ran out into the first mysterious light of the morning. The disturbed dogs began to bark. He flung himself into his wife's yurt, and found it full of ministering women. Bortei, spent but tranquil, lay exhausted on her couch, and watched a serving-woman as she anointed the squirming naked body of the baby. It was a strong child, and shouted indignantly, though he was barely an hour old. By the light of the tallow lamps Temujin looked at the child, and saw an angry red face, a big round head covered with wet black hair, and the broad chest of a future soldier. He thought to himself: Is this my son, or the son of another? He knew he would never know. But all at once this was insignificant. It was a child, and probably the fruit of his own loins, and a fine fellow. That was sufficient to the man-hungry Mongol.

He seized the child from the arms of the woman and gazed at him with humorous delight. The baby stopped his shouting; his voice died to a whimper. He was as blind and unconscious as a new-born kitten, but Temujin was certain that he looked directly at him, and with recognition.

"What shall we call my son?" he cried.

The serving-women exchanged furtive and knowing glances, but were silent. Bortei smiled languidly. And then Houlun's voice came strongly and harshly from behind her son, and every one was startled and taken aback, for no one had heard or seen her enter.

"Call him Juchi!" she exclaimed.

Juchi! The Shadowed! They stared at her. She stood near the flap of the yurt, seemingly unusually tall and passionate, her face white with scorn, her eyes blazing. Bortei made a muffled sound of distress, and turned her head aside. The serving-women cowered before their mistress. But Temujin looked steadfastly at his mother over the squirming body of the child. His eyes were as green as grass in the lamplight.

"Yes, it is Juchi," he said in a quiet voice.

He laid the child on the bed. Bortei's arm flung itself protectingly about the child. Houlun, breathing rapidly and audibly, smiled maliciously as with some curious excitement, and stepped aside. Temujin laid his lips against his wife's damp forehead, to which tendrils of dark moist hair clung childishly.

"Do thou nurture my son in all diligence, my wife," he said.

And then, without a glance at his mother, he left the yurt.

The serving-women, embarrassed and afraid, began their clucking ministrations again. Houlun stood alone. She had pressed her hands against her breast as if to quiet some mortal pain. Her eyes were dark, and all the blaze had left her face, so that it was as cold and colorless as death.

She waited until the women had done, then approached Bortei's couch. The two women looked long and unshakingly at each other. Bortei smiled faintly. She had conquered. In her smile there was something triumphant and mean. But Houlun, whose lips were white and pinched, did not smile. She lifted the child in her arms, and gazed at it piercingly, with a sort of fierce sorrow.

"My grandson is a beautiful boy," she said.

And in Houlun's bitter but proud surrender, Bortei could find no further triumph.

The first sight that met Temujin's eyes as he left his wife's yurt was the arrival of the noisy messengers and the three hundred stallions. Warriors and women and children and herdsmen and shepherds came pouring excitedly out of their yurts to exclaim and wonder and shout with exultation. For it was a wonderful gift. The messenger proudly delivered the silver casket full of its treasures, and Temujin bellowed when he saw the contents. He commanded that Jamuga be sent to him, and went to his yurt, unrolling the sheet of parchment which contained Toghrul's message.

The sun was now a ball of flaming red on the eastern horizon. The campfires were lighted. The herds were being driven together in preparation for pasture. It was very cold, for winter had come, and now they must be underway for the new pastures.

The sky was already wan and high and chill. No longer were there geese travelling in a long line before the endless wind. The pools were heavily webbed with gray ice, and the river was silent. Over the rounded black tops of the city of the tents the smoke hung low and thick, like a cloud.

Jamuga came at once, reserved and quiet. He found Temujin eating noisily and vigorously, and was invited to join him. While a servant filled bowls with hot millet and milk, and covered a silver platter with steaming mutton, Temujin gave the parchment to his anda and impatiently waited to have it read to him.

Jamuga read in silence. When he had done he looked at Temujin with a strange expression. "I have been told that thou hast a son," he said.

Temujin was taken aback. He had forgotten, momentarily, though the knowledge of his paternity had hung like a rich warm curtain at the back of his exultant thoughts. "Yes, yes," he said, hastily. His smile was a little sheepish. To cover his embarrassment, he pointed at the parchment with a hand that clutched a huge fragment of mutton. "Read the letter," he commanded.

"Let me offer my felicitations," said Jamuga.

Temujin stared. "Eh?" he said. For a moment he wondered what delightful news the letter contained, that made Jamuga give vent to this sentiment. His face shone with egotism. And then it occurred to him that Jamuga meant the birth of the child. He colored. Then he laughed outright.

"It is a fine fellow," he said. He laughed again. And Jamuga, who had dreaded this morning for Temujin, began to laugh, also. They laughed together as at some vast joke, as only friends who understand each other can laugh.

"I have called him Juchi, the Shadowed," said Temujin. He grinned broadly. For a moment Jamuga became suddenly serious. And he thought to himself that he really did not understand Temujin at all, and the thought saddened him heavily again.

"But read the letter!" exclaimed Temujin. "I shall expire with curiosity."

Jamuga began to read in his low toneless voice:

"Greetings to my beloved son, Temujin.

"Thou hast accomplished great things, and the heart of thy foster father beats with pride and joy. Never has it expected less of thee, but it is good for an old man's heart if he be justified in his faith in his children.

"The gifts I am sending thee are poor in comparison with

the things thou hast done. The new caravan routes shall be opened immediately, and I know that these shall have thy protection also."

Temujin, chewing prodigiously, nodded. He said in a muffled tone: "The old buttocks! When a man no longer findeth a comfort in a woman's warm belly he doth satisfy his lust with gold. Let him have it!"

Jamuga's smooth brow wrinkled at this, but he went on evenly:

"In every city, in every bazaar, in every merchant's shop, in every palace and counting-house, the fame of Temujin doth rise like incense."

"Ha!" snorted Temujin. He spat out a morsel with a noise of contempt. "What a fame is this! To be sung of in the reedy voice of a castrated trader!" He had seized another chunk of mutton, and he waved it in Jamuga's fastidious face. "Dost thou know what I think? I think I shall have to boot these merchants about some fine day for the good of my soul!"

Jamuga sighed. "Dost thou wish to hear the rest or not?"

Temujin shrugged. "Oh, go on." He stuffed his mouth full, and looked at Jamuga with bulging eyes.

Jamuga's thin nostrils drew themselves in distastefully. He stared fixedly at the parchment, and proceeded:

"Even in the marts of Cathay have I heard praise of the dauntless Temujin, the friend of the merchant, the protector of the peaceful trader." Jamuga looked at his anda coldly. "Temujin, I must ask thee not to make such disgusting noises. Doubtless thou dost mean to convey an honest contempt. But my stomach is squeamish this morning."

Temujin chuckled. "I ask thy pardon. I shall listen to the rest in decorous silence. But who could help breaking wind at such hypocrisy?"

"I do not think Toghrul is hypocritical," said Jamuga in an icy voice. "He is truly grateful. After all," he added bitterly, "thou hast killed many men to make the caravans safe for the good traders." He rattled the parchment. His hands had begun to tremble, but his voice was still even when he continued:

"Thou hast given me great opportunity for rejoicing. And I have still another reason. Before the next full moon my daughter Azara will be wedded to the Caliph of Bokhara. I, therefore, for the sake of the joy which thou wilt give mine old eyes, invite thee to the wedding. Then shall my cup indeed be full."

Jamuga paused. He waited for some comment from Temujin. When it did not come, he glanced up in surprise. Temujin had paused in the very act of chewing. His face was bulging and expressionless. But he had turned ghastly. His eyes, fixed and brilliant, were the color of blue stone.

Finally he turned aside his head and spat out the food his mouth contained. He kept his head averted. He had fallen into an ominous silence. Jamuga saw his profile, ravenous like that of a bird of prey's. He saw the under lip caught in glistening teeth. His jaw jutted harshly, and the muscles about it were strained.

Jamuga was alarmed. He cried out: "Temujin! What ailest thee?" He put out his hand to his anda.

Temujin slowly turned his face to him. He smiled. He was still excessively pale, and his eyes gleamed and flashed. But he said placidly enough:

"We shall go to this famous wedding. But is there nothing more?"

Jamuga, disturbed, still stared at him, then reluctantly returned to the letter. "There is nothing else, except effusive assurances of his love and gratitude and his longing to see thee again."

Temujin filled his cup with wine and drank deeply. He again filled it, and drank. Then he stood up. "Yes, verily, we must go to this famous wedding."

chapter 13

He made all his preparations the next day, after the riotous feast of rejoicing over the birth of his son. He had drunk mightily, and had had to be carried to his yurt. But the next day he showed no signs of his dissipation either on his face or in his manner.

He consulted all his noyon, and his nokud. But every one knew, by now, that this was pure courtesy. He made all his decisions himself.

With him he would take Chepe Noyon and Kasar. He would leave Jamuga as khan in his place, ably assisted by Subodai. He would also take a few of his nokud, and a detachment of picked warriors. All at once he seemed in an enormous hurry. His voice became quick and strong and impatient. Sometimes he appeared to sink into profound and oppressive thought, from which he emerged with renewed irritation.

Kurelen said: "But is it not strange that thou dost leave Jamuga Sechen in thy place? Thou knowest his incompetence in the matter of organization and the understanding of men."

Temujin shrugged. "It is the least I can do for him," he answered.

Kurelen raised a brow at this extraordinary remark, but made no comment.

"Besides," added Temujin, "Subodai is here, and most of the nokud. Jamuga's part will be merely the place of honor. I have given orders that he is not to be taken too seriously, though treated with the most elaborate respect and reverence, as my representative. Subodai is subtle; the nokud are intelligent. Jamuga will never guess but that he hath supreme authority."

Kurelen smiled. Temujin, with his customary generosity, had given away all the coins in the silver basket. He had kept only the cloth of silver for Bortei. Kurelen had had a large share of the gift. Also, his pick of the white stallions. Kurelen brooded happily on all this. He had almost forgotten what he was talking about to his nephew, and heard him say, with surprise:

"Too, there is no one less vulnerable to the suggestions of a priest than Jamuga."

Then Temujin went to Kokchu, who had taken on flesh the last few months, and had become exceedingly fat.

Kokchu now had half a dozen younger Shamans to assist him in the mysteries of religion, and he had convinced them of his utter sanctity and omnipotence. His yurt was as big as Temujin's, and far more elaborately and richly decorated and filled. His women were quite as pretty and desirable, his robes woven of silk and embroidered wool, his chest crowded with treasures. He received Temujin with great ceremony and respect.

But Temujin spoke, as always, without preamble:

"Priest, stick to thy gods, and let better men manage worldly affairs. Dost thou understand?"

Kokchu affected at first to be bewildered, and then, seeing that Temujin only grinned at him, affected to be deeply wounded.

"Thou dost not trust me, lord," he said, in a low grieved voice.

Temujin laughed. "The day a king trusteth a priest that day must he look under his bed for an assassin." He tapped Kokchu on his fat chest. "Remember, no tricks."

There was a grim excitement about him, and soon it had infected the entire city of the yurts. The normal uproar became a long roar of confusion, in which every living thing attempted to be heard over all the others. Yet discipline was never relaxed. The nokud came separately, heard their brief orders, saluted, retired before the entrance of another. Subodai came and listened gravely, his beautiful face intent, his eyes fixed on his lord's stern lips. There was to be a high full moon tonight, and so Temujin intended to leave shortly after twilight.

Jamuga was the last to come. He seemed disturbed. He said: "Temujin, we should have left many days ago for our winter pastures. Now, we must wait thy return, no matter how long it be. This will work hardship on our people."

"I think not. They have plentiful supplies. The herds may not remain so fat. But that will soon be altered when I return. Besides, three caravans are to pass this way from Samarkand, and I have promised to protect them. But see that thou dost collect the reward before extending the protection."

Jamuga said nothing. But his perturbation seemed to grow. Temujin observed him with a quizzical smile. Finally Jamuga said with a burst of bitterness:

"Art thou not afraid to trust me?"

Temujin stared, then burst into laughter. He thrust Jamuga roughly in the belly with his clenched fist. "Cease thy childishness, Jamuga!"

The other man flushed painfully. Temujin looked at him, his whole face sparkling with savage mirth. He seemed about to say something more, but evidently thought better of it. So he merely laid his arm for a moment on his anda's shoulder and remarked that he still had considerable to do.

Jamuga left the yurt and pondered to himself the reason for Temujin's acceptance of Toghrul Khan's invitation. At this time of the year, and so soon after a precarious victory, it was a dangerous matter. Too, he was puzzled by the strange violence he had easily detected under Temujin's easy laughter and careful orders. His eyes, sharpened by love, had seen that violence, seething, throwing up gleams into Temujin's eyes, like the light that was thrown upward by troubled waves. Others might be deceived into believing that nothing disturbed the young khan, but not Jamuga. There was a wildness and madness beneath the surface of his competent manner.

Jamuga retired to his yurt, sat down, and pondered. He knitted his thin light brows, and returned to the past, when Temujin had been the guest of Toghrul Khan. Carefully, he went over each day. He remembered the night of the feast, and the appearance of Azara, with her soft black eyes and golden hair. Suddenly, his heart quickened. It was true that Temujin was susceptible to women beyond the susceptibility of other men, and he had openly and shamelessly betrayed his desire for the daughter of Prester John. His companions had joked about it, later. But there was nothing to wonder at in this memory, Jamuga decided.

But stay: perhaps there was. All at once he remembered yesterday, and the reading of the letter. He remembered Temujin's sudden pallor and the malignancy of his eyes, when he had listened to Toghrul Khan's invitation to the marriage of his daughter. "We must certainly attend this famous wedding!"

With a cry of alarm, Jamuga flung up his head. This whole foolish expedition had something to do with the beauty of a once-seen woman. What mad folly was Temujin contemplating? What suicidal plotting? What did he intend to do? Jamuga had long suspected the envy, the malevolence and hatred, of Toghrul Khan, and the foul hypocrisy. He had been afraid, all during that visit, that Temujin was in some monstrous danger. Some prescience had made him hear evil intonations beneath Toghrul's sweet and paternal voice. And now Temujin was risking the existence of his people, their safety and security, his own life and the lives of his friends, for some incredibly foolish plan of his own. What could he do? Jamuga knew him well enough to know that nothing would stop him once he had started, no advice, no pleading, no calling to reason. Did he contemplate seizing the daughter of the mighty Toghrul

Khan right from under her father's nose, in his own palace, among the thousands of his retainers? No, this was beyond even Temujin! But was it?

Jamuga hurriedly got to his feet and ran out, seeking Temujin. The blue and saffron twilight had fallen. The earth was swept in shades of umber, rose and yellow. In the distance, towards the east, there was a cloud of dust. Temujin was already gone. Jamuga stared at the cloud of dust, his throat drying, his heart beating with sickening pressure. Then he turned and went to the yurt of Kurelen.

Kurelen, he observed with distaste, was eating again, sopping up rich dark gravy from a bowl with a wedge of bread, and sucking noisily and with enjoyment as he did so. The faithful Chassa, a stout middle-aged woman now, with a big bosom and graying hair and a round placid face, was watching Kurelen's feasting with the indulgent smile of a mother. At intervals, she refilled the bowl with gravy and morsels of good mutton, and also refilled his silver goblet with excellent wine. She kept making solicitous noises, urging him to eat more, when he lagged in repletion. She frowned at the wan Jamuga when he entered, indicating by her manner that, now he had interrupted, her child would no longer stuff himself, to his sad lack of nourishment.

Seeing Jamuga, Kurelen invited him to join him. Jamuga refused shortly. He glanced sternly at Chassa, who stubbornly refused to see his glance, and again refilled Kurelen's bowl. Kurelen smiled, patted her cheek.

"I have enough, Chassa. And now, do thou leave us for a moment. But not for long."

After Chassa, with a scowl, had retired, Jamuga still refused to sit down and join the feasting. He stood beside Kurelen, and looked down at him with feverish eyes. Kurelen, for his part, looked up at the thin slight body of the young man, and also studied his pale and rigid countenance.

"What ailest thee, Jamuga? What misery is burning thy bowels now?"

He chuckled a little. He was increasingly amused by Jamuga. He was an old man now, more emaciated than ever, more bent and twisted. His straight black hair had turned a dull gray. His features were sunken. But his black eyes were as vivid and malicious as in his youth.

Jamuga said abruptly: "I do not know what assistance thou canst give me. But I must tell thee the truth: Temujin is enamored of the daughter of Toghrul Khan. He lusted after her openly, when we visited the camp of the Khan. Yesterday I read him the letter of Toghrul, in which he was invited to the marriage of this girl to the Caliph of Bokhara."

Kurelen cocked an eyebrow. "If I remember rightly, Temujin is continually becoming enamored of some wench or other. He hath a harem to inspire the respect of a minor sultan. I see no reason for thy perturbation."

Jamuga said inexorably: "When I read him the letter, he suddenly turned white as bleached wool. His eyes became full of violence, and evil. He was like a madman, trying to hide his madness. I am convinced he is going to this wedding in order to seize this girl."

He waited for Kurelen to make some exclamation or remark. But Kurelen merely fixed his eyes piercingly on his and said nothing. His expression was inscrutable. All at once, Jamuga was driven to frenzy by this silence and calm. He squatted down beside the old man, and gripped him by the arm.

"Dost thou not see everything?" he cried fiercely. "Toghrul Khan, the mighty ruler of the Karaits! The Caliph of Bokhara, lord of military legions and a hundred cities and limitless power and wealth! These are to be affronted, to be made the remorseless enemies of a small barbarian chieftain with a handful of warriors and a roaming band of women and children! They will kill him, and destroy us, as easily as a man steppeth on a hill of ants. Let Toghrul Khan give the word, and in a day we shall drown in our own blood. The whole Gobi will be on us like a sea of steel! All that we have gained through such suffering and hardship, such enormous pain and fortitude, lost for a woman's pink body and a man's uncontrollable lust!"

Kurelen turned aside his head and gazed thoughtfully at his bowl. After a long moment, during which Jamuga's thin panting filled the yurt, Kurelen picked up another wedge of bread, sopped it, lifted it to his mouth, and chewed. Then he slowly, still chewing, turned his face on Jamuga again, and the inscrutable expression was thicker in his eyes. But now there was a penetrating gleam in them, also.

He spoke softly: "Jamuga Sechen, Temujin hath made thee temporary khan in his place. What orders thou dost give shall be obeyed. Thou canst, for instance, give orders that we leave immediately for the winter pastures. If we move rapidly, and at once, we can be far from here by daybreak, and immensely far by the time Temujin doth commit his—folly. So far, indeed, that it would be hard to find us." He added, even more softly: "Thou art the khan, Jamuga Sechen."

A silence like that following a flash of lightning and a deafening crash of thunder filled the yurt. Kurelen's eyes shone like fire as they fixed themselves on Jamuga's rapidly paling face. He saw the sudden convulsive lift of Jamuga's thin and pallid lip. He saw the sudden flash of Jamuga's light blue eye. The student of men felt nothing but the most intense curiosity and speculation. He leaned forward a little, the better to see the young man in the gloom of the yurt. He smiled slightly. His whole expression became subtle and dark and watchful. He thought to himself: I have not been mistaken. In that cold and dedicated breast is the bloodless man's insane passion for power and mastery, which he believeth can avenge him on the world of warmer men.

Suddenly Jamuga stood up, as though pricked by an intolerable pain. He turned his back to Kurelen, as though he could not endure the reflection of himself in the knowing eyes of the old man. He leaned heavily against a high chest. His head was bent on his breast.

Kurelen huddled deeply in himself, as he squatted on his cushions on the floor. He began to smile with irrepressible amusement and enjoyment. He asked himself: Will Jamuga, in his aroused lust, find some noble excuse to follow my suggestion? He will always need a noble excuse, this man without violence and loins, to accomplish the passion of his pale but vitriolic heart! Never again shall he have this opportunity, and he doth know it! He must decide between a love and loyalty which have never brought him anything but humiliation and bitterness and envy, and a last chance of seizing what he hath dreamed in his soul in his nights of impotence and livid longing.

To Kurelen, the conflicts and struggles and battles that raged in a man's spirit were more entertaining and more exciting than those that raged about him in the external world. He knew to the utmost what Jamuga was suffering in his temptation, and he understood that if love and loyalty prevailed it would only be because Jamuga had finally conquered, subjugated and destroyed himself. And this death of the inmost heart would be a death indeed.

But he felt no pity, only amused curiosity and wry mirth.

At last he heard a deep, almost shuddering sigh. Slowly, Jamuga turned back to him. His thin and ghastly face was bedewed with cold moisture. His eyes were those of a drowned man, who had died in agony and despair. He staggered a little. He had to catch hold of the chest beside him to keep from falling. But his expression was quite calm, and when he spoke, his voice was also controlled and calm.

"Perhaps what thou hast suggested is the wisest course for all of us, Kurelen. But it cannot be. If Temujin doth perish in his folly, then we must perish, also. There can be no life for us if he doth die. He is our heart; we are only his body."

Kurelen smiled ironically. He studied Jamuga's face with a curious mixture of contempt and respect. He shrugged imperceptibly. He filled a goblet of wine and held it up to the young man. Jamuga took the goblet. It almost slipped from his nerveless fingers, and he had to seize it in both his trembling hands. He put it to his lips and drank deeply and desperately, as a man must drink the poisoned cup of execution. And all the time Kurelen watched him with his venomous and speculative smile.

When Jamuga had handed back the goblet, Kurelen said coldly, noting the utter exhaustion and prostrated pallor of the young man: "Jamuga, torment thyself no longer, and take a little comfort to thyself. Thou hast thought of the danger which Temujin may bring down upon himself and upon his people. Do not underestimate him: he hath, doubtless, already thought of this, himself. I grant thee that he is reckless and violent throughout all his nature. But he is no fool. Thou dost grant he is no fool?"

He waited, smiling, for Jamuga's answer. But Jamuga was beyond speaking, beyond noticing the sardonic lift of Kurelen's brows. He merely nodded.

"Women are precious and delightful to Temujin. But not so precious nor delightful as himself, and his own life. I can assure thee that he will return to us safely, perhaps a trifle scarred, but return he will. And he will still have the friendship of Toghrul Khan. So, comfort thyself, and be at peace."

Jamuga bowed his head. He seemed utterly broken. He turned towards the door of the yurt, as if to go. Then he halted. He suddenly turned back to Kurelen. Something appeared to have snapped in him. He began to speak in the incoherent and rapid voice of a man who cries out because of his inner torment:

"How can we understand such a man as this? He doth understand nothing of us!"

Kurelen laughed, lightly and derisively. "Do not deceive thyself, Jamuga! He understandeth us, but we do not understand him."

Jamuga made a disordered and abandoned gesture, the gesture of one who is utterly prostrate and broken.

"But who can read his thoughts—the thoughts of such men? They are cruel enigmas, stony faces of eternal mystery, brutal visages without tenderness or mercy!"

And then Kurelen understood that the icy fastnesses of

Jamuga's spirit had been shattered, and that he stood before him, naked and terrified and despairing, as he had never stood before another man. For a moment Kurelen was filled with rare compassion and pity. His expression became gentle and a little sad.

"Surely, Jamuga Sechen, we can never understand such men by attempting to decipher their souls by our own code. If we do, we come upon confusion. We cannot use their own code, because it is a secret one, never to be understood by us. If we even vaguely guessed, we would be stunned and incredulous, and believe that we are having a bad dream, where shadows have become light, and light, shadows. But do not try to comprehend, lest thou go mad."

Jamuga suddenly sat down beside him, as though his legs could no longer support him, and also because he must speak now or lose his mind because of the old pressure upon it.

"I do not comprehend! I cannot understand! I have tried to, for years, and only the gibbering face of madness hath confronted me! But what can I do?"

His words were a cry of misery and despair. He looked at Kurelen with the stark and naked face of a man whose last defenses have gone down, and who must turn to any one for help, no matter whom.

Kurelen looked at him intensely in a long silence. Pity rose in his dark and twisted heart. He no longer felt contempt for Jamuga, nor amusement.

Finally he asked gently: "What dost thou want?"

Jamuga gazed at him with dreadful despair, without speaking. And then, because he could no longer endure the understanding in the eyes of the old man, he dropped his head on his chest.

Kurelen laid his hand affectionately on his thin shoulder. It moved under his hand, and then was still.

"Jamuga, thou hast been born either too late, or too early. If the former, seek comfort in the Persian poets. If the latter, hang thyself. But, if both, go to Cathay. For what Cathay hath been, so must the world of the future be, if men are to survive."

Jamuga, without lifting his head, asked dully: "And what hath Cathay been?"

Kurelen, without answering, reached over and opened one of his chests. He withdrew an ancient manuscript, tied with a ribbon of gold. He unrolled it. It crackled dryly. Kurelen drew a silver lamp closer on its tabouret.

He began to read quietly and slowly:

"Where is the perfect State, where man's heart shall be at

rest, and his soul at peace, and where he can live with his fellows and not long to destroy them?

"Seek this State in thine own heart, O Man, and when thou hast found it then shall it exist in all the world.

"What shall be its attributes?

"The condition where all men shall pursue perfection, but never fully attain it. Where there is gentleness with dignity, kindness with reason, learning with aristocracy, love with pride, peace with strength, mercy as wide as the earth, wisdom with humility, and knowledge with wonder.

"Respect another's soul, O Man, and demand respect for thine own. Despise a fool above all other men. If thou be a ruler, be the first servant of thy people, without hypocrisy. Delight in what is beautiful, and be horrified by what is evil. Discipline thyself gladly for the sake of thy fellows. Love truth, for falsehood is the tongue of the slave. Speak not of money, but of friendship and God. If thou be a priest, serve God, and not men.

"Dishonor not thy soul, and thou shalt dishonor no other. Have faith, for without faith a people must perish.

"Be at peace. Be just. Remember that the world before thee is only thine own dream. Thus can no man injure thee, though he doth destroy thy body.

"Love God, and seek Him ever, with thine every breath and thine every thought and thine every word and act. He alone will not betray thee nor fail thee. In Him is the only reality.

"Believe all these things, and the perfect State is thine, and the whole world's."

Kurelen had finished. He waited for some word from Jamuga. But none came. But on the young man's face there had come a quietness, like that of a man who is sleeping after great pain.

When he had finally gone away, Kurelen thought:

"Jamuga hath lost the whole world, but hath finally found his soul."

chapter 14

Jamuga was not the only one who wondered why Temujin was making this long journey to attend the marriage of Azara, daughter of Toghrul Khan, to the Caliph of Bokhara. Chepe Noyon speculated, cynically, Kasar, with simple bewilderment. Chepe Noyon, finally, was no longer deceived. The fair Azara was the lodestar that drew the susceptible Temujin. After a while, Chepe Noyon was alarmed, but excited. What did Temujin wish to accomplish? What did he hope to accomplish?

Temujin was also wondering this. At times, he berated and ridiculed himself. But these were on the rare times when he momentarily forgot Azara's charms. But he could not resist the impulse that drew him so inexorably to the girl. His passions were brief, wild and violent, and this passion was the wildest and the most violent he had ever experienced. The closer he came to the Karait towns, the madder he became, until finally all his thoughts, his desires, the beat of his heart, the pound of his pulses, his soul and his very breath, were entangled like helpless flies in the web of Azara's pale bright hair. He was helpless, now, to summon his own will power, even had he desired to summon it. He could think of nothing. He was like a man dying of thirst, who sees no desert about him, no valleys, no hills, is conscious not even of his own being, but whose glaring vision is fixed only on a distant oasis. He saw Azara's face everywhere. He heard her voice in every wind. When the sky turned pink at sunset, he saw her lips. Finally, his thirst for her became so consuming that he could barely speak, and sank into a deep moroseness and silence that no one could break.

He was not the slow-planning man who carefully lays his plots far in advance. The plots are there, shimmering but nebulous in the distance, and he was content to approach them hourly and steadily, trusting to circumstance and fate and luck to aid him, to guide him when the moment to seize has arrived. Details were not cautiously plotted for the future. The city stood before him on a hill, the thousands of cities of his life, shining and glorious but shadowy, and it was always enough for him, and would always be enough, to ride towards it inexorably, armored with luck and desire and relentlessness, and to wait until he was at the very gates before planning the last decisive campaign. Thus, he never spent himself in advance, and arrived at the last moment fresh and enthusiastic and irresistible. Neither was he hampered nor distracted with previously laid plans, and could proceed brilliantly, taking advantage of every new circumstance which presented itself, and which he could never have foreseen. Historians were later to say that every campaign he conducted was planned far into the future, to the last detail. But that was not true. Like every great man he vaguely saw the vast and glorious future, but was wise enough to conduct the immediate skirmish only, trusting to destiny to lead him on to the next, and then the next, closer at each hour to the ultimate goal. Thus he lived always in the element of surprise, both for himself and others. Not knowing exactly what he would do on the morrow, his enemies could never know, either.

Once Kurelen had told him: "He who plans for tomorrow completely is a fool. He hath failed to take into his calculations the human equation, which must always frustrate and baffle him. Too, Fate is a knave of many tricks, and delighteth in nothing more than in presenting to the plotter new labyrinths and new passes, which his plotting had not dreamed existed."

He did not know what he would do when he arrived at the palace of Toghrul Khan. But he did know that he must see Azara, that he must hold her in his arms, that he must possess her. The ultimate stood before him in its veils. He had no doubt that he would be able to tear aside these veils, and conquer the ultimate to his own satisfaction. But just at this time he did not know how. Nor did this worry him overmuch. If Fate were a knave, it was also a capricious woman, who loved the reckless man.

Therefore, though he was reckless, he was also bold. Never did he doubt for an instant that he was irresistible.

He rode ahead of his companions and his warriors, his heavy brown coat fluttering in the cold gales, his fox-skin cap on his head, his lance in his hand, his green-blue eyes steadily but excitedly fixed forward. He did not notice the long and arduous journey. At night, he scarcely slept. He was like a man entranced, but with a deadly entrancement. His mood infected those with him. They became reckless and somber by turns, and quarrelsome.

They passed several caravans, and these Temujin encountered, egotistically satisfied when he discovered that these caravans were under his protection, and that they carried gifts for him. Those in charge, seeing the Mongols riding up to them, were at first alarmed, then deliriously happy upon learning their identity. On these occasions, the Mongols were received like princes, and dined and wined to stupefaction, the leaders slavishly doing them honor, and bending before them like serfs.

Among the gifts, which Temujin ordered to be delivered to his encamped people, was a necklace of glittering onyx disks set in a chain of bright pale gold and pearls, and also a bracelet. He no sooner saw them than they reminded him of Azara with her black eyes and golden hair and little white teeth. He would present them to her, himself! He took the golden casket, lined with white silk, which contained them, and carried it jealously with him. At night, he looked at them, letting them fall slowly through his fingers. They seemed warm and voluptuous to his touch. He would kiss them over and over, with mounting passion and aching desire, catching the dim lamplight on the glittering black disks, watching the reflections of the campfire on the round lustrousness of the pearls. They seemed living things to him, the holders of his love, the crystallizations of his adoration. Some alleviation of his burning torment would come to him, as he slept with them against his breast and his lips.

But when he arrived at the large Karait town, he was pale and grim with inexorable purpose. He felt that even death could not frustrate him. And he was completely certain that in some way Azara knew of the purpose of his coming, and that she awaited him, as aching and desirous and passionate as himself.

It was high noon when he and his warriors rode into the town. He had seen smaller villages, but no city like this. When he rode through the gates, he was amazed at what seemed to him countless multitudes, feverishly going about the inexplicable business of townsmen. He clattered through the narrow twisting streets, with their fetid gutters and low, flat-roofed white houses and gardens, and looked about him with the stern fierce glances of the steppe-dweller. The crowds drew back against walls to let him and his warriors pass, admiring their carriage, their horses, their rope-lariats and their sabers, but also amused at their wildness and their bronzed faces and their acrid smell. But they were more used to barbarians than the barbarians were accustomed to cities, and therefore were not unduly excited by their appearance. Hardly a week passed without some desert chieftain coming to pay his court and allegiance to the mighty Toghrul Khan. But they had never seen one with such a face and such eyes and hair as this Temujin, and he aroused comment as he passed.

Temujin, though he despised townsmen, and all the things

of which the townsmen were the symbols, was nevertheless slightly embarrassed by the hugeness of the city and the elegant people he passed. All at once he realized what he must look like in their eyes, with his rough brown coat and fox-skin cap and naked saber. So he glared fiercely ahead, and affected to despise them, rearing his horse, and roaring angrily when some silk-curtained litter suddenly appeared from around some corner and confronted him. Once an especially large entourage encountered him, attended by vast eunuchs. The scarlet curtains, embroidered with golden crescents, were drawn about the litter. Before the litter, and ahead of the eunuchs were two slight youths in scarlet silk robes, carrying golden bells, which they rung imperiously. They advanced with arrogant insolence, and Temujin involuntarily drew aside, motioning to his followers to do likewise. When the litter was abreast of him, the curtains were discreetly parted, and the gay delicate face of a lady peered forth, all white skin and black eyes and black, elaborately dressed hair. The cloudy veil across her face did not conceal her features, nor the provocative smile and glance she directed upward at the young Mongol. He looked down at her, and could not help returning the smile, which was an ardent tribute to himself. He watched the litter out of sight, well pleased with himself, and idly speculating about the lady, whom he had readily seen would not be unapproachable.

He was in high good humor when he arrived at the palace gates. Some prescience had already assured him that he had not seen the last of the delicate lady. He had some idea that she would see to this, herself.

He and his companions were received with some astonishment by the attendants, who apparently had not been prepared for so large a company. He was informed, by a haughty and supercilious steward, that he, and possibly his noyon, Chepe Noyon and Kasar, would be housed in special apartments in the palace, already prepared for them. But the warriors would be quartered out in near-by dwellings, which were waiting to receive them. As he gave this information, in high languid accents, the steward kept wrinkling his exquisite nose and fingering the golden chain on his breast.

Temujin looked about him. He was standing in a large court paved with blocks of white polished stone, formally bordered with grass and flowers and palm trees, and sparkling with drops of water from numerous fountains. Here the air was balmier than the desert air, and scented with a thousand delicious odors. Beyond the court, in its luxurious gardens, was the palace itself, white and shining and splendid. Temujin was aghast at all this luxury and beauty, but also enormously excited. He swung down from his horse, and threw the reins in the steward's face. A servant deftly caught them. The steward backed away, openly touching his nose with a white finger. Chepe Noyon smiled, but Kasar was enraged. When he got down from his horse, his hand was trembling on the hilt of his saber.

The steward, disdainfully walking ahead, led them through a white wall into the purlieus of the palace. They followed him through long white corridors, whose arched doorways were discreetly filled with blue or scarlet or yellow curtains, embroidered grotesquely with crosses and the Moslem crescent and stars. This intimacy, delightful and gay, of the symbols of two hating religions, was lost on Temujin. But it was not lost on the more sophisticated Chepe Noyon, who found it intriguing. Some archways were open, and revealed glimpses of brilliant green gardens and blazing blue pools of water, and hot noonday sky. From behind the curtained doorways came the soft laughter and voices of women, and snatches of light dancing music of flute and stringed instruments. Sometimes the raucous shrieking of parrots could be heard, as some girl teased them. Here the air was cool and dim and sparkling with reflections. The smooth white floor bore scattered crimson and flowered Persian and Turkish rugs upon it. Everywhere were the intoxicating fragrances of flowers and exotic scents, and the languorous warmness of spices, and everywhere, even through the noonday quiet, could be heard the murmur of the comfortable palace life, and the invisible coming and going of a multitude of servants. And at every few feet, enormous eunuchs, fat and naked to the waist, and turbaned, and holding bare blades in their hands, stood like colored statues, on guard. Each was smooth of cheek, wore golden rings in his ears, and broad golden bands on his upper arms, and jewelled sandals on his feet. The dim yet sparkling light flashed on wet belly and smooth hairless chest and gemmed belt, and lavishly embroidered silken trousers. Their eyes, fixed yet remote, did not seem to see Temujin and his companions, yet they had the impression of unclean and avaricious watchfulness.

Finally, the voices of the women were left behind. The steward paused disdainfully by a large archway, and held aside the thick silken curtains with gilt fringes. Temujin and his companions found themselves in a beautiful cool apartment, all white walls and white floor and silken couches and Chinese tables. Crimson panels of embroidered silk appeared at intervals on the walls, and the floor was covered with brilliantly colored little rugs. The far archways opened on the gardens, glittering and green in the sunlight. Motionless, with arms folded on their breasts, three servants, clad in blue and scarlet, waited to serve the guests.

With a shout of pleasure, Temujin pulled off his cap and tossed it onto a table. He loosened his belt, with a sigh of relief. He flung himself boisterously on a soft couch, and threw out his legs in their barbarous deerskin boots. Chepe Noyon sat down on another couch, and investigated the contents of a silver box of sweetmeats. Kasar gingerly seated himself on a pile of cushions. The servants began to bring in enamelled bowls of fruit, meat and delicate white bread, and basins of water, and fine white towels. In the water, subtly scented, floated rose petals. Crystal and silver decanters of wine were placed on the tables.

Temujin sat up and scratched his head. He laved his hands and wiped them on a towel. He pursed his lips disdainfully.

"What luxury!" he exclaimed, in a loud, hectoring voice. "No wonder these townsmen are soft!"

Chepe Noyon raised his eyebrows. He knew that Temujin was only seeking to impress the servants, with their downcast eyes and pale, inscrutable expressions. The servants did not show by any look or gesture that they were impressed. Only their nostrils quivered. As for Kasar, he was wretched. He scowled at a servant who offered him a bowl of water, and abruptly waved him away. But Chepe Noyon daintily washed his hands, and daintily drank wine. The dimples came and went in his gay face.

"I was born for this," he remarked, holding a crystal goblet for a servant to fill. "I am hoping, most ardently, that thou wilt be able to secure such as this for all of us, lord."

Temujin shouted contemptuously. "I have never cared for effete luxury," he said. Chepe Noyon glanced at him quizzically. And then he knew that Temujin spoke the truth, however he was impressed by his surroundings.

Temujin went on: "Nay, I have never cared for it. Nor desired it. I prefer the wind and the desert. There, one is not a eunuch, either in body or spirit. But, I promise thee, I shall get all this for you, if it is desired." He laughed. "But I cannot understand the desire."

Chepe Noyon regarded him placidly. "I do desire it. I prefer a soft couch, to one of earth and horsehair. I prefer this good spiced wine, to kumiss. My stomach doth respond gratefully to this sweet white bread, instead of boiled millet and crusts. Moreover, my body yearneth for silk, instead of harsh wool. Too, I think I should prefer a scented and anointed woman to one of our rough-skinned desert wenches. Towns-women are less direct in love, it is said, but much more subtle."

Temujin shrugged. "If I did not know thee so well, Chepe Noyon, I would say thou art no soldier."

Chepe Noyon laughed. "I do not think a man is less a soldier if he doth prefer fragrances to stenches, lord. Nor is he less skilled in killing, if, after battle, he doth delight in sweet music and the soft hands of a dainty woman, and the sleek comfort of a silk couch."

Kasar grunted angrily, out of his misery. "I prefer the open wind, and the desert moon, and the saddle, always."

Temujin, who had begun to walk about like a lithe feline animal, stopped beside his brother, and clapped his hand roughly on his shoulder. "Spoken like a true soldier, Kasar, and not like a libertine, such as our Chepe Noyon!" And he laughed boisterously.

He lay down again on a couch, sprawling, and eating prodigiously. On the high white ceiling the trembling shadows of the trees outside were reflected. Music was borne on the soft wind, and the faint far laughter of women. The servants noiselessly ministered to the guests. The dim mutter of palace life was all about them, like the murmur of contented bees.

The curtains parted and a eunuch entered, salaaming. He addressed himself to Temujin, who was drinking noisily. "The lord Taliph, son of the khan, doth desire the presence of the noble lord, Temujin, whenever he hath sufficiently refreshed himself."

Temujin sat up, wiping his mouth on his sleeve, and disdaining the towel distressedly offered him by one of the servants. "Hah!" he said. He stood up, shaking himself, fastening his loosened belt. He smoothed his fiery red hair with his palms. Then he looked at Chepe Noyon, luxuriously lounging on his couch, and laughed.

"Guzzle, Chepe Noyon, and sleep. And thou, too, Kasar. I go to pay my respects."

Kasar eagerly scrambled to his feet, scowling. "I will go with thee, lord, to protect thee. One never knows about these townsmen."

But Temujin shook his head. "Nay, stay thou with Chepe Noyon, and guard him, lest he go exploring among the women, and so violate the hospitality of the khan. Nay, Kasar, I do mean this. Protest not."

chapter 15

He followed the scornful eunuch out of the apartments, leaving Kasar muttering and scowling behind him. He followed him down winding corridors, and then up an immense white staircase to the upper floor. The eunuch stopped at an archway, and held aside the curtains.

Temujin entered an elegant and even more luxurious apartment than that assigned to him. Here Chinese and Persian and Turkish art treasures crowded the great sparkling rooms. Vases, silver lamps, carved tables, statuettes, painted silken panels, fringed rugs, couches, columns, chests and silver mirrors, encountered the eye in bewildering profusion. In the center of the room was a fountain made in the form of a jewelled green dragon, out of whose mouth poured scented water. In the marble-bordered pool, in which the dragon crouched, white water lilies floated, like alabaster flowers with golden hearts. The walls were covered with exquisite Persian tiles, brilliantly colored and decadently designed, with an intricacy of line and form. On a marble pedestal stood a rearing bronze horse of ancient Persian artistry, and on other pedestals stood ceramic statuettes of old Persian kings, exquisitely colored and glazed. Though at first glance there was a redundancy of color and form and complexity of design, in painting, tile, curtain and carpet, a bewildering and crowded array of ceramic, bronze, ivory and silver, the whole effect was charming in its Persian, corrupt air and elegance. The room appeared to be formed of jewels, so brilliant and incisive were the many colors, so lovely the tints of enamel, so lustrous the gleam of tile and rug. The draped curtains at the end of the apartment were drawn theatrically, in order to bring in the hues of garden and sky and pool outside. On one tabouret stood a huge smiling Buddha of pink jade, from whose lips issued a slow coiling smoke of incense.

Temujin blinked at all this brilliance and liveliness of color, which gleamed and glittered and sparkled on his eye. And then he saw that two people awaited him, reclining on a wide silken divan, one a young man of great elegance, and with a dark, long, subtle face, and the other a veiled lady. Instantly, Temujin recognized the lady. It was the provocative lady of the scarlet litter. He forgot the gentleman at once, and smiling, concentrated on the woman, who modestly bent her head and drew her transparent veil more discreetly across her features. She made a motion as though to rise and flee, but the young man negligently laid his hand on her bare white shoulder, and she subsided beside him. He regarded Temujin with amiable languor, and waved his hand in the direction of another divan near by.

"Greetings, my lord," he said, in a low dulcet voice, faintly edged with irony. "It doth give me intense pleasure to welcome thee to the abode of my father, the khan, who doth beg to be excused for an hour or so. He is an old man, and is over-fatigued after a long audience with the envoys of the Caliph of Bokhara."

Temujin sat down with his swift feline movement, and stared openly at Taliph. The two young men regarded each other in a slightly smiling silence, one, the elegant and poetic townsman, the other the virile barbarian from the desert and the barrens. Temujin thought: He speaketh like a man, but hath the soul of a woman. A most dangerous combination! And Taliph thought: He hath the green eyes of a serpent, and the body of a Persian king. But, Allah! How he doth smell!

They liked each other at once.

Temujin said: "It is my sincere hope that the khan will soon see me, for I am athirst for the sight of my foster father again."

Taliph replied with filial regret: "He doth fatigue himself too much on behalf of others."

And then they smiled at each other broadly, and understood each other with the most complete perfection.

During this time, the lady of the scarlet litter had been peeping decorously but licentiously at Temujin. Her lashes fluttered as his eyes suddenly turned upon her, and she blushed as though at an urgent physical contact. But her pink lips, faintly seen through the veil, parted, and there was the swift gleam of her white teeth.

Taliph clapped his hands delicately, and a slave-woman entered, bringing with her a silver bucket full of cool water, in which stood a jewelled jug of spiced wine. The two young men drank, slowly. The lady picked up a large fan of white ostrich plumes, and began to fan Taliph with languid, flexible movements of her gemmed hand. The plumes, at moments, half hid her face, and through the fronds she darted glances of invitation at Temujin, who had again begun to stare boldly at her.

Taliph put aside his cup, and smiled at his guest.

"I have heard much of thy valor and wisdom, my lord," he said. "I, myself, am only a poet, and know nothing of military prowess. But I enjoy hearing about it. Thou hast a reputation for immense sagacity, and a genius for organization. All speak with enthusiasm of thy many successes. Canst thou tell me how thou hast been able to do so much in such a small space of time?"

Temujin grinned. His eyes turned the color of innocent turquoises.

"I proceed always on the premise that men are stupid," he answered, his strong steady voice in startling contrast to the musical tones of Taliph.

Taliph seemed amused. He regarded Temujin with a respectful admiration that was only partially affected.

"But dost thou not occasionally encounter men who are not stupid?"

"Yes. But these men are leaders, and so I work with them, and not against them. That is, when it doth serve my purpose. But always, I remember that men are stupid, and differ only in degree. So far, I have not had to revise mine opinion, nor have I suffered reverses for judging wrongly."

Taliph sighed lightly. "I would like to disagree with thee, but experience doth tell me that thou art only too right. My father is sometimes not so wise. Sometimes he is guilty of believing that his opponent hath as much intelligence as he."

And now he looked directly and ironically at Temujin, who began to smile, and then to laugh silently, his teeth flashing in the colored light of the great room. And then Taliph's long dark face began to smile, also, and he bit his lip in a futile effort to suppress that smile. They gazed into each other's eyes, and suddenly they laughed outright, hugely, again understanding each other.

They drank another goblet of wine. Taliph shook his head as though in ribald denial as he drank.

He asked, in a voice both frank and artless, and full of friendliness:

"Men like thee always want something, consumingly, my lord. What dost thou want?"

Temujin assumed an expression of youthful innocence. "I? I love nothing but order and peacefulness, my lord. I am the servant, as well as the son, of thy father. I live only to serve such as he."

Taliph pursed his lips. He shook his head with a regretful smile.

"Ah! I thought we understood each other. I thought thou mightest be candid with me."

But Temujin merely inclined his head, narrowing his eyes, and smiling. He said at last: "I am only a soldier, my lord. And soldiers are notoriously devoted, and stupid."

Taliph was delighted. Among his friends he found only a decadent intelligence, an affectation of cynical worldliness and disillusion. He had discovered, in Temujin, an intellect beyond any he had ever encountered before, and a wryness and irony which was not affected, but rooted in reality and comprehension, and vigorously refreshing.

"Ah, ye military men! Your devotion to those who—hire—you is remarkable. Ye serve your masters with a loyalty that might in truth come from the heart, instead of the pocket."

Temujin grimaced with amusement. "Thou dost speak as though this loyalty of the soldier to him who doth hire him is somehow shameful. I, myself, think not. I believe it is the sign of the soldier's superiority to other men. Loyalty because of love, or idealism, is silly, because it is based on that which doth not exist. But money is always the first and last reality, the rock on which a man can build his house and know that none can assail it."

Taliph clucked sardonically. "What a realist thou art, my lord Temujin! And thou dost truly believe in the immense superiority of the military man?"

Temujin was no longer smiling. He regarded Taliph with open contempt. "Yes. Look thou, my lord: I have often said before that men are incapable of thought and reason. What happiness they feel is only the happiness of an animal who eateth well, and doth excrete, and hateth fiercely and briefly, and whose whole nature is full of simple ferocity and the desire for strife. Life hath designed him to be only a military tool, and when he hath become this tool he is completely happy, for he hath all the opportunities to fulfill all the demands of his inherent nature. And so, because he is completely himself, he is the perfect tool in the hand of his master, and being completed, he is superior to those men who languish in the cramped pattern they have stupidly designed for themselves."

Taliph listened intently. This barbarian, he thought, doth express himself like a poet, or a philosopher! He did not smile, as he pondered Temujin's words. He recalled that he had heard his father say that Temujin was illiterate, yet he spoke as a man of great learning. Truly, the barrens were a mighty school!

He curved his thin hand like a dark bird's wing over his mouth, to conceal his surprised thoughts. Over its edge he regarded Temujin with intense thoughtfulness and some perturbation. The bending fronds of the ostrich fan threw alternate shades of light and shadow over his elegant face. The fountain sang softly in the warm stillness. The lady's black eyes shone upon Temujin with a sort of fascinated lewdness and adoration.

At last Taliph dropped his concealing hand, and a smile covered his thoughts. "Thou hast little love for thy fellow man, my lord! I do not blame thee. But still, the philosophers, for all the bitterness of their tongues, do exhort us to mercy and gentleness. I fear thou art no philosopher. But surely, thou dost believe in something?"

"In myself." Temujin's voice was quiet and strong. Taliph arched a brow sarcastically. But Temujin's voice had had no arrogance, no egotism in it. He was like one who had stated a self-evident truth, simply and with forthrightness. "I also believe in force," he added, after a moment. "Argumentations and philosophy are weak reeds in battle. The sword doth ask no questions and replieth to none. All men understand the sword, but their ears are like the ears of donkeys, which are deaf to words."

Taliph sighed, lifted his hands, dropped them with a graceful gesture of ironic futility. "I am afraid that thou must despise me then, Temujin. I believe in the Word. I believe that it will conquer the Sword, at the last. I believe in gentleness and philosophy. I believe in beauty."

He stopped, for Temujin had burst into a roar of laughter. He was slapping his thigh. "Thou didst accuse me of hating my fellow men, my lord!" he shouted. "Do thou turn thine accusation upon thyself!"

Taliph paled. His lip lifted coldly with affront. Then, because he never lied in his heart to himself, he suddenly colored brightly. He began to smile. Finally he laughed outright, his eyes glittering, his slender body shaking with his huge laughter at himself. And the lady laughed with the sound of tinkling bells, though she had understood nothing.

Exhausted, finally, by his laughter, Taliph said: "I fear thou art too much for me, Temujin." His voice was gay and light. "Thou are disconcertingly shrewd. Moreover, I do suspect thou art a poet, also, however thou wouldst repudiate this."

Temujin, pleased by the appreciation of this accomplished townsman, was ready to be gracious and accommodating. "Nay, I am no poet, my lord. But I love it. Wilt thou not honor me by reciting some of thine?"

Taliph was also pleased. He had been writing poetry all morning, poetry only faintly suggestive of Omar Khayyam.

He stretched out his long jewelled hand, and took a rolled manuscript from the table beside him.

"This is only a fragment of a kind of Rubaiyat, Temujin," he said, sighing daintily. "An expression of boredom and weariness, and the resignation of despair. I dislike most intensely inflicting it upon thee, but thou hast a fresh outlook, and mayhap thou canst tell me what is wrong with it."

The lady, well schooled in what she must do, lifted a small stringed instrument from the table, and ran her white fingers over it delicately. It emitted a poignant and melancholy tremor of sound, which seemed to quiver on the warm and scented air like a sigh. Taliph leaned back against his cushions, and began to recite softly and feelingly:

"Ah, with the wine my fainting life provide,
And lave my flesh from which the soul hath died,
And lay me, shrouded with the living vine,
Beneath the shadow of some mountain-side.

"Alas! the gods that I have loved so long,
Have done my honor in this land much wrong,
Have quenched my spirit in a goblet bright,
And sold my wisdom to the market throng!"

The music trembled into melancholy silence. Taliph's voice dropped, full of musical sorrow. It was a long moment before he glanced up at Temujin, for his comment. He was disconcerted and angered to discover that Temujin was grinning shamelessly and openly. And then his anger flamed to cold rage when Temujin began to applaud loudly, with unconcealed irony.

"I have always loved those verses!" he exclaimed. "But methinks they were slightly different. Shall I repeat them to thee, my lord?"

Taliph turned the color of the blue-white kumiss. His lips became the very hue of lead.

Temujin, still grinning, nodded to the lady, who struck up a louder and more rollicking air. Then the young Mongol sat upright, assumed an attitude:

"Ah, with the Grape my fading Life provide,
And wash the Body whence the Life has died,
And lay me, shrouded in the living Leaf,
By some not unfrequented Garden-side.

"Indeed the Idols I have loved so long
Have done my credit in this World much wrong:
Have drowned my glory in a shallow Cup,
And sold my Reputation for a Song!"

Taliph was astounded. His lips opened, dropped, giving him an idiotic expression. He had lived long enough not to be surprised overmuch at anything, but now he was utterly nonplussed. He thought that he must be dreaming. He incredulously refused to believe that this illiterate barbarian had actually recited the verses of the over-civilized and decadent Persian poet, Omar Khayyam. This barbarian, in his rough woolen coat, his deerskin boots, his bronzed face and emerald eyes, his dazzling, animal teeth, his smell and his beastlike virility! It was a nightmare, a grotesque dream, from which he must awake, gasping and laughing. He could only stare at Temujin with staring eyes, all his elegance somehow absurd, his hands fallen, lax, beside him.

Temujin was openly enjoying his triumph. He winked at the lady, mockingly, and she incontinently winked back, delighted.

Taliph uttered a strangled murmur. He forced himself to smile. Temujin smiled at him, without malice.

"Thou dost see, my lord," he said, in a tone that Taliph could hardly endure, "mine uncle, Kurelen, is well-versed in poetry and philosophy, and can recite verses unendingly. Omar Khayyam is one of his great favorites. I have heard him recite the whole Rubaiyat many times. I know it almost by heart. But I congratulate thee: it would take a very careful ear, indeed, to detect it in thy verses. And I must confess that I believe thou hast improved upon it."

Taliph found this the most unendurable of all. He inwardly writhed. His tinted nails bit into his soft palms. His smile was the smile of some venomous reptile. No one in all the world would have dared so to affront him. But at last he made himself laugh, thinly, raspingly.

"I am afraid thou art too much for me, Temujin!" he exclaimed, affecting to wipe tears of mirth from his eyes. He looked at Temujin with a twinkling expression. "And I am also afraid that I have underestimated thee. Accept my apology."

Temujin laughed a little. But his eyes were no longer gleaming with mockery and merriment. For now he understood that he had made his most deadly enemy, who would stop at nothing to destroy him.

At first, he was disconçerted. He told himself that he was a fool, that he had long ago learned that unnecessary enemies were made only by stupid men, or men too strong to care. But the wise man, Kurelen had told him often, strives to make friends, if only to betray them the more completely in the future. He had made an unnecessary enemy, where he might have made a friend who would not overly oppose him. And then, he was contemptuous. At least, let me honor a worthy foe, he thought. What have I to fear from this flabby townsman, whose neck I could wring as easily as I could wring the neck of a lamb?

His broad dark face became cold with arrogance and disdain.

He took his leave soon thereafter, abruptly, without asking the permission of his host. Taliph again expressed his pleasure in Temujin's presence in the palace, and promised that they would have plenty of conversations together. But the air was full of poison during the last few moments they were together, and Taliph's face was still pale with his malevolent humiliation.

Temujin had no sooner gone than the young lord made his way at once to his father, who had just awakened from his afternoon sleep.

"My father," said Taliph, with an air of regretful honesty, "I have spoken to thy barbarian vassal. I have but one thing to say to thee, at this moment: he is a dangerous animal, and must die. But not immediately. We must choose the correct hour."

chapter 16

Chepe Noyon could see at once that his lord was perturbed, for he was frowning, and answered questions with a short irritability.

"I have made a fool of myself," he said, after some time, to Chepe Noyon. And then he told what had taken place between himself and Taliph. Chepe Noyon listened with a quizzical expression and a half smile. Kasar, whose simple mind could understand no subtleties, merely gathered that Taliph had annoyed his adored brother, and he exclaimed that he would go immediately and teach the effete young lord proper manners. This outburst restored Temujin's good humor, and he rallied Kasar and teased him until the poor youth was completely bewildered, and on the verge of enraged tears.

"But seriously, my lord," said Chepe Noyon, who always took more liberties with Temujin than any one else, because he understood him more, "thou wert exceedingly indiscreet." He coughed delicately. "I confess that I do not understand what hath brought us here, but whatever thou hast in mind is endangered by thy desire to ridicule the lord Taliph. Kurelen once told us that thou mayest rob a man, betray him, worst him in any encounter, and thou mayest at some time obtain his forgiveness, and even his friendship. But if thou dost humiliate him, and laugh at him, he will never forgive thee, but will always remain thy remorseless enemy."

Temujin frowned. He suddenly remembered that Taliph was the brother of Azara, and the son of Toghrul Khan. He had most certainly done his plans no good. His annoyance with himself grew rapidly. But he exclaimed:

"I could not resist it, I tell thee! But what have I to fear from a man who writeth poetry, and bad poetry at that, and stolen?"

Chepe Noyon shrugged. "If he had written good poetry, and his own, and even then thou hadst ridiculed him, he would have forgiven thee, for he would have known that thou art only an illiterate barbarian, and nothing better could have been expected of thee. Therefore, thou hast much to fear from him."

"Oh, thou art an old woman!" Temujin said, with contempt. Chepe Noyon was not offended. He merely shrugged again, yawned, lay back on his cushions and blissfully closed his eyes. Temujin scowled at him, began to pace the floor, muttering under his breath. Kasar watched him with humble and eager eyes. He was willing to engage the whole palace in defense of his brother.

A eunuch entered and announced that the great lord, Toghrul Khan, requested the presence of his noble foster son, Temujin, at the evening meal. On his arm the eunuch disdainfully bore a robe of soft white silk, a girdle of twisted silver, a necklace and arm-bracelets of heavy silver and turquoises, and sandals made of the softest blue leather. These, he remarked in his high womanish voice, were garments selected by the khan, himself, for his guest. While Temujin, with grunts of laughter, was examining these beautiful garments, and vowing he would not wear them, servants entered and informed him that his bath was ready.

"They apparently do not like the way we smell," remarked Chepe Noyon, enviously fingering the silk, and rattling the necklace and bracelets.

"I shall not wear them!" repeated Temujin. And then he bit his lip. He had a premonition that Azara would be present, however Eastern and Moslem etiquette forbid the presence of women. He examined the garments with a sudden interest, then tossed them from his disdainfully. "Perhaps, however, it would be discourteous for me to refuse the gifts of my foster father."

"Are we not to accompany thee, lord?" asked Kasar, in dismay.

The eunuch answered him with lofty coldness: "The invitation is only for the noble lord, Temujin."

Temujin followed his attendants into the bathroom. There, in a room of chastest marble, was a sunken pool of warm and perfumed water. He threw off his brown coat and rough under-garment of wool, and tugged off his boots, refusing the assistance of the servants. He stood naked before them, and they were amazed at the milky whiteness of his skin, which had been protected from the desert sun. Pagan admirers of physical perfection, they stood in astounded silence, gazing at his lean and beautiful body, muscled and firm, like a statue. His flesh rippled and shimmered like silk. Only his throat and face and arms were brown. He unbraided his hair, and it hung to his shoulders, red as new gold, and as bright. He was a young god, utterly splendid. He leaped into the water and splashed vigorously, aware of the admiration of the slaves, and pretending to ignore them. When he emerged from the pool, the drops of water clinging to his skin and glittering like quicksilver, they wiped him with soft linen towels and anointed him with perfumed ointment. Then they brought his new garments to him.

But before dressing him they shaved away the red stubble on his cheeks and chin. He emerged from their ministrations, clean-skinned and fresh. They brushed and combed his hair until it shone, and suggested that he leave it unbraided. He thought this effeminate, but they assured him that the finest gentlemen of Bokhara, Baghdad and Samarkand left it so, and after a while he was persuaded. He looked in the silver mirror held up to him, and conceded to himself that his rippling locks gave him a certain irresistible air.

When he emerged, with a faint swagger, into the presence of Chepe Noyon and Kasar, they could only gaze at him with open-mouthed incredulity. The soft white silken garment draped itself lovingly about him. His narrow waist was encircled with the silver and turquoise girdle. About his brown neck was the heavy necklace, and clasped about his brown bare arms were the shining bracelets. From under the robe peeped his blue sandals. His red hair curled daintily on his shoulders, and was as bright as the sun, and its very color at sunset. Moreover, he moved in an aura of perfume.

At last Kasar found his voice, and he wailed: "They have made a woman of my lord!"

But Chepe Noyon paced reverently about the flushing young man, and admired him from every angle. "I would not have believed it!" he murmured in hushed tones. He sniffed audibly. "Roses from dew-wet gardens! Ah, I was made for this!"

Temujin felt foolish. He scowled forbiddingly. But this was mere pretense. He was exceedingly proud of himself. He kept thinking that no woman could resist him now. He ran his hands over the encrusted turquoises on his belt, and smiled.

"Thou wilt outshine any fine gentleman at this court!" exclaimed Chepe Noyon. "But I trust that the khan will not allow any of his women to see thee!"

Temujin bridled egotistically, while Kasar watched him with distended and stricken eyes, speechless, certain that his lord was completely ruined. Temujin was amused. He made a frank and obscene gesture.

"Do not be so disturbed, Kasar. I assure thee I am still a man!"

Chepe Noyon shrieked with laughter. Even the attendants smiled. But Kasar gingerly lifted the hem of Temujin's robe, and when he saw the bare legs underneath, he lifted his voice in such acute lamentation that Temujin flung himself on a divan and laughed himself into helplessness, and Chepe Noyon, convulsed, rolled on the floor.

Temujin was still laughing as he followed the eunuch through the winding corridors to Toghrul Khan's apartments. The eunuchs on guard in the corridor admired him with their eyes, but reproached his levity with severe expressions. His leader moved aside heavy scarlet draperies, and he found himself entering the lofty white room of his foster father.

Now that the sun had fallen the evening had become swiftly cold. Smoking braziers stood in each of the four corners of the room. The crystal and silver lamps had been lighted, and stood, beaming and soft, on the many tables. Very low divans had been drawn in a semicircle in the center of the room, and on these divans sat Toghrul Khan, Taliph and his favorite wife, the lady of the scarlet litter, and Azara, and an old man clad in simple white and crimson garments. Before them were low tables, covered with gleaming white cloths, and set with enamelled Persian plates, Chinese silver platters, golden cups, and bowls of jewel-like fruit, dates and figs and pears and apples.

The scarlet curtains fell behind Temujin, and he stood, a white statue, before them, no longer laughing. His eye had gone swiftly over all of them. But now he saw only Azara, clad in silver, and veilless. He saw at once that her face was as white and cold as marble, and thin, and that her eyes were shadowed with violet. But she, of all of them, did not look at him. Her head was slightly averted.

Toghrul Khan regarded Temujin with smiling surprise. "Ah! My son, welcome to the home of thy father." He extended his claw of a hand to Temujin, who advanced, took the hand, knelt, and touched his forehead to the khan's feet.

"I would not have known thee," said Toghrul Khan, admiringly. "What a change white silk and perfume can make in a man. Stand, and let me gaze my fill of thee."

Temujin stood up. And now Azara slowly lifted her head and looked at him, and he looked only at her. She did not smile. Her black eyes dilated. Her lips were pale and chill and dry as a leaf. They regarded each other as from an immense distance, rapt and entranced and sorrowful. Temujin thought to himself: I never knew how much I love her! There is no other woman in all the world for me. But what grief hath so darkened her eyes and rendered white her lips?

Toghrul Khan was indicating a seat beside him for his foster son, and Temujin sat down. Now, for the first time, he turned his attention to the others. Taliph was a picture of affected Persian elegance, wearing a short embroidered coat of red silk, high-collared and tight and jewelled, coming only to the knees. Below the coat were elegant trousers of pale yellow silk, which ended in narrow boots of red leather. On his head was a high twisted turban of yellow silk, through which was thrust a white plume. His hands blinded the eye with the splintering light of many rings. Under the turban, which greatly became him, his dark thin face was more subtle and sensitive than ever. He smiled at Temujin with a gay and comradely air, and lifted a cup to him in a silent toast.

Beside him sat his lady, complementing his costume by being dressed in yellow silk also, with a loose red scarf over her black hair. She, too, was veilless, and her small white face with its full pouting lips and dark eyes was quite entrancing. She gave Temujin a coquettish but ribald smile, and tossed her head. He smiled in return, as they both shared a delightful secret, which they would discuss at a more propitious and private moment.

Toghrul Khan, bald and little and emaciated, was clad in blue and white, and a white turban had been wrapped about his head. His old wizened face smiled sweetly; his eyes beamed with paternal affection upon Temujin, and his voice was soft. But never had he appeared so evil to the young man.

And then his attention was caught by the old man in his white and crimson robes, and Temujin, startled, told himself that never had he seen so beautiful and gentle a face, so illuminated and kind, despite its furrows and its weary expression. The skin was as yellow as ancient ivory, and the bare skull was quite bald. But the eyes, shining as though with some inward light, were gentle and peaceful, and full of wisdom and ancient tenderness. It was evident that he was a Chinese, for his attitude was intensely quiet and infinitely calm. He was like an ivory statue of a Buddha, who had witnessed centuries in understanding silence. He wore no jewels. On his right hand sat Azara.

Toghrul Khan turned to him and said: "This is one of my most promising vassals, lord, a young man of parts and valor. It is he who hath made our caravan routes safe, over the territory he hath conquered. I owe him much."

He laid his hand affectionately on Temujin's shoulder, and in a voice of reverence he said:

"My son, this is a prince of Cathay, to whom I am only a son in the faith. He is Chin T'ian, brother to the Chin Emperor, and the Nestorian Christian Bishop of Cathay. He hath done me the most awesome honor of partaking of my poor hospitality, while he doth discuss with me the welfare of my Christian subjects in my domains. He is also one of my most honored guests at the wedding of my daughter."

He bowed his head reverently on his breast. The bishop smiled sweetly at Temujin. The smile seemed to run like rays of light over his yellow face. But he did not speak. Temujin stared at him frankly, his heart faintly stirring in a strange emotion. Because of the strangeness of this emotion, he did not know whether he was annoyed or pleased.

After a few moments, he was embarrassed, aware of his staring. His eye shifted. It was caught by a blaze of light. Chastely but magnificently, on an otherwise empty wall, hung the gemmed golden cross he had seen in Toghrul Khan's tent. Below it stood a table with a great lamp upon it, like a moon. There was something ostentatious in this lighting, and Temujin observed it, though without understanding. The crescents-and-stars were conspicuously absent from the room.

He said: "Among my people there are many Christians."

The bishop spoke. His voice was gentle and low, like music. "And thou dost not interfere with their religion, my son?"

Temujin frowned a little. "Why should I?" he asked, bluntly. "I ask nothing of any man but that he serve me first, above all other men, and all gods."

The bishop's face changed a trifle, became faintly sad. But his eyes, earnest and tender, fixed themselves upon Temujin's face.

"Men must serve God first, and if they do so, with faith and sincerity, they cannot but serve men."

Temujin thought this somewhat obscure. While he was pondering this, the bishop spoke again:

"Hast thou a Christian priest among thy people?"

"Nay, I think not. My Christians are not overly devout. They attend the sacrifices, though I have been told that sacrifices are an abomination in their sight. If this is so, then they conceal their aversion very cleverly." He laughed. Taliph laughed, and also his lady. But Toghrul Khan affected to be severe, and pursed his lips. But Azara, who could look at no one but Temujin, did not appear to have heard his words, but only his voice.

Temujin, suddenly remembering that this bishop was a great prince of a great house in a great empire, ceased to laugh, and was filled with wonder. It amazed him that such a man could sit like this, humbly and quietly, among such as Toghrul Khan and Taliph and himself, and the two women. He began to doubt the authenticity of his princehood. He looked sharply at the bishop, who, alone of the men, was not smiling. He seemed to be filled with sorrow and meditation. But he said nothing.

Still puzzled, it was a relief to him to concentrate his attention upon Azara. And again, across a space that was as wide as eternity yet no more distant than the close beat of their hearts, they gazed long and strangely at each other. There was no one else in the room, in the world. Azara's pale face grew even paler; her lips parted with the anguished grief of a child; her nostrils distended with quickened breath, and her eyes widened with a silent and desperate prayer to him for help. Once her hands fluttered, as though they were about to extend themselves to him, and her lips trembled, as though she were about to cry out. There was no decorous and maidenly modesty in her manner now, no coquetry, no blushing coyness, such as he had remembered from their last meeting. Now she was merely a woman, agonized and full of despair, calling to her beloved, believing that he would not fail her nor betray her, calling simply and pleadingly, without shame.

Temujin's face darkened, his nostrils flared. He heard the call throughout his body and his mind, and understood it. Now he comprehended the reason for her pallor and thinness, the wide and suffering misery in her eyes. He fixed his gaze upon hers, calling to her, promising her, assuring her that his love was her sword and her shield, and that nothing should come between his heart and hers. And as he so called, he was filled with exultation, an ecstatic joy. But part of his mind stood detached, wondering, telling him that never had he felt so about any other woman, and would never feel so again for any but Azara. He was amazed. Even though he saw the delicate pulsing of the violet veins in Azara's throat, saw the transparency of her young shoulders and the wondrous pale brightness of her hair and the light in her great black eyes, he felt no urgency in his body, no lust for her, no burning desire. He felt only a great and passionate tenderness, a profound and shaking love. And then he knew that in all the world before he had never really loved any woman but this, and with this surety came another: that he would never love so again.

His eyes glowed with his thoughts, and Azara saw them. Her fluttering hands grew still, and lay in her silver lap. A faint color, like dawn, came into her white lips. The anguish abated in her eyes. She smiled, and Temujin heard the faint indrawing of her breath. And now she looked at him as a woman might look at a god, all her soul shining in her face.

The lady of the litter had, of all of them, observed this deep and passionate interchange between the barbarian from the desert and her husband's beautiful sister. At first an expression of outraged jealousy flashed in her eyes. This subsided. Now she began to smile evilly, and beneath her black lashes she thoughtfully regarded her father-in-law, and then her husband. Her smile deepened. She seemed about to laugh aloud. The evil brightened in her eyes until it became like the gleam of a sword. Mirth quivered over her features like the reflection of sunlit water.

In the meantime, the servants had been bringing in the feast: delicate lamb stewed in rich and spicy sauces; tender fowl swimming in boiled cream; bread as tender and white as milk. And mounds of figs and dates, combs of golden honey, pastries full of almonds and thick Turkish preserves, bowls of tinted fruit, jugs of spiced wine and strong bitter Turkish spirit. Temujin, accustomed to the coarse boiled mutton and horseflesh and boiled millet and sour kumiss of his people, ate ravenously, though assuring himself scornfully that the riders of the steppes and the barrens could never survive on such decadent and luscious fare, fit only for women and poets and eunuchs.

As usual, he drank too much. It seemed to him that the cool wine might drown out the wild exultation, rapture and passion that threatened to break from the confines of his flesh and ignite the air. He could hear the violent hammering of his heart, the singing pulses in his temples and throat. But the wine did not cool him. It merely inflamed him. The atmosphere began to swim in ecstatic light, which brightened like a halo about the head of Azara and filled her eyes with radiance. Now he felt that old and intoxicating conviction that he held the world in the palm of his hand, that he was taller in stature than the highest star, that the secrets of heaven and earth were his, that he was invincible, omnipotent and clothed in terror and power.

Something of this terrible conviction seemed to emanate from his body, flame from his eyes. Taliph, in his suave and smiling hatred, had plotted to humiliate him, to reveal him to his womenfolk and his father as a boastful and ignorant barbarian, who must be squashed under the heel like a poisonous worm. But though the malignant smile remained fixed on his features, he was possessed with a sort of horror, as though he were laboring through the mazes of an appalling nightmare. For this young Mongol, sitting there on the divan in his borrowed finery, had a splendor and frightfulness about him which was evident even to the envious eyes of a mortal hatred.

Taliph, aghast, looked about him at the others. And he

saw that his father was regarding Temujin with the narrowed eyes of unnerved speculation, that the bishop was gazing at him with fascinated absorption, that his own lady was staring at him with open lewdness and desire, and that Azara was looking at him like a woman transfixed by the awful majesty of a god.

The young Karait noble shook his head, as though to free his eyes from blinding cobwebs. He said to himself: I have been put under a spell. I am dreaming. This man is a wild-eyed serpent, a ravening wolf, from the barrens, illiterate and uncouth and odoriferous, an empty whirlwind which will leave nothing behind.

It humiliated and enraged his cool heart that he, son of the mighty Toghrul Khan, gave this barbarian the honor of his smallest thoughts.

Yet, when Temujin smiled at him with open friendliness, his teeth and green eyes blazing in the light of the rosy lamps, Taliph felt a stir in him, a swift and astounding response, a hypnotized tremor of his veins. He thought: he is a wizard, who can seize men's souls in his hands. For one sharp instant, he felt regret that he hated him. And the next moment, scornful amusement that he could experience this magnetic and mysterious pull.

Temujin continued to drink and gorge himself. He assured himself solemnly that before retiring that night he must remember to thrust his finger far down his throat. Otherwise, he would be sick on the morrow. Now his thoughts swam in colored and brilliant circles through the room, visible to his inflamed eyes. Blue and scarlet and moonbright and golden, they moved with concentric motions, spinning about Azara's head, about the head of the bishop. Finally he saw no one but these two.

Suddenly it seemed to him that the bishop's face shone like the moon at midnight, soft and beaming and gently resplendent, filling all space with a luminous brightness. And though the bishop was not speaking, it seemed to Temujin that he had spoken, and that the warm air of the room was full of the ringing of muted bells. He put down his cup, and openly, for a long time, stared at the old man.

Toghrul Khan had been speaking to his son in his low honeyed accents. He was in the midst of some long involved sentence, when Temujin's voice, harsh and loud and barbaric, pierced through Toghrul Khan's words like a sword through silk.

"My lord," he said to the bishop, "thou art not like other men. There is a beam on thy face, like the beam of the sun."

The bishop smiled. His eyes burned with gentle tenderness.

Toghrul Khan was affronted. But Taliph laughed lightly and derisively at this vulgarity, and his lady, who now hated every one in the room, including Temujin, joined him in his laughter.

"Nay, my son," said the bishop, gently, "I am but a mortal man, no greater than the least. If there is a beam upon my face, the beam cometh from thy heart. Before God, there are no princes, illuminated and splendid, no beggars, with sores and rags. There are only men."

He turned to Azara, beside him, and touched her cheek with his hand.

"Thou dost believe me, my daughter?"

She smiled at him, her whole face alight with modest love. She bent her head.

Temujin stared. Through his own excitation, through the fog of the wine he had drunk, he could still think. Now he understood many things. He understood why the two women were veilless, and why they sat openly with men at their meal. To this strange priest, women were equal with men, and all men were equal with each other. They were all but common humanity, without distinction. And then he also understood why the Moslem envoys of the Caliph of Bokhara were not at this meal.

He was astounded, and disconcerted. He blinked, believing that he had heard something fantastic, and that laughter must follow. But no one laughed. Toghrul Khan had bowed his turbaned head modestly. Taliph was fixedly regarding his folded hands. The lady of the litter had bowed her head, also, with becoming humility. But Azara gazed trustfully at the bishop, as a child might gaze at her father.

Then Temujin burst into a loud and contemptuous laugh. He shook his red head at the bishop.

"Thine are strange words, lord, exceedingly strange words to come from the lips of a prince."

The bishop smiled upon him. "Nay, I am no prince, Temujin."

So! thought Temujin, suddenly, angered and derisive. This was no prince, but only a beggar priest, no better than his own Shaman Kokchu! His anger rose to rage against Toghrul Khan, who had humiliated him, by making him sit down with a beggar. Perhaps the old khan believed that such was good enough for his vassal! His vassal! Temujin's fists clenched. His face became purple with his violence, and his eyes shot forth red flames. His vassal! The day would come when the khan would bow before him, and kiss his feet!

Toghrul Khan turned affectionately to his foster son. "Temujin," he said, in his sweet voice, "thou dost not understand. Among us, the Christians, there are no distinctions among men. The prince doth regard himself as the least of his subjects, and only a man in the sight of God. Our beloved bishop is brother to the Chin Emperor, yet he believeth that he is no better than the humblest slave that walketh in the halls of his royal brother's palace. A great general is ofttimes less than his meanest soldier, in the eyes of the Lord. Only he is great who is lowly and good and full of virtue and kindness."

Temujin stared at them all, incredulous, disbelieving. He shook his head as though benumbed. Then he said again, loudly, repudiatingly: "This is madness! I have not heard aright!"

The bishop leaned towards him, and laid his withered old hand on his knee. "Let me tell thee, my son.

"I see thou knowest who and what the Christians are. Thou shakest thy head. Thou dost mean thou knowest they call themselves Christians, but do not know why? I will tell thee.

"Many centuries ago, twelve long centuries ago, there lived in a certain small nation, and born to a certain small people, a Man. But he was not like all other men. God had sent Him as His messenger of love and pity and mercy to all the world. He came to us, not blindly, not without understanding, but attended by angels, knowing Who He was, and why He had come. He lived but a little while, hardly to become much older than thee. But in those short years He laid a cross of Light upon the dark face of the earth, and it was never again to be the same. For He had given it His blood, and had redeemed it from the blackness of death, and brought man from out the tomb into the light of the eternal Day.

"He had said unto all men: 'Ye are my brothers, my children, flesh of My flesh and soul of My soul. I am yours, and you are Mine. I have shown ye the Way. Follow Me, and ye shall not die, nay, not even though the world perisheth, and the stars of the heavens are rolled up like a scroll, and forgotten.' "

Temujin listened, his mouth fallen open, the wine-filled goblet tipped in his hand, and spilling. His brows had drawn together. His expression was one of profound incredulity and bewilderment.

Then, when the bishop had finished, he exclaimed: "This is a mad story! If a great Spirit had indeed come upon this earth, then surely all men would have known it, and there would be but one faith, and one joy, and one peace!"

The bishop shook his head sorrowfully. "Nay, that is not the way of God. For such would have destroyed the free will with which every man is born. Each man must find his way to the Cross of Light himself, stumbling through the caverns and the darkness of the world on his own lonely journey, guided only by faith and love and hope. Each man must undertake his own pilgrimage, for only he can save his own soul."

Temujin laughed derisively. "It is a mad story! And only madmen can believe in it! It is a story that must be told at midnight, in the darkness, for in the light of full day it doth ring foolishly on the ears, refuted by all the things in the world."

"Nay," almost whispered the bishop, looking at him with his illumined eyes, "the world is refuted by it. All its institutions, its cruelties, its violences, its hatred, its death and its agony, its ignorance and its blindness, its monstrousness of man against man—all these are refuted and destroyed by the story of the coming of God."

Temujin told himself that he was listening to the words of a madman, and that because of these words the earth was shaking under his feet, and that its face had assumed a grotesque and insane expression.

He said suddenly: "This story is the story of a slave!"

The bishop bowed his head. "The story of a slave who was a King," he said, and his voice trembled.

Temujin gazed at him, fascinated. The story of a slave who was a King! The bishop's attitude, his bent head, his humble folded hands, his gentleness and meekness, were those of the poorest slave. Yet, he might have been a king. The blood of the world's mightiest kings ran in his veins. Again, the young Mongol shook his head, utterly dumfounded.

He said again, in a voice loud and protesting: "If every man believed like this, there would be no kings, no generals, no rulers, no wars, no conquests!"

The bishop lifted his head, and he smiled, and it seemed to Temujin that the room was flooded with light.

"True," he said, softly, "there would be none of these things!"

All at once Temujin was possessed by a veritable fury of impatience.

"Thy faith would emasculate the strength of men! it would reduce the world to a maudlin house of slaves! It would rob man of his greatest joy: war and glory! It would take the beard from the face of manhood, destroy the roughness in its voice, set men to spinning and plowing, and break down the walls of the strong cities! What could survive of joy and jubilation and courage, in such a congregation of eunuchs?"

The bishop looked at him, and could not look away. For Temujin's face was full of fire and power, full of savage splendor and violence. The very air vibrated about him; the very walls resounded with his voice. And the others looked at him, and suddenly Taliph felt that his own limbs were soft and weak, his own body without manhood, his own loins without potency. And Toghrul Khan thought, with thin and acrid hatred: I am an old man, accursed be I, and accursed be he! But the lady of the litter breathed heavily, and with lust, and Azara gazed at Temujin with a sort of terror, as though the golden god had begun to exhale lightning and speak in thunder.

The bishop spoke, gently and with sorrow:

"My son, what dost thou believe?"

Temujin laughed aloud, exultantly, contemptuously. He lifted his clenched fist.

"In myself, and what I can do! I believe in force and strength, in power and conquest! In the stupidity of men, in their hatred and their lust, their inability to think! I believe that they were created for such as I to conquer, and that in their conquest they feel a voluptuous surrender, and an adoration for their conqueror! Only he who is strong can lead other men! Only he who can wield the sword is worthy of worshippers! Men deserve a god, but he must be a god of power, not one who doth go about mewling like a new-born lamb."

The bishop said painfully, paling, his face shrinking:

"And thou hast no regard for the souls of men?"

Temujin shouted. "What souls? I have regard for the strong man's body, for his arm and his fearlessness. But beyond that, there is nothing."

And then the bishop asked with increased painfulness:

"What dost thou want, my son?"

Temujin smiled, and his smile was terrible.

"The world!"

At this, Taliph covered his mouth with his hand, and behind it he smiled. Toghrul Khan sighed, inclined his head, like an old father of obstreperous sons, whose opinions he must repudiate. The lady of the litter laughed lightly. But Azara gazed at Temujin with her heart in her eyes, again hearing only his voice.

And the bishop gazed at him, also, white sorrow on his face, and a sort of horrified understanding, the contemplation of which petrified him. He was like one who had been confronted with an appalling vision, too dreadful for the sight of men. He closed his eyes. He shivered. He spoke, his eyes still closed:

"And thou shalt have it! I have seen a vision, and before it, I am stricken down, and cry out to God: 'Why hast Thou willed this thing? Why hast Thou so afflicted Thy children?' I see the earth desolated and laid waste. I see the walls of cities crumbling, and the cities enveloped in flame. All the world is full of lamentation and despair and ruin, and the riding of enormous dark hordes. And beyond these hordes come others, endlessly, eternally, their horses shod with death, their swords sheathed in fire. On they come, over the rim of the world, spewed up by the centuries, riding forever, until the last man goeth down in agony, and never riseth again!"

He lifted his hands, and in a voice full of terror and anguish, he cried:

"Why hast thou done this thing, O Lord? Why hast thou created these monsters out of the womb of darkness, and flung them upon the fair and helpless earth? Why hast thou let them ride over our hearts?"

Only his voice filled the room. The servants in the archways looked at the old man, unable to move. And Taliph stared at the bishop as at a madman, and Toghrul Khan smiled a pale and vitriolic smile, and shook with silent mirth. But Temujin, scowling blackly, stared at the bishop, biting his lip, believing that he was being ridiculed, and that momentarily the old man would burst into mocking laughter, in which all would join.

Then the old bishop dropped his hands slowly. His white and deathlike face became gray with weariness and suffering. He dropped his head on his breast. He seemed to be listening.

He began to speak again, his voice low and weak, but slowly gathering strength.

"I hear Thy voice, O Lamb of God! Faintly, I hear it! But it is becoming stronger, and lo! I hear Thy words! For Thou sayest that the earth is Thine, until all eternity, though red-mawed tigers come out of the centuries, to ravage and tear and kill, and leave their imprints on the souls of men! And Thou sayest that always, until the end of time, the Earth is Thine. Eternally, forever, Thou sayest that they shall not conquer!"

Now his voice was strong, ringing like a trumpet. He lifted his head. His face was full of mysterious and unearthly joy, and his eyes blazed like the sun.

"For the Earth is the Lord's! The Earth is the Lord's! Forever and ever, the Earth is the Lord's!"

Some mystical strength seemed to lift him, to stand him upon his feet. He lifted his arms. He seemed to listen to a terrible Voice, coming out of the tumbling chaos of space and time.

He turned, and before any one could move, he had left the room, like a ghost, like a specter, like some visitation. And they watched him go, not moving, staring after him, disbelieving.

The curtain dropped behind him. And then, one by one they looked at each other. Taliph began to smile. He laughed aloud. He pointed a delicate finger at Temujin.

"What thou hast done to our saintly Christian prince, Temujin! Thou red-mawed tiger! But just at present, there is only sauce upon thy chin, and an idiot look in thine eye!"

His lady began to laugh. Toghrul Khan smiled viciously. He shook his head. But Azara did not smile nor laugh. Her head had fallen upon her breast. Then she stood up, and her brother's wife, angry, stood also. Azara turned away. She left the room, and the lady was forced to follow her. The men watched them go. And after they had gone, Taliph laughed again, uproariously.

Temujin glared. He felt that in some way he had been made a fool of, and he lusted for vengeance. But when he saw that Taliph was not malicious, but only full of pure enjoyment, and that Toghrul Khan was smiling forgivingly, his rage subsided.

He began to laugh, at first surlily, and finally, with full appreciation and pleasure.

chapter 17

But when he returned to his apartments, and found his companions sleeping the early and healthy sleep of the steppe-dweller, he was no longer amused.

"I have been insulted by a mean priest!" he said aloud. He dropped the curtains that hid the bedchamber of Chepe Noyon and Kasar, and went to his own bedroom. He sat down on his couch, and resting his hands on his knees, supported his chin, and glowered before him. The immense amount of wine he had consumed made a singing in his ears like a thousand gnats. But he was not jubilant and excited as he usually was when he had drunk too much.

Then he had forgotten the bishop. He could think only of Azara, and suddenly all his body was pervaded with an anguished desire for her. Unable to sit still now, he stood up and paced up and down the room with rapid and feverish steps. He could not understand himself. He had desired women before, but never like this, with a sort of terror and feeling of doom, of agony and tenderness and love. Her face, pale with fear and suffering, stood before him. He could see it, though he closed his eyes, and clenched his fists convulsively. "What aileth me?" he asked himself aloud, as though frightened. "This is only a beautiful woman, after all!"

But then he knew again that no other woman would be to him as Azara was. She seemed to be flesh of his flesh, part of his breath and his heart. Her thoughts of him appeared to enter the room and mingle with his, like living exhalations.

He had come to the palace. But he was no nearer Azara than before. The bride of the Caliph of Bokhara was being guarded like the most precious treasure, in order that she be delivered up to her lord like a pure and unsullied jewel. He realized, with an exclamation of mingled wrath and despair, that he did not know what to do next. But see her he must, though he had to strike down every guard in the palace.

He forced himself to sit down. "This is madness," he groaned. To attempt to see her, to force himself past her guardians, would be to make a mortal enemy of Toghrul Khan, and the mighty Caliph. There would be no spot on earth where he could hide from them, and he would bring ruin down upon his people.

All that he had gained, at such cost of blood and death and fortitude and torment, would be lost.

But somehow he could only look at the cost, and not feel it in his mind. In his terrific effort to realize it, to pierce through the numbness in his brain, he seized his head in his hand and feverishly ran his fingers through his thick red hair. He rolled his head from side to side. He sweated. He gasped. But still nothing mattered but Azara. The world was well lost for her.

But, strangely, he could not make himself completely believe this, either. Nothing mattered, however, but the consuming passion and mournful desire for her which now convulsed him. His thoughts ran out to her like winged messengers of fire. His whole flesh trembled, was bathed in cold dew. He recalled to himself that he had always done as he wished, and evaded the cost later.

Once Kurelen had said: "Bite off more than thou canst chew, and then chew it." All at once he laughed a little, but the laugh was like a groan.

Should he finally, by some miracle, see her, what could he do after the brief assauging of his passion in the cool waters? How could he rescue her from the arms and harem of the old Caliph?

"I shall not think of that, yet," he said, still speaking aloud. He got up and tore off the white silken finery of Toghrul Khan. He flung it from him with a grimace. He dressed himself in the only other garment he had brought with him, a loose tunic of red-and-white striped linen. He pulled on his deerskin boots. He thrust his dagger through his belt, and took up his saber. He ran his finger delicately along its edge. In the mingled moonlight and lamplight of his bedroom, the broad curved blade glimmered like pale lightning. He flung his cloak over his shoulders, pulled the hood over his head. From its dark depths his eyes shone like those of a wild and ravenous beast's.

Then he stopped, motionless, like a statue, all his savage mind concentrated on a faint sound. He heard it again, the soft slithering of muted footsteps. He tore aside the draperies. A huge eunuch stood before him, and when he saw the young Mongol, he bowed deeply. He put his finger to his lips.

"Come with me, my lord," he whispered.

Temujin regarded him piercingly. "Who hath sent thee? Where art thou to take me?" he asked in a low and imperious voice.

But the eunuch merely bowed again, and whispered: "Come with me."

Temujin hesitated, biting his lip. He scowled forbiddingly at the eunuch. But the man's expression, faintly seen in the dimness, was amiable, though somewhat frightened. He kept glancing over his shoulder. Temujin felt for the dagger on his belt. He lifted his saber from the bed, and gripped it tightly in his hand.

His heart was beating wildly. Had Azara sent for him? There could be no other explanation. Suddenly every pulse in his body was singing, every vein trembling with a savage joy. He was incredulous, however. She would not do this thing, however she desired him. It was not in her to do this thing.

"Let us go," he said abruptly. The eunuch reached out and quenched the lamp. Now only pale bright moonlight filled the rooms. Temujin could hear the deep breathing of his sleeping companions.

He followed the eunuch out into the long dark corridor. No one was about. This section of the palace was quiet and sleeping. But at the far end of the corridor a eunuch was leaning on his long saber, and drowsing, his head bent. Again, Temujin's guide fearfully put a finger to his lip, and tiptoed ahead. Temujin followed, holding his saber tightly. The eunuch pushed aside a heavy crimson curtain, and Temujin found himself in a tiny private court, filled with tremendous vases of flowers. The moonlight flooded the court, and the warm night wind dried the sweat on Temujin's face. The air was pervaded with a thousand flower scents, and he could hear the musical and drowsy twinkling of the distant fountains. Beyond the courts were the gardens, dark and still, though glow-worms flashed their eerie lights continually in the grass.

He followed his guide, the hood pulled far down over his face, his naked saber still in his hand. They walked over the grass, drifting like shadows. Now they rounded a wall, and a flood of yellow lamplight streamed far into the darkness. Toghrul Khan and his son had joined the envoys of the Caliph of Bokhara for a late festivity. Temujin could now hear the tinkling of instruments, the gay muted sound of cymbals, the licentious laughter of dancing women and the hoarse roaring of men. Temujin felt a momentary rage and affront that he had not been invited to join this festivity. The barbarian from the barrens was no fit company for the elegant men from Bokhara, the soft Persian gentlemen of the great city! He ground his teeth. He halted, and stared up at the flooding yellow light.

He felt a tug at his cloak. The eunuch, alarmed, was motioning him to continue. He flung off the man's hand, his heart beating with outraged fury. Again, the eunuch tugged at him and whispered: "Lord, we must go! If we are found here by the guards, they will run us through at once!"

Temujin gave a last ominous scowl at the light, and followed again. The eunuch approached the end of the low wall, and held up his hand warningly. Soldiers, carrying torches, armed and alert, were pacing up and down near the entrance to the palace. As they passed each other, they challenged, went on. The eunuch, peeping around the wall, watched them intently. Temujin peeped, also. "Only four!" he whispered. "I can attack them, myself."

Terrified, the eunuch shook his head. "Nay, wait, lord. We must wait. There is no other way."

An unusually loud burst of laughter and song and music issued from the palace. The great brass doors opened, and several gentlemen came out into the coolness of the night for refreshment. One of them called to the soldiers, jingling coins in his hand. A soldier ran to him, his torch streaming red in the darkness. But the gentleman, with a contemptuous laugh, flung the coins in the air, where the torchlight caught them, glittering. The red light shone on his dark and exquisite Persian face, and on his jewelled turban, jewelled belt and jewelled hands. Now the other soldiers, with laughter, tried to catch the coins before they fell.

It was an auspicious moment, and the eunuch signalled to Temujin. They fled through the shadows, only a few paces from the shouting soldiers and the laughing gentlemen. They reached the safety of a thick copse of rustling trees. There they stopped, panting, listening. But the soldiers had not seen them. They resumed their pacing, carrying their torches, in high good humor. The doors closed again after the Persian gentlemen. The night resumed its close warm heaviness. Temujin was conscious of the thick and slumbrous odors of roses.

Now they wound their way through the trees, emerged into the gardens where the fountains sang. A nightingale suddenly broke out into lustrous song, filling the night with the purest and most poignant of notes. Another joined him. The moon span over the treetops like a silver wheel, emitting beams of argent light.

Temujin felt a fresh dark coolness on his face. They were descending into a grotto, where water dripped. The odors of tree and flower were overpowering. Here were silence and dampness, and complete darkness. He could hardly see his guide, though he was but a pace ahead.

The eunuch stopped. "I go no farther, lord," he whispered.

"But I shall wait here for thee. Go ten steps more, and then halt."

Temujin hesitated again. Was this a trap? But why should Toghrul Khan go to such secrecy? There were easier and less involved ways to kill a man. He gripped his saber more tightly, then passing the eunuch he walked slowly, counting to ten paces. Then he stopped. He could see nothing but complete darkness, and hear nothing but the sighing of the heavy trees, and the singing of the nightingales, who were filling the night with a thousand aching songs.

He felt a touch on his arm, like the touch of a falling leaf. He started, reached out and seized some one's arm. But the arm was soft and covered with a silken veil, and he knew he held a woman. He pulled her to him roughly. He caught her in his arms. "Azara!" he whispered. His body swelled as though his blood had become hot and his veins could no longer hold it.

He heard a soft laugh, felt veiled lips touch his own. It was a lewd laugh, and the breath caught. He felt the pressure of a woman's firm soft breast against his own, the pressure of desirous limbs bending against his thighs. His nostrils were full of the scent of a woman's flesh, perfumed and warm. But he knew now that it was not Azara, but only the lady of the litter.

His heart plunged sickeningly. He thrust her roughly aside. He could see a little. A few wan beams of moonlight were struggling through the thick shade. He saw the veiled form before him, and heard a light amused laugh. The form approached him again. She was standing on tiptoe, and her lips were against his ear.

"Fear not, my lord! I am a virtuous wife, but could not resist embracing thee. Ah, thy lips are like fire! It is enough. I have come to lead thee to thy love, who awaiteth thee."

His heart was still plunging. His senses swam. He felt his arm taken, but he could not move a step for several moments. But his mind was as clear and sharp as ice. He put his hand to the lady's throat. She drew a sharp breath, and trembled, and pressed her warm tender flesh against his hard fingers. But they were not closing desirously on her throat, but only on a necklace which he remembered she had worn, a necklace of pearls and gold. He jerked at it fiercely; there was a slight breaking sound, and the necklace was in his hand. She cried out, faintly, fell back from him. But he suddenly seized her by the hair. One soft strand curled on his fingers. He lifted his saber and slashed it free from her head. She saw the flash of the blade in the moonlight, and uttered a muffled scream.

He smiled grimly. He caught her in his arms again, and pressed his mouth savagely upon hers, partly to stifle her cry, and partly because he remembered that she was very desirable, and that she had desired him for all her virtue. She subsided in his arms, and lay quietly, returning his kisses with a lustful passion. She put her soft palms against his cheeks, in order to hold him to her. His hand closed over her breast, and held it. She panted a little. Her breath was hot and perfumed. She seemed almost fainting in his arms, and moaned under her breath. And again Temujin's pulses sang, and his senses were caught up in a silver spinning cloud.

But finally, after a long time, he thrust her from him again. His teeth flashed in the gloom.

"And now I have thy necklace, and a lock of thy hair, to remember thee by," he whispered, mockingly. "A sweet remembrance! I shall treasure them forever, remembering the lovely moments I dallied with thee! But I shall also hold them as ransom, in order that thou shalt play me no tricks, my delicious one."

He heard her panting. He knew she was full of rage. He laughed a little. "If I did not love a woman so deeply that my blood is cold to another, I should remain with thee," he said. "But, who knoweth? Mayhap tomorrow night, in this selfsame spot?"

Now she began to laugh, almost silently. "I did not bring thee here for myself, Temujin, but to lead thee to Azara, who doth languish for thee. Have I not told thee I am a virtuous woman? But who knoweth if I shall not be here tomorrow?" She added, in a quieter tone: "Follow me."

But he caught her arm again. "Why dost thou do this thing?"

She laughed, with a low vicious note in her laughter.

"Because I hate Toghrul Khan, and my husband, who treateth me like a dog, the Moslem serpent! And because I hate Azara, too! It will be a happy remembrance in the days to come, to know thou didst tarnish the gem reserved for the great Caliph of Bokhara, and to conjecture if Azara's son is not the fruit of thine own loins!"

"Thou art a Christian?" Temujin was beginning to understand.

"Yes, a virtuous Christian woman, my lord." And she laughed again, with that cold vicious laughter.

Temujin was silent. A sick spasm of contempt twisted his stomach. These women! Crafty as serpents, cruel as death, cold-hearted as stone! He, who had killed his own brother with his own hand, felt repulsion at such treachery, such lewdness and wickedness. Then he laughed to himself, with amusement at his own thoughts.

The lady was moving away. He saw her dimly beckoning. He followed, cautiously. He could hardly see her, for the light was so wan, and her movements were so spectral. They emerged from the thicket. Before them stood a long flight of white steps, shimmering in the moonlight. They mounted the steps. They reached a narrow colonnade, unguarded. They entered a faintly-lighted room, the bedchamber of the lady. No one was about. It was apparent that she had dismissed her attendants. She looked at him, and he could see her clearly. Her lips laughed at him through her veil, and her dark eyes sparkled wantonly. He thought swiftly: "My love for Azara will lead me to doom and ruin. Mayhap I could quench my desire in this golden bowl, and no longer yearn after a woman whom I dare not touch?"

She read his thoughts in his flaming eyes and suffused face. But she shook her head at him archly, and lifted a dainty warning finger. "Not tonight!" she whispered. "But who knoweth what tomorrow might bring?"

She lifted the curtain, and led him through a series of empty, lamplit luxurious rooms. She reached a tall narrow doorway of bronze, intricately chased. She opened it without a sound, and motioned him through.

On the threshold he stopped, looked at her, then seized her in his arms, and covered her mouth with his lips. She struggled a little, then sank against him. Then, after an instant or two, she pushed him away, and laughed at him with her gay and beautiful eyes.

"Save thy passion for Azara," she said, mockingly, "or I shall be denied my revenge."

"Tomorrow night?" he asked urgently, convinced that he must have her.

She nodded. Her teeth gleamed through her veil. "Tomorrow night, my lord, my panther!" She added: "And fear no intrusion. I have guarded against this."

She pushed him through the doorway, then closed the door after him. He found himself in a little narrow corridor. At the end, a blue-and-gold curtain wavered in a faint wind. Now he forgot the lady of the litter, Taliph's wife. Behind that curtain Azara waited for him, and again his heart pounded and there was no one else in all the world. He walked swiftly down the corridor, tore aside the curtain.

He had expected to find Azara standing there, awaiting him, her arms outstretched, a smile of langurous desire upon her lips. But instead, he found himself standing only in her bedchamber, lighted only by the moon. It was a vast room, and the floor was covered by Persian carpets. A delicate scent, fragile and illusive, filled the warm dim air. For a moment he could see nothing, then slowly the objects in the room took vague form. Near a distant wall was Azara's couch, and she was lying upon it, asleep.

chapter 18

It appeared to him that the sudden thundering of his heart must sound through all the palace like arousing drums, and would instantly bring armed guards with torches, shouting. In a moment he would be surrounded, he would be overpowered and murdered. His breath came loudly. He trembled.

But there was no sound. The arousing drums were only his own body. The moonlight streamed into the apartment, bringing with it the dark and scented night wind and the singing of the nightingales. Beyond the doors he knew that guards paced, alert and listening, for he could hear the faint slithering of their steps. The lock on the casket was well guarded, but the hinges had been broken, by a treacherous and vengeful woman.

He knew that he must move with the utmost silence. And so, shaking in every limb, he approached Azara's couch, and stook there, looking down at her.

She slept like a child, her cheek in her curved hand, her wondrous hair streaming over her shoulders and breast like a gleaming cloak. The moonlight bathed her with its pallid light. She lay in a circle of dreamlike radiance, breathing softly and gently. He saw the circles of her yellow lashes, closed and tender and innocent. He saw the movement of her pure and youthful breasts, the curve of her hip and thigh under the coverlet of cloth-of-gold. But he saw also how pale she was, how marked with suffering her gentle and beautiful young face.

He stood there, gazing at her, thinking to himself that he was looking at all the world, and that all his life and desires were centered in that sleeping girl. The hotness of his blood subsided, became cool, and he was filled with an infinite sadness and love, and a passionate tenderness. He wanted to kneel beside her, and gently kiss her hand, which hung down over the side of the couch. He wanted to bury his face in her hair, and forget everything but how much he loved her. It seemed to him that if he did so, all the pain and fever in his heart would subside, and he would be at peace.

He knelt beside her, not touching her, only filling his eyes with her nearness. He knew that she had not sent for him, and that she slept, trusting in him to help her, how, she did not know. Some of the acute prescience of love told him that she slept so for the first time in many nights, trusting in him, resting in the knowledge that he was under the same roof that sheltered her also.

He thought to himself: Shall I go? Without disturbing her, without alarming her? He felt in his breast. The gold-and-jet necklace he had brought for her moved into his hand. He could lay this on her pillow, and tomorrow she would know he had been there, and that he had given her a promise. But what promise would it be? What could he do?

He was drowned in a wave of despair. In quarters outside the palace his warriors waited. He could call them. But they would be overpowered by the soldiers in the palace and the city. He could wake her, take her from her father's house, and ride away from this accursed place, into the desert and the mountain and the barrens. But what then? Vengeance would ride after him. He did not know what to do!

The young Mongol, who had never been truly desperate before, truly impotent, could only kneel there, trembling, enraged at his own helplessness, biting his lips, clenching his fists. And Azara continued to sleep, smiling trustfully.

He said to himself: I came only to possess her, to quench my lust in her, and then to abandon her to whatever fate her father had designed for her. I came only for a day, and then to ride away, satisfied, forgetting. But I cannot do this, now. I do not desire this. For, no matter how long I live, or where I go, I shall never forget her, and my life shall be an everlasting torment without her. And he was consumed with an objective wonder.

He was brought out of his despair, for Azara was stirring. She was sighing deeply. Her hands moved. Then she smiled again. He bent over her. His breath touched her cheek. Then simply, without a sound, as though she had not really been sleeping, she opened her eyes, and fixed them fully on his face.

He lifted his hand quickly, as though to put it over her mouth if she were about to utter a startled cry. But she did not cry out. She did not move. Only her eyes widened, but not with surprise. It was as if she believed she was still dreaming, and that her dream had become reality. She smiled, a smile of infinite joy and peace and love. Tears welled up into her eyes, spilled onto her cheeks, swiftly. Then she turned to him as a child who has been in pain turns, and held up her arms to him.

He hesitated. He could not move! Lustful and exigent with women, responding savagely to them, he could not touch this girl, who looked at him like this, innocently and simply, with an unawakened passion of rapture. An enormous shame fell over him. He felt that it would be sacrilege to touch her, a blasphemy for which the spirits would blast him to dust. He could only look at her, all his soul despairingly, hungrily, in his eyes.

"I knew thou wouldst come," she said, and again, with joy: "I knew thou wouldst come!"

Then suddenly he buried his face in her breast, holding her as though he would never let her go. He could hear the swift rising beat of her heart, beating with mingled terror and ecstasy. Her flesh was as soft as velvet, and scented. He felt her hands fluttering on his head, and then they were still, like birds that had come to rest. He heard her murmuring and sighing, and then he knew she was weeping.

"I shall never leave thee, my love," he said. "I have come, and shall never leave thee again."

In the warm swimming moonlight outside, drenched in the perfume of roses, the song of the nightingales rose triumphantly, but with an unbearable sound of rapture and joy.

chapter 19

Impotence was a new sensation for the young Mongol. Especially was it unendurable when that impotence was forced upon him by those he despised.

He was torn by alternate gales of despair and rage. The night with Azara had merely intensified his desire for her, and his love. He had promised her that he would never leave her. He had promised this to other women, also, and lightly, never meaning it. But now he meant it. When he thought of her innocence and beauty, and gentleness of spirit, he was forced to rise, though already exhausted, and pace up and down in a veritable fever of anguish, clenching his fists and rolling his head from side to side. The wildest plans rushed through his mind, but his reason rejected all of them with passionate contempt. If he only had time! Then he might force matters, become increasingly powerful, and boldly demand the girl from her father, and not be refused. But he had no time. In less than seven days Azara would be the bride of the Caliph, who was already on his way to claim her.

What could he do? He did not know. He might flee with her, but even if he were able to get beyond the city, his days with her would be brief. Then utter ruin, and death, not only for himself and Azara, but for all his people. Even his love and passion were not able to blind that cold dispassionate part of his spirit which was never deceived. Therefore, he knew the cost was too great for that brief ecstasy.

He seemed to see himself wandering in a labyrinth, returning only to the place where he started. But his agony would not let him rest.

When Chepe Noyon and Kasar awoke, refreshed, when the dawn was pink in the eastern skies, they found Temujin still walking back and forth, alternate light and shadow falling on his haggard face. Chepe Noyon was surprised.

"What, my lord! Hast thou risen so early?"

Temujin regarded him in dark and gloomy silence, resumed his pacing. Then, because much of his self-control was shattered, he burst out into incoherent speech. Chepe Noyon listened, at first indulgently, then with active horror. The pure gem for the crown of the Caliph was tarnished! Temujin had committed the unpardonable crime, had ravished the lily and desecrated the fountain. Chepe Noyon stood up and exclaimed in a low rapid voice:

"We must leave at once, my lord, and pray to the eternal spirits that we be clear of the city before this hath been discovered!"

Temujin stared at him with bitter anger. He watched Chepe Noyon dress, buckle on his sword. The gay humorous face of the young nokud was grim and tense, such as it had never been in battle.

"Hark thee, Chepe Noyon. We shall not go. I have never been balked before, and I shall not be balked now!"

Chepe Noyon was aghast. He actually stammered when he spoke:

"My lord! Thou art not serious? What canst thou do? What wouldst thou do?"

Temujin shook his head with despairing fury. "I know not. I know not why I have told thee, for thou hast nothing to offer. But this I do know: I shall not leave this girl."

Dumfounded, Chepe Noyon sat down and gazed at him with distended eyes.

Kasar, who had been listening, open-mouthed, looked helplessly from one to the other. His slow mind was a long time in absorbing what he had heard. When he did so, he uttered a wild cry.

Temujin regarded them with the utmost black contempt and anger.

"Ye sit there, gaping at me, and have nothing to offer but flight! Flee then. I shall remain."

Chepe Noyon, slightly recovered, answered gravely: "Lord, thou knowest we cannot leave thee, even if we desired to do so. Thou art our khan. If thou dost remain, to thy death, then we must remain, also.

"Forgive me if I attempt to reason with thee. Think me not insolent. But thou hast said, thyself, that thou dost not know what to do. The maiden is beautiful, but so are thousands of other women. And all women are the same, in the blindness of night. Thou knowest this. Thou hast gone too far to bring ruin upon thyself for the sake of one woman out of a world of women."

Suddenly the young man, always so gay and cynical, burst out grimly:

"A curse on the wench! She hath bewitched my lord!"

Temujin put his hand to his aching forehead. "Thou art

right," he said, with simple anguish, "she hath bewitched me. My heart is gone."

"But I have another suggestion, my lord: a woman's bed is a cure for a man's passion. Enjoy her all thou wilt, and then, when the moment cometh, thou wilt leave her, and forget."

Temujin's brows drew together. "I shall never forget. I love her."

Chepe Noyon suppressed a smile. He was greatly relieved, for he saw that Temujin was weighing his advice.

But now the faithful Kasar burst out vehemently: "My lord, if thou wishest this woman, then I shall seize her for thee with mine own hands, and defy a whole garrison!"

Temujin laughed drearily, but some of the tension relaxed in his face. He put his hand on his brother's shoulder.

"I believe thou wouldst really do this, Kasar! But the matter is not so simple." He looked at Chepe Noyon. "Thou hast spoken with judicious wisdom. I shall visit her for the whole seven nights. Perhaps then I shall be released from the spell. If not, at least I shall have some small measure of self-control. Just at this moment, I cannot think at all."

He bathed, combed his red hair, partook of the breakfast brought to him and his companions. His expression was lighter. But he was thinking.

Then he recalled the bishop. The skeptical Mongol, derisive of priests and their magical deceptions, yet began to wonder if this old man with the illuminated face might not be able to conjure, to create miracles. But more than this, he was brother to the world's mightiest emperor, who was lord of a thousand walled cities and countless legions of cavalry and soldiers. Who was Toghrul Khan compared to this man? A pretty chieftain, a rabbit! Temujin suddenly shouted aloud, with exultation.

He clapped his hands. A servant appeared at once. Temujin told him imperiously to go to the bishop and request that he grant the lord Temujin an audience as soon as possible. Chepe Noyon listened to this extraordinary command with raised eyebrows, but made no comment.

The servant returned and announced, with open surprise, that the bishop would see the noble lord Temujin at once.

Temujin's spirits rose hilariously. Without a word to Chepe Noyon, he followed his guide to the austere and simple apartments of the bishop. The old man was lying on his couch, and a servant was rubbing his tired and twisted feet. But he greeted Temujin with a smile of the purest sweetness, and was apparently neither surprised nor curious at this visit. Temujin bowed low before him, as one bowed to a great prince, and then seated himself on the floor beside the old Chinese.

He had already decided on his method of attack. He said, looking at the bishop with a frank smile which did not deceive him at all:

"Thou must wonder why I have come to thee, my lord. But it is to ask thy pardon for any affront I offered thee, and beg indulgence for myself."

"There is nothing to forgive," answered the old priest, very gently. He paused. Now his eyes became piercing from under the jutting shelves of his brows, and he regarded Temujin with a passionate earnestness and sorrow. In himself was a confusion: Men like this are scourges, sent by God. Yet, perhaps I could soften his heart, that terrible heart of the barbarian. But would that not be interfering with the plans of God?

He knew that signs are always given to those who trust God, so he waited, praying for that sign.

Temujin's spirits rose. He had made an auspicious beginning. But as he studied the old man's yellow face, he hesitated. He could not understand that deep and earnest look, such as a man directs down into an abyss whose bottom is hidden. He could not understand the grave sorrow.

He assumed an expression of complete candor.

"I have come to thee for help, my lord," he said, shrewdly judging the priest.

"For help?" The sorrow lifted from the bishop's eyes, and was replaced by the light of simple eagerness. "Be assured, my son, that I shall help thee to the end of my poor power."

Temujin shook his head. "It is not a poor power, my lord. And I wish to invoke it. Against Toghrul Khan, who is my enemy, and thine."

The bishop's first expression was amazement, and then distress.

"I do not think he is my enemy, nor thine, my son," he said, in a low voice. "But even if he were, no malignity could touch us except by the will of God."

Temujin leaned towards him and spoke quickly: "Thou knowest the daughter of Toghrul Khan, Azara. She hath told me that thou didst secretly baptize her into the Christian religion. She hath also told me that she is in despair because of her coming marriage to the Moslem, the Caliph of Bokhara, who hath many wives and concubines. She hath asked me for help."

The bishop uttered a faint exclamation of pity and grief, then was silent. His intuition made him fix his eyes upon Temujin, and then he knew all he needed to know.

He said, still in that low voice: "She hath asked me for help, also. I can offer her nothing but resignation and humility, obedience to her father. I have told her that life is short and bitter, but it endeth like an evil night, and the sun riseth. What doth come in the night is only a dream, and then there is the awakening."

Astounded, Temujin stared at the priest. His look of candor and young eagerness disappeared, as though wiped away by a revealing hand. Now the savage face of the barbarian glared out, violent and infuriated, and full of black amazement.

"Thou wouldst condemn this girl to a life of misery?" he cried.

"But misery is short, my son," replied the bishop, with a faint sigh. "And a small payment to make for the glory of the sunrise."

Unable to endure this foolishness, Temujin sprang to his feet, and began to walk up and down the room, trying to hold back the flood of his rage and disgust. His veins thickened in his throat. For several moments he thought he would choke. And the bishop watched him as he paced back and forth, and the sorrow returned to his eyes, and with it, great compassion.

Finally Temujin stopped beside him, and his voice was hoarse and muffled:

"Thou art a Christian, and Toghrul Khan, on occasion, is a Christian, also. Canst thou not appeal to him?"

Again the old man sighed. "I have already appealed. But he hath told me that he, too, is helpless. He dare not oppose the Caliph of Bokhara. If he did, he would bring disaster upon his own people."

"That is a lie! He exhibited the girl to the Caliph, like a slave-woman! And he is to give her a huge dowry! Azara hath told me that she appealed to him only recently, and he threatened her with death if she spoke of the matter again."

The bishop was silent. His face had paled excessively. He clasped his hands together and wrung them.

Temujin lifted his clenched fist, and pointed with it at the old man.

"Thy God is a poor God if he cannot rescue this miserable girl!"

But the bishop said in a voice of infinite pity: "Thou dost love Azara."

Temujin replied: "She doth love me, also. I shall not abandon her."

The bishop gazed at him and marvelled at the power of love, which could subdue even this terrible barbarian with the violent green eyes. Verily, he thought, love is the mover of men and worlds, and the walls of darkness fall before its singing voice.

Temujin resumed: "I have never felt impotence before. I feel it now. Therefore, I am forced to appeal to thee. She doth reverence thee; thou darest not betray her."

"What can I do?" asked the bishop, lifting his hands helplessly.

Temujin was suddenly encouraged. He smiled.

"Much, my lord. I shall take Azara away with me. There will be an uproar. Toghrul Khan will set out in pursuit, for vengeance. Then thou canst tell him he must not lift his hand against us, for it he doth, thou wilt invoke the power of thy brother, the Emperor."

The bishop listened, aghast.

But Temujin had not finished. "Last night, thou didst say I would have the world. But I need time. Thy brother, the Emperor, will listen to thee when thou dost tell him what thou hast told me. He will value a strong ally, such as I, for his empire is rotten, and decaying, and must fall without assistance. It is already threatened, as thou dost know, thyself. But tell him what thou hast told me, and he will rejoice."

Still, the bishop could not speak.

Temujin laughed aloud, exultantly. "I am called a barbarian. Oh, I know what the townsmen say of the desert hordes and clans! We are animals, without civilization, marauders, bandits, robbers, murderers. But I tell thee now that a new civilization shall come out of the barrens, stronger, fiercer, more powerful, more virile, more orderly and invincible, than was ever begotten by the weak loins of the cities in the bed of decadence. Nothing but disease hath issued from this civilization of thine, nothing but degeneracy and wantonness and greed, men like eunuchs, and women like wantons. All your philosophy is only a plaint of impotence; all your religion is only the wail of the slave. Ye preach the creed of hopelessness in your academies. Ye fashion delicate things, which are in themselves shameful and unmanly. There is no health in your institutions.

"But we are strong and living. We shall conquer. For you of the cities gasp on your fetid deathbed, while we thunder at your doors.

"Tell this to thy brother, my lord, and he will listen. For he is wiser than thee."

The bishop was still silent. Temujin waited. He saw the furrows deepen on the yellow face. He saw the old man become older and more haggard, as though he had just awakened from an appalling nightmare, which he knew was a prophecy.

Then the bishop lifted his eyes, and Temujin was amazed to see how quiet and still they were, how calm with suffering.

"My son, I cannot help thee. Even if I could, I would not." He lay down and turned his face to the wall. "Leave me," he said.

Temujin looked at that thin bent back and shoulders, and all at once, with rage, he knew that the body of the old man was a wall he could not scale, a fortress he could not take, a river he could not swim. The power of all the world was in that feeble and dying flesh, and before it he was completely impotent.

I have failed, he thought. But failure never filled him with despair, but only with anger and greater determination. It was like strong wine which renewed his vitality.

He left the apartments, not cast down, but only the more resolute, only the more inexorable.

chapter 20

He returned in gloom to his splendid chambers. But Chepe Noyon and Kasar were not there. A slave told him that they were amusing themselves in the garden, with the women graciously assigned to them by their host. Temujin stood on the open colonnade, and somberly surveyed the greenness and beauty of the gardens. But he did not see them. He saw only Azara. His heart was like a great burning coal.

Apparently, he admitted, there was no hope. But he did not believe this. Never, in his life, did he ever truly believe there was no hope for him. But he fumed. He bit his lip. He looked at the blue and shining sky, and remembered the evil gods of his ancestors, who lived in the mongke tengri, the Eternal Blue Sky. He remembered the stories of the black and frozen gods, who lived in the kanun kotan, the land of everlasting ice. He invoked their aid, with mingled anger and derision, for he did not believe in them. He wanted only their wicked and mysterious power. He inhaled deeply, feeling that he inhaled with his breath the power of the gods of his people.

Everything was smooth and quiet and in order. But suddenly he knew that an extensive search had been made of these quarters, minutely, and that Chepe Noyon and Kasar had been lured away so that the search could be thorough. His keen animal instinct smelt the subtle odor of the enemy. He smiled darkly, knowing for what the searchers had been seeking. He put his hand to his breast and felt in it the lock of black hair and the necklace of the Taliph's favorite. So long as he had these talismans she dared not betray him. But he needed a better hiding place. He might be overpowered in some corridor and forcibly searched by some of the lady's servants, or he might be drugged, and robbed in his sleep. That night he would give them to Azara, and she would conceal them in her own chamber.

The thought of Azara came to him like a sharp and bitter pang, compounded of despair and longing and love. He stood motionless, enduring the onslaught of his pain. He tried to reason with himself. She was only a woman. Kurelen had told him that the Chinese regarded women as the world's greatest danger, an immortal threat to the peace of men and empires. It was said that he who looked too long on a woman's face lost his manhood, and became, thereafter, a weak slave in silk, her handmaiden. Too, the Mongols despised women, though they lusted after them as no other men lusted. They were valuable only as breeders of men, as servants, as weavers and makers of felt. All at once he had a vision of Azara milking the mares, and the vision was grotesque. He laughed aloud, shortly. She was not even valuable for that small and domestic purpose. If she bore sons, they would be lords of the cities, sitting in their gardens, and watching the sun on their foolish artificial lakes, and listening to music, and delighting in the shameful contortions of dancing women. He felt the hatred and contempt of the desert-dweller for those who lived in the cities, painting flowers and leaves on silken panels, and mouthing their little philosophies of impotence and corruption. "The hat-and-girdle men" were not men, but deformed women dressed in men's garments.

He remembered what his father had said: that men should lust for women, but never love them. A man might love his horse, his saber, his strong-bow, his sons, his friends. This love added strength to his strength. But should he love a woman he was lost. His strength left him like water. He was bound with chains of bright hair, and lacked even the will to break them.

So he reasoned with himself, muttering aloud his disgust for his own folly. Walking up and down the room, his cat-green eyes blazing, he stamped his feet in their boots of hide. He loathed himself for his weakness, for his captivity to a woman, which could bring only death to himself and annihilation to his people. He was a traitor.

Yet, the great burning coal in him brightened and smoldered only the stronger. The more he argued against Azara, the sweeter and clearer became the image of her face in his thoughts. He was full of helpless and infuriated wonderment. For now he dimly perceived that a man might feel something more for a woman than lust, and this thing he felt was more terrible than an army, more powerful than the gods themselves. It was a mystery, not to be defined. But it was the life-giving air of all the world, the passion before which other passions were small and worthless.

"I have been bewitched," he thought, and knew that there was no potion that could relieve his hunger, this sweet and painful thirst of his heart.

He sat down, and thought with fury. He must take Azara. Without her, there was nothing he desired.

Once his final decision was made, he felt strength, and was amused. The old men were wrong: those who loved women were made doubly strong, and felt no fear. He would take Azara to his own people, and she would bear his sons. She would learn to milk the herds, and would sit at his left hand, his favorite wife. Bortei would serve her, and his mother. He would heap her chests with treasures. He would cover her beautiful body with the finest furs and the softest silk. He would hang jewelled necklaces about her white throat. Her sons would be his bodyguard, his keshik. The world would give them honor. He would make them kings over many nations. This Persian girl, who was a Christian, would be the goddess of the Mongols, and from her womb would come a race of warriors and khans. He woud guard her like a precious gem.

He trusted to his destiny. The spirits who loved him would find a way for him. Perhaps in Azara's body the seed of his first son was already swelling. Her mother was a princess of a noble people, her father a mighty kahn. Destiny had given her to him. Destiny would not betray him, nor mock him.

The curtain was drawn aside, and Taliph, elegant in a tunic of golden silk and red silken trousers and silver boots, his turban nodding with plumes, stood there, graciously smiling at him. Temujin scowled, then his annoyance evaporated. For he saw, in Taliph's smile, a strange resemblance to Azara, whose smile was radiant.

"Greetings, my lord," said Taliph, his face humorous. "It is sunset. I thought thou mightest desire to accompany me through the city. I love the city at sunset, more than at any other time."

Temujin was pleased at his coming. He felt a kindness for the brother of Azara, and a lofty contempt for the man whose favorite wife was a wanton. Kurelen had once told him that the best kindness was that which was tinged with a secret sense of superiority. He was prepared to be amiable.

He accompanied Taliph to the courtyard, where two immense white camels were waiting, surrounded by servants in scarlet-and-blue garments. The western sky was deepening into a crimson hue. The air was warm, scented with jasmine and roses, and full of voices and bustle. But its perfume, Temujin perceived, was the perfume of the city, compounded of the stench of decay and the odor of sweet corruption.

They majestically lumbered through the narrow streets, rolling in slow dignity from side to side. They were shielded from the hot late sunlight by small red awnings fringed with gold. About them moved the camel-drivers, uttering shrill or hoarse cries to clear the way, carrying staffs in their hands.

Temujin stared with interest at the low white houses with

their flat roofs, their white walls protecting gardens of which nothing could be seen except the fronds of palms. The sunlight splashed the walls with feathers of orange. Now they were entering the streets of the more luxurious inhabitants. Here the houses were built on the opulent Persian pattern. Black-and-brown pillars, enormous and intricately carved, guarded doors of bronze and bright brass. The walls were low, in order to afford the passerby the glimpse of great green gardens, blue artificial lakes and ponds. But the large latticed windows were all closed to the street. Guards, trousered and turbaned and dark of face, stood by each gate, with bare swords. The air was increasingly filled with flower scents and the clashing of the palm leaves in the wind which was coming strongly from the west.

Near the western gates of the city was the great bazaar, open to the winds and the burning sunlight. Temujin's keen nose discerned it by its mighty stench at some distance, long before his sharp eye saw it or his ears heard it. This stench overpowered the sweet odors of the orchards he was passing, the fresh odor of fountains and grottoes. But he was excited by it, for it was pungent and strong, and lusty with life.

The bazaar, sprawling for many acres, did not disappoint him. He had heard much of the bazaars of the cities, but his imagination had not encompassed them. The noise was deafening, though they were merely approaching the outskirts. The last sunlight glared down upon it. As though they realized that religion must share in life and lustiness and noise, the colorful vivid bazaar was surrounded by mosques with gilded domes and minarets and the slender towers of the muezzin, the small squat austerity of Jewish synagogues, the curious pagoda-shapes of the Buddhist and Taoist temples, and the little nondescript churches of the Nestorian Christians. Beyond these crowded temples lay the bazaar, veiled by clouds of golden dust, odoriferous, rowdy, clanging and filled with noise of cymbals and laughter and multitudinous voices.

The ground was hard-packed clay, beaten into smoothness by thousands of feet. The bazaar seemed a small town in itself, threaded by crooked narrow streets, which were lined with the open booths of busy craftsmen and raucous traders, by tall flimsy structures of cheap gay brothels, by slave markets and horse and mule and camel stalls, by open shops selling carpets, jewelry, poultry, fruit, silken shawls and garments, musical instruments, sweetmeats, wines, military weapons, games, sandals, leather girdles, turbans, fans, and a thousand other articles. The uproar was deafening, the stench overpowering. Flies swarmed in black insistent clouds over displayed dates and figs, grapes and sweetmeats, and other delicacies. The tradesmen, wearing monstrous turbans, their dark faces shining with sweat, their avaricious eyes glinting over the throngs, sat crosslegged in the doorways of their tiny shops, or by their open stalls, haranguing and wheedling or insulting the passersby, and hoarsely laughing at some sally of a neighbor or a young man or impudent girl. Here and there a shouting youth sauntered on the outskirts of the crowds, carrying on his shoulders, his arms, and even his head, brilliantly colored birds, attached to him by strings. The birds squawked, lifted their red, blue, white and yellow wings, flapped them in the faces of unwary passers. Girls, insolently unveiled, or very nebulously veiled, held out baskets of flowers and dates, and called in ribald words to possible customers. Here, too, were snake charmers and magicians and conjurers, and even a whirling dervish.

There were discreet shops, rather haughty, selling Persian, Turkish and Chinese manuscripts to the discerning. The proprietors did not sit outside, but waited inside, like erudite spiders among their busily copying clerks. The perfume shops were also discreet and withdrawn, but from their dark low doorways issued the hot and swooning aura of their precious scents.

But few walked in the streets of elegance. The crowds were concentrated in the rowdier streets, where slave-girls with naked breasts contorted on platforms, to the licentious music of flute, drum and cymbal, flinging out their arms, shaking their anointed torsoes, and tossing their long black hair. Their masters kept up a discreet but insistent harangue, offering strange pleasures for a small sum within the curtained purlieus. At intervals they struck small cymbals of their own, and eyed the dancing maidens with well-feigned expressions of delight and sly lust. There were puppet-shows also, surrounded by crowds of laughing men and boys, who watched the antics of the puppets with glee. The slave-markets attracted considerable attention also. Here pretty girls, guaranteed to be virgins by their turbaned and black-faced Turkish proprietors were discreetly and modestly stripped at intervals, but only a little, in order to whet the appetites of potential purchasers. The girls were very young, most of them only children, and much frightened. They had been seized in raids, and one saw strange faces here, fair or golden, with dark curls or yellow hair, brown, gray, green and blue eyes. Some of them bore an Egyptian stamp on their delicate features, though their skins were black and polished as ebony.

But Temujin found the brawling throngs themselves worthy

of observation. Motley, composed of many races, they moved, sweating and pushing, through the streets. Here were tall fierce Afghans, mustached and hugely turbaned, and stinking; here were Buddhist and Taoist monks, in red and yellow garments, their wide-brimmed hats throwing purple shadows on their cool ivory faces, their hands holding prayer-wheels; here were subtle, severe-lipped and burning-eyed Jews, carrying their manuscripts of prayers, and glancing about them shrewdly or austerely; here were visiting desert-dwellers in their deerskin boots and fur caps; here were dignified Chinese, Tibetans, Hindoos, Karaits, Uighurs, the Merkit, Turks, and even tall blue-eyed men from the frozen wastes, the reindeer people. There were Persians, also, elegantly clad and bored, feeling vastly superior to these mongrel crowds. Here all Asia met its neighbor, and despised him, especially his religion. In a certain section swine were slaughtered and sold, but this section was far from that occupied by Moslems and Jews. Temujin found them fascinating, for he was interested in mankind, and these alien faces excited him. He even liked the monstrous stench and the dust. When he passed the horse-stalls, he insisted on stopping and getting down. The seller could not understand his language, nor he, his, but that did not prevent them from getting into fierce arguments and scornful exclamations, as Temujin expertly examined the animals. The argument must have been more vehement that ordinarily, for a crowd gathered, gleefully ribald and full of suggestions, while Taliph sat on his camel and watched with enjoyment. Finally Temujin pushed his way contemptuously through the crowd and mounted his camel again. "Not even fit to eat," he said disdainfully, departing in a shower of curses and imprecations from the owner of the beasts.

He stopped at the camel stalls, and looked them over with a critical eye. "Fly-blown," was his verdict. He insisted upon stopping at a wineshop, and went within, though Taliph would not accompany him. There he drank quantities of wine and rice-wine, and had to come out, asking for payment from Taliph, for he carried no coins with him. At his heels, darkly suspicious, came the proprietor, deftly catching the money tossed him by Taliph, and thereafter bowing deeply to the ground in the wake of the contemptuous white camels.

Now there was a sudden uproar, and the confusion of a fight. It appeared that some gay young men had bought a pig, and were dragging the squealing animal through the streets occupied by the booths of some Moslems and Jews. This was a sacrilege. The younger Jews and Moslems came roaring out of their stalls and set upon the youths, who soon had delighted allies. Most of them were Christians and Buddhists. It was a religious and racial row, now, and fought with gusto, and a hearty lack of discrimination. Now police appeared, armed with staves, and laid about them with democratic impartiality. The pig, in the meanwhile, had been discreetly stolen by some one who had no objection to the meat of pigs. Within a few minutes, the merchants had retired to their stalls, and had resumed their shouting, the fighters settled their hats and turbans on their heads, the crowds moved on. Peace was restored, and every one was happy.

They came upon an open space where three gray elephants, gigantic and solemn and obviously filled with ennui, were performing lumbering tricks under the whips of their trainers. Crowds of children watched. Their parents indulgently tossed coppers to the trainers, who caught them in the air without ceasing their hubbub for an instant. The elephants performed with philosophic detachment; their tiny eyes were bored and sardonic, their great heads covered with little caps fringed with bells. They were females, and very superior. Temujin found them vastly amusing. He rocked with laughter on his perch. But it was not their solemn tricks which he found so titillating. They reminded him of fat old women.

Beyond the crowded domes, minarets and palms and flat white roofs of the city, the western sky was blood-red. The sun was an immense crimson ball, slowly drooping. Temujin had bought a silver necklace and bracelets for Bortei, a woolen cloak for his mother, and a Chinese manuscript for Kurelen. All with Taliph's freely given money. "Baubles," said Temujin, disdainfully, but watched them with a wary eye as a servant carried them.

He was beginning to be fatigued by the clashing of the cymbals and the shrilling of the flutes, and the hubbub of the marketplace. But he was not tired of looking at the strange alien faces.

When they arrived back at the palace of Toghrul Khan, Taliph asked him what had impressed him most in the sight of the crossroads of the world. Temujin considered a moment, then answered:

"The facelessness of the people."

Taliph was surprised, but awaited enlightenment.

"In the barrens," said Temujin, "every man hath his soul. It doth look from his eyes and speaketh distinctly in his voice. His face is his own. But in the cities every man speaketh with the voice of his neighbor, and looketh through his eyes. There is no strength in him. He is not a soldier."

"Perhaps the cities despise the soldier," remarked Taliph.

Temujin shrugged. "That is because of their envy. Only the soldier knoweth life in its richness and excitement. The townsman must have strange pleasures and vices in order to make his drab life endurable. His soul is the anonymous and mean soul of all his neighbors."

And then he said something which made Taliph think for a long time:

"Cities should be easy to conquer, for no man hath in them anything of value, and nothing to defend."

But he was already distrait. For tonight he would see Azara again.

chapter 21

The hot white moon came through the latticed windows and lay upon the dark floor in little circles, crescents, stars and lozenges. They glittered as with a pale luminous light of their own, like fireflies. The cool night wind entered also, filled with fresh odor of flowers and fountains. Beyond the locked doors the guards paced. But within, there were silence and rapture.

Azara lay with her head on Temujin's breast. He held her hands against his heart, and his lips against her hair. They did not speak, even in a whisper. They felt that they lay in a citadel of peace and joy, and utter contentment. There was no tomorrow for them. There was nothing but this night, which stood suspended in time, complete in itself, an eternity of ecstasy, without danger or suffering. Beyond this night the world lay, predatory and threatening, and full of death. They forgot it. They felt only each other.

And then, very slowly, though the moon sank, reality began to enter the thoughts of Temujin. It was as though he had opened the door of his mind, and had allowed men with swords to enter. He must deal with them. Tomorrow stood on the threshold, and must be fled from or attacked.

He stirred. But Azara was asleep. He could see the curve of her cheek, the closed lashes of her eyes. His hand touched her hair. She sighed. Her breast was pearly in the dimly translucent light. Her flesh exhaled warm but intangible perfume.

All at once his heart contracted with a fierce pain. He thought: Mayhap it would be better if I should rise now, and leave her forever. I can bring her nothing but suffering and terror. I have been a black shadow falling across her life. Shall I depart like that shadow, and leave the clear sun to shine again upon her?

But he knew that there would no longer be a clear sun for Azara. She was too young; she had loved too utterly. Had she loved less, she might have recovered. He had put aside himself; the ferocity of the barbarian was held at bay by the angel of self-obliterating love.

Wherever I must go, there she must go, he thought.

Azara moved, sighed, smiled in her sleep, and awoke. She looked up at him. An expression of ineffable delight passed over her beautiful face like a beam. She wound her arms about his neck and lay on his heart. It seemed to him that his heart opened to receive her with passionate tenderness.

"My beloved," he whispered, "it is almost dawn. I must leave thee. But hearken unto me for a moment. Thou knowest we are in terrible danger. Tonight I will come to thee again. But when I leave at dawn, I shall leave with thee. We shall flee together to the steppes, and my people shall receive thee as their queen."

She listened, her eyes fixed on his shadowy face with grave earnestness. The beam had left her own face. Then she raised herself and sat on the edge of her couch, gazing down at him with such intense and sorrowful concentration that he was startled. Her pale bright hair fell over her shoulders and her breast.

"My warriors will be ready," he went on. "We have the fleetest horses in the world. Before the palace is aroused, and thou art missed, we shall be leagues away."

The sorrow made a whiteness over her face. Then she whispered: "Temujin, we have five nights more. Let us take them."

He frowned, raised himself on his elbow.

"And then?"

She was silent. Her head dropped on her breast.

He was filled with anger against her. "And then thou wilt become the bride of the Caliph."

"Nay," she murmured, "I shall be the bride of no other man but thee."

"Thou meanest that after five nights thou wilt come with me?"

She lifted her head and smiled at him with mournful passion.

"Remember this, my lord: Whether in death or life, I shall be with thee always."

She shivered; she drew her thick hair over her naked flesh as though it were a garment. But her smile remained, fixed and sad.

He pondered on her words. For some unknown reason a chill ran over his body. He gazed at her intently, trying to read her thoughts.

She began to speak again, in a low murmur.

"Temujin, I can bring thee only death or torture. My father would not dare to forgive me, for fear of the Caliph. He would hunt me down, no matter where thou didst hide me, and thee, also. I care not for myself. I care only for thee. If thou lovest me, thou wilt go after these five nights, and never return, and try to forget me."

He listened, and slowly rage turned his face black. He seized her by the wrist.

"Art thou a wanton? Art thou weary of me?"

She did not answer, but only gazed at him with such grief and torment that he was ashamed. But he continued to hold her wrist.

She said, weeping: "If I brought ruin upon thee and thy people, there would be no joy in all the world again for me."

He said, after some moments: "I cannot leave thee. Either thou dost flee with me to my people, and hope for the best, or I shall remain here. I shall go to thy father and demand thee for my wife, telling him thou art no fit bride for the Caliph."

She put her slender hands over her face, and the tears ran through her fingers. He rose and put on his garments, watching her gloomily. When he was about to go, she withdrew her hands, and smiled at him through white lips.

"I have told thee, Temujin: where thou dost go I shall go forever." She held up her arms and he caught her fiercely to him, burying his face in her shoulder. She held him as a mother might hold her son, sorrowfully and with aching tenderness.

"Thou wilt say nothing at all about me to my father, Temujin?" she asked.

"Nothing," he answered, his lips against her flesh.

"Thou wilt swear it? Swear it by all thou dost reverence, and by all thou dost believe?"

He was startled, even in his passion, by the sharp earnestness of her words.

"I swear it," he answered. He smiled. "I swear it by myself, for that is all my belief."

She gazed at him, as though trying to pierce into his spirit, and piercing, willing him to remember.

He picked up a strand of her hair and pressed it against his mouth. She watched him, smiling mournfully.

"Take thou a lock of my hair, Temujin," she said faintly. "Take it for a talisman and a reminder of me."

"I can remember thee without a talisman, Azara. But if thou dost wish it, I shall take a lock."

He cut loose a long length of her hair. It curled about his fingers as though it loved him. It was as warm and soft as silk, and as radiant.

Again she held up her arms to him, and her lips. He held her to him, and it seemed to him that her flesh merged with his and became part of it. He could taste the saltiness of her tears, but she continued to smile.

The eastern sky was pricked with pale pink fire. He must

go. He kissed her hands slowly and passionately, and she watched him, hardly seeming to breathe. When he left the room, she gazed at him to the last, as though wishing to remember everything about him.

He was quite jubilant when he reached his own chambers. Chepe Noyon and Kasar were just awakening. They were relieved to see him once more, but said nothing. He lay down, after greeting them jovially, and fell instantly asleep.

"What can we do?" asked the simple Kasar, with despair.

"I know not," replied Chepe Noyon, shaking his head. "But I believe this: that nothing in heaven or earth can harm Temujin. The gods are his protectors, and he is the instrument in their hands."

"Dost thou truly believe this?" said the superstitious Kasar, looking furtively at his sleeping brother.

Chepe Noyon smiled. "I believe in no spirits, but there are men born for destiny. Such is our lord."

chapter 22

As he slept, Temujin had a strange and terrible dream.

He dreamed that he lay on this very couch, sleeping, and that he felt a touch on his shoulder. He dreamed that he awoke, and found Azara standing beside him in the brilliant sunlight. But she was as white and cold as ice, even though she smiled down at him with infinite love. He was extremely frightened, and thought: This is madness, that she hath come to me in these chambers.

She bent over then, and kissed him on the lips. A cold thrill ran through him, for her lips were chilled and stiff. He uttered an exclamation, and tried to seize her in his arms. But she shook her head, and stepped backwards, still smiling at him. Tears ran over her face.

Then, still gazing at him, she moved backwards towards the doorway. She lifted the curtains, and to the last she gazed at him. Her lips moved, but he could hear nothing. The curtain dropped behind her, and she was gone.

An ironlike paralysis encased his body. He struggled with it. He could feel the sweat running down into his eyes. At length he was able to throw it off. He sprang from his couch. The strong sunlight streamed through the latticed windows into the room, but it did not warm him. He was shuddering violently. He ran through the doorway, out into the corridor, shouting and calling for Azara. He passed the guardian eunuchs, with their naked torsos and bared swords, but they did not seem to see or hear him. He ran into the gardens, bright and brilliant with flowers and sunlight, and saw the glittering of the lakes and the fountains. A group of girls were laughing and disporting themselves. He spoke to them, asking them if they had seen Azara. But they did not answer. He might have been a shadow for all that they noticed him.

He ran through the gardens, calling. Then, through an aisle of bending and clashing and fluttering palms, he saw Azara, running like a flash of sunshine. He pursued her. But he could not overtake her. His legs felt weak, his body fainting. He implored her to wait for him. But she did not look back.

All at once he saw before the girl a tall, smooth white wall. He could not remember having seen it before. There was a huge door in it, made of gold and intricately chased. Azara approached the door. It opened as though by invisible hands. She stood on the threshold, and now she turned, and looked back at Temujin. Her face was the face of death, but she smiled at him. And now he heard her voice, like a faint echo.

"Go back, Temujin. Thou canst not enter here. Go back, beloved."

She pressed her hands to her lips, and blew him a kiss. Then, bending her head, she passed over the threshold, and the door silently closed after her.

Panting and weeping aloud, he reached the door. The sunlight fell on it in golden tremulous waves. He beat upon it, imploring, calling, shouting. But it did not open.

"Azara!" he cried. "It is I! Come back to me!"

Then he was aware of the profound and shining silence about him. He saw no one. The gardens were empty. The earth and the sky were empty, and full of warm brilliance and peace. He looked about him, despairing. There was not even the note of a bird, or a voice. To his left the palace rose, serene and silent, glittering in the intense light.

In his heart was a wound of bleeding desolation. It seemed to him that life was leaving his body. He sank on the earth beside the door, and darkness fell over his eyes.

He awoke suddenly, trembling and sobbing aloud. No one was near him. He lay alone in his room. A warm sunlit wind was stirring the draperies in the archways, and he could hear the dim murmuring bustle of the palace life.

He sat up on his couch, trying to control his trembling, and the horrible nausea in the pit of his stomach. He dressed himself. His arms were cold and nerveless, and suddenly he retched, ignominiously.

When he had done, he lay back on his couch, as weak as an infant. Complete desolation and despair overwhelmed him. It was a long time before he was able to fight his way out of the darkness of his sensations. At last he thought: It was an omen. We cannot wait. We must flee tonight.

The draperies were lifted, and Chepe Noyon and Kasar entered, laughing youthfully together. But when they saw Temujin's face, they were silent and alarmed.

He spoke at once, in a hoarse, weak voice:

"See to it that our warriors are prepared to leave tonight, at midnight."

An expression of intense relief appeared on the faces of the young men.

"It shall be done, lord," said Chepe Noyon. He glanced at Kasar, and nodded his head.

Temujin sat up, and put his hands to his aching forehead. "Azara doth leave with us," he said.

Chepe Noyon paled. He compressed his lips. Kasar uttered a faint cry, and then was silent.

"It shall be done," repeated Chepe Noyon. He inhaled a deep breath, and then held it. His hand touched the hilt of his sword.

They knew now what faced them. Most certain death, if not immediately, in the near future. But they could do nothing but obey. Temujin was their khan. His word was their law. A pinched maturity and resolution appeared on Kasar's doglike face.

Neither of them attempted to dissuade Temujin.

A black gloom had settled upon him. He could not eat the food the servants brought him. He was feverish. Chepe Noyon suggested a walk in the gardens, but he shook his head. His bronzed skin was pale and damp. His red hair rose on his head like the mane of a lion. He was like a man obsessed with some terrible premonition.

Chepe Noyon, who was of a sensitive nature, tried to arouse him with gay chatter, but Kasar was unable to speak. Temujin listened to Chepe Noyon, but in reality all his attention was strangely trained on the tranquil noises of the palace. In the midst of Chepe Noyon's words, he suddenly raised his hand sharply.

"Hark!" he exclaimed. "Didst thou hear a woman scream?"

Chepe Noyon listened, then shook his head. "Nay, there was nothing." Then he listened again, more intently. The tranquil noises of the palace had been hushed, as though cold hands had been laid upon a multitude of mouths. An awful silence seemed to have descended upon everything. There was not a single sound. Even the birds appeared to have been struck into that silence, and the wind, and the trees.

Temujin sprang to his feet. He stood before his noyon like a wild beast suddenly affrighted. But he did not look at them. He stared before him, listening, his head bent, his whole body visibly trembling. And they, too, caught by his attitude and his look, listened, also, their hearts beating heavily.

Then, as though a gale had struck the palace, it appeared to shudder, and resound all through it with aching cries and shrieks. It was like a wind, sweeping through every corridor, battering at every door, shaking every column and every wall. It rose to a frightful crescendo, deafening.

Temujin's face had become like stone. His arms hung nerveless at his sides. But Chepe Noyon ran out into a corridor. It was swarming with eunuchs and women, slaves of both sexes, running blindly to and fro. He caught a woman by the arm, and looked into her dazed face. Her mouth was open, and emitting shriek after shriek. He shook her. But she continued to glare blindly at him, shrieking. He struck her across the face, and again demanded the reason for all this tumult.

She burst into tears, seeing him for the first time. "The Princess Azara!" she cried. "She hath been found in her chamber, hung with her own girdle!"

Horror turned Chepe Noyon to marble. He released the woman, and stood among the rushing throngs like a slender tree in a flood. He thought only: Do they know about Temujin? And: We must flee at once.

He swung about, struggled through the weeping and wailing throngs, and returned to his apartments. He found Temujin still standing there, stonelike, not moving nor breathing. Only his green eyes were horribly alive in his ghastly face. And then Chepe Noyon knew that he had heard, that he knew everything.

He spoke very quietly, without inflection in his steadfast voice:

"She did this for me. She sacrificed herself for me."

But he did not weep, nor cry out. He seemed like a man who now understood everything.

chapter 23

The palace sank into a black apathy of grief, terror and despair. Silence again descended upon it, but it was a disorganized silence. The servants moved about like stunned shadows, unspeaking. Even the eunuchs, who hated all women, had loved Azara. They leaned on their swords, and wept silently, their heads bowed.

It was said that Toghrul Khan had collapsed, and lay in a stupor. Only his son Taliph was with him. His physicians would admit no others. They would not allow even a Moslem or Christian priest to see him. He lay on his couch, his old withered face empurpled and swollen, as rigid as a corpse. The Caliph's envoys whispered behind his shut doors, and shook their heads ominously. The ambassadors of sultans whispered, also. There was a muted coming and going. Statues were draped in black. Within the purlieus of the palace dark shadows lay, for the sun was shut out.

Within her own bedroom, attended only by Taliph's weeping and terrified wife, lay Azara, smiling palely and serenely in her final sleep. A silver scarf was wound about her throat, hiding the horrid marks of her death. Her hands were folded on her breast; her hair streamed over her shoulders and her limbs. She was strangely alive, and appeared to glitter with a golden light of her own, in that shadowed and shuttered room. Beyond the doors whispered and shivered the wives of Toghrul Khan and Taliph, their faces and heads draped in black veils. They whispered that Azara had been seized with madness; that she had died rather than marry the old Moslem Caliph. There was an avid and excited gleam in the eyes of these women, who had hated Azara.

The corridors were full of motionless groups, silent or whispering.

Chepe Noyon marvelled at the composure of Temujin, who gave his orders for their departure that night. His face was gray and expressionless. His eyes were like bits of dead green stone. He did not speak of Azara. Chepe Noyon was intensely relieved. Temujin, the realistic and the exigent, would expend no energies in this deathly place any longer. He would keep his emotions at a minimum, never extravagant nor dangerous. What he had come for had gone. He would leave. He was a wise man. Chepe Noyon knew that he would never hear Azara's name on Temujin's lips again. She had vanished like an ominous dream, like the shadow of death over a multitude of people.

Chepe Noyon thought: If there are gods, I thank them that this girl hath died. This is but another evidence that they are concerned with Temujin's destiny.

The cynical young man was suddenly superstitious and taken aback. But he was also joyous. He did not fear death, but neither did he court it. He preferred to live. Now he was being allowed to live.

No one noticed their departure at midnight, for every one was occupied with the tragedy which had occurred, and the grave state of Toghrul Khan. Their absence would not be missed for several days. Then they would be forgotten. They were only stinking barbarians from the steppes, covered with grease, slightly bowed of legs from the curve of their horses' bellies, wearing strange garments. Chepe Noyon saw himself as these townsmen saw him, and was happily grateful.

They left the city, and were only perfunctorily challenged at the gates. The moon was dissolving into a pale mist, and earth and sky were swimming in nebulous clouds. The warriors rode behind their lord, the sound of their horses' hoofs the only echo in a profound stillness. Temujin spurred his horse; the others followed at this quickened pace. All about them stretched the dark plains, motionless under the moon.

Chepe Noyon rode only slightly behind Temujin. He could see Temujin's face clearly. It was gray-colored, yet shining, like steel. His eyes were fixed ahead. Of what is he thinking? thought Chepe Noyon. Of Azara, for whom he had been prepared to risk everything, even those who had loved and served him? But Chepe Noyon decided this could not be so. A man did not remember his dead love and have such a face. There was no despair in it, no anguish. It was the face of a falcon, seeking for prey, and hating it with a curiously human hatred.

Now they were out upon the barrens, black and endless. The moon came out more clearly. The air was very cold and still as death. They dismounted, and prepared to camp for the night. Chepe Noyon, seeing that Temujin would give no orders, gave them himself. There would be no fires. They would eat their dried Mongol beef, which they had carried under the saddles of their horses, against the latter's warm flesh, so that it should be softened. They would drink water. Every one spoke and moved about warily, as though expecting enemies.

Temujin ate nothing. He sat apart with his brother and Chepe

Noyon. His hands hung between his knees. He appeared absorbed in some profound melancholy of his own. But surely it was not grief. It was too somber, too menacing, for that.

The men wrapped themselves in their cloaks and lay down to sleep near their horses. Temujin lay down, with Chepe Noyon beside him. Chepe Noyon was peacefully tired. But still he could not free himself from a vague uneasiness.

Then Temujin spoke, as though aloud, and to himself, quietly and deeply:

"I shall be avenged."

Chepe Noyon was startled. Avenged? Upon whom? He puzzled this to himself, with growing alarm. But in the very midst of his perturbation he fell asleep.

He awoke instantly to full consciousness later, aware that he must have slept for some time. The moon had vanished. Now there was only darkness. But Chepe Noyon sat up, intently listening, straining all his power to hear. He could see nothing, but knew that no one had stirred, not even Temujin, wrapped in his cloak beside him.

He decided that he must have dreamed the sound that had awakened him: the sound of a man's weeping, broken and dry, and muffled.

chapter 24

Each morning Jamuga searched the pink horizon, and each evening he searched the hyacinth horizon, desperately hoping to see Temujin returning. His alarm and perturbation were increasing as the days passed. Each night he reassured himself that Temujin was sagacious; each morning his old patronizing underestimation of his anda returned, and he was positive that the end lay crouching somewhere behind those horizons he searched so desperately.

He was not too happy in his position, for he was no fool. He saw that his khanship was not only temporary, but negligible. The true rule of the tribe was in the hands of the silent and beautiful Subodai. It is true that Subodai consulted him with great respect, and at frequent intervals, but it was only lip service. He felt himself dragged helplessly along, as usual, on a current decided by another. To a man of his cool and hidden vanity, this was intolerable. The pale stern line between his brows deepened. He became petty in small matters, and irritable, in order to display to others that he was in truth the khan, and not Subodai. He was guilty of small tyrannies and caprices. But even this did not give him pleasure. He felt a hidden disdain beneath the respect accorded him, a sly amusement at his pallid arrogance. Had Temujin detected this against himself, he would have come savagely out in the open and fought it down into genuine respect and fear. But Jamuga was at once too proud, too timid, too egotistic, to force an open struggle in which he doubted that he would be victor.

He was too fastidious to be cruel; he did not possess any real warmth nor kindness, and because of this he could not win affection if not respect. He was either embarrassed, alarmed, uneasy or nervous among his fellows. Had he possessed potential ferocities and power, his aloofness would have inspired awe and even worship. But uncertain, cold, filled with shadowy arrogance, proud and vain, he lacked strength and exigency, and consequently was regarded with contempt. As the days passed, the stern but gentle Subodai found it all he could do, by prodigious will power and low warnings, to compel the people to heed Jamuga and at least allow him to believe he ruled them. The sensitive Jamuga soon detected it, and a thin venomous hatred rose in him against Subodai, who ruled wherever he desired without apparent effort. At night, he wept bitter tears and could not sleep.

Once he was guilty of a grave error. This error was the seed which was to bear terrible fruit for him, in the years to come.

He had told himself that during his khanship he would rectify many "injustices" among the people, in order to have an arguing-point against Temujin when he returned, and to demonstrate to his anda some of the errors of his rule.

The nokud each had absolute life-and-death control of those members of the tribe assigned under their jurisdiction. The nokud made all decisions, judged all quarrels, punished all offenders. If a man were condemned to die, no one could appeal the judgment of the nokud.

It happened that at one sunset Jamuga was walking gloomily through the tent city to take up his customary vantage point where he might watch the evening horizon for Temujin. It was far from his own yurt and household. This section was under the jurisdiction of a stern middle-aged man by the name of Agoti, whom Jamuga knew slightly and disliked for his inexorable stolidity. Too absorbed in his own dismal thoughts, he did not at first hear the wailing of women and children coming, muffled, from a certain large yurt. But at last he heard it. He was sensitive, rather than compassionate, and the noise made him wince. He went to investigate. He found, in the yurt, about twenty young women, two older women, and two crones, and at least twelve children. They were packed in the smoke-filled musky confines of the yurt, squatting on their haunches, their heads covered by their garments. All wept and moaned in unison, rocking back and forth.

Jamuga's light low voice could not at first penetrate the wall of grief, but at last a boy noticed him and called his mother's attention to the khan. At the sight of him she screamed aloud, flung herself upon her face before him, and grovelled at his feet, kissing them, drenching them in her tears, and crying for mercy. In a few moments all the other women had followed her example, and the evening was hideous with their cries and screams and imploring broken voices. A small crowd gathered outside, ejaculating and conjecturing.

Jamuga finally was able to gather that their lord, Chutagi, had been condemned to death. None of them appeared to know why. But he was to be strangled at midnight by orders of Agoti. Only Jamuga Sechen, the great khan, could save him. They knelt about him or lay prostrate, clutching his garments, weeping. The dim light fell on their haggard wet faces and disordered hair. One of the older women was the mother of Chutagi, and one his grandmother. All the others were his wives, daughters and sons.

Jamuga looked at them; his pale face changed, and he compressed his lips. He remembered Agoti with hatred and anger. Finally he was able to tear himself loose from the clinging women. He promised them that he would consult with Agoti and see what the crime of Chutagi had been, and what could be done.

He went back to his own yurt, burning with a strange and fiery emotion, his heart beating painfully. He did not know why he felt so. He knew that the laws of the tribe were immutable, and that Chutagi had apparently violated one of them, and gravely. He did not know why he wished to interfere. He did not try to analyze what he felt, nor what he might do. But he seemed to see the face of Temujin, and all his thin and acid gorge rose. He began to tremble violently. But still, there was no pity in him for the man who was to die, nor even for his women.

At the door of his own yurt, he paused. Then still obeying his strange impulse, he went to Temujin's yurt. Standing on the platform, he commanded a servant to bring Agoti to him at once. Then he entered Temujin's yurt and sat down on his smooth and empty couch. He looked about him, breathing very hard. The palms of his hands were wet. His flesh shook, and his mouth was dry. Now he began to understand some of his emotion. It was rage that had him, but an obscure if mortal rage that he had never felt before. Behind him hung the banner of the nine yak-tails, and beneath it one of Temujin's drawn sabers. He picked up the saber and laid it across his knees. Then he waited, breathing thinly and with difficulty.

Many had seen him enter, and were outside, whispering excitedly together. Soon they were joined by others. Within a few minutes nearly five hundred men were gathered in the section surrounding Temujin's yurt. Jamuga Sechen had entered the house of their lord and was sitting on his couch, holding Temujin's sword!

When Agoti, summoned, approached the yurt, a huge throng was at his heels. Something portentous was afoot, every man knew. But Agoti walked stolidly, looking ahead with complete indifference and even contempt. Occasionally, he spat, glowered at the men, who shrank back and dropped their eyes.

When he reached Temujin's yurt, he said in a loud voice: "So!" And smiled with dark grimness. Then he entered the yurt, and bowed low and ironically before Jamuga Sechen. He waited in silence for Jamuga to speak.

Jamuga's white face glistened with sweat; his light blue eyes were brilliant with emotion. But he spoke quietly:

"Agoti, I am informed that thou hast condemned one Chutagi to death. Why was I not informed of it?" Quiet as his voice was, it reached the nearest of the keen-eared Mongols, who quickly relayed it to their companions.

Agoti stared. Then his face became thick and congested. He could not keep the disdain and arrogance from his tones, when he answered:

"Lord, I am a nokud. I need to report to no one, not even the lord Temujin, about the disposition of the law among those under my command. Such hath he decreed."

The strange choking emotion that was afflicting Jamuga rose to a mad point. Everything turned black before him for a moment. Hatred seized him by the throat, but like his rage it was an obscure hatred.

When he spoke, his voice was faint and choked:

"Thou hast forgotten that I am khan, until our lord doth return. I tell thee now, and shall tell the others, that I am to be the final voice until that time. If thou dost make such momentous decisions in the future without my permission, thou shalt suffer the same fate."

The whispering throngs outside were struck with dumb amazement. As for Agoti, he stared at Jamuga as a man might stare at a madman. But he was not unintelligent. He recovered quickly. He said in a voice of calm dignity:

"Am I to understand that thou, Jamuga Sechen, art abrogating the laws laid down for us by the great lord, Temujin?"

A moment's reflection might have saved Jamuga from committing his greatest folly. But he did not reflect. His heart was beating with a sensation like mortal anguish. For the first time in his life, he desired to kill. His fingers gripped the hilt of the saber until they turned white. Even the stolid Agoti was startled by his face, and retreated a step, uneasily, after his bold words.

Then Jamuga said: "Thou art so to understand."

This was repeated outside, and struck the listeners mute with horror and excitement and glee, for they all despised him.

Agoti smiled ironically, and to conceal that smile, he bowed again.

Jamuga went on, in his choked failing voice: "The law of yesterday is not of today, or tomorrow. What hath this man done?"

Agoti spoke in a voice of mock respect: "Lord, he hath committed treason."

"Treason!" A pale shadow, inscrutable and dim, passed over Jamuga's face.

"Yes, lord. He was overheard to say many times these last days that our great khan hath deserted us incontinently for some trivial reason, delaying our departure to our winter pastures, leaving us open to attack in his folly." Agoti spoke slowly, as though relishing each word. He fixed his bland eyes upon Jamuga's. "He also said, as though this were not bad enough, that the people should elect a new khan, who will give them orders to take us away from this place of danger at once."

Jamuga listened. He moistened his dry and withered lips. He did not look away from Agoti. His eyes were the fixed glazed eyes of a blind man. Then, very slowly, he dropped his head forward, and seemed to sink into profound thought.

When he spoke his voice was like that of a man who speaks in his sleep:

"Is it treason, then, to deny a free man bold and open expression of his opinions?" He looked up sharply, and again his face was brilliant. "Nay, it is not! This man is no slave; he hath not been purchased and chained. It is an evil thing if he cannot speak as his mind doth dictate. Free him at once."

The sardonic and heavy-lipped Agoti turned the color of old wax. He drew a sharp loud breath, and held it. He regarded Jamuga incredulously. He was unable to speak, and sweat burst out over his skin as he made the attempt. Outside, the people suddenly murmured to themselves, and their voices rose like a wind.

Seeing Agoti standing before him, rooted, his nostrils distended, Jamuga became wildly enraged. His voice became high and hysterical like a woman's when he exclaimed:

"Art thou an imbecile? Art thou deaf? Thou hast heard me! Release Chutagi immediately, or thou shalt suffer dire consequences!"

Agoti was no longer satirical nor ironic nor amused. He was shaken to the heart. He could not orient himself. Dumfounded, he could still not move. I have not heard aright, he seemed to be saying over and over, to himself, repudiating his own ears.

Jamuga glared about him. Drops of cold dew stood out all over his pale face. His eye fell on a yak whip close to his hand, and he seized it. He swung it in the air; he brought it full across Agoti's face; it hissed like a snake in its passage, and when it had fallen, a scarlet welt rose where it had struck.

"Now, go!" said Jamuga, hoarsely, panting. And send Chutagi to me."

Agoti had not winced nor fallen back when the whip had struck him. He had received it full, unflinching. He stood before Jamuga, and his stature seemed to increase. He was clothed in grave dignity, and looked at the other man with pride and courage.

"Thou art the khan," he said, quietly. Then instantly he was no longer a nokud, but a man, and his eyes blazed murderously. He bent his head in salute, wheeled, and left the yurt.

Alone in the yurt, Jamuga's panting breath filled the ominous silence. His darting eye fell on the whip in his hand. He uttered a faint exclamation, and flung it from him with loathing. But in an instant later, he drew his lips together, and clenched his narrow hands. His breath grew more quiet; the violet pulse in his temples abated. He heard nothing from the people outside, and assumed they had gone. He did not know that they were completely shocked and stunned at what they had heard.

The flap of the yurt opened, and Agoti came in, accompanied by Chutagi. Chutagi moved like a man in a fantastic dream. He looked at Jamuga as one hypnotized. He kept blinking his eyes and wetting his lips with the tip of his tongue. He was a tall man, bronzed and lean, with strong squat legs; his height was in his torso. His expression was bold and somewhat insolent, his eyes protruding with a bellicose look. Jamuga studied him in silence. Here was a man of courage and strength, who spoke his mind in the face of death, and could not be awed even by such a one as Temujin, before whom the people trembled.

Here is one, at least, who doth not adore Temujin, thought Jamuga, and even in his disordered state he was conscious of a strange acrid thrill of satisfaction. He motioned to Agoti brusquely. "Go," he said.

Agoti hesitated. The whip had torn across his lower lip, which was swollen and bleeding, and his chin, which was broken and discolored. Then he saluted, and withdrew.

Jamuga and Chutagi regarded each other in silence. Chutagi was not afraid. He held his shoulders arrogantly. Then Jamuga was conscious of disappointment. Here was no intelligent rebel, speaking as he wished with dignity and understanding. He was only an urchin in soul, perpetually discontented, a malcontent seeking only to stir up trouble. Jamuga saw this, however, only dimly; his disappointment rose from the fact that Chutagi wore no look of gratitude and joy, respect and reverence. He regarded Jamuga with the boldness of complete impudence, and, seeing this lack of veneration, Jamuga's anger obscurely rose again. He had expected Chutagi to kneel before him, acknowledging both his power and his mercy.

Jamuga said curtly: "I have heard that thou hast expressed disrespect for our khan, Temujin. I deplore thy foolishness and lack of discretion. We are in no position, at this time, to have our people divided, no matter what thine opinion. Nevertheless, thou hast spoken boldly, like a free man. Bold speech is never a reason for death. Go; thou art free, but mind thy silly tongue in the future."

Chutagi stared. But his expression did not change. It merely grew a trifle bolder and more impudent. Then, incredible to Jamuga, this look was gone, and was replaced by one of uncertainty and bewilderment.

"I am free, my lord? Free to go, after my treason?"

Jamuga's thin fury rose like the thrust of a blade once more. "Thou fool! Hast thou heard nothing I have said?"

Chutagi was silent. He was no longer courageous and defiant. He seemed thoughtful; he brooded. Then his features wrinkled, and Jamuga, disbelieving, saw that he was about to burst into tears.

"But, lord, I urged the people to rebellion. I am guilty of treachery and disobedience. I must die. I have violated the first law of my people; I deserve punishment."

It was Jamuga, now, who stared, as at a madman. He choked. He dared not speak for some time, lest he burst out into wild vituperation, and strike the other man down. His arms lifted, waved incoherently. Then he cried:

"Thou idiot! Get out of my sight!"

Complete bewilderment had Chutagi; he was entirely disorganized. He was like one who sees the ground open before him, who sees the aspect of the world change into something nightmarish and appalling, wherein he is a complete and terrified stranger, and all safe and established things have vanished. Then he stumbled backwards, blinking his eyes. He almost fell out of the yurt.

Jamuga groaned over and over: "Oh, these animals! These animals!"

He buried his face in his hands; he felt mortally sick. He retched, drily.

The listening people outside gazed at each other. Each man's face was a replica of Chutagi's, baffled, frightened, wrinkling at the contemplation of a world that was no longer firm and secure and orderly. Then one by one they drifted away, returned to their yurts. Soon the whole city of the tents was silent and breathless, as though it mourned. The campfires died down;

the women gathered together and whispered. Many caught their children to them, as if to protect them.

Jamuga, recovering a little, said to himself: It is Temujin's fault. He hath taken the manhood from his people, and hath made them fools and beasts.

chapter 25

Jamuga lay on his couch, but could not sleep. The whole city seemed sunken into sleep. But this was an illusion. Never had a night found it so awake. It blew with rumors. Temujin had been killed; Jamuga had been appointed khan in his place. Temujin was alive, and returning immediately; upon his return, he would personally dispatch his anda. Tomorrow Jamuga would give the order to leave for the winter pastures; tomorrow he would do nothing. Perhaps he might commit suicide, when he finally reached sanity. But every one knew that something terrible and momentous had happened. And never had the city been so restless, so frightened, so rebellious.

Jamuga, sensitive and subtle, felt these winds of rumor and terror. But he was horribly bewildered and disgusted. The more he tried to understand, the more nebulous did things become. What had he done? Merely freed a man unjustly and absurdly sentenced to death for no valid reason! He had defied a barbaric law laid down by Temujin. At times a knife-blade of exultation made him smile in the darkness; he had successfully defied that law. He had employed reason instead of imbecility. Surely Temujin would acknowledge that.

At the thought of Temujin, Jamuga felt a contraction of his heart. But the contraction was not fear. Rather, it was compounded of uneasiness, anger, scorn, and sadness, and something else which he refused to examine.

He saw the faint bright shadow of a torch. Some one was plucking at the flap of his yurt. He got up and opened it. Kurelen stood there, wrapped in his black cloak. The old cripple smiled at him reassuringly, handed the torch to a warrior who guarded the yurt outside, and entered.

"I thought mayhap thou wert sleeping. Forgive me, if this is so," said Kurelen. His words were gentle, and his smile paternal. But his sharp eyes studied Jamuga's colorless narrow face with close attention.

"I was not asleep," replied Jamuga, bitterly. He was resentful. He had some idea why Kurelen had come. The old man sat down on Jamuga's tumbled couch. He fitted his fingers together, and again smiled at Jamuga. "Ah," he said, thoughtfully. Apparently, he was in no hurry to begin. And Jamuga, obstinately refusing to go on the defensive, waited in embittered silence.

Kurelen continued to scrutinize the young man. He kept smiling to himself; once he curved his twisted dark hand over his mouth to hide his smiles. At last he said:

"I commend thy compassion and thy sentiments. But not thy discretion, Jamuga."

Jamuga regarded him with proud offense and weary disdain.

"My discretion! Are men logs of wood, or lumps of dried dung, to be thrown into a fire at the capricious will of a stupid petty lord?"

Kurelen shrugged. "I am not prepared to argue about the intrinsic value of any human being. I do not know whether any of us have any value. Certainly not, in the light of eternity." He lifted his hand. "Please, Jamuga, let me speak.

"I do not know this Chutagi, nor do I care to know. I have heard he spoke foolishly. But not more foolishly than thou didst act. However, it seemeth we have laws against this kind of foolishness of his. Now, I am not prepared to argue about the validity of these laws. The fact is, there are such laws. By abrogating them, thou didst commit a grave folly. The people know this. Thou hast sinned against them. They know not where they can turn. Thou hast terrified them——"

"But why?" Jamuga's voice rose hotly. He stood up, as though burned. He began to pace up and down with disordered steps; a flush rose over his face. "Why should they be terrified? Because I was merciful, and just, and reasonable?"

Kurelen shrugged again, spread out his hands.

"Because thou hast violated a law, and when a khan doth violate a law he soweth confusion among his people. He hath taken security from them, and given them anarchy." And then he knew it was useless, that Jamuga could not understand, would never understand.

Jamuga was regarding him with venomous scorn. "And I thought thou wast a just and reasonable man, sometimes compassionate!" he exclaimed.

"Nevertheless," said Kurelen, mildly, "I do not advocate the sudden and violent abrogation of law, without preliminary preparation and education of the people. They are children. They must be taught slowly. They are incapable of long reasoning, but simple facts, constantly reiterated, can sometimes penetrate to their primitive minds and be received with security and satisfaction."

"I do not understand!" cried Jamuga, violently.

"I see thou dost not. And, Jamuga, I fear thou wilt never understand. Thou wilt never understand other men. Thou dost judge them by thyself. That is fatal."

Jamuga was silent. Tears of impotence and despair rose to his eyes.

Kurelen leaned towards him and put his hand on his arm.

"Thou hast courage, but thou art a dreamer, Jamuga Sechen. This is no world for dreams. We must accept facts."

"What shall I do?" asked Jamuga, despairingly.

"Tomorrow, direct Agoti to take Chutagi into custody again. Tell the people that thou hast finally decided to wait the return of Temujin for decision, saying the matter is too grave for thy responsibility. Jamuga," he urged, "thou hast no right to do this to our people. thou must restore their security immediately. Otherwise, dire things will come about."

Jamuga flung off his hand hotly. "Thou talkest like a fool, Kurelen! I shall not do this thing! I shall not debase myself so, before——"

"Before Temujin?" asked Kurelen, slyly.

Jamuga's face turned crimson with mortification and fury.

"Before the people! I shall not retract. I offer no apology. I have done what I considered right." He glared at Kurelen wildly. "Dost thou not understand? This Chutagi is a man, not a beast! He cannot be disposed of like an animal awaiting slaughter."

Kurelen raised his brows. "I say again, that I am not prepared to discuss the value of human beings. I know that something portentous will result from this. I know that I am giving you sound advice."

"Thou art advising me to crawl back on my footsteps, and destroy a fellow human being!"

Kurelen stood up. "It is hopeless, then. Thou wilt never understand." He paused. He gazed at Jamuga for a long moment. A curious change came over his sunken and withered features. A flicker as of regret and sadness touched his eyes. He put his hand for a moment on Jamuga's shoulder.

"Jamuga, the first thing a wise king must learn is never to destroy authority, never to cast doubt in the minds of a people about the sacrosanct quality of law. If he doeth these things, he, himself, will be destroyed by the destruction he hath created. Authority and law maketh a world of men; their abolition doth return the world to darkness."

Jamuga made a gesture of wounded contempt.

"Must laws be immutable? Must an heir to a throne retain the laws of those who hath died? May not he make others, more suited to present circumstances? We cannot live under the shadow of the hand of the dead, always!"

Kurelen smiled inscrutably.

"But Temujin is not yet dead, Jamuga."

He put on his cloak.

"Nevertheless, Jamuga, I again commend thy compassion, though I do not agree with thee." He added: "I am an old man, now."

He went out, leaving Jamuga alone with his angry misery.

But he was not alone very long. Again, some one moved aside the flap of his yurt, and this time Subodai, grave and beautiful, and gently smiling, begged permission to enter. His manner soothed Jamuga, though he suspected why Subodai had come, for it was respectful and calm.

"Permit me to speak, lord," he said.

Jamuga nodded curtly, bracing himself. He was jealous of Subodai, but no one could really hate this handsome and gentle youth with the shining and straightforward eyes.

Subodai hesitated for only an instant. All his nature was full of clarity; there was no deviousness, no servility nor fear in him.

"Forgive me, lord, if I speak straightly, out of my apprehension. If thou dost desire to punish me for my candor, I still cannot refrain from speaking. This is a sad thing thou hast done."

Now he showed his anxiety fully. Jamuga waited, biting his lip, and frowning.

"Thou hast taught the people to despise obedience, Jamuga Sechen."

Jamuga groaned in exasperation. "Obedience! Obedience to savage laws! Are the people not capable of recognizing an evil law?"

Subodai compressed his lips for a moment. "I cannot argue with thee about this, my lord. I only know that obedience must be enforced. I ask no questions; the people must realize they must ask no questions. Discipline and obedience and loyalty are the foundations of any tribe, of any nation. That is all my concern."

Feeling exhausted, Jamuga sat down. He fixed his tired eyes on Subodai's intelligent face. But all at once he knew that that very intelligence was his enemy. He saw that an intelligent man could deliberately will himself to disregard reason, and that this disregarding was exceedingly dangerous, more so than in a stupid man. Impotence rolled over him like dark waves.

"Thou hast taught the people to despise obedience," repeated Subodai. "Unless thou dost retract, I cannot promise to hold them together until the return of the lord, Temujin."

Jamuga bent his head. He sank into profound thought. Subodai waited. Then Jamuga spoke slowly and heavily, as though thinking aloud:

"Let us suppose that Temujin doth not return. In that event, I shall be khan until another is elected. I shall then abrogate many of Temujin's laws, which I believe are cruel and stupid. Will this cause the disintegration of our people?"

Subodai said softly: "But our lord is still alive, and the people know it. Thou hast flouted his laws of obedience and authority. But I cannot argue with thee. I know only obedience."

Jamuga cried out: "Canst thou not reason, Subodai?"

"I know only obedience," repeated Subodai gravely. "Only by obedience can a people survive."

"If Temujin commanded thee to commit a folly, to destroy wantonly, to kill thyself, to lead our people to death, wouldst thou obey?"

"I would," replied Subodai, simply.

"O God!" groaned Jamuga. He rubbed his forehead distractedly. "We are a generation of fools!"

Subodai said nothing.

Jamuga stood up and paced the floor. His face grew more pinched and haggard. Finally he stopped before Subodai, and spoke in a fainting voice:

"I cannot retract. That is my final word."

Subodai saluted. "So be it, lord," he said quietly.

Alone, Jamuga said aloud: "I have done what is right! I am certain of this."

He lay down and tried to sleep, but it was no use. Temujin entered his thoughts. What would he do? What would he say?

He was so accustomed to visitors now that it did not surprise him when another entered. This time it was Houlun, accompanied by several grave-faced nokud. The old woman stood before him, gaunt, gray-haired, but magnificent, a matriarch of power and dignity. She spoke without preamble:

"Jamuga Sechen, thou hast committed a terrible folly. I have come to ask thee to retract immediately."

As she spoke, she looked at him with her fierce gray eyes, and they were full of angry scorn.

For some reason the sight of her infuriated Jamuga. His nostrils flared out in his pale drawn face. He looked her fully in the eye.

"I shall not retract," he said.

She smiled darkly. "Dost thou realize thou hast abetted treason against my son?"

Jamuga's heart turned cold. He looked into her eyes, and tried to keep his flesh from trembling.

"I have committed no treason, and thou dost know it, Houlun. I have merely used my best judgment. If I have been wrong, let Temujin decide that for himself. But I do believe I have done no wrong."

She studied him in silence, then she spoke curiously:

"If thou couldst retract without making a fool of thyself, thou wouldst do so. But thy vanity is greater than thy discretion and thy sense, and thine envy of my son is even greater than thy vanity. In breaking one of his laws thou dost feel thou hast triumphed over him. In destroying his discipline and abetting treachery against him, thou dost have the silly joy of feeling momentarily stronger than he. But surely even thou dost realize that the personal gratification of one man is nothing compared with the unity and integrity of a whole people!"

Jamuga listened to her, and it seemed to him that his heart burst into devouring flames. He turned scarlet; his lips shook. His voice died in his throat. His struggles were visible, and Houlun observed them with dour satisfaction.

Finally he could speak: "I am khan until Temujin doth return. Go thou to thy yurt, Houlun, and do not leave it until I give thee permission."

She smiled with dark amusement. "Thou dost imprison the mother of Temujin? O Jamuga, thou art a greater fool than even I suspected!"

She inclined her head towards the nokud, who followed her from the yurt. She left him with pride and dignity. Then, from a little distance, he heard her laugh, loudly, again and again.

Jamuga's fury filled him like a poison. He walked up and down, distraught. He muttered to himself; sometimes he exclaimed aloud, flung himself on his bed and clutched his head in his hands. But the steel core of his obstinacy and belief in himself could not yield. Towards dawn he fell into an uneasy and nightmare-ridden dream.

He dreamed that he saw Temujin advancing towards him, smiling, his hand extended in friendship. He heard Temujin say: "This is mine anda. He hath done what I would have commanded to be done."

Jamuga felt an almost intolerable relief. He took Temujin's hand. He felt something hard in it. He recoiled, and saw that the hand held a dagger directed at his own heart. Temujin still smiled, but he held out the dagger inexorably, and now the smile was terrible.

Jamuga awoke with a cry. The dawnlight was pale and gray outside. Some one was fumbling again at the flap. Utterly distraught now, and nerveless, Jamuga gave vent to an involuntary shriek.

Subodai was entering, and with him was Agoti. Both men were very white, and breathing audibly. Jamuga saw that something awful had happened. He sat up in his bed, supported by a trembling arm. He glared at them from the extremity of his terror and exhaustion.

Subodai saluted. "Lord," he said gravely, "Agoti hath just told me Chutagi hath strangled himself with the girdle of his first wife, in his own yurt."

Jamuga was speechless. He could not remove his distended eyes from Subodai's pale calm face.

Agoti spoke respectfully, but with an undertone of small triumph:

"He told the woman that he must die for his treason against our lord."

Subodai, seeing Jamuga's sinking distraction, felt a qualm of pity.

"It is better so, Jamuga Sechen," he said gently. "We shall give it out to the people that he died by thy will."

"No!" screamed Jamuga. "I shall not have it so!"

The two men saluted in silence, and left him.

Jamuga flung himself face down on his bed. He groaned. He rolled from side to side. He was the prey of the most dreadful thoughts and suffering. He vomited. Pain ran through his body, and he thought: I am dying. He lusted after death with a piteous lust.

But after a while, he lay motionless, his eyes closed.

He thought: I have done the right thing. I did the only thing I could do.

chapter 26

As though fate wished to show Jamuga that she had been merely playing with him heretofore, she now seemed to devote herself to tormenting him in earnest.

Every one avoided him, except Kurelen. No one troubled to salute him with respect or reverence. Had he been invisible, he could have been no more ignored. At first he was angered; then, finally, he was alarmed. His influence and discipline were gone. The people seemed restless and undecided. They muttered openly. They searched the horizons with fierce and rebellious eyes. They spoke loudly about the increasing cold, and the thickness of the ice on the river in the morning. Now the women, always more bold and voluble than the men, were heard to criticize Temujin without restraint. Temujin's women complained to Bortei, saying: "Our lord is no longer mindful of us. It is said he is pursuing a Persian woman, and hath forgotten us, even thou, his first wife, and the mother of his son."

Bortei looked at her lusty child, and set her teeth. If she were only certain, she thought to herself somberly, she would never have let Temujin go. Or, rather, he would have stayed. So she deceived herself. Her blood burned hotly with jealousy and hatred. Was the Persian woman more comely than herself? She ran her small fingers through her long black hair with its touches of bronze; she regarded herself piercingly in her polished silver mirror. She could not help smiling vainly as she saw that she was more beautiful than ever. Her gray eyes were lustrous; her little nose was sharp and clear, and her mouth was a dark rose. The old minstrels often sang of her at twilight, declaring that no woman could surpass Bortei the Beautiful. She believed it. How, then, had Temujin been seduced?

She laid down the mirror, and drawing her brows together, scowled thoughtfully. Then she began to smile, slowly and voluptuously. She preened her head; she lay back on her couch, and smiled even more, studying the rounded lines of her breast, her hips and thighs. She no longer thought of Temujin.

Jamuga became more conscious every hour that disorder was imminent in the city of the tents. He watched Subodai going about, silently, but with a grave alert face. When the handsome young paladin appeared, the people saluted, for they feared him. But when he had gone, they muttered more loudly than ever. Lines of sleeplessness appeared on his face. He dared not sleep. But when he encountered Jamuga, he did not reproach him either by glance or word. His manner, if anything, was more respectful than ever, and gentle. He kept in constant communication with the nokud. At first he was inclined to give severe orders and punishments, but he soon saw that this would only make the rebellion flare out fatally. Each day he told the nokud to give out that Temujin would appear soon, that he had already left the Karait city. Once he gave it out that Temujin had greatly pleased his foster father, and that he was returning with a new horde of warriors and much riches. The mentioning of the name of the mighty Toghrul Khan brought the people temporarily to their senses. They became uneasy. If they rebelled, or muttered more, they would probably have to answer to Toghrul Khan.

Nevertheless, the situation was acute. And no one knew this more than the subtle old Chief Shaman, Kokchu. Subodai could not be sure of this, but he suspected that much of the unrest came from the conjurer. So he visited him one evening.

Kokchu had no particular dislike for Subodai. In fact, he admired him, as he admired all beauty. And like many evil men, he appreciated virtue, though he mocked it. Subodai was both beautiful and virtuous, and had only one wife, whom he loved dearly. So Kokchu greeted him with pleasure, making a place for him at his side, and dismissing his women and his young shaman. He was not surprised at this visit; in fact, he had expected it. But he had expected Jamuga in Subodai's place.

Subodai sat down. He smiled quietly but radiantly. He drank the good wine offered him, and partook of the evening meal. Kokchu was in a sly and amiable mood.

"I watched thy cavalry formations today, Subodai. Thou art truly a genius and a valiant man. What would Temujin do, these days, without thee?"

Subodai inclined his head with grave dignity at this flattery. "It is little enough," he answered. "Kokchu, I have come to thee for advice. The people mutter. Thou art the Chief Shaman, and they revere thee. I ask thee now to order them to cease their muttering, under the threat of dire penalties. After all, it is treason."

Kokchu threw up his eyes and his hands. "So I have told them! But, my son, thou must remember they have justification for their complaints. The winter is almost upon us. We should have been long gone to our winter pastures. The people are full of fear. Is it their fault that Temujin hath deserted them?"

Subodai regarded him steadfastly. "Thou knowest our lord hath not deserted us, Kokchu," he said, coldly. "He was invited to the wedding of Toghrul Khan's daughter. To have refused would have been a serious matter. He had to go."

Kokchu smiled, lifted his shoulders. "They say it is the woman that hath drawn Temujin, and not the wedding. I have heard it said that he will steal her, and bring her here, thus invoking the rage and vengeance of Toghrul Khan."

Subodai bit his lip. "It is a lie. I know not where this rumor doth arise. But it is a lie. He will return without her."

"How dost thou know?" asked Kokchu, with an insinuating smile.

Subodai got to his feet. "I know," he answered with a quiet and positive air. Kokchu regarded him keenly. But Subodai's eyes did not shift. Then Kokchu sucked in his lips and frowned. Perhaps Subodai did know, in truth. In that event, matters would not be comfortable for those who whispered treason to the people. Kokchu's cheek twisted. But he made himself smile gently.

"I will do what I can," he said. He sighed. "But it will be a hard task. But I will do what I can."

"I thank thee," said Subodai, gravely, without a smile. "And when our lord doth return, I will speak to him of thy great loyalty."

Kurelen was alarmed at what he heard and saw. He communicated this to Jamuga, maliciously. He said: "I say again, Jamuga, that thou wast born either too early or too late. In any event, thou hast committed a monstrous folly."

But Jamuga's own alarm and apprehension had made him excessively irritable, and he shrilled at Kurelen with such venom that the old man let him alone henceforth.

And it was at this time that fate struck him again.

He could not sleep. He could hear the redoubled guards pacing and moving about in the darkness of the night. He heard Subodai's low voice challenging them, and consulting with them. The sentinels, too, were redoubled, sitting motionless on their horses in the face of the enormous midnight moon, wrapped in their blankets and their thick coats, their lances or sabers held ready in their hands. But Jamuga obstinately clung to his belief that he had been right. But when he saw Subodai's uncomplaining and haggard face, and noticed that his gentle smile never failed him, he was filled with a personal remorse, not for what he had done, but for what he had made Subodai suffer.

His own sleeplessness became a torment. One night he

got up, desperately. Subodai had just passed in the darkness; Jamuga had heard his voice. He decided he would go to the young paladin and talk to him, seeking comfort in that steadfast virtue and lack of panic.

He followed Subodai's shadowy figure in the light of the waning moon. Subodai walked with his own graceful dignity, unhurried and calm. Jamuga was so weak with fear and sleeplessness that he could not overtake him. Subodai was making his rounds; he was approaching the section where Temujin's deserted yurt stood, with its guards. When Subodai reached the kibitka, the guard spoke to him. Subodai bent his head and listened intently; he appeared surprised. Then he nodded. He sprang up on the platform and went within. The guard then walked away, leaving the yurt unguarded, apparently by order.

Jamuga sighed. He quickened his steps. He knew that Subodai would be alone and now he could talk with him freely. He climbed slowly and heavily upon the platform, and reached out to draw aside the flap. And then he stopped, his hand outstretched, his nerves thrilling. For he saw that there was dim lamplight within, and he heard the quick whispering of voices.

Had Temujin returned? His heart beat violently, and then sweat of profound relief and weak joy burst out all over him. He bent his head, listening intently.

But he did not hear Temujin. He heard Subodai.

"I have come," the young paladin was saying. "What dost thou wish of me, Bortei?"

Jamuga heard Bortei's laugh, rich and languid.

"I am afraid, Subodai. I have no one to whom to turn for comfort and protection. My lord's mother, Houlun, is a prisoner in her yurt, and is forbidden visitors, by that fool, Jamuga. I am only a woman, and a mother, and frail of soul and heart. Forgive me that I have troubled thee."

There was a little silence. Outside, Jamuga's senses reeled; he almost fell off the platform.

Then Subodai spoke slowly and gravely: "Thou hast not troubled me, Bortei. Whatever I can do for the wife of my lord is thine to command."

Again, Bortei laughed her seductive laugh; then she sighed audibly.

"I know thy loyalty, Subodai. Sit beside me. Hold my hand. Thou art a brother to our lord, and I take comfort in thy touch and the sight of thee."

Jamuga knelt down on the platform. He lifted the flap a mere slip, in a wet hand. He peered within. He saw that Bortei was sitting on her couch, dressed in a white wool robe, elaborately embroidered. Necklaces of turquoise and gold were hung about her throat, and his wrists jingled with bracelets. Her black hair hung heavily over her shoulders, and the dim lamplight threw rosy shadows on her face, making her dark eyes inscrutable, swimming with radiance, and her lips like red flowers warm in the sun.

Subodai stood before her, tall and slender and silent. His blue eyes caught the light, and they were the color of the sky, vivid and shining. He made no effort to sit beside her. He was exceedingly pale.

"I must not linger," he said calmly. "I must complete my rounds, over and over. But speak quickly, Bortei: what can I do for thee?"

Her face changed. She looked at him in silence. Her breast rose, then began to heave with quickened breath. Her eyes moved from his lips, and thenceforth down his body in its long embroidered coat and woolen trousers, tied tightly about his ankles against the cold. Suddenly her cheeks flushed; her wet lips parted; her eyes swam in hot languor. She held his eyes with hers; she rose. She smiled seductively. She laid her hands on his shoulders, and threw back her head. Her white throat glimmered in the lamplight. And he looked down at her face, with its humid, half-opened smiling mouth, and did not move. But he did not seem amazed, nor even taken aback.

She began to whisper, thrillingly, and brought her face closer to his so that her hot breath touched his lips.

"Subodai, my lord hath deserted me. Thou knowest this. Soon the people will rise up and elect thee khan. Subodai, I have always loved thee. Thou wilt take me as thy wife. But I cannot wait. Take me tonight, Subodai! Take me tonight!"

Still, he did not move. His face was as composed and expressionless as that of a stone image's. She studied him; her breast rose swellingly. The throat of her garment was open, and now it parted, and her bosom was revealed shamelessly. She laughed, low and triumphantly. Her hands slipped from his shoulders, found their way under his coat; she clasped him about the waist. Then she leaned against him, putting her head on his breast. Her body pressed against his; her thigh clung to his. Her eyes half-closed in the languor of lust, and she smiled.

They stood like this for a long moment, like one body. In the darkness outside, Jamuga began to shudder violently. He felt mortally sick. His sight failed him, and he thought he was dying. When he opened his eyes, he believed that he had fainted. But when he looked within the yurt again, he saw that only a little time had passed. The man and the woman still stood together, immobile.

Then, gently but firmly, Subodai disengaged himself. Bortei attempted to cling to him, but his hands were inexorable. He seemed to push her away without violence, but this was just seemingly, for when he had released himself from her last clutch, she staggered backwards and fell on her couch. She sat there, panting, her hair disordered, her lips open, showing the glisten of her teeth.

Subodai smiled whitely; he bowed to her. "And that is all thou dost wish of me, Bortei?" he asked in a quiet and ironic voice.

She glared at him, and did not move. He bowed again. "If it is so, then I must refuse. Thou wilt forgive me, tomorrow, I know. But spare me thy gratitude."

He turned away, still smiling that strange fixed smile. He took a step from her. She watched him. Then she uttered a shrill and savage cry. She flung herself upon her knees; she tore her garments from her shoulders and her breast. Her bosom was like twin moons, and glimmering. She grasped him about the knees, and laid her cheek fiercely to them.

"Thou darest not leave me! I shall not let thee go, Subodai! I love thee; I cannot live without thee!"

He struggled to release himself. His face was damp with sweat and horror. He closed his eyes, to shut out the sight of her nakedness. She clung to him like a serpent; she began to laugh, deeply, in her throat.

Suddenly they heard a muffled cry, the sound of some one entering. Subodai stood upright, glaring and breathing heavily. But Bortei, too paralyzed with terror, did not move. Her arms still clutched the young paladin; she looked over her shoulder at Jamuga, standing there, his face ghastly with fury and hatred and loathing.

"Thou foul wanton!" he exclaimed. "Thou iniquitous whore!'

Now Bortei's arms fell from Subodai's knees. She squatted there before Jamuga, her hair on her shoulders, her breast exposed. Her face was idiotic with fear and rage and shame.

Jamuga, trembling, turned to Subodai. "Leave us!" he commanded. In those moments he was a khan in truth, no longer proud and timid and haughty. Subodai, white as death, inclined his head. He hesitated. Then, after a long deep look into Jamuga's distended eyes, he left the yurt, moving without haste, but in his own quick way.

Alone with the woman, rage fell on Jamuga. His eye sought out Temujin's whip. He bent and seized it. Bortei watched him, unable to rise. She saw Jamuga lift the whip; she winced. Her mouth opened in a soundless scream. She heard the whip whistle, and felt its searing tongue on her bare shoulders and breast. She rolled from her knees and lay on the floor, trying to protect herself with her arms. But the whip was relentless. It fell again and again, cutting her flesh, leaving scarlet ribbons on her white body. But there was no sound from either her or Jamuga, just the mad flailing of the whip and its whistling.

Then he had done. She lay motionless on the floor, gasping, her head hidden in her arms. Jamuga flung the whip from him.

"Bitch!" he said in a low voice. And that was all.

He left her, stumbling blindly through the night. Reaching a sheltered spot, he fell down, moaning with tearing anguish.

Bortei, alone, began to sob. She writhed in her torment. She sat up, putting aside her hair. She glared about her. Her eyes fell on the whip, in which strands of her hair were entangled. Suddenly her face became distorted with fury and hatred. She pushed herself slowly to her feet, her head hanging, her breath hoarse in her throat. Swaying, as she stood, she examined her injuries. They were many.

Her arms dropped to her sides. Then she smiled evilly.

Jamuga did not yet know it. But he had marked himself for death. It would take some time. But inevitably, he had marked himself.

Subodai found Jamuga, almost at dawn, lying prostrate in the shadow of his yurt. He had been unable to summon the strength to climb upon the platform. Without speaking, the young paladin helped him inside, and laid him upon the couch. He poured wine, and forced Jamuga to drink it.

"What shall we do?" he asked, when Jamuga seemed to have recovered some part of his strength.

Jamuga shook his head. He said, grimly: "Nothing. The woman will never dare to speak. As for us, we must keep our silence."

Then suddenly he began to weep, like a woman.

chapter 27

Shortly after dawn, Jamuga, finally overcome by exhaustion, fell asleep. He did not dream. His collapse was too profound. So it was that Subodai had to call him several times before he awakened. He sat up. The sunlight was warm and brilliant as it streamed into the yurt.

Subodai's pale face was shining with joy. "Our lord hath returned!" he cried. "Our sentinels have sighted him to the east!"

Jamuga stood up; he staggered. He almost fell. Subodai helped him to put on his coat and buckle his belt. The young paladin's hands were sure and calm, and he smiled. They went out together.

The camp was already in a state of intense excitement and joy. Everything was forgotten, save that Temujin had returned. The people thronged the narrow winding streets between the yurts. The dogs barked furiously. The women began to sing and the minstrels strummed their fiddles, and boys began to beat drums. Kokchu emerged from his yurt, attended by his young priests. He was gorgeously arrayed. Kurelen, smiling wryly, stood beside him. Only Houlun was not there, nor Bortei. But finally Bortei appeared, clothed and tranquil, but colorless. Even in his fury, Jamuga had remembered to spare her face, and it was untouched. She held her child in her arms, wrapped in a white fur robe.

On the eastern horizon was a cloud of swiftly approaching dust. It caught the sun and shone, a golden halo of drifting light. They could hear the faint drumming of hoofs.

"The lord hath returned!" chanted the minstrels and the women. "He hath come unto his people, like the sun out of the heavens! He hath given us the light of his countenance, and the glory of his smile! What have we feared in the darkness? What have we dreaded? We do not remember; we have forgotten! The lord hath returned!"

The yellow river glinted in the sunshine. A string of gray geese moved across the sky. The herds were excited, and bellowed,and the horses neighed.

The people surged out to meet their khan. The warriors held their lances, and sat monumentally on their horses, their faces graven. The children screamed.

The simple people had indeed forgotten. But there were a few who had not. Kurelen, Subodai, the nokud, Bortei and Kokchu, waited, watching. Was the Persian woman with Temujin? They were chill with fear and alarm. If so, then this joy was but a respite before horrors and death and endless flight from vengeance.

Now, through the golden dust they could see the galloping horsemen, and the glittering tips of the lances, and the fluttering of the banners. But no woman was with the horsemen. They rode alone.

Kurelen drew in a deep whistling breath of thankfulness. He turned to Jamuga, rigid and gray-lipped, beside him. "Our fears were groundless," he said in a low voice.

But Jamuga said nothing. He had fixed his eyes ahead.

Temujin and his warriors were greeted with shouts and cries of joy, which the brown and purple barrens flung back, ringingly. The whole earth seemed to rejoice. The people surged about the returning men; women seized the bridles of the horses, and looked up, their faces streaming with tears and bright with happiness. The warriors, laughing, dismounted, and embraced their women and their children. The air resounded with the babble of voices and the great excitement. The minstrels shouted louder, and the drums beat on the ears.

Temujin, dust-stained and unsmiling, dismounted from his horse. Kurelen and the nokud, Jamuga and Subodai and Kokchu, approached him, pushing their way through the excited throngs. Kurelen looked at Temujin, and thought: He hath aged. His flesh hath dissolved from his bones. This is a man who hath suffered awful agony, and who will never rid himself of its scars. But he smiled at his nephew and embraced him.

"Welcome, my nephew. Never have I rejoiced more than now."

Bortei approached. She smiled languidly, and laid her hand on Temujin's arm. He looked down at her as though he did not see her. His lips moved in a slight convulsion. Then he received the greetings of his nokud and his paladins. He seemed bemused, and though he kept inclining his head it was evident that he heard little. Before Kokchu had finished his elaborate speech of greeting, Temujin began to push his way towards his yurt. Chepe Noyon and Kasar remained behind.

Kurelen plucked at Chepe Noyon's sleeve. The others gathered about, furtively, making a small island of conspiracy in the midst of the colorful and laughing people.

"What!" whispered Kurelen. "No woman?"

Chepe Noyon shook his head. He glanced swiftly after Temujin's retreating back. The young noyon did not smile.

"No woman," he said briefly.

But Kasar, the simple, was not so taciturn. He was caught up in the general excitement and glad to be at home.

"She killed herself," he said loudly and frankly. "She sacrificed herself for our lord."

"Hush!" said Chepe Noyon sternly. "Hush!" cried the others, glancing fearfully over their shoulders. The people near at hand, sensing some drama, looked at them hopefully and curiously.

Chepe Noyon spoke in a loud and casual voice.

"Toghrul Khan gave us no women. But he filled our hands with treasures. Is that not enough?"

The people laughed pridefully. They forgot the small group standing together, with stiffly smiling faces.

Kurelen said: "Come with me." Subodai, Chepe Noyon, Jamuga, and Kasar, followed him. They did not speak until they were inside Kurelen's tent, and then they sat down and drank his good wine.

"Now, tell us," said Kurelen, briefly.

Chepe Noyon told them in short words, Kasar excitedly supplying any missing details. When he had finished they all sank into silence. Kurelen appeared much moved, and enormously relieved. He shook his head.

"From what thou dost tell me, Chepe Noyon, this was a beauteous and wise woman. But tell me this: is Temujin inconsolable?"

"He hath not spoken her name since she died."

Kurelen sighed deeply. "Ah, that is bad. His eyes are sleepless. He hath been stricken to the heart. I doubt he will fully recover."

"The world is full of beautiful women," said Chepe Noyon.

Again, Kurelen shook his head. He seemed to speak to himself:

"But there doth come a time in a man's life when there is only one woman. Temujin hath known this one. He will have many others, but none shall take her place. I suffer with him."

Chepe Noyon, who believed this pure sentimentality, raised his brows and shrugged.

"She had hair like the morning sun," said Kasar, with solemn relish. "Her face was like a flower, in the spring, when the desert doth bloom. I saw her but once, and I knew that she was a dream among women."

"Oh, thou art a chattering and vulgar goat!" remarked

Kurelen, absently. "But tell me, Chepe Noyon: who doth know of this besides thee, and Kasar?"

"None. The warriors know only that Azara died, and there would be no wedding."

Kurelen regarded Kasar sternly, and the young man winced like a child.

"Hold thy tongue, Kasar, thou babbler! Tell no one of this."

Jamuga, despite his own preoccupation with his miseries, felt a deep sadness and compassion. Now that Azara was no longer a menace, he could regret the death of so much beauty and love, and he could feel an answering anguish for Temujin. He wanted to go to Temujin, but remembered that Temujin had spoken to no one, and had gone to his yurt like an animal that has been mortally stricken. And then he remembered his own precarious and wretched state, and was again preoccupied.

Bortei gave it out that the young khan was greatly tired from his journey, and wished to sleep. Even she was forbidden his yurt. A double guard was posted about the tent, to warn away exigent visitors. But Temujin was not sleeping. He was not even lying down. The guards could hear his hurried and stumbling footsteps within, going back and forth for hours. They could hear his sighs, his low incoherent exclamations. They exchanged impassive glances, but no words.

At sunset, he called for food, but ate it alone, inside his yurt. When the sun finally stood like a red plate on the horizon, he sent for Subodai and his nokud, for their reports. They found him pale and worn, but calm. His feverish eyes sparkled greenly in the lamplight. He noticed Jamuga's absence, and inquired the reason. It was Subodai who replied, tranquilly and straightly:

"Much hath happened in this time, my lord. And Jamuga hath requested me to tell thee, myself."

Temujin stared. He gazed at Subodai over the lip of his goblet.

"What is the matter? And why is Jamuga such a coward?"

Subodai hesitated. "Jamuga is no coward. It might have been better had he been so."

Temujin grunted. He put down his goblet. "Well, speak," he said shortly.

Alone in his yurt, Jamuga waited. The sun fell, and darkness came out with its bristling stars. The moon rose, filled with light. The howling of distant wolves came on the endless wind. The campfires blazed, then died down to smoldering ruins. The city of tents fell into silence.

Jamuga's heart was beating now with a cold terror and despair. He still waited. The hours were filled with menace. He did not know what he feared, but he was paralyzed with his fear. Now he was sure that Temujin would never forgive him, and that he was torturing him tonight as a prelude to worse torture.

Some one was plucking at the flap of the yurt. Jamuga started, and his face streamed with sudden water. Subodai stood there, smiling.

"Our lord doth request thy presence in his yurt, Jamuga Sechen." And then seeing Jamuga's agony, he laid his hand on his shoulder.

"Calm thyself, Jamuga. It is not so very bad."

chapter 28

Jamuga found Temujin among three or four of his nokud, and Chepe Noyon. They sat in silence, and every eye was fixed on the wretched young man as he entered. Temujin's eyes, sunken and febrile, regarded him piercingly. He did not smile. Jamuga thought that he had never seemed so ferocious, so inhuman, so relentless, as he did at this hour.

Temujin did not ask him to sit down. And so Jamuga stood before him, waiting. His fear and despair had gone. He was prepared for the worst. This was not his anda who sat before him, not his brother, not his friend. It was an inexorable monster, without mercy, gray-lipped like stone, and full of terribleness. Expecting nothing but death now, Jamuga could be calm.

He made himself speak: "I do not know if they have told thee, Temujin, but I have ordered the imprisonment of thy mother, Houlun, for insolent language and defiance."

He was appalled at his foolish words, and wondered if it had been his own voice which had uttered them. And then, to his intense amazement, he saw that Temujin had begun to smile, as though with involuntary amusement. The smile darkened rather than lightened his face, but it was actually a smile, and Jamuga, with the keen instinct of the sensitive man, knew it was Temujin's first smile in many days. The others were surprised, and exchanged glances. Then, they, too, smiled, with immense relief. The air of tension in the yurt relaxed. Chepe Noyon even chuckled.

"Well, then, Jamuga Sechen, it doth seem thou art less of a coward than I," said Temujin, with grim jocularity. "I would never have dared to do so. I salute thee as a courageous man."

Jamuga, completely bewildered, could only stare in miserable silence. He did not understand Temujin's amusement. And then he was completely undone when he heard Temujin's hard and bitter laughter, which came reluctantly, pushing itself up like water through layers of congealed rock. He heard the laughter of the others; he saw Subodai nodding to him encouragingly, and sensed his relief. Baffled, he could only stare at Temujin, dumbly, wondering what had occasioned all this.

The icy torment on Temujin's face had lightened when he

had done. Even when the sternness had returned to it, the darkness had lifted measurably.

"Jamuga Sechen, it is not my way to condemn any one without hearing his own defense." He paused. He fixed his eyes inexorably on Jamuga's, and Jamuga's heart sank again, for Temujin had not called him his anda. "Speak; what hast thou to say?"

Jamuga sighed; his colorless lips parted. "Only this, Temujin: that I believe I did no wrong. I would do it again."

The others exchanged looks of consternation, and Subodai seemed alarmed and regretful at these quiet but bold words.

"Ah," said Temujin, thoughtfully. He held out his goblet, and Chepe Noyon filled it. He drank slowly, not removing his eyes from Jamuga's face. Jamuga sighed again, as though his heart were bursting. He looked away from Temujin. He encountered the unfriendly and stolid countenance of Agoti, who sat in smug triumph and satisfaction. I am undone, he thought.

Temujin put aside his goblet. He licked his lips. At the corners of them there was a slight twitching. His eye slowly travelled about his nokud.

"I know ye have your own opinions as to the wisdom of what Jamuga Sechen hath done," he said indifferently. "But I am glad that ye obeyed him. Had ye not, I would have visited my vengeance on ye."

Utter amazement seized them. They looked at one another with expressions of imbecility, and blinked. Only Chepe Noyon and Subodai smiled, and Chepe Noyon winked at the other man. Temujin observed all this, and again his lips twitched.

"Go, now, all of ye, and accept, again, my thanks for your obedience and loyalty."

In the profound silence that followed his words, they got to their feet, saluted, and left the room. None looked at Jamuga, except Subodai, and his smile was sweet and encouraging.

Alone with his anda, Temujin smiled again, that hard and reluctant smile. He reached for another goblet, filled it. "Sit thee down beside me, and drink," he said.

Jamuga's trembling legs collapsed under him. He sat down. He took the goblet in his nerveless fingers. He put it to his lips. But he could not swallow. And Temujin watched him with those green unwinking eyes.

He spoke in a casual and humorous voice: "Thou knowest thou art a fool, of course, Jamuga?"

"Why didst thou speak so to them?" whispered Jamuga, still disbelieving.

Temujin shrugged. "Wouldst thou have me confess to them that the man I appointed in my place was a fool, and incompetent?" He grunted in amusement. "What would they think of mine infallible judgement, then?"

Desperate anger, thin but exhausted, turned in Jamuga's weary heart.

"Do with me as thou wilt, Temujin, but do not mock me. I have endured enough."

Temujin stared at him curiously. He seemed more amused than ever. "I can believe that," he said. And then again he laughed aloud. "Drink thy wine. Go on; I command it."

Jamuga forced himself to drink. He choked. The wine ran through his vitals like fire.

"No," said Temujin meditatively, "it would never have done for me to confess that. That would have undermined authority. And that is something a ruler must never permit himself."

He regarded Jamuga in a sudden silence, as though he could never be done staring at him in his curiosity and cold wonder.

"Thou art a fool, Jamuga," he said at last, but there was no malignancy in the words, but even a glimmer of affection. "Dost thou not understand what thou didst? Dost thou not know that we are constantly surrounded by enemies, who hunger to destroy us, and that obedience and merciless discipline are our only protection, and unity our only invincibility? Weakness and disunity are always the signal for stronger enemies to attack. Dost thou not know this?"

Jamuga sighed. "I do not see that strength and unity are dependent upon cruelty, Temujin. Why is mercy to be forbidden in the name of unity?"

Temujin smiled, as at a silly child. "Mercy is the luxury of the strong. We are not strong enough yet."

Jamuga's head fell on his breast with a movement of complete collapse. But his whisper was steadfast: "I believe I did what was right, though idiots deny it. The wrong is not in what I did, but what thou hast done in the past. Thou didst make animals and babes out of thy people."

He expected, now, that Temujin's full wrath would fall on him. But only silence answered his fainting words. He looked up. Temujin was looking at him, smiling, and often affection was on his face, as well as amusement.

"I see thou wilt never understand, Jamuga. But thou art mine anda. I must forgive much, though I shall never be able to teach thee. Only to thee will I confess that I was a fool in leaving thee in my place."

Jamuga listened in astonishment. He was not to die then,

not to be punished. His astonishment and incredulity stood out on his tired face.

Temujin leaned his arm on Jamuga's shoulder and looked into his eyes. "Thou art mine anda," he repeated. "Twice thou didst save my life." And he smiled.

When Jamuga was alone, his first emotion was one of almost hysterical relief and joy. It was not until he was lying on his couch that his heart grew cold again.

He hath not truly forgiven me, he thought. But why did he spare me?

And he knew that matters would never again be as they were before between him and Temujin. And it seemed to him that he had never before realized the full terribleness of Temujin, who had called himself his anda.

chapter 29

They were soon on the way to the winter pastures, moving with great speed, for hourly, now, the wind grew harsher and the air more bitter. Sand mixed with snow flayed their faces. The women and children huddled in the yurts, wrapping themselves against the cold. Temujin rode at the head of his people, carrying his ivory baton, the mace of the general or leader. About him rode his nokud, his paladins, Subodai, Chepe Noyon, Kasar, Jamuga Sechen, Arghun, the lute player, Muhuli and Bayan and Soo, generals of great craft and masters of battle, and Borchu, who has almost as prodigious a crossbowman as Kasar, who disliked him. There were many others also, but these were his favorites.

On the way, they were joined by hundreds of other men and their families, wandering clans who were former enemies, but who now were struck with awe and admiration of this young Yakka Mongol who had conquered Targoutai and his brother, and many other former khans. Despite the fact that some of these clans were poorly supplied with food, and even hungry, and badly armed, Temujin, against the demurs and suggestions of his nokud and noyon, welcomed them with hearty eagerness. He said:

"I measure strength not by treasure nor gold, nor the crafty politics of townsmen, but in man-power. Loyal numbers, at the last, are more powerful than paid mercenaries bought with the gold of cities, and stronger than the walls of Cathay."

He looked at the new members of his tribe, and said: "A leader must be successful if he is to merit loyalty. Only fools and dreamers follow lost causes and weak generals. At the end, he who feedeth his people and giveth them pastures is he who deserveth their love."

"It is not so simple," protested Jamuga.

"In what way?" asked Temujin.

But Jamuga was unable to answer, though he set his mouth stubbornly.

Once Jamuga asked Kurelen if there was any manner in which he could show his sympathy for Temujin, because of the death of Azara. Kurelen only smiled and asked if Temujin were displaying any prostrating grief. Jamuga was forced to admit that he was not. "Perhaps thou art fanciful, then," said Kurelen.

Jamuga felt disappointed, and somehow cheated. For, as the days passed, the darkness on Temujin's face lifted, and he went about his business with his usual sureness and invincibility. His strong voice was as quick and brief as ever. He smiled as ever, shortly and sardonically. If he laughed less, he had never laughed much, and only a very acute ear could have detected this. Jamuga was angered at this insensitiveness, and though he told himself that Temujin never valued women as human beings, he ought, at least, to have shown in some way that he remembered the girl who had died because of him.

Sometimes they rode by the sparsely grassed edges of a yellow river, and Temujin turned his head to watch the cold sun glittering brightly on it. Jamuga thought: Is he remembering Azara's hair? And sometimes, when the western sky was radiant with rose-tints, he thought: Is he remembering her mouth? But if Temujin were remembering, nothing in his calm and immobile face showed that this was so. He looked at the river and sky as always, dispassionately.

Only Bortei and the other women uneasily suspected what Jamuga now doubted. For since his return, despite his susceptibility to women, and his need of them, he had remained in his own yurt, night after night, alone.

Behind Temujin rumbled his city of carts, and his thousands upon thousands of warriors rode steadily. Behind them all came the herds and the herdsmen, shouting and driving. At night, the campfires burned boldly, for by now few would dare to attack them. Occasionally they would encounter caravans. Most of them were under Temujin's protection, and he would stop only long enough to greet the traders and collect his tribute of money, jewels, woolens, horses, or slaves. He acquired a troupe of gay painted dancing-girls, and at night they would dance in the open, for the air was becoming softer each day. But though he apparently enjoyed watching them, and openly admired some, he still slept alone in his yurt. This, his other wives conceded, was at least a small satisfaction, though they gossiped and complained among themselves enough.

Temujin's greatest amusement at this time was Kasar's growing arrogance. Others were not quite so amused, but Temujin indulged his brother and encouraged him to display this arrogance. For Kasar, the simple and not too discriminating, had suddenly begun to realize that he was brother and noyon to a great khan. The other noyon and paladins were annoyed by his childlike insolence, especially when he affected an air of being close to Temujin's counsels, and nodded his head with superior mystery on occasion. "Ah," he would say, during a discussion, "I know something ye do not know! I have heard my lord speaking, as if to himself!"

They did not really believe him, but were irritated. Some of them mocked him, and one or two hardy ones challenged him to a wrestling match. But he was exceedingly strong, and none too fair, and so there were no more challenges. He bragged; he strutted; he preened; he nodded his head with cryptic smiles, until they began to look at him murderously. Some of them questioned if there were any truth in what he said, and felt themselves affronted and hurt.

"Oh, let him alone," said Chepe Noyon, laughing. "He is only an ox, and hath no wit. Our lord would certainly not consult him in anything more important than the breeding of a mare, or the flight of an arrow."

They admitted they did not believe him, but they longed to kick him heartily. Jamuga complained contemptuously, as did Borchu and Bayan and two or three others, but Temujin only laughed. It amused him to see Kasar strut and posture, and strike heroic attitudes before the women. When they raided a caravan not under his protection, Temujin, with a solemn face, announced that Kasar was to have the first choice of the spoils. He did it only to encourage Kasar to fresh amusing displays of mysterious arrogance, but the others were silently enraged.

Houlun, infuriated that Temujin had not reprimanded or punished Jamuga for her imprisonment, was by now openly hostile to him, and railed at him even when he was among his noyon.

"Thy brother, Kasar, is a fool," she said angrily. "But folly is like a crippled limb, and should inspire only contempt and sympathy in others. Thou dost encourage his folly as though it were some fine mark of character, superior to that of other men."

"He doth amuse me," replied Temujin, with a rare display of good temper. "And at present, I desire to be amused. Tomorrow, perhaps I may not laugh. Let me laugh tonight." And he made Kasar sit at his right hand, though he had never done this before.

There was some wanton and womanish perversity in him these days, and he seemed to laugh silently in himself when he saw the glum faces of the others.

The days did not pass peacefully all the time. During the long march they encountered hostile clans, who assaulted them, or were assaulted. But these Temujin was able to subdue with appalling ease. Before the winter had ended, one hundred thousand yurts followed the young khan, and countless herds. Before the spring had really come, he had called Bortei to him, and when the summer migration started, she jubilantly knew she was with child again.

The city of the tents moved north once more behind Temujin. His dream of a confederacy of the nomad clans had begun to take definite shape. The old men had warned him that this would never take place. He had told them: "A great king is he who doth begin a task that can never be accomplished, and doth accomplish it."

The people worshipped him. They said of him that he was the Hawk of Heaven, the Falcon of the Eternal Blue Sky, the Subduer of all men. His terrible courage, his ferocity, his cunning and his resistless power dazzled them. They knew he was feared on the Gobi, and they held up their heads, proud to belong to the ordu of such a khan.

"I shall extend my rule over all my neighbors," he said to his noyon. "I shall make the Gobi one empire. And then——"

"And then?" asked Chepe Noyon.

But Temujin only smiled, and looked eastwards. It was noticed when he did so that hatred was like a cold light on his face.

Book Three

THIS DAY'S MADNESS

Yesterday This Day's Madness did prepare;
Tomorrow's Silence, Triumph, or Despair:
Drink! for you know not whence you came, nor why.
Drink! for you know not why you go, nor where.

—RUBAIYAT OF OMAR KHAYYAM

chapter 1

"When we attain union, then we can afford peace," said Temujin. "For when a people is united, then its will can be forced upon weaker and inferior peoples ofttimes without war, and many times by mere intimidation and terror."

He knew, now, the paralyzing psychological force of terror. His spies went among weaker, and even stronger, tribes, and whispered that there was something supernatural, something mystical and not to be resisted, in Temujin, khan of the Yakka Mongols. The tribes of the Gobi were fierce men and indomitable fighters; they never hesitated to attack or ferociously defend, when necessary, even if outnumbered. But they felt helpless before a man whom heaven itself seemed to help, and before whom the most selfless courage and strength were impotent. A feeling of doom pervaded them, like a noxious gas, chilling their blood and slowing down their hearts. Even when the spies were exposed, and murdered, their whispers went among the people like phantoms.

"Temujin hath no quarrel with you," went the whispers. "He doth love you all like a father. His only wish is to make you kings among lesser men. Submit yourselves under his standard of the nine yaktails, and he shall lead you to victory, to riches and treasures, to countless fair women and many herds."

"If you do not submit," went still another whisper, "then he shall set upon you with remorseless terror and death, because you are traitors unto him, and his enemies. Struggle against him, and you shall surely die, for the lightnings have leaped out of heaven at his bidding, and the avenging waters have arisen to do his will."

The superstitious tribes listened, wrinkling their dark bronzed faces. "It is the will of heaven that there be a confederacy of the clans of the Gobi," said the spies. "For the gods have a mighty mission for the hordes, for the noble and irresistible people who range the barrens. The empires are in a state of decay; their men are eunuchs, their arms fat and feeble. God hath called us to destroy the abomination of this rottenness, this swollen greed which hath condemned the people of the steppes to poverty and hunger and hardship. The wealth and the treasures of the city-empires have been denied us, and starvation doth dog our heels through the long winters. We alone are good and strong, healthy and full of virility. We are called to deliver the earth from the stench and the disease of the bloated cities, and drive the trader-eunuchs from their warm cushions and their feasts."

But Temujin had underestimated the intelligence of the nomad peoples, who loved their freedom even more than they loved their feasts and their women and their horses. Some of the bolder khans and chieftains spoke of the beastlike enslavement of those Temujin had conquered. "It is said that he doth regard men as animals, and doth bend them to his will without consulting them, and without their consent. 'Go,' he sayeth, and they have no choice."

The spies laughed scornfully. "This is but for the moment. The confederacy of the Gobi is his first goal. To attain it in our lifetime he must be ruthless; he must be judge and general, lord and leader, without question. He must move rapidly. Countless wills and countless dissenting voices are delaying and dangerous, and render peoples impotent. For a time they must say 'aye,' in order to conquer. But when they have conquered, then their freedom shall be restored to them, and they shall rule the earth."

"I wish to know what it is I die for, or fight for," grumbled the older chieftains, who were too proud to follow and had a high respect for their own judgment. "I wish to be consulted. I wish to know where I must lead those who trust me."

Again the spies laughed derisively. "In long argument is long weakness. When men quarrel over a campaign, the enemy rides in and overtakes them in the midst of their womanish gabble. But Temujin, himself, is only an instrument in the hands of destiny; he, too, serveth. What are you, that you dare defy the gods?"

But still many resisted, among them the dour Merkit, and the Uighurs, who were strong, proud men, willing to serve the tribe but jealous of their own individual freedom and wills. But many listened to the spies, plucking their lips, thinking that the loss of individual will was a small price to pay for glory and conquest, for dedication and the service of the gods. Romantic and worshippers of the hero, they listened eagerly to the tales of the red-haired young khan who had been known to smite down fifty men with his own sword, and emerge, scratchless. And then, too, he was foster son of the mighty Toghrul Khan, and it was whispered that Prester John loved him more than he did his own son, Taliph, and would make Temujin his sole heir. The myths attending his birth went about. Many of the spies were shaman, and they whispered of the frightful auguries of this birth, and the spirits who had visibly tended his mother in her travail.

Over the vast expanse of the Gobi went the whispers, over the green-gray steppes, across the slow-winding yellow rivers, over the chaotic mountains and the dead sand. Men spoke doubtfully of them by campfires, and uneasily glanced at the horizon.

And now the younger men, the youths and the boys, became restless. Their hearts yearned towards one who was immortal youth to them, splendid and conquering, resistless and full of power. "The graybeards sit by the fires," they said resentfully, "content to dip mutton in herb sauces and chew millet. The flame of strife hath gone out of them; they speak of freedom as though it were a joy, instead of an invitation to starvation and cold and danger."

The graybeards shook angry withered fingers at them, and shrilled:

"Are we men, or cattle? We have our independence and our liberty, for which our fathers died, and ye young fools wish to destroy them for a fistful of gold and the pleasure of murder! Have ye no pride in yourselves as men, that ye must lay your heads down before such as this man, and ask him to put his foot upon them?"

But the young knew that only the old appreciate freedom and independence. Youth longs only for authority and obedience, for the privilege of being commanded and scorned, led and whipped. And the old men knew that maturity loves its pride and its manhood, its privilege of gazing into any man's eye and saying, I am equal to thee, and thou art no greater than I.

Of this privilege in the years to come, the young were contemptuous.

The old men spoke of the glories of their tribe, and said scornfully of Temujin that he was of the Yakka Mongols, who were beggarly murderers and thieves. But the young had no pride of race, and said that Temujin was wise, in that he wished to consolidate all the peoples of the steppes and the barrens.

"Once he fled from us," chuckled the old men of the Merkit. "He abandoned his women and the children to us. He ran into the barrens, and we hunted him."

"Ye think only of killing," said the old men. "We think only of peace." And they mourned among themselves that discipline had not been enforced, and a proper respect for age had not been inculcated in their children. "In our youth," they said, "our fathers were our gods. We respected them and bowed before them. Woe unto us, that we have begotten a race of impudent liars and scorners of authority."

All through the Gobi the spirit of unrest ran on red feet, whispering and condemning, urging and promising. And wherever it whispered, there disunity resulted, and angry voices, and confusion. Long before the hordes of the Yakka Mongols appeared, the people were disorganized, quarrelling and vacillating, and many tribes laid down their arms and gave the oath of fealty without the loss of a single life.

"Confuse a people in their own midst, and thou shalt take them without a blow," Temujin said.

But still, there were many peoples remaining, much stronger than Temujin's, and derisive in their strength. "Let him take the weak," they said scornfully. "But us he shall not take."

They listened to the tales about Temujin, and laughed, and went about their business. They made jokes about Temujin's theory that there must be among all peoples one supreme people. "What!" they exclaimed, "doth he think his Mongols superior to us—doth he truly believe they were born to be kings over other men?"

Among the mightiest of the people of the Gobi were the Karait and the Tatars, and before them, in their pride, their ferocity, and in the case of the Kerait, their civilization, Temujin was only a prowling petty chieftain afflicted with a dream. They laughed at him and forgot him, letting him conquer weak peoples, and even telling themselves that at least he had made the caravan routes safe, at a price. For this, they said, they owed him a measure of gratitude.

chapter 2

Deep in the barrens, in the wastes and steppes of the Gobi, Temujin sleeplessly busied himself with his consolidation of the little peoples and tribes whom he had absorbed. It was nothing to him that the mighty Karait and the Tatars laughed at him, and forgot him. "Let them laugh, and forget," he said, when it was reported to him by his spies. "Laughter and forgetfulness are mine allies. But some day they will not laugh, and never again will they forget."

In the meantime, more and more traders paid him tribute to protect their caravans. The Chinese paid him huge sums and gave him vast treasures for this protection. "At last," many of them said, "we have some semblance of order in the heart of the horrible Gobi. This man hath made men of ravaging beasts, and it is nothing to us how he hath accomplished this. He hath created order out of a jungle." And now their historians deigned to give him a line or two in their recordings.

But for the most part, the mighty and the rich, the secure and the fortressed, had never heard of him. Behind the great wall of Cathay, built less to keep out barbarian invaders than to keep the flower of civilization within, the enormous empire went about its business and knew nothing of a young Mongol khan and his petty confederacy in the lost barrens of a desert of which they had only vaguely heard, and shuddered delicately upon hearing.

Temujin, indeed, was only a little savage chieftain lost in the wastes, busy about his own tiny affairs, his antlike manipulations. The Chinese were more aware of the mighty Tatars, beating like sullen but still inoffensive waves against the Great Wall. "Their women give birth to litters," complained a Cathayan noble. "Some day we shall have to reckon with sheer weight of numbers."

But the others laughed. "The barbarians are armed only with bows. They are only lumbering bears, these Tatars. In the meantime, our horsemen ride the tops of our walls, and our gates are guarded by the best soldiers in the world."

So civilization slept and dreamed, and the Tatars muttered and quarrelled near the walls, or rode out in vast armies to plunder the surrounding country. And occasionally, their elegant and civilized masters, the Chinese, had to send, with immense boredom, some expeditions against these barbarians, merely to call attention to their own might, and the inadequacy of the Tatars, much in the fashion of a father languidly disciplining one of his many and annoying sons.

But the Tatars received these expeditions with less and less respect, and even showed much fight and resistance. And finally, the Chinese, annoyed and detesting, decided something must be done once and for all, against them, in order to teach these stinking barbarians their proper place in the scheme of things.

History, who had yawned for a thousand years in Asia, stirred on her dust-covered couch, and opened her eyes. And when she opened them, an ominous sound struck upon her ears—the long subterranean mutter of barbarians at the gate of civilization. She sighed, sat up, shook the dust from the pages of brittle manuscript, and reread the ancient story. And then she took up her pen and moistened it, and waited. "It is an old tale," she said, and her old bones moved wearily, for she had thought to sleep forever.

"What shall be the name of the monster in this hour?" she thought. "From whence will he rise again? From the east, from the west, from the north, from the south? A thousand times he hath risen and conquered, and at the end is conquered. But always he doth come, and always the old tale is rewritten."

She yawned wearily, and wondered whether the day would ever come when the monster would be forever destroyed, and she could sink into eternal sleep.

Among those who did not laugh at Temujin, the little forager of the barrens and the steppes, was Toghrul Khan, who had his own spies.

"Men make a great error when they hear a man boasting, and say that because he boasteth he will never act," he said, to his son, Taliph. "That is a vicious aphorism. Men who act first talk. I fear talkers."

"But do not think so much of this Temujin," said Taliph. "I confess I used to think of him. But now he hath sunk back into his proper perspective—an ambitious little ant-king surrounded by thousands of empty miles. Let him have his small day among the other ants. Think, this day, of the Tatars."

But some strange obstinacy made the old khan think of Temujin.

"History is always contemporary," he observed.

Taliph was impatient. "If that is so, then it hath begun to sing of the Tatars."

But still Toghrul Khan thought of Temujin, and he could not shake it off. "I should have killed him when I had the opportunity," he said. "Who knoweth? Maybe men might have been grateful for this killing."

Taliph thought his father in his dotage. It seemed folly to him to waste a thought on such an insignificant insect as Temujin, who was certainly no menace to the great Karait peoples. One single army of the Karait could destroy him overnight, and leave no trace even upon the Gobi. Indeed, his father was in his dotage. But he had not been quite the same since the death of Azara, that idiot girl who had nestled so deeply into her father's heart. For months the old man had cried without ceasing: "Why did she do this thing? Was I a harsh father? Did I strike her down and despise her? Nay, I loved her. She was my heart's darling. She was the spark of mine old eyes. I had given her as bride to a great prince of her mother's people, and she would have been a queen. Why did she do this thing, my child, my lovely one?"

Taliph thought this incessant mourning indecent, for Azara had only been a woman, after all. It was obscene for a man to lament like this for cheap girl-flesh, however beautiful. It was comtemptible even to seek for a reason for this suicide. Any clever man knew that women were unpredictable cattle, and only fools tried to fathom the reasons for their blind follies.

Taliph was glad, however, that his father had begun to speak of something else besides Azara. The endless chant had disgusted him. So he talked of the Tatars, who were a real menace, by reason of their very numbers, to the peace of the cities.

"They need discipline again," he said.

But Toghrul Khan spoke only of Temujin. "I should have killed him," he repeated.

"Thou wasteth too much time in thinking of one of the least of thy vassals, my father."

Toghrul Khan gazed deeply before him with sunken and feverish eyes.

"He is a shadow of fire on the black dawn of the future," he murmured. "I dreamed last night that he rode out of that black dawn, and he and his horse reached from the earth to the sky. I could not remember his name, and some one whispered to me that he was immortal, and had had many names, and would have many more."

But Taliph was wrong in assuming that his father was in his dotage. Never had the old man been so aware of events. He listened closely to the reports of his legions of spies, who were everywhere in Asia. And that strange prescience of his made him listen even more attentively to the reports of Temujin. He even knew that Temujin had another son now, and would soon have another. Three sons, then. "The litter of the Beast," he said aloud, and was terrified at the involuntary words.

He knew the names of Temujin's chief noyon, his half-brother, Belgutei; his brother, Kasar, and Subodai, Chepe Noyon, and Jamuga Sechen. They were not the names of ants to him, despite the occasional arguments of his reason. They were names of visitations.

And then one day he had a summons from a great Chinese general to appear at the latter's court within the Wall.

chapter 3

Toghrul Khan was the close friend of the general, who was of the formidable Chin Empire, which did not particularly like the Empire of the Sung, the Kingdom of Hia, and the Empire of Black Cathay. These various Chinese Empires were jealous of each other, though they maintained a more or less civilized tolerance and elegant exchange. They were all united in their love for their own civilization and contempt for what they called the nameless hordes beyond the Wall. But hatred was brooding in their garden, like a crimson flower, awaiting only the moment to burst into full and dreadful bloom out of the corruption and decadence of the thronged cities.

The general was languidly annoyed. "We have been negligent," he said. "Now it is time to discipline the barbarians again. I call upon thee, Toghrul Khan, to summon the best among thy vassals and give us assistance against the Tatars." He yawned. "It is very boring," he added.

He privately thought Toghrul Khan himself a barbarian, only partly civilized, in spite of his Karait cities and his Persian palace. He had been a graduate of a military school, in which he had learned that civilized gentlemen use their barbarian allies to subdue other barbarians. It was much easier on the gentlemen, and when barbarians fought, gentlemen could return to their own pursuits, happy in the fact that the others were murdering each other, and thus rendering themselves mutually less a menace to their masters. It was all very neat, and every one was satisfied.

"What shall I get out of this?" asked Toghrul Khan.

The general stared, but was polite enough, after a moment, to stop staring. He was much younger than the Karait Khan, and he passingly wondered what more the old man wanted, for surely he was on the verge of the grave, with his death's head and shaking hands.

He smiled gently. "We shall give thee the Chinese title of Wang, or prince, my good old friend," he answered, "and the first share of any spoils thou dost seize. All of them, if thou canst so persuade thy vassals."

"Not enough," said Toghrul Khan. "I want a palace and a permanent income within the Wall."

The general raised his brows delicately. "But why, my friend?"

Toghrul Khan said stubbornly: "That is my desire."

And then the general saw that deep within the sunken and crafty eyes there was the pale shadow of fear. But fear of what? Surely his own Karait cities were fortressed and guarded enough?

Toghrul Khan repeated in a dull but obstinate voice: "A house within the Wall."

The general shrugged, and frowned a little to himself. He knew the emperor disliked any alien becoming entrenched within the empire. Aliens, he had said, bring other aliens, and aliens are always enemies. But, this time— It was better for the Karait barbarians to die rather than Chinese.

"Very well," he said, cordially, "thou shalt have it. And let me extend to thee, at this time, my own personal welcome."

At home, Toghrul Khan muttered to himself: "Wang. Wang Khan. A prince of Cathay! And a house behind the Wall. The beautiful Wall! The invincible Wall!"

For the first time in long and anguished months, he slept and did not dream.

On the day of the birth of his third son, Ogotai, Temujin received the summons from Toghrul Khan. He now had three sons, Juchi, the Shadowed, and Chutagi, and Ogotai. He made no distinction between Juchi and the two younger children; they were all children of the body of Bortei, whom he loved, and whom he understood. He delighted in the boys, all dark and sturdy and gray-eyed, like Bortei; he especially delighted in Ogotai, who had his red hair. Houlun, in her rare moments of affability, told her son that Ogotai might have been himself at his own birth.

But these affable moments became more infrequent. For Houlun could not speak to Temujin without irony, scorn, condemnation or anger. She and Kurelen were the only ones who did not appear to fear him. She openly disliked Bortei, and as she was still mistress of the yurts, she made Bortei's life miserable on occasion, telling her that she knew as little as a mere virgin serving-girl of the care of children, that she was vain and silly and full of greed, and, in short, no fit wife for a Yakka Mongol khan. Between the two women the hatred had become malignant, and part of Houlun's hatred was because of her lost influence with her son. She well knew that the woman who shared a man's bed also had his ear, and she suspected, with truth, that Bortei spoke slightingly of her husband's mother, and all in a voice of indulgent amusement. So wounded pride and loneliness sharpened the older woman's tongue, and even when she spoke in rage there was a hurt sadness in her eyes.

She, herself, had no love for Jamuga Sechen, whom she vigorously and audibly considered a fool. But she did not subscribe to the malicious reports that he was disaffected, though she, herself, had occasionally declared he was. In her reason, which was vigorous and cool, she knew that Jamuga was no traitor, that he was merely cursed with a peculiar conscience, the like of which she had never known before. But being clever and subtle, herself, she understood his conscience, though she derided it. She knew, too, of Jamuga's passionate love for Temujin, and knew that he suffered, as she did, because of it. Jamuga found himself with an unexpected ally in this lonely mother of his anda, and though by nature cold and suspicious of every one, he began to feel a shy gratitude. He knew that this alliance was rooted in her suspicion and hatred for Bortei, but he was also aware that it was genuine. They spoke to each other occasionally, in short guarded words, but what they said was heavy with meaning and anxiety.

"Jamuga Sechen," she said one day, "be on thy guard. Thou hast a most vicious enemy, Bortei, wife of my son. She will not rest until she hath destroyed thee."

"I know," he said, in a low voice. But in his own mind he discounted the power of Bortei, for all her three sons.

"What I tell Temujin in the day is destroyed at night," she observed.

"Temujin believeth nothing but what he desireth to believe," said Jamuga, sadly. But in fact, he felt little disturbance with regard to his own relationship with Temujin, for the young khan showed him, these days, nothing but friendliness.

"I will give thee advice, Jamuga: hold thy tongue. Whatsoever Temujin doeth, do not cross him. Assent by silence, if thou canst not with words."

But this Jamuga found it impossible to do. His inner tortured drive forced bitter words to his tongue; had he not spoken he would not have had even a small peace. He expelled protests as a volcano expels spent fire and steam, lest it explode all at once, and destroy itself. What Kurelen had given him to read a long time ago had stiffened the bewildered integrity in him, so that he knew that a man's life was a small price to pay for his peace.

And now a fatherly and affectionate summons had come to Temujin from the old Karait, Toghrul Khan, saying that he needed his foster son in a war against the Tatars, who menaced the tranquillity of the Chin Empire. Temujin responded at once, with his usual vigor. He called all his priests to him, the red-and-yellow-clad lamas, the two Nestorian Christian pastors, the three Moslems, and his own Shaman. They must speak to their followers that night and tell them that the khan was leading them to war in a noble cause, and to prepare themselves for victory or death.

Temujin had great religious tolerance, and one of the major crimes he would not countenance was any strife among the religious groups that formed his people. Once a Moslem had taken violent issue with a Christian, and both had drawn sabers and were trying to kill each other with immense heartiness. He had taken up a club, stepped between them for all the flashing steel, and had beaten both into insensibility. In fact, the Moslem died the next day from his injuries.

"In the cause of unity, there must be peace between religions," he said. "He who doth quarrel because of his gods shall go to them with dispatch and there settle the argument." He added: "A leader who doth stir up religious strife among his people, or doth countenance it, is no true leader, but a quarrelsome and stupid woman doomed to death."

Jamuga would have approved of this religious tolerance and equality, had he not known that in truth Temujin cared nothing for real tolerance, but only for unity among the many different peoples who now formed his tribe. When they quarrelled about their doctrines, they deprecated his supremity and their own loyalty to him. This he would not allow, and death or the next severest punishment was his law.

"Serve your gods in your souls, but serve me first in your arms," he said. "He who sayeth his god is the only true god, and so stirreth up dissension, hath done me an unforgivable injury."

So when the Moslems knelt down to pray at sunset, he commanded that the Christians kneel also, and his own people, and the Taoists and Buddhists. "Prayers in unity do no harm," he said, but he commanded that the Moslems whisper their invocation: "There is no God but Allah, and Mohammed is His prophet," so that the others would not overhear it. When the Christians began their celebrations of the Mass, he commanded the Moslems to stand near-by and observe it with reverence, saying: "There is but one God of all men, and answereth to all names, as a woman answereth to the many endearments of her husband, remaining always the same woman."

When the Buddhist priests spun their prayer-wheels and

chanted, he said to the others: "Observe how wonderful is God, that He understandeth the language of all men!"

But he was sternest with the priests, who he knew were the seeds of bitterness and dissension. "Teach your people that God is the father of all mankind," he said, "and that he who sayeth God is only his father, and not the father of others, is a liar."

He, himself, killed a priest who did not obey him.

"Keep your opinions to yourselves," he said, "and speak aloud only one law: obedience to the khan, who is the audible voice of the gods."

Being wise, he rewarded the priests richly, knowing that a fat priest is a good servant of masters. He treated all priests with absolute impartiality and friendliness, and settled all quarrels among them with fairness and good sense.

As a result, the priests obeyed him and loved him. The night before the warriors set forth to this supreme battle, the priests were very busy, invoking and praying and counselling their followers.

Jamuga, despite Houlun's and Kurelen's urgent advice, could not keep still. When he heard of the expedition, he went to Temujin, full of anger.

"This is a foreign and distant war, Temujin," he cried, "and hath nothing to do with us, who live deep in the heart of the Gobi. What quarrel have we with the Tatars?"

"They killed my father," said Temujin, with a faint sardonic smile.

Jamuga looked at him in scornful silence, and Temujin grinned.

"In wars, men grow strong. I need to strengthen my people," he added.

"For what? Other wars?" asked Jamuga, angrily.

"Yes. Thou hast hit it. For other wars."

Jamuga drew a deep breath. "I have no quarrel with wars of necessity, and survival. But neither necessity nor survival is threatened by the Tatars, whose near-by tribes live at peace with us. Thou hast two Tatar wives. Last week a Tatar khan was thy guest. Why send forth our people now to kill them, leagues away, at the desire of the Chinese and Toghrul Khan? Toghrul Khan will benefit. But what benefit wilt thou obtain? Are our people paid mercenaries?"

Temujin looked at him inscrutably.

"Every war is the story of one man's revenge," he said at last.

Jamuga was baffled. "But this revenge is not thine," he stammered.

Temujin shrugged. His eyes glinted. "How dost thou know that?" he asked. "Go away, Jamuga, thou dost weary me. Thou dost look at today only. I look at tomorrow."

"Tomorrow!"

"Dost thou think I plan only for today? I see the future. Every war leadeth me closer to it."

But Jamuga was excited. This expedition seemed cruel and foolish to him, and shameful in that Temujin was to lead his people into a war for the profit of others. Again, he underestimated his anda, because he always saw things straightly and simply.

"He who selleth his birthright once hath sold it for all time," he said.

"That is not bad, if the price be high enough," replied Temujin, smiling. Then he smiled no longer. "I do not know why I endure thy reproaches and thy gabbling, Jamuga Sechen. None other would dare speak so to me. I have commanded thee: Go; thou dost weary me."

But still, Jamuga would not be silent. With tortured bitterness he said:

"If thy people were still free, instead of the slaves thou hast made them, thou wouldst not dare do this thing. A free man fighteth noble wars, he having chosen to defend what is precious to him. But in this war we defend nothing but the profits of others."

Temujin did not reply. But he looked at Jamuga in a thoughtful and peculiar way, and his smile was cruel and dark.

Jamuga's quarrel with Temujin was soon open camp story. That night Bortei, while she lay in Temujin's arms, said:

"I have told thee, my lord, that this is a traitor. He is going among the people, urging rebellion."

But Temujin laughed. "I do not believe that, Bortei. The people are laughing at him. And he is incapable of treachery."

But Bortei was not to be set aside. "A dissenting opinion is always dangerous," she said. "The people know that thine anda hath quarrelled with thee, and so they wonder if the quarrel were not justified. So long as this man liveth, there will be discussion as to his opinion." She began to weep. "Thy love for him blindeth thee, and doth endanger all of us. In such a vast number of people there must be many who disagree with thee, but in silence. But this man doth make their dissent articulate."

Temujin agreed with her in his mind. But he told her curtly to hold her tongue. He had his own plans. And he could not forget that Jamuga had saved his life twice, and had for him a deep and passionate love, and a loyalty that sprang from the soul and was unafraid.

But Bortei had one more thing to say: "There are traitors in every people, and whatever Jamuga's loyalty to thee, he is simple, and can become the tool of ambitious and unscrupulous men."

And again Temujin agreed with her in his mind, but he struck her across the mouth and dismissed her from his bed.

chapter 4

The obstinate Jamuga would not let go without one final desperate effort: he consulted Kurelen without knowing his own reason, but feeling numb conviction that at least he would be understood. Kurelen listened thoughtfully. Then he said:

"Jamuga Sechen, hath it occurred to thee that perhaps Temujin is merely returning a favor? Toghrul Khan responded to his cry for help, generously and unstintingly. Temujin is his vassal, and now Toghrul Khan hath only requested that Temujin live up to his agreement with him, and render the same aid which had been given by his foster father."

"That was different, Kurelen. Then, Temujin's call for help was desperate, and necessary for the survival of a people. It was life or death. But in this war of Toghrul Khan's and his Chinese masters against the Tatars, there is no such condition. Toghrul Khan will be generously rewarded for his aid in destroying a hungry and wandering people, whose only crime is that they have never had enough to eat. He will generously throw a bone to Temujin, whose warriors will have no reward but the remembered misery of a destructive war, and death, and the exhaustion and futility of a quarrel not their own."

"And thou dost think this war will be such a misfortune for them?" Kurelen went out and stood upon the platform of the yurt and watched the clamorous gathering of the warriors. Jamuga stood beside him. They listened to the fierce shouts of exultation and excitement, the happy laughter, the gay quarrels and arguments. Horses stamped, reared and neighed and wheeled. The confusion was tremendous. The face of every horseman and warrior shone with delight under its layer of grease and dust. Many swung their lariats, practicing, catching the neck or body of a near-by friend, and dragging him from his horse, with shouts of merriment. Many, on foot, engaged in mock battle, and the clash of steel added to the din. The whole scene, colorful, active, seething, confused the eye.

"I do not seem to remember them so gay for a long time," said Kurelen. "They are jubilant, drunk with joy, riotous in anticipation."

"That is because they are intoxicated with dreams of glory and conquest, and have been seduced by the mysticism of the crafty priests."

Kurelen continued to watch the warriors. "I wonder," he said meditatively. "I have lived long enough to know that nothing is so simple as the intellectual man would have us believe. I believe that the love of war doth reside, not in any king's or priest's artful lies, but in the nature of man himself. The bloodless and the pale will deny this, but it is so."

"Thou dost believe men would prefer blood and death and torture and hatred, to peace and security and friendship?" asked Jamuga, incredulously.

Kurelen nodded, slowly. "Yes, because peace and security are monotonous and maddening. They insist that strength devour itself behind safe walls, like a chained animal. But the steel and blood and death of war doth answer to the adventurous and virile spirit of man, and to his mystic urge for self-sacrifice and self-abnegation. And so he doth feel a greater security than peace can bring, the security of being part of one enormous purpose and universal urge, and of having served something greater than himself."

He smiled at Jamuga's pale and repudiating face.

"The problem of the ages, if there is ever to be peace, is to make that peace, not drab and monotonous and stagnating, an affront to the rebellious and active spirit of man, but adventurous and exciting, calling forth all the self-sacrifice and virility of his nature. And Jamuga, this will not be found in books or in philosophies, which are dry dust settling on dead faces."

He laughed. "Our learning doth belittle men. War doth exalt them. It is we who are dying, not they. We discourse, and they live!"

But Jamuga was silent. He was watching something else, with a sad intentness. Then he said suddenly:

"Observe the faces of the women. These are not gay nor jubilant, but only wretched and full of grief and fear."

Kurelen looked at the women. And then he answered in a low voice: "It is part of our decadence, Jamuga Sechen, that we consider women."

Jamuga, caution lost, went to Subodai, Chepe Noyon, and Belgutei. They were standing alone, with the simple Kasar, for a last consultation about formations. Belgutei greeted him with a smile, but said in an envious voice: "Fortunate art thou, Jamuga, to be going with our lord on this expedition. I have been commanded to remain here, and Kurelen is to be lord in Temujin's place."

This was news to Jamuga, who had thought that he was to remain behind. A dull flush rose to his colorless cheek, and he bit his lip. His anger made his last shred of caution disappear.

Had he taken counsel with himself, he would have spoken to each young noyon separately, but now he burst out recklessly, stung:

"What think ye of this expedition? Are ye men, or unthinking beasts? Do ye not know that we fight a battle not ours, for the sake of an old man's greed?"

They stared at him, astonished. Then, slowly, each man dropped his eyes after a glance at his neighbor. But no one answered Jamuga. Only Kasar, of them all, looked at Jamuga, and then with snapping eyes and a malicious half-smile.

"Subodai," said Jamuga, desperately turning to the young paladin. "Hast thou nothing to say?"

Subodai looked up, and his face was cold and stern. He answered quietly: "My lord's will is my will. I live only to obey him. I have told thee this before, Jamuga Sechen."

Chepe Noyon smiled, and asked curiously and lightly: "What wouldst thou have us do? Defy our Khan, and refuse to go with him?"

Belgutei laughed. He liked Jamuga, and he saw that this might become serious. He glanced swiftly at Kasar, who he knew was madly jealous of Temujin's anda. So he tried to pass the whole matter off as a huge joke.

"Jamuga doth not like us, apparently. He doth wish to destroy all of us and become our lord's first adviser as he is his first friend."

Subodai and Chepe Noyon understood him immediately. They looked at Kasar, then exchanged significant glances. "Ah," said Chepe Noyon, laughing, "I know! Thou art just jealous of us, Jamuga. But we go, too, as well as thou."

Jamuga was silent. He saw something subterranean was going on. He looked from one to the other, baffled. Then affronted, he turned and walked away, full of wretchedness.

Kasar said nothing to any one, which Chepe Noyon remarked was unusual. They watched him walk away, casually. Belgutei said, narrowing his eyes: "I distrust Kasar, for all his simplicity. Simple men are always dangerous, for they get a single idea and act on it stubbornly, like a mule. And we all know he is insanely jealous of Jamuga. Where do ye think he is going, now?"

Chepe Noyon shrugged. "I have made it a rule in my life to worry about nothing that doth not concern me."

"Jamuga is a fool," said Subodai, uneasily.

Kasar walked aimlessly. But once out of sight of the others, he began to hurry. He went to Temujin's yurt, and found him embracing Bortei for the last time. Kasar's original admiration for Bortei had become worship. She could do with him as she would. Now she smiled at him graciously. Kasar was pleased that she was there, for he knew how she detested Jamuga.

He spoke to his brother in an eager voice: "My lord, I have just come from consulting with Subodai and Chepe Noyon and Belgutei about our formations. And then, while we were talking, Jamuga Sechen, thine anda, came up to us, all in a sweat and a fever, and urged us to disobey thee, saying that this war is none of ours, and a foolish one, and only to be waged for the profit of thy noble foster father, Toghrul Khan."

Temujin stared, incredulous. But Bortei gleefully clapped her hands.

"Have I not told thee, my lord, that this man is a traitor? But wouldst thou listen to me? Nay, thou didst merely send me from thy presence with a blow. Now thou dost hear it from thine own brother." She looked at Kasar briefly, with sparkling eyes.

"I cannot believe this!" exclaimed Temujin. All his blood rushed to his head and his face, and his color turned purple. His expression was full of murderous rage. "But if it is so, what did the others say?"

"They laughed at him," admitted Kasar.

Temujin clenched his teeth. "They saw he was a fool."

"But fools are dangerous," said Bortei.

"He hath gone too far," muttered Temujin. He put his hand on the hilt of his sword. He breathed hoarsely and audibly.

Some one was plucking at the flap of the yurt, and Kurelen entered. He was smiling, but one quick glance around told him that something portentous was going on here. He had come to ask Temujin to allow Jamuga to remain at home, saying that he might need the young man. He had done this out of pity. But now what he had come to say died on his tongue, as he felt the black atmosphere in the yurt.

"What is wrong?" he asked quickly.

"I have just heard that Jamuga Sechen is a traitor, and is trying to stir up dissension among my noyon, saying this is no war of ours," answered Temujin, his face swelling. "I shall kill him now, with mine own hand."

Oh, the fool! thought Kurelen. He glanced piercingly, not at Temujin, but at Kasar, who was beginning to look sheepish. For Kasar, who was only simple and jealous, had only wanted to force Jamuga out of Temujin's affections, but certainly had not desired his death. Alarm appeared in his doglike eyes.

Kurelen sat down and assumed a negligent attitude. He

smiled. Now he would need all his skill to turn aside this wrath from Jamuga.

"Thou dost know how Jamuga doth talk, Temujin. And thou knowest he is no traitor. He hath only a loose tongue, and many foolish ideas."

Temujin's lips twitched, and his eyes became fiery.

"Well, then, in justice to him, I shall ask Subodai, Chepe Noyon, and Belgutei to come here, and they shall tell me, themselves."

Kurelen sighed, as though exasperated at such childishness in a grave hour. "I can tell thee, myself, Temujin: Jamuga came to me. Thou dost know what a womanish conscience he hath. He asked me if I thought this war were righteous. Men like this prefer to fight in righteous wars. They like to believe they choose what they shall do. It doth give them a feeling of self-will and independence. So I told him that whatsoever thou doeth is always righteous."

Temujin tried to keep his face black, but involuntarily he began to smile. Bortei was infuriated. She looked at Kurelen with vicious eyes.

"We all know, Kurelen, what affection thou hast for Jamuga Sechen," she said, mockingly. "Then dost always defend him, even against our lord."

Kurelen put his hand meditatively to his lips, and looked over it at Bortei. "Hast thou personal occasion to dislike Jamuga, Bortei?" he asked gently. "Hath he injured thee irrevocably? And if so, why not summon him here, and ask him what there hath been between ye both?"

Bortei paled. Her heart almost stopped. She regarded Kurelen with the intent and piercing gaze of a cornered animal. And then, with sickness, she realized that Kurelen, in some mysterious way, knew of what had transpired between herself and Jamuga. Her lips dried with terror.

"There hath been nothing between us," she stammered, trembling.

Kurelen continued to regard her with merciless thoughtfulness.

"Bortei," he said quietly, "thou art a wise woman. I have always admired thee, and thought of thee as a daughter, knowing thou art full of sense. If thou dost truly believe Jamuga is a traitor, then it must be because of some secret knowledge of thine, and I shall insist he be brought here and confronted by thee, and accused by thee."

No one but Bortei heard the menace and threat in his affectionate voice.

"By all means," said Temujin, impatiently, "summon him here. Bortei hath often warned me against him, and she shall accuse him, herself."

Bortei was as white as the chalked walls of the yurt. Her eyes, enormous, glittered with terror. She swallowed, moistened her parched lips. She began to stammer. almost incoherently:

"Perhaps we have been too hasty. Perhaps he is not a traitor —"

Now Kasar, indignant, interfered: "But I heard him myself!"

Kurelen, satisfied with the effect of his words on Bortei, turned to his younger nephew. "Kasar, I have always admired thine intelligence. Thou art clever enough to know that Jamuga is not traitor. If thou dost insist he is, then I shall know mine opinion of thee is false."

"But I heard him say this thing to the others," said Kasar, coloring uneasily.

"But thou art discerning enough to know that Jamuga is only a fool," urged Kurelen, as one clever and amused man to another.

Kasar was silent a moment. He was enormously flattered, for he had believed that Kurelen had considered him foolish in the past. Then, trying to keep the conceit from his voice, he said: "Thou art right, Kurelen. I have always thought Jamuga a fool. He merely likes to talk loosely."

While all this had been going on, Temujin, looking closely from one to the other, had sensed some undercurrents.

"Apparently it hath now been settled that Jamuga is a fool and no traitor," he said ironically. "However, I shall summon the others and ask them what Jamuga hath said."

Kurelen shrugged, sighed as at the words of an impetuous child.

"Temujin, hath it occurred to thee that at this time, when there is a war in prospect, this is no good moment to raise the question about a traitor in the camp? An accusation of treason doth make the people think. And Jamuga hath many friends here."

He stood up. He placed his hand on Temujin's shoulder. "Ask thyself in thy heart, Temujin, if thine anda is a traitor to thee."

Temujin glowered, but he was silent.

Kurelen smiled. "Thou dost see, thou canst not answer. But I shall speak to Jamuga myself, and tell him to hold his tongue. Like all men of thought, he doth talk too much. But let him ride at thy side; perhaps he will save thy life again. Thou knowest he would die for thee."

And so it was that Jamuga, to his surprise, and to the sudden glad aching of his heart, was summoned to ride at Temujin's side, and he alone. When he heard the summons, he could not speak, for he was afraid that he would burst into tears.

Despite the uneasy throbbing of his integrity, his doubts and angers were swallowed up in his love.

Kurelen knew what Temujin had not forgotten, however. He only hoped that Jamuga would distinguish himself again. For he knew, with fateful prescience, that the young noyon was in the most terrible danger, and only some miracle could save him now.

chapter 5

Jamuga wondered what thoughts haunted Temujin in the palace of Toghrul Khan. Did he see Azara in the corridors and the gardens? Did he think of her in the moonlight? He could never know. Baffled, he watched Temujin's face, and saw there nothing but indifferent calm. Once, he pointed to the long vista of the gardens in the moonlight, and said to Jamuga: "One night I dreamt that there was a high white wall there, reaching to the heavens, with a golden door set in it. I tried to force the door, but it would not open."

"That was an omen," answered Jamuga, who did not know the rest of the dream. "It doth mean there are gates which men can never force, and walls through which they cannot pass."

Temujin looked at him with a long and dreamy thoughtfulness. He smiled, then, and Jamuga, puzzled, thought he saw both pain and irony in that smile.

"I believe thou art right," said the young khan. He walked away then, and Jamuga saw him moving back and forth in the garden, restlessly, as though searching for something.

One night Jamuga was awakened by some strange sound, like a sigh or a muffled groan. But when he sat up and listened, he heard nothing. Temujin was sleeping peacefully beside him, the pale shadow of the moon on his quiet face.

Toghrul Khan and Temujin had greeted each other affectionately. Temujin was surprised to see how the old man had aged; he had shrunken, and his face was like a withered nut, and carved with a thousand hairlike lines. But his greed and craftiness glowed in his quenchless eyes, and his voice was as sweet as ever.

Neither of them mentioned Azara, for to both it was a name not to be borne. They spoke only of the coming campaign, and Toghrul Khan expressed his gratification at the good size and appearance of Temujin's warriors. "We shall soon defeat these Tatar animals," he said. He smiled at his foster son, and was surprised that Temujin did not smile back.

"The Tatars are not animals," said Temujin, tranquilly. "They are merely annoyances to the princes of Cathay. Thou hast been induced to assist the princes. Thou wilt receive thy reward. I ask only for the captives, and their wives, their children, their horses, their herds and their yurts." And when he had said this, he would say no more. Taliph, amiable and friendly, was puzzled. But Toghrul Khan, his evil old eyes glittering, was not puzzled in the least.

A great feast had been prepared in honor of Ye Liu Chutsai, the Cathayan prince and general. It was very elaborate, licentious and extravagant. Toghrul Khan thought it only a fitting feast for so illustrious a guest, and hoped that the general would find things congenial and familiar. Ye Liu Chutsai's father had been a Taoist, and he, himself, subscribed to this religion's austerity and simplicity, though, as a gentleman, he loved restraint and cultured elegance. He found Toghrul Khan's feast and palace barbarous and revolting. But, as he often said, a gentleman never allows religion or delicacy to interfere with graciousness, and so he professed to be overwhelmed and delighted by this orgy of women and color, wine and laughter, richness and vulgarity.

He was most interested in Temujin, and gazed at him with frank wonder and admiration. He had never seen red hair nor sea-green eyes before, and he thought them fascinating. Too, he was intrigued by Temujin himself, and his face and manner. He said, shortly after their first meeting: "We have a plant in Cathay, called Mon Nin Ching, an evergreen, which blooms but once in ten thousand years, and doth signify the coming of a great king or a great spiritual leader, or, sometimes, a terrible pestilence. Heaven hath given a sign in this flower, we believe. This morning, two of my evergreens burst into bloom, and tonight, I see thee."

He smiled as he said this, gently, as though amused by his own words, and as if he were sharing an amiable joke with Temujin. Temujin smiled back. But Toghrul Khan said nothing; he looked from one face to the other like a rat that hears and sees everything in a world both hating and hated.

Ye Liu Chutsai was a handsome middle-aged man, with a voice as deep and resonant as a muted cymbal. His skin was clear ivory, and his eyes were lustrous with the light of intellectual and bodily vigor. Through his long beard, reaching beyond his middle, his lips were red and full, and given to ironic or affable smiles. His fingernails were long, thin and curved, and lacquered, and on his fingers sparkled clusters of jewelled rings. He wore only white silken robes, except when in battle. He held his head proudly yet simply. He was the first gentleman Temujin had ever seen. Between the two men, barbarian and noble, there rose a warm feeling of complete friendship and trust.

Temujin was interested in the story of the evergreen. All at once, the Chinese gentleman laughed lightly.

"This morning I pointed this flower out to my mother's old cousin, who hath taken up some barbarous religion or philosophy. He is an old man, and wise, for all his separation from the faith of his fathers. He turned excessively pale at the sight of it, and said: 'This flowering doth portend the coming of the ancient monster from the darkness of the past into the bloody light of the present.'

"He doth believe that the calamities that visit men are immortal, that the monster may be killed, but he doth rise again in future generations, to harass, destroy, scourge and punish men for their evil deeds and forgetfulness of God."

He looked at Temujin with gay and dancing eyes, and laughed very heartily, but without malice.

"And then, when I told him of thy coming, he wept and said: 'The Monster hath come again! I knew this from the beginning.' Thou dost see Temujin, that my old cousin hath met thee before."

Temujin stared. And then he knew. He was nonplussed, and embarrassed, and thrown into a turmoil of thought.

"Thy cousin, the great lord, doth flatter me," he said.

Toghrul Khan laughed, also, but he chewed his sunken nether lip, and looked only at Temujin.

Ye Liu Chutsai was enjoying his joke. He saw nothing formidable in this young Mongol in his ill-smelling rough woolen clothes and lacquered leather armor. He told himself that he must remember to repeat the joke to his mother, who laughed little since the death of her husband.

Toghrul Khan spoke maliciously to the Chinese officer, but looked at Temujin as he said: "Perhaps thy cousin was credulous, as many of the old are, my lord. For, thou dost see, Temujin told him once that he wished for the world."

Ye Liu Chutsai laughed again, but without malice. He regarded Temujin with mirth-filled eyes. "Nay!" he exclaimed. "What for?"

Temujin, stung, said: "Dost thou not desire glory and conquest, my lord?"

Ye Liu Chutsai raised his eyebrows with immense surprise. "I? Most certainly not! Why should I?"

"Thy people are decadent," said Temujin.

The Cathayan was deeply entertained. "What dost thou call decadence? Civilization? The cultivation of the arts, of music, of gracious living, of peace, of philosophy and books, and all the things which distinguish men from beasts? It seemeth to me I have heard this threadbare theory before."

"But all these things steal away the strength and virility of men," answered Temujin.

Ye Liu Chutsai regarded him as a teacher might regard an obstreperous but lovable child.

"Dost thou think it necessary for virility to smell of manure and go about marauding and killing? Can a man be literate and not be virile? Doth the ability to wield a pen nullify the ability to wield a sword? I do not agree with thee." He was more amused than ever.

Jamuga, who had been listening in silence at a little distance, leaned forward eagerly. With some obscure satisfaction, he saw the dark flush rising to Temujin's hard and arrogant face.

Temujin said: "Suppose thy great Golden Emperor were attacked, and countless besiegers had nothing to lose but their lives, and counted them as cheap. Would thy people be able to withstand such fury, as they sit in their gardens and listen to women tinkling silver bells?"

Ye Liu Chutsai gazed at him thoughtfully, with a half smile. "Thou art very subtle, my young friend. I do not underestimate thee. And thou dost not think that gardens and peace and silver bells would be worth fighting for?"

"No, because too much thought maketh men regardful for their lives, and doth inspire in them the belief that life at any price is worth the having. But my people, and peoples like them form the steppes and the barrens, hold life in small regard. Between the man who loveth life, even as a slave, and a man who loveth life only because he can lose it in battle, there can be no question of the victor."

Ye Liu Chutsai pursed his lips and considered this. "Thou dost mean, I see, that only a man who is willing to sacrifice everything can win in the end. Perhaps thou art right. But I believe that if the empires of Cathay were threatened, we should find enough men who would prefer death to slavery. There are enough of us who love our civilization sufficiently to prize it above life."

"Dost thou?" asked Temujin, quickly.

Ye Liu Chutsai smiled. He shrugged. "If I died, then civilization would cease to exist for me," he answered, and at this sophistry he could not help laughing outright.

But Temujin, who understood him, felt no anger at the laughter. They regarded each other with great friendliness. Jamuga was astonished and chagrined. He could not understand the reason for the friendliness between this great cultivated gentleman and the rough, illiterate petty khan from the barrens.

Toghrul Khan told Ye Liu Chutsai of Temujin's demand that his own spoils of the coming war be only the persons of the Tatars and their belongings. He spoke of this in a voice of gentle ridicule, for he was infuriated with jealousy and contempt. But Ye Liu Chutsai did not seem to be either contemptuous or amused. He merely gazed at Temujin with a sort of amiable surprise.

Later, he sought Temujin out, and invited him to stroll with him in the gardens. There he told the young Mongol much of the history and grandeur and civilization of his own people. Before Temujin he spread out the vast empire ruled by tradition and culture, poetry and music, philosophy and learning. As on an endless plain he saw silver rivers, mighty cities where men discussed Buddha and Lao-tse, and thought that a stanza of golden words was more of worth than the taking of loot. He heard voices, raised not in fury nor vengeance, but in long arguments as to the meaning of an obscure philosophic phrase; he saw temples and heard cymbals, and the learned discussions of priests. He heard that poets were more revered than princes, and pride of family was greater than pride in wealth. "Songs of war are no longer heard among us," said Ye Liu Chutsai, smilingly. "We regard the soldier as lower than an animal, and hear of his exploits with disgust. When we engage in war, and rarely, we do it with dispatch, holding our noses. We prefer the comtemplation of nature, the beauty of our land. For in these things are no madnesses; madness liveth only in the minds of sick men. We love epigrams, for they are our revenge on the many insupportable things of living. We are both desperately and calmly sad, and the gayest of all people. We know that man is by nature evil, and because we are gentlemen, we cover that evil with flowers, preferring perfumes to stenches."

"Nevertheless," said Temujin cynically, "ye are noted for the craftiness of your traders, and the great wealth of your merchants."

Ye Liu Chutsai laughed, and admitted: "This is so. Beyond the music of our tea-houses our merchants jingle their change. But these are not gentlemen. I am speaking only of mine own kind."

Then, very frankly, as a philosopher cynically tolerant of all evils and nastinesses, and holding his nose, he told Temujin of the corruption of government officials, of the hatred between classes behind the great Wall, of oppressive taxes and the bitternesses between Buddhists and Confucians, of the misery of the men in the streets, of disillusion and disheartenment among thinking men, of drunken lords and lazy stupid princes, of bureaucrats and democrats in unceasing warfare of words, of bankruptcy and despair and the hopelessness of the poor. "But none of these are gentlemen," he added, and made a faintly wry face as though his own words embittered him.

"Among such hatred and confusion, there can be no unity in the face of war and aggression," said Temujin. He seemed to be thinking aloud.

"But the nature of the Chinese is merry, gay and passionate. Above all things, he hateth slavery."

"Ye have gone far from your nature," said Temujin, "and so, are ripe for destruction."

The prince found Temujin refreshing, as a strong wind is refreshing. He wanted to hear about Temujin's own life, and his people, and listened with intense interest, though he could not repress a private shudder.

"What do ye do in your spare time, when ye are not breeding, nor slaughtering nor quarrelling?"

"We sleep," said Temujin, and laughed.

At this, the other man shook his head without comment, and only smiled.

Temujin was surprised at the cunning and dexterity of the Cathayan soldiers, fighting side by side with his own warriors and those of Toghrul Khan. They had no aversion to killing, he saw, but they killed as though it were an unpleasant necessity, which gave them no joy. Moreover, they defended themselves sedulously, and retreated, instead of fighting to the death. It was his own men, and the Karait, who fought with shouts of exultation and pleasure, and who died without regret or groans. He stored what he had learned away in his mind, and never forgot it. He learned that gallantry and intelligence could defend themselves poorly in the face of ferocity and recklessness. A gentleman, at the last, was no match against the fighting machine. He had too much imagination. Even when he was cornered, one could tell that he feared more than death the sharp bite of steel in his vitals, and was sickened by the sight of his own blood.

The Tatars, ferocious and wild, fought with the simple frightfulness of simple beasts. But they were soon overcome by superior numbers. Even while dying, they rose to a knee, and struck out. This, Temujin could understand, and honor.

The Tatars were driven back from the wall and fled in disorder, pursued. They left behind them their yurts and their women and children. These, Temujin confiscated. In the meantime, the men were pursued by his warriors, and captured. That night, in the midst of the huge disorder, he spoke to the Tatars and invited them to join him.

They looked at him, and knew him for one of their own. They hated, with passionate hatred, the Cathayans, and the Karait, who they felt had betrayed them. But they looked at Temujin, and loved him. They knelt before him and offered their fealty.

Toghrul Khan was elated. He boasted to Ye Liu Chutsai of his victories. He was given the title of Wang, as had been promised to him, and much of the loot. Temujin desired only the men and their families and their herds and yurts. Quietly, among the Tatars, he slected two of the most beautiful maidens, and made them his wives. They felt, now, that he was their ally, and that he hated their enemies as they hated them.

"Patience," he said to them privately. "Patience. We shall be avenged."

Ye Liu Chutsai regretted that Temujin must now part with him.

"Do not be too dismayed," said Temujin, with an odd smile. "We shall meet again."

Ye Liu Chutsai insisted upon giving him a necklace of pearls and opals for Bortei, and many bamboo cases of tea and spices, and many lengths of silken cloth. They parted with expressions of mutual affection and many promises.

Temujin began the long journey homeward. Behind him trundled the vast new city of his vassals. The Tatars rode beside his own warriors, and shared their blankets and food.

Jamuga did not like the Tatars. He distrusted them. He had talked with several of the Cathayan officers at night, between battles, and he felt that here was his own people. When he rode home with Temujin, he fell behind, feeling that his anda was now a complete stranger to him, and that all love was dead between them.

"I shall go away," he thought miserably. "Surely, my mother's people will take me unto them. There is no place for me with Temujin."

chapter 6

During all the long ride homewards to the Gobi, Temujin did not speak to Jamuga, nor Jamuga to him, except on one occasion.

They had circled about, the Mongols and the Tatars, and at one twilight they suddenly entered a region familiar to Jamuga, one of low terra-cotta hills carved by the wind into strange and fantastic shapes, nightmarish and grotesque. They descended into a narrow twisting valley, reddish and dry, where a river had run. Now the sun was setting, and the earth swam in unearthly colors of violet, yellow, bronze and scarlet, in which the hills drifted, lit into pink clarity by the last bloody light. The silence of the barrens, empty and motionless, fell over the whole world. Even the horsemen made no sound, as they moved down the valley, winding past colored hills in the forms of pillared temples and flattened volcanoes.

Then, suddenly, in the distance, the Lake of the Damned could be seen, dimly bluish and purple in its shores of pallid shadows. There it lay, immobile, stark and mystic, a dream drifting on the desert. Many of the horsemen had never seen it before, and they uttered faint cries, believing this to be a natural inland sea, promising coolness and rest. But they thought this only a moment, for then the awfulness, the silence, the unearthly quality of the Lake bore in upon their senses, and they were terrified. The sun had fallen, and the earth was alone, spinning in a nightmare of foglike colors and soundlessness, with the Lake in the distance, spreading into infinity, and the sky above, lost in dusty rose and fading fire.

Temujin, on his horse, stood a little in advance of the others, his lance in his hand. He faced the Lake. He looked at it a long time, and the ghastly last light of the earth and the heavens lay on his face and in his eyes. He heard some one move up to him, to his side, and after a moment, he turned his head and looked at the other man. It was Jamuga, pale and silent, who was gazing at the Lake. Behind them, the thousands of warriors waited, uneasily, wrapped in their cloaks, dark-faced and intent.

Then Jamuga spoke, pointing to the Lake: "The Lake of the Damned! The Lake of those who would conquer and destroy for their own lust and vanity! As surely as this is a frightful mirage, so is the tyrant's dream of power, and so shall his dream end, in waste and wilderness, in illusion and death."

Temujin looked at him with an inscrutable expression, then, very slowly, be began to smile. To Jamuga, it was a most terrible smile. Then Temujin looked over his shoulder at his people, and said in a light voice:

"This is only a mirage. Nevertheless, let us pursue it, and see what doth happen."

The men laughed with a sound of release. Temujin spurred his horse, and, with a wild hoarse shout, he rushed down towards the Lake. The others followed, shouting and screaming, brandishing their spears and lances as though in pursuit of a foe. And, after a few minutes, Jamuga followed.

The Lake lay before them, visible and mysterious, but as they thundered down upon it, it retreated, never coming nearer. They reached a region of white and acrid borax, which rose up about them, disturbed, in clouds of choking, smarting dust. But, always retreating, always frightful and unearthly, the Lake stood in the desert.

Darkness came rapidly, and all at once the Lake had vanished, and now there was nothing for endless miles but purple shadows, like sheets of water. The sky was the color of amethysts. And now the wind rose, fierce and irresistible, sweeping over the wastes with the sound of low drumming thunder. The hills had vanished. There was nothing but the purple gale, and the immense loneliness of a dead land.

Temujin, laughing and panting, reined-in his horse, and the others did likewise. He looked at them, and they looked at him. And then he stared beyond them, at Jamuga, slowly cantering up with a sad face.

"Let us be on," said Temujin, turning about. "We must camp very soon, for the night."

The moon rose behind the western ramparts of the templed hills, and soon flooded earth and heaven with a milky luster. The wind was stronger, now. They were obliged to camp sooner than expected, in the shadow of a bleached wall.

But Jamuga and Temujin slept apart that night, as they had never slept before, and they did not speak for the rest of the journey.

chapter 7

Jamuga did not like the young Juchi, the Shadowed, for he was much like Bortei, with sullen gray eyes and a petulant red mouth. Moreover, he was both arrogant and intolerant, exigent and angry. He seemed to be Temujin's favorite, for all his doubtful birth, for the boy was fearless and handsome, and, even while still a little child, would insist upon riding wild horses and subduing them with cruel blows.

But the lonely Jamuga, despairingly pondering his own escape, but not moving in that direction for a long time, loved the three younger children of his estranged anda, Chutagi, Ogotai and the young Tuli, still only an infant in the arms of his mother. These four boys were the sons of Bortei. Temujin's children by his other wives, beautiful Turkish, Naiman, Merkit and Uighur women, were regarded by their father with fond indifference and indulgence. But the children of Bortei were his heart's darlings. He loved their gray or green-blue eyes. Tuli, especially, was his love, for the baby had bright red-gold hair and a sweet laugh.

It was the wretched Jamuga who taught Chutagi and Ogotai the art of riding on a ram, clutching the dirty wool in sturdy little fingers. As he watched the two small boys riding the bucking animals, side by side, and shouting with glee, he would smile sadly, remembering the days when he and Temujin rode like this, laughing into each other's faces, and understanding everything between them. It was Jamuga who taught them strange short songs. He also taught them to box and wrestle fairly, and to cast a lance with telling effect. Sometimes he wondered why Bortei, his old enemy, allowed the children to be with him so much. He did not know that this was by Temujin's command.

Sometimes he would carry Tuli on his shoulder, and the two older boys would accompany him on foot as he led them to the water and taught them to swim. Still celibate and childless, he found an aching joy and wistfulness in the touch of these children, in the affection he saw for him in their young eyes. He told them stories, and gave them wise counsel beyond their years. Chutagi and Ogotai would listen respectfully, for this pale gentleman was their father's anda, but they hardly understood. Tuli would gurgle in Jamuga's arms and poke fingers into his eyes and mouth, and shriek with glee at Jamuga's gentle bite and ferocious growls.

Kurelen watched all this with a sad wryness. Once he said to Jamuga: "Thou art no longer very young. Why dost thou not marry, and have sons of thine own?"

Then Jamuga answered sorrowfully: "I cannot marry. I cannot beget children. For I am only a pusillanimous slave. When I escape, when I am free, then shall I have peace, and a wife, and children."

This Kurelen told Temujin. He knew that there had been only silence and avoidance between the two men for a long time, that Jamuga never was invited to the councils of the tarkhans, the orkhons and the divisional commanders, nor was he called to the feasts. Worse than all, he remained at home, obscurely and shamefully, during raids and battles. He was forgotten. Only Kurelen saw his sorrow and misery, saw the look on his face as he watched Temujin at a distance. Only Kurelen suspected that in spite of his patience Jamuga was not a meek man, and he was afraid and distrustful of the time when that patience would break and Jamuga would emerge.

So one day Kurelen said to Temujin: "Thou hast been cruel and merciless to Jamuga, because never hath he lied to thee, nor flattered thee for his own ends, nor bowed before thee. I cannot think thou dost hate him, in spite of what thou art. Let him go."

Temujin listened with a dark and averted face. Then he said: "Go? Where can he go?"

"Let him return to his mother's people, the Naiman. Thou hast a huge conquered tribe of the Naiman, under thy banner, loyal and devoted to thee. Let him be thy nokud, the commander of that tribe."

Temujin snorted. "And let him preach treason to them?"

"He will never preach treason. This tribe is a quiet one, composed mostly of herdsmen and shepherds, peaceful and docile. He will be at home with them, as he never is with thee. Let him have peace. His only crime against thee is that he loveth thee, as no one else loveth thee."

"But he is such a fool!" exclaimed Temujin, impatiently. His face was darker than ever, as though with some obscure pain and uncertainty.

"He is not a fool, Temujin. He hath only ideas alien to thee. These ideas will do no harm among the Naiman. Let him go. Thou knowest how brave he is. If thou dost need him, he will respond with selfless joy to thy command."

Temujin promised nothing. A long time passed, and Kurelen thought that he had forgotten.

In the meantime, hundreds of other clans joined Temujin's standard. Now there was no one stronger in the Gobi, nor had more influence, except Toghrul Khan. Because of his strength, and his protection, the caravan routes were crowded, and his own wealth grew. His name was magic in the barrens and the desert. Every caravan brought flattering and loving letters to him from Toghrul Khan. He would have the letters read to him, then he would seize them with an oath, spit upon them, and toss them into the fires. When he did this, it was noted that his face became demoniacal, like that of a madman. And he would look to the east, his mouth moving in silent imprecations.

Jamuga, by now, had been stripped of all power, silently and relentlessly. He lived alone in his yurt, served by an old woman, a relative of his mother's. He thought he had been completely forgotten, and daily his despair and hopelessness grew. Though still young, there were streaks of premature gray in his light hair, and two deep furrows had appeared beside his patient and rigid mouth.

Then one day he received a summons from Temujin. Trembling and bewildered, he went to the yurt of his anda, his heart beating with dread. But his manner was composed. He found Temujin alone, lolling on his couch and drinking hot tea. When he appeared before Temujin, the latter smiled at him with an aspect of such friendliness and affection that Jamuga stood dumb, unable to move. Temujin motioned him to take his place by his side, and silently Jamuga obeyed, his underlip shaking.

Temujin drank noisily. He filled a steaming cup for Jamuga. "A vile brew, but an inspiring one," he said, laughing. His green-gray eyes began to soften into a soft blue. His red hair seemed to crackle on his head with vitality.

Jamuga drank. The hot liquid burned his throat. He could hardly control his trembling. Temujin watched him with an amiable and affectionate smile.

"Thou needest a family, and authority, Jamuga," he said.

"I need nothing," stammered Jamuga, in a low stifled voice.

Tears rose to his eyes. He clenched his teeth to control his emotion.

Temujin bent towards him, and laid his arm on his shoulder in his old way. He looked deeply into Jamuga's face. What he saw seemed to amuse him, but without malice, and even with compassion.

"Thou hast deserted me, Jamuga," he said gayly.

They might have seen each other, in friendship, but a day before. But Jamuga, with his rigid integrity and hurt, could not accept this. He was silent. He bent his head and gazed before him, tight-lipped and sad.

After a moment, Temujin removed his arm. There was a little silence between them. Jamuga, miserably, knew he ought to unbend, that he ought to look at Temujin with his old openness, accepting his anda's mood. But he was unable to do this; he did not know how to dissemble or pretend.

Temujin spoke again, lightly and artifically, "I say, thou needest a family, a wife, or wives. Is there none among these women that doth entice thee?"

"No," murmured Jamuga. Again, he felt the weight of tears in his eyes.

"Yet, thou dost love children."

Jamuga was silent.

Temujin began to eat. His relishing manner was a little too obvious. He was ill-at-ease, and truth to tell, he was embarrassed and a trifle ashamed.

"I have thought matters over, Jamuga. I have decided to make thee nokud of one of the tribes of the Naiman. Quiet, peaceful people, herdsmen and shepherds."

Jamuga lifted his head, astounded. Now his heart began to beat wildly. Color came into his pale face. He stared at Temujin, who pretended to be engrossed in dismembering meat from a small bone.

"Yes," said Temujin, nodding his head. "I think thou wouldst be an excellent commander. And these are thy mother's people. The present nokud is an old man, in his dotage. I know I can rely upon thy wisdom and discretion." Now he looked at Jamuga with a brilliant smile. "What dost thou think?"

"I can only obey. And thank thee," said Jamuga, through trembling lips. The blood was deep in his cheeks. He was like a man promised life after a threat of death.

"Good!" exclaimed Temujin, heartily. "I knew thou wouldst obey me without question." He paused. "Jamuga, I have never forgotten thou art mine anda."

Jamuga could only gaze at him, luminous-eyed, unspeaking.

Temujin could not endure that look. Shame smote him. He turned his head away. He could not bear the sight of such love, such humility and such joy. His hard heart twisted in his chest.

"Tomorrow, thou shalt take thy pick of the stallions, and with thee shall go one hundred men of thy choice, among the Naiman."

He hesitated. He reached out to a tabouret, on which stood

a brass box. He opened it, and withdrew a large gold ring, set with a dull red stone. He put the ring on Jamuga's finger, and smiled into his eyes.

"I shall never forget thee, Jamuga. This is my gift to thee. Wear it to thy death, and bequeath it to thy first son. It is a talisman. If thou needest me at any time, send it with a messenger, and I shall come at once."

Jamuga looked at the ring. He tried to speak. And then, to his own shame, he burst into tears.

The next day the city of yurts hummed with the excitement of the news. Bortei was enraged. She argued with Temujin that he was putting power into the hands of a traitor. But Houlun, despite the humiliation she had suffered long ago at Jamuga's hands, upheld her son vigorously. Kurelen was delighted.

Temujin gave a tremendous feast in honor of Jamuga. And Jamuga sat at his right hand, with Temujin's ring on his finger. His face was white with joy, and full of peace.

It was the last time they would ever sit so. It was the last time they would look at each other like this. Years later, Temujin remembered, and the memory never gave him anything but the strongest pain and sadness.

chapter 8

Jamuga, by nature apprehensive and doubtful, did not expect, at the last, too much of the Naiman whom he was to rule. The Naiman who had been absorbed directly into Temujin's people had not been distinguished by gentleness of soul, or less ferocity, than their new masters. The nomad peoples, of whatever tribe or origin, were singularly alike, both in nature and feature. Realists all, knowing with sensible clarity that the only thing worth fighting for was sustenance and pastures, they were expedient and direct.

However, from the first moment of his arrival, after a long journey, at the site of this camp of the Naiman, Jamuga's joy was tinged with incredulity. For here there was little outward ferocity or truculence. The camp was situated in a warm and gentle valley, sheltered by the bare white sides of enormous sterile mountains which guarded it from the more fierce winds and the sharper cold. Through this narrow green valley, level and grassy, ran a smooth and quiet river, and along the banks of this river the Naiman had planted slender fields of millet and corn and wheat. Oftentimes, when a winter was somewhat mild, they did not leave this site, but remained the year around. The nomad people rarely planted anything, and this, perhaps, was the true source of their ferocity, restlessness, and the hunger which was both physical and spiritual. But by planting, this tribe had become less warlike and brutal. Having to guard their fields, and till them, they were not often induced to go hunting or marauding. Civilization, by way of the growth of the earth, had begun to pervade them, and a sort of calm peacefulness had already settled over their bronzed faces.

The plow, thought Jamuga, with a sudden sense of refreshment, is the weapon of the civilized against the uncivilized, the first stone in the wall raised against barbarism. For the man who plowed the earth, and tended it, had no desire to heap it with corpses. The first step towards chaos, too, was the huge paved city, which removed its people from the earth, and filled them with the restless and rapacious spirit of the nomads. Between the barbarism of the city hordes, and the barbarism of the desert hordes, there was no difference. Ferocity and brutality sprang from homelessness, whether it be on barren or city street. The barbarian urbanite and the barbarian desert-dweller were blood brothers, having nothing to lose but their miserable lives, and having everything to gain by murder and cruelty and rapacity.

Peace cometh from the earth, Jamuga had read. He had read it, but had not understood it. But now, looking at the yellow heads of the grain, watching them ripple like a golden sea in the wind, he understood. The man who raised bread was the man of peace, but the homeless man who hated and sharpened his sword was the enemy of all other men. Wars and oppressions would end on the day when every man had a plot of earth to call his own. Who could watch the sun rising and setting on his own plowed land, and observe how the rains and the snows came to make fertility, and bear upon his hands the darkness of his own soil, and then lust to go forth and subjugate and destroy others?

Not far from this valley was another, in a long chain of valleys, and in this particular spot lived a tribe of the Uighur, whom Jamuga knew and respected as an able and responsible people, probably one of the first to become settled and agricultural, as well as highly civilized. Even those who developed and lived in cities did not forget their tie with the land. Between this tribe of the Naiman and the Uighur was a very friendly fraternalism, and they intermarried and held mutual celebrations. Manichaeism, Buddhism and Christianity were practised among them with fine impartiality and tolerance.

Jamuga was received at first with reserve, for every one knew of the exigency and relentlessness of Temujin, their feudal lord. They had awaited Jamuga's arrival with apprehension, believing that Temujin would send some one like himself, who would despise their agricultural life, and whip them into militarism. It was said among them that he would immediately instill hostility in them against the Uighur, who lived such a proud and independent life, and who hated to pay tribute to any one. Because of this rumor, the Uighur had, for some weeks, kept to themselves, with sad cautiousness, and their friends, the Naiman, were miserable in consequence.

But when the old men saw Jamuga, and observed his gentle hesitant manners, and saw his blue eyes and his smile, their hearts lifted with joy. Here was one they could understand, and who would understand them. "The lord Temujin," they cried, "is a lord of great wisdom!"

On the second night of his arrival, the old man who had been the previous nokud suggested, with a simple forthrightness, that Jamuga marry his granddaughter, Yesi, and become in truth, one of the Naiman.

"I have no desire to marry," replied Jamuga abruptly. "There are men who are celibate, and live only for their own thoughts, and service."

The old man spread out his hands with deprecating gentleness. "But how can a man serve men unless he giveth sons to serve his people, also?"

"Thou dost mean, to serve Temujin," answered Jamuga, with bitterness.

The old man sighed. "It is the will of God. We must give tribute to our lord, not only in corn and horses and herds, but in soldiers, also. But peace is precious, and no price is too high to pay for it."

He urged Jamuga to look at Yesi at least, who was skilled in all womanly duties, a gentle Christian woman who knew her place and had a soft tongue. At first Jamuga, remembering Bortei, and recalling that women were at best a danger to men, refused. But later, he reconsidered. Perhaps the old men were right; perhaps it would be comfortable to have a wife, whom he need not look at except at night. She would bear him children and tend his fires and his yurt. Suddenly he was conscious of his great loneliness. A wife became a warm fire in the midst of strangers. If he truly wished to be one of this people, he must marry one of their women.

He sent for Yesi and her grandfather. The old man came at once, gleefully, leading the girl by the hand. Jamuga saw that she was tall, and that she kept her head modestly bent, covered by a striped shawl. She stood before him, trembling a little, her head hidden.

Jamuga felt a great tenderness and gentleness. He stretched out his hand and removed the girl's shawl. He looked long at her blushing face. And then he knew that never again would he be lonely and homeless, without a friend and without love.

Then man and woman regarded each other in a deep silence. The girl had a sweet and tinted face, full of honesty and innocence and fearlessness, with a pale rosy mouth, a small straight nose, and the bluest eyes he had ever seen. In her eyes he saw courage and gentleness and modesty, and a steadfast intelligence. Her hair, pale brown and smooth and straight as silk, hung to her knees in shining braids, and gave her a look of proud meekness and aristocracy. Her figure was slender and exceedingly beautiful in its robe of rough white wool. She had tied a scarf of multi-colored striped silk about her narrow waist, and a silver cross hung between her breasts.

Jamuga's heart turned over with a sensation of infinite sweetness and pain. For a moment he thought that she resembled Azara, who had so bewitched and changed Temujin.

He extended his hand to her, and said: "Come." She hesitated; color flooded her cheeks. Her eyes filled with tears. Then she smiled, and gave him her hand, bending her head to hide her face. He felt her hand tremble, then nestle closely in his.

There was a great marriage feast. The Uighur came, singing hoarsely, and stamping their rough deerskin boots in an uncouth dance. The Naiman rejoiced. The fires burned until dawn, and there was more wine than any one man could drink. The old men sang songs, not of warlike heroes, but of sunlight and earth, wheat and rain, peace and love.

Yesi sat by the side of her husband, and received, with him, the homage of their people. And Jamuga, listening and looking and smiling, with Yesi's hand in his, thought at last that he had come home, and that never again for him would there be unrest and misery, homelessness and sorrow.

When he slept that night with Yesi beside him, he had a strange dream, which, upon waking, seemed an omen not only of the present, but of the world to come, still in the embryo of the future.

He thought that he stood on the white crystalline shores of the Lake of the Damned. He was filled with his old pain and sadness, his old sensation of imminent death and disaster and complete hopelessness. The sky was as red as blood, and streaked with yellow fire. The Lake lay in its awful mystery of purple shadows and silence. And then, all at once, he heard a dim far shout, and saw an army of men approaching the Lake, on foot. But they were not armed with swords. Their horses went before them, dragging plows. And they drove these horses and plows over the terrible Lake, shouting and singing and calling to each other in voices of jubilant triumph. The ominous silence of the red-lit air was broken, and echoes flew through it, like white doves. And then, in the wake of the plows rose the wheat, wave upon wave, resistless and golden, the sound of its growing like a loud and rustling wind. The bloody sky faded; it was sunset, and the sky was a deep shadowy blue, full of peace and promise. And the men continued to plow until all the earth was waving with grain, and the Lake was gone. Then, the plowers rested on their plows, and looked back at what they had done. And their faces were filled with the peace of the fertile land.

Jamuga sighed in his dream. It seemed to him that all the hot anguish flowed out of him and was lost in the fruitful silence. Some one was speaking to him, but he could not see the speaker.

"The earth is the Lord's," said the unseen one. "Always, and forever, the earth is the Lord's!"

chapter 9

Temujin's face was inscrutable as he was read the letter from his anda. It was Kurelen who read the letter to him, and in all its words Temujin heard peaceful joy and contentment.

"This year I can send only forty young men to thee, for the winter was cold and the last harvest was meager. This spring we are planting many more acres of reclaimed earth, and as the river overflowed and fertilized the land, we expect that we shall have more wheat than ever. Therefore, because of the last harvest, I regret that I cannot send thee the usual amount of grain. What I am sending is all I can spare, both of grain and men, for our people need every hand to bring forth an abundance of harvests."

Temujin looked at the forty young Naiman. They were strong and comely young men, with calloused hands and sun-blackened amiable faces. Their military equipment was poor and neglected. Temujin frowned. Jamuga had said these men were unmarried; they had not brought wives or children or yurts with them. But the horses they rode, and the stallions and mares they had brought as tribute, were fat and sleek, and oversized.

"These are not soldiers," he said contemptuously. "They are herdsmen and farmers." He added, with a vicious undertone: "How can men who have planted grain learn the arts of war?"

"Nevertheless," said old Kurelen, "planters are needed, as well as destroyers."

He continued to read the letter, and as he did so, he seemed pleased.

"I ask thee, as mine anda, to rejoice with me in the birth of my first children, twins, a son and a daughter, Yuzjani and Khati. The old men say they are the sun and the moon, which is an extravagance. However, pardon the prejudice of a father when I tell thee that the boy is as strong as the girl is beautiful. I do not know which I love the better. But the girl hath the beauty of her mother, my beloved Yesi, and is already showing the artfulness of her sex. She can do with me as she wilt. The boy shall be a Buddhist, like Yesi's grandfather, and the girl shall be a Christian. It was a beautiful sight to see the Buddhists and the Christians celebrating their individual masses in the names of my children. My wife and I feel that God hath given us every blessing, and there is nothing more we can desire."

Kurelen looked at Temujin's dark face with its obscure and brooding expression. He saw there contempt and envy, and a somber restlessness.

"Jamuga never desired the world," he said to his nephew.

Temujin snorted. "He who desireth little is content with nothing," he replied. "A woman, children, herds and grain! What a small soul he hath!"

Kurelen shrugged, but said nothing. However, he was alarmed. For he saw that some rage had Temujin, and he was afraid for Jamuga, who had been indiscreet enough to be happy in the face of a man who would never be happy.

Finally the old man said: "Thou art right, Temujin. The little life led by Jamuga would never appeal to thee. Thou wert made for destiny, for the conquest of the earth, not its meager cultivation." He made a wry mouth as he said this, and watched Temujin keenly.

But for some reason Temujin did not look soothed nor placated. He walked away, scowling right and left, and, even his warriors and officers fell back, uneasily, at his look. He had his favorite white stallion brought to him, and then rode off furiously into the barrens. He mounted a low gray hill, which was strewn with tamarisk and dead thorn-bushes, and descended another side. There he was alone, in a frozen sea of such low gray hills, lifeless under a sky the color of dull silver. Here the wind stung his face with mingled dust and sand, the erosions of the ages. There was no sound, but this wind, and the impatient snuffling of his horse. He sat, huddled in his saddle, gloomily staring off into the distance, not moving, a cloaked statue, immobile and somber, his thoughts as lifeless and dark as the barrens and the skies.

He had come here to sort out his restless emotions and dull angry thoughts. But as he sat on his horse, his mind took on the color of this dead world, this empty and dusty space. The gale moaned heavily about him, and all at once it seemed to him that it was freighted with a multitude of lost voices, desolately speaking of what had once lived in this world, which had gone forever.

Kurelen had long ago told him the legends of these barrens, that once a mighty empire of mighty cities had stood here, blazing with life and color and movement, restlessly seething with a thousand dynasties. Here had been temples and market places, academies and schools, fountains and thronged streets, palaces and endless houses, gardens and pools and terraces. Here had been walls and bronze gates, and the hubbub of caravans and commerce, countinghouses and traders and merchants from a hundred towns. Where had they gone? This world had rolled up like a painted scroll, and had vanished into dust.

Kurelen had said this was the inevitable fate of all empires and all glories—dust and laden wind and eroded emptiness. The banners of triumph had crumbled and been blown away. The halls where conquerors had walked had become heaps of stone, covered by the ages. Kings had ridden down streets now buried in sand, and sand drifted where their generals had stood in a forest of lances. Oppressor and oppressed lay side by side now, in the tomb of nothingness, their mouths filled with earth. Those who had loved and those who had hated were alike in that they had gone, leaving no trace behind them. Multitudes had wept here, and rejoiced, and there was nothing left of them but this wind and this enormous death.

A horrible pang went through Temujin, and he spoke aloud, simply and harshly:

"What does it matter, then, what I do, and what I covet, and what I seize? I may gain the world, and tomorrow, there shall be nothing left but desert and silence, and the laden wind! What doth drive me? Revenge? But Kurelen hath said to me that a man who longeth for revenge, and taketh it, is still defeated. Envy? But such is the end of envy—this barrenness and this gray sand-filled void! Power? But the end of power is surely waste and nothingness!

"Death, then, is the end of everything. What doth anything matter, but today? And even today is lost, if there be no love in it."

He heard his own words, and was aghast. A dreadful sense of emptiness and hopelessness swept over him. He could taste the dry sand and dust in his mouth, and it appeared to him that the taste was on the lips of his soul. His heart ached and throbbed, and his eyes went blind.

"Azara!" he cried in anguish. "If thou wouldst have remained with me, if we could have been together, then every day would have been a day of life, and not of death! There would have been depth in every hour, and every night would have had its meaning. But now, there is nothing for me!"

He bent his head. His hands fell from the reins. The stallion, feeling his thoughts, began to tremble. The sky darkened, and the hills became lost in shadow and grayness. The whole desolate landscape was flooded with a wan and macabre light, in which there was no outline of any living thing, and the world became a dream still held in chaos. And in the midst of this dream of dead ages stood the horse and the man.

Why do I go on? thought Temujin. What is there on the earth for me? Why cannot I have rest, and love, as lesser men have them?

He lifted his head. He looked about him. He could feel his warm heart beating painfully in this universal death. He thought of the things he had done, and which he must do, though he did not know why. He was suddenly permeated by an enormous weariness.

Why must I do these things? I know not. I only know that there is an impelling force in me, as mysterious as the lights of the North, as resistless as the hurricane, as wild as the desert, as savage as the wolf, as terrible as life and death. There is in me an awful hunger. I am filled with voices and a sense of limitless power.

But after all I am a leaf in the wind, a feather upon the river. I am blown and driven, and I know not where. I only know I must do as I must do.

I am not a man, but only violence and chaos. I am part of the universal upheaval. Such as I am one with the volcano and the wave, the earthquake and the storm. I am part of the furious destiny of the earth, and have no more volition or will than any other part, and am as helpless.

If I leave behind me the shattered and blackened walls of cities—if my path is heaped with victims—this do I know in truth: My spirit is no less shattered and blackened. I am the first victim.

chapter 10

A servant came hurriedly to Jamuga.

"Lord, there is a caravan coming, and one doth carry the banner of the nine yak-tails!"

Jamuga's heart alternately sank, then rose. "Temujin!" he said aloud. His breath came fast. He did not know why he was at once filled with apprehension and joy. He went out to greet his visitors, and brought his wife with him.

But the visitor, accompanied by a detachment of warriors and servants, was not Temujin. Jamuga, seeing this, was conscious of a sinking disappointment, then relief. The visitor was Kurelen, so wrapped in furs that he resembled an old dejected bear. Seeing Jamuga, he shouted and waved.

Jamuga helped him to dismount, then embraced him. "How glad I am to see thee!" he exclaimed. He had never been overly fond of the old cripple, but now his face was lighted with pleasure and affection.

Kurelen spat. "My mouth is as dry as a withered sack!" he said, "and my old bones rattle. Well, Jamuga! Thou hast not aged a day! Such is a result of joy. And a good wife," he added genially, seeing Yesi, who was gazing at him with a modest and innocent smile.

She bowed before him. "My husband's friend is as a father to me," she answered in a low voice, and kissed his dark and twisted hand.

Kurelen was touched. To cover his emotion, he looked about him. He saw throngs of smiling and contented faces. Then Jamuga led him to his yurt, and ordered wine and food. Kurelen ate with his old gusto, and commented on the good bread and mutton.

"We grew the corn ourselves," said Jamuga, proudly.

Then there was a sudden silence between them. At last Jamuga asked diffidently: "And how is Temujin?"

Kurelen laughed. "He hath a score of children. Thou, I presume, hast only one wife, but Temujin hath a harem. His little daughters are very beautiful, and though he doth make a huge fuss over Bortei's sons, I suspect he loveth his girls the best. He is already talking about marrying the oldest to princes of Cathay. What an ambition doth consume him!"

Jamuga was yearning to ask if Temujin ever spoke of him, but instead he said: "But is he happy? And well?"

Kurelen shrugged. "Sometimes he doth complain of his liver, but I believe he doth eat too much, and is too fond of wine. But that is a family failing. Happy? I do not think so. How can a man be happy when he hath a fire in him? Sometimes he doth look despairing, as though seeking help. I ofttimes wonder if that Persian girl, the daughter of Toghrul Khan, did not eat too deeply into him. Yet, he never speaks of her."

Jamuga said, with a touch of his old bitterness: "Temujin never loved any one."

Kurelen raised an eyebrow quizzically. "I do not agree with thee. He loved thee, Jamuga. I believe he doth love thee still."

Jamuga looked up with involuntary eagerness. But he said: "I cannot believe it." His face darkened sadly, and he looked away.

Kurelen laid his hand on his arm. "Thou wert always suspicious, and a cold doubter. Nevertheless, when I asked permission of Temujin to visit thee, he seemed pleased. And in my bags there are gifts for thee and thy wife."

He had his bags brought into the yurt, and opened them like a jovial pasha. Yesi, who had been serving them, stopped near by, a plate in her hand, and a look of young anticipation on her face. Kurelen produced a fine Chinese dagger for Jamuga, with a handle of gold encrusted with turquoises. There was also a pair of deerskin boots, as fine and soft as silk, and elaborately embroidered. And best of all, there were several Chinese manuscripts of poetry and philosophy, seized from a luckless caravan. For Yesi, there were lengths of yellow and scarlet silk, a shawl of the finest crimson wool, a necklace of opals and silver, bracelets of carved green jade, and a silver box of attar of roses. For her children, there were a cloak of white wolfskins and a cluster of jingling silver bells.

Jamuga was so moved by these rich gifts that he could not speak, but Yesi took them with cries of joy. Jamuga watched her with a sad and loving smile. She held the fur up to her face; she thrust the bracelets upon her arms. Then she looked at her husband, pleading for his admiration. But again his expression darkened.

"Did he send me no message?" he asked.

Temujin had sent no message, but this did not prevent Kurelen from lying jovially. "Certainly. He wished me to tell thee that he is well pleased with the young men thou hast sent him."

Now Jamuga was intensely interested. "Are they happy, these young men of mine?"

Kurelen could answer with truth, though he knew the truth would not overly please Jamuga: "They seem to be very—enthusiastic. They soon learn to be excellent soldiers. Temujin hath remarked, with apparent surprise, that they take readily to war."

Jamuga sighed. "I was afraid of that."

"Thou dost remember, Jamuga, that I told thee that war is in the nature of men!"

"But not here!" cried Jamuga, passionately. "Here, they are content!"

Kurelen nodded gravely. "I believe thee. But perhaps thou hast here something that Temujin hath not. That is why I have come: to see for myself what thou hast."

But Jamuga eyed him with pale suspicion. "Art thou not sure that Temujin hath sent thee to spy on me?" Instantly, he was remorseful. But Kurelen was not offended.

"Nay, thou doubter, I have come for mine own curiosity."

He continued to eat. "Temujin hath done well. His dream of a confederacy of all the tribes is within realization. That is why I fear for the enmity of Toghrul Khan, that old prayer-singing vulture. I should not be surprised if open war is not soon declared between them. But no: it is not Toghrul Khan's way to be open at any time. I suspect that we shall soon experience treachery."

"I have done well, too," replied Jamuga. "Many of the clans hereabouts have joined me. Peaceful and friendly people, content with our way of life."

Again, Kurelen nodded. Now he could speak with truth. "Temujin is pleased with thee for this. Thou hast done good work, in this country. But now, thou canst show me thy secret."

It was sunset. The two men, the old and the young, rode through the city of tents, towards the river and the pastures and the fields of grain. Kurelen looked about him, keenly. The people seemed gentle yet proud, with calm faces and amiable eyes. Every one busy, coming and going, without haste, but intent. The herds were coming in from pasture. The women were going out with pails, followed by the young and playing children. Campfires were beginning to burn high. Kurelen heard the singing of young girls, the laughter of young men. He was conscious of contentment and peace and strong purpose. When the people greeted Jamuga, it was with mingled pride and love, and the respect one gives honestly. It was evident that their salutes to the khan came from their hearts, without servility or fear. And Jamuga returned their salutes with grave dignity, sometimes calling a man or child by name, and stopping to exchange a word.

Kurelen was impressed by the lack of turbulent or violent faces, by the absence of discordant and angry voices, and furious cries. Children were not dispatched with blows, nor did the women cast sullen glances at the men. Even the dogs trotted about playfully, and their barking was jovial. A man stroked the neck of an ox; a woman leaned against the side of a mare, talking to her affectionately. Other women gossiped near a campfire, the old women with the young, without surliness.

This is a different people, thought Kurelen, with incredulous wonder. This is a race I have never encountered before.

They came to the river. The sun had fallen behind the distant purple ridges. The water was the color of saffron, in which the low violet hills were reflected. The east was already the hue of hyacinths, cool and remote. But the west was a vivid scarlet, in which flakes of fire drifted. In the zenith, golden and vast, trembled the sickle of a new moon. Near by, along the river, moved and shook the yellow grain. Over everything stood a calm peace and silence, full of fruitfulness, and the tranquillity of eternity.

Jamuga looked at the saffron river, then at the hills, then the sky. His face glowed with the bright golden light. His eyes were full of rest. He seemed to have forgotten Kurelen, and to be absorbed in thoughts as large and calm as the landscape. Behind them was the city of black tents, interspaced with the red campfires.

Kurelen sat on his horse in silence, breathing in the universal peace. He looked at Jamuga, sitting so upright and straight on his narrow gray mare, and he thought that this was a new Jamuga, imbued with dignity and quiet splendor. A sudden sense of loneliness and nostalgia descended on the old cripple, and all at once he felt small and dark and mean, like a reptile from another and more violent world, intruding furtively on a planet floating in blue still heavens.

"What is thy secret, Jamuga?" he asked, in a voice of new gentleness.

Jamuga did not answer for a moment, and then he turned his head, smiling, his eyes full of the radiance of the skies.

"It is no secret," he answered. "Peace and justice and mercy and reason are simple things. Here, they are not a theory; they are a way of life.

"Here, every man hath dignity. None is a slave, but a person of respect. If he is virtuous, brave and kind, he doth receive honor. Rapacity is a crime, punished severely. Treachery and meanness, cruelty and selfishness, are wanton things, enemies of a good society. Violence is a shameful sin committed against all the people, and punished by ostracism.

"No man worketh constantly, but only long enough to tend his own herds, his own plot of ground. We have gaiety, and many amusements: races, contests of strength and agility, contests of skill with the bow and the staff. We have contests to produce the best horses and the best sheep and cattle. Every man can read, and story-tellers are in much demand. If a man lacketh anything, his neighbor doth hasten to supply it. There is no rank, save in virtue and accomplishments and service. We like each other. Yet, we are not weak. We are strong with our dignity, and our health, and the knowledge that we are important to each other."

He smiled, with a sort of joy.

"Here, I stress the relationship of man with man, and of man with the earth. The priests tell them that man hath a destiny, one with God and the future. What is to come is a mystery, but we are part of it. We are one with the past, but we are one with tomorrow, and who knoweth but that the morrow is ours, also? Life is a river, coming from yesterday into today, and into the ages to come, and we are that river of life, reflecting the hills and the skies of today's sun, but unchanged in ourselves, and eternal. Our people feel that though the heated moment is theirs, eternity is also theirs. We have an adventure, but it is an adventure in God and the nature of man and the earth. They experience a mysterious joy, as vast as time, and boundless as the heavens. When they die, they say to those they are leaving: 'Until tomorrow!' And they know that tomorrow cometh, and know no grief."

He was silent. He looked at Kurelen with a transfigured face, but Kurelen knew that he did not see him, but some unearthly scene.

"We have a vision," he said. "A vision of God, without which man must perish, and leave no trace behind."

Kurelen could not speak. He heard, but was incredulous. He told himself that he was hearing mad words from the lips of a madman. A vision of God! What insanity was this! A revelation of eternity, in which everything changed, except God and man, which were eternal, and one together! It was not to be understood. It was a violation of reality, which was exigent and bloody, standing in a real today.

And yet, the dark old cripple could not speak. He saw, suddenly, with a blinding clarity, what this could mean, this awareness of God, this awareness of His imminence and presence. For a long time, he stood in this clarity, and it seemed to him that his body and his soul were dissolved in it, and he was aware of a joy and a peace that were almost annihilating. Self was gone, and he floated in an element lighted with rapture, in which fear had vanished, and man's stature was limitless, his vision piercing eternities.

He shook his head, and closed his eyes. When he opened them, he had the sensation that he had fallen from great and radiant heights, into a dark abyss, where terrible things lurked and obscene figures moved wantonly. Some of that darkness had drifted over Jamuga's face.

"I can understand, now," he said, in a low voice, "why my young men take so easily to war and violence, with Temujin. They have lost the vision. They have forgotten the adventure."

When Kurelen returned to Temujin, and was asked by his nephew how Jamuga was faring, his first impulse was to say: "I have come from another world, and because of what I have seen, this world of ours is disjointed and disgusting, and vicious and petty."

But instead, with an eye to Jamuga's peace, he said: "Jamuga is doing well, and cultivating in his people love and loyalty to thee."

He no longer feared for Jamuga. For he knew that Jamuga was shielded against tragedy and misfortune. Or, at least, he hoped so.

chapter 11

Kurelen, Chepe Noyon and Subodai were the tutors of Temujin's sons. The children must learn all the lore which these three men had gathered. They must learn to draw the strange characters of the Cathayans, and must read much of the Golden Emperors of Cathay, the sons of heaven.

Juchi was Kurelen's pupil, a moody and rebellious child, with surly eyes and a low guttural voice, which he used rarely. Kurelen was not overly fond of the boy, but he taught him as well as he could, and had occasion to be proud of him. For Juchi learned easily, and had hard logic. From childhood, he hated his father, Temujin, and was bitterly envious of any slight privilege of his brothers. He was Bortei's favorite, as he was Kasar's.

Temujin was absent from his ordu very often. The king on horseback rode through his vast new domains, stopping briefly to converse with his tarkhans, and give commands. Everywhere his fierce eye darted, and everywhere, to his satisfaction, he saw order. There was personal liberty no longer for any man. There was only obedience, swift, slavish and unquestioning. But there were discipline and loyalty, and these were the things he desired. Ferocious, exigent, inexorable and turbulent of nature, he was regarded with superstitious terror and awe by his clans, the new confederacy of the Gobi.

Over the barrens he cast his mighty figure, and to the very feet of Toghrul Khan's people, the Karait Turks, he flung his shadow. Between him and Toghrul Khan there was voluble peace, and the frequent exchange of affectionate letters and gifts. But Toghrul Khan looked over the steppes and the desert and barrens, and he knew his enemy. The two peoples were facing each other across the tremendous spaces, like two armies ready for combat.

Toghrul Khan called all his sons to him, and also his favorite, Taliph. He looked at them closely for a long time, pursing up his shrivelled old lips and wrinkling his sunken ancient eyes.

"What shall we do about Temujin, that green-eyed dog of a Mongol?" he asked.

"Declare war on him, and destroy him at once!" exclaimed one of his sons.

"Demand his immediate obedience and subordination," said another.

The others cried out, vehemently and contemptuously. Who was this illiterate cur who had suddenly become a menace?

But Taliph grimaced. He said: "We have let him become too strong. Because the merchants and the traders loved their profits, we have encouraged him, loudly admired him, made him rich, let him go his way. Now the dog which served us and which we condescendingly admired and petted, hath become a wolf, and he is showing his teeth. It is our own fault."

Toghrul Khan turned to him. He took no one's advice but Taliph's.

"What shall we do?" he asked.

Taliph considered. "To declare open war on him would be very bad. We must undermine him, destroy his influence. Or at least, limit it. He must be shown, immediately, that he hath gone far enough. A gentle threat, perhaps."

Toghrul Khan sniffled. "Threats! Hast thou forgotten him, Taliph? Threats are spurs to such animals."

Taliph spread out his hands elegantly. "Then undermine him. Send secret emissaries to his clans. Seek the co-operation of his tarkhans and noyon. This will take a long time. But treachery is much better than open warfare, which may—" and he paused significantly, "profit us nothing.

"The Merkit hate him, though he hath absorbed many of their people. The Naiman hate him also, though he hath also absorbed much of them. The Taijiut would rejoice in a chance to betray him. The Tatars have no love for him. Send emissaries to them.

"I, myself, offer my services. I shall go to the more intelligent tarkhans. Send my brothers to the lesser. This will all take a long time, and a difficult one. But it is the best way."

He added: "Sow discontent, dislike and suspicion among the clans. Thus will we disintegrate them, destroy the unity he hath built up. And when that is destroyed, he will be a fugitive, and helpless."

Toghrul Khan's face became a mask of ancient evil. "How I should rejoice in having him brought before me, in chains!" He pondered. "This is a dangerous and difficult business, and will require all our cleverness and subtlety. What fools we were! We hired him to protect us, and now we must protect ourselves against his growing menace. Thou art right, Taliph. I shall take thine advice."

Another thought made him uneasy. "Among our own people there are those who admire and love him. Upon my death;

the heritage of my sons will be scattered, unless he is overcome. We must act! The dog must die."

Taliph had another hopeful thought to combat this. "East of Lake Baikul, the people are already arming against his western confederacy. Send messengers to them at once! They will join us against him. They have always been our enemy, and now they can be induced to become our ally. Hah! The more I think of it, the easier it doth seem! I am afraid we have conferred too much importance on our Mongol brother."

So, Toghrul Khan took his clever son's advice. The emissaries rode forth, secretly, to those unconquered among the Merkit, the Tatars and the Naiman and Taijiut, and others. They found these very easy to convince. But the task was not so easy among the clans of the confederacy, who were passionately loyal to Temujin. In fact, the emissaries had to be exceedingly careful, loudly admiring the loyalty and devotion to Temujin, and declaring they came only as visitors, to see what had been done.

Nevertheless, among many of the clans they were able to sow distrust and doubt and uneasiness.

The people east of Lake Baikul were only too eager. It took but a short time to secure them as allies.

To Taliph, Toghrul Khan left the Naiman, the more civilized of the peoples of the Gobi.

Taliph was well informed about Jamuga Sechen, through spies. And Jamuga was one of the first tarkhans he visited.

chapter 12

When the rich and resplendent caravan halted at the Naiman camp, Jamuga did not at first recognize his distingushed visitor. He had seen Taliph only once, years before. But his memories of an amiable and gracious prince had been pleasant.

He apologized for the simplicity and austerity of his camp, but Taliph waved away his apologies with an elegant hand.

"I assure thee, Jamuga Sechen, that I am a man of inherently simple tastes. Thou dost smile. But it is so."

His good manners, his affable smiles, his aristocratic gestures, won Jamuga, whose experience among gentlemen had been little. Taliph admired Jamuga's treasures. And indeed he was surprised at their good taste. He saw that Jamuga had delicacy and refinement. Best of all, he discerned that Jamuga was honest and clear as water, without deviousness or craft. He was greatly encouraged. No one was so easy to deceive as such men.

"I have not travelled much over the steppes," he said, frankly. "This is a rare surprise and delight, to find a civilized man among savages and barbarians." He spoke cunningly, aware that such praise was as honey and rich wine to Jamuga, whom he well suspected of being vain and conceited by nature, as were most diffident and silent men, and he knew that such men loved nothing more than being treated as equals by those they secretly envied and admired.

He told his host that he was on the way to Bokhara. Jamuga was charmed by the open democracy of so great a prince. His vanity was soothed. Taliph put on no airs. He laughed and conversed as to an equal in birth and position. Jamuga, always sensitive to condescension, found nothing to suspect. His heart opened. He talked with eagerness and pleasure, feeling that some old hard lock had been removed from his tongue. And like most men of his kind, once the lock had been removed he spoke of much which more experienced men would have kept silent.

That night they sat by Jamuga's fire, eating and drinking. Yesi was surprised to hear Jamuga's frequent and open laughter. She saw, too, that her husband, who was not overly fond of wine, drank a great deal. For some reason, she was uneasy, with the uneasiness of the innocent and inexperienced woman who suspects some danger.

She wished to stay near Jamuga, fearful, in her timidity, that if she were not there he might be indiscreet, though what he would be indiscreet about she did not know. But she did not like Taliph, and something rebelled in her quiet heart when his eye touched her as though she were a dog or other animal, and not a human being. When she served him, he would impatiently watch her, and then motion her aside. Her presence irritated him. It was evident that he thought her a slave-woman of less importance than a fly.

Her slender body was swelling again with child, and her face was pale with strain and weariness. But she resolutely sat in the dim background, her eyes gleaming feverishly in the light of the fire, her thin hands clasped rigidly on her knees. She listened with painful attention, moistening her lips, which were colorless with a nameless fear.

She could not look away from Taliph, with his narrow elegant face and subtle eyes and gay smile. He wore a red fez, which gave him a crafty and sinister look. His blouse was of the finest white silk, and about his neck hung a golden chain. His trousers were scarlet, and at his belt there was a jewelled dagger. He was highly perfumed, and at intervals he touched his long thin nose with a scented kerchief. When he moved his feet, his gemmed boots, of soft red leather, caught the light and sparkled. Jamuga, sitting beside him, in his blue-and-white-striped woolen coat, his trousers thrust into crude deerskin boots, was as simple and elemental as the earth. For he wore no jewels, and his hands were stained with soil. But his head rose on his throat, proud and quiet, and his eyes were blue as hyacinths in the firelight.

Nothing could be gentler nor more intimate than Taliph's sympathy, as he listened to Jamuga, who was telling him of the peace and sweetness of his life, and the pleasant ways of his people. But Yesi saw how the Turk's black eyes gleamed and shifted with sardonic amusement, for all his attentive smiles and bent head. Sometimes, for a fleeting moment, he gazed at Jamuga with the incredulous grin of one who regards a madman.

But when Jamuga had finished, Taliph sat in silence for some time. He seemed to be deep in thought. An expression of grave regret appeared on his face.

"Jamuga Sechen," he said at last, in a sad voice, "many have had thy dream, and the dream hath been shattered in blood and darkness. As thine must be shattered."

"What dost thou mean?" asked Jamuga, in alarm.

Taliph sighed. He looked at Jamuga with apparent surprise. "Dost thou not know? A war such as the Gobi hath never seen before is about to break out. At least, so I have heard. It is rumored that the people east of Lake Baikul are fearful of Temujin's rising power and new confederacy of the Gobi, and that they will attack him imminently, or that his own lust and ambition will force him to strike the first blow. At any rate, there will be a terrible conflict. Then Temujin will demand of all his tarkhans that they join him in the struggle, and give not only their own services but those of all their men."

He shrugged regretfully. "In the universal horror and strife, thy dream of peace and contentment in this valley will die. For clan will be against clan, and brother against brother, and people against people. The barrens and the steppes will resound with battle. Multitudes will perish, and terror will ride over the Gobi. Perhaps Temujin will conquer. But of what use is conquest, when men are dead? And if he should conquer, it will but whet his desire for new struggles, new victims, new power."

Jamuga sat like a statue, pale and motionless, and listened. He knew that Taliph spoke the truth, and he knew, too, that he had been expecting this in his soul. It had been the ominous storm on the horizon of his quiet and shining life. Now it was imminent. He paled even more. A look of death stood in his eyes.

He thought of the thousands of his contented and happy people, living in peace and fellowship. He thought of their wives and children. He thought of the fields of corn newly planted, and the herds, and the green pastures. And then he was seized with a dreadful internal convulsion, in which his heart was squeezed in iron hands. Sweat burst out over his white face.

He cried convulsively: "No matter what the call, I shall not sacrifice my people! I have no quarrel with any man! I shall help no one, no, not even Temujin, to destroy and ravish, to seize and lay waste! He hath a mad vision, and my people shall not die for it!"

He sprang to his feet. He flung out his arms wildly, and his distended eyes burned.

"Always, he hath had this madness, this craving for limitless power! He is filled with hatred and lust. He doth need victims to satisfy them. Never hath he loved nor served, nor wished peace and goodness. There is a fire in his heart, which shall inflame the world and fill it with death.

"He is all that is evil and deadly, a pestilence of the soul and a famine of the spirit. He hateth every man and every living thing. His happiness is to crush the helpless, to steal their herds and their treasures, to hear the weeping of their women. Terror is his sword, and madness is his horse!"

He began to weep, with terrifying dry sobs, and Yesi, in the background, put her hands to her mouth to stifle her own cries.

"Why hath God sent this monster to afflict the earth? Why is he not stricken down and stamped out?"

Taliph listened to all this, and was highly gratified at the result of his words. But he made his face somber, and averted his head.

"I know not," he said, sadly.

Jamuga stood in trembling silence, glaring about him as though in terror of unseen enemies. Then he began to speak again, in the low shaking voice of a man unendurably stricken to the soul:

"I have lived only for peace and happiness, for love and contentment. My people want nothing but the bread they eat, and the wives and children in their yurts. What have they done to be so afflicted?"

He paused, then resumed with a wild passion:

"They shall not die for this madman! They shall not help him seize and ruin and murder! I shall take them far from this place——!"

Then the artful Taliph said, insinuatingly:

"But ofttimes men must fight for peace and for safety. Would ye hesitate to join those who would rescue the people from Temujin's sword?"

Jamuga was stricken dumb. He panted. But his febrile eyes fixed themselves on Taliph's face.

Taliph continued softly: "Are there no battles worth the fighting?"

Jamuga's lips shook; he was like a man afflicted with the palsy.

Taliph said: "He must be halted. It is now or never. The history of tyrants is the history of the pusillanimous who will not oppose them."

Jamuga spoke in a low and fainting voice:

"I shall take my people away. But if we are attacked, then we shall fight."

"Alone? Why not join those who will challenge Temujin? That is your safety. What can you do alone against him?"

"I said, we shall flee. We shall fight only when attacked."

Taliph pursed his lips with contempt. "A useless and sacrificial gesture! He will destroy you all in an hour."

Then Jamuga's fury, settling on a new thought, burst forth:

"It is ye who have brought this down upon the peoples of Asia! Ye have encouraged him, assisted him, aided him, for your own gains! Ye have allowed him to ravage and pillage and shared the loot with him, so long as ye received your share and he protected your caravans and your treasures! When he seized and subjugated weaker peoples, ye shrugged your shoulders and did not oppose him, believing that the more he annihilated and absorbed, the safer you would be.

" 'He is our friend, the guardian of our interests', ye said. And now, with your aid, he hath grown powerful. The dog who guarded your gates is threatening your own house. I see it all now! He hath flung his shadow of hatred and conquest into your cities; he doth stand at your walls!

"Ye are the guilty! It is you who have opened the cage and sent forth the monster!"

Taliph, alarmed at the face and words of Jamuga, involuntarily rose to his feet. He looked steadily into Jamuga's wild and glittering eyes. He compressed his lips. Then he spoke brutally and quietly:

"And if thou art right, what then? Shall we allow him to continue, even though, in our folly, we aided him? It is too late for reproaches. The hour of decision is at hand. The beast we set free is bent on the destruction of the world. Even though the imbecility was ours, the struggle must now be yours, also."

Jamuga dropped his head on his breast. He groaned aloud.

"But my poor people are guiltless!"

Taliph laid his hand on his shoulder with a sad and commiserating gesture.

"But the guiltless have their guiltlessness to console them. It is too late for reproaches. We are guilty of folly. Thou must now aid us to undo this folly, to restore and protect the peace of the world. We must wash out our greed and shortsightedness and complacency in our own blood. And we ask the blood of the guiltless in the universal sacrifice."

He added somberly: "If we do not fight, we shall all be overwhelmed, guilty and innocent alike. It is we who have created the menace; thou dost see how frank I am. But the menace doth threaten thee now, as well as ourselves. Thine is the choice: thou wilt join us in opposing and subjugating him, or thou wilt join him, and aid in the end of the world."

He went on: "A foolish man doth free a tiger. The tiger

goes forth, devouring. He will devour the wise as well as the foolish, now that he is free. Is it wisdom for the wise to say: 'This tiger is none of ours; we did not release him'? The fact remains that the tiger is at large, and will enter your own city as well as ours. Your wisdom will not soften his ferocity."

Jamuga did not speak. Then Taliph said, after a silence:

"Help us to destroy the tiger."

Jamuga's features withered in the flame of his anguish. But he looked at Taliph straightly.

"I will help thee to destroy him," he said.

Taliph smiled. He extended his hand. "Thou art a brave as well as a wise man."

Jamuga looked at the hand. He shuddered. He struck it aside.

"Thy hand is as guilty as his! I want none of it."

All at once he seemed to be overwhelmed with a terrible and mysterious sorrow, which Taliph could not understand.

chapter 13

Nomad by nature and ancestry himself, Toghrul Khan, or Wang Khan, as he was now known, was well aware of the strange and uncanny way in which the most hidden rumors passed like the wind over the barrens and the desert.

He knew that it would not be very long before Temujin became conscious of his treachery. So now his emissaries and spies worked feverishly. And it was only a short time until Toghrul Khan knew that Temujin understood everything, and was aware that the peoples to the east of Lake Baikul were ready to strike in concert with the Karait Turks, and the rest of the unconquered peoples of the Gobi.

Toghrul Khan waited, gloating but tense. Would Temujin strike first, seeking a sweeping offensive which would demoralize peoples not yet conditioned to wholesale war? Or would he hold back, watching for the first move of his enemies?

Then one day Toghrul Khan received a letter from his foster son. It was brought by three warriors, dark-faced sturdy men with the fierce eyes of falcons.

"On a day when thine own brother pursued thee, with intent to kill thee, O my foster father, mine own father aided thee and gave thee shelter, and protected thee. And did thou not become his anda, and did thou not sleep under the same blanket with him, swearing eternal friendship for him and his children?

"Did thou not swear to me by the holy Black River that thou wouldst never hear evil of me, thy foster son, but that we would meet at all times and settle all misunderstandings between us?

"Am I not one of the wheels of thy kibitka? And doth not only the man of folly quarrel with that which doth move his house, and carry it from danger?

"It is said that thou dost suspect me of enormous ambition. It is true that I have boasted before thee, but I thought thou didst listen indulgently, as a father doth listen to the words of a favorite son, knowing that youth is prone to brag overmuch. But have I ever given thee reason to suspect that I lust after thy power, and would seize the heritage from thy sons? Have I not come at thy word, with all my warriors, asking only to serve thee?

"Have I not made safe thy roads and thy caravans, and filled thy coffers with riches? And have I asked more than thy love and help, and a mere handful of coins?

"And now I have heard thou art inflamed against me, that thou art raising up the people against me, that thou wouldst cast me down and trample me underfoot. Why is thy rage rising like a fire against me; why is thy heart darkened and poisoned against thy son?

"I am filled with sorrow. I sit in my yurt, given up to grief.

"I have only one hope: that thou wilt send me a message that all that I have heard, of spies and plots, of treachery and hatred, are lies, and that thy love for me is unshaken and full of trust."

Toghrul Khan could hardly believe his eyes. He squealed and chuckled with joy and gloating.

He continued to read:

"With thy help I have become strong and most powerful in the Gobi. My warriors stand like giants on the barrens and the steppes. Their hoofbeats are like thunder, and the earth is darkened with their passage, so many are they. Where they ride, the multitudes bow before them, acknowledging their resistless might. They are loyal and fearless, and full of ferocity, and would die for me.

"They live but to serve me, these many thousands of mighty men. And I live but to serve thee, to maintain the order which is necessary for thy welfare."

Wang Khan shrilled like an exultant monkey. "The dog is trembling in his own offal! He cowers before me, with a servile whining! Never have I read so cowardly and slavish a letter! This is more than I dared hope. We have him in the hollow of our hands!"

One of his sons, Sen-Kung, cried out in fury: "How dare this pig call thee, my father, 'father'! It is an insult which can be washed away only in his own blood!"

But Taliph reread the letter. When he had done, he rolled and unrolled it in his hands, narrowing his eyes.

"Do not exult prematurely, my father. I read many things in this letter which thou hast not apparently read. For instance, I read a threat. A most ominous threat. This is not the letter of a coward, but a most dangerous and merciless enemy."

Wang Khan gaped at him, incredulous, his mouth falling open. His other sons muttered disparaging and scornful remarks.

"Threats!" cried the old man. "Thou art mad, Taliph."

Taliph shook his head and smiled thinly. "Nay, I only read what is meant to be read. He hath recounted to thee the might, the number, and the ferocity of his warriors. In other words he doth say: 'I am powerful. I have the best fighters in Asia, ready to die for me. I have built up an army of fighters which none can resist. Strike at me, and I shall strike back, and thou shalt fall, not I!"

"Give me that letter!" exclaimed Wang Khan, and snatched it from the other's hand. He reread it, his face wrinkling and grimacing like that of an ape's.

"He doth also say," remarked Taliph, calmly, "that thou must hasten to reassure him of thy goodwill and affection, lest he lose patience and teach thee a lesson. In other words, he doth demand thy peaceful gestures, and a cessation of plots and treachery against him. A most ominous letter! I like it not."

Wang Khan flung the letter from him upon the floor. He trampled on it with the acid venom of the old. He spat at it. Then he raised his fist and shook it in the air.

"He dares to threaten me, me, Toghrul Khan, Wang Khan! I shall show the dog! We must strike immediately! Each day that we do not strike is a day of added danger!"

His aged face was suddenly contorted with his old fear. It shrank beneath his bald skull, so that he resembled a death's-head. Now he gave himself up to his ancient dread, his own sick superstitions and nightmares. He wrung his hands; he glanced from side to side like a weasel threatened by wolves. Then his buried eyes lightened malignantly.

"Where are his messengers? Seize them. Cut off their heads. Then send their heads to Temujin! That will be my answer to his lovenote!"

He began to laugh, with a dry crackling sound, mad and evil.

Taliph looked at his father with a grave face.

"Thou dost realize this is a declaration of open and relentless war?"

The old man nodded fiercely. He grinned.

"I do! Allah, have I not waited for this day!"

His sons left him, to give orders.

He sat, huddled on his pillows, his hand sunken between his bony shoulders. He alternately chuckled, then shivered. His eyes roved wildly, from side to side. He was the personification of ageless wickedness, contemplating all evil and all violence.

Then he was still, staring rigidly before him, slowly blinking with eyelids of stone.

"I have a house, behind the Wall," he muttered.

chapter 14

Yesi, in her extreme terror, spoke to her husband.

"That man, that Turk, is evil," she said. "He doth speak words of reason and understanding and nobility. Nevertheless, he hath them not in his heart. He desires thy help because he is afraid, and not because the welfare of men is dear to him."

Jamuga, who had been white and distraught for many days, was forced to admit the wisdom of his wife's words. He looked into her clear blue eyes, so innocent, so full of anguish for him, and he felt a pang of almost unendurable love for her.

"Thou dost speak the truth, beloved," he answered gently. "Nevertheless, though he hath no goodness in his soul, yet his words are true. The tiger is at large; we must cage or destroy him."

Yesi said quietly: "This tiger is thine anda."

A look of torment flashed over Jamuga's thin face. "I know!" he cried. He wrung his hands. "I know! But he is also a tiger."

"He hath been good to thee, my lord."

"I know! But nevertheless, he is a monster." He took his wife by the hand, imploringly. "Yesi, my sweet, wouldst thou have me join him in his crusade against the world?"

She suddenly pressed herself against him in the extremity of her fear. "Nay, my lord! I must confess I think only of thee: if Temujin doth hear of this, he will kill thee at once."

He put his arms about her tenderly. His expression was both sorrowful and dark. "I know this. I have only two choices: to join the ravager, or to help stop him. Thou knowest which I must choose. Everything else must be forgotten." He sighed. "Would I that I had never known thee, and that thou hadst not borne my children! Now, I must be haunted by fears of thy fate, if I am overcome."

She saw his suffering, and now had only one desire, to ease it. She smiled at him with passionate love. "Surely, thou shalt not be overcome! God is in His heaven, still, and surely He will not allow goodness and sweetness and peace to pass away from the earth. Thou shalt conquer, my dearest one; thou shalt overcome the evil."

He nodded his head. "I must have faith in this."

He took his horse and rode away to an open space near

the river. And as he rode, he was conscious again of the old painful loneliness and bitter longing. For years he had, riding like this, imagined Temujin beside him, and speaking, as they had always ridden and spoken in their youth, understanding each through the medium of a word, and sometimes by only a touch or a glance. These years of solitary riding had not been empty, for now he could speak in his mind to his anda, and all the old misunderstanding had vanished, and only the love and friendship remained. He would return, satisfied and at peace, like one who has conversed with a beloved brother, and knew he would see him tomorrow again.

But today he rode alone indeed, and there was no shadowy companion with him. And he knew that never had he been so alone, so solitary. Some psychic amputation in him bled and ached. The mournful realization came over him that a death had taken place, some beloved had died, and that he would henceforth be unutterably lonely and lost.

Now he was no longer enraged against Temujin. The suffused features of the monster had disappeared, and only the face of his anda was left, young and gay, violent and turbulent, vehement and generous. He thought of Temujin as one thinks of the dead. The creature which had taken his place was an enemy, as much Temujin's enemy as his own.

His heart shook with his anguish. His eyes gazed blindly at the green and flowing river, and the golden grain.

O Temujin! he cried silently, where art thou? Why hast thou left me, abandoned and alone, never again to see thee nor to hear thy voice? Never again shall we sleep under the same blanket under the stars. Never again shalt thou smile at me, and call me friend! Thou hast died. The world is as empty as a broken cup. It is a desert where no thing grows.

And then he was still, thinking only of the things which he must do. Some prescience told him that death would be his reward, and that all that he had done must fall into ruins.

But surely, he thought with sudden strength and courage, the things of hope and peace and love shall not die, nay, though the darkness and fury shall come, they shall live! It is in the nature of the world that though the storm cometh and the forest is broken, that though the volcano pour its lava over the vineyards, that though the winter blacken the pastures, there is a spring of the earth and the soul, and all things shall rise and bloom again.

This must be my faith. This must be the faith of all men.

Otherwise, the earth and all the peoples must forever die, and God Himself must pass as a shadow.

chapter 15

"And now," said Temujin, quietly, looking at the bloody heads of his messengers, "the time hath come."

Many of his people thought that he meant the time had come for vengeance. But he knew that the time of his destiny had come.

By some strange accident, the disaffection of Jamuga Sechen had not reached him. Had he heard the rumor, he would not have believed it. For rooted in him was the conviction that Jamuga would never betray him. Paradoxically, it was he, rather than Jamuga, who believed in the sacredness of the true oath of friendship, which must never be violated. He would have more readily believed in his own betrayal of himself than believe in Jamuga's betrayal.

It is true that he had often been enraged with Jamuga, had often insulted and affronted him. It is true that he had banished him, and laughed at him, and spoken with open contempt of him. But nevertheless, he believed in his loyalty. Even so late as this day, he told himself in his heart that he had no other friend but Jamuga, no real friend of the spirit.

The memory of their years of conflict was forgotten. Like Jamuga, he rode with a shadow at his side. Never had he so loved Jamuga as he did in these dark and ominous days of approaching conflict. He spoke to that shadow frankly, hearing no dissenting nor criticizing word. He was more candid with the shadow of Jamuga than he had been with the substance.

There are those that argue that the things that are, are the things that must be, he would say to his invisible companion. But when the wheels stop the cart goes nowhere. There are those that say that change is but another face belonging to a single entity. But the face at least is new. Man cannot stop motionless, gazing at the moon, forever. He must move, if only in a circle. Otherwise his heart and his blood must halt. They say there are no tomorrows. Perhaps, in eternity, this is true. But for every living man there is always tomorrow.

To each man of courage and vision, tomorrow doth wait. And tomorrow is mine. The empires of Cathay have fallen in the swamp of yesterday; the Golden Emperor is crumbling into dust. Each day doth call to a single man. Today it doth call to me.

The hour of conflict is here. And I know in my soul that I shall conquer.

He was filled with a wild exultation. He laughed aloud, in the solitary spaces where he rode with the shadow of Jamuga. He clenched his fist, and gazed arrogantly at the pale heavens.

Men shall say of me: Here was the greatest of all warriors, of all emperors. Here was he whose vast army roamed the steppes and the barrens, and the eyes of men fell away in fear before it. Above the low anonymous mass of the centuries, the head and shoulders of Temujin shall rise, like a peak over monotonous plains, illuminated by the light of deathless ages!

And the shadow of Jamuga answered: I have always believed in thee.

But Kurelen, for one, was not so easily convinced. He was alarmed. He said: "Perhaps it is because I am old. But I believe thou art going into certain disaster. Toghrul Khan is still the mightiest of the nomad khans, and he hath invincible friends among the princes and the politicians of Cathay. Who art thou, to challenge him? An unwashed baghatur of the steppes. A young illiterate man who doth not know the strength of his mature enemies. Draw back before it is too late. Keep silence. And perhaps Toghrul Khan will forget thee."

Temujin listened to this with incredulous fury. "Once thou didst say, mine uncle, that I was made for destiny."

Kurelen shrugged. "That was because I wished to have enough to eat, and flattery was the spur I used to get it." He added: "But what canst thou do? Thou art outnumbered by Toghrul Khan by twenty to one. Thou hast gained much. Do not sacrifice it by one mad gesture. Look at thyself! Look, without delusion. And thou wilt know I have given thee good advice."

Houlun, too, was aghast. "Thou wouldst attack Toghrul Khan? My son, thou art a mad fool. He will crush and annihilate us before the first snow falls!"

She added with bitter dismay: "Thou art a fox that wouldst challenge a tiger. I grant thee that he hath treated thee with abomination, and murdered thy peaceful messengers. I grant thee that this is so, on the surface. But I know deeper things than this. I know that thine increasing arrogance hath angered thy foster father. Thy boastfulness and ruthlessness have given him grave doubts about the enduring peace of the Gobi. I have but one advice to give thee: write to him at once. Acknowledge thy foolishness. Ask his forgiveness, and promise him thy continuing obedience and fealty."

Temujin looked long and slowly over his tremendous city

of yurts, and he smiled darkly. He looked at the herds, and the many people. He said: "I have done all this. I have brought order where bandits and robbers roamed before. I have brought peace to warring clans, and ended feuds. I have introduced stern discipline, and given strength to hundreds of helpless tribes. I have guaranteed safety for the caravans, and added to mine own wealth and strength. All this have I done myself. And now Toghrul Khan is envious and alarmed." His voice suddenly rose with wild ferocity: "For he doth know that I am his enemy! That between us a conflict must come, for control of the Gobi! I have known this always. I have kept the peace until I was strong enough to attack. Now, I am strong. Now, we must fight for the lordship of the Gobi. And I tell thee that I shall not be the defeated. Fate and the spirits are with me. It hath been said before. Now I know it is true."

Old Kokchu was demoralized with fear. But when Temujin came to him, and he saw his face, he concealed what he thought. He knew what Temujin wished him to say, and being a wise priest, he said it:

"Lord, for many nights I have made divinations. Last night, at midnight, a new star appeared in the heavens. It brightened; it grew large. It blazed. It was the color of a conflagration, and the black skies about it trembled as though with the shadow of fire. And all the other stars paled and faded beside it. And I knew that this star bore the name of Temujin, the mighty warrior."

Temujin listened to this with a surly half-smile. When the priest had done, he said: "See to it that the people hear of this. Keep thy prophecies for them."

Nevertheless, he was oddly heartened, though he chuckled to himself. That night he took a furtive look at the skies, himself. And to his amazement, he saw the red blazing of the new star. Perhaps it is true, he thought. But before he allowed Kokchu to speak of it, he waited several nights, to see if the star remained fixed in its place, and to be certain it was not a mere meteor to disprove the divinations, and thus to dismay his people. The star remained fixed, and the people were filled with superstitious joy and awe.

Bortei was not alarmed. She was exultant. She cried to Temujin: "Have I not always told thee this, my lord, that thou art the mightiest warrior of the ages, and that no man shall stand before thee?"

Chepe Noyon, who believed in no divinations, and privately thought that this approaching war would mean the end of everything, merely shrugged and smiled, and accepted everything with the indifference of the true fatalist. But he said to Temujin: "It is given only to thee to see the end. And to lead us."

Subodai said simply: "We live but to obey thee, lord. Where thou goest, there shall we go. And we shall fight beside thee, worthy warriors of thy banner. We are thy Raging Torrents, thy paladins. We have no will but thine."

Kasar merely looked at his brother with his heart in his simple eyes, and laid his hand on his sword. Belgutei, his half-brother, was dismayed. And then he thought to himself that when Toghrul Khan annihilated Temujin, perhaps the old khan might make him vassal lord over the remnants of the Mongols. He was much cheered at this logic. Therefore, he regarded the coming conflict with enthusiasm.

So Temujin was satisfied. He sedulously avoided Kurelen and Houlun, whom he called old crows croaking of disaster. He sent out swift-riding messengers to call in the various tar-khans of the tribes, to give them instructions and to mobilize their warriors. When he had sent forth the messenger to Jamuga Sechen, his heart strangely lifted.

Tomorrow, he thought, I shall see Jamuga!

Then, for the first time, he fully realized how lonely he had been, and how rusty his tongue had become. Now his thoughts and his words arched behind the dam of silence, waiting for release. He waited for Jamuga as a bridegroom waits for his bride, conscious of past emptiness and loneliness.

With the messenger to Jamuga, he had sent rich gifts for Yesi and the children, and a letter full of friendship and anticipation.

When Jamuga received the gifts and the letters, he burst into tears.

chapter 16

The wildest excitement spread over the clans of the western confederacy of the Gobi, and the most feverish activity.

The Mongol tarkhans and the nokud came, furrowed and dark of face, their bodies wrapped in long woolen coats and girdled with painted leather, their fur caps and tall pointed hats shadowing their glittering eyes. Temujin's ordu rang with strange hoarse shouts; the women cooked over their pots unceasingly. Messengers came and went in a general hubbub of confusion and excitement. The fattest of the herds was killed, and the odors of cooking meat and spices hung in the dusty air.

It was a most momentous gathering, one of the most important in the history of the world. Hourly, a new chieftain arrived, roaring up on his horse, surrounded by his officers and generals, their lances glittering in the sun. The children peered eagerly from the yurts at the unceasing flow of newcomers. The dogs barked fiercely. Camels shrieked in the uproar. Everywhere, there was a constant coming and going, the delivering and the sending of messengers. The prettiest girls coquetted from the safety of the platforms of their family yurts with the strange young officers, who pretended to ignore them. Women screamed at their children, and bustled to and fro in the preparation of the gigantic feast, carrying sacks of wine and cups, and throwing dung upon the high hot fires.

Every chieftain, immediately upon his arrival, went to Temujin's yurt, to pay his respects and renew his oath of fealty. Temujin sat on his royal white-horseskin, with his banner hanging over his head. Each chieftain knelt before him, or near him, and remained there, waiting for the arrival of the others.

As each chieftain entered, Temujin glanced up with hidden eagerness, and as he saw the newcomer's face, a faint darkness of disappointment passed over his eyes. He had sat like this since the dawn. Now, it was almost sunset, and Jamuga had not come.

He looked at the bronzed and somber faces about him; he saw the fierce, falconlike eyes fixed on him. Some of the eyes were gray, for the owners were members of his own people, the Bourchikoun. Some of the khans were still unconquered by Temujin's arms. But they had come to him at his summoning, swearing allegiance, and declaring their enmity for Toghrul Khan, the Karait Turk.

The hoarse voices of these men filled the hot and stifling confines of the huge yurt. The smell of their bodies was acrid and pungent. The sunlight that struggled into the gloom through the flaps made luminous their wild barbarian eyes, made their bronzed skins shimmer with a metallic reflection. They drank wine with Temujin; they glanced about them with untamed ferocity. More and more came, until the yurt was crowded to the walls, and the air was fetid.

It was sunset. Now the last came, one by one. The uproar of the camp made the cooling atmosphere vibrate. And each time a shadow darkened the aperture, Temujin stopped in the middle of a sentence, and glanced up with intense eagerness.

But still, Jamuga did not come.

Now the air was redly aglow with the fires, and a servant lit the lamps in the yurt. The lamps added to the heat. The smells grew stronger. Temujin panted. His face shone with sweat, and those about him saw how his green eyes glowed in the hot semidarkness, like the eyes of a tiger. And they saw how pale he was.

They became restive. Temujin had spoken only casually of irrelevant things, though hours had passed. They exchanged impatient and furtive glances. Why did he not speak of the thing most important to them? They drank, to cover their barbarian impatience, and finally, they too watched the empty aperture, expecting they knew not what. They became hungry. They loudly sniffed the odors of good cooking food which entered the yurt. But they dared not rise and excuse themselves until he gave the word.

At last a shadow appeared at the doorway, and Temujin glanced up with a passionate expectancy. But it was only a frightened messenger with a letter from Jamuga Sechen. Temujin seized it; they saw how his hands shook. He looked about him fiercely, and his lips parted. Then he rose, and ordering them to remain where they were, he left the yurt rapidly.

He strode out into the cool dim twilight, which was filled with the leaping firelight. He passed unseeingly through the throngs. He went to Kurelen's yurt. He found the old cripple dozing on his couch. Old Chassa sat near by, fanning him, absorbed, all her soul visible in her wrinkled face.

"Wake!" cried Temujin in a peculiar, stifled voice. He flung the letter at his uncle. "Read this to me immediately!"

Kurelen, blinking and groaning, sat up. He looked at Temujin, and was about to speak. But when he saw his nephew's face, he could not speak. He lifted the letter, and saw that it was from Jamuga. Instantly, his heart failed him.

He began to read, slowly:

"Greetings to mine anda, and wishing him all the health and happiness which a sincere heart can offer."

He paused.

"Read!" cried Temujin.

Never had Kurelen seen such a face and such eyes. For the first time in his life, he quailed before the younger man.

"I have the summons of mine anda, and I have read it with despair and sorrow, and I have written this letter, knowing what anger it will provoke, but daring to write nothing else.

"For I can write nothing but this, and praying for forgiveness and charity and understanding.

"Thou hast summoned me to the gathering of the khans, to lay before me the plans for the bloody war of conquest which thou hast long ordained. But I cannot come. I shall not come. And neither can I promise thee the aid of my people, nor mine own. To do so would be to violate all that I believe and hold dear.

"Instead, with prayers and grief, I can only beg thee to reconsider, before thou dost plunge the peoples of the Gobi into death and ruin. I ask thee to consider that thou canst not overcome Toghrul Khan, and the end will be nothing but famine and torment and flight. My love for thee imploreth thee to halt before it is too late. If thou shouldst die, there would no longer be joy in the world for me.

"I cannot believe that this is a just war. Thou hast spoken of conquest from thine earliest youth. I know that this ordained war is but the expression of thy lust for power. Surely thou canst not believe thou art justified in destroying thousands of men, and laying waste their lives, for thine own vanity and madness. Surely thou dost not believe that victory is more than peace, and tranquillity less than conflict.

"Therefore, I cannot come. And again, I implore thy forgiveness, and pray thee to remember that it is not treachery that hath prompted my words, but only love and sorrow. To mine anda, I, as always, swear fealty to the death. But to Temujin, the murderer and the warmaker, I point my sword."

Kurelen slowly rerolled the letter. His heart was beating with a deathly pain. He hardly dared look at Temujin.

But Temujin stood before him, in a terrible silence. He did not seem to breathe. Not a finger moved. His lips were folded like stone. Only his eyes, frightful and blazing, were alive.

Kurelen wet his trembling old lips. "Temujin," he faltered, "this is not the letter of a traitor. It is the message of the man who hath loved thee more than life, more than all else."

An indescribable expression appeared on Temujin's face. Then, without a word, he wheeled and left the yurt.

chapter 17

But nothing could have been calmer than Temujin's manner when he re-entered his great yurt, and resumed his place on the white horseskin. If he were ordinarily livid, if there were a look of rigor on his face, no emotion was apparent either in his gestures or his voice.

He began to speak quietly, but in resonant tone that filled the whole yurt, and engaged every man's acute attention:

"I have many times said unto ye that the land between the three rivers must have a lord. Ye have dwelt in anarchy, in purposeless turbulence, in restless comings and goings. So, ye have had no safety, no wealth, no permanent pastures, until I came unto you, and gave you a vision of unity and strength. We have dwelt in harmony, we khans, like brothers ruling separate kingdoms, and consulting each other. We are a confederacy of many tribes and small nations."

He looked at them for a silent moment. They bent forward in order to listen more attentively, and the lamplight gave them the appearance of bronze statues.

"Ye know how well we have lived, since ye followed my vision. Ye know how strong we are. For the first time in many ages, the nomad people who have followed me have known no famine, no disorder, no violence. We have learnt order and discipline confining authority to ourselves, and quelling the individual and presumptuous quarrels of those under us.

"The world has admired us. But like all those who are admired, we have inspired hatred and envy and fear. There are those, now, powerful and mighty, who wish to destroy us."

The khans exchanged significant and somber looks. Some of them knew why they had been summoned, and their faces darkened with sullen gravity and uneasiness. No man spoke, yet a deep murmur, guttural and fierce, seemed to blow through the yurt.

Then they looked intently again at Temujin, seeing how his eyes sparkled with ferocity and excitement.

"I have been betrayed, and through my betrayal, all of you, all our people, are threatened to their death."

He paused. "My foster father, Toghrul Khan, humorously called Wang Khan, by reason of his abject and crawling slavery to the people of the Golden Empire, hath repudiated his vow of friendship with my father, and his oath of paternalism to me. He hath observed that we have become strong and formidable. He hath seen that we are no longer slaves under the whim of elements and stronger men. And so, he hath conjured up the idea that we are a menace to him and his profits and his lusts. He would reduce us again to starving hordes, dependent upon his bounty, and, compelled by hunger and weakness, to serve him whenever he doth call."

Most of the khans flushed with rage. Their faces took on his own wild excitement. But quite a few looked disturbed and more uneasy. They dropped their eyes; they fumbled with their garments or the rings on their fingers. The first exclaimed hoarsely; the latter were silent.

"We shall not endure this ignominy, this slavery, this threat!" cried one of the khans, who worshipped Temujin. His companions muttered angrily in affirmation. But the others were silent, and stole furtive glances at each other. Among them were Temujin's own people, the gray-eyed Bourchikoun, who, like all kinsmen, were jealous and suspicious of gains and powers attained by those of their blood. Many of them had been forcibly subjugated by Temujin, and compelled to join the confederation by threats. Had he been a stranger, they would have felt little animosity. But because he was a kinsman, they secretly resented or hated him, felt humiliated and dishonored.

Temujin's glittering eye, passing from face to face, saw this incipient resentment or disaffection. He picked out a forceful man among the dissenters, and fixed him with a fiery glance.

"Borchu! Thy father was my father's cousin! Thou art my kinsman. What hast thou to say?"

Borchu, a middle-aged man, lean and black of hair, and quite without fear, lifted his eyes to Temujin's face and spoke quietly, with an aspect of reason:

"What can we gain by resistance or attack? Toghrul Khan is the mightiest of the Karait. He hath armies much vaster than all of ours put together. Thou hast said, Temujin, that Toghrul Khan is enraged against us. Thou knowest full well that only a miracle could permit us to be successful against him. And I," he added wryly, with a long humorous glance at his companions, "do not believe in miracles."

There was a sharp silence. The disaffection of the Bourchikoun made them a separate and hostile camp, eyed by the others with rage and mortification.

"This is cowardice!" cried one of the khans, at last.

Borchu turned his slow intent eye upon the speaker. "Cowardice?" he asked softly. He made a movement as though to rise, his hand on his saber. "Who sayeth cowardice?"

The khan was a young man, full of eagerness and anger. "I!" he cried, his cheeks burning red with loyalty to Temujin. "And treachery! Whoever doth disagree with our lord is a traitor!"

The yurt was suddenly filled with the more acrid pungency of the sweat of excitement. Every man moved and murmured. Every nostril distended, as though smelling blood. Every eye gleamed with the lust for battle. For several moments violence seemed about to break out openly in the yurt.

Then Temujin laughed, loud and ringingly, and the sound was like cold water flung into each fierce and congested face.

"What fools ye are, quarrelling among yourselves in this hour of terrible danger! I have asked ye to come to me for discussion and planning, not for petty fights under my very eyes. I will talk. I will fling accusations of treachery or cowardice!" He held them with his glance, so hypnotic and inexorable. "But, so far as I can see, there is no traitor here, no coward. Unless he so brand himself."

He waited. The Bourchikoun were still infuriated and resentful. But before that compelling look, that implacable glance, they sank into silence, and turned their eyes away. They hated Temujin more than ever, but for some mysterious reason, they dared not murmur nor return gaze for gaze.

Every man subsided, sighing audibly. But the division between the two camps remained.

Temujin resumed: "Borchu, speak freely. I wish thine opinion."

Borchu hesitated. Then, after gathering in the supporting glances of his kinmen, he regained courage. He spoke boldly and quietly:

"It is my sincere opinion that we can gain nothing by open conflict with Toghrul Khan. Everything we have gained, under thy most wise leadership," and again his face and voice were wry and ironical, "will be lost. Who are we, to challenge Toghrul Khan? We are outnumbered. We have no battle bases, except our own tribes. And Toghrul Khan hath not only the weight of his own tremendous paid armies, but the support of the Turkish towns behind him. And perhaps even the awesome empires of Cathay." He paused. "We are a handful of men challenging a whole world," he added, gloomily. "A cloud of gnats shrieking defiance to a flock of hawks!"

Again, Temujin's camp muttered loud and wrathfully, handling their sabers. But Temujin held up his hand for silence. He looked only at Borchu.

"And," he said, in a voice heavy with mocking deference, "what wouldst thou do in the face of his threat to us?"

Borchu shrugged, and once more looked at his kinsmen for support.

"I suggest that we immediately submit to the overlordship of Toghrul Khan, renew our vows of fealty to him as our kha khan, and promise obedience to his will, assuring him that we are no threat to him, but only his servants."

Now Temujin's camp raged furiously, and many of them started to their feet. But again he subdued them with a gesture and a look.

Borchu continued, gaining strength from the conviction of his own wisdom: "A reasonable man will easily perceive this is the best way. War will destroy us. In peace, we can gain strength. We have all that we wish. Now, we must lose all by one reckless and stupid gesture. An oath of fealty costs nothing. A bare sword is the signal for our complete destruction."

There was a sudden heavy silence after he had ceased to speak. Temujin sat quietly on his horseskin, seeming to ponder. His face was calm, his manner quiet. He appeared to be weighing every one of Borchu's words, and his camp breathlessly gazed at him and awaited his verdict.

Finally, he turned to those loyal to him, and said:

"What is your opinion?"

They burst out in a furious chorus: "We say, let us have battle! And we extend to thee, our lord, the baton of leadership, to lead us as thou wilt!"

"Yes! Yes!" shouted their followers.

The wildest excitement prevailed. Men started to their feet, exultantly brandishing their sabers. They laughed shortly and excitedly. They surrounded Temujin, knelt before him, touching his feet with their heads. They seemed possessed. They flung arms about each other in rough fellowship. Their eyes blazed.

But Borchu's camp were uneasily and sullenly silent.

Temujin smilingly acknowledged the vows and eagerness of his followers. Then he rose and faced all of them, lifting his hand for silence. He began to speak in a low and penetrating voice, fixing each man separately with his glowing eye:

"It was prophesied at my birth that I would be emperor of all the peoples of the barrens, the desert and the steppes. It was said by the priests that the Eternal Blue Sky had given me the destiny of those who live in the felt yurts. It was ordained that I would lead them victoriously, and establish them as lords over all of High Asia, that empires of men, wheresoever they dwelt, would be subject to me and my people. That I would be the mightiest of all the lords of all generations, the Perfect Warrior, the Mighty Manslayer."

He paused. His kinsmen exchanged glances of dark furtive amusement at this boastfulness. But they were uneasy. There was such a fateful and formidable look about this young Mongol, standing tall and slender before them, his body like an upright flame, vibrating and shaking, for all his stillness.

"I believe this!" he cried strongly. "I believe that no one can oppose me! My life is a vindication of the prophesies! I was a fugitive beggar, cast out, and now I am lord of all those who dwelt between the three rivers!

"Who dareth challenge the prophecies? Who dareth mock the Sky?

"And now, I swear unto you that though we are challenged, that though others would destroy us, I shall maintain for you the places of our ancestors, the customs of our peoples, the lands of our fathers, and will add unto them the empires of the world!"

His flaming exaltation infected his followers. They groaned; they laughed; they wept. They seized on each other, flinging their arms about their neighbors' shoulders. They looked at Temujin with exultant eyes, and screamed out their defiance of all those who would oppose him.

And the Bourchikoun, doubting and fearful, were mesmerized and shaken. They wet their silent and fallen lips. They breathed heavily.

Temujin lifted his arm. Every man was transfixed by that awful and luminous face, in which the eyes flamed like coals.

"Ye shall be my lords, my paladins, my Banners, my Torrents! Wheresoever we ride, there shall we subjugate! Wheresoever we put our feet, there shall the historians and the poets sing to the future ages of our conquest! We shall not lose! We shall conquer! The world is ours!"

The Bourchikoun, who were reasonable and intelligent men, were incredulous and disordered. Their minds told them that they were listening to the words of a shaggy and homeless fool, infected with insanity. Their reason assured them that they were hearing the cries of one afflicted with madness. They felt their stable world caught up in a whirl of unreality and murderous folly, in which all values were changed by some supernatural horror and imbecility.

And yet, their hearts shuddered. Their reason was stricken into silence by the look and the manner of this adventurer, this febrile screamer of mad words. Despite themselves, their souls were seized in the furious and violent dervish-dance of his visions. What if he doth speak the truth? they asked themselves, dumbly. What if all things are known to him? What if the world is indeed standing on its head, and he can accomplish this incredible miracle, this reasonless plot? What if madness is more valid than reason, and facts less than prophecies?

They looked at him, disturbed and shaken to the soul. They bit their lips; they audibly panted; sweat covered their faces. And Temujin, seeing all this, with an ironical and mocking smile, waited.

Then, very slowly, as though hypnotized, Borchu rose, not removing his fixed and glaring eye from Temujin. He stood before the young Mongol, swaying slightly. And then, as a loud shout broke from all the others, he knelt before Temujin, and, like a man moving in a reasonless but impelling dream, he touched Temujin's feet with his forehead. And then he knelt like this, as though asleep, or dead.

The others fell into silence, stopping where they were, with upraised hand or open mouth, overcome with the awesomeness of what they saw. And the Bourchikoun gazed at their leader, like those who were seeing something portentous and not to be believed, overcome with a sort of incredulous horror. But the spell was upon them, the mad enchantment. One by one they rose, and one by one, in utter silence, they knelt before Temujin, and touched his feet with their foreheads.

Then the maddest exaltation seized every man. The yurt trembled under the fury of the shouts and cries, under the din of stamping feet. The lamps leapt on their tables. The felt walls vibrated. Every man wanted to touch Temujin, to partake of his mystical strength, to be infected with his indomitable courage and power. And he stood among them, smiling faintly, looking at them with his fiery green eyes, submitting to their touches, their embraces, their screamed vows of obedience and fealty.

He accepted the baton of leadership. He had hoped, in the violent excitement, to be named their kha khan, the Emperor of All Men. But the lords of the barrens were still jealous of their individual authority and their independence. However, he was content. All the rest would come later, when he was victorious. He was content, now, just to be their leader. He knew the fierce pride of each small khan, and was wise enough to know that this was not the time to violate it.

When some measure of sanity and order had been restored, he sat among them and laid before them his plans.

"Only one course is open to us. We must rely upon lightning

battle, upon surprise, upon swift mobility. We must strike unexpectedly and with all our strength, thus demoralizing our enemies. Audacity and boldness are our allies. We must risk everything upon a few disintegrating blows, hurled with all our power.

"We must attack our foes in their own provinces. There, we have nothing to lose, but they will fight cautiously. For they will be among their own treasures, and will fear ruthlessness which will mean destruction of their treasures. Men fighting among their own possessions are already half beaten. We have nothing to lose, and can fight with every atom of our bodies.

"When men see their treasures destroyed, they are stricken to the heart, and their arms are weakened. Cities fall more easily than battle camps. We must count upon demoralization. Too, our foes are already fat and decadent. We are hardened by our hardy life, and by strife. But they will prefer the sparing of their possessions to a ruinous victory."

"Again, I say we have nothing to lose, and everything to gain. And being of one mind and soul, and having only one resolution: to conquer, we shall be victorious."

And then he laid before them, with a meticulous detail, all the amazing plans he had previously outlined to himself. They listened, overcome with amazement and admiration, their excitement renewed. They already felt like conquerors. They found difficulty in restraining themselves. But Temujin was as cold as ice, and inexorable as death. He felt no excitement. He was too sure of himself.

In that yurt, in that tent upon the empty and limitless barrens, the fate of a whole world was decided, and history, standing, waiting, lifted her pen and began to write. She marvelled to herself that these barbarians could so decide the destiny of millions of men, and then she recalled to herself that it was only the same old story, the same old bloody tale.

It was much later, when the moon was beginning to wane upon the exhausted but still febrile men, that Temujin spoke of Jamuga. And his khans listened, aghast, at the story of this betrayal of their lord by his own anda, his own sworn brother. They watched his face, so pale and composed, and listened to his calm emotionless words.

"If there is one treacherous general in an army, one traitorous officer, that army is already in danger. Jamuga Sechen hath not only betrayed me, he hath betrayed you, and all our people. He is our danger, our rotten spot, our enemy. And so, he must die. Our first campaign must be an assault upon him. It will be a speedy victory, for he will have no one to help him. Again, surprise and swiftness must be our guide. When he is destroyed, we can then proceed."

There were many, remembering the stories of the love between the two men, and the passionate devotion, who listened and watched curiously.

But if they expected to see any sign of grief or sorrow upon Temujin's face, they were mistaken. For they saw no emotion there, no torment. He spoke of Jamuga as he would speak of a dog who had attacked him.

And then they knew that there was more to this plan of campaign against Jamuga than the mere destruction of a traitor.

There was some dark and agonized vengeance to be attained, some violation to be washed out in blood, and that there was no joy, but only anguish, to be gained by Temujin.

chapter 18

Bortei's triumphant malice was unrestrained, when she learned of the treachery of Jamuga Sechen.

"My lord!" she cried to Temujin, laughing so that her two rows of white teeth glistened like those of a she-wolf's. "Did I not tell thee so? But thou wouldst not listen to me. Thou didst think I had some secret antagonism against thy beloved anda. I was a fool, thou didst say! But lo! it is not I who am the fool!"

Hatred for Jamuga was a vivid glare in her eyes. The prospect of revenge on this man maddened her, as the sight of blood maddens a wild beast. She could hardly contain herself for glee.

"Thou wilt bring him here, to suffer his punishment?" she implored, eagerly. She imagined Jamuga being boiled in hot oil, being torn apart by plunging horses, and her face flamed and swelled, and her nostrils flared wide.

Temujin looked at her, but said nothing. She could see no answer to her words in his secret and inscrutable expression. But something in his regard of her gave her a momentary qualm.

It was then that Kurelen and Houlun entered Temujin's yurt. Temujin was closely examining his articles of warfare. Kurelen noted that he seemed abstracted. He had heard Bortei's last words, and Temujin's manner sent a pang of new hope through the old cripple. His sister had heard too. The magnificent and aging woman cast a contemptuous and loathing glance at her son's wife, and said:

"Temujin, send this woman hence. We would talk with thee."

Bortei was infuriated at this assault. She turned upon Houlun and Kurelen, all her naked hatred, and all the years of smothered resentment, in her face.

"If Jamuga Sechen hath been a traitor to our lord, and is punished, ye two should be punished also! For always ye did say that he was no traitor, and were always protecting him against just wrath."

Houlun looked at her with cold dignity and scorn. "I still say, he is no traitor. Leave us, woman. I command thee."

But Bortei looked at Temujin, smiling triumphantly.

Then, for the first time, he pretended to be aware of them.

"Ah," he said, thoughtfully, laying down his sword. He even smiled slightly, and Kurelen, with renewed hope, saw how strained were his features, in spite of his calm, and how feverishly bright his eyes. He turned to his wife, and said good-naturedly: "Leave us, Bortei."

She was aghast and outraged. She pointed her finger at the old man and woman. "But these are traitors, my lord! They come to plead the cause of a traitor!"

Kurelen smiled a little. But Houlun's glance at Bortei was full of fiery contempt. She said nothing.

Temujin put his hand on his wife's shoulder, and gave her a rough push. "Leave us, Bortei," he repeated.

She burst into tears of rage and frustration. She looked pleadingly at Temujin, but something in his face quelled her. She left the yurt, giving Houlun a vicious but triumphant glance as she passed her.

That glance amused Houlun, and her stony features relaxed into a fleeting smile. Then her stern expression settled again on her face, and she gazed at her son like a haughty priestess about to utter words of condemnation.

"Thou goest to murder thine anda?" she asked brutally.

Temujin regarded her reflectively, and his mouth took on an inimical aspect.

"Once he did imprison thee for talking too much," he said. Suddenly he laughed shortly, and loudly, and turned from her.

Houlun flushed, but she said steadfastly: "Thou goest to murder him?"

Temujin looked at her idly, over his shoulder. "Subodai, and some of his warriors, go to seize him. They shall bring him here."

"Thou art not going?" asked Kurelen, in surprise.

"Nay. If I went, it would confer importance upon the traitor. He will be brought here for judgment, as an insignificant but venomous prisoner."

Relief filled Kurelen. Seeing this, Temujin smiled malignantly. He said:

"He was never my friend. He violated the most sacred oath which men can swear. Nevertheless, I shall be merciful to him." He paused, and the malignant smile widened. "I shall give him two choices: to die either by strangling, or by fire."

The old man and woman paled until they were ghastly with horror. Houlun burst into tears, not of weakness, but of proud despair and bitterness.

"It is not less than I expected of thee," she said in a low voice.

But Kurelen saw that taunts would not move Temujin. He approached his nephew; he laid his hand on the rigid and repudiating arm. He said gently:

"Temujin, thou knowest in thy heart Jamuga is no traitor.

He saved thy life twice. Ye did both sleep under the same blanket. He was thine only friend. If he criticized thee, because of the burning of his bowels, it was because he is a virtuous man, and a narrow one. He knoweth no compromise. He wished thee to fill out the lofty pattern he had designed for thee, without pettiness or cruelty or violence. If he were wrong to have such a pattern, it is his judgment which is at fault, not his loyalty."

Temujin listened. His eyes fixed themselves inscrutably on his uncle's face. He began to speak quietly:

"These are ominous times, mine uncle. I owe thee no explanation, but I will give thee one: because of the danger to us all, no traitor, or one who doth utter traitorous things, must survive. Otherwise, we are weakened. Terror must be stricken to the heart of every potential traitor, for the sake of unity and strength." He paused a moment, then added in a softer voice: "I have no personal enmity towards Jamuga. Necessity alone impels me."

Kurelen was silent. He searched Temujin's face for a long moment. Then he said, almost with compassion:

"Thou art sorely wounded. It is a personal revenge which thou dost seek, feeling thyself violated, and thy love for Jamuga made a mockery. Oh, my nephew, have mercy on this unfortunate man! Bring him here; temporarily imprison him for indiscretion. If thou dost not, if thou dost murder him, never more shall peace come unto thee, no, not even if thou dost gain the world."

But a ruthless and inexorable look made Temujin's eyes take on the appearance of polished blue-gray stone. He smiled almost pityingly at his uncle.

"I have said: I dare not spare him. Leniency will only give potential traitors boldness."

Houlun had listened to all this, breathing heavily. Then she could no longer control herself. She cried out, fiercely: "Thou art a hypocrite! Murder is a joy to thee! Thou didst murder thy brother, Bektor, and now thou wilt murder Jamuga! Thou art no man; thou art a foul beast!"

Temujin ignored her. He said to his uncle, quietly: "Thou dost see? I must do this thing."

Despairing, Kurelen meditated. Then he asked: "And Jamuga's people?"

Without emotion, Temujin answered: "I have given orders to Subodai that none are to be spared among the men, either young or old. No child is to be spared who is taller than a cart wheel, and no old woman. The young women, and the very small children, shall be brought here, with Jamuga."

Kurelen stared at him, disbelieving. A horrible sickness seized upon his vitals. He stammered: "But this is not thy usual custom. Thou didst formerly absorb conquered people into thy clan——"

Temujin shook his head. "Not these. They are all traitors. Moreover, they are soft. I cannot have them amongst us, spreading disaffection, and hindering our movements."

A momentary darkness passed over Kurelen's vision. Through it, he heard Houlun's wild cries and bitter reproaches and epithets. He struggled to regain himself, feeling that he must momentarily collapse.

"Thou canst not do this," he whispered.

Temujin shrugged. He picked up his saber again, ran his finger delicately along its glittering edge. Then he looked at his uncle blandly:

"Please leave me. I have much to consider, and much to plan. I am weary."

Then Kurelen, knowing all was lost, began to speak in a subdued and meditative voice:

"The guilt is also mine. I imbued thee, from thy childhood, with a mocking contempt for gentleness, and laughed lightly at honor which would impose a burden. I said all things were justified in the name of expediency, that men who considered were weaklings, and exigency was the mark of a strong man. I was a fool. Because I was impotent, I admired the potency of ruthless men. Because mine arm was feeble, I expressed contempt for the defenseless, and exalted brutality. The frail and sickly man, the dwindled eunuch, is always the exponent of cruelty and ruthlessness. It is he who doth create tyrants and murderers. It is the man without loins who doth loudly sing of the virile. It is the man without courage who doth put a sword in the hand of the merciless."

Temujin listened to that slow, almost droning voice. His lips jerked; he smiled, as though with intense amusement.

Kurelen lifted his sunken eyes to Temujin's face, and there was a spark in them, like sudden fire.

"I sought a revenge on the world which had denied me strength and manhood. I have gained it. And through my gain, Jamuga Sechen must die."

He trembled violently. Then, all at once, he flung himself upon his knees and seized Temujin about his legs with his twisted arms.

"Temujin! I have never asked anything of thee. I ask thee now, to give me Jamuga's life!"

Temujin looked down at him. He was amazed. He saw the

huddled and contorted form of the old cripple at his feet; he saw the dark and misshapen face, with its long beaklike nose and winglike eyebrows. But more than anything else, he saw, with profound astonishment, that there were tears in his eyes. Houlun, too, gazed at her brother, and as she did so, she felt that her heart had melted into streams of blood, and was draining from her body.

Perhaps Temujin was touched. In any event, his voice was almost gentle when he said: "Kurelen, ask me anything else, and it is thine."

Kurelen tightened his frenzied grasp on the other man's knees. "No!" he cried, "I want only this! And I shall not release thee until thou dost promise!"

Temujin seized him; he dragged him to his feet. His face had become dark with violence. "Thou fool!" he exclaimed. He shook the old man savagely. "Get thee hence! I have wasted time in listening to thy nonsense. Get thee hence, lest I do thee a mischief!"

He flung Kurelen from him. The old cripple staggered. He threw out his arms, and churned the air with grotesque swimming gestures, in order to regain his balance. His face took on a ludicrous expression of intense concentration. Houlun tried to seize him, to save him, but his momentum tore him from her grasp, sent him spinning, his feet pounding on the floor. He whirled, finally, and fell backwards, abruptly. As he collapsed, the back of his head struck the edge of a teakwood chest, and his head was thrown forward sharply on his chest. And then he lay still, in that twisted position, motionless, sprawled out like a boneless heap of clothes, his eyes, horribly rolled up, fixed upon Temujin.

Houlun, after a long and dreadful silence, wherein she and her son stared, mesmerized, at Kurelen, uttered a series of high piercing screams. She flung herself beside her brother. She lifted his head; blood poured over her hands. Her screams abruptly ceased. She gazed into the dead and distended eyes. Then her cries were renewed. She pressed her brother's head to her breast, and her flesh became wet with his blood. She seized his hands; she pressed them to her lips, and kissed them with abandoned passion. She kissed his hair, his cheek, his cooling and fallen lips. Her long gray-black hair fell over him, mercifully hiding the horror of his look, and his eyes. She seemed to become mad. She cradled him in her arms; she moaned, she rocked on her haunches, she gave vent to strange and mournful words:

"My beloved! My heart's darling! Who have I loved but

thee? Who hath been part of my flesh, part of my soul? Only thou, my beloved, only thou! Speak to me; tell me again that thou dost love me, my brother, my lover, my dearest one!"

And Temujin stood like a statue, watching this dreadful scene, hearing the words of his crazed mother, listening to her cries. Her crooning and passionate voice filled his ears. She was a woman whose lover had been murdered; she was a mother mourning wildly over her dead son. She was all grief and all despair, all that had ever loved and ever lost. Temujin closed his eyes on a spasm. The moaning, love-filled, mad voice seemed to invade his brain. It was more than he could endure.

He went out into the cold blue air of the day. His legs turned to water. A swimming sickness made everything dim before him. His heart lunged in his chest.

He found his way to Kokchu's yurt.

He spoke hoarsely and falteringly:

"Mine uncle, Kurelen, was in my yurt, and he was taken with a fainting spell, and did fall and crush his skull. Go thou to him, and to my mother, who needeth thee."

Kokchu, who had been reclining on his couch, being fanned by his favorite young dancing girl, slowly rose. He stared at Temujin. He saw that gloomy, blue-lined face, those savage eyes. He saw how the khan was trembling, and that there was a drop of blood on his bitten lower lip.

"I go," he said, in a voice of silken compassion. He picked up his small silver box of amulets. But still, his curious gaze fixed itself on Temujin.

And then, all at once, the crafty priest knew everything. A malevolent light flashed across his face. But he bowed his head with an affectation of sorrow and humility, and went to obey Temujin's command.

He found Houlun lying prostrate, unconscious, across the body of her brother, and stained with his blood. When they tried to disengage her arms, they were like stone. They carried her to her yurt, and gave her to the care of her women.

When she recovered consciousness, at midnight, they saw, with horror, that she was hopelessly mad. She raved, screamed, laughed incessantly, struggling with her women, who tried to hold her down upon her couch. All through that night, the city of tents resounded with her cries, and the women shuddered and held their children to them.

At dawn, overcome with exhaustion, she became quiet, and seemed to sleep. But when her women, thankful and prostrated with weariness, went to cover her with her furs, they saw that she was dead.

chapter 19

Jamuga called all the men of his clan to him, the old and the young. He looked at them with pale and sorrowful love, and, seeing this, they knew that he was greatly disturbed. They looked back at him, trying to reassure him with their resolute expressions.

He told them of Temujin's command, and his own answer. And then he waited, gazing at them with imploring anxiety. Alarm, anxiety, courage, bewilderment and apprehension ran over their faces. They murmured to each other. And Jamuga still waited, openly wringing his hands.

Then an old man voiced the thoughts of the others:

"Lord, thou hast done the only thing thou couldst have done, and thy people honor and love thee for it."

Jamuga smiled. Tears filled his eyes.

"I thank ye all," he said, humbly. He took comfort from their smiles. They crowded about him, like a wall of flesh, timidly and awkwardly touched him, to impart their own virtue to him.

Then he spoke again, and this time with increasing and despairing sadness:

"Once an old man told me that it took more than a mere disgusted convulsion of the belly to save the world. I did not believe him. I thought there was sufficient defense in a people which willed peace, and loved peace. I thought if a people were good, and committed to the ways of friendship and tranquillity, and sought no quarrels, nothing evil would threaten them, and they would need no arms nor training in the arts of war. If they regarded their neighbors with benevolence, I thought, and treated these neighbors with justice and honor and mercy, these neighbors would never assault them, but would leave them in peace. A man who sought no war or conquest, who was content, was a man who would remain unmenaced. He needed only to attend to his own household and his own flocks, to turn aside lustful eyes, and to be forgotten, he needed only to mind his own business."

He sighed mournfully. "I was wrong, my brothers. I see now that peace must be defended as resolutely as any other treasure. The answer to tyrants is an army stronger than theirs.

To remain safe from attack, it is first necessary to become too strong for attack. Sometimes, to bring peace to the earth, men must fight to the death. To establish justice and liberty and tranquillity, men must sometimes take up arms to the very end, and give up their lives for their children's security.

"In my dreaming folly, I did not know this. If we desired peace, that was sufficient: we would have peace. Because I have believed this, I have exposed you to grave danger. I have given you up, defenseless, to the enemy. I have destroyed peace, because I hated the sword. I have exposed your wives and your children to the prospect of death or slavery. I am your real foe; I am your guilty betrayer."

He stood before them, and wept.

"I have deprived ye of the means of defending your homes and your pastures. I have filled your hearts with softness, and deprived you of the knowledge of the ways of war. Therefore, we are a fat worm, defenseless, awaiting the beak of the vulture."

The old man, who was the spokesman, knelt before Jamuga, and lifted his hands.

"Nevertheless, lord, we are willing to fight for peace now."

Jamuga laid his hand on his shoulder.

"Nay," he said sadly, "it is too late. With what will ye fight? With your bare hands, accustomed only to the plow? Will ye expose your defenseless breasts, unavailingly, to the swords of the avenging enemy? Do you think all your courage is sufficient to protect you from the trained and bloodthirsty hordes of the approaching foe? A man may have the courage of a tiger, and the fearlessness of a falcon, and they will avail him nothing if he hath no arms."

He looked at them and cried: "I shall not sacrifice you! I shall not see you slaughtered like defenseless cattle! I shall not urge you to a struggle which can result only in your death and agony!"

"We have no defense. Surrender is our only choice. It is too late for anything else. Today, my spies tell me that Temujin is sending a vast and murderous horde to destroy us. If we resist, with our naked hands, we shall all be slain. If we surrender, they will spare you, for Temujin's first wish is always to absorb the conquered, in order to make himself the more strong. We can do nothing else but submit."

He raised his voice and cried out with anguish: "Surrender is always the necessity of those who cannot defend themselves. Slavery is always the lot of the man who hath not valued peace enough to prepare to fight for it!"

The men listened, and paled. They could not speak. They glanced fearfully at the horizon, from whence would come the avenging hordes of Temujin.

Then the old man spoke once more:

"And what of thee, lord?"

Jamuga smiled drearily. "I shall ride forth, today, to meet the army of Temujin. I shall surrender, before they come here. Then all of you will be saved from death, and not one unavailing blow will be struck."

The old man asked: "And what guarantee have we that they will spare thee?"

At this, the other men burst out into a loud cry of agreement.

"If the guarantee is not given, we shall not surrender! We shall fight, if only with our bare hands!"

Jamuga was alarmed. He knew Temujin, and realized that he could expect no mercy from a man who would never forgive opposition or rebellion. But if his people knew this, then they would die for him, and be slaughtered to the last man. So he said, trying to smile lightly:

"I am Temujin's anda. He hath great respect for oaths. He may discipline me, but that is all. I can swear this to you." He paused, then added: "If I meet them, they may not even come here. After all, I am the one who defied Temujin, not you. I shall return with the officers, for my discipline. In the meantime," and he turned to the old man, "I leave thee in my place. If I do not return, and this is improbable, administer my laws with justice and mercy, and do nothing that I would not do. Save this: teach the young men the arts of war. Beat your ploughshares into swords. Prepare to defend that which is dear to you."

He went to his wife's yurt. There, he knelt before her, and kissed her hands. "Forgive me, my beloved," he said, "for not being able to defend thee."

She knelt beside him and kissed his forehead and his lips.

He dared not tell her of the approaching enemy, and that he was going out to meet them, and surrender. But he called for his children, and he kissed them with consuming and despairing passion. He was devoured with remorse.

He went out and called for his horse, and, without arousing attention, he rode quickly away.

He reached the brow of a low hill, and looked back at what he was leaving, probably forever. He saw the golden river and the golden grain, and the peaceful village of the tents. He saw the distant herds grazing tranquilly. He saw the men and the women going about their work, unthreatened.

"It is little I am doing," he said aloud, and now there was joy on his face. "It is little enough, to give my life for them. If I can do this, perhaps I have not lived in vain."

chapter 20

Jamuga rode in the direction from which the enemy would come. He rode without haste, and his countenance was full of an austere peace, like that of a man who had died. For he had renounced everything, even life itself.

The vast ruined landscape of the desert enhanced his calm, his feeling that he had already departed the world of the living. All about him, in awful loneliness and immobility, stood cream-colored crumbling walls, cliffs, terraces, plateaus and enormous pedestals, upon which giant statues might have stood. He thought to himself, in a dreamlike meditation, that perhaps, ages past, giants had indeed inhabited these regions, and that these hills, shaped like temples, with faint outlines of disintegrating columns upon them, might have been their dwelling-places. Above him, the sky was the color of pale silver; under the feet of his horse, the earth was rutted and rippling, formed of mingled dust and sand and dry bleached earth. Nothing grew here but thorns and tamarisk bushes, covered with a whitish deposit. Nothing warm and living ran here, or moved, except Jamuga, a quietly-moving insect wandering through the tremendous ramparts of a dead world. He heard no sound; even the wind was still. He crept through silence, as through a tomb.

On the second day, towards sunset, he thought he saw the thin distant file of approaching horsemen. He reined in his horse. The bleached hills were a clear pink, and the sky was a brilliant polished blue. Jamuga waited; his hood lay on his shoulders. He waited without fear or despair, following the movement of the far horde with his calm blue eyes, and the fiery sunset light carved his face.

It was quite a while before he was certain that this was the enemy he expected. He spurred his horse, and rode towards them. He heard a faint horn blowing, and knew that he had been seen. He saw the banner of the nine yak-tails curving in the wind. Now, as he approached the army, he was amazed at its number, and smiled drearily to himself, and thought of his defenseless people. Would Temujin be here? Was he leading this regiment?

A horseman rode out to meet him, and he saw that it was Subodai. The Mongol then reined in his horse, and waited for Jamuga. He was a beautiful sight on his horse, though he was no longer very young. There was an ageless quality in his beauty which nothing would ever destroy. For it was compounded of nobility and dignity and pride, of virtue and steadfastness. He stood, sharp and vivid, against the red sky, his face turned towards Jamuga.

Seeing him, Jamuga's heart rose on a wave of joy. Here was one without ferocity or cruelty, without vengeance and hatred. It was a good omen that he had come!

He rode up to Subodai, lifting his hand in greeting, and Subodai gravely returned the salute. They looked at each other in an intense silence, facing each other. Then Jamuga extended his hand to his old friend, and Subodai, without a moment's hesitation, took that hand.

"Greetings to my lord, Subodai," said Jamuga.

"Greetings to thee, Jamuga Sechen," responded Subodai. His voice was so low that it was almost inaudible. And then for the first time Jamuga became conscious of the heavy pallor on Subodai's face, and the troubled look in his eyes.

"I have come to surrender myself to Temujin," said Jamuga, "and to return with thee."

Subodai was silent. Then he glanced at the sky. "It is evening," he said. "We shall camp here for the night."

One of his officers rode up for orders, and received them. Jamuga looked curiously at the great army which had come to capture one helpless man. He saw their dark and threatening faces; he saw that when he looked at them, they turned their eyes away.

Jamuga's nostrils distended; his heart rolled in his chest. A sudden wind of terror and foreboding blew over him. He turned to Subodai, and saw that the other was seemingly intensely preoccupied in unsaddling his horse. There was no sound of any voice as the army prepared to camp for the night.

Panic and fear clutched Jamuga. He could hardly breathe. He approached Subodai, and said:

"Why camp here? We have an hour or two of daylight left. And the way back is much easier."

Subodai looked at him for a long moment, and his expression softened.

"My men are tired. I think it best we sleep before proceeding."

Their gaze held. Subodai's pallor appeared to increase, and for an incredible instant, Jamuga thought that there were tears in his eyes. But this could not be; it was but the reflection of the burning sunset!

Subodai laid his hand gently on Jamuga's shoulder. "Thou wilt dine with me, Jamuga, and we shall sleep in the same tent. I have much to tell thee."

Jamuga took hope again; his vague wordless terror blew away. Quiet comfort came to him. Subodai was his friend, and his trust in him was implicit.

Neither of the two men could eat much when it was brought to them. But Subodai drank, and Jamuga followed his example. The bitter cold of the desert night was about them. But the campfire was warm, and beyond its light lay the dark cloaked shapes of the sleeping men, and beyond them, the tethered horses. Of all the men and the beasts, Jamuga and Subodai were the only ones awake, except for the sentries, who could not be seen in the darkness.

The wine, and the presence of his friend, made Jamuga more voluble than usual. He told Subodai of his people, his wife and his children. And then, as he talked, he was like a man pleading before a judge for all that he held dear. Subodai listened, his wine cup in his hand, his head bent a little so that Jamuga could see only a portion of his handsome face.

"I believe I have found a way of life which is true and beautiful," said Jamuga. "I have given my people peace and contentment. They are harmless and faithful and generous. They desire nothing of their neighbors but friendship. I am sorry, Subodai, that thou wilt not see them."

Subodai stirred. "Didst thou speak?" asked Jamuga, bending forward, trying to see the other's face.

Subodai lifted his cup and drank. Then he looked at Jamuga, and his expression was grave and gentle. "I said nothing, Jamuga."

Jamuga continued to speak of his people, and Subodai listened. At moments, Jamuga's voice broke with emotion, and he involuntarily wrung his hands. His was the only sound under the moon, and it seemed that all the earth listened to him.

After a while he ceased to speak. He was inexpressibly weary, but again, peace was on him. For, with the telling of what he loved, he felt again the loveliness of self-sacrifice and renunciation.

Still, Subodai said nothing. And after a little, Jamuga inquired of news from his former people. But he had asked nothing yet of Temujin, and Subodai had not spoken of the khan.

Subodai seemed overwhelmingly relieved at Jamuga's question. He said: "A few days ago, I am sorry to tell thee, Kurelen died, and also Houlun."

Jamuga was stricken with grief and regret. And then, simply, he spoke of his old anda: "Temujin will have a heavy heart, now, for Kurelen was like a father to him, and in spite of many things, he loved his mother."

He waited, eagerly, for Subodai to speak of Temujin. He could not understand, himself, why his pulses began to pound like those of a man who awaits the name of someone overwhelmingly precious.

But Subodai said nothing. The strangest look was on his face. Jamuga could not understand this look. Despite himself, he spoke again of Temujin: "He is well, is he not?"

"He is well," replied Subodai, almost inaudibly.

Then another silence fell upon them. The campfire was low. The moonlight lay over the whole gloomy landscape, like spectral water. The air became colder, and a horse or two neighed uneasily near-by. And the two men sat side by side, plunged in melancholy meditation, the faint crimson light lying in the folds of their coats and on their features.

Then Jamuga became mysteriously conscious that some enormous struggle was taking place in Subodai, something which was like a convulsion of his whole being. Not by a look nor a motion did he give Jamuga this impression, but in his soul Jamuga was aware of this struggle. His own spirit sprang up, trembling, as if seeing relentless enemies. His flesh became rigid as iron; he could not have moved even if he had desired it. But a horrible sweat burst out over him, and there was a poisonous taste in his mouth.

And Subodai, sitting beside him, his head bent and averted, might have been asleep.

Several times, Jamuga tried to speak, but each time his voice died in his throat. Finally, in a faint voice, and through stiff and icy lips, he said: "Subodai, there is something thou hast not told me!"

Subodai sighed. He seemed to shrink in his garments. Then he lifted his head and looked full at Jamuga. Nothing could have been more despairing, more grief-stricken than his expressions.

"Thou art right, Jamuga, I have not told thee all."

Jamuga clenched his hands so that the nails tore into his flesh. But he said calmly: "I am not a woman. Tell me what thou hast to say." The tint of death itself spread over his face.

Subodai said gently: "I have come to take thee prisoner, Jamuga, to deliver thee, unharmed, to Temujin, for punishment."

Jamuga nodded. He felt that he was smothering. "I know that!" he cried. "But, what else?"

Subodai wet his shaking lips. "And this, Jamuga: I have been bidden to kill all thy people, except the young women, and the children no taller than the wheel of a cart, and to bring these back, with thee."

Jamuga's face withered and collapsed visibly, so that it was corpselike. Then all at once, he uttered a frightful cry, incoherent, the cry of an animal wounded mortally. At that sound, the horses near-by awoke, and neighed frantically, and several men rose to their elbows, blinking, and fumbling for their weapons.

Jamuga seized Subodai by his arm, and shook him violently.

"Thou art lying! Even Temujin would do no such monstrous thing! Thou art lying, Subodai!"

Subodai looked at the hand on his arm, and, after a moment, he placed his own over it. He felt its deathlike sweat, its straining tendons, which were like those of a man in extremis.

"Jamuga, I am not lying," he said, in a pitiful tone. "I would to all the gods that I were."

Jamuga bent his head, and burst into loud weeping, most dreadful to hear. Subodai put his arm about him. Compassion and sorrow ran through him like a knife. He had no comfort to offer; he could only embrace his friend dumbly.

Then, with a sudden violent movement, Jamuga shook off his arm. Again, his fingers gripped Subodai's flesh.

"Surely, thou art no monster, Subodai! Surely thou couldst not, in cold blood, murder these defenseless people!"

Subodai sighed. "I have my orders. I must obey. I must always obey."

"But not in this!" cried Jamuga, feverishly, clutching his friend with both his hands, and shaking him. "Thou canst tell Temujin that when thou didst come to the place where my people were, thou didst discover they had fled, and left no trace behind!"

Subodai felt the grip on the other's hands, which were like tendons of biting iron. But he could only look at Jamuga with bitter sorrow in his face.

"I have mine orders, Jamuga, and thou knowest I have lived only to obey."

Jamuga stared at him, madness in his eyes. Then he lifted his hand and struck Subodai savagely across the face. He struck him again and again. And Subodai did not move. He merely gazed at Jamuga with grief and gentleness, though his cheek turned scarlet, and blood appeared at the corners of his lips. Finally, he caught Jamuga's hand by the wrist, and held it firmly.

"Jamuga," he said sadly, "thou knowest this will do no good."

Jamuga, crushed and collapsing, wept again. His head fell on his chest. Subodai released his hand, and listened to that awful weeping. Emotion of various kinds raced over his bruised and bleeding face. He sighed deeply, again and again. Once he put up his hand and wiped the blood from his lips, and stared at it, on the back of his hand, as though wondering what it was.

Then Jamuga was still, overcome with his tragic despair. He sat motionless, his head on his breast. Subodai glanced about him cautiously. He hesitated. Then he put his lips to Jamuga's ear and whispered:

"Harken unto me, Jamuga: Thou hast said thy people are defenseless. They do not expect us; they would be slaughtered like lambs. I will allow thee to send a messenger unto them, this night, warning them of our approach, and imploring them to prepare to defend themselves. At least, then, they will die like men, fighting for themselves and their families."

Jamuga lifted his head. He looked at Subodai with dying eyes.

"They have few weapons," he said, his voice broken.

"Nevertheless, they will fight, with whatever weapons they have." He paused, and added wearily: "This is all I can offer thee. It is no joy to me to kill unarmed men."

He stood up and went to a sleeping man, and kicked him with unaccustomed savagery, then bade him rise and saddle his horse. Then he returned to Jamuga, and sat beside him again. He opened his pack, and withdrew a coarse sheet of Chinese paper, and a pen. These he laid on Jamuga's knee. Jamuga stared at them blindly, not moving.

"I have but one request, Jamuga," said Subodai gravely, "and that is this: that when we approach the camp of thy people thou wilt not attempt to aid them. For I have mine orders to bring thee safely to Temujin. Thou must give me thy word; otherwise, I withdraw my offer."

Jamuga picked up the pen in his numb fingers. All life and substance seemed to have left his face. He said: "I give thee my word." He began to write. The characters were fumbling and tremulous.

He urged his people to prepare to defend themselves to the death, for the murdering enemy was approaching.

"I know ye have little with which to defend yourselves; but I implore you to fight like men for all we have held dear, for all we love. This is all I can do for you. And I implore you to forgive me for my part in your tragedy. On my knees, I implore you, asking you not to think of me with bitterness, but with the knowledge that I share your grief and your death."

He lifted the pen. It almost slipped from his fingers. But it was evident that he had not yet finished.

He resumed his writing, and now his hand shook so that the characters were barely legible:

"To my wife, Yesi: My heart's beloved, forgive me for thy fate. I know that the women of our people, and the children, are to be carried back, as slaves, to the camp of Temujin. And I implore thee now, not to let this happen to thee and my children. We shall meet again, beloved. Thy Christian faith hath taught thee so. Beyond this darkness, I shall embrace thee once more, and my children. Until tomorrow, my sweet, my wife."

He handed the paper to Subodai, who read it without hesitation.

The illiterate warrior now presented himself for orders. Subodai handed him the letter, and fixing his eyes on him, he said slowly and clearly:

"This is a message to the people of the tarkhan, Jamuga Sechen, urging them to surrender without a struggle. Do thou ride with the wind, and present this message to the old men who can read."

The warrior saluted, wheeled, and left them. In the profound silence, they heard his horse gallop away into the night.

chapter 21

Because of his great pity, Subodai decided not to allow Jamuga to accompany him and his warriors to the camp of the Naiman. He knew the sight of what would take place would be too much for this wretched man.

So, he left Jamuga with a small number of warriors, to await his return.

Jamuga wept no more. He listened to Subodai's last pitiful words, but gave no sign that he heard. He seemed already dead. A great dull calm was upon him. Subodai thought that his soul had died, and only the feeble flesh remained, in its last agonies of unconscious dissolution. His eyes were glazed; he breathed slowly and irregularly. He sat in the midst of the group of warriors, his gaze fixed on the ground, his hands hanging lifelessly on his knees.

Subodai gave orders that Jamuga was to have any comfort he desired. But he knew, as he rode heavy-hearted away, that Jamuga would eat no more, nor would he ever rest again.

The warriors left behind with him were disgruntled, and complained among themselves, casting resentful looks at Jamuga, who was the cause of their loss of anticipated sport. They feared that they would receive only the remains of the loot, and the ugliest of the women. But finally his aspect made them uneasy. It was like guarding a corpse, they muttered to each other. Some of them whispered that his spirit was gone, and perhaps a strange and malevolent spirit would take its place. So they looked at him with fear.

The day passed. The restless warriors hunted for near-by game. They offered Jamuga food and wine. But he looked at them unseeingly. Hour after hour wheeled by, and he sat, unmoving, his eyes glazed and fixed, his under lip fallen, his chest hardly moving. The warriors played games of chance about him, and laughed and sang hoarsely. But he did not hear them, and at last, they were silent with him, superstitiously afraid.

The night came. The warriors slept. One kept awake, to guard Jamuga. But still he did not move. Still he sat like a man who had died in a sitting posture. He did not lie down. He did not utter a single word, or even a sigh. When the dawn came, it threw its brilliant light on his cold and sunken face.

The warriors marvelled that he still lived. One or two, less ferocious than the others, were moved to an alien pity. Never had they seen such despair. They hoped he would begin to wail, or weep. Thus, they would have relief.

The whole day passed, and again the night, and still Jamuga waited, like an image. No one could guess if he were awake or sleeping or unconscious, or if he thought anything at all. When the dawn came again, those who had pitied him felt a thrill of disappointment that he was still alive.

Now they began to expect the return of their general and their brother warriors. One or two took places on a high piece of land, and gazed towards the east. In their excitement and speculation, they forgot Jamuga, and their fear and sullen pity. They complained again, because they had been left behind, and some of them mocked the others, prophesying that they would receive only the old hags and the leavings of the victorious warriors. They discussed the possibilities of the beauty of the Naiman women. They made coarse and obscene jokes. One man complained that his wives resembled donkeys; he had hoped that he might get a handsome girl or two from the Naiman.

"I am certain that thou wilt get another donkey," mocked one of his companions.

To relieve their tedium, they wrestled and had bouts with their sabers. Now a note of real quarrelling was heard in their voices. Their restlessness grew. They lost their fear of Jamuga. Loudly, in his presence, they mocked him, prophesied his fate.

"If his wife is beautiful, she will sleep with our lord, and will forget this pallid shadow," said one. "She will breed real sons, instead of goats."

But still Jamuga heard nothing, and saw nothing. The bellowed laughter did not move him. Hourly, his features sank, and he took on more and more the aspect of a corpse.

And then, at sunset on the third day, a watcher shouted exultantly. The warriors were returning. The watcher reported that behind them trundled a vast number of yurts, and that there was a great number of horses and a large herd. His companions joined them. They shouted and stamped with glee.

They did not hear Jamuga's faint thrilling cry. They did not see him rise, and his legs tottering, lean heavily against the side of the white cliff which had sheltered them from the incessant wind. His ghastly and haggard face was convulsed; his cracked lips worked. He gasped hoarsely; his emaciated fingers gripped the crumbling stone, and he swayed.

Subodai rode ahead of the immense congregation of victorious warriors, yurts, herds and horses. And as he rode, his head was dropped, and he seemed to move in a mournful bemusement. From the yurts behind him there came a constant howl of wailing and weeping.

He glanced up, as he approached the rise of ground, and he saw Jamuga. He bit his lip. He spurred his horse, then arriving at the rise, he sprang down to the ground, and ran forward. The warriors rushed forward, shouting, to join those who were returning. In the confusion, Subodai approached Jamuga, glanced swiftly and compassionately at him, and put his arm about his shoulders.

Jamuga drew a deep and shuddering breath. He clutched his friend desperately, and in a voice full of broken anguish, he cried: "My wife? My children?"

Subodai closed his eyes; he could not endure the sight of that face.

"Be comforted," he said, gently. "They are not here."

Jamuga collapsed against him; his body shook with his sobs. From his breast there came a long groan, as though his heart was breaking. Subodai tightened his arm about him, and his beautiful face became dark and grim, as though with some deep anger.

"Thou art ill," he said, compassionately. "Come; thou must lie down in one of the yurts."

Jamuga shook his head. His exhaustion increased, so that Subodai was compelled to support the whole weight of his body.

"Then, thou shalt ride beside me."

His plan was that Jamuga should ride at the head of the caravan, in order that he would hear very little of the constant lamentation from the yurts. Jamuga understood him, and again he shook his head.

"I shall ride behind," he murmured faintly. "I am guilty of this. I must fill mine ears with the cries of those I have so frightfully wronged."

Subodai's next fear was that Jamuga would die before he could be delivered to Temujin. He forced his own flask of wine against Jamuga's lips. Jamuga automatically swallowed. But he looked beyond Subodai with his agonized eyes, and was aware of nothing but the yurts and the sorrowful wailing.

Half-dragging, half-carrying, the stricken man, Subodai led him to a horse, and helped him climb upon it. Jamuga sat there, bent forward, in a dream of numb anguish. Subodai sprang up on his stallion, and took the reins of Jamuga's horse in his hand. His anxiety became acute. At all costs, he must arouse him.

"Thy people fought and died bravely," he said. "So well did they fight that I lost a goodly number of my best men."

Jamuga looked at him. "That is no joy to me," he said faintly.

The huge caravan began to move.

Jamuga, huddled in his saddle, heard nothing, was aware of nothing, but the wailing of the women and children, trundling behind him in the yurts.

And Subodai, riding beside him, holding the reins of his horse, looked ahead, bitterly and somberly.

"I live only to obey. Only to obey," he said to himself, over and over, in a hypnotic litany, as though he was trying to dim the sound of his clamorous thoughts.

chapter 22

An officer ran to Temujin's huge yurt, in the dawn.

"Subodai is approaching!"

Temujin, who had been sleeping, was instantly awake. He buckled on his coat and pulled on his boots. He went out into the lucent morning light, his head uncovered, and his red hair was like a fire, a lion's mane on his shoulders. The caravan could be plainly seen on the flank of a scarlet hill. Temujin, shading his eyes, watched it for a long time. Then he returned to his yurt and sat down on his couch.

He did not stir, staring unseeingly before him. But a hard purple vein pulsed violently in his forehead, like a thin writhing snake.

After a long time, the flap of his yurt opened, and Subodai entered, pale and calm. He saluted, stood stiffly before his khan.

"I have returned," he said quietly. "I have conquered the Naiman, and obeyed thine orders. I have brought Jamuga Sechen as prisoner."

"Thou hast done well," replied Temujin mechanically, after a pause. Then he was silent again, staring at Subodai.

Subodai spoke: "Jamuga Sechen is a dying man. I have had him carried to my yurt, for a rest he doth sorely need. But he will not sleep."

Temujin rose, and turned his back upon Subodai.

"Let him rest," he muttered. "But at noon, bring him to me."

Subodai saluted again, and went towards the flap. He had reached the flap when he heard Temujin call him. He turned slowly. Temujin fixed his gaze upon him without speaking, and his look was strange.

"My lord?" said Subodai, composedly.

But Temujin merely stared at him, and his strange look became more intense. Then he made an abrupt gesture.

"Nothing. It is evident thou art weary, Subodai. Seek rest, thyself, until thou dost bring Jamuga to me."

Subodai departed. There was a cold fine sweat upon his forehead. And once more he resumed his litany: "I must obey!"

He went to his yurt. The camp was in the wildest excitement, and full of jubilation. Many warriors of distant clans had arrived in Subodai's absence. The camp was thronged with strangers. But he passed among them, not looking at them. When he entered his yurt, Jamuga was lying prostrate on his couch, and one of Subodai's women was washing his hands and face. Jamuga submitted; he seemed not to be conscious of his surroundings or of the woman. But when Subodai stood beside him, life came back to his dying eyes, and he smiled faintly, his hand moving towards his friend. Subodai took that fumbling hand and held it strongly in his.

"The end of the journey is in sight," he said, trying to smile. "Be of courage. Thou wast ever a valiant man."

Jamuga tried to speak, but his last strength was gone. A sudden hope rose in Subodai that he might expire before the ordeal.

"It is not thee I pity," he said.

Jamuga closed his eyes; he either fainted or slept. Subodai did not know. After a long time, he gently released Jamuga's hand, and laid it down. It lay there, relaxed and open, as if dead. Subodai continued to stand by the couch, and he sighed deeply, at intervals.

Some one was entering the yurt. It was Chepe Noyon, alert and eager. But when he saw Jamuga, he was silent, and a curious gleam passed over his eyes.

At last he whispered to Subodai: "I am sorry. Thou shouldst have slain him mercifully."

Subodai turned his heroic head, and answered: "I could only obey."

Despite his compassion, Chepe Noyon smiled involuntarily at Subodai, with a kind of mockery and wonder. "Art thou a fool?" he asked. "Ofttimes, I have asked myself this, but still, I do not know the answer."

Subodai was silent. He stood, gazing down at Jamuga.

Some one else was entering. It was Kasar, avid and uncouth. "Ha!" he snorted, seeing Jamuga. "So thou hast brought the traitor safely to his judgment, Subodai! I hope only that his punishment is in proportion to his crime." He looked at Jamuga venomously, all his old hatred and jealousy black on his simple broad face. He was filled with exultant satisfaction.

Chepe Noyon was about to reply with his customary jocular contempt, when he was compelled to pause, in amazement, his mouth dropping open. For an astounding transformation had taken place in Subodai. All his calm was gone, all his statue-like composure. He was a man aflame. His blue eyes blazed like lightning, and his teeth flashed between his lips. He seemed to bound towards Kasar. He seized the heavy shortish man by the throat, and shook him violently. His thumbs pressed into his neck, and he uttered savage and guttural sounds. Kasar struggled to free himself; his eyes opened and glared in his terror. His lips swelled. His hands tore at the choking fingers on his throat. He staggered. Subodai forced him to his knees, and increased the pressure on the other's throat. Kasar turned his head from side to side. His face became purple, and his black tongue appeared between his lips, and he uttered strangled brutish whimpers. His eyes rolled up; his chest arched out in his desperate attempts to gain a single life-saving breath.

Chepe Noyon watched. He smiled with bright viciousness, his nostrils widening. He peered forward, in order to see the better in the half-gloom of the yurt. Then he spoke, conversationally:

"I would not kill him, Subodai, though I regret to give thee this advice. Temujin would not like it at all."

But Subodai seemed oblivious to this advice. His handsome face was black with an awful rage. He seemed absorbed in some ghastly and terrible enchantment. The animal-like sounds continued to bubble from his throat. He bent over Kasar. His thumbs were sunken deep in the other's flesh. He swung Kasar from side to side, bending him backwards. A thin line of bloody foam appeared on Kasar's blackening lips. Now the pupils of his eyes could not be seen, and only the whites showed, glaucous and threaded with scarlet.

Chepe Noyon seized his arms. "I love thee too well to see thee murdered," he said calmly. Then he took Subodai by his own throat, and tightened a steely grip upon it. But he might have held a man under a spell. Subodai was not even aware of him. He was laughing deeply, with a mad sound. Then, quite casually, Chepe Noyon bent down and fastened his teeth in Subodai's hands. His teeth sank into the other's tendons, deeper and deeper. He did not relax his grip until he felt Subodai's hands release Kasar. Something heavy rolled against him, and he knew it was the body of Temujin's brother. Then, smiling, he looked up, and wiped Subodai's blood from his lips. Kasar lay writhing on the floor, tearing at his tortured throat. He sobbed and gasped, drawing in deep and tormented breaths, with a whistling groan.

But Subodai had collapsed on the couch at the unconscious Jamuga's feet. He had covered his face with his bleeding hands. But he made no sound.

Chepe Noyon deftly seized Kasar by his arms, and dragged the half-dead man to his feet. "Thou art a dog," he said amiably.

"But thou wert fortunate in not sharing a dog's fate."

He observed Kasar's purple face with pleasure. Then he dragged him to the flap of the yurt and calmly threw him out.

"I never liked him," he remarked. He began to chuckle.

But Subodai seemed as unconscious as Jamuga.

chapter 23

At noon, Subodai awakened Jamuga. This was not easy to do, for the wretched man had sunken into a deep stupor. But Subodai rubbed his hands and held wine to his pale lips, and finally he awoke. He came out of his stupor as one coming out of death, slowly and heavily.

"Our lord hath commanded that thou be brought to him now," said Subodai. He helped Jamuga to put on his coat and boots. Jamuga still did not appear to be wholly conscious. Subodai thought that he had not heard, but after a little, he answered faintly:

"He might have spared me this."

Subodai was silent, but his smile was gentle and encouraging. He put his arm about Jamuga, and helped the tottering man out of the yurt, and literally lifted him down from the platform. The sun was blindingly brilliant, and the whole yellow and reddish landscape shimmered in its cataracts of light.

Subodai said, simply: "Forgive me."

Jamuga's brows drew together in a painful effort at concentration, and he stared at Subodai in bewilderment. Then he said mournfully: "No man can do other than what is in his nature to do." And he pressed Subodai's hand feebly.

He gazed about him, blinking in the strong light, and for the first time was aware of what was taking place. Thousands of warriors had arrived, preparing for the campaign against Toghrul Khan. The camp resounded with confusion. The narrow passageways between the yurts were crowded with strange men, armed and fierce and black of face. Subodai was glad of this. Jamuga would take his journey to Temujin's yurt comparatively unmarked. He tried to hurry Jamuga a little, but Jamuga's faltering steps could not be hastened. Then Subodai considerately pulled Jamuga's hood over his face, so that he might not be recognized by the Mongols, who had already forgotten the campaign against the miserable Naiman, and were enthusiastically preparing for the larger struggle.

Jamuga paused. He lifted his hood and said imploringly: "Subodai, let me pause a moment to say farewell to the women of my people."

Subodai answered sorrowfully: "This hath been forbidden."

Jamuga sighed; he bent his head and the hood fell over his face. Like a man in a dream, he allowed himself to be led by his friend, and again, sunken in his despair and anguish, he was hardly aware of his own movements.

Subodai had brought him to a halt. He lifted his hood and gazed about him with red-rimmed eyes. He was standing before Temujin's enormous yurt, and here everything was quiet, save for two stonelike guards on either side.

"I can go no farther with thee, Jamuga," said Subodai. He hesitated, then forced himself to smile. "Above all things, thou wert famous for thy courage."

In spite of his suffering, Jamuga smiled ironically. "The lowest animals have courage. Men should have something more," he said, in his dwindled voice.

Subodai moved aside the flap, and Jamuga bent and entered. He moved with a new strength and composure.

Temujin sat in the dimly lighted yurt, in the center, on his white horseskin, his arms folded across his chest, his head dropped forward. He seemed to be under the influence of some narcotic, for he did not move nor look up as Jamuga entered. And Jamuga stood before him, upright now, all the herioc nobility of his nature shining on his white and emaciated face. Moments passed, and neither of the men spoke or moved. Jamuga's look of exaltation quickened, until he seemed to throw out a pale and mysterious light.

Then, very slowly, Temujin lifted his eyes, and they were no longer green, but a cloudy gray. He fixed them upon Jamuga's, and he seemed to contemplate the other in some extraordinary detachment. And Jamuga looked at this man who had so foully wronged him and broken him, and as he did so, life came back to his body with his bitter wrath and sorrow.

Neither spoke. In this intense silence they were aware of nothing but themselves, these men who had loved each other more than anything else in the world, who had slept under one blanket and had sworn the oath of sacred brotherhood. There was something more profound between them than the mere accident of blood or chance. There was complete understanding, a bond of spirit which could never be broken, not even now.

Then Temujin spoke, his lips barely moving to emit the sound of his distant voice: "Jamuga Sechen, thou hast been guilty of treason against me."

Jamuga stirred, and his own voice answered Temujin, clearly and bitterly and full of torment:

"If that be treachery, I would do it again, and again, unto the end of the world!"

His heart seemed to be dividing in his chest with an unendurable pang, mysterious and not to be understood. All that he had suffered before was as nothing to this suffering, which was inexplicable.

And again they gazed at each other in that intense silence.

Then Jamuga, for the first time, saw that there was some change in his anda. Temujin was more gaunt, more gloomy, more inscrutable than ever. Some misery had given a rigor to his face, a somberness without ferocity to his eyes. Something was torturing him beyond human endurance. His gray lips were bitten and distorted. And Temujin saw all the marks of suffering on Jamuga's face, all the white exaltation of approaching death in his eyes.

Jamuga then heard strange words from this terrible man:

"I would have spared thee this, for the sake of our old oath."

Jamuga's lips parted in a deep and trembling sigh. The pain in his heart increased. But he could not speak.

Temujin looked away from him, and his somber gloominess became more marked.

"But thou hast become mine enemy, and I have learned that I must allow no enemy to live. I dare not let him live, if I wish to survive."

"I was never thine enemy," replied Jamuga, in a faint clear tone. "Thou knowest this, in thy soul. When we became anda, our hearts were as one, and we communed together in words that only death can obliterate, and mayhap, not even death. Rarely did I agree with thee, and ofttimes we did quarrel and upbraid each other, but thou knowest my loyalty and my love, and that for thee I would have died a thousand deaths, and suffered a thousand wounds."

His voice broke. Tears ran over his face. Temujin moved, as though tormented. He covered his eyes with his hand, to shut out the sight of Jamuga.

"Nevertheless," he muttered, "thou didst, as ever, go thine own way, and I received a mortal wrong from the man I least expected it from. Thou didst violate the oath; thou didst turn away from me, intoxicated with thine own folly."

"I never turned from thee," said Jamuga, brokenly. "But thou didst command me to do a thing I could not do. Thou hast hurled me down, and murdered all that I have loved, but still, I would do as I have done as long as there was life in me."

Temujin dropped his hand, and gazed fully at Jamuga. He

seemed about to speak again, with passion, and then could only be silent. Reflections of the sunlight outside came through the flap, and filled the yurt with rippling waves of subdued radiance. They rippled over Jamuga's tragic face and steadfast, heroic eyes. Temujin continued to gaze at him, and an expression of deep sadness appeared on his features.

"Jamuga, thou hast suffered much, but I know thou art no traitor. Thou wert ill-advised by thy vanity and thy narrow virtue; thou hast never learned to compromise. To have done this would have been to destroy thy whole nature, and death alone can do this."

He paused, and resumed in melancholy tones: "Because thou hast suffered, because of our old oath, I offer thee now, not death, but peace."

Jamuga smiled wildly and terribly. "Peace!" he murmured. "What peace for me? Behind me, there is darkness and ruin, and all that I have loved. My life is water that hath run into the sand. It is blood that is spilled, and vanished. Before me, the future is like a grave, without hope or joy or forgetfulness, lighted with no vision, and filled only with the shadows of what I have lost. I would move among the living like a ghost, forever homeless, forever despairing." He sighed, and the sound was full of anguish.

"How can I live in such a world which thou art making? There is no place in that world for me. The contemplation of it is unendurable, the sight of it too awful for mine eyes. I prefer to die, to leave it behind, and forget it in eternal darkness."

Temujin listened, and something of his old implacability returned to his face. But he said nothing.

And now a sudden supernatural passion seemed to seize Jamuga, mystical and awful. He seemed to expand; the blazing light brightened in his dying eyes. He pointed his shaking finger at Temujin, who involuntarily recoiled:

"But the world which thou wilt make shall pass in a red mist, and the world which others like thee shall make shall also pass, and there shall be no trace of you! For yours is the way of death, and all that lives must repudiate you. The tyrant is crushed, at the end, by the weight of his victims. The cities he hath broken down shall rise again. The grain he hath burned to the ground shall be replanted, and the fountain he hath polluted shall flow purely once more. Where he hath planted his banners the pastures will once more be at peace, and where his hordes have ridden, the grass will grow and obliterate his footsteps.

"I have dreamed a dream, and I have seen a vision, and they are the way of life! They are the way of the forest which groweth, and the way of the living river. A thousand times thou shalt afflict the earth, and a thousand times thou shalt be forgotten, and men will survive, to plant the ground and build upon it. For that which is good endureth forever, but all that thou doest shall be as trickling sands in thy fingers, dropping again to the desert."

His voice, strong and fervent, died away, and the glow remained on him. And once again, that prolonged silence filled the yurt.

Then Temujin rose. He stood before Jamuga, and then he extended his hand and laid it on his anda's shoulder. "Peace be with thee," he said gently.

He withdrew his own dagger and put it in Jamuga's icy hand. He looked long into his eyes, and there was no savagery in his own, but only sorrow and weariness.

Then he turned and went out of the yurt, leaving Jamuga alone.

chapter 24

Temujin's spies told him that Toghrul Khan, or Wang Khan, with his son, Sen-Kung, and a mighty array of Karait warriors, were advancing down the long slope of the Lake Baikul towards him. He knew that Toghrul Khan had aroused the people east of Lake Baikul, and they were ready for attack and offensive, and were moving down behind Toghrul Khan, to assist him.

Temujin realized that once Toghrul Khan was defeated, disorder and panic would spread among the old Karait's own people, and this disorder and panic would be communicated to the tribes east of Lake Baikul, and all the other unconquered tribes of the Merkit, Naiman, Uighurs, Ongut, and the other western Turks. The first necessity, then, was the conquest and death of Toghrul Khan.

He called his khans to a kuriltai. A letter was thereafter sent to Toghrul Khan, purported to be written by the terrified Kasar, brother of Temujin.

"My brother Temujin, the khan, hath been sorely stricken with a mysterious illness, and I have been summoned by our people to take his place. I, in turn, summoned a kuriltai, and the khans have persuaded me that to oppose thee would be to court certain ruin. Moreover, I am convinced that no good will be accomplished by any challenge between the Yakka Mongols and the people of my brother's foster father, and that it is my duty to offer thee, in Temujin's name, his expression of remorse and promises of filial obedience."

Sen-Kung, the suspicious, argued with his father that this letter was written in duplicity, but Toghrul Khan, who now could remember Temujin only as he had last seen him, a petty noble whose very existence depended upon the largesse of the towns, was exultant. "I know this dog!" he exclaimed. "Always expedient, always crafty, never overestimating nor underestimating. Look thee, Sen-Kung: what is he compared to us? A miserable vagabond, a shabby baghatur of the steppes, a bandit and a robber. Moreover, he is very intelligent. He knoweth now that he dare not oppose us."

That night, several horsemen galloped into Toghrul Khan's camp, declaring themselves, panting, to be deserting khans from the western confederacy. They were deserting Temujin, they said, with angry contempt. His pretensions had disgusted them; he had violated the free pride and independence of the members of his confederacy, by his arrogance and assumption of absolute authority. Moreover, he was now exposing them to great danger, which their people would not survive. They could endure this no longer; they had no quarrel with the mighty Wang Khan, and placed themselves, therefore, at his command.

"Send thou a messenger to Temujin, saying we are here, and have come to our senses, and that if he doth attack thee, we will fight with thee against him."

Toghrul Khan, made a trifle suspicious by the suspicions of Sen-Kung, listened carefully. Then he was pleased and reassured. He knew the haughty and ferocious pride of the nobles of the barrens, and he knew how they must resent Temujin's overlordship. He knew their jealousy for their independence. Nevertheless, he asked cautiously:

"Do ye know of any illness of Temujin's? I have had word that he is stricken."

They shook their heads, and one sheepishly admitted that they had left Temujin several nights ago, and knew nothing of any alleged illness.

Toghrul Khan's last suspicions disappeared. If these khans were treacherous, and inspired by Temujin, they would have known of any so-called illness, and would have enlarged upon it. Their ignorance argued for their good faith.

"Where are your people?" asked the old Karait.

"Waiting. Just beyond the eastern hills."

"Then summon them."

The khans hesitated. "We must be assured that thou dost mean to keep faith with us," they said.

Toghrul Khan laughed. "Ye have my promise. Tomorrow night, I shall give you all a feast."

He was very cordial to the traitors, who roamed over the camp, and carefully noted everything. His suspicions might have been aroused again, had they continued to berate Temujin loudly and insistently, but they were silent. When Sen-Kung tormented them for their former idolatrous faith in Temujin, two or three vehemently exclaimed that he was a mighty warrior, and they would regret that new allegiance to Wang Khan if Temujin were further ridiculed. So even Sen-Kung's suspicions were allayed.

Toghrul Khan sent word to Temujin, ironically commiserating with him because of his illness, and telling him of his khans' desertion.

"Thou hast not been able to convince these men of thy power,

O my doughty foster son! They have deserted thee like weasels; they have run from thy tracks, howling like sick dogs. Thus, they have shown their wisdom. But wisdom is not thine. I therefore call upon thee to humble thyself, to offer thyself up for discipline, and to promise me that thou wilt disband thy silly and infamous petty confederacy. If thou dost not, within three days, I shall order an attack, and thou shalt not be spared, nor one of thy people."

Temujin, who had been impatiently awaiting this very message, called the remaining khans into counsel.

"Our brothers have arrived in the camp of Toghrul Khan, and I have received word. Now, we will await further information."

Within a few hours, another message arrived for him from the khans.

"We beseech thee, Temujin, to obey the generous offer of the great Toghrul Khan, and deliver thyself up to him, before the full height of the moon on the third night. We shall be beside him, to receive, with him, the pledge of the disbanding of the confederacy. Do not dream of opposing him. We have only four thousand warriors at our immediate command, and he hath six thousand. Moreover, these warriors are skilled bowmen, and dexterous with the saber, and need no large cavalry to protect themselves. Because of their indomitable spirit, our cavalry will be impotent before them. We urge thee, therefore, to send him an immediate message of thy capitulation."

Temujin had the letter read to him, and shouted aloud in his exultation. "So!" he cried. "They have six thousand warriors, about half of which are mounted! Write, thou, Subodai." And he dictated another letter; purporting to come from the terrified Kasar:

"My brother, the khan Temujin, still lyeth in unconsciousness, but I am empowered to offer thee, most glorious Wang Khan, on oath of fealty, humility and obedience. I shall arrive on the morning of the fourth day, with Temujin's sword."

And with this message, he enclosed Temujin's most beloved treasure, a huge gold ring set with a single brilliant blue stone.

Toghrul Khan read the letter to the treacherous khans. But they snorted. "It is a trick," they said. "If Temujin had been ill, we should have known it. He is merely frightened, and hath used a pretense of sickness in order to escape complete humiliation."

A letter was dispatched to Kasar, graciously accepting the surrender, and informing him that Toghrul Khan would receive him with honors upon his arrival.

In the meantime, the khans studied the position of their host's camp, and laid their plans.

Toghrul Khan, even on a campaign, lived luxuriously. His tent was hung with cloth-of-gold. His officers were quartered in pleasant yurts, filled with treasures, such as goblets and plates of engraved silver and rich carpets. The horses were draped with silk, and saddled with fine red leather. The hilts of the officers' swords were encrusted with gold and gems. There were many women in the camp, singing girls with pretty painted faces, and other girls who were licentious dancers. Musicians, skilled with the flute and the fiddle, made the nights pleasant. The khans moved about, enviously eyeing the treasures, and choosing what would most please them when Temujin arrived.

On the third night, when the moon was full, there was still another feast, and the khans pretended to drink themselves into a stupor. They had to be carried to their yurts. Beyond the yurts, the singing and the dancing and the revelry went on. When they were certain they were no longer watched, the khans gathered together in a place previously designated, and waited. The one with the keenest eyesight crept like a shadow to a rise of ground, and gazed to the south, from which direction the Mongols would come. The others crouched in the darkness, armed and vigilant, not even daring to whisper. At a little distance the sentries paced slowly, yawning, and listening resentfully to the music and laughter. The Karait, who were partially civilized, were not exceedingly well-disciplined, and the sentries took occasion to gather together and exchange bored words.

The moon flooded the landscape of fir and poplar, of plain and hill, of river and great rock, with a white and spectral light. But now it was waning; moreover, to their satisfaction, the Mongols saw that the sky was clouding, and the moon rolled behind these clouds, and her light became nebulous and wandering.

Suddenly, the Mongol sentinel writhed down the rise of ground on his belly, to his companions below. He put his lips to each ear in turn and softly whispered:

"Our lord is approaching. Within the hour, he will be here."

They waited, holding their breath, their hawk's eyes fixed on the yawning Karait sentries, who had begun their languid march again on the rim of the higher ground, moving like shadows against the marbled sky.

Then, a signal, barely perceptible, passed among the Mongols. They dared wait no longer. Even the sentries would soon notice the ghostly approach of the enemy. So, moving on silent feet, they sprang upwards, each toward the sentry previously chosen, and flung themselves upon the Karait. They struck their short daggers up to the hilt in each unsuspecting back, and with only the faintest sigh of a groan, the sentries sank to their knees, and then to their faces. It took only instants to divest them of their headdresses, which the Mongols placed upon their own heads. Then, wrapping themselves in their cloaks, the Mongols, carrying naked swords, took the places of the dead men, and paced silently back and forth.

Sen-Kung, in whom the wary instinct of the nomad was well developed, in spite of his civilization, was suddenly uneasy. He sat by his father, drinking and watching the dancing girls. Then he could no longer stand it. He said:

"My father, for some reason my soul is disturbed, and smelleth danger. Permit me to leave thee for a moment, while I consult with the sentries."

Toghrul Khan, who was just then absorbed in the skillful and obscene contortions of his favorite dancing girl, nodded indifferently, and Sen-Kung rose and started to mount the long swell of ground towards the sentries. He saw them pacing stiffly back and forth, saw them keenly watching the horizon. Still, he was not satisfied.

He approached one of them, who was closely muffled in his cloak.

"All is well?" he asked curtly.

The man nodded. The other sentries, hearing voices, glanced back over their shoulders. They stiffened; their eyes glinted in the wan moonlight. Now the approaching Mongols could be clearly seen, moving like bodiless specters on horseback towards the camp, completely visible from this position.

Sen-Kung breathed deeply through his wide nostrils. He glanced about him; he started to approach another sentry. Then he happened to look southwards and saw the enemy, for the moon suddenly rolled behind her cloud and showed all that was to be seen as clearly as though it were day.

Sen-Kung started violently, his breath loud and harsh in the quiet. Then, with a swift motion, he tore aside the cloak of the sentry nearest him, and saw, fully, the face of one of the khans. The face glared at him, inimical and savage, and now the other sentries ran swiftly towards him, their swords held low.

The hapless Karait looked at the assumed sentries, and saw that death was upon him. But his last thought was for his people. He opened his mouth to utter a loud desperate cry. But at that instant the sentry at his side thrust his sword deeply into his bowels, and pressed his hand over his lips. But the Karait, even in his extremis, strove to call out his warning to his people. He bit the hand over his mouth with teeth like a wolf's; dying as he was, and spouting blood from his vitals, his strength was the strength of three men. In a moment he would be free; he could see the legs of the others surrounding him. He tore the hand from his mouth; he bent his knee and thrust it into the belly of the sentry who was bending over him.

Then one of the others, just as he was about to scream out his warning, kicked him violently in the temple, not once, but several times. The dying man's body arched up; his arms flayed the air. A boot was pressed firmly over his face, and the heel crushed into his eyes. At last, he was still, and did not move again.

The others, panting, smiled grimly at each other. Now they dropped their cloaks. Together they moved down the slope towards the camp, not caring if they were seen. For Temujin and his warriors were almost at hand.

The Mongols no longer moved quietly. They spurred their horses, and with thundering hoofs and screams of exultation, they rode down upon the camp.

Toghrul Khan, who was half asleep, was suddenly awakened by the frenzied shrieks of the girls and the shouts of his warriors. He staggered to his feet, steadying himself against the crouching body of one of the women. He looked down at the plain, and saw the Mongols, saw the curving standard against the moon. He glared about him; he cried out, feebly. His voice, numbed and despairing, called to his officers, who were arousing themselves, blinking in the firelight.

The utmost confusion immediately prevailed. The camp was thrown into panic. Warriors rushed about, as though blind, snatching at the panic-stricken horses that lunged past them. The woman gathered together, and filled the night with their screams and lamentations. Men and beasts plunged through the campfires, scattering red sparks and blazing embers. The officers tried to restore order, to bring the ranks together, buckling on the belts they had loosened at the feast, and kicking savagely about them at the distraught warriors. In the meantime, Temujin's khans ran among them, taking advantage of the noise and disorder to use their swords deftly, darting away, from one murder to another. Some of them, however, actually paused to snatch up a silver plate or a cup, and conceal it skillfully under their clothes. Horses, riderless, flung themselves up against the moon, careering around in circles, while their owners impotently snatched at the bridles.

Toghrul Khan, overcome with terror, rushed into his luxurious yurt, and tried to burrow under the bodies of two girls who had taken refuge there. And thus, Temujin was to find him within a few moments.

In the meantime, the Karait, disordered and dispersed though they were, were brave and resolute. The Mongols roared into the camp like an irresistible wave, slashing about them indiscriminately with their curved sabers, racing about through the aisles of the yurts on their fleet and dexterous horses, avenging shadows with the terrible faces of exalted madmen. They left behind them paths strewn with dead. Unprepared, the Karait tried to hold them back, without avail. The groans and shrieks of the wounded and dying added to the indescribable confusion. Men huddled over their bleeding vitals, trying to stem the blood. The moon looked down at the black and writhing disorder, at the flight and the panic, at the slaughtering Mongols racing back and forth on their horses. Some of the Karait tried to escape, struggling to climb up the slope of land. But every man was pursued and cut down ruthlessly, his sword flung from his hand.

In an incredibly short space of time the Karait were completely demoralized. But still the slaughter went on until every man was dead, and the broad white plain was strewn with the heaps of the dead, including men and horses.

Temujin finally sprang down from his horse. His khans gathered about him, laughing and blood-covered. He congratulated them, slapping them on their backs and shoulders. In the meantime, the wailing and weeping of the terrified girls filled the air.

"Ye have done well," said Temujin, his green eyes and wolfish teeth flashing in the moonlight. "I have lost barely one quarter of my warriors. But I could not have done this without your help."

Subodai rode up, with Chepe Noyon, and informed Temujin that the Karait had been completely annihilated. Temujin nodded; he wiped his blood-wet sword on the side of his boots. Then he frowned.

"Silence those women," he ordered. He glanced about him. "But where is my foster father, and his son?"

Every one clamored that the old Karait had disappeared, and that his son was dead. Temujin stamped his foot savagely.

"I must have him. I must deal with him myself. If any of ye have killed him, I shall inflict the direst punishment upon him. For I have ordered before that none must have him but myself."

They began to search among the dead, flinging aside arms and cloaks, to stare at the white fixed faces. Then Temujin's eye fell on the tent hung with cloth-of-gold, and he strode towards it. He thrust his head through the flap.

He saw a most ludicrous sight. Three girls were sitting on the prone body of the old prince, striving to hide him with their legs and their hair. They looked at Temujin with the wild distended eyes of hunted animals, and kept up a constant thin moaning, wringing their hands, and loudly bewailing the death of their lord.

Temujin burst into loud laughter, and the others came running, their hands full of loot. Temujin pointed at the girls, not able to speak for laughter. Then he flung them aside as though they were dogs, and kicked them in the rumps as they fell, sprawling. He seized Toghrul Khan by the nape of the neck, and dragged him out into the moonlight.

The old man was beside himself with terror. He fell on his knees and clasped Temujin about the knees.

"I abjure thee to spare thine old father, my son!" he wailed. "I abjure thee to remember thine oath of fealty! Do not kill me. I am old, and my years are many. The days before me are few, and my sorrows are as thick as flies. If ever thou didst love me, spare me, and send me hence."

Temujin looked about him at his officers and men, and grinned.

"Listen closely to the bleatings of this old goat! Yesterday, he trumpeted in triumph, and was full of boastfulness and threats against me! Today he doth grovel at my feet, imploring me to spare his goathood, and to send him back to his ewes!"

The others shouted with raucous laughter. Temujin bent over the whimpering old man and struck him across the face. Toghrul Khan fell flat on his face, and lay there, writhing humbly and imploringly, filled with the terror of death. He tried to kiss Temujin's feet, uttering, meanwhile, thin sobbing bleats. Temujin watched him, smiling broadly, his face black and evil.

"I have heard the story," he said. "I have heard that thou didst send thy son, Taliph, unto mine anda, Jamuga, and there did seduce him and make him a traitor. For this treachery he died. But now, I shall avenge him."

He seized the old man once more by the neck, and dragged him to his feet, and literally let him hang from his hand as a boy would hold a rabbit. He hung grotesquely, his feet, in their boots of glimmering gold, pointing downwards, limply. But he looked at Temujin cravenly, his hands folded together in mute and shameful pleading. His attitude, his look, excited renewed laughter among the Mongols.

Temujin, playing with him, swung him to and fro, as though he were a mere bag of clothes. Slobber dripped from the old man's blubbering lips; his eyes rolled up. "Spare me! Spare me!" he whimpered. "Jesus! Allah!"

Then, holding Toghrul Khan a little distance from him, Temujin deliberately thrust him through the body with his sword. He plunged the weapon again and again through the cringing belly of the old man, until he was dead, and Temujin dropped the sword, black and wet with blood in the moonlight. Then he flung the body from him and kicked it in the face.

"I have been avenged," he said. But he no longer saw Toghrul Khan. He saw Jamuga and Azara.

The looting went on, systematically. Just as dawn came up, the Mongols turned homeward, their loot on their saddles, and the dancing girls, weeping, riding behind them.

When Taliph heard the news, he fled to his father's new house behind the Wall.

chapter 25

It was in the year of the Leopard that Temujin defeated Toghrul Khan, and murdered him, thus, as he thought, avenging both Azara and Jamuga.

But the battle was not yet won.

Now he set out, with unrelenting ferocity, savagery and speed, to subjugate the rest of the Karait. Never allowing them to rest, he pursued them to their very stronghold, the city in the desert, Karakorum, or the Black Sands. The Karait were resolute fighters, and contemptuous of the nomad "beggar," but all their resolution and contempt could not withstand the lightning assaults, the almost supernatural tirelessness of the enemy. And now it happened that it needed only the word that the red-haired Mongol was approaching, with his Raging Torrents, his Terrible Riders, to throw panic among the proud Karait. For it was said that spirits rode with him, and none could oppose him, that his warriors, cut down, rose again, unwounded. More than his hordes and vicious fighters, superstition and terror defeated his enemies. Among the Moslem Karait, it was said that God had unloosed a scourge, which could not be held at bay, could not be defeated.

The priests in the mosques cried out: "We have sinned, and forgotten God and His prophet! And so He is punishing us, sending an invincible Terror to destroy us, and none can withstand it!"

The Christian priests exclaimed: "This is the prophecy of the unloosing of Satan, and the end of the world! Against the whip of the Lord, every man is powerless."

The frightful hordes rode like lightning, preceded by a ghostly army, armed with supernaturalism. It was said that Temujin was everywhere. He was striking at the unconquered Merkit and Karait and Uighur and Naiman, in a hundred different places at the identical time, hundreds of miles apart. It was whispered that he rode on the whirlwind. Complete frenzy and demoralization flew over the Gobi. At the last, it was not the hordes of Temujin that defeated the enemy. It was his very name, terrible and mystic.

Men may struggle against a human foe, said the terrified whisper, but how can men oppose the will of God?

One by one, the tribes fell and surrendered, expecting annihilation. But Temujin again displayed his great wisdom. As each tribe surrendered, he said to them: "Ye are heroes, for ye have fought like demons, like faithful men. I need you. Come unto me, and enter my nation, and serve me. Once, the Yakka Mongols were a tribe. Now we are a nation, and ye may be part of it, sharing in our glory and our triumphs, riding, invincible with us, before the shadow of God."

Hypnotized by his power, his strength, his generosity, his very appearance, not a tribe refused to join him. And they joined him wholeheartedly, caught up by the mysterious spell, willing to die for him, fixing their eyes upon him as men fix their eyes upon an altar. The murderer of the steppes seemed, indeed, imbued with the lightning of the heavens. Eventually, other tribes laid down their arms without a single blow given or received, and crowded about the standard of the nine yak tails.

Again, in these days of overwhelming triumph, Temujin showed his wisdom. For he set over each conquered people a ruler picked from among themselves, whom they trusted, and whom he could trust. Thus, reconciled and stabilized, he could leave each conquered tribe, and launch himself into new struggles and new conquests. With each victory, his strength increased. He never rested. He told his paladins: "The success of an action lies in completing it, and consolidating it. Never leave a position until you are certain that it is yours forever."

Town after town fell, often without an attempt at resistance. When this happened, his warriors could pick from the loot, but were not allowed to molest the inhabitants, nor strip them completely. First, above everything else, he needed allegiance. By his generosity, he turned terrified enemies into passionate friends.

Within three years, his hordes conquered the valleys and towns of the Western Turks, the towns and pasturage and lands and rivers of the Taijiut, the Naiman, the Uighur and the Merkit. Down the writhing flank of the Great Wall of Cathay, his mounted warriors rode, and along the sides of the low bleached mountain of the north, driving like living battering-rams through the old towns of Khoten and Bishbalik, galloping like the whirlwind, leaving complete subjugation and demoralization behind them, setting up their standard in the palaces of sultans and princes, and leaving their banners in mosques and temples and churches.

Adoring tales were told of his green eyes and his red hair,

his blazing smile and his generosity, his courage and his invincibility. Subtle as always, he first made rulers and priests his vassals and friends, and left the rest to them.

He knew that strength lay in men and superstition and terror. He tried to win allegiance with promises, which were always kept. If these failed, he had no mercy. Every man was hunted down and killed, the women enslaved, the children adopted by the Mongol women, and the pastures and towns turned over to alien owners.

Mysteriously, he seemed to know the right thing to do, and never made a mistake. Thus, the tales of his supernatural power became stronger, and often, he had only to ride towards a site or a city to have its rulers come forth, offering surrender and allegiance.

No longer were mere hordes added to his empire. Rich men, merchants and traders, nobles and lords, surrendered to him, and even philosophers and teachers from the academies joined him with idolatry. Wisdom seemed no shield against his might. Those who had taught the dignity of men, and the learning of the ages, were often the first to drivel of "the hand of God, and the glory of Temujin." Now, to his entourage, he added learned men, scholars and savants, astrologers and scientists and physicians, who rode with him in litters, and sat with him about the council fires. Among his favorites was a physician, who was his personal attendant. Chepe Noyon and Subodai smiled to themselves, and mentioned the strange resemblance of this physician to the dead Kurelen.

The ancient feuds of the Gobi were stamped out in the hoofprints of Temujin's hordes. The old independence was gone, the old liberty of the nomad. The peoples of the Gobi were welded together in a feudal system where there was only one law: the will of Temujin.

Cathayan scholars had said that liberty was dearest and nearest to the heart of all men. This was proved to be a bitter lie. For Temujin knew that above liberty, men loved a whip, above freedom, they worshipped a sword, above an elected leader, they adored a tyrant, who discounted their ability to think, and commanded instead of consulted. He knew that men voluptuously revel in complete surrender, as women secretly revel in rape. In surrender, men experienced a sensual orgasm. And as he conquered, and saw the grovelling and adoration of the people, his hatred and contempt for all mankind grew.

He said to himself: "These are soulless beasts. If they were not, they would prefer death and endless struggle to servitude." But this was a counsel he kept to himself. He preferred to tell the conquered that they were heroes, that he subjugated them only to add to their own strength, and set them as kings upon the earth. More and more he despised and loathed the priests, who persuaded the people to give up their liberties and their independence. Buddhist and Christian, Shaman and Muhammadan, Confucian and Taoist, he could depend upon the priests to deliver the people into his hands, bound and helpless. And so, to the end of his life, he believed that priests were the enemies of all men, and was careful to guard himself against them as against serpents.

Now he was master of the Gobi. But he was not yet satisfied. He called a kurultai, a council of the khans, knowing that the hour had come, which would give him his most coveted honor.

chapter 26

The khans came, a separate horde in themselves, coming as priests to a god. It was a tremendous gathering, that council in the Gobi.

By this time, the Mongol horde was no loose confederacy. It had a hard nucleus of organization, its permanent central unit, which was divided into units of ten thousand, the tuman, each commanded by a Mongol officer. It was purely a military organization, in which the warrior was the first and last authority. From this organization, headed by Temujin, issued all the commands and laws of the Gobi empire. The Mongols were the lord-people, set over all other tribes and races.

But still, among the peoples of the Gobi, custom and tradition died hard. Temujin was wise enough to know this. He wanted to be named emperor. But he knew that should he announce himself emperor, he might violate the old quarrelsome right of the khans to elect a leader themselves. He dared not violate this tradition. They must elect him, with due process.

That gathering of the khans was the most momentous event in the history of Asia, and the most splendid. There, in the midst of the barrens, the mountains and the desert, they came, resplendent and arrogant, jubilant and proud, knowing why they had been summoned. They came like free men, displaying mighty accoutrements, attended by slaves and warriors, arrayed in silks and armor. They set up their yurts about the council fires, yurts hung with cloth-of-gold and cloth-of-silver, and filled with treasures and dancing girls. No longer were they shabby baghaturs. Temujin had made them arrogant kings, gorgeously clad, followed by retinues.

There was a glorious feast, in the Gobi, that night. The looted treasures and luxuries of a thousand cities added to the splendor of the scene. Jewels glittered in the red light of the campfires. Women and old minstrels sang, and girls danced. And Temujin sat in the midst of them all, on his white horseskin, simply clad in a white wool coat, belted with silver, his hair the color of fire.

The khans knew why they had been summoned; they knew what they were to do. But they pretended not to know. They affected to believe this was merely a feast prepared for them by the leader, in acknowledgment of their victories. They drank deeply; they laughed and shouted. They ate until they could eat no more, and then watched the dancers and listened to the singers, their dark faces shining with grease and surfeit. And servants piled high the fires, and brought fresh food and wine in silver cups and silver platters.

Then, at midnight, there was a sudden awesome silence. The khans sat like bronze statues, clad in silks and gold, their savage faces intent and fixed. Every eye gazed steadfastly and expectantly at Temujin.

He looked from one to the other, slowly, gathering in every glance, every thought, every soul. Then he rose. He stood among them, tall and broad, his greenish eyes shining and sparkling in the light of the fires. He began to speak, quietly and forcefully:

"The time hath come to us when we must name an emperor, a lord of all men. Our power is great; our conquests dazzle the hearts and minds of humanity. But, we must name an emperor, who must be the supreme authority, the fountain-head of all law. For we have greater things to do, greater conquests. The world lies before us, from the sunrise to the sunset. To seize it all, there must be one lord, one guiding voice, to whom all khans must offer allegiance and obedience. We are a nation. The nation needs its emperor."

The khans listened, in somber silence. When Temujin had finished, and stood among them, waiting, they affected to be considering the momentous decision. They glanced about them, at their brothers, as though awaiting a name, or names. But they knew the name, had always known the name. It was part of their pride that they pretended to be in doubt.

Then one of the khans rose, and made obeisance to Temujin, kneeling before him.

"This is my choice: that the lord Temujin be named emperor."

The khans broke into a tumultuous confusion of voices, and pretended to consult among themselves. And Temujin watched and waited, smiling darkly. His swift and ruthless nature made him feel an overwhelming contempt and amusement for all this pretense, but still, he knew he dared not violate the ancient law.

Then one by one the khans rose and knelt before him, proclaiming him emperor. They seized his rough garments; they wept. They laid their swords at his feet. A tumult broke from their throats, an acclamation which was like the roaring of beasts.

Temujin affected to be stunned, to be overcome. He bowed his head. His eyes, filled with tears, moved from face to face. His chest heaved. He affected to be unable to speak. This pleased the khans, who loved ceremony and pretense, and the observance of tradition. Their love and adoration poured out to him like wine from golden goblets.

Kokchu had been waiting in his yurt. The old Chief Shaman already knew his part. Now he advanced into the circle of the fires, attended by his young shaman. In his hands he bore a golden circlet, part of the loot of a rich city. Seeing this, Temujin pretended to start, to be completely overwhelmed and swamped with emotion. The hands of the khans seized him, and forced him to his knees.

He knelt before Kokchu, who was arrayed like the rainbow, his fat old hands covered with jewels. And Kokchu raised the circlet solemnly aloft, and appeared to consult the terrible spirits of the Eternal Blue Sky. His lips moved; his eyes distended. He trembled, and tears ran over his face. Temujin knelt before him with bent head, and now even the clamorous khans were silent.

Then Kokchu, dropping his eyes, surveyed the kneeling Mongol. His lips shook. In a strangled voice of awful emotion, he cried out:

"The spirits have spoken, and the kings of the earth! And it hath been declared that Temujin, son of Yesukai, shall be named Emperor of All Men, Genghis Kha Khan, the Mighty Ruler, the Rider of Heaven!"

And slowly, with elaborate gestures, he placed the golden circlet on Temujin's red head.

chapter 27

"I have only begun!" said Temujin to himself. He sat alone on his horse, and waited for the morning.

Behind him, the exhausted and resplendent khans were asleep in their yurts. He was completely alone. Even the horses and all the beasts slept, immobile.

He gazed at the east. There the sky was a pale and luminous silver, a throbbing pallor. But along its lower edges the frail fire of the dawn was running. The desert lay in purple mystery and silence to the west. The distant mountains, fanged and chaotic, were black with night, but their upper reaches were flaming with gold and scarlet. The endless wind rushed like torrents of water over the world, and blew into Temujin's face.

He smiled no longer, with his usual dark cynicism. His red hair lay on his shoulders. In his eyes was a vast deep shadow, and his expression was somber and fixed. His hands lay along the neck of his white stallion, who stood like a marble statue, only its snowy mane, rippling in the gale.

Then Temujin looked to the east, where lay the empires of Cathay. He looked to the west, at the Moslem provinces and kingdoms, and beyond them, to Europe, adrift with the fogs of the unknown, which he was to conquer. He looked at the world. A frightful exultation suddenly filled him, and his spirit seemed to expand, to grow as large as eternity. He lifted his clenched fist, and held it rigid in the air. His nostrils flared in his brown face. His eyes sparkled, as though with the reflection of a conflagration, and the shadow of a mysterious fire fell over his face. There was something dreadful, something ghastly, in his aspect. Asia slept still, in its immense reaches, to west of him, to east and north and south of him. But its emperor, its destroyer, its builder and its devastater, stood alone, with his lifted fist and his appalling face, confronted only by God and death. "I have only begun!" he said again.

He was suddenly aware of some terrible Presence, of some unsleeping Eye, some most ominous regard. For an instant, his heart quailed, and his hand dropped. Then, lifting his eyes, he gazed at the brightening immensity of the skies, and his whole spirit was filled with triumph and defiance, fury and savage joy.

"I have the world!" he cried, and his voice seemed to sound

like a trumpet note in the silence. "I, Genghis Khan, am the world!"

Only silence answered him, unbroken and contemptuous and awesome. Only the silence of God replied. The sun rose above the broken horizon. It fell with a bloody light upon the face and the figure of Genghis Khan. And suddenly, about him, there seemed a spectral horde, the shadows of the past and the shadows of the future, the shadows of the enemies of men.

They stood about him, silent and fierce, seeing, but unseen.

And the eyes of God saw everything, and the silence of God swallowed up the universe, and the spirit of God seemed to flow out upon the earth, invincible, conquering, and ever victorious.